READER'S DIGEST
CONDENSED BOOKS

With the exception of actual personages identified as such, the characters and incidents in the fictional selections in this volume are entirely the product of the authors' imaginations and have no relation to any person or event in real life.

www.readersdigest.co.uk

The Reader's Digest Association Limited 11 Westferry Circus Canary Wharf London E14 4HE

For information as to ownership of copyright in the material of this book, and acknowledgments, see last page.

Printed in France
ISBN 0 276 426754

READER'S DIGEST CONDENSED BOOKS

Selected and edited by Reader's Digest

CONDENSED BOOKS DIVISION

THE READER'S DIGEST ASSOCIATION LIMITED, LONDON

CONTENTS

Nick Stone is far from happy with the latest assignment from his intelligence service bosses but, under duress, he flies to Panama to carry out his orders. Once there, he finds himself caught up in a high-level conspiracy that could result in the deaths of thousands of innocent people. Vivid, authentic action, set in the sweltering jungles of Central America, from former SAS soldier and best-selling author Andy McNab.

PUBLISHED BY BANTAM PRESS

For years, the US Government has been wanting to catch a ruthless smuggler of illegal immigrants known as the Ghost, and now at last they have their chance. Calling on the skills of forensic expert Lincoln Rhyme, the authorities pursue their quarry to New York's Chinatown, where a tense cat-and-mouse chase ensues. A superb, exotic new thriller set in the labyrinthine Chinese underworld.

PUBLISHED BY HODDER & STOUGHTON

DYING TO TELL

page 299

Robert Goddard

When Lance Bradley's old friend Rupert Alder disappears, he leaves behind him a tantalising trail of clues stretching from London to Berlin, Tokyo and San Francisco. As Lance retraces Rupe's movements, he discovers that his friend had unearthed a sensational secret from the past, forcing him to go on the run. Before long Lance, too, is in grave danger. An intricate and atmospheric mystery from the highly acclaimed Robert Goddard.

PUBLISHED BY BANTAM PRESS

FALLEN ANGEL

page 445

Don J. Snyder

The popular summer resort of Rose Point is always deserted in winter, so when caretaker Paul McQuinn hears that the Halworths plan to spend Christmas there, he is surprised. As he and his young son, Terry, trudge through the snow to open up the house for the family's arrival, they have no idea how profoundly the events of the next few days will change their lives. A beautifully told story of love, forgiveness and the courage to begin again.

PUBLISHED BY POCKET BOOKS (USA)

ANDY McNAB
LAST LIGHT

Nick Stone can't help feeling he's not getting the whole picture. He's been recruited by the intelligence services to assassinate 'a key player', but the fact that the target is a teenage boy makes him deeply uneasy about the whole mission.

And when he discovers that he's being used as a pawn in an extremely ruthless political game, Nick knows for sure that it's time to take matters into his own hands . . .

ONE

Sunday, September 3, 2000

I didn't know who we were going to kill—just that he or she would be among the crowd munching canapés and sipping champagne on the terrace of the Houses of Parliament at 3.00pm, and that the Yes Man would identify the target by placing his hand on their left shoulder when he greeted them.

I'd done some weird stuff over the years, but this job was scaring me. In less than ninety minutes, I was going to be shitting on my own doorstep big-time. I only hoped the Firm knew what it was doing, because I wasn't too sure that I did.

As I looked down yet again at the clear plastic lunch-box on the desk in front of me, three torch bulbs sticking out of holes I'd burnt in the lid stared back up. None of them was illuminated; the three snipers were still not in position.

I stared through the net curtains across the boat-filled river. The Houses of Parliament were some 350 yards away to my half left. The office I'd broken into was on the top floor of County Hall, the former Greater London Council building. Now redeveloped into offices, hotels and tourist attractions, it overlooked the Thames from the south side. I was feeling rather grand sitting behind a highly polished, dark wood desk, as I looked out at the killing ground.

Parliament's terrace spanned the whole of its river frontage. Two prefabricated pavilions with candy-striped roofs had been erected at the far left end, for use throughout the summer months. The Department of Trade and Industry's guests today were a group of businessmen, plus some family, from Central and South America. Maybe the DTI was trying to sell them a power station. Who cared? All I knew was that one of them would be getting dropped somewhere between the vol-au-vents and the profiteroles.

Three torch bulbs were still unlit. I wasn't flapping, just concerned.

At either end of the row of lights was a white, rectangular bell-push, glued in position, the wires curling into the box. The one on the left was covered with the top from a can of shaving cream. It was the detonation pressel for the device that I'd set up as a diversion. The device was basically a black powder charge, designed to give off a big enough bang to grab London's attention but not to kill anyone. There'd be the odd cut or bruise, but there shouldn't be any fatalities. The shaving cream top was there because I didn't want to detonate it by accident. The pressel on the right was exposed. This was the one that would initiate the shoot. Next to the box I had a set of binos mounted on a mini-tripod and trained on the killing ground.

The lunch-box contained a lithium battery, and a mess of wires and circuit boards. Two plastic-coated wire antennas stuck out of the rear of the box, trailed along the desk, over the windowsill I'd pushed it up against, then dangled down the outside wall.

Big Ben struck two. I knew the snipers wouldn't move into their fire positions until the last moment so as not to expose themselves longer than necessary, but I wanted those lights to start flashing.

At last. The middle bulb, Sniper Two's, gave five deliberate, one-second pulses. I put my thumb on the send pressel and depressed it three times in the same rhythm, to say that I had received the signal.

I got three flashes back immediately from the middle bulb. Good news. Sniper Two was in position, ready to fire, and we had comms. All I needed now was One and Three, and I'd be cooking with gas.

I'd put everything these snipers needed to know—where to be, how to get there, what to do once in position, and how to get away afterwards—with the weapons and equipment in their individual dead letterboxes. The three had different fire positions, each unknown to the others. None of them had met or even seen each other, and they hadn't met me. That's how these things are done: operational security. You only know what you need to.

I'd had a busy ten nights of close target recces to find suitable fire positions in the hospital grounds this side of the river and directly opposite the killing ground. Then, by day, I'd made the keys for the snipers to gain access to their positions, prepared the equipment they would need, then loaded the dead letterboxes. Tandy, B&Q and a remote-control model shop in Camden had made a fortune out of me once I'd hit ATMs with my new Royal Bank of Scotland Visa card under my new cover for this job, Nick Somerhurst.

Operational security was so tight that the Yes Man had briefed me personally. Tucked in an attaché case, he had a buff folder with black boxes stamped on the outside for people to sign and date as they authorised its contents. No one had signed any of them, and there was no yellow card attached to signify it was an accountable document. Things like that worried me: I knew it meant trouble.

As we drove along Chelsea Embankment towards Parliament in the back of a Previa MPV with darkened windows, the Yes Man had pulled two pages of printed A4 from the folder and briefed me.

I didn't like the condescending wanker one bit as he told me I was 'special' and 'the only one capable'. Things didn't improve when he stressed that no one in government knew of this job, and only two in the Firm: 'C', the boss of the Secret Intelligence Service (SIS), and the Director of Security and Public Affairs.

'And, of course,' he said, with a smile, 'the three of us.'

The driver, whose thick blond side-parted hair made him look like Robert Redford when he was young enough to be the Sundance Kid, glanced in the rearview mirror and I caught his eye for a second.

It was blindingly obvious to me that the reason no one knew about this operation was because no one in their right mind would sanction it, and no one in their right mind would take the job on. Maybe that was why I'd been picked. Then, as now, I comforted myself with the thought that at least the money was good. Well, sort of. But I was desperate for the eighty grand on offer, forty now in two very large brown Jiffy bags, and the rest afterwards. That was how I justified saying yes to something I just knew was going to be a nightmare.

We were now on the approach road to Westminster Bridge with Big Ben and Parliament to my right.

'You should get out here, Stone. Have a look around.'

The Sundance Kid kerbed the Previa, and I slid the door back and stepped out. The Yes Man leaned forward in his seat and took the door handle. 'Call in for what you need, and where you want the other three to collect their furnishings.'

With that, the door slid shut and Sundance cut up a bus to get back into the traffic stream heading south across the river.

From the moment the Yes Man dropped me off with my two Jiffy bags, I'd started protecting myself far more than I normally would. I knew that if I got caught by Special Branch the Firm would deny me, and that was part and parcel of being a K (deniable operator). But there was more to it this time. The stuff I did normally didn't happen in the UK. Everything felt wrong, and the Yes Man would never want to be on the losing side. He'd knife his own grandmother if it meant promotion; in fact, since he took over the Ks Desk from Colonel Lynn, he was so far up C's arse he could have flossed his teeth. If things didn't go to plan, he wouldn't hesitate to fuck me over if it meant he could take any credit and pass on any blame.

I needed a safety blanket, so I started by noting down the serial numbers of all three snipers' weapons before grinding them out. Then I took Polaroids of all the equipment, plus the three firing positions. I had a full pictorial story of the job, together with photocopies of each set of sniper's orders. It all went into a bag in Left Luggage at Waterloo Station, along with everything else I owned: a pair of jeans, socks, pants, washing kit and two fleece jackets.

After loading the three snipers' dead letterboxes, I should have left them alone—but I didn't. Instead I put in an observation post on Sniper Two's dead letterbox, just outside the town of Thetford in Norfolk, the nearest of the three to London. The other two were in the Peak District and on Bodmin Moor. All had been chosen in uninhabited areas so that once they'd got the weapons they could zero them to make sure the optic sight was correctly aligned to the barrel, so that a round hit the target precisely at a given distance.

Inside the dead letterbox, a forty-five-gallon oil drum, was a large black Puma tennis bag that held everything needed for the shoot and was totally sterile of me: no fingerprints, certainly no DNA. Dressed like a technician in a chemical warfare lab, I had prepared, cleaned and wiped everything down so many times it was a wonder there was any parkerization (protective paint) left on the barrels.

Jammed into a Gore-Tex bivi bag and dug in among the ferns in drizzling rain, I waited for Sniper Two to arrive. I knew that all three would be extremely cautious when they made their approach to lift the dead letterboxes, to ensure they weren't followed or walking into a trap. I had to keep my distance, which meant choosing a telephoto lens on my Nikon for more photographic evidence of this job.

I waited, throwing Mars bars and water down my neck, and in the end it was just over thirty boring and wet hours before Sniper Two moved in. At least it was daylight. I watched the hooded figure check the immediate area around a collection of old, rusty farm machinery and oil drums. It edged forward like a cautious cat. I brought up the telephoto lens. Tapered blue jeans, brown cross-trainers, beige waterproof jacket. The hood had a sewn-in peak, and I could see the label on the left breast pocket: L.L. Bean. I'd never seen one of their shops outside the US.

What I'd also never seen outside the US was a woman sniper. She was maybe early thirties, slim, average height, with brown hair poking out of the sides of the hood. She reached the oil drums, and carefully checked inside hers to make sure it wasn't booby-trapped before lifting out the bag. She turned in my direction, taking the weight of it in both hands, and threw it over her right shoulder. I hit the shutter release and the camera whirred. Within seconds she'd melted into the trees.

I was still staring at the three bulbs, waiting for One and Three to sign in. A helicopter clattered overhead, following the river bank on the north side. My paranoia was working overtime. For a moment I thought it had found the explosive device I'd placed on the roof of the Royal Horseguards Hotel in Whitehall the night before. The hotel was behind the Ministry of Defence building across the river to my half right. Seeing the three service flags fluttering on its roof prompted me to check the wind indicators. Keeping the row of torch bulbs in my peripheral vision, I looked down at the river.

In urban areas the wind can move in different directions, at different levels, and in different strengths, depending on the buildings it has to get round. Sometimes streets become wind tunnels, redirecting and momentarily strengthening the gusts. The wind can blow a round off course. Indicators were therefore needed at different distances from the killing area, so the snipers could compensate by adjusting their sights. Flags are useful, and there were more around here than at a UN summit. On the water were boats with pennants at the stern. On both ends of Westminster Bridge, tourist stalls were selling plastic Union Jacks and Man United streamers. The snipers would use all of these, and they would know where to look because I'd keyed them onto the maps supplied in the dead letterboxes. The wind condition at river level was good, just a hint of a breeze.

I checked out the terrace with one eye on the binos, the other ready to pick up any flashes from the torch bulbs. Catering staff were streaming in and out of the pavilions, laying out ashtrays and placing bowls of nibbles on tables.

At least the weather was on our side. Taking the shot through one of the pavilion windows would have made things even more difficult.

The sniper positions were all on my side of the river; three Portakabins in the grounds of St Thomas's Hospital. Three different positions gave three angles of fire, and therefore three chances of getting a round into the target.

This would be the first time the snipers had ever been to the fire position, and it would also be the last. Soon after the shoot they'd be heading for Paris, Lille or Brussels on Eurostar trains, which left from Waterloo Station just ten minutes' walk away.

I thought about Sniper Two. She would have moved cautiously into the fire position after clearing her route, employing the same tradecraft as at the dead letterbox, and probably in a simple disguise. A wig, coat and sunglasses do more than people think, even if Special Branch racked up hundreds of man-hours poring over footage from hospital security, traffic and urban CCTV cameras.

Having first put on her surgical gloves, she would have made entry to her Portakabin with the key provided, locked the door and shoved two rubber wedges in the frame to prevent anyone entering. Then she'd have opened the sports bag and put on her work clothes, a set of hooded and footed coveralls from B&Q. It was imperative that she didn't contaminate the area or the weapon and equipment that were going to be left behind with clothing fibres or other personal sign. Her mouth would now be covered by a protective mask to prevent leaving even a pinprick of saliva on the weapon as she took aim.

The coveralls and gloves were also there to protect clothes and skin. If she was apprehended immediately after the shoot, residue from the round that she'd fired would be detectable on her skin and clothes. I was also wearing surgical gloves, but just as a normal precaution. I was determined to leave nothing, and disturb nothing too.

Once she'd got covered up, with just her eyes exposed, it would have been time to prepare the fire position. She'd have dragged the desk away from the window. Then she'd have pinned a net curtain into the ceiling, letting it fall in front of the desk before pinning it to the legs. Next, she'd have pinned up the sheet of opaque black material behind her, letting it hang to the floor. The combination creates the illusion of a room in shadow. Anyone looking through the window wouldn't see a rifle muzzle being pointed at them.

The weapon, issued to me by the Yes Man, was 'take down'. So, once she had zeroed it in Thetford Forest, it had to be taken apart for concealment, and carried as if it was fine china—the slightest knock could upset the optic sight and wreck the weapon's zero—before being reassembled at the firing point.

This bolt-action model only had to be split in two at the barrel, and because they were brand-new they wouldn't have suffered much wear and tear on the bearing surfaces. But there only had to be a slight difference in the assembly from when it was zeroed for the weapon to be inches off where she was aiming. This isn't a problem when firing at a body mass at close range, but these boys and girls were going for a catastrophic brain shot, a single round into the brain stem or neural motor strips. That meant they had to aim at either of two spots—the tip of an earlobe, or the skin between the nostrils.

Some fifteen minutes after arriving, Sniper Two would be sitting in the swivel chair behind the desk. Her weapon would be assembled and supported on the desk by the bipod attached to the forward stock. To deaden the sound of the shot, each weapon was fitted with a suppressor. It wouldn't stop the bullet's supersonic crack, but that didn't matter because the noise would be downrange and well away from the fire position; it would stop the weapon's signature being heard by hospital staff or tourists on the embankment below.

The Portakabin's windows had to be slid open. Firing through glass would not only alert the tourists but would also affect the bullet's accuracy.

Her binos, mounted on a mini-tripod, would also be on the desk, and in front of her would be her plastic lunch-box. It would only be once she was happy with her fire position, and her hearing aid was in place under her hood, that she would sign on. Her box of tricks didn't have lights, just a wire antenna. A copper coil inside the box emitted three low touch tones; when I hit my send pressel, they picked that up through the hearing aid.

There was one other wire coming out of the box, leading to a flat, black plastic button; this would now be taped onto the weapon wherever she had her support hand in position to fire.

Hitting the pressel five times, once she was ready to go, was what lit up my number-two bulb five times.

There was nothing left for her to do now but wait. If anyone from hospital security attempted to be the good guy and close her window, a woman dressed like an extra from the *X-Files* would be the last thing they ever saw as she dragged them inside.

I was going to control the snipers and tell them when to fire using this method: whenever any of the snipers had a sight picture of the target and felt confident about taking the shot, they'd hit their pressel and keep it pressed. The corresponding bulb in front of me would stay lit for as long as they could take the shot. If they lost their sight picture, they released their pressel and the bulb would go out.

Once I'd made the decision when to fire, I'd push my send pressel three times in a one-second rhythm. The first press would tell the firer or firers to stop breathing so their body movement didn't affect the aim. The second would tell them to take up the first pressure on the trigger, so as not to jerk the weapon when they fired. As I hit the pressel the second time, I'd also trigger the detonation. The third time, the snipers would fire as the device exploded on the roof of the hotel. The device would not only disguise the sonic cracks, but also create a diversion on the north side of the river while we extracted.

None of the snipers would know if the others had the target. They'd know the option was going ahead when they heard the three tones in their ear. If they didn't have a sight picture themselves, they wouldn't take a shot.

After the explosion, whether they'd fired a round or not, they would all exit from their positions, stripping off their outer layer of coveralls and leaving the area casually and professionally with the protective clothing in their bag. The rest of the kit, and the weapons, would be discovered at some point by the police, but that wouldn't matter as I'd handed it over sterile, and these people ought to be professional enough to leave it in the same condition as they'd received it.

Another light flashed. Sniper One was in position, ready to go.

I hit the send pressel three times, and after a short pause Sniper One's bulb flashed three times in return.

Different colours of clothing were moving among the black and white of the catering staff now. I put one eye to the binos and checked them out. The new arrivals seemed to be the advance party, maybe ten suited men, all of them white. Dark, double-breasted suits with a polyester mix seemed to be the order of the day. The jackets were mostly undone, revealing ties that hung either too high or too low. They had to be Brit politicians and civil servants.

There was a flash in my peripheral vision, and I looked down. The third bulb. I concentrated on the box as I replied to the flashes. Sniper Three duly acknowledged. Big Ben chimed three times.

Relief washed over me. Now I just wanted this thing over and done with, and to slip away on Eurostar to the Gare du Nord, then on to Charles de Gaulle. I should make the check-in nicely for my 9.00pm American Airlines flight to Baltimore, to see Kelly and finish my business with Josh.

I got back on the binos. Human shapes were pouring out into the killing area. The South American contingent was easy to identify because they were far better dressed, in well-cut suits and expertly knotted ties.

The Yes Man was due to arrive ten minutes after the main party. The plan was that he'd spend five minutes by the door, making a call, which would give all four of us time to ping him. From there he would move off and ID the target.

More people cut across my field of view, then the Yes Man appeared in the doorway. He was five foot six tall, and wearing a dark, ill-fitting business suit and a scarlet tie—his main visual distinguishing mark. The rest of his kit and his physical description had also been given to the snipers, but he was easy enough to identify from his permanently blushing complexion.

Producing his mobile, the Yes Man moved to the right of the doorway, keeping his back against the wall so that we could check the tie. A young waiter came up to him with a tray of full glasses, but was waved away. The Yes Man didn't drink or smoke.

Phone conversation over, he wove through the crowd, stopping eventually by a group of maybe ten men, gathered in an informal circle. I could see some of their faces, but not all. Two were white-eyes, and four or five Latino faces were turned towards the river.

The older of the two white-eyes smiled at the Yes Man and shook his hand warmly. He then began to introduce his new Latin friends.

I'd assumed they were all South Americans, but as one of their number turned I saw that he was Chinese. He was in his fifties, and taller than the Yes Man. Why he was part of a South American delegation was a mystery to me, but I concentrated on how he was greeted. It was just a normal handshake. The Chinaman, who obviously spoke English, then introduced a smaller guy to his right, who had his back to me. The Yes Man moved towards him, and then, as they shook, placed his left hand on the small guy's shoulder.

I hated to admit it, but he was doing an excellent job. He even started to swing the target round so he faced the river, pointing out the London Eye and the bridges either side of Parliament.

The target was also part Chinese—and I had to double-take because he couldn't have been more than sixteen or seventeen years old. He was wearing a smart blazer with a white shirt and blue tie, the sort of boy any parent would want their daughter to date. He looked happy, exuberant even, grinning at everyone and joining in the conversation as he turned back into the circle with the Yes Man.

I got a feeling I was in worse trouble than I'd thought. But I forced myself to cut away. I'd worry about it on the flight to the States.

The conversation on the terrace carried on as the Yes Man said his goodbyes to the group, waved at another, and moved out of my field of view. He wouldn't be leaving yet—that would be suspicious—he just didn't want to be near the boy when we dropped him.

Seconds later, I had three bulbs burning below me. The snipers were waiting for those three command tones to buzz in their ear.

It didn't feel right but reflexes took over. I flicked the shaving cream top from the box and positioned my thumbs over the two pressels. I was about to press when all three lights went out.

I got back on to the binos, just with my right eye, thumbs ready over the pressels. The group was moving en masse from left to right. The Chinaman's arm was round the boy's shoulders—it must have been his son—as they approached a table laden with food.

I was having doubts, I didn't know why, and tried to get a grip. What was happening in my head was totally unprofessional.

The boy started to help himself to some food, looking back at his dad to check if he wanted anything. I watched him pick at the canapés on the silver trays. I studied his shiny young face as he wondered what would best complement his glass of Coke.

All three lights now burned. How could they not?

In that instant, my plan switched to screwing up the shoot and finding something to blame it on. I couldn't stop myself.

The snipers wouldn't know who else had a sight picture, and it wasn't as if we were all going to get together and have a debrief over coffee the next morning. I'd take my chances with the Yes Man.

The boy moved back into the crowd, towards his dad. The three lights went out. Wrong or right, now was my time to act.

I pushed the send pressel once with my thumb, keeping my eyes on the boy. Then I pressed it again, and at the same time hit the detonation button. The third time, I pushed just on the send pressel.

The explosion on the other side of the Thames was like a massive clap of thunder. I watched the boy and everyone around him react to the detonation. As panic broke out on the terrace, his father bustled him towards the door. Then the Yes Man came into view. He had a concerned look on his face, which had nothing to do with the explosion and everything to do with seeing the target alive.

The Yes Man looked up and across the river at me. He didn't know exactly where I was in the building, but I felt as if he was looking straight into my eyes.

I was going to be in a world of shit about this, and knew I had to have a really good story for him. But not today: it was time to head for Waterloo. My Eurostar left in an hour and five.

I opened the window a fraction to retrieve the antennas. Pedestrians were rooted to the spot as the cloud of black smoke billowed over the rooftop of the MOD building. I closed the window and packed away all my gear as quickly as I could, then put the dirty coffee mug, Wayne's World coaster and telephone back exactly where they'd been before, using the Polaroid I'd taken as a reference.

My brain started to bang against my skull. There was something strange about what I had seen outside.

I looked back out of the window and it hit me in an instant. Instead of looking at the column of smoke to my right, the crowd's attention was on the hospital to my left. Now they were looking towards the sniper positions, listening to the dull thud of six or seven short, sharp, single shots . . . There were screams below the window, mixed with the wail of fast-approaching police sirens.

I opened my window and pushed the net curtain aside, sticking out my head and looking towards the hospital. A fleet of police cars and vans with flashing lights had been abandoned along the embankment, just short of the sniper positions, their doors left open. At the same time I saw uniforms hastily organising a cordon.

This was wrong, very wrong. The event I was witnessing had been planned and prepared for. The frenzy of police activity down there was far too organised to be a spur-of-the-moment reaction to an explosion a few minutes earlier. We had been stitched up.

Three more shots were fired. Then I heard the heavy thuds of a flashbang going off. They were hitting Number Three's position.

Adrenaline jolted through my body. It'd be my turn soon.

I slammed the window down. My mind raced. Apart from me, the only person who knew the exact sniper positions was the Yes Man, because he needed to position the target well enough for it to be identified. He didn't know precisely where I was going to be, because I hadn't known myself. But he knew enough. Messing up the shoot was the least of my worries now.

Helicopters were now rattling overhead as I closed the door gently behind me and moved out into the wide, brightly lit corridor.

Timberlands squeaked on the polished stone floor as I headed towards the fire-exit door at the far end, forcing myself not to quicken my pace. There might be a time to run, but it wasn't yet.

There was a turning to the right that led to the stairwell that would take me to the ground floor. I reached it and froze. Between me and the stairwell was a wall of six-foot-high ballistic shields. Behind them were a dozen police in full black assault gear, weapon barrels pointing at me through the gaps in the shields.

'STAND STILL! STAND STILL!'

It was time to run.

As I zeroed in on the fire-exit door, the corridor ahead filled with more shields. Police emerged from the offices on either side, their weapons pointing at me at far too close a range for my liking.

'STAND STILL! STAND STILL NOW!'

Coming to a halt, I dropped my bag to the floor and put my hands in the air. 'Not armed!' I yelled. 'I'm weapons free! Weapons free!'

I pivoted slowly so they could see my back and check I wasn't lying. As I faced the corridor junction, I heard more boots thundering towards me from the stairwell corridor, closing the trap.

A shield slammed into position on the floor at the corridor junction. A muzzle of an MP5 came round the side of it, and I could see a sliver of the user's face as he took aim on me.

'Weapons free!' My voice was almost a scream. 'I'm weapons free!'

Keeping my hands in the air I stared at the unblinking eye behind the weapon. The eye didn't move from my chest. I looked down as a red laser spot the size of a shirt button splashed on it dead centre.

A voice shouted, 'Keep your hands up! Get down on your knees!'

Keeping my hands up, I lowered myself slowly. The firer in front of me followed my every move with the laser splash.

The voice shouted more orders from behind. 'Lie down, with your arms spread out to your sides. Do it now.'

I did as I was told. There was total, scary silence, broken by the squeak of rubber-soled boots approaching me from behind. Then my hands were pulled up in front of me. I felt the metal bite into my wrists as the handcuffs were ratcheted tight. They were the newer style, police issue: instead of a chain between them they had a solid metal spacer. Once these things are on, just one tap against the spacer with a baton is enough to have you screaming in agony as the metal gives the good news to your wrist bones. I was in enough pain already as one man pulled at the cuffs to keep my arms straight, and someone else's knee was forced down between my shoulder blades.

A pair of hands were making their way over my body. My wallet, containing my Eurostar ticket and my Nick Somerhurst passport, was taken from the inside pocket of my bomber jacket.

I made out three pairs of jeans emerging from behind the shield at the junction. One pair of jeans passed me by, but the other two moved in close: a set of trainers and a pair of light tan boots, their Caterpillar label just inches from my nose.

Hands went under each armpit and hauled me onto my knees. I saw the face of the man wearing the Cats.

His hair wasn't looking so neat today: the Sundance Kid had been running about a bit. Above his jeans he was wearing a green bomber jacket and heavy blue body armour with a protective ceramic plate tucked into the pouch over his chest.

There wasn't the slightest trace of emotion in his face as he stared down at me. Probably he was trying to hide from the others that his part of the job hadn't gone too well. I was still alive; he hadn't been able to make entry into the office with the help of his new mates here and claim self-defence as he shot me.

My documents were handed to him and they went into his back pocket. Sundance and his mate, Trainers, were joined by the third pair of jeans, who had my bag over his right shoulder. It was pointless appealing to the uniforms for help. They'd have heard it all before from drunks claiming to be Jesus and people like me ranting that they'd been stitched.

Sundance spoke for the first time. 'Good result, Sarge.' His thick Glasgow accent was directed to someone behind me, before he turned away with the other two. I watched them walk towards the stairwell, to the sound of Velcro being ripped apart as they started to peel off their body armour.

I was dragged to my feet by two policemen. With their strong grip under each of my armpits, I followed them towards the corridor junction. As we made our way down the stone stairs, Sundance and the boys were about two floors below. We exited the building. White-shirted police officers were running about, yelling at pedestrians to clear the area.

In front of me, at the kerbside, was a white Mercedes estate, engine running, all doors open. One of the pairs of jeans was in the driver's seat ready to go. A hand pushed down on top of my head and I was quickly bundled into the back.

The guy with the trainers sat on my left and attached one end of a pair of handcuffs to the D ring of the centre set of seat belts. He flicked the free end round the pair that gripped my wrists.

Sundance got into the front passenger seat and closed his door. Retrieving a blue light from the floor and slapping it onto the dashboard, he plugged the lead into the cigarette-lighter socket. The light started flashing as the car moved off.

We came out of the County Hall approach road and onto the main drag, opposite the hospital. The road was cordoned off and surrounded by every police vehicle in the Greater London area. We wove round the obstacles in the road and through the cordon. Once we were over the large roundabout, Sundance removed the flashing light from the dashboard. We were heading south.

I looked at Sundance's face in the wing mirror. 'This isn't going to work. I've got on tape the orders you drove for and I—'

There was an explosion of pain as Trainers' hand chopped down on the spacer bar between the cuffs, but I knew it was nothing compared with what would happen if I didn't buy myself some time.

'Look,' I gasped, 'it's me stitched today, it could be you lot next. No one gives a damn about people like us. That's why I keep records. For my own security.' I nodded to give Trainers the message that I was going to shut up. I wanted them to feel I was confident, and that they would be making a big mistake if they didn't pay attention.

Sundance sparked up. 'What do you know, then, boy?'

I shrugged. 'I taped the briefing that you drove for.' Which was a lie. 'I've got pictures of the locations.' Which was true. 'And pictures and serial numbers of the weapons. I've got all the dates, all diaried, even pictures of the snipers.'

I glimpsed Sundance's face in the wing mirror. He was looking dead ahead, his expression giving nothing away. 'Show me.'

That was easy enough. 'Sniper Two is a woman, she's in her early thirties and she has brown hair.' There was silence, which I took as my chance to carry on. 'You need to tell him,' I said. 'Frampton won't be first in the queue for taking the blame. It'll be you lot who get that for sure.' The message had at least got through to Trainers. He was swapping glances with Sundance in the mirror.

We approached a retail park. Sundance pointed at the entrance. 'In there.' The indicator started clicking and we cut across the traffic.

We stopped near a bacon roll and stewy tea van, and Sundance got out. He walked out of sight somewhere behind us, dialling into a StarTac that he'd pulled from his jacket.

The rest of us sat in silence. The driver just looked ahead through his sunglasses and Trainers turned round in his seat to try to see what Sundance was up to, taking care to cover my handcuffs so the shoppers couldn't see that we weren't there for the sale.

Sundance slumped back into the Merc and slammed the door. The other two looked at him expectantly, probably hoping to be told to drive me down to Beachy Head and give me a helping hand in my tragic suicide.

He looked at the driver. 'Kennington.'

I felt a surge of relief about the change of plan. Whatever had been going to happen to me had been postponed.

At length Sundance muttered, 'If you're messing with me, things will get hurtful.'

I nodded into the rearview mirror. There was no need for further conversation as we drove back up the Old Kent Road. I was going to save all that for later, for the Yes Man.

Somebody turned on the radio and the soothing sound of violins filled the Merc. The music finished and a female voice came on with an update on the incident that had shaken London. There were unconfirmed reports, she said, that three people had been killed in a gun battle with police, and that the bomb blast in Whitehall had produced ten minor casualties, who were being treated in hospital. No one had claimed responsibility for the blast.

We passed Kennington tube station, then took a right into a quiet residential street. We turned again, then stopped. Sundance hit his key fob and a graffiti-covered double garage shutter started to roll up. Inside was completely empty. We drove in.

The shutter door rattled and squeaked its way down behind me. The engine was cut and the three of them started to get out.

Sundance disappeared through a door, leaving it open behind him. Trainers leaned down and undid the cuffs pinning me to the seat. Then he and the driver dragged me out. They hauled me through the door and into a windowless, rectangular space with dirty white-washed brick walls and a harsh fluorescent unit in the ceiling.

On the floor in the left-hand corner was a TV. Facing it was a worn three-piece suite. Plugged into adapters in the same socket as the TV were a plastic kettle, a toaster, and battery chargers for three mobiles.

Sundance was finishing another call on his mobile. He looked at me and gestured towards the corner. 'Keep it shut, boy.'

The other two gave me a shove to help me on my way. I slid down the wall and slumped onto the floor, facing the TV.

I guessed this place had been a temporary set-up for the duration of the job—and the job, of course, was preparing to kill me. No doubt there was a similar set-up elsewhere in London where a whole lot of the boys and girls had prepared for the hit on the snipers.

As the other two headed back into the garage, Trainers lined up two mugs. He threw a tea bag into each, splashed milk on top, then dug a spoon into a bag of sugar, tipping heaps of it into the mugs.

In the garage area I could hear the Merc door slam, the engine turning over, and more squeaking and grinding as the shutter lifted. Then the car backed out into the road and drove away.

Sundance appeared at the office door, his back to us, checking that the shutter had fully closed. As the steel banged onto the floor, he walked to the settee and threw his green cotton bomber jacket onto the armrest of the nearest chair, revealing a sweaty maroon polo shirt and a chunky Sig 9mm, holstered just behind his right hip.

He stripped off his polo shirt and used it to wipe the sweat from his face, exposing a badly scarred back. Two indentations were gun-shot wounds, and someone had also given him the good news with a knife, some of the slashes running the whole length of his back.

Trainers, who'd just finished fishing out the tea bags, lifted up a brew for Sundance. 'Want one?' His accent was 100 per cent Belfast.

'Right enough.' Sundance sat down in the chair nearest the TV.

Trainers sat on the settee and pulled out a packet of Drum. He took out some Rizlas and started to make himself a roll-up.

Sundance didn't like that. 'You know he hates that—just wait.'

'Right enough.' The Drum packet was folded and stashed.

The Yes Man must be on his way. Even though I'd never smoked I'd never been a tobacco Nazi, but Frampton certainly was.

Sundance got up, walked to the TV, and hit the power button then each of the station buttons till he got a decent picture.

Trainers sparked up, 'I like this one. It's a laugh.'

Sundance shuffled backwards to his chair, eyes glued to *Antiques Roadshow*. I waited for the Merc to return.

Whoever had christened Frampton the Yes Man was a genius: it was the only word he said to any of his superiors. In the past this had never worried me because I had nothing to do with him directly, but all that changed when he was promoted to run the UK Ks Desk in SIS. The Firm used some ex-SAS people like me as deniable operators. The Ks Desk had traditionally been run by a member of Intelligence Branch, the senior branch of the service.

The Yes Man had been to university, but neither of the right two. He had never been one of the elite, a member of Intelligence Branch, but had probably always wanted to be. His background was the Directorate of Special Support, a branch of wild-haired technicians and scientists working on electronics, signals, electronic surveillance and explosive devices.

I didn't know why the Firm had let a non-IB take command. Maybe with the change of government they thought they should look a bit more meritocratic. So, who better to run the Desk than someone who wasn't an IB, arse-licked his way from breakfast to dinnertime, and would do whatever he was told?

The shutter rattled and I heard an engine rev outside.

They both stood up. Sundance put his wet shirt back on and turned off the TV. The engine noise got louder. Doors slammed and the shutter came down again.

The Yes Man appeared at the door, still in his suit. Trainers slipped dutifully out of the room, like the family labrador.

The Yes Man's face was an even brighter red than usual. He was under pressure. 'What happened, Stone?' he shouted. 'Can't you get anything right?'

What was he on about? Only two hours ago he'd wanted me killed, and now he was telling me off like I was a naughty schoolboy. But it wasn't the moment to point this out.

'I just don't know, Mr Frampton. As soon as I had three lights up I sent the fire commands. I don't know what happened after that. It should have worked, all four of us had comms up until then but—'

'But nothing!' he exploded. 'You don't understand the importance of this operation that you have completely scuppered, do you?'

Scuppered? I tried not to smile but couldn't help it. 'Fucked up' was how his predecessor, Colonel Lynn, would have put it.

The Yes Man was still playing the schoolteacher. 'There's nothing to smile about, Stone. Who, in heaven's name, do you think you are?'

'Just someone trying to keep alive,' I said. 'That's why I taped our conversation, Mr Frampton.'

He was silent for a few seconds while that sank in. Ah, yes, the tape and pictures. He must have remembered why I was alive and he was here. But his brain switch was set to Transmit rather than Receive.

'You've no idea of the damage you've done. The Americans were adamant that this had to be done today. I gave my word that it would. You have let a serious problem develop in Central America, Stone. Because of you, we, the Service, are not influencing events in a direction favourable to Britain.' He thumbed behind him in the direction of Sundance. 'Now, go with this man to collect the tape and all the other material that you claim to have on this operation, and I'll see about trying to save your backside.'

'I can't do that, sir.'

He stiffened. He was starting to lose it. '"Can't do that, sir?"'

'I'm sorry, Mr Frampton, but I need to make sure you don't have a change of heart about me. I like being alive. I understand the reasons why the snipers were killed. I just don't want to join them.'

The Yes Man crouched down so that his eyes were level with mine. He was struggling to control a rage that was threatening to burst out of his face. 'Let me tell you something, Stone. Things are changing in my department. A new permanent cadre is being installed, and soon all the dead wood will be cleared away. People like you will cease to exist.' He was shaking with anger. He knew I had him by the bollocks, for now. He stood up abruptly, and stormed from the room. Sundance shot me a threatening glare and followed him.

I tried to listen to the mumbling going on in the garage, but with no luck. A few seconds later car doors slammed, the shutter went up, and the car reversed out. The shutter hit the floor once more, and then Trainers and Sundance reappeared.

The first kick was aimed at my chest. My body reflexed into a ball but Sundance's boot connected hard with my thigh. By now my chin was down, my teeth were clenched, and I'd closed my eyes. There was nothing I could do but accept the inevitable, curled up like a hedgehog, my hands still cuffed, trying to protect my face.

They grabbed my feet and dragged me to the centre of the room. I kept my legs as bent as I could, fighting against them being stretched out to expose my stomach and bollocks. I opened one eye in time to watch a Caterpillar boot connect with my ribs. I brought my head down further to cover my chest, and another boot swung into my arse. The pain was off the scale and to counteract it I tried to clench my cheek muscles together—but to do that I had to straighten my legs a little.

The boot flew into the pit of my stomach. Bile exploded from me, the acid taste in my mouth and nose almost worse than the kicking.

IT WAS PAST MIDNIGHT and I was curled up back in my corner. At least they'd taken the cuffs off now. The lights were off and the TV flickered away. They'd had pie and chips earlier and made me crawl over to wipe up my bile from the floor with the used paper.

Sundance lay asleep on the settee. Trainers was awake, draped across an armchair, making sure I didn't have any stupid ideas.

I stretched out flat on my stomach to lessen the pain from the kicking, and rested my face on my hands, closing my eyes to try to get some sleep. It was never going to work: I couldn't stop thinking about what might happen to me next. My Beachy Head trip could still be on the cards with these two; it all depended on the Yes Man.

I thought of Kelly. I hadn't spoken to her since this job started. Not because there had been no opportunity—I had agreed timings with Josh last month—it was just that I was too busy with preparations, or sometimes I just forgot.

Josh was right to tell me off when I did get through: she did need a routine and stability. I could see his half-Mexican, half-black shaved head, scowling at me on the phone like a divorced wife.

Apart from Kelly, Josh was the only living person I cared for. Would he miss me, or just be pissed off that we had unfinished business? And what about Kelly herself? She had a new start now. Would she forget about her useless, incompetent guardian in a few years?

THREE

Monday, September 4, 2000

Sundance's StarTac's short, sharp tones cut the air after a long, painful night. He opened up his phone. He knew who it was. There was no preliminary waffle, just nods and grunts.

Trainers hit the kettle button as the StarTac was closed down and Sundance rolled himself off the settee. He gave me a big grin. 'You have a visitor, and d'ye know what? He doesn't sound too pleased.'

I sat up and leaned into the corner of the brick walls. It wasn't long before I heard a vehicle and Trainers went out to open the shutter.

The slamming of car doors drowned out the sound of Kennington's morning commute. Before the shutter had come down, the Yes Man was striding into the room, dressed in a light grey suit.

He was still in enraged-teacher mode. He stopped a couple of paces short of me, put his hands on his hips, and looked down at me in disgust. 'You, Stone, are going to be given one chance to rectify matters. You don't know how lucky you are.' He checked his watch. 'The target has just left the UK. You will follow him tonight, to Panama, and you will kill him by last light Friday. Are you listening?'

Nodding slowly, I rubbed my sore eyes.

'FARC are waiting for the delivery of a missile launch control system—a computer guidance console. One antiaircraft missile is already in their possession. It will be the first of many. If FARC have a complete weapons system in their hands the implications for Plan Colombia will be catastrophic. There are six hundred million dollars' worth of US helicopters in Colombia, with crews and support. FARC must not get the capability to shoot them down. They must not get that launch control system. You don't need to know why, but the young man's death will stop that happening.'

He hunched down and thrust his face close to mine. 'You will carry out this task in the time specified. If not? We will kill her. You know who I'm talking about, that Little Orphan Annie of yours. She must be about eleven now, eh? I've been told that she's settled in very well back in the States. It seems that Joshua is doing an absolutely sterling job. It must be hard for you now, eh? Missing her growing up, turning into a fine young woman . . .' His knees cracked as he straightened up and hovered above me once more.

'Why kill the boy?' I said. 'Why not the father? I presume he's the one moving this system.'

He kicked my thigh with his shiny toecap. It was pure frustration. 'Clean yourself up—look at the state of you. Now go. These gentlemen will collect you from your . . . residence . . . at three.'

I hauled myself to my feet, the muscles in my stomach protesting badly. 'I need money.' I looked down as I leaned against the wall.

The Yes Man sighed with impatience and nodded at Sundance.

The Jock dug out his wallet from the back of his jeans, and counted out eighty-five pounds. 'You owe me, boy.'

I took it, not bothering to mention the US $600 he'd already liberated from my pocket. Jamming the notes into my jeans, I walked to the door. Trainers hit the shutter, but not before the Yes Man had the last word.

'You'd better make good use of that money, Stone. There is no more. Think yourself lucky you're keeping what you already have.'

FIFTEEN MINUTES LATER I was on the tube from Kennington, heading north towards Camden Town. The front pages of the morning papers were covered with dramatic pictures of the police attacking the sniper positions. I just held on to the handrail, trying to get my head round what had happened, and getting nowhere.

What could I do with Kelly? Nip over to Maryland, pick her up, run away and hide in the woods? Taking her away from Josh would screw her up even more than she was already. In any event, it would only be short-term. If the Firm wanted her dead, they'd make it happen eventually. What about telling Josh? No need: the Firm wouldn't do anything unless I failed.

I didn't know if the Yes Man was bluffing—any more, probably, than he knew if I was. But it made no difference. Even if I did expose the job, that wouldn't stop Sundance and Trainers taking their trip to Maryland. No matter which way I looked at it, my only option was to kill the boy. No, not a boy, let's get this right: just as the Yes Man said, he was a young man.

I should have killed him yesterday when I'd had the chance. If I didn't do this job, Kelly would die, simple as that. So I'd go to Panama and do what the Yes Man wanted, by last light Friday.

Kelly had been living with Josh and his kids since mid-August, just a couple of weeks after her therapy sessions had ended prematurely when the Yes Man handed me the sniper job. She hadn't fully recovered from her post-traumatic stress disorder; I didn't know whether she ever would. Seeing your whole family murdered took some recovering from. But she was a fighter, just like her dad had been, and had made some dramatic strides this summer.

Since March I'd had to commit myself to being with her during the therapy sessions three times a week in Chelsea, and on all the other days had visited her at the private care home in Hampstead where she was being looked after. Kelly and I would tube it down to the plush clinic, the Moorings.

Dr Hughes was in her fifties and looked more like a newsreader than a shrink. When Kelly said something that Hughes considered meaningful, she would tilt her elegant head and look at me over the top of her gold half-moons. 'How do you feel about that, Nick?'

My answer was always: 'We're here for Kelly, not me.' That was because I was an emotional dwarf. I must be—Josh told me so.

The train shuddered to a halt at Camden Town. I rode the up escalator, crossed the road to Superdrug for some washing and shaving kit, then walked along Camden High Street to get something to eat.

The caff was full of construction workers. I put in my order and settled down at a table. For some reason I remembered being seven years old, afraid of the dark, petrified that the night monster would come out from under the bed and eat me. The same feeling of terror and helplessness was with me again, after all these years.

I was jolted from my trance. 'Set breakfast, extra egg?'

'That's me.'

I sat back and threw coffee, bacon, sausage and egg down my neck and started to think about my shopping list. I wouldn't need much clothing for my Central American trip. There now, maybe things weren't that bad: at least I was going somewhere warm.

I'd never been to Panama, but had operated on its Colombian border against the Revolutionary Armed Forces of Colombia—FARC—while in the Regiment in the eighties. We were part of an American-funded operation to hit drug manufacture at source, which meant getting into the jungle for weeks on end, finding the drug-manufacturing plants and destroying them. FARC had their fingers in a substantial amount of the drug-trafficking pie.

Now Plan Colombia was getting into full swing. Clinton had given the Colombian government a $1.3 billion military aid package to combat drug trafficking, including over sixty of the Yes Man's precious Huey and Black Hawk helicopters.

I knew that, for most of the twentieth century, the USA had paid for, run and protected the Panama Canal and stationed the US army's Southern Command, SOUTHCOM, in-country. Thousands of US troops and aircraft stationed in Panama had been responsible for all the anti-drug operations in Central and South America, but that had stopped at midnight on December 31, 1999, when the US handed back control of the canal to the locals, and SOUTHCOM and all American presence was withdrawn.

From what I'd read, when the American public discovered that a Chinese company, not American, had been awarded the contract to operate the ports at each end of the canal and take over some of the old US military facilities, the right wing went apeshit. I hadn't thought of it at the time, but maybe that was why the Chinaman had been in the delegation, as part of the new order in Central America.

I felt a little better after some death-by-cholesterol, and left the caff. A fifteen-minute shopping frenzy in the market bought me a new pair of rip-off Levi's for sixteen quid, a blue sweatshirt for seven, a pair of boxers and three pairs of socks for another five. I carried on to Arlington Road, and turned right by the Good Mixer pub. I was just a few minutes away from a hot shower. A hundred yards ahead was my impressive Victorian redbrick residence.

Walking past the graffiti-filled walls of the decaying buildings, I approached the front entrance. Two worn stone steps took me to a set of glazed wooden doors, which I pushed my way through. I buzzed to be let through the second lot of security doors, pressing my head to the glass so whoever was on duty could check me out.

The door buzzed and I pushed through. I got a smile off Maureen at reception, a huge, fifty-year-old woman who looked me up and down with an arched eyebrow. 'Hello, darling, what you doing here?'

I put on my happy face. 'I missed you.'

She gave her usual loud bass laugh. 'Yeah, right.'

'Any chance of using a shower? The plumbing in my new place has gone on the blink.' I held up my bag of washing kit for her to see.

She rolled her eyes at my story and sucked her teeth, not believing a word of it. 'Ten minutes, don't tell.'

'Maureen, you're the best.'

'Tell me something I don't know, darling.'

I walked up to the second floor, where the decor was easy-clean, thick-gloss walls and a grey industrial-lino staircase, then walked along the corridor, heading for the showers. To my left were rows of doors to bedrooms, and I could hear their occupants mumbling to themselves, coughing, snoring. The corridor smelt of beer and cigarettes, with dog-ends trodden into the threadbare carpet.

The council-run 'hostel' was what we used to call a dosshouse when we were kids. Nowadays it was filled not only with homeless men of every age, but also Bosnian, Serbian and Kosovan refugees.

The showers were three stained cubicles and I got into one, peeling off my clothes. Once undressed, I pulled out the washing and shaving kit, turned on the water and got to work. After I'd cleaned myself up I used my old clothes to dry myself. I threw on my new jeans and sweatshirt; the only old things I put back on were my Timberlands, bomber jacket and belt. I left everything else in the shower.

I walked back along the corridor, passing the closed door to my old cell-like room. I'd only left the previous Saturday but it already had a new occupant; I could hear a radio.

I made my way down the stairs. In the reception area, I picked up the wall-mounted phone, shoved in six quids' worth of coins, and started dialling Josh, trying desperately to think of an excuse for calling him so early. The East Coast of the US was five hours behind.

The distinctive tone rang just twice before I heard a sleepy American grunt. 'Yeah?'

'Josh, it's me, Nick.'

'What do you want, Nick? It's just after six.'

'I know, I'm sorry, mate. It's just that I can't make it until next Tuesday and I—'

There was a loud sigh. He'd heard my I-can't-make-it routine so many times before. Then the earpiece barked: 'Why can't you get your life in good order? We arranged this Tuesday—that's tomorrow, man. She's got her heart set on it. She loves you so much, man, so much—don't you get it? You can't just breeze in and—'

I cut in, almost begging, 'I know, I know. I'm sorry . . .' I knew where the conversation was going and also knew that he was right in taking it there. 'Please, Josh—can I talk with her?'

He lost his cool for once and went ballistic. 'No!'

'I—'

It was too late; he'd hung up.

ON THE DOT of 3.00pm the Merc cruised past and found a space further down the road. Trainers was at the wheel, Sundance next to him. I unstuck my arse from the steps where I'd been slouching, and dragged myself towards them. They gave me no acknowledgment as I got into the back.

Sundance threw a brown envelope at me as we drove off. 'I've already taken five hundred out of the account, so don't bother trying again today. That covers the eighty-five sub—plus interest.'

They grinned at each other. The job had its compensations.

My new passport and credit card were hot off the press but looking suitably aged, along with my new PIN number and open-return air ticket, leaving Miami to Panama City, 7.05am tomorrow.

I flicked through my visas so I knew that I'd been on holiday for two weeks in Morocco in July. I had been there, just not as recently. But at least it meant I could bluff my way through a routine check at immigration and customs. The rest of my cover story would be the same as ever, just travelling after a boring life selling insurance; I had done most of Europe, now I wanted to see the rest of the world.

I wasn't impressed by my cover name. Hoff. It didn't sound right. Nick Hoff. It would be difficult not to get hesitant when signing it.

Sundance didn't ask for a signature, which bothered me. I got pissed off with bullshit when it was official, but even more so when it wasn't.

'What about my CA?' I asked. 'Can I call them?'

Sundance didn't bother to look round. 'It's already done.' He dipped into his jeans and brought out a scrap of paper. 'The mini-roundabout has been built at last, but everyone is still waiting on the decision about the bypass. That comes through next month.'

I nodded; it was an update on the local news from what the Yes Man had renamed the Cover Address. James and Rosemary had loved me like a son since I boarded with them years ago, or so the cover story went. I even had a bedroom there, and some clothes in the wardrobe. These were the people who would both confirm my cover story and be part of it. They'd never take action on my behalf, but would back me up if I needed them to. 'That's where I live,' I could tell whoever was questioning me. 'Phone them, ask them.'

I visited James and Rosemary whenever I could, so my cover had got stronger as time passed. They knew nothing about the ops and didn't want to; we would just talk about what was going on at the social club, and a bit of other local and personal stuff. I needed to know these things because I would do if I lived there all the time.

Sundance started to tell me how I was going to make it to Miami in time for my flight to Panama. Within four hours I'd be lying in a sleeping-bag on top of some crates of military kit stuffed into an RAF Tristar, leaving RAF Brize Norton, near Oxford, for Fort Campbell in Kentucky, where a Jock infantry battalion was having a joint exercise with the 101st Airborne Division. There were no commercial flights this time of day that would get me where I needed to be by tomorrow morning; this was the only way. I was getting kicked off in Florida, and a US visa waiver would be stamped in my passport at the Marine base. I then had three hours in which to transfer to Miami Airport and make the flight to Panama.

'Once you get there you are being sponsored by two doctors.'

Sundance glanced at his notes again. 'Carrie and Aaron Yanklewitz. There will be no contact with Mr Frampton or anyone here. Everything to, or from, is via their handler. They'll be at the airport with a name card and a pass number of thirteen. You got that?'

I nodded, not bothering to look at him.

'They'll show you the wee boy's house, and should have all the imagery by the time you get there. They don't know what your job is. But we do, don't we, boy? You're going to finish what you were paid to do. And it's going to be done by Friday, last light. Do you understand, Stone? Kill the boy.'

As we joined the A40 out of London and headed for Brize, I tried to focus on the job. Easier said than done. I was penniless. I'd sold the Ducati, the house in Norfolk, the furniture, everything apart from what I could shove into a sports bag, to pay for Kelly's treatment. Twenty-four-hour private care in Hampstead and regular trips to the Moorings had cleaned me out.

The A40 opened up into motorway and Sundance decided it was time for a bit of a performance.

'You know what?' He looked over at Trainers.

Trainers swung into the outside lane. 'What's that, then?'

'I wouldn't mind a trip to Maryland. We could go to Washington and do the sights first. I hear Laurel . . .' Sundance turned to face me. 'That's where she lives now, isn't it?'

I didn't answer. He knew very well it was. Sundance turned back to face the road. 'I hear it's very picturesque there—you know, trees and grass and all that. Anyway, after we finished up there in Laurel, you could take me to see that half-sister of yours in New York . . .'

'No way you're getting near her!'

I had a terrible feeling in the pit of my stomach and had to breathe out quickly as I thought about what might happen if I didn't get the job done. But I was damned if I was going to play their game. Besides, I was just too tired to react.

JUST OVER AN HOUR later the Merc pulled up outside the air movement centre at Brize, and Trainers got out to organise the next stage of my life. He came back with a nervous-looking RAF corporal. He was told to wait short of the car as Trainers came and opened the rear kerbside door. I climbed out and nodded a greeting to the corporal.

We'd only gone a few paces when Sundance called to me. I went back and poked my head through the rear door, which Trainers had kept open. 'I forgot to ask, how is that wain of yours? I hear you two were going to the fruit farm before she left. Little soft in the head as well, is she?' He grinned. 'Maybe if you mess up it'd be a good thing for the wee one—you know, we'd be doing her a favour.'

I couldn't hold it any longer. I launched myself forward and gripped his head with both hands. In one movement I put my head down and pulled his face hard towards the top of my crown. I made contact and it hurt, making me dizzy.

Once outside I looked in at Sundance. He was sunk into the seat, hands covering his nose, blood running between his fingers. I started towards the RAF corporal, feeling a lot better.

Trainers looked as if he was trying to decide whether to drop me or not. He still hadn't made up his mind as I virtually pushed the frightened corporal into the building with me.

FOUR

Tuesday, September 5

We had just hit cruising altitude on the four-and-a-bit-hour flight from Miami to Panama City, scheduled to land at 11.40am local. My window seat was next to a Latino woman with big hair.

I read the tourist-guide pages in the in-flight magazine. I found them invaluable for getting an idea of wherever I was going on fast-balls like this. I'd tried to buy a guidebook to Panama in Miami Airport, but it seemed there wasn't much call for that sort of thing.

The magazine showed wonderful pictures of exotic birds and smiling Indian children in canoes, and stuff I already knew but wouldn't have been able to put so eloquently. 'Panama is the most southern of the Central American countries, making the long, narrow country the umbilical cord joining South and Central America. It is in the shape of an S bordered on the west by Costa Rica, on the east by Colombia, and has roughly the same landmass as Ireland.' It said that most people thought that Panama's land boundaries were north and south. That was wrong: the country runs west to east. Facts like that were important to me if I had to leave in a hurry.

The three pages of bumph and pictures went on to tell me that Panama was best known internationally for its canal, joining the Caribbean and the Pacific, and its 'vibrant banking services'. Not surprisingly, it didn't say anything about Operation Just Cause—the US invasion in 1989 to oust General Noriega, or the drug trafficking that makes the banking system so vibrant.

Looking down at the endless blue of the Caribbean Sea, I thought about Kelly. Josh was right. She did need stability. That was precisely why she was there with him, and the not-calling-when-I-should, calling-when-I-shouldn't thing wasn't helping her at all.

I should have been there today to sign over my guardianship of Kelly completely to him, to change the present arrangement of joint responsibility. In her father's will, Josh and I had both been named as guardians, but I was the one who'd landed up with her. I couldn't even remember how that had come about, it just sort of had.

Food was being served and mine turned up in its prepacked tray. I peeled back the foil to see a breakfast of pasta. As I threw it down my neck, I thought about the job and the information Sundance had given me. The pass number for the meet with the Yanklewitzes was thirteen. Pass numbers are good for people who aren't trained in tradecraft or who, like me, are crap at remembering confirmation statements. These people could be either. I didn't know if they were experienced operators or just contacts helping me out with bed and breakfast.

I didn't like anyone else being involved in anything I did, but this time I had no choice. I didn't know where the target lived or the target's routine, and I didn't have a whole lot of time to find out.

THE FLIGHT TOUCHED DOWN early, at eleven thirty local time. One of the first off, I followed the signs for baggage reclaim and customs.

After four hours of air conditioning, the heat hit me like a wall. In my hand were the two forms we'd been given to fill in on the aircraft, one for immigration, one for customs. Mine said that Nick Hoff was staying at the Marriott—there is always a Marriott.

Apart from the clothes I stood up in—jeans, sweatshirt and bomber jacket—the only items I had with me were my passport and wallet containing $500. It had come from an ATM in Miami departures, courtesy of my new Royal Bank of Scotland Visa card in my crap cover name. But passing through immigration turned out to be a breeze, even without any luggage. I also shot through customs. I should really have bought a piece of hand luggage in Miami to look normal, but my head must have been elsewhere. Not that it mattered; the Panamanian customs boys were obviously in the same place.

I headed towards the exit, fitting my new Leatherman tool kit onto my belt. I'd bought it in Miami and airport security had taken it off me and packed it into a Jiffy bag in case I tried to use it to hijack the plane. I'd collected it from the luggage service desk when we landed.

The small arrivals area was hosting the noise-and-crush Olympics. Steel barriers funnelled me deeper into the hall. At last, among the surge of people, I spotted a square foot of white card with the name YANKLEWITZ in marker pen. The man holding it was slim, about my height, maybe five ten, and probably in his mid-fifties. He was dressed in khaki shorts and a matching photographer's waistcoat over a faded blue T-shirt. His long salt-and-pepper hair was tied back in a ponytail, away from a tanned face that had a few days' silver growth. His face looked worn: life had obviously been chewing on it.

I walked straight past him to the end of the barrier, wanting to tune in to the place first, and watch this man for a while before I gave myself over to him. I carried on towards the glass wall and sliding exit doors. I leaned against the glass and watched my contact getting pushed and shoved in the melee.

Now and again I caught sight of his tanned, muscular legs. The soles of his feet were covered by old leather Jesus sandals. He looked more like a farm hand or hippie throwback than any kind of doctor.

The heat was getting to me. I took off my jacket and leaned back against the glass. Sitting on a bench was the only person here who wasn't sweating. A thirtysomething white woman, she looked like GI Jane, with short hair, green fatigue cargos and a baggy grey high-necked vest. She had sunglasses on and her hands were wrapped round a can of Pepsi.

After about a quarter of an hour the crowd started thinning. Aaron was standing with the remaining few people still waiting at the barrier. I had one last check around the hall for anything unusual, then I started my approach.

I must have been about three steps away from his back as he thrust his card under the nose of an American business suit pulling his bag on wheels behind him. 'Mr Yanklewitz?' I called.

He spun round, holding the card against his chest. He had blood-shot but very blue eyes, sunk into deep crow's-feet.

I was supposed to let him initiate conversation with a story that involved a number, something like, 'Oh, I hear you have ten bags with you?' to which I would say, 'No, I have three.' But I couldn't be bothered: I was hot and tired, and I wanted to get on.

'Seven.'

'Oh, that would make me six, I guess.' He sounded disappointed.

I smiled. There was an expectant pause: I was waiting for him to tell me what to do next.

'Er, OK, shall we go, then?' His accent was soft, educated American. 'Unless of course you want to—'

'I don't want to do anything, apart from go with you.'

'OK. Please, this way.' He started towards the exit and I fell into step on his left. He folded the card as he went, moving faster than I'd have liked. I didn't want us looking unnatural, but then what was I worrying about in this madhouse?

On the other side of the exit doors was the service road for drop-offs and pick-ups. Beyond that was the car park, and in the distance were lush green mountains. Out there was virgin ground to me, and I never liked entering the unknown without having a look first.

'Where are we going?'

'That kinda depends on, er . . . my wife is—'

'That's Carrie, right?'

'Yes, Carrie.'

I'd forgotten to introduce myself. 'Do you know my name?'

He turned towards me, his blue eyes focused slightly to one side of mine. 'No, but if you don't want to tell me, that's fine. Whatever you feel safe with, whatever is best for you.' He didn't look scared, but was definitely ill at ease.

I stopped and held out my hand. 'Nick.' Better to be friendly to the help rather than alienate them: you get better results that way.

There was an embarrassed smile from him, displaying teeth discoloured by coffee or tobacco. He held out his hand. 'Aaron. Pleased to meet you, Nick.'

It was a large hand with hard skin, but the handshake was gentle. Small scars covered its surface; he was no pen-pusher. His nails were dirty and jagged, and there was a dull gold wedding band.

'Well, Aaron, as you can see, I haven't packed for a long stay. I'll just get my job done and be out of the way by Friday. I'll try not to be a pain in the arse while I'm here.'

'Hey, no problem. You did kinda throw me, you know. I wasn't expecting an English guy.'

I smiled. 'I was expecting to see Carrie as well.'

He pointed behind me. 'She's right here.'

I turned to see GI Jane approaching us. She greeted me with a smile and an out-thrust hand. 'Hi, I'm Carrie.'

Her hair was jet black, cut into the nape of her neck. She was maybe mid- to late thirties, just a few years younger than me. Her skin was only lightly tanned, not dark and leathery like Aaron's.

I shook her firm hand. 'I'm Nick. Finished your Pepsi, then?'

'Sure, it was good.' Her manner was brisk, sort of aggressive, and wouldn't have been out of place on Wall Street.

She stood by Aaron and they certainly made an unusual pair. He had a slight pot-belly and showed his age; she had a body that was well toned and looked after.

Carrie shrugged. 'What happens now?'

They were waiting for instructions.

'You haven't done this before, have you?'

Aaron shook his head. 'First time. All we know is that we pick you up and you tell us the rest.'

'OK—do you have any imagery yet?'

She nodded. 'It's satellite, I pulled it off the Web last night. It's at the house.'

'How far away is that?'

'If the rain holds off, four hours maybe. We're talking boondocks.'

'How far to the other guy's house?'

'An hour thirty from here, maybe two. It's the other side of the city—it's in the boonies, too.'

'I'd like to see his place first, then back to yours.' There wasn't enough time to spend maybe ten hours on the road, or even prepare myself for a day under the canopy. I'd have to get on and do the close target recce of the house first, since it was so close, and then, on the way back to their place, get planning what I was going to do next, and how.

She nodded, turning to Aaron. 'You know what? I'll go pick up Luce from the dentist and meet you two at home.'

There was a pause as if she expected me to pick up on what she'd said. But I didn't care that much who Luce was. It wasn't important at the moment, and I was sure to be told soon anyway.

We headed outside and into the oppressive heat. She walked the other side of Aaron. The sunshine felt as if I had a searchlight pointed straight into my eyes. I squinted like a mole.

Aaron pulled a pair of sunglasses from a pocket of his waistcoat and put them on as he pointed to our half right. 'We're over here.'

We crossed the road to what might have been a parking lot in any US shopping mall. Japanese and American SUVs were lined up alongside saloons and people-carriers, and none looked more than two years old. It surprised me: I'd been expecting worse.

Carrie broke away from us and headed towards the other side of the car park. 'See you both later.'

I nodded goodbye. Aaron didn't say a word, just nodded with me.

The ground was wet with rain and sunlight glinted off the tarmac. My eyes were still half closed when we reached a blue, rusty, mud-covered Mazda pick-up.

'This is us.'

This was more what I'd been expecting. It had a double cab, with an old Fibreglass cover over the rear that turned it into a van. Aaron was already inside, leaning over to open my door.

It was like climbing into an oven. I was just pleased that there was an old blanket draped over the seats to protect us from the almost molten PVC upholstery.

'Will you excuse me, Nick? I need a moment. Won't be long.'

I kept my door open, trying to let some air in, as he closed his and disappeared behind the Mazda.

I caught four Aarons and Carries in the broken wing mirror, and standing next to her, four wagons. It was also a pick-up, but a much older style than the Mazda, maybe an old Chevy, with a rounded bonnet and wings and a flat-bed that had wooden slats up the sides. They were arguing as they stood by the opened driver's door. She waved her hands in the air and Aaron kept shaking his head at her.

A minute or two later he jumped into the cab. 'Sorry about that, Nick, just some things I needed from the store.'

By the way she'd reacted they must have been expensive. I nodded as if I hadn't seen a thing. We closed our doors and he started up.

Having kept my window shut to help the air conditioner spark up, I saw Aaron winding his down as he manoeuvred out of the parking space. Glancing at my closed window he said, 'Sorry, no air.'

I wound it down and then lowered the sun visor as we drove out of the airport and along a dual carriageway. The exhaust rattled under the wagon as we picked up speed, and the open windows made no difference to the heat.

Less than two minutes later we had to stop at a tolbooth and Aaron handed over a US dollar bill to the operator. 'It's the currency here,' he told me. 'It's called a balboa.'

I nodded as the road became a newly laid dual carriageway. The sunlight rebounded off the light grey concrete, giving me a headache.

Aaron could see my problem and rummaged in his door pocket. 'Here, Nick, want these?'

The sunglasses must have been Carrie's, with large oval lenses that Jackie Onassis would have been proud of. They covered half my face.

The jungle was soon trying to reclaim the land back from the pampas grass either side of the carriageway, at least on the areas that weren't covered with breeze block and tin shacks.

I decided to warm him up before I asked the important ones. 'How long have you lived here?'

'Always have. I'm a Zonian. I was born here in the Zone, the US Canal Zone. It's a ten-mile-wide strip that used to bracket the whole length of the canal. The US controlled the Zone from the early 1900s, you know.' There was pride in his voice.

'I didn't know that.' I thought the US just used to have bases there, not jurisdiction over a whole chunk of the country.

'My father was a canal pilot. Before him, my grandfather started as a tug captain and made it to tonnage surveyor—you know, assessing the ships' weights to determine their tolls. The Zone is home.'

'But you're an American, right?'

He gave a gentle laugh at my ignorance. 'My grandfather was born in Minneapolis, but my father was also born here, in the Zone. The US have always been here, working for the canal authority or in the military. Southern Command had up to sixty-five thousand troops stationed here. But now, of course, everything's gone.'

The scenery was still very green, but now mostly grass. Much of the land had been cleared. When the trees did come, they were the same size as European ones, not like the 100-foot-tall buttress trees I'd seen in primary jungle further south in Colombia. This low canopy of leaf and palm created secondary jungle conditions because sunlight could penetrate so vegetation could grow between the tree trunks. Tall grass, large palms and creeping vines of all descriptions were trying their best to catch the rays.

'I read about that. It must be quite a shock after all those years.'

Aaron nodded as he watched the road. 'Yes, sir, growing up here was just like small-town USA,' he enthused, 'apart from no air in the house—there wasn't enough juice on the grid in those days. But it didn't matter. I'd come home from school and wham! I'm right into the forest. Building forts, fishing for tarpon. We'd play basketball, baseball, just like up north. Everything we needed was in the Zone.' A smile of fondness for the good old days played across his face. 'I went north, to California, for my university years, came back with my degree to lecture at the university. That's where I met Carrie.'

'What do you teach?'

'Plant biodiversity, forestry conservation, that sort of thing.' He looked past me at the distant grass-covered mountains. 'Panama is still one of the richest ecological regions on earth, a mother lode of biodiversity . . . But you know what, Nick, we're losing it . . .'

Ahead, I began to make out a high-rise skyline that looked like a mini-Manhattan—something else I hadn't been expecting.

'Does Carrie lecture too?'

'No, we have a small research deal from the university. That's why I still have to lecture.' He wanted to get off the subject. 'You heard of FARC? The Fuerzas Armadas Revolucionarias Colombianas?'

I nodded. 'I hear they're crossing into Panama quite a lot now, with SOUTHCOM gone.'

'Sure are. These are worrying times. It's not just the ecological problems. Panama couldn't handle FARC if they came in force. They're too strong.' There was a pause. Something was bugging him. 'Nick, I want you to know, I'm not a spy, I'm not a revolutionary. I'm just a guy who wants to work and live here peacefully. That's all.'

FIVE

I nodded. 'Like I said, I'll be out of here by Friday and try not to be a major pain in the arse.' It was somehow good to know that someone else was unhappy with the situation.

We hit a wide, tree-lined boulevard, then passed through mini-Manhattan—a trendy area with Japanese restaurants, designer clothes shops and a Porsche showroom—and hit the coastline, following the sweep of the bay.

We stopped to let a line of schoolkids cross the road. The girls were all in white dresses, the boys in blue shorts and white shirts.

Aaron grinned as he watched them. 'You have kids, Nick?'

'No.' I shook my head. I didn't want to get into that sort of conversation. The less he knew about me the better. A proper operator wouldn't have asked, and it was strange being with someone who didn't know the score.

'Oh. We have a girl, Luce. She'll be fifteen this November.'

'Oh, nice.' I hoped he wasn't going to get photos out of his wallet.

We fought our way through the traffic along the boulevard. To the right was a run of Spanish colonial-type buildings, all flying the red, white and blue squares and stars of the Panamanian flag. Laid out between them were public parks with statues of sixteenth-century Spaniards pointing their swords heroically towards the sea.

Soon we were passing the equally impressive American and British embassies. Inside each compound, the Stars and Stripes and Union Jack fluttered above the trees and high perimeter railings.

It's always good to check on where your embassy is, to know where to run to if the wheels fall off. Ambassadors don't take too kindly to deniable operators begging for help. I'd have to jump the fence; they wouldn't let people like me in through the front door. But once I was inside, it would take more than the security to get me back onto the street.

We reached the end of the bay and what was obviously the rougher side of town. The buildings were flat-roofed, decaying tenement blocks, their once multicoloured façades bleached out by the sun.

We passed through a street market. 'This is El Chorrillo. Remember Just Cause—you know, the invasion?'

I nodded.

'Well, this was ground zero when they—we—attacked the city. Noriega had his command centre here. It was bombed flat.'

Very soon we were out of the slums and moved into upscale residential. One house we passed was still under construction and the drills were going for it big-time. All the power was coming from a generator that belonged to the US army. I knew that because the camouflage pattern and the US ARMY stencilling told me so.

'See that?' Aaron pointed at the generator. 'When SOUTHCOM couldn't clear out the five remaining bases by the December deadline, they decided to abandon items valued at less than a thousand dollars. To make life easier, nearly everything was valued at nine hundred and ninety-nine bucks. It was supposed to have been given to good causes, but everything was just marked up and sold on, vehicles, furniture, you name it.'

Rising into the sky ahead, and looking like three towering metal Hs, were the stacks of container cranes. 'Balboa docks,' he said.

'They're at the entrance to the canal. We'll be in the Zone'—he corrected himself—'the old Canal Zone, real soon.'

Soon afterwards we hit a good-quality, grey concrete road that bent right round an airfield full of light aircraft and private and commercial helicopters. 'That used to be US Air Force Albrook.' We passed a series of boarded-up barrack blocks, four floors high.

As soon as we cleared the air base, we hit another row of tolbooths, paid our few cents and moved through.

'Welcome to the Zone. This road parallels the canal, which is about a quarter of a mile that way.' He pointed over to our left and it was as if we'd just driven into a South Florida subdivision, with American-style bungalows and houses, rows of telephone booths, traffic lights and road signs in English. A deserted high school on the right looked like something straight out of an American TV show. Beside it squatted a massive white dome for all-weather sports. A golf course further up the road was advertised in English and Spanish. Aaron pointed. 'Used to be the officers' club.'

We were most definitely where the other half lived.

'How long till we get to the house?'

'Maybe another forty, fifty minutes.'

It was time to talk shop. 'Do you have any idea why I'm here?'

Aaron shrugged and used his gentle voice that was hard to hear above the wind. 'We only got told last night you were coming. We're to help you in any way we can and show you where Charlie lives.'

'Charlie?'

'Charlie Chan—you know, the guy from that old black and white movie. That's not his real name, of course, just what people call him here. Not to his face, God forbid. His real name is Oscar Choi.'

'What do you know about him?' I asked.

'He's really well known here. He's a very generous guy, plays the all-round good citizen thing—patron of the arts, that kind of stuff. In fact, he funds the degree course I get to lecture on.'

This wasn't sounding much like a teenager. 'How old is he?'

'Maybe a bit younger than me. Say early fifties.'

I started to get a little worried. 'Does he have a family?'

'Yeah, four sons and a daughter, I think.'

'How old are they?'

'I don't know about the older ones, but I know the youngest son has just started university. Chose a good course—environmental stuff is cool right now. I think the others work for him downtown.'

Aaron obviously had views on the Chinaman. 'It's strange that men like him spend all their lives slashing, burning, pillaging to get what they want. Then, once they've amassed all their wealth, they try to preserve everything they used to try to destroy, but underneath never change. Very Viking, don't you think, Nick?'

'What is he, a politician?'

'Nope, doesn't need to be, he owns most of them. His family has been here since the labourers started digging the canal in 1904, selling opium to keep the workers happy. He has his fingers in every pie, from construction to "import and export".' Aaron lifted two fingers to give the quote sign. 'You know, keeping up the family tradition—cocaine, heroin, even supplying arms to FARC or anyone else who has the money. He's one of the very few who are happy about the US stand-down. Business is so much easier to conduct now we've gone. It's a well-known story round here that he crucified sixteen men in Colombia. They were trying to cut him out of a deal he'd made with them for moving coke. He had them nailed up in the town square.'

A chain-link fence line started to appear on the right.

'This is'—he corrected himself once more—'was Fort Clayton.'

The place was deserted. Through the fence was a line of impressive military buildings. As we drove further on, I could see the same accommodation blocks that were at USAF Albrook.

'Nick, do you mind if we stop for a Coke? I'm feeling pretty dry.'

'How far is it to Charlie's place?'

'Maybe another six, seven miles after the Coke stop. It's only a few minutes off the route.'

Sounded good to me: I was going to be having a long day.

We stayed on the main drag for maybe another half-mile before turning left onto a narrower road. Ahead of us in the distance, on the high ground, I could just make out the superstructure and high load of a container ship, looking bizarre as it cut the green skyline.

'That's where we're heading, the Miraflores Locks,' Aaron said. 'It's the only place round here to get a drink now—everyone moving along this road comes here; it's like a desert watering hole.'

As we reached the higher ground of the locks a scene unfolded that made me wonder if Clinton was about to visit. The place was packed with vehicles and people. A line of brightly coloured buses had brought an American-style marching band and baton twisters. Red tunics, white trousers and feathered hats were blowing into trombones and all sorts as the baton girls, squeezed into red leotards and white knee-high boots, whirled their chrome sticks and streamers.

'Uh-oh,' Aaron sighed, 'I thought it was going to be on Saturday.'

'What?'

'The *Ocaso*. It means sunset. It's a cruise liner, one of the biggest. Two thousand passengers plus. It's been coming through here for years, runs out of San Diego to the Caribbean.'

While trying to find a parking space, he checked out some posters stuck up along a chain-link fence. 'Yeah, it's this Saturday, the four hundredth and final transit. It's going to be a big deal. TV stations, politicians. This must be the dress rehearsal.'

I caught my first glimpse of the enormous concrete locks, just past the chain-link. Manoeuvring into the first lock was the ship, five storeys high and over 200 yards long, powered by its own engines but being guided by six stubby locomotives on rails, three each side. Six cables slung between the hull and the locos, four at the rear, the other two up front, helped guide it between the concrete walls.

Aaron sounded off with the tour-guide bit as he squeezed between two cars. 'Four per cent of the world's trade and fourteen of the US's passes through here. From the Bay of Panama here on the Pacific side up to the Caribbean, it only takes eight to ten hours. Without the canal you could spend two weeks sailing round Cape Horn.'

I was nodding with what I hoped was the required amount of awe when I saw where we'd be getting our Cokes. A truck-trailer had grown roots in the middle of the car park and become a café. White plastic chairs were scattered around tables shaded by multicoloured umbrellas. We found a space and got out. It was sweltering.

Aaron headed towards the side window to join the line of tourists and red tunics. 'I'll get us a couple of cold ones.'

I stood under one of the parasols and watched the ship inch into the lock. A four-tier grandstand was being erected on the grass facing the lock, supplementing the permanent one to the left of it, by the visitors' centre. Saturday was going to be very busy indeed.

The ship was nearly into the lock, with just a couple of feet to spare each side. Tourists watched from the permanent viewing platform, clicking away with their Nikons, as the band drifted onto the grass. Some of the girls practised their splits, professional smiles, and top and bottom wiggles as they got into ranks.

The only person at ground level who seemed not to be looking at the girls was a white man in a flowery pink Hawaiian shirt. He was leaning against a large, dark blue GMC Suburban, watching the ship as he smoked, using his free hand to wave the bottom of his shirt to circulate some air. His stomach had been badly burned, leaving a large scar the size of a pizza that looked like melted plastic.

Apart from the windscreen, all the windows had been blackened out with film. I could see it was a DIY job by a clear triangle in one of the rear door windows where the plastic had been ripped.

Then, as if he'd just realised he'd forgotten to lock his front door, he jumped into the wagon and drove out.

Aaron came back with four cans of Minute Maid. 'No Coke—they've been overrun today.'

We sat in the shade and watched the hydraulic rams slowly push the gates shut, and the water—27 million gallons of it, according to Aaron—flooded into the lock. The ship rose into the sky before us as the scaffolders downed tools and took seats for the girls' rehearsal.

Aaron was soon waffling on. 'The canal isn't just a big ditch cut through the country, like the Suez. It's a complicated piece of engineering. The Miraflores, and the other two sets further up, lift these ships eighty feet. Once up there, they sail on over the lake and get lowered again the other side. It's like a bridge over the isthmus.'

I nodded towards the lock. 'Bit of a tight fit, isn't it?'

He responded as if he'd designed the thing himself. 'No problem—they're all built to Panamax specifications. Shipyards have been keeping the size of the locks in mind for decades now.'

The vessel continued to rise like a skyscraper in front of me. Just then, the trumpets, drums and whistles started up as the band broke into a quick-tempo samba and the girls did their stuff.

Ten minutes later, when the water levels were equal, the front gate was opened and the process began all over again. It was like a giant staircase. The batons were still getting thrown into the air and the band were marching up and down the grass.

A black Lexus 4x4 with gold-mirrored side windows pulled up opposite the café. The windows slid down to reveal two shirt-and-tied white-eyes. The front-seat passenger, a muscular, well-tanned twentysomething, got out and went straight to the trailer window, ignoring the queue. One of the new small, chrome-effect Nokias glinted from his belt along with a weapon holstered on his right hip. I thought nothing of it—after all, this was Central America. I just tilted my head back to get the last of the drink down my neck.

A young American voice called out from the Lexus as the twentysomething went back with the drinks. 'Hey, Mr Y!'

Aaron's head jerked round, his face breaking into a smile. He waved. 'Hey, Michael, how are you? How was your break?'

I turned as well. My head was still back but I instantly recognised the grinning face leaning out of the rear passenger window.

Finishing the drink, I brought my head down as Aaron moved over to the car. This was not good, not good at all. I looked at the floor, pretending to relax, and tried to listen above the music.

The boy held out a hand for Aaron to shake, but his eyes were on the girls. 'I'm sorry, I can't get out of the car—my father says I have to stay in with Robert and Ross. I heard they'd be here today; thought I'd get a look at the pompom girls on the way home, know what I mean, Mr Y?'

The two bodyguards weren't distracted by the girls or the infectious Latin tempo. Their faces were impassive behind sunglasses as they drank from their cans. The engine was kept running, too.

Michael jabbered on with excitement, and something he said made Aaron arch an eyebrow. 'England?'

'Yes, I returned yesterday. There was a bomb. Some terrorists were killed. My father and I were close by, in the Houses of Parliament.'

Aaron showed his surprise as Michael pulled back the ring on his can. 'Hey, Nick, did you hear that?' He pointed me out to the target with a cock of his head. 'Nick—he's British.'

Shit, shit, Aaron—no!

Michael's eyes turned to me and he smiled, displaying perfect white teeth. The bodyguards also moved their heads casually to give me the once-over. This wasn't good.

I smiled and studied the target. He had short black shining hair, side parted, and his eyes and nose looked slightly European. His smooth unblemished skin was darker than most Chinese.

Aaron had realised what he had done and stammered, 'He kind of hitched a lift from me in the city to take a look at the locks—you know, and check out the chicks . . .'

Michael nodded, not really that fussed. I turned back to the ship, wanting to walk over and ram my can in Aaron's mouth.

After a minute or so of university stuff, Michael got a nod from the bodyguards and started to wind down the conversation. As he held out his hand again for a farewell he glanced once more at the leotards and pompoms. 'I have to go now. See you next week, Mr Y.'

'Sure.' Aaron gave him a high five. 'You get that project done?'

'I think you'll like it. Anyway, catch you later.' Out of politeness he nodded to me over Aaron's shoulder, then the Lexus moved off.

Aaron waved, then spun towards me, his face abject. 'Nick, I'm really sorry.' He shook his head. 'I just didn't think. I'm not really cut out for this kind of thing. That's Charlie's son—did I tell you he's on the course I teach? I'm sorry, I just didn't think.'

'It's OK, mate. No damage done.' I was lying. The last thing I needed was to be introduced to the target and, even worse, have the bodyguards knowing what I looked like. There was also the connection with Aaron. My heart was pounding. All in all, not a good day.

'Those guys with him—Robert and Ross? They're the ones who hung up those Colombians. They're Charlie's special guys.'

I swallowed the last of the juice and started to walk towards the trailer window. 'What about another drink while we wait for Michael to get home and settle down?'

We spent the next forty minutes killing time at the plastic table. Aaron took the opportunity to explain about the US stand-down the previous December.

In total, more than 400,000 acres of Canal Zone and bases, worth more than $10 billion, had been handed over—along with the canal itself, which had been built and paid for by the US to the tune of a further $30 billion. And the only way they could come back was under the terms of the DeConcini Reservation, which allowed for military intervention if the canal was endangered.

It was all interesting stuff, but what was more important to me was confirming that Michael would be at university this week.

'For sure.' Aaron nodded. 'They'll all be headed back. The semester started for most folks last week.'

We headed for the house, driving through Fort Clayton and into the mountains. The jungle closed in on both sides of the narrow, winding tarmac road. I could only see about five yards; after that everything blurred into a wall of green. This was secondary jungle; movement through it would be very, very difficult. I preferred primary, where the canopy is much higher and the sun finds it difficult to penetrate to ground level so there's less vegetation.

Grey clouds were covering the sky, making everything darker. I thought about all the months I'd spent living in jungles while on operations. You'd come out two stone lighter, your skin as white and clammy as an uncooked chip, but I really liked it. Tactically, it's a great environment to operate in. Everything you need is there: shelter, food, and, most importantly, water.

Aaron leaned forward and peered up through the windscreen. 'Here they are, look—right on time.' The grey clouds had disappeared, pushed out by blacker ones. I knew what that meant and, sure enough, the sky suddenly emptied on us. We hurriedly wound up our windows, but only about three-quarters of the way, because humidity was already misting up the inside of the windscreen. Aaron hit the demister, and its noise was drowned as the roof took a pounding.

Lightning cracked and sizzled, splashing the jungle with brilliant blue light. An almighty clap of thunder boomed above us.

I shouted at Aaron, above the drumming on the roof. 'Does this road go straight to Charlie's house?'

'No—this is a loop, just access to an electricity substation. The private road to the house leads off from it. I thought I could drop you off where the two join, otherwise I'd have nowhere to go.'

That seemed reasonable. 'How far to the house from the junction?'

'If the scale on the imagery is right, maybe a mile.'

The deluge continued as we crawled uphill. I leaned down and felt under my seat, trying to find something to protect my documents. I wasn't going to leave them with Aaron: they were going with me.

Aaron looked at me. 'What do you need?'

I explained.

'You'll find something in the back, for sure.'

We followed the road as it curved to the right, then Aaron moved over to the edge of the road and stopped. He pointed just ahead of us. 'That's the road that goes to the house. They say from up there Chan can see the sun rise over the Caribbean and set in the Pacific. What do you want me to do now?'

'First, just stay here and let me get into the back.'

I got out and put my jacket back on. Visibility was down to maybe twenty yards. I went to the rear of the wagon and opened the tailgate. I was soaked to the skin before I got halfway.

I rummaged around in the back. Four five-gallon US army jerry cans were fixed with bungees to the far end of the flat-bed, adjacent to the cab. At least we wouldn't run out of fuel. Scattered around them were a jack, a towrope and all the associated crap that would be needed for a wreck like this. I found what I was looking for: two plastic carrier bags, empty apart from a few bits of mud and leaves. I shook them out, tucked my passport, air ticket and wallet into the first and wrapped them up. I put that into the second, gave it a twist, and placed it in an inside pocket of my jacket. Slamming the tailgate,

I went to Aaron's door and put my face to the gap in the window.

'Can you give me that compass, mate?'

He unstuck the floating ball compass from the windscreen, and passed it through. 'Sorry, I didn't think about it. I should have brought a proper one, and a map.'

I couldn't be arsed to say it wasn't a problem. My head was banging big-time and I wanted to get on. I pressed the illumination button on my Baby-G wristwatch. 'When's last light?'

'Six thirty, or thereabouts.'

'It's just gone three thirty. Drive well away from here, back to the city, whatever. Then come back to this exact spot at three a.m.'

He nodded without even thinking about it.

'OK, park here, and wait ten minutes. Keep the passenger door unlocked and sit in the car with the engine running.' If you switch the engine off on a job, Sod's Law says it won't start up again. 'You also need to think of a story in case you're stopped. Say you're looking for some rare plant or something.'

'Yes, that's a good idea. In fact the barrigon tree is common in—'

'That's good, mate, but make sure the story's in your head by the time you pick me up, so it sounds convincing.'

'OK.' He nodded, still thinking trees.

'If I'm not here by ten past three, drive off. Then come back round again and do exactly the same every hour until it gets light, OK?'

He nodded sharply. 'OK.'

'At first light, stop doing the circuit. Come back for me at midday, but not here—at the locks, by the trailer. Wait for an hour, OK?'

He nodded some more.

'Got any questions?'

He hadn't. I figured I'd given myself enough time, but if there was a cockup and I didn't make this RV, all was not lost. I could get to a river, clean all the jungle shit off and, with luck, dry myself off if the sun was shining tomorrow morning. Then I wouldn't stand out too much once I got among the real people at the locks.

'Now, worst-case scenario, Aaron—if I don't appear at the locks by midday tomorrow, then you'd better call your handler, all right?'

'Why's that?'

'Because I'll probably be dead.'

There was a pause. He was obviously shaken: maybe he hadn't realised what game we were playing here.

'Have you got that?'

'Sure.' He was looking through the windscreen, frowning.

I tapped on his window and he turned his head. 'Hey, don't worry about it, mate. I'm just planning for the worst. I'll see you here at three.' I tapped once more on the glass. 'See you later, mate.'

Aaron drove off. The engine noise was drowned by the rain. I walked off the road into the murky, twilight world of the jungle. At once I was pushing against palm leaves and bushes.

I moved in a few yards to get out of sight while I waited for Aaron to get well away from the area, and plonked down in the mud and leaf litter, resting my back against a tree trunk as more thunder erupted. Water still found me as it cascaded from the canopy.

Underneath my jacket, my left arm was being chewed. I gave the material a good rub and attempted to squeeze to death whatever had got up there. I should have looked out for some mozzie repellent in the Miami departures lounge instead of a guidebook.

My jeans were wet and heavy, hugging my legs as I stood up. I wasn't exactly dressed for crawling around in the jungle, but I'd just have to get on with it. I headed back to the loop. For all I knew it might have stopped raining out there by now; inside the canopy the water still falls for ages as it makes its way down leaf by leaf.

I turned right onto the single-track metal road: it was pointless moving through the jungle from this distance. The downpour had eased a little, but it was still enough to mean that a vehicle wouldn't see me until it was right on top of me.

As I started to walk up the road I checked the ball compass. I was heading uphill and west, as we had been all the way from Clayton in the Mazda. I kept to one side so I could make a quick entry into cover, and didn't move too fast so I'd be able to hear any approaching vehicles above the rasping of my soaked jeans.

SIX

For the best part of a mile of uphill slog I was deluged with rain. Then it subsided, and the sun emerged between the gaps in the clouds, burning onto my face and making me squint as it reflected off the mirror of wet tarmac. The Jackie O sunglasses went back on but I knew there was more rain to come. The dark clouds hadn't completely dispersed, and thunder still rumbled in the distance.

Humidity oozed from the jungle. Birds began to call from high up in the canopy and, as ever, there was the blanket noise of cicadas.

I rounded a gentle bend and a pair of iron gates came into view, blocking the road about 400 yards ahead. They were set into a high, whitewashed wall that disappeared into the jungle on each side. Once I'd confirmed that I was still heading westish, I eased back into cover, moving branches and fronds carefully aside. I didn't want to mark my entry point with top sign—sign made above ground level. A large rubber leaf or a fern, for example, doesn't naturally expose its lighter underside; that only happens if it's disturbed by someone or something brushing past. The leaf will eventually turn back its darker side to gather light, but in the meantime, in this case, it might be seen from the road if these people were switched-on enough.

Once under the canopy, I felt like I was in a pressure cooker; the humidity has nowhere to go, and it gives your lungs a serious workout. Rainwater still fell in bursts as unseen birds took flight from the branches above.

Having moved maybe thirty yards in a direct line away from the road, I stopped to check the compass. My aim now was to head west again and see if I hit the perimeter wall. If I encountered nothing after an hour I'd stop, move back, and try again. The wall of green vegetation was maybe seven yards away, and that was where I would focus my attention as I moved, to detect any hostiles and find the house.

As I moved off, I felt a tug on my sleeve and realised I'd encountered my first batch of wait-a-while. It's a thin vine, studded with tiny barbs that dig into clothing and skin, much like a bramble. Every jungle I'd been in was infested with the stuff. Once it's caught you, the only way to get clear is to tear yourself free. If you try to extricate yourself barb by barb, you'll be there for ever.

For the next half an hour or so I headed uphill and west. My hands were soon covered with small cuts and scratches. I thought about the close target recce. Under ideal conditions, I'd take time to find out the target's routine, so I could take him on in a killing ground of my choosing. But I didn't have time, and the only thing I'd learned from Aaron about Michael's movements was that he would be going to college at some point this week. It's easy enough to kill someone; the hard bit is getting away with it.

I saw open space ahead, just beyond the wall of green, flooded with sunlight and awash with mud. I moved slowly back into the jungle until it disappeared from sight, and stood against a tree. Taking deep breaths and wiping the sweat from my face, I felt the first of what I knew was going to be a whole colony of itchy bumps on my neck, and quite a big one coming up on my left eyelid.

A lot of questions needed answering. Was there physical security? If so, were they young or old? Did they look switched on and/or armed? If so, what with? If there was technical security, where were the devices, and were they powered up? The best way of finding answers was just to observe the target. The longer I stayed there, the more information would sink into my unconscious for me to drag out later. What I needed to do was get my arse up to that mud a few yards away and have a look at what was out there.

Concentrating on the green wall, I moved carefully forward. I saw the sunlight reflecting off the puddles in front of me and dropped slowly onto my stomach in the mud and rotting leaves. Stretching out my arms, I put pressure on my elbows and pushed myself forward on the tips of my toes, lifting my body just clear of the jungle floor, sliding about six inches at a time, trying to avoid crushing dead palm leaves as I moved. They always make a brittle, crunching noise, even when they're wet. I stopped every couple of bounds, lifted my head from the mud, looked and listened.

The first thing I spotted of any significance was wire fencing along the edge of the tree line. I moved carefully towards the most prickly and uninviting bush at the edge of the clearing and wormed my way into it, cutting my hands on the barbs that covered its branches.

Lying on my stomach, I rested my chin on my hands and raised my eyes. I found myself looking through a four-inch chain-link fence, designed more to keep out wildlife than humans. The house was obviously very new, and by the look of things Charlie Chan had been so keen to move in he hadn't waited for proper security.

The open space in front of me was a gently undulating plateau covering maybe twenty acres. Tree stumps stuck out here and there like rotten teeth, waiting to be dragged out or blasted before a lawn was laid. Caterpillar-tracked plant was scattered about, lying idle, but business at Choi and Co. was obviously booming in every other respect, now that the US had gone. The house looked more like a luxury hotel than a family hideaway. The main building was sited no more than 300 yards to my left. I had a clear view of the front and right elevation. It was a massive, three-floor, Spanish-style villa with brilliant whitewashed walls, wrought-iron balconies and a pristine terracotta roof.

Other pitched roofs radiated in all directions from the main building, covering a network of verandahs and archways. A swimming pool sparkled to the right of the main house, surrounded by a raised patio. Four tennis courts stood behind a line of fencing. Nearby, three large satellite dishes were set into the ground.

Including the Lexus, there were six shiny SUVs and pick-ups parked outside a large turning circle that bordered a very ornate stone fountain, then led down to the front gates. I looked back at the vehicles. One in particular had caught my eye. A dark blue GMC with blacked-out windows.

Most impressively, there was a white and yellow Jet Ranger helicopter using some of the driveway in front of the house as a pad.

I lay still and watched, but there was no movement, nothing going on. There was no need to do a 360-degree tour of the target: I could see everything I needed from here. Getting close to the house in daylight would be impossible—there was too much open ground to cover. It might be just as difficult at night; I didn't yet know if they had night-viewing facility, or closed-circuit TV with white light or an infrared capability covering the area, so I had to assume they did.

Two white, short-sleeved shirts and ties came out of the main door with a man in a pink Hawaiian shirt who climbed into the GMC. My friend the Pizza Man. The other two got into one of the pick-ups and a fourth, running from the main door, jumped onto the back. Standing up, leaning forward against the cab, he looked like he was leading a wagon train as the pick-up rounded the fountain and headed for the gates with the GMC following. He wasn't dressed as smartly as the other two: he was in black wellies and carried a wide-brimmed straw hat and a bundle under his arm.

Both wagons stopped for maybe thirty seconds as the gates swung open, then drove out of sight as they closed again behind them.

A gust of wind made the trees sway at the edge of the canopy. It wouldn't be long before the next batch of rain. I'd have to get going if I wanted to be out of the jungle by last light. I started to shift backwards on my elbows and toes, got onto my hands and knees for a while, and finally to my feet once I was behind the wall of green. I gave myself a frenzied scratch and shake, and tucked everything back in. My left eyelid had swollen up and was starting to close.

Baby-G told me it was just after five: maybe an hour before last light, as it gets dark under the canopy before it does outside.

My plan now was to move south towards the road, turn right and parallel it under the canopy until I hit the edge of the cleared area again nearer the gate, then sit and watch the target under cover of darkness. That way, as soon as I'd finished, I could jump onto the tarmac to meet Aaron down at the loop at 3.00am.

I headed off. Wet tarmac and a dark, moody sky soon came into sight through the foliage. A distant rumble of thunder resonated across the treetops, and then there was silence, as if the jungle was holding its breath. Thirty seconds later, I felt the first splashes of rain, then the thunder roared directly overhead. Another thirty seconds and the water had worked its way down from the canopy and back onto my head and shoulders.

I turned right and picked my way towards the fence line, paralleling the road about seven or eight yards in. Mentally I was preparing myself for a miserable few hours in the dark. However, it was better to kill time watching the target while I waited for Aaron than do nothing down at the loop. Time in reconnaissance is seldom wasted.

I moved forward. At one stage a large rotted tree trunk blocked my way. I couldn't be bothered working round it, so I just lay across it on my stomach and twisted myself over. As I got to my feet, looking down, brushing off bark, I caught a glimpse to my right of something that shouldn't have been there. In the jungle there are no straight lines and everything's random. Everything except this.

The man was looking straight at me, rooted to the spot five or six yards away. He was wearing a green US army poncho with the hood over his head. Rain dripped from the wide-brimmed straw hat perched on top of that.

He was a small guy, about five five, his body perfectly still, and if I could have seen his eyes they would probably have been wide and dancing around, full of indecision. Fight or flight?

My eyes shot towards the blade that protruded from his green nylon poncho—six inches of what was probably a two-foot machete. I could hear the rain pounding on the taut nylon, before it dripped down to his black wellies.

We stood there. I didn't know what he was going to do but I wasn't going to be this close to a machete and not do something to protect myself, even if it was with just a pair of pointed pliers. The knife on my Leatherman would take too long to pull out.

I reached for the soaking leather pouch. My fingers fumbled to undo the retaining stud then closed around the hard steel of the Leatherman. All the time, my eyes never left that still-static blade.

He made his decision, screaming at the top of his voice as he ran at me. I made mine, turning and bolting in the direction of the road.

I was still fumbling to get the Leatherman out of its pouch as I ran, folding the two handles back on themselves, exposing the pliers as he followed in my wake. He was shouting stuff. What? Shouting for help? Telling me to stop? It didn't matter, the jungle swallowed it.

I could hear the nylon poncho flapping behind me. I could see tarmac . . . once on that he wouldn't be able to catch me in those wellies. I lost my footing, falling onto my arse but gripping the Leatherman as if my life depended on it.

I looked up at him. He stopped, eyes wide as saucers as the machete rose into the air. I slipped and slithered, moving backwards, trying to get back onto my feet. The blade flashed through the air.

It must have been a cheap buy: the blade hit a sapling and made a tinny sound. He spun round, still screaming and shouting as he, too, slipped on the mud and onto his arse.

As he fell, the rear of the poncho caught on some wait-a-while and was yanked vertically. With the Leatherman still in my right hand I grabbed the poncho with my left and pulled back on it as hard as I could, not knowing what I was going to do next. All I knew was that the machete had to be stopped. This was one of Chan's men, those boys who crucified their victims. I wasn't going to join the queue.

I grabbed another handful of cape and pulled again, constricting his neck by bunching the nylon of the hood as I got up. He kicked out as I dragged him back into the jungle. He couldn't see me behind him, but still he hit out, swirling around in desperation. The blade slashed the poncho. His arse bulldozed through leaves and palm branches. I was just concentrating on getting him back into the jungle and making sure the whirling blade didn't connect with me.

But then it did—big-time—sinking into my right calf.

I screamed with pain as I held on, still dragging him backwards. I had no choice: if I stopped moving he'd be able to get up.

I didn't see the log. My legs hit it and buckled and I fell backwards. The guy felt the material round his neck relax, and scrambled to his knees. I crabbed backwards on my hands and feet, trying to get myself upright again, trying to keep clear of his reach.

Cursing and screaming in Spanish, he lunged. I thrashed backwards and managed to get to my feet. It was time to run again.

I felt the machete whoosh through the air behind me. This was getting outrageous—I was going to die. I had to take a chance.

I turned and charged straight at him, face down, bending forward so that only my back was exposed. If I wasn't quick enough, I'd soon know because I'd feel the blade slice down between my shoulders.

The Leatherman pliers were still in my right hand. I got into him and felt his body buckle with the impact as I wrapped my left arm round him and tried to pinion his machete arm.

Then I rammed the pointed tips against his stomach.

Both of us moved backwards. We hit a tree. His back was against it and I used my weight to force the pliers to penetrate his clothing.

He gave an agonised howl, and I felt his stomach tighten. I kept on pushing, using my weight against him with the pliers between us. At last I felt his flesh give way. It was like pushing into a sheet of rubber.

He screamed and collapsed forward. Only then did I withdraw my hand. As the Leatherman emerged, he fell into the foetal position.

I picked up the machete from where he'd dropped it, and went and sat against a tree, fighting for breath. As my body calmed down, the pain came back to my leg. I pulled up my slashed jeans on my right leg and inspected the damage. It was to the rear of the calf; the gash was only about four inches long and not very deep, but bad enough to be leaking quite badly.

I used the knife blade of my Leatherman to cut my sweatshirt sleeves into strips. With these I improvised a bandage, wrapping it round my leg to apply pressure on the wound.

I stared at the man, still lying in a foetal position, covered in mud. I felt sorry for him, but I'd had no choice. Once that length of razor-sharp steel started flying around it was either him or me.

I could see that this wasn't exactly the local woodcutter I'd stumbled across. His nails were clean and well manicured, and though his hair was a mess of mud and leaves, it was well cut. He was young, good-looking and clean-shaven. He had one unusual feature: instead of two distinct eyebrows he had just one big one. This guy wasn't a farm hand, he was a city boy, the one who'd been standing in the back of the pick-up. As Aaron had said, these people didn't mess about and he would have sliced me up without a second thought. But what had he been doing in here?

It got darker and the rain did its thing above the canopy. This episode spelt the end of the recce, and both of us were going to have to disappear. He would be missed. They would come looking for him, and if I left him here it wouldn't take them long to find him.

I folded down my bloodstained Leatherman and put it back in its pouch. I guessed that the fence must be closer than the road now: if I headed for that, at least I'd have something to guide me out of the jungle in the darkness.

Unibrow's breathing was shallow and quick, and he was still gripping his stomach with both hands and mumbling weakly to himself. I went in search of his hat, wondering what to do with him once we were out of here. If he was still alive I couldn't take him to a hospital because he'd talk about me, which would alert Charlie. I couldn't take him back to Aaron and Carrie's place because that would compromise them. All I knew was that I had to get him away from the immediate vicinity. I'd think of something later.

Hat retrieved, I got hold of Unibrow's right arm and hoisted him in a fireman's lift over my back and shoulder. Then, machete back in hand, I checked the compass and headed for the fence line. Within minutes I came to it. Ahead of me, in the open, semidark space, was a solid wall of rain. Lights were already on in the house. The fountain was illuminated but I couldn't see the statue. That was good, because it meant they couldn't see me.

I followed the fence for a few minutes, my passenger's poncho constantly snagging on branches of wait-a-while. All the time I kept my eyes glued on the house. I came across what looked like a small mammal track, paralleling the fence and about two feet in. I followed it, past caring about leaving sign in the churned-up mud. The rain would sort that out. I'd gone no more than a dozen steps when my limping right leg was whipped away from under me and both of us went crashing into the undergrowth.

My right foot was stuck fast. I looked down and saw a glimmer of metal. It was wire: I was caught in a snare. It was simple enough to ease open the loop. I got to my feet and heaved Unibrow back onto my shoulders, then set off along the track.

Just another five minutes of stumbling brought us to the start of the whitewashed rough-stone wall and, ten yards or so later, the tall iron gates. It was good to feel tarmac under my feet. I turned left and moved as quickly as I could to get away from the area. If a vehicle came I'd just have to plunge back into the undergrowth.

It took an hour but I finally got us both into the canopy at the loop. The rain had eased but Unibrow's pain hadn't, and neither had mine. For an hour or so I sat, rubbed my leg, and waited for Aaron.

Unibrow's groans faded, and eventually disappeared. I crawled over to him. All I could hear was weak, wheezy breath. I pulled out the Leatherman and jabbed his tongue with the blade. There was no reaction. He was definitely on his way out.

Rolling him onto his back, I lay on top of him and jammed my right forearm into his throat, pushing down with all my weight, my left hand on my right wrist. There was little resistance. His legs kicked out weakly, and a hand came up to scratch at my face. I simply moved my head out of the way and listened to the insects as I cut off the blood supply to his head, and oxygen to his lungs.

SEVEN

Wednesday, September 6

There was a crash of branches, followed swiftly by a thud on the jungle floor, close enough that I felt the vibration in the ground. Two tonnes of dead tree had just given up the will to stay upright.

A few gallons of canopy-held rain followed the deadfall. I wiped the water from my face and stood up.

Deadfall was a constant problem in the jungle, and checking to see if there were any dead trees or branches nearby or overhead when basha'ing up for the night was standard operating procedure.

According to Baby-G it was 2.23, not long to pick-up. I'd been here among the leaf litter for nearly six hours.

I'd fought off jet lag, but my body still wanted to curl into a ball and sink into a deep sleep. I felt my way back down against the hard rough bark of a tree. As I stretched out my legs, the soles of my Timberlands pushed against Unibrow. I'd searched him before we went into the tree line, and found a wallet and several lengths of copper wire tucked into a canvas pouch on his belt. He'd been setting traps. Maybe he was into that sort of stuff for fun: it wasn't as if the lot up at the house would be in need of the odd wild turkey.

I thought back over the stuff I'd done over the years, and right now I hated all the jobs I'd ever been on. I hated Unibrow for making me kill him. I hated me. I was getting attacked by everything that moved, and I'd still had to kill someone else. One way or another that was the way it had always been.

Until midnight I'd heard only three vehicles moving along the road, and it was hard to tell if they were heading towards the house or away from it. After that, the only sounds were the buzzing of insects. At one point a troop of howler monkeys passed us by, their booming barks and groans reverberating through the jungle.

At 2.58 I heard the low rumble of a vehicle. This time the noise didn't fade. The engine note took over gradually from the cicadas and stopped just past me, with a squeak of not-too-good brakes. The engine ticked over erratically. It had to be the Mazda.

I got to my feet, felt around for Unibrow, took hold of an arm and a leg, and heaved him over my shoulder. With the machete and hat in my right hand I made my way towards the edge of the tree line, my eyes half closed to protect them from the unseen wait-a-while. I might as well have closed them completely: I couldn't see a thing.

The moment I emerged from the forest, I saw the Mazda, bathed in a glow of white and red reflecting off the wet tarmac. I laid Unibrow down with his hat in the mud and tall grass at the jungle's edge, and squelched towards the passenger side, machete in hand, checking there was only one body shape in the cab.

Aaron was sitting with both hands gripping the wheel, and in the dull glow of the instruments I could see him staring rigidly ahead. Even with the window down, he didn't seem to register I was there.

I said quietly, 'Seen any of those barry-whatever trees yet?'

He jumped forward in his seat as if he'd just seen a ghost.

'Is the back unlocked, mate?'

'Yes.' He nodded frantically, his voice shaking.

'Good, won't be long.' I walked to the rear, opened the tailgate, then went back to fetch Unibrow. The suspension sank a little as I dumped the body on the crap-strewn floor. His hat followed, and I covered him with his poncho before shutting the tailgate. The back window was covered in grime. Nobody would be able to see through.

I went round to the passenger door and jumped in. 'Let's go then, mate. Not too fast, just drive normally.'

Aaron pushed the selector into Drive and we moved off. I leaned down and placed the machete under my feet.

Aaron at last found the courage to speak. 'What's in the back?'

There was no point beating about the bush. 'A body.'

'God forbid . . . What happened, Nick?'

'I'll explain later—it's OK, it isn't a drama.' I tried to keep my voice slow and calm. 'All we need to worry about is getting away from the area, and then I'll sort the problem out, OK?'

Switching on the cab light, I fumbled for Unibrow's wallet in my jeans and pulled it apart. He had a few dollars, and a picture ID that called him Diego Paredes and said he had been born in 1976.

Aaron's head was obviously full of things he wanted to say. 'Can't we take him to hospital? We can't just keep him in the back.'

I tried to sound relaxed. 'We have to—for now. He belongs to Charlie. If they find his body, it could put all of us in danger. Once we're out of the area we'll make sure we dump him so he's never found.' Or at least, as far as I was concerned, not before Saturday morning.

There was a long, awkward silence as we drove along the jungle-lined tarmac and through Clayton. Then we turned a corner and I could see the high-mounted floodlights of the locks in the distance.

We were driving alongside a very wide, deep, U-shaped concrete storm trench. I got Aaron to stop and turn off his lights.

I nodded towards the locks. 'I've got to clean myself up before we hit all that.' I wanted to look at least a bit normal, in case we were seen or stopped as we went through the city. Being wet wasn't unusual here; it rained a lot.

'Oh, OK.'

I forced my aching body out of the Mazda. The glow from the powerful arc lights gave us just enough light to see what was going on about us. I went to the rear and lifted the tailgate to check Unibrow. He had been sliding about and the stench was so strong I had to move my head away. It smelt like a freezer after a power cut.

Leaving the tailgate up, I scrambled down the side of the concrete ditch and into the surging storm water. I pulled the plastic documents bag from under my jacket and wedged it above the water line.

I squatted in the edge of the flow and washed off all the mud, blood and leaf litter that covered me. As I took off my jacket, I heard Aaron's door open. By now I was rinsing my jeans in the trench before wringing them out and throwing them up onto the grass. I watched as he stuck his head slowly into the back of the wagon. He recoiled and turned away, vomit already exploding from his mouth. I heard it splatter against the side of the vehicle and tarmac above me, then the sounds of him retching.

I scrambled up onto the grass and hurriedly dressed in my wet clothes. Aaron walked back to the cab, wiping his face with a handkerchief. Sidestepping the pool of vomit on the tarmac, I covered Unibrow again with the poncho, lowered the tailgate, and climbed in next to Aaron, ignoring what had just happened. 'Back to your place, then, mate.'

We left the lock behind us, travelling in silence. Before long we approached the floodlit tolbooths by the old Albrook air-force base. Aaron spent the best part of a minute fumbling in his pockets and the glove compartment at the tolbooth. A bored, middle-aged woman just stared into space with her hand out.

I let my head bob about as we bounced along the potholed road and into the sleeping city via El Chorrillo. I looked out at the rubbish overflowing from the piles of soaked cardboard boxes that fringed the market square, and cats fighting over the scraps.

Aaron broke the silence. 'Nick? Is that what you do—kill people? I mean, I know it happens. It's just that—'

I pointed down at the machete in the footwell. 'I nearly lost my leg with that thing, and if he'd had his way it would have been my head. I'm sorry, mate, there was no other way.'

He didn't reply, just stared intently through the windscreen.

We hit the bay once more. Then I realised Aaron had started to shake. He'd spotted a police car at the roadside ahead, with two rather bored-looking officers smoking and reading the papers.

I kept my voice calm. 'Don't worry, just drive normally, everything's OK.' It wasn't, of course: they might stop a beaten-up Mazda just to relieve the boredom.

As we passed, the driver glanced up from his newspaper, and said something to his mate. I kept my eyes on the cracked wing mirror, watching the police car. 'It's OK, mate, there's no movement from behind. They're still static. Just keep to the limit and smile.'

We splashed through mini-Manhattan. Aaron gave a small cough. 'You know what you're going to do with that guy yet, Nick?'

'We need to hide him somewhere on the way to your place, once we're out of the city. Any ideas?'

Aaron shook his head. 'We can't leave him to rot . . . He's a human being, for God's sake. Look, I'll bury him for you. There's an old tribal site near the house. No one will find him there.'

I wasn't going to argue with that. If he wanted to dig a hole, that was fine by me.

We came to the airport road tolbooth the other side of the financial district, and this time I got out a dollar of my own money. I didn't want us standing still any longer than we had to. Diego would take quite a bit of explaining. Aaron paid the woman and the lights faded behind us as we hit the road out of town.

The wind through my window got stronger as we gathered speed. I wound it up only halfway to keep me awake, and I tried to concentrate on what I'd seen on the close target recce and get back to work.

'NICK! THE POLICE! Nick, what do we do? Wake up! Please!'

Before I'd even opened my eyes I was trying to calm him down. 'Don't worry, it'll be OK.' I focused on the vehicle checkpoint ahead, set up in the middle of nowhere: two police vehicles blocking the road. I could see silhouettes moving across the two sets of headlights. Aaron's foot had frozen on the accelerator pedal.

'Slow down, for fuck's sake. Calm down.'

He came out of his trance and hit the brakes.

There was a torrent of shouts in Spanish, and the muzzles of half a dozen M-16s came up. I placed my hands on the dash so they were in clear view. Aaron killed the lights and turned off the engine.

Three torchbeams headed our way, three men in olive-green fatigues with M-16s at the ready. They split up, two going left, to Aaron, the other towards me. Aaron started to wind down the remaining half of his window. His breathing was becoming rapid.

There was an abrupt command in Spanish. Aaron lifted his arse from the seat and searched around in his back pocket.

A green baseball cap and bushy black moustache shoved its way through Aaron's window and demanded something from me. I saw sergeant's stripes and POLICIA badges on his sleeve.

'He wants your ID, Nick.'

Aaron presented his own. It was snatched by the sergeant, who stood back from the window, using his Maglite to inspect the docs.

I pulled my plastic bag from under my jacket and rummaged in it.

I heard boots behind the wagon, but couldn't see anything in the mirror. My heart-rate pumped up a few more revs per minute, and I made a mental note of where the door handle was, and checked that the door-lock knob was up. If I heard the squeak of rusty hinges from the tailgate I'd be out and running. I handed my passport over.

The sergeant was gobbing off about me as he looked at my passport with his Maglite. I only understood the odd word of Aaron's replies. '*Británico . . . amigo . . . vacaciones . . .*' Straining my ears, I waited for the tailgate to open, visualising my escape route: three steps into the darkness to my right.

The sergeant bent down once more and pointed at my clothes as he rattled off something to Aaron. He replied with a funny, and forced a laugh, as he turned to me. 'You're a friend and I picked you up from the airport. You wanted so much to see the rain forest so I took you in at the edge of the city. Now you never want to go in again. It was so funny, please just smile.'

The sergeant had joined in the laughter and told the other guy behind him about the dickhead *británico* as he handed back the IDs. Then he banged the roof of the Mazda and followed the others towards the blocking wagons. There was a lot of shouting, followed by the roar of wagons being manoeuvred clear of the road.

Aaron was shaking as he turned the ignition, but managed to appear relaxed from the neck up for the police's benefit. He even waved as we passed. Our headlights caught five bodies lined up on their backs at the roadside. Their clothes glistened with blood. One of the kids was still open-mouthed, eyes staring up at the sky.

Aaron said nothing for the next ten minutes as we bounced along the potholed road. Then he braked suddenly, pushed the selector into Park, and jumped out. I could hear him retching.

The suspension creaked as he closed the door, wiping his water-logged eyes. 'I'm sorry, Nick, I saw a couple of guys blown away a few years ago. I had nightmares about it. Then, seeing the body and now those kids back there, hacked to death, it just . . .'

'Did he tell you what had happened?'

'It was a robbery. FARC.'

'Look, mate, I think we'd better get rid of the body. As soon as it's light we'll find somewhere to hide him. We can't go through that again.'

He nodded slowly. 'Sure, sure, you're right.'

We drove on. Neither of us wanted to talk about bodies any more.

'What road are we on?'

'The Pan-American Highway. Runs all the way from Alaska to Chile, apart from a ninety-three-mile break in the Darien Gap, the jungle area bordering Colombia.'

'Is that where we're going, to the Gap?'

He shook his head. 'We're heading off the road at Chepo, maybe another ten minutes or so.'

First light was starting to edge its way past the corners of the sky. The headlights exposed nothing but tufts of grass, mud and pools of water. This place was as barren as a moonscape. Not much good for hiding a body. 'There's not a whole lot of forest here, mate, is there?'

'Hey, what can I say? Where there's a road, there's loggers. They keep on going until everything's levelled.'

Ahead and to our left I could see the dark shadows of trees, and I pointed. 'What about there?'

'I guess so, but it's not that far to where I could do it properly.'

'No, mate, no. Let's do it now.' I tried to keep my voice level.

We pulled into the side of the road and under the trees. 'Want to help?' I asked, as I retrieved the machete from under my feet.

He thought hard. 'I just don't want the picture of him in there, you know, in my head. Can you understand that?'

I could: there were a whole lot of pictures in my own head I wished weren't there. I climbed out, held my breath, opened the back, and pulled Diego out, dragging him into the tree line.

About ten yards inside the gloom of the canopy I rolled both him and the wiped-clean machete under a rotted deadfall, covering the gaps with leaves and debris. I only needed to hide him until Saturday.

Having closed down the tailgate I got back into the cab and slammed the door. He turned. 'You know what? I think maybe Carrie shouldn't know about this, Nick. Don't you think? I mean—'

'Mate,' I said, 'you took the words right out of my mouth.'

Aaron nodded and steered back onto the road. Maybe fifteen minutes later he spun the wheel to the right, and that was us quitting the Pan-American Highway.

I saw a huddle of corrugated roofs. 'Chepo?'

'Yep, the bad and sad side.'

We passed a rectangular building made from unpainted breeze blocks. Through the windows I could see shelves of tinned food. Further up the road was a large wooden shack on stilts. A sign said it was a restaurant. As we drew level I saw, chained up in a cage on the verandah, the scrawniest big cat I'd ever seen. There was only enough space for it to turn round.

Aaron shook his head. 'Shit, they've still got her in there! They can't do that. You're not even allowed to have a parrot in a cage, man, it's the law . . . But the police? Shit, they just spend their whole time worrying about narcos.'

He pointed ahead of us. We were driving towards what reminded me of an army security base in Northern Ireland. High, corrugated-iron fencing protected whatever buildings were inside. Sandbags were piled on top of each other to make bunkers, and the barrel of an American M-60 machine gun jutted from the one covering the large double gates. A big sign declared this was the police station.

We left Chepo behind us and the road got progressively worse, until finally we turned off it and hit a rutted track that worked its way to some high ground a couple of miles away.

Aaron pointed ahead. 'We're just over that hill.'

We ploughed on through the mist, finally cresting the steep, rugged hill. A valley lay below us, and as far as the eye could see the landscape was strewn with felled, decaying wood. It was as if somebody had tipped an enormous box of matchsticks all over a desert of rust-coloured mud. Then, at the far end of the valley, where the ground flattened out, was lush green jungle. I couldn't work it out.

Aaron must have sensed my confusion. 'They just got fed up with this side of the hills,' he shouted above the wagon's creaks and groans. 'There wasn't enough hardwood to take, and it wasn't macho for the *hombres* to take these little things away.'

We reached the valley floor, and carried on through the tree graveyard for three or four miles until we were rescued by the lush canopy at the end of the valley. Here we were back in secondary jungle. The trees were engulfed in vines, all sorts of stuff growing between them.

Forty minutes later we emerged into a large clearing, most of it lying behind a building that was side on and directly in front of us, 200 yards away. It looked like the house that Jack built.

'This is us.' Aaron didn't sound too enthusiastic.

To my left, and facing the front of the house, was a steep hill covered with more fallen trees and rotten stumps, with tufty grass growing between them. The rest of the clearing was rough, but fairly flat.

We followed the track towards the building. The main section was a one-storey, terracotta-roofed villa, with dirty green plastered walls. There was a covered verandah out front, facing the high ground. Behind the main building, and attached to it, was a corrugated-iron extension maybe twice as big as the house itself.

On my right were row upon row of white plastic five-gallon tubs, hundreds of them, about two feet high and the same in diameter. Their lids were sealed, but sprays of plants of all colours, shapes and sizes shot from a circular hole cut out of the middle of each. Past the tubs was a generator under a corrugated-iron roof with no side walls. As we got closer I could make out a pair of satellite dishes on the roof of the house. I could also see the other pick-up truck, parked on the far side of the verandah. Aaron hit the Mazda's horn, and Carrie emerged from the verandah, putting on her wraparounds.

'Please, Nick—not a word.'

The wagon stopped and he jumped out as she stepped down from the verandah. I got out, squinting to fight the glare, and took a few steps towards them, then stopped to give them some space. But there weren't any greetings, kisses or touches, just a strained exchange.

I put on my nice-and-cheery-to-the-host voice. 'Hello.'

She noticed my hobble and ripped jeans. 'What happened? You OK?'

'I walked into some sort of animal trap or something. I'm—'

'You'd better come and get cleaned up. I've some porridge fixed.'

'That sounds wonderful.' It sounded shit.

She turned to walk back to the house, but Aaron had other ideas. 'I'm going to clean the truck. There was a fuel spillage in the back.'

Carrie turned. 'Oh, OK.'

I followed her towards the house as Aaron went back to the wagon. Just short of the verandah she stopped and turned.

'Luce, our daughter, thinks you're part of a UK study group, and you're here for a few days to see how we work. OK?'

'Sure, that's not a problem.'

'She knows nothing about why you're really here. Nor do we, come to that. She's asleep, you'll see her soon.'

I was so tired I could hardly keep my eyes open as we stepped across cracked, faded terracotta tiles, past two rocking chairs and an old rope hammock. The front door was open, and Carrie pulled open a mesh mozzie door with a creak of hinges. To the left, above a meshed window, was a wall light, its bowl full of dried insects, fatally attracted to its glow. I caught the screen before it sprang back, and followed her inside.

Carrie was heading straight to another door, painted a faded yellow. I followed. To our left were armchairs arranged round a coffee table. Trained over the table and chairs were two freestanding electric fans. The wall to the left had two more doors. The furthest one was partly open and led into what I presumed was their bedroom. A headboard held one end of a mosquito net; the other was suspended from the ceiling. Men's and women's clothes were thrown over a chair. A rifle hung on the wall to the right of the bed.

On my right, the whole wall was covered by bookshelves. The only break was a window, also covered with protective mesh, which seemed to be the only other source of natural light.

In the corner was the kitchen area, with a small table and chairs.

Steam rose from a large pot sitting on one of the units to the side of the cooker. Next to it lay a big bunch of bananas.

Carrie disappeared through the yellow door, and I followed her into the larger, corrugated-iron extension. The walls were lined with plyboard, and there was a rough concrete floor. Hanging down from the high ceiling were two old and very dirty overhead fans, both stationary. Large sheets of clear corrugated plastic high up in the walls served as windows.

The extension might be cheap and low-tech, but what it housed wasn't. Running the length of the wall in front of me was one continuous desk unit, formed out of trestle tables. On it were two PCs with webcams attached to the top of the monitors; in front of each was a canvas director's chair. The screen of the PC on the right was displaying an image of the Miraflores Locks. It must have been a webcam online, because the screen was just at the point of refreshing itself to show a cargo ship halfway out of one of the locks.

The PC to the left was closed down, and had a set of headphones with the mike attached hanging over the camera. The desk against the wall to the left housed a third PC, surrounded by schoolbooks.

Carrie turned immediately to the right through the only other door and I followed. We entered what looked like a quartermaster's store. Rows of grey angle-iron shelving lined the walls left and right, stacked with all sorts—cartons of tinned food, hurricane lamps, torches, packs of batteries. On pallets on the floor were bags of rice, porridge oats and milk powder the size of coal sacks. Laid out in the corridor was a US army cot bed and dark green US army lightweight blankets still in their plastic wrapping. 'That's for you.'

She nodded towards a corrugated-iron door facing us as she quickly closed the one to the computer room behind us, plunging this area into near darkness. 'That'll take you outside. You'll be able to see better out there. I'll bring out the first-aid kit.'

I walked past her, dropped my jacket on the cot, then turned back to see her climbing up the shelves. 'Could I see the imagery, please?'

She didn't look down at me. 'Sure.'

I went outside. The massed ranks of white tubs lay 200 yards in front of me. The generator chugged rhythmically. Aaron was in the distance, where the tubs met the track, a hose in his hands, flushing out the back of the wagon.

I slumped down on the concrete foundation that protruded along the wall, my back against a green water butt, and opened the hole in my jeans to inspect the wound. Carrie appeared from the storeroom with a suitcase and a sheet of A4 paper. She placed both on the concrete and lifted the suitcase lid to reveal a basic medical pack.

Her voice was clear, concise. 'So, what is it you're here for?'

'To give Charlie a reminder. There's something we want him to do.'

'What?'

I shrugged. 'I thought maybe you might know.'

'I was told nothing except that you'd be coming and we were to help.' She sounded almost sad about it.

I pointed to the medical kit. 'I need to clean myself up before I dress the wound. I'm afraid I don't have any other clothes.'

She stood up. 'You can use some of Aaron's. The shower is out in back.' She pointed behind her. 'I'll get a towel.'

Before reaching the door she turned to me. 'We have a two-minute rule here. First minute for soaking, then turn off the hose and soap yourself down. The second minute is to rinse. We get a lot of rain but have trouble capturing it.' She gripped on the handle. 'Oh, and in case you're tempted, don't drink from the shower, only from the hoses marked with a D—that's the treated water.' There was a smile as she disappeared. 'Otherwise it'll be giving you a pretty big reminder of why it needs to be treated.'

I took a look at the print-out of the satellite imagery. Its grainy reproduction covered the whole page and was zoomed right into the target, giving me a plan view of the house, the more or less rectangular tree line and the broccoli patch of jungle surrounding it. I tried to get to work, but I just couldn't get my head to do it.

Instead, my eye caught one of the dark brown bottles of pills. The label said dihydrocodeine, an excellent painkiller, especially when taken with aspirin, which boosts its effect. I shook one out and dry swallowed as I sorted in the case for an aspirin. Eventually I pushed one out of its foil and got that down my neck as well.

I placed one of the bandages on top of the paper to hold it down, got up and limped round the back in the direction of the shower. Maybe it was just that I was knackered, but I was feeling very woozy.

Hobbling past the storeroom entrance, I looked in and saw that the computer-room door was still closed. I went in and shut out the daylight, then stumbled to the cot, still in my damp clothes, and lay down on my back, my heart pumping as my head filled with Kelly, bodies, Diego, more bodies, the Yes Man, even Josh. And why had I told Carrie I was here to give Charlie a reminder? Shit, shit, shit . . .

I had pins and needles in my legs and my skin tingled. I turned over and curled up, my arms holding my shins, not wanting to think any more, not wanting to see any more.

EIGHT

Thursday, September 7

I walk into the bedroom, Buffy and Britney posters, bunk beds and the smell of sleep. I move towards them in the dark, kicking into shoes and teen-girl magazines. She is asleep, half in, half out of her duvet, stretched out on her back like a starfish, her hair spread over the pillow. I put her dangling leg and arm back under the duvet. Something is wrong . . . my hands are wet . . . she is limp . . . she isn't sucking her bottom lip, isn't dreaming of being a pop star. The lights go on and I see the blood dripping from my hands onto her face. Her mouth is wide open, her eyes staring at the ceiling.

Sundance is lying on the top bunk, a bloodstained baseball bat in his hands, looking down at me, smiling. 'I wouldn't mind a trip to Maryland . . . we could go to Washington and do the sights first . . .'

I cry, fall to my knees, pins and needles.

I pull her from the bed, trying to take her with me.

'It's OK, Nick, it's OK. It's just a dream . . .'

I opened my eyes. I was kneeling on the concrete, pulling Carrie towards me.

'It's OK,' she said again. 'Relax, you're in my house, relax.'

I quickly released my grip, climbing back onto the cot.

She stayed down on the floor. The half-light from the living room illuminated a concerned face. 'Here, have some of this.'

I took the half-empty bottle of water from her and started to unscrew the top, feeling embarrassed, my legs stinging with pins and needles. I cleared my throat. 'Thanks, thank you.'

'Maybe you have a fever—picked up something in the forest yesterday. See what it's like in the morning and we'll take you to the clinic in Chepo.'

I nodded as I drank. 'How long have you been here?'

'You just woke us, we were worried.' She put the back of her hand to my forehead. 'These fevers out here can make you maniacal.'

'I was having a nightmare? I can't even remember it.'

She started to get up. 'It happens. You OK now?'

I shook my head to try to clear it. 'I'm fine, thanks.'

'I'll see you in the morning, then. Good night.' She walked back into the dark computer room, closing the door behind her.

I checked my watch: 12.46am. I had been out for over fourteen hours. I ripped the plastic from the blanket, lay down and covered myself, blaming the drug cocktail for my doziness. Dihydrocodeine does that to you. I tossed and turned. My body was telling me I still needed sleep, but I really didn't want to close my eyes again.

HALF AN HOUR LATER I checked Baby-G and it was 3.18am. So much for not closing my eyes. The pain had gone, and I didn't feel as groggy as before. I felt around below the cot for the water bottle. Blinking my eyes open, I drank to the noise of the cicadas.

I didn't want to lie and think too much, so decided to have a walk-about to keep my head busy. Besides, I was nosy.

Pushing myself upright, I sat on the edge of the cot for a while, rubbing my face back to life before standing up and reaching for the light switch. I couldn't find it, so felt for the door handle instead and bumbled into the computer room, water in hand. The switch in here was easy to find. As the strip lighting flickered I saw that the living-room door was closed. I checked the darkness on the other side.

Behind the two blank screens nearest me was a cork board with a montage of photographs. All of them seemed to be of the extension being built, and of the clearing behind. A few showed Aaron up a ladder hammering nails into sheets of wriggly tin, some of him with what looked like a local, standing next to craters in the ground with half-blown-up trees around them.

Taking a swig of the water I walked over to what I assumed was Luce's PC. I looked down at the desk and noticed her name on an exercise book. Her name was spelt Luz. I remembered from my Colombia days that their Z is pronounced as S. So her name was the Spanish for 'light'—it wasn't short for Lucy at all.

I headed for the living room, checking their bedroom once more before hitting the brass light switch on the other side of the door.

The room was lit by three bare bulbs. The cooker was a chipped white enamel thing. There was a coffee percolator on the cooker, and various family-hug photos fixed to the fridge with magnets.

I pulled two bananas from the bunch and looked idly at the photographs. The pictures were of the family having fun about the house, and some of an older guy in a white polo shirt, holding hands with Luz on the verandah. I peeled the second banana as my eye fell on a faded black and white picture of five men. One of them was most certainly the older guy with Luz. All five were in trunks on the beach, holding up babies for the camera. The one on the far left had a badly scarred stomach.

I leaned forward to get a closer look. His hair had been darker then, but there was no doubt about it. The long features and wiry body belonged to Pizza Man.

Finishing off the water, I got up and dumped the banana skins in the plastic bag under the sink and headed for the cot. I'd had a long rest but I still felt like more.

I OPENED MY EYES to the sound of a vehicle engine. I stumbled over the medical case as I made my way to the outside door.

Blinding sunlight hit me, and I was just in time to see the Mazda heading into the tree line. As I held up my hand to shield my eyes, I saw Carrie at the front of the house. She turned to me.

'Morning.'

I nodded a reply as I watched the wagon disappear.

'Aaron's gone to Chepo. There's a jaguar that's been caged up for months. I'll get you those clothes and a towel. You OK?'

'Yes, thanks. The fever's gone, I think.'

'I'm fixing breakfast. You want some?'

'Thanks, I'll have a shower first if that's OK.'

She moved back towards the verandah. 'Sure.'

The hardstanding at the rear of the extension was covered by an open-walled lean-to. It was obviously the washing area. In front of me was the shower, three sides formed out of wriggly tin, and an old plastic curtain across the front. A black rubber hose snaked down from a hole in the roof. Beyond it was an old stainless-steel double sink unit fed by two other hoses, with wastepipes disappearing into the ground. Further back was the toilet cubicle. The ground to the rear of the house sloped gently away so that I could just see the treetops in the distance.

I pulled back the plastic shower curtain, took off all my kit and dropped it on the hardstanding, but left the sweatshirt bandage in place round my leg. I stepped into the cubicle, a concrete platform with a drainage hole in the middle, and a shelf holding a bottle of shampoo, and a half-worn bar of soap.

I soaked the sweatshirt material with lukewarm water to try to soften up the clotting, then, holding the hose over my head, I counted off my sixty seconds. Closing off the flow, I lathered myself down with the flowery-smelling soap and rubbed shampoo into my hair. When the water had had enough time to do its stuff with the dressing, I bent down and untied the sweatshirt.

As I gritted my teeth and rubbed soap into the gash to clear out the crap, there was a noise from the sink area. I poked my head out to say thanks to Carrie for the clothes and towel, but it wasn't her, it was Luz—at least, I presumed it was. She was dressed in a worn-looking blue nightgown, and had the wildest black curly hair I'd ever seen. Near her on the drainer was a pile of clothes and a blue towel. She stood there, staring at me with big dark eyes above high, pronounced Latin cheekbones. '*Hola*,' she said.

That sort of Spanish I understood. 'Oh, *hola*. You're Luz?'

She nodded. 'My mom told me to bring you these.' She spoke American, tinged with a hint of Spanish.

'Thank you very much. I'm Nick—nice to meet you, Luz.'

She nodded—'See you'—and left.

I got back to business. The wound was about four inches long and maybe an inch deep, but at least it was a clean cut. Letting loose with the hose, I rinsed off for my allotted sixty seconds.

I towelled myself dry, then got dressed in Aaron's clothes, khaki cotton trousers with two map pockets either side, and a full-sleeved, faded grey T-shirt. The trousers were too big round the waist, but a couple of twists of the waistband tightened them up. The trouser pockets had good Velcro seals, so I put my wallet, passport and air ticket, still in their plastic bags, in the right-hand one.

After slicking back my hair I took my Leatherman out of its case to wash off Diego's blood, then put it into my pocket. I hung the wet towel on the line. Carrying my old clothes and my Timberlands, I walked back round to the storeroom, picked up the medical kit and satellite picture, then, after crawling about under the cot, Diego's wallet, and sat outside on the foundations again.

Looking at the sat image I could clearly see the road from Charlie's house down to the gate, wagons parked, diesel fumes belching from a JCB as it dragged a tree stump out of the ground, bodies by the pool. This was good stuff, but told me nothing I didn't already know.

I found antibiotic powder in a puff bottle, doused my wound with it, then applied a gauze dressing and secured it with a crepe bandage.

Carrie hadn't provided any socks, so I put my own back on. They were the consistency of cardboard, but at least they were dry now. I pulled on my boots, rubbed antihistamine cream over the lumps on my face, then packed everything back into the case. I found two safety pins to secure the map pocket, and took the suitcase back to the storeroom. I dumped all my old kit under the cot and rummaged about for matches, then gouged a hole in the earth with the heel of my Timberland, and emptied the contents of Diego's wallet into it, less the thirty-eight dollars. I watched his picture ID curl and turn black as I thought about what I was going to do with Michael.

It was going to have to be a shoot. Nothing else would work with such little time, information and kit: at 300-ish yards, and with even a half-decent weapon, I should be able to drop him. No fancy tip-of-an-ear stuff, just going for the centre mass of his trunk. Once he was down I could get another few rounds into him to make sure. Afterwards, I'd stay in the jungle until Sunday, then pop out and get myself to the airport. Even if I didn't find an opportunity until last light tomorrow, I could still be at Josh's by Tuesday.

After pushing mud over the pile of ash, I headed for the kitchen, throwing the wallet onto a shelf as I passed through the storeroom. The fans in the living area were turning noisily. Carrie was at the cooker with her back turned; Luz was at the table, eating porridge. She was dressed like her mother, in green cargos and T-shirt.

I put on my cheerful voice again and gave a general, 'Hello, hello.'

Carrie turned and smiled. 'Oh, hello.' She ladled porridge into a white bowl and I hoped it was for me. 'Sit down. Coffee?'

I did as I was told. 'Please.' By the time I'd pulled up my chair, the porridge and a spoon were on the table in front of me.

She tapped the top of a jug on the table. 'Milk. Powdered, but you get used to it.' Then she joined us with two mugs of coffee.

Luz was just finishing her food as Carrie checked the clock by the sink. 'You know what? Just leave your plate on the side and go and log on. You don't want to keep Grandpa waiting.'

Luz nodded with delight, got up with her plate, and put it down next to the sink before disappearing into the computer room.

Carrie called out, 'Tell Grandpa I'll say hello in a minute.'

A voice drifted back from inside the computer room. 'Sure.'

Carrie pointed at the pictures on the fridge and one in particular, the guy in a polo shirt with grey-sided black hair, holding hands with Luz on the verandah. 'My father, George, teaches her math.'

'Who are the ones holding the babies?'

She turned back and looked at the fading picture. 'Oh, that's also my father, he's holding me—we're on the far right. It's my favourite.'

'Who are the ones with you?'

Luz stuck her head round the corner, looking and sounding worried. 'Mom, the locks picture has closed down.'

'That's OK, darling, I know.'

'But, Mom, you said it must always be—'

Carrie was sharp with her. 'I know, I've changed my mind, OK?'

'Oh, OK.' Luz retreated, looking confused.

'We home-school everything else here. This keeps her in contact with her grandfather; they're real close.'

'Sounds good,' I said, not that fussed she hadn't answered my question. There were more important things on my mind. It was time to cut to the last page. 'Is that rifle in the bedroom working?'

'You don't miss much, do you, fever man? Of course . . . why?'

'For protection. We can call your handler for one but I haven't got much time and I want to get going as soon as I can.'

She stood up and walked towards her bedroom, disappearing behind the door. I could hear working parts moving back and forth, and the chink of brass rounds. I'd supposed they'd have it loaded and ready to go, otherwise why have it on the bedroom wall?

She reappeared with a bolt-action rifle in one hand, and a tin box with webbing handles in the other. It didn't have a lid, and I could see cardboard boxes of ammunition. My eyes were drawn to the weapon, a very old-style piece of kit. The wooden furniture stretched from the butt all along the barrel to just short of the muzzle.

She put it down on the table. 'It's a Mosin Nagant. My father took it from the body of a North Vietnamese sniper during the war.'

I knew about this weapon: it was a classic.

Before passing it across, she turned it to present the opened bolt and show me that the chamber and magazine were clear. I was impressed, which must have been plain to see. 'My father—what's the use of having one if you don't know how to use it?'

I took the weapon from her. 'What service was he in?'

'Army. He made general before retiring.' She nodded over at the fridge pictures. 'The beach? Those are his army buddies.'

'What did he do?'

'Technical stuff, intelligence. There's one good thing that can be said about George—he's got smarts. He's at the Defense Intelligence Agency now. There's a senior White House adviser and two other generals, one still serving, in that photograph.'

'That's some bad scar on the end. Is he one of the generals?'

'No, he left the service in the eighties, just before the Iran-Contra hearings. They were all involved in one way or the other, though Ollie North took the heat. I never did know what happened to him.'

If he was part of the Iran-Contra affair, George would know all about jobs like this one. Black-ops jobs that no one wanted to know about, and people like him wouldn't tell anyway.

The connection between these two, George and the Pizza Man, was starting to make me feel uncomfortable. But I was a small player and didn't want to get involved with what was going on down here.

Luz called from the other room, 'Mom, Grandpa needs to talk with you.'

Carrie got up with a polite 'Won't be long,' and disappeared into the next room.

I examined the weapon, which looked unsophisticated compared with the sort of thing around nowadays. But I was familiar enough with the Russian weapon's history to know that these things had sent thousands of Germans to their graves on the eastern front in the forties. The one I had in my hands had been beautifully maintained. The wooden furniture was varnished, and the bolt action had been lightly oiled and was rust-free. The optic sight was a straight black tube about eight inches long and an inch in diameter mounted on top of the weapon. There were two dials halfway along the sight—the top one to adjust for elevation (up and down), and the one on the right-hand side for windage (left and right). The dials had no graduation marks any more—the top discs were missing—just some scratch marks where it had been zeroed.

Looking into the sight, I could see I had a post sight to aim with. A thick black bar came up from the bottom of the sight and finished in a point in the centre of the sight picture. Just below the point was a horizontal line that crossed the whole width of the sight. There were also conventional iron sights on the weapon.

I placed the gun on the table and was helping myself to more coffee when Carrie returned. 'Do you know how to adjust the sights?'

'No.' It would save me a lot of time if I didn't have to experiment.

'It's got a point blank zero at three hundred and fifty yards,' she said. I nodded as she picked up the weapon and turned the dials.

I could hear the clicks even above the noise of the fans before she handed it to me. 'There, the notches are in line.' She showed me the score marks levelled off against the sight on both dials to indicate the correct position for the sight to be zeroed.

I checked out the score marks. 'Anywhere I can go to check zero?'

'Take your pick. There's nothing but space out there.'

I picked up the ammunition tin. 'Can I have some of your printer paper and a marker pen?'

She knew exactly what I needed it for. 'Tell you what,' she said, 'I'll even throw in some tacks for free. See you outside.'

She went into the computer room and I went out through the mozzie screen and onto the verandah. Even in the shade it was much hotter out here. I was glad I was beginning to feel better, because it was an oppressive heat. My dizziness had all but disappeared.

Carrie came out carrying a paper bag. She handed it over. 'I've told Luz you might go hunting later, so you want to try out the rifle.'

'I'll be over there.' I indicated the tree line about 200 yards away, to the right of the house. It was on the opposite side to the track, so if Aaron came back early from rescuing jaguars he wouldn't get a 7.62 in his ear. 'See you in a bit.' I left the verandah.

Carrie called out from behind me. 'By the way, only load up four rounds. You can place five in the magazine OK, but can't close the bolt without stripping off the second round—got it?'

I lifted the weapon as I walked. I'd keep the point blank zero (PBZ), if it still existed. Why mess with something that might already be right? I might cock it up by trying to improve it.

PBZ is just a way of averaging out the averages to ensure the round hits the target in the vital area. Over a range of 350 yards the round won't rise or fall more than seven inches. My shoot should be from a maximum of 300 yards, so if I aimed at the centre of the target's sternum, he should take a round somewhere in the chest cavity.

I wandered to the tree line and put down the ammunition box. Then I set off towards the rising ground. I found a suitable tree and pinned a sheet of paper to the trunk. With a marker pen I drew a circle about the size of a two-pound coin and inked it in. I then pinned a sheet above and another below the first, then turned and walked back with the weapon and rounds, counting out a hundred one-yard paces. At that range, even if the sight was wildly inaccurate, with luck I would cut paper to see how bad it was.

A hundred paces later and still in the shade of the tree line, I sat against a tree and slowly closed the bolt action. Before I fired this weapon I needed to find out what the trigger pressures were. Correct trigger control will release the firing pin without moving the weapon.

I placed the top pad of my right index finger gently against the trigger. There was just a few millimetres of give as I squeezed until I felt resistance. This was the first pressure. The resistance was the second pressure. I gently squeezed again, and instantly heard the click as the firing pin pushed itself out of the head of the bolt.

Pulling the bolt back once more, I took one of the boxes of 7.62 rounds out of the ammunition tin, and fed in four, from the top of the breech, into what should have been a fixed five-round mag. Then I slid the bolt home, watching as it pushed the top round into the chamber. The on/off switch was at the back of the cocking piece, a flat circle of metal at the rear of the bolt about the size of a fifty-pence piece, and turning it to the left I applied Safe.

I looked for a small mound in the rough ground to double as a sandbag, and lay prone behind it. The weapon butt was in my right shoulder and my trigger finger ran over the trigger guard. I looked through the sight, taking aim at the centre of the not-too-circular black circle, then closed my eyes and stopped breathing. I relaxed my muscles slightly as I emptied my lungs. Three seconds later, I opened my eyes, started to breathe normally, and looked through the sight once more. My point of aim had shifted to the left-hand edge of the sheet of paper, so I swivelled my body to the right, then did the same thing twice more until I was naturally aligned to the target. It was pointless trying to force my body into a position that it didn't want to be in: that would affect the round when I fired.

I took three deep breaths to oxygenate my body. The weapon sight moved up and down as I sucked in air, and settled to a gentler movement as I started to breathe normally. It was only then that I took off the safety. Acquiring a good sight picture once more, I aimed before taking up the first pressure. At the same time I stopped breathing, to steady the weapon.

One second, two seconds . . . I gently squeezed the second pressure.

I didn't even hear the crack, I was so busy maintaining concentration while the weapon jumped up and back into my shoulder. All the time I kept my right eye open and followed through the shot, watching as the point of aim came back to settle on the centre of the target. That was good: my body was correctly aligned.

I looked through the sight to check where my round had fallen. I'd hit the top of the main sheet of paper: about five inches high. That was OK, it should be high at this close range: the optic was set at 350. The problem was that the round had gone to the left of the centre line by maybe as much as three inches. At 300 yards that would become nine inches. That wasn't good enough.

I waited maybe three minutes before reloading because I needed this to be a cold barrel zero. Variations in the barrel's temperature will warp the metal. It would be stupid to zero with a warm barrel, since it would be cold when I took the shot.

I took another shot. My round cut paper less than a quarter of an inch in from the first. The shots were well grouped, so I knew that the first round wasn't just a wild crazy one; the sight did need adjusting.

I sat up and waited for the barrel to cool. It was then that I saw Carrie making her way towards me from the rear of the house.

NINE

She was swinging a two-litre bottle of water in her right hand. I waved. She waved back.

When she got closer, she asked, 'How's the zero going?'

'Fine, just off a bit to the left.'

She held out the bottle with a smile. The condensation glistened on the plastic: it had come straight out of the fridge. I nodded my thanks, unscrewed the top and took some long, hard swallows.

She stayed above me, hands on hips. 'The sight might've taken some knocks over the months.' She put out her hand for the water. 'Question. If it's just for protection, how come you're checking the scope?' She pointed into the jungle. 'No good in there, is it?'

I smiled. 'Just like to be prepared, that's all. Want to help me?'

She caught my tone and went with it. 'Sure.'

'All I want you to do is aim dead centre into the black circle. I just want to adjust the sights.'

'One shot zero, right?'

'Right.'

'OK, tell you what—you aim, you're stronger. I'll adjust.'

I opened the bolt, ejecting the empty case, reloaded and applied Safe. 'I want the same elevation.'

She raised her eyebrow. 'Sure.' I was telling her how to suck eggs.

I pushed the stock into the mud and packed mud around it: the weapon needed to be locked tight into position for this to work. Once that was done, I checked that the score marks were still in line on the sight, and aimed dead centre of the black circle. 'OK.'

There was an 'Affirmative' from above as she pushed down on the mound with her sandalled foot, compacting the earth around the stock as I held it firmly in position. My arms strained as I tried to keep the weapon in a vicelike grip to ensure the post sight stayed dead centre. I could have done this on my own but it would have taken a whole lot longer.

She had finished packing the soil over the weapon and I still had a good sight picture, so I told her this and moved my head to the left so she could lean over and see the target through the sight. Our heads touched as her right hand moved onto the windage dial on the left side of the optic, and started to turn it. I heard a series of metallic clicks as she moved the post left until the point of aim was directly below the two rounds that I had fired while remaining in line with the centre of the black circle.

She moved her head back and squatted on her knees. 'OK, done.'

I dragged my Leatherman out of my pocket and passed it up to her, glad that I'd cleaned it. 'Score it for me, will you?'

She opened out the knife blade and leaned over to scrape a line from the dial onto the metal housing of the optic, so I'd be able to tell if the dial had been inadvertently moved, knocking the zero off.

She stood up to get out of the way. 'Ooookay . . .'

Pulling the weapon from the mud, I recocked and went through the firing sequence, aiming at the centre of the circle. The zero was good; the round went in directly above the point of aim, roughly in line with the other two rounds to the left. At 300 the round should cut paper slightly above the circle, but I'd soon find out.

I felt Carrie's knees against my arm. 'Is it OK?'

'Yeah, it's fine. Dead on.' I ejected the round.

We stood up together and walked back into the shade as I cleaned the mud off the rifle's furniture. She sat down under a tree.

I worked hard to think of something to say. 'How did the house come to be here? I mean, it's a bit off the beaten track, isn't it?'

'A rich hippie guy built it in the sixties. He came here to escape the draft. He died nine years ago and left the house and land to the university. We've been here nearly six years now. Cleared the land out back for helicopters. Even put up the extension ourselves.'

'Aaron told me you met at the university . . .'

She nodded. ''Eighty-six. Without him I'd never have had the stamina to get my PhD. I was one of his students. Staying here to study while the folks went back up north and got divorced was great. You know, straitlaced Catholic family gone wrong—the rebellious teenage years, father not understanding—that sort of stuff.'

'How does Luz fit in here? I mean, she isn't your natural child, is she?' She might have been: she could have had her with somebody else. 'What I mean is, she isn't—'

She cut in. 'No, no, you're right, she isn't. She's kind of fostered. She was my dearest and only friend really, Lulu . . . Luz is her daughter . . . Just Cause. You know what that is?'

I nodded. 'The invasion. December '89. Were you here?'

She shook her head sadly. 'Months before the invasion things were getting tense. Riots, curfews, people getting killed. It was only a matter of time before the US intervened, but nobody knew when. My father wanted us to move north, but Aaron wouldn't hear of it—this is his home. Besides, the Zone was only a few miles away, and whatever happened out here, in there we'd be safe. So we stayed. On the morning of the 19th, I got called by my father telling us to get into the Zone because it was going down that night. He was still in the military then, working out of DC.'

She gave a fleeting smile. 'Knowing George, he was probably planning it. God knows what he gets up to. Anyways, he'd arranged accommodation for us in Clayton. So we moved into the Zone and, sure enough, we saw enough troops, tanks, helicopters, you name it, to take on Washington state.' She shook her head slowly. 'That night the first bombs hit the city. They were taking out Noriega's headquarters, just a few miles from where we were. It was terrible—they were bombing El Chorrillo, where Lulu and Luz lived.'

It wasn't until the day after Christmas that Carrie and Aaron managed to get back to their house near the university. 'It was fine. It wasn't even looted, but the whole area was an occupation zone, checkpoints, troops, they were everywhere. We were so worried about Lulu and Luz, we went to El Chorrillo. There were bombed-out buildings, troops with machine guns cruising round in armoured vehicles. Lulu's walkup was just a heap of rubble. Her neighbours told us she'd been inside. Luz had been sleeping over at Lulu's sister's place in the next block. That was bombed, too, and the sister had been killed, but there was no trace of Luz. We found her eventually in one of the reception camps, in a crèche area with all the other parentless kids. The rest is history. From that day till this, we've looked after her.'

'Do you think the US did the right thing?' I asked.

'How could we just sit and watch Noriega—the deaths, torture, corruption? We should have done something sooner. Not that it's done any good. With the stand-down from the Zone, we've given everything away. I feel so sad that we could just give away everything that people died for back then. Can you understand that, Nick?'

Yes, I understood, but if I went there I wasn't sure I could navigate my way out again. I got to my feet. I filled the space with business. 'I've been thinking. I need to be back at Charlie's by four tomorrow morning, so I'll have to leave here at ten tonight—and we're going to need to work out how I can return this.' I held up the weapon. 'I presume you want it back?'

'Sure do. It's the only present my father ever gave me.' Carrie looked at me. 'Do you know how you're going to do it yet—you know, give him a reminder?'

'I've had one or two thoughts . . .' I looked out at the clearing, then had another. 'You got any explosive left? I saw the pictures, on the cork board.'

'You are nosy, aren't you?' She pointed towards the tree line that faced the rear of the house. 'There's a stash down there in the shack.'

I was amazed. 'You mean you've just left it there? In a shed?'

'Hey, come on. Where are we? There's more to worry about round here than a few cans of explosives. What do you want it for, anyway?'

'I need to make a lot of noise—to remind him.'

I couldn't see any outbuildings, just greenery: because of the downhill slope the bottom third of the tree line was in dead ground.

She pointed towards the dead ground. 'I'll take you down there after we've—'

'Mom! Mom! Grandpa wants to talk!' Luz was yelling for her from the rear of the house.

Carrie put her hands to her mouth. 'OK, baby.' She sounded quite concerned as she put down the bottle and ammo box. 'I've got to go.'

Jogging out into the sun towards the house, she pointed once more towards the invisible hut in the tree line. 'You can't miss it. Later.'

I LEFT EVERYTHING where it was and headed for the trees at the bottom of the cleared patch, eventually getting to what looked like an outdoor privy. Grass grew high right up against the door. I looked through the gap in the broken door, but didn't see a toilet. Instead I saw square metal boxes with red and black stencilling.

This was a gift: four boxes, eight kilos in each. I couldn't understand the Spanish, but made out what was important: it contained 55 per cent nitroglycerine, a high proportion. A high-velocity round would easily detonate this stuff, which wouldn't have been the case with military standard high explosive, which is shockproof.

I wrenched open the door and stepped inside. Pulling off the opening key from the side of the top box, I saw the date on the pasted-on label, 01/99, which I presumed was its Best Blown-up-by date.

I got to work, peeling the sealing strip of metal just below the lid exactly as if I was opening a giant can of corned beef. A plan was forming in my mind to leave a device by Charlie's gates. If I couldn't drop the target as he moved outside the house, I could take him out while his vehicle waited for the gates to open by getting a round into this shit. My fire position would have to be in the same area I'd been in yesterday to ensure a good view of the front of the house and the road to the gate. I'd have to rig the device so it was in line of sight of the fire position, but I couldn't see that as a problem.

Inside the tin container I found five sticks of commercial dynamite, wrapped in dark yellow greaseproof paper, some stained by the nitro, which had been sweating in this heat for years. A heavy smell of marzipan filled the air.

I took three of the eight-inch sticks and wandered back to the firing point, pulling back the greaseproof paper as I walked to reveal sticks of light green Plasticine-type material. Passing the weapon and ammo box, I continued the other 200 paces to the target area, where I placed them side by side at the trunk of the thickest tree I could find. Then, back at the 200 point, I got into my firing position and took a shot at the black circle. The zero was good: it went in directly above the one-shot zero round I'd fired—just as it should.

Now came the acid test, for both the zero and explosive. Picking up the ammo, weapon and bottle, I took another 100 paces to roughly the 300-yard mark, lay down, checked to make sure Carrie or Luz hadn't decided to wander from the house towards the target area, then aimed at the sternum-sized target of green dynamite.

I had one last check around the area. 'Firing, firing!' The warning shout had become a habit from years of playing with this kit.

Aiming centre of the sternum, I took a slow, controlled shot.

The crack of the round and the roar of the explosion seemed to be as one. The earth surrounding it was dried instantly by the heat of rapid combustion, turned to dust by the shock wave, and sent up in a thirty-foot plume. Slivers of wood were falling around the high ground like rain. The tree was still standing, and so it should be considering the size of it, but it was badly damaged.

'NIIICK! NIIICK!'

I jumped up and waved at Carrie as she ran from the back of the house. 'It's OK! OK! Just testing.'

She stopped at the sight of me and screamed, 'YOU IDIOT! I THOUGHT—' Abruptly she turned and stormed back inside.

Luckily there was no need to do anything more: the zero was on for all ranges, and the dynamite worked. All I had to do now was make a charge that'd take out a vehicle. Clearing the weapon, I picked up all the other bits and pieces and headed back to the house.

WITH THE HALF-EMPTY water bottle in my hand, I knocked on the door of the computer room as I entered. Carrie was sitting in the director's chair on the left, bent over some papers.

It was Luz who saw me first, seated at her desk further down the room. Swivelling in her chair to face me, she gave a '*Booom!*' with a big smile spread over her face and an apple in her hand. At least she thought it was funny. I shrugged sheepishly. 'Yeah, sorry about that.'

Carrie turned in her seat to face me. I gave her an apologetic shrug too and pointed at the storeroom. 'I'm going to need some things.'

She hit a final few keys on her PC and stood up. We headed for the storeroom. Carrie closed the door behind us. The outside entrance was open, and I could see the light fading on the rows of white tubs. The sky was no longer blue; clouds were moving across the sun.

I picked up a cardboard box that told me it should be holding twenty-four cans of Campbell's tomato soup, but in fact had only two. I took out the cans and stacked them on the shelf.

Carrie walked towards the outside door and gazed out at the white tubs. I looked at her framed in the doorway, then walked over to join her, carrying the water and soup box. 'What exactly do you do here?'

She pointed to the tubs. 'We're searching for new species of endemic flora—ferns, flowering trees, that sort of thing. We catalogue and propagate them before they disappear for ever.'

I moved outside and sat on the concrete, putting the soup box down beside me and untwisting the bottle top. As I took a swig she came and sat beside me, putting her glasses on.

'We go into the forest for specimens, cultivate them, and send samples to the university. So many of our medicines come from those things out there in the tubs. Every time we lose a species, we lose a potential cure for HIV, Alzheimer's, ME, whatever. The drug companies provide grants for the university to find and test new species for them. But they're closing us down next year. We're doing great work, but they want quick results for their buck.'

'How do you reconcile what you do here with what you're doing for me? I mean, the two don't exactly stand together, do they?'

She kept looking out at the tubs. 'It's helped me with Luz.'

'How's that?'

'Aaron's too old to adopt, and it's complicated getting things done here. So my father came up with the offer of a US passport for her, in exchange for our help. Sometimes we do wrong things for right reasons—isn't that true, Nick whatever-your-name-is?' She gazed out at the tree line. 'Aaron doesn't approve of this. We fight. He wanted to keep hassling for an adoption. But there's no time, we need to head back to Boston. My mother went to live there again after the divorce. George stayed in DC, doing what he's always done.'

'Why go after so long—because you're being closed down?'

'Not only that. The situation is getting worse down here. And there's Luz to think about. Soon it'll be high school, then college. She's got to start having a normal life.' She smiled. 'Hey, she wants to go, like yesterday.' The smile died. 'But Aaron hates change—just like my father. He's just hoping all the troubles will go away.'

I knew I was supposed to say something, but I didn't know what. I felt that the mess I'd made of my own life didn't exactly qualify me to sort out hers.

'I love him very much,' she said. 'It's just that I've gradually realised I'm not *in* love with the man, I guess . . . There are times when I feel so terribly lonely.'

She used both hands to put her hair behind her ears then turned towards me. 'What about you, Nick?' she said. 'Do you get lonely?'

I couldn't help myself . . . I told her that I lived in sheltered housing in London, that I had no money, had to line up to get free food from a Hare Krishna soup wagon. I told her that all my friends were dead apart from one, and he despised me. Apart from the clothes I was wearing when I arrived at their house, my only other possessions were in a bag stuck in left luggage at a railway station in London.

I also told her the only reason I was in Panama was that it would stop a child being killed by my boss. I wanted to tell her more, but managed to force the lid back on before it all came flooding out.

When I'd finished, I just stared out at the tubs again.

She cleared her throat. 'The child . . . is that Marsha or Kelly?'

I spun my head round and she mistook my shock for anger.

'I'm sorry, sorry . . . I shouldn't have asked, I know. It's just I was there, I was with you all night, I hadn't just appeared . . . I had to stay. Don't you remember? You kept on waking up shouting, trying to get outside to look for Kelly. And then you were calling out for Marsha. Somebody had to be there for you. Aaron had been up all night and he was out of it. I was worried about you.'

I felt very hot. 'What else did I say?'

'Well—Kev. I thought it was your real name until just now and—'

'Nick Stone.'

A smile returned to her face. 'That's your real name?'

I nodded. 'The girl's name is Kelly. Her mother was Marsha, married to my friend, Kev. Her little sister was called Aida. They were all murdered, in their house. Kelly's the only one left. I was just minutes too late to save them. She's why I'm here—she's all I have left.'

She nodded slowly, taking it all in. 'Why don't you tell me about her?' she said quietly. 'I'd love to hear about her.'

I felt the lid forcing itself open, and I had nothing left to control it.

'It's OK—it's OK, Nick. Let it out.' Her voice was cool, soothing.

And then I knew I couldn't stop it. The lid burst open and words crashed out of my mouth, hardly giving me time to breathe. I told her about being Kelly's guardian, being totally inconsistent, going to Maryland to see Josh, the only friend I had left, signing Kelly over permanently to Josh's care, Kelly's therapy, the loneliness . . . everything. By the end, I felt exhausted and just sat there with my hands covering my face.

I felt a hand gently touch my shoulder. 'You've never told anybody that before, have you?'

I shook my head and tried to smile. 'I've never sat still long enough,' I said. 'I had to give the therapist a few details about the way Kev and Marsha died, but I did my best to hide the rest of it.'

I stared at the tubs for a long while. Eventually she gave a theatrical sigh. 'What are we going to do with you?' She got to her feet and clipped me playfully across the ear. 'Well, recess over, back to work.'

'Yes, right. I need one of your tubs—I saw some empties near the sinks.'

'Sure, we're maxed out. They won't be needed soon, anyway.'

I held up the box. 'I'm going to play with that explosive down in the shack for a while, and I promise, no more bangs.'

She nodded. 'That's a relief. I think we've both had quite enough excitement for one day.' She turned towards the storeroom but then paused. 'Don't worry, Nick Stone, no one will know about this.'

I nodded a thank you, not just for keeping quiet, as she headed for the storeroom. 'Carrie?' She stopped and half turned. 'OK if I take some stuff with me? Food and equipment for tonight.'

'Sure, but just tell me what you've got so we can replace it, OK?'

'No worries.'

She gave a rueful smile. 'As if, Nick Stone.'

I watched her disappear into the store before heading across the open ground to the shack, swinging the tub I'd just collected in one hand, the box and water bottle in the other.

SITTING IN THE SHADE of the hut, I tore off the top and bottom flaps of the Campbell's box, scrunched them up in the bottom of the tub, and was left with the main carcass, a four-sided cube, which I ripped apart at a seam and opened out so that I had one long, flat section of cardboard. I started fitting it into the tub, running it round the edges then twisting it until I'd made a cone with its apex about a third of the way up from the bottom. If I let it go now the cone would spring apart, so I started to pack high explosive, still in its wrappers, around the base to keep it in place. Then, with the cone held fast, I peeled open the other boxes, unwrapped more explosive and played with the puttylike substance, packing it into the tub and around the cone.

I was trying to make a French off-route mine. These are the same shape as the tub, but a little smaller, and designed so that, unlike a conventional mine, they don't have to be directly beneath the target when detonated to destroy it. It can be concealed off to one side of a road or track, hidden in the bushes or, as I was planning, up a tree.

One version of the mine is initiated by a cable as thin as a strand of silk that's laid over the tarmac and crushed. I was going to detonate it with a round from the Mosin Nagant.

Once triggered, the manufactured ones instantly turn a cone of copper into a hot, molten slug, propelling it at such speed and power that it penetrates the target's armour. I didn't have any copper; in its place, and shaped very much the same way, was the cardboard cone, but there should be enough force in the explosive alone to do the job.

I continued squashing down the explosive, trying to make it one solid mass over the cone. My hands stung as the glycerine got into cuts. When I'd finished, I sealed the top on the tub, left the device in the shed, and started back to the house.

The sky had turned metallic and there was a rumble of thunder in the distance as I crested the slope. Aaron and Carrie were by the sinks, and I could see they were arguing again. Carrie's arms were flying about and Aaron's head was jutting forward like a rooster.

I slowed down, lowered my head, and hoped they'd see me soon.

They must have spotted me, because the arms stopped windmilling. Carrie disappeared into the storeroom as Aaron dried himself. I got to him as he retied his hair, clearly embarrassed.

'Sorry you had to see that.'

'None of my business,' I said. 'Besides, I'll be gone tonight.'

'Carrie told me you'll need dropping off—ten, right?'

Nodding, I released the water pressure and soaked my hands before cutting the supply and soaping up to get all the nitro off me. 'You said you had a map? Is it on the bookshelf?'

'Help yourself, and I'll get you a real compass.' He hung the green towel on the line. 'You feeling better now? We were worried.'

'Fine, must have picked something up yesterday. How's the jaguar?'

'They promised they're going to do something this time, maybe the zoo, but I'll believe it when I see it.' He headed for the door.

TEN

Now that the sky had greyed over completely the storeroom was almost dark. I eventually found the string-pull for the light and a single fluorescent strip flickered on.

The first thing I saw was that the weapon and ammunition had been placed on a shelf for me, along with a Silva compass and map.

I needed to make some 'ready rounds', so ripped about six inches off a roll of one-inch gaffer tape, placed a round on the sticky side, and rolled. As soon as the round was covered I placed another, rolled a little, then another, until four rounds were in a noiseless bundle, easy to fit into my pocket. I folded over the last two inches of tape to make it easier to pull apart, then started on another.

I had to prepare for as much as four nights in the field—up to two on target and two in the jungle—before popping out once the dust had settled and making my own way to the airport.

I found an old bergen in the storeroom, and lobbed it onto the cot with a spare box of ammunition, three litre bottles of Evian, nine cans of tuna and an assortment of honey sesame bars that looked as if they'd get me through daylight hours.

Judging by what was on the shelves, they had certainly got their hands on enough of that military giveaway. I grabbed a poncho, some new blankets, and some dark green mozzie nets. I could make a shelter from a poncho with the hood tied up and a couple of yards of string through the holes at each corner, and the mosquito nets would not only keep the beasties off me at night, but also act as camouflage netting. I took three.

Most importantly, I found a machete, an absolute necessity for the jungle because it can provide protection, food and shelter. This one was US army issue and much sturdier than the one Diego had been swinging at me. It had a canvas sheath with a light alloy lip.

Otherwise, all I needed was the wet clothes I'd be standing up in, plus a dry set, and a hammock. All this would be kept dry in plastic in the bergen, and by the poncho at night. I already had my eye on the string hammock on the verandah.

I carried on rooting around, and was happy to find the one thing I was desperate for, its clear thick liquid contained in rows of plastic bottles. The label said it was 95 per cent proof. Diethyl-m-toluamide—I just knew it as Deet—was magical stuff that would keep the mozzies and creepy-crawlies away from me. Some commercial stuff contains only 15 per cent, and is crap. The more Deet the better. I threw three bottles onto the cot.

I started to pack the bergen. Having removed the noisy wrappers from the sesame bars and put them all into a plastic bag, I stuffed them into the large left-hand side pouch for easy access during the day. I shoved a bottle of Evian into the right-hand one for the same reason. The rest of the water and the tuna went into the bottom of the pack, wrapped in dishcloths to muffle any noise. I'd only pull that food out at night when I wasn't in my fire position.

Into a large plastic laundry bag went a mozzie net and the blankets. The hammock would join them once I'd nicked it from the verandah later on. All the stuff in this bag needed to be dry at all times. Into it also would go my dry clothes for sleeping in, the same ones I'd wear once out of the canopy and heading for the airport. I'd get those from Aaron when I got the hammock.

I laid the other two mozzie nets beside the bergen, together with some four-inch-wide, multicoloured nylon luggage straps. Any colour but this collection would have been better to blend into a world of green. I placed them inside the top flap, ready to make a simple but effective sniper seat.

I sat on the cot, and thought about any other stuff I could use. First up was a shade for the front of the optic sight, so that sunlight didn't reflect off the objective (front) lens and give away my position.

I got a container of antifungal powder, again US army issue, in a small olive-green plastic cylinder. Emptying the contents, I cut off the top and bottom, then split it down the side. After wiping away all the powder on the inside, I put it over the front of the sight. It naturally hugged the metal cylinder as I moved it back and forth until the section protruding in front of the lens was just slightly longer than the lens's width. The sunlight would now only reflect off the lens if the sun itself was visible within my field of view.

Next I needed to protect the muzzle and working parts from the rain, because wet ammunition and a wet barrel will affect the round's trajectory. I fed a plastic bag over the muzzle and taped it to the furniture, then loaded up with rounds, pushed the bolt action forward to make ready the weapon, and applied the safety.

I ripped open the bottom of one of the clear plastic bags that had held the blankets, then worked it over the weapon until it was covering the sight, magazine and working parts, using gaffer tape to fix each open end to the furniture. Then, making a slit in the plastic above the sight, I pushed it down so that the sight was now clear, and gaffer-taped the plastic together underneath to keep the seal. Everything in that area, bar the sight, was now encased in plastic. The safety could still be taken off, and when the time came I could still get my finger into the trigger by breaking the plastic. If I needed to fire more than one round, I'd just quickly rip the bag to reload.

Next, I used the clear plastic from the last of the blankets on the shelf to protect the map, which said it had been compiled by the US army's 551st Engineer Company for the Panamanian government in

1964. A lot would have changed on the ground since then—Charlie's house and the loop road being just two of them. That didn't concern me too much; I was interested in the topographical features, the high ground and water features. That was the stuff that would get me out of there when I needed to head towards the city.

The compass still had its cord on, so I could put it over my head and under the T-shirt. The map, compass, machete and docs would stay on my body at all times once under the canopy. I couldn't afford to lose them.

The last thing I did before getting my head down was thread the end of a ball of twine through the slit drilled into the butt designed to take a webbing or leather sling, and wrap about four foot of it round the butt, cut it and tie it secure. The weapon would never be over my shoulder unless I was climbing a tree. Only then would I tie the string into the slit in the stock and sling it.

I pushed everything that was left off the bed, and gave the light cord a tug. It wasn't that I was feeling antisocial, just that when there's a lull before the battle you get your head down.

I WAS WOKEN SUDDENLY. I snapped my wrist in front of my face to check Baby-G, and calmed down: it was just after a quarter past eight. I didn't need to get up until about nine.

The rain played a low, constant drumroll that accompanied the low thud of the fans next door. I turned onto my stomach. It was then that I heard some conspiratorial-sounding murmurs.

The cot creaked as I slowly swung my feet over the side and stood up. The sound was coming from the computer room, and I felt my way towards the door. A sliver of light from beneath it guided me.

I put my ear to the wood and listened.

It was Carrie. In a whisper she was answering questions I couldn't hear: 'They can't come now . . . What if he sees them? . . . No, he knows nothing, but how am I going to keep them apart? . . . No, I can't. He'll wake up . . .'

My hand reached for the door handle. Gripping it tightly, I opened the door half an inch to see who she was talking to.

The six-inches-by-six, black and white image was a little jittery and fuzzed around the edges, but I could clearly see whose head and shoulders were filling the webcam. Wearing a checked jacket and dark tie, George was looking straight into his camera.

Carrie was listening via the headphones as his mouth moved

silently. 'But it wouldn't work, he won't buy that . . . What do you want me to do with him? . . . He's next door asleep . . . No, it was just a fever . . . Christ, Dad, you said this wouldn't happen . . .'

George pointed at her through the screen.

She answered angrily. 'Of course I was . . . He likes me.'

My face began to smart and burn as I rested my head on the door-frame. It was a long time since I'd felt so massively betrayed.

I knew I shouldn't have opened up to her, I just knew it.

'No, I've got to go get ready, he's only next door . . .'

When I pulled the door open Carrie jumped out of her seat with shock, the headset wire jerking tight as the headset pulled down round her neck and the screen closed down.

She recovered, bending forward to take them off. 'Oh, Nick—sleep better?' She knew, I could see it in her eyes.

I checked that the living-room door was closed and took three paces towards her. I slapped my hand over her mouth, grabbed a fist-ful of hair at the back of her head, and lifted. She let out a whimper, her green eyes bigger than I'd ever thought eyes could be. Her nos-trils snorted in an attempt to get some air into her lungs. Both her hands were hanging on my wrists, trying to release some of the pres-sure from her face. I dragged her into the darkness of the storeroom, her feet scarcely touching the ground. Kicking the door shut so that we both became instantly blind, I put my mouth to her ear. 'I'm going to ask questions. Then I'm going to let go of your mouth and you'll answer. Do not scream, just answer. Nod if you understand.'

She gave a succession of jerky nods into my hands.

Taking a slow, deep breath, I whispered into her ear once more. 'Why are you talking to your dad about me? Who is coming?'

I released my grip from her mouth a little so she could suck in air, but still gripped her hair. 'I can explain, please, just let me breathe—'

Both of us heard the noise of a wagon approaching as it laboured up the muddy track.

'Oh God, oh, please, Nick, please just stay in here. It's dangerous, I'll explain later, please.'

I hit the light and it started to flicker above us as I grabbed the weapon from the shelf, ripped the plastic from the bolt and rammed the two bundles of ready rounds into my pockets.

She was still begging as the engine got louder. 'Please stay here, don't leave the room—I'll handle this.'

I moved to the exit door. 'Turn the light off, now!'

She pulled the switch.

I eased the door open a couple of inches and looked to the right, towards the front of the house. I couldn't see a wagon, just the glow of headlights bouncing off the verandah through the rain.

I slipped through the door and closed it gently behind me. Turning left, I made for the washing area just as two vehicle doors slammed in quick succession, accompanied by shouts—not aggressive, just communicating, I guessed in Spanish, though I couldn't tell from this distance. As soon as I'd rounded the corner I set off towards the shack in the dead ground, using the house as cover.

I moved for maybe 200 yards before risking a glance back. The house was silhouetted in the glow of headlights, and the engine noise had faded. I moved on another twenty paces; the lights, too, slowly disappeared as I gradually dropped down into the dead ground, heading towards the hut. Turning right, I ran for the other tree line.

Once I'd got halfway towards the trees I turned right again and started moving up the crest, back towards the house. I'd been concentrating so hard that I hadn't realised the rain had stopped.

I slowed when I was maybe 150 yards behind the house, and started to move more cautiously, keeping my body as low as possible.

My angle of view gradually changed. I could see the area in front of the verandah, caught in the headlights of a large 4x4 parked next to the Mazda. On the roof, upside-down and strapped on tight, I could see a Gemini, an inflatable rubber boat.

The low revs of the engine became audible as I finally reached the rows of white plastic tubs. I got onto my knees and right hand and, with the weapon balanced in my left, moved between the rows.

The scene on the verandah slowly came into focus. I could see two male figures with Carrie, but I couldn't hear their voices. One was quite a bit shorter and fatter than the other.

Keeping the weapon in my left hand and out of the mud, I eased myself down into a fire position between the tubs. I got a blurred sight picture owing to the rain on the lenses.

Carrie's head filled half the optic. I focused on her face, trying to read it. She didn't look scared as she spoke, just serious.

I panned and picked up the taller of the two men. He was Latino, with a crew cut and rough-looking beard, and wearing a black collarless shirt. I panned down to see muddy green fatigue bottoms tucked into equally dirty boots. He was quite animated, pointing first at Carrie, then at the shorter man. Something was wrong.

The movements stopped and he looked at Carrie again, expecting some sort of answer. I panned onto her. She nodded slowly, pulled open the mozzie screen and shouted into the house, 'Aaron!'

I looked over at the vehicle. It was a GMC, its block shape high off the ground and its bodywork splattered with mud. All the doors were closed and the engine was still running, probably for the air.

The mozzie screen slammed shut. I aimed back towards the verandah and saw Aaron. There weren't any greetings for him: Carrie just spoke to him for less than a minute, then with a nod he went back into the house, a worried-looking man. Carrie and the other two followed. The short guy carried an aluminium briefcase that I hadn't seen until then. I watched as they passed the bookshelf window, heading towards the computer room.

All of a sudden, to my left, there was a flash in my peripheral vision. I turned to see the last of a match burning in the dark of the GMC's interior.

I brought the weapon back into the aim, and saw a bright red glow from the rear seat. I ran the optic down the side windows of the GMC, but couldn't tell whether or not they were blacked out until another drag was taken. That wasn't long in coming; I couldn't see anything from the side apart from a gentle red triangular glow in the rear door window. It had to be the GMC from the locks. What was the chance of the same visual distinguishing mark?

I watched as the cigarette was sucked to death, and the glow disappeared, then the rear door furthest from the verandah opened and a body stepped out. I could see the top half of a man taking a piss. I recognised the long features and nose.

This wasn't good. The Pizza Man had been at Charlie's; I was on my way there now. He knew George; George knew about me.

He jumped back into the wagon as the mozzie screen opened and the two guys stepped down from the verandah. The shorter one was still clutching his briefcase. Carrie followed them out and watched as they both climbed in.

The engine revved and headlights flooded the area around me as the wagon turned. I hugged the ground, waiting for the light to wash over me, then got onto my knees and watched and listened as the engine noise and taillights faded back into the jungle.

Pulling myself out of the mud, I moved towards the house. The light in the storeroom was on, and I placed the weapon gently on the cot as Carrie came into the computer room, sat at the PCs, and buried her head in her hands. I closed the door behind her. 'Tell me.'

She looked scared as her face came up to look at me. 'This whole thing is creeping me out—have you any idea how crazy those people are? I hate it when they come.'

'I can see that, but who are they?'

'They work for my father. They're doing some sort of operation against FARC, on the Bayano somewhere. It's a drugs-surveillance thing . . . we have the relay board for their communications. It's secure, so it comes through us, then to George. He said to keep it from you for operational security.'

'So why did they come when I was here?'

'The webcam. . . they're monitoring any ships suspected of drug-trafficking. I was told to close it down before you arrived, but I forgot. Good spy, huh? When I eventually did close it down, it messed up their other communications, something to do with the relay.' She pointed to the wires under the tables. 'They had to come and fix it. That's what George was telling me when you came in. We didn't want it to get mixed up with the job he's sent you to do—'

'Hold on—your dad sent me?'

'Didn't you know? He's controlling both operations.'

Aaron came into the room, his eyes darting between the two of us.

'I've told him,' she said. 'I've told him everything.'

Aaron looked at me and sighed. 'I've always hated all this. I told her not to get involved.' He turned to Carrie. 'It isn't worth it for what you want, Carrie. There has to be another way.' Taking two paces forward, he threw his arms round her, stroking her head.

I walked through the living room to the verandah and joined the mozzies by the wall light as I untied the hammock.

Everything she'd said would have made sense, if it weren't for the Pizza Man. If he had seen Aaron or the Mazda at the locks, it explained why he bolted so quickly: if Aaron and Carrie didn't know he was on the ground, he wouldn't want to be seen by them. I was tempted to tell her, to pump her for more information on him. But that would stay in my pocket in case I needed it—and there was still the question of his going to Charlie's that I couldn't work out.

I stepped off into the mud, opened up the back of the Mazda and saw in the light from the verandah that everything had been packed into an old canvas bag. I dragged out the blue towrope, which reeked of petrol, and walked back towards the house.

I stepped up onto the verandah and as I bent down to gather up the hammock I realised what I was going to do about it. Nothing. Absolutely nothing. I didn't have the luxury of doing anything other than what I'd come here to do: keep Kelly alive.

I had to keep mission-orientated; that was the only thing I had to concentrate on. My sole focus had to be keeping the Yes Man happy.

With the hammock and towrope gathered in my arms I pulled the mozzie screen open just as Aaron tiptoed out of Luz's darkened bedroom and gently closed the door. He walked towards me.

I kept my voice low. 'Listen, I didn't know anything about Carrie, her dad, or any of the other stuff until today. I'm sorry if life is shit, but I've come to do a job and I still need to be taken to do it.'

He drew a long, deep breath. 'You know why's she doing this?'

I nodded and shrugged. 'Something to do with a passport?'

'You got it. But you know what? I think she would have done it anyway. No matter how much she hates to admit it, she's just like George, takes the Stars and Stripes gig to the max.'

He held up his wrist to show his watch. 'Anything you need?' He was right: it was nearly ten o'clock, time to go.

'There is. I put all of that explosive from the hut in one of your tubs, and I've left it down there.'

'You taking it with you?'

I nodded.

He took another deep breath. It seemed there were many things that Carrie didn't talk to him about. 'OK, gimme five.'

We parted, him to his bedroom and me to the storeroom. Carrie was still sitting on the director's chair, elbows on the desk, cradling her head. I left her to it and packed the hammock and other stuff into the bergen.

The mozzie screen slammed as Aaron left to collect the device. Remembering that I still needed dry clothes, I went back to the computer room. 'Carrie?' There was no reply. 'Carrie?'

She slowly lifted her head as I walked into the room.

'I need some more clothes.' I pulled at my mud-covered sweatshirt. 'A complete set of stuff.'

'Oh, right. I'll, um . . . Sure.' She stood up and left the room.

I rummaged around under the cot and shelves for more polythene blanket wrappers. With several ripped ones in my hands, I picked up the rifle and swathed the muzzle and working parts in polythene again, completing the seal with tape.

Carrie reappeared with a thick brown cotton shirt and matching canvas trousers. They went into the protective plastic in the bergen, which I then closed down with the other two mozzie nets on top.

I gave my trousers a good squirt of Deet before tucking them into my socks, then doused them as well. Then I got to work on my forearms, hands, neck and head. I wanted to be armour-plated with the stuff, and I'd go on replenishing it all the time I was on the ground. I carried on squirting it over my clothing and rubbing it in. I threw her one of the bottles as she stood, zombie-like. 'Do my back, will you?'

It seemed to snap her out of her trance. She started rubbing it roughly into my sweatshirt. 'I'm taking you.'

'What?'

'It's my job, I'll take you. I'm the one who wants the passport.'

I nodded. I didn't want to talk about it. All I wanted was the lift.

The rubbing stopped. 'We ought to be going.'

The half-used bottle appeared over my shoulder.

She walked out, and I packed all the Deet bottles in the top flap and started to wrap the weapon in the blanket for protection.

THE ATMOSPHERE WAS STRAINED as Carrie and I shook around in the cab, following the beam as it bounced off the jungle around us. I kept a hand on the rifle between my knees to protect the zero.

We eventually emerged from the forest and passed through the valley of dead trees. At last she cleared her throat. 'Am I forgiven?' She glanced at me to check that she really was before her eyes darted back to the track as we tilted left.

'Can't your dad just give Luz a passport? Surely he can sort it out?'

'Sure he can. But I've never had anything from him for free. I always had to earn it first. It was only going to be for locating the relay board. Then it got worse, some food and stores, a few gallons of two-stroke. They didn't want to go to Chepo in case they got recognised, I suppose . . . Then you came along. Aaron told me that once it started it'd never stop, he'd keep using me. Maybe he's right, but as soon as the passport comes we'll be out of here.'

'You'll go to your mum's? Boston?'

'She's got a house in Marblehead, on the coast. I have a job waiting at MIT and Luz is set for school.'

'What's the score with your dad? I can't work out if you hate him, love him or what.'

'I can't either. I never knew who he really was, what he really did. He just went away, came back sometimes with something he'd pick up for me last minute. Then he left again as soon as I'd got used to him being around. He's a cold man, but still my father.'

'Aaron said you're like him—something about Stars and Stripes?'

She laughed. 'Aaron only thinks that because, for once, I agree with George on what's gone wrong in this country. Aaron's too stubborn to see it, that's why he wants to stay. He's hoping for a brighter future but it ain't coming on its own. The Zone as he remembers it has gone. We, America, let that happen. It's disgusting.'

'You guys could come back if the canal was threatened. Isn't there a clause in the treaty, something in the small print?'

'Oh, yeah, sure—like the Russians are going to invade. I'm not planning my future around it.'

'You lot gave the thing back, didn't you? What's the big deal?'

'OK, there are two major problems to address.' Her right index finger sprang up from the bucking steering wheel. 'SOUTHCOM's drugs eradication capability is about a third of what it was before '99. People like Charlie and FARC are getting a free run. So the only answer was what Clinton did—throw a billion plus at Plan Colombia, with troops, hardware, all to kick ass down there.'

She fought with the wheel. 'Without the Zone, we had no alternative but to project further south, take the fight to them in their back yard. But it ain't going to work. We're just getting dragged into a long, costly war that's going to have little impact on the drug trade. Because we've given away the Zone, we've created a situation where we now need it more than ever. Crazy, no?'

It made sense to me. 'Otherwise it'll be like launching the D-Day invasion of France from New York?'

She gave me a smile of approval, between fighting the ruts.

'Panama's going to be needed as a forward operating area from which to project our forces, as well as a buffer to stop the conflict spreading into Central America. What Clinton has done is a very dangerous alternative, but without the Zone he had no choice.'

We finally hit the road to Chepo.

'And the most scary thing is that China now runs the canal. We let the very country that could back FARC in the war take control.'

'Come on, it's just a Hong Kong firm who got the contract. They run ports worldwide.'

Her jaw tightened as she gritted her teeth. 'Oh, yeah? Well, ten per cent of it is owned by Beijing—they operate the ports at each end of the canal and some of our old military locations. In effect, we've got

Communist China controlling fourteen per cent of all US trade.'

I was beginning to see her point.

'Charlie was one of the group pushing the Chinese deal. I wonder what his kickback was—freedom to use the docks for business?'

I started to see pinholes of light penetrating the blackness ahead: we were approaching Chepo. She kept glancing over at me as we rumbled over the gravel, waiting for some kind of response.

'I guess this is where I fit in,' I said. 'I'm here to stop Charlie handing over a missile guidance system to FARC so they can't use it against US helicopters in Colombia.'

'Hey, so you're one of the good guys.' She'd started smiling again.

'That's not the way it feels.' I hesitated. 'Your dad wants me to kill Charlie's son.'

She jolted the wagon to a halt on the gravel. I could see her full face in red shadow. I couldn't make out whether the look in her eyes was shock or disgust. Maybe it was both.

'I couldn't tell you because of operational security.' I tried to fight it but couldn't, the lid was still completely off. 'And also because I'm ashamed. But I've still got to do it. I'm desperate, just like you.' I glanced out at the expanse of muddy potholes caught in the headlights. 'His name is Michael. Aaron teaches him at the university.'

She slumped in her seat. 'The locks . . . he told me about—'

'That's right, he's just a few years older than Luz.'

She didn't respond. Her eyes fixed on the tunnel of light.

'So, now you have the misfortune of knowing all that I know.'

It was time for me to shut up. I turned and watched as she pursed her lips, shook her head and drove as if she was on autopilot.

ELEVEN

Friday, September 8

We had hardly exchanged another word as we bounced around in the cab for the next couple of hours.

I finished getting the bergen out of the back.

'Nick?'

I leaned down to the half-open window.

'Michael is dying to save hundreds, maybe thousands of lives. It's the only way I can deal with it. Maybe it'll work for you.'

I nodded, concentrating more on protecting the zero than trying to justify myself. Charlie should be getting the good news, not his boy.

'It's certainly going to save one, Nick. One that you love very much, I know. Sometimes we have to do the wrong thing for the right reasons, no?' She held my gaze for another couple of seconds, then glanced down at the selector, chose Drive, and hit the gas.

I stood and watched the red taillights fade into the darkness, then waited for my night vision to kick in. When I could see where I was putting my feet, I tied the machete round my waist, shouldered my bergen, heaved the tub on top, and held it with a straight arm, my left hand gripping the handle. With the rifle in my right, I moved down to the road junction, then headed west towards the house.

Only three and a half hours of darkness remained, by the end of which I needed to be ready at the gate. As soon as it was light enough to see what I was doing, I needed to place the device and find a firing position in the opposite tree line.

I pushed on, listening and looking for vehicles.

After a few changes of arm supporting the weight of the tub, I was finally at the gates. Keeping to the right, in cover, I dumped the tub while I caught my breath. When eventually I looked through the railings of the gate, the fountain was still lit, and I could see the glint of light on a number of vehicles parked in the drive beyond it. The gold side windows of the Lexus winked back at me. The house was asleep, no light shining out apart from an enormous chandelier, which sparkled through a large window above the main entrance.

There wasn't going to be any finesse about this device, but it had to be set precisely. As the vehicle moved through the gates, the force of the shaped charge had to be directed exactly where I wanted it.

I collected the tub, then stumbled along the animal track that ran between the wall and the canopy. The wall ran out after just seven or eight yards, and at that point I moved a few feet back into the trees to wait for first light. Keeping the bergen on my back, I sat on the tub with the weapon across my legs to protect the zero.

Eventually I began to see an arc of pale light rising above the tree line. The birds took their cue to get noisy. I made out a low mist lying on the mud of the clearing and, higher up, grey cloud cover.

Another ten minutes and light was penetrating the canopy. I could just see my feet. It was time to start rigging the device.

I moved slowly towards the gate. I dropped the tub and bergen about two yards short of it, and lay the weapon on the ground.

It didn't take long to find a tree of the right height and structure to take the charge. I took the nylon towrope out of the top pouch of the bergen, tied one end to the tub's handle and gripped the other between my teeth while I worked out how to climb my chosen tree.

It was a noisy ascent but now was the moment to get on with it, before everybody in the house began to stir.

At last I could just see over the wall to the house, and to the other tree line to my half right. My firing point was going to be somewhere along that tree line; it was maybe 300 yards away and the tub should be easy enough to find from that distance with the optic.

I was working out how I was going to strap the tub in position when I heard an engine start up in the driveway. I turned towards the source. There were no lights from any of the vehicles, just the low, gentle sound of a petrol engine ticking over.

I had to act. This might be the only chance I got.

I opened my mouth to release the rope, and scrambled down the trunk. I grabbed the weapon and ran back to the end of the wall, frantically tearing at the plastic, feeling for the ready rounds.

Dropping onto my right knee, I brought the weapon up and looked through the optic, gulping deep breaths to oxygenate myself.

An oldish guy moved around in the low light, a cigarette glowing in his mouth. He was wearing flip-flops, shorts and a polo shirt, and was wiping the night's rain off the Lexus with a chamois leather.

I sat back on my right foot and braced my left elbow on my left knee, butt pulled firmly into the shoulder. I visualised the target coming from the front door, heading for the Lexus.

The old guy made his way conscientiously along the wagon with his chamois. Then the two huge doors at the front of the house opened and I was aiming into a body, the chandelier backlighting him perfectly. The post sight was in the middle of a white, short-sleeved shirt-and-tie, one of the bodyguards, either Robert or Ross, whichever had gone out for the drinks. He was standing in the door-frame, talking on his Nokia and checking progress with the wagon.

My heart-rate soared, then training kicked back in: I controlled my breathing and my pulse started to drop.

The bodyguards disappeared back into the house but the front door was still open. I waited in the aim, feeling the pulse in my neck.

There he was. Michael stepped outside, green on blue, carrying a rucksack, smiling, talking with Robert and Ross either side of him. I got the post on him, centre of the trunk, got it on his sternum, took first pressure. Shit . . . A white-shirt moved between us.

Keeping the pressure, I followed the group. I got part of his face, still smiling, chatting. Not good enough, too small a target.

Then someone else, a dark grey suit, blocked my view completely. This wasn't going to work—too late, too many bodies blocking.

They were at the wagon. Shit, shit, shit . . .

I released first pressure, ducked back behind the wall, and ran for the gate while applying Safe. Fuck the off-route mine now, I just wanted an explosion. I grabbed the tub.

Gasping for air, I reached the gate and dropped the tub against the wall, the towrope still attached, the rest trailing behind.

The engine note of the Lexus changed as the wagon started down the drive towards me. It got louder as I picked up the bergen and sprinted along the edge of the trees by the road. I launched myself into the foliage at a point about thirty yards from the gate.

The electric whine of the motor opening the gates drowned out the noise of the Lexus as it came nearer and then stopped.

To get muzzle clearance, I jumped up in a semi-squat, legs apart to steady myself, butt of the rifle in my shoulder as I got the safety off.

I could see the wraparounds of the two white-shirts in front as we all waited for the gates to open, and knew I was exposed to them. I kept as low as I could, my chest heaving up and down as the Lexus finally started to roll forward. Just twenty feet to go.

The wagon stopped so suddenly the rear bucked on its suspension.

Shit! I stopped breathing and fixed both eyes on the tub. I brought the weapon up to refocus into the optic, and took first pressure.

The engine went high-pitched into reverse. I saw the blurry whiteness of the tub and the post clear and sharp in the middle of it, then fired. I dropped the weapon as I hit the floor, and the shock wave surged over me. It felt like I'd been freefalling at 100mph and was suddenly stopped by a giant hand in midair, but my insides kept going.

Grabbing the rifle, I reloaded and got to my feet, checking the battle sight. There was no time to watch out for the debris falling from the sky: I had to confirm he was dead.

The wagon had been pushed back six or seven yards on the tarmac. I started towards the dustcloud as shattered masonry and bits of jungle fell back to earth, butt in the shoulder, ears ringing, vision blurred, my whole body shaking. Rubble and twisted ironwork lay where part of the right-hand wall and gates had once stood.

I closed in on the mangled wreck, running in a semi-stoop, and took up a position by the remains of the wall just forward of a smouldering crater. The Lexus looked like a stock car, its side windows missing, the windscreen safety glass shattered and buckled.

I took aim with the battle sights through the driver's window. The first round thudded into the bloodstained white-shirt who was slumped but recovering over the steering wheel. *Two!*

Maintaining the weapon in the shoulder and supported by my left hand, I reloaded and took another shot into the second slumped, bloodstained white-shirt on the passenger side.

Three! With only four I had to remember my rounds fired.

I moved, weapon up, towards the rear door. I saw two slumped bodies covered in shattered glass: one the green T-shirt and blue jeans, the other the dark grey suit. I closed in. The suit was Charlie.

The target was more or less collapsed in the footwell, with his dad draped over him. Both were badly shaken, but alive. There was some coughing from Charlie and I could see the target moving.

Mustn't hit Charlie . . . I rammed the weapon through the window gap. The muzzle was no more than two inches from the target's bloody, glass-covered and confused head.

The target moaned and groaned, pushing his father off him. His eyes were closed; fragments of glass were trapped in his eyebrows.

I felt the second pressure on my finger pad, but it was refusing to squeeze further. Something was holding me back.

The muzzle followed his head as it moved about, turning over onto his side. It was now virtually in his ear.

It wasn't happening, my finger wouldn't move. COME ON, DO IT! DO IT! I couldn't, and in that instant I knew why.

My brain filtered out almost everything, but it let in the shouts; I turned to see men pouring from the house, carrying weapons.

I withdrew the rifle, reached in the front, and pulled the Nokia off the bodyguard's belt. Then I wrenched open the buckled metal and seized a fistful of suit. I dragged Charlie onto the tarmac, virtually running with him to the other side of what was left of the wall. 'Move! Move!'

I kicked him to his knees and he fell forward onto his hands. Stepping back, I aimed at his head. 'Can you hear me?' The shouts were getting nearer. 'The missile guidance system, make sure—'

'What is wrong with you people?' He shouted angrily. 'It's been delivered—last night! You have the launch control system—you have everything! The Sunburn is complete! What more do you want?'

'Delivered? This is about getting it delivered?'

'Last night! You people use my son to threaten me, demanding it by tomorrow night, you get it and still—' He saw my confusion. 'Don't you people know what each other is doing?'

'Tuesday—the guy in the pink shirt. He was here—has he got it?'

'Of course! The deal is done, yet you still threaten my family . . . Remember the condition—no Panamanian targets. You said it would move straight to Colombia—not use it here.'

'Fatherrrrr!' Michael had seen us. 'Don't kill him. Please!'

Charlie yelled something in Spanish, probably telling him to run, then fixed his glare on me once more. 'Well, Englishman, what now? You already have what you came here for.'

I turned and ran along the tree line, back towards the bergen. I grabbed it in my spare hand, looked back and saw Michael limping towards his dad as people and vehicles converged.

That was the problem. Michael was real people. He was a kid with a life, not one of the shadow people I was used to, the sort of target I'd never thought twice about killing.

I hurled myself into the jungle, crashing through wait-a-while, not caring about sign. I just wanted to get my arse out of here and into the wall of green. The commotion behind me faded as I penetrated deeper—but I knew it wouldn't be long before they came in after me.

There was automatic fire. They were firing blindly, hoping to zap me as I ran. That didn't bother me, the trees would take the brunt.

I pulled out my compass and headed east for about twenty yards, taking my time, trying not to leave upturned leaves or broken cobwebs in my wake. Then I turned north, then west, doubling back on myself but to the side of my original track. After five or six yards I stopped, looked for a thick bush, and wormed my way into it.

Squatting on my bergen, butt in the shoulder, safety off, I fought for breath. If they were tracking, they would pass right to left, seven or eight yards in front as they followed my sign. The rule about being chased in the jungle was that when the enemy are coming fast you've got to sidestep and creep away. Don't keep on running, because they'll just keep on following.

Slowly peeling open one of the ready rounds I pulled back the bolt. I caught the round it was about to eject, then fed the four rounds into the mag before pushing the bolt home.

I sat, watched and listened as I got out the blood-smeared mobile. No matter what was going on down here—stop delivery, guarantee delivery, whatever—I'd failed to do what the Yes Man had sent me here for, and I knew what that meant. I had to make a call.

There was no signal.

I played with the phone, finding vibrate, and put it away again.

A frenzied exchange in Spanish brought me back to the real world. They were close. There were more shouts from under the canopy. I sat motionless as seconds, and then whole minutes, ticked by.

I had fucked up, I had to accept that. But what was more important, at this moment, was getting a signal on the mobile, and that meant going back uphill towards the house, where I'd seen it used.

There was movement to my front, the crashing of foliage as they got closer. I held my breath, butt in the shoulder, pad on the trigger as they stopped on my trail.

Three voices gobbed off at warp speed, maybe deciding which direction to take. I could hear their M-16s, that plastic, almost toy-like sound as they moved them. A burst of automatic fire went off in the distance and my three seemed to decide to go back the way they'd come. They'd obviously had enough of this jungle lark.

I got just short of the edge of the tree line, all the time checking the signal bars on the mobile. Still nothing. I heard the heavy revs of one of the bulldozers and the squeal of its tracks. Moving forward cautiously, I saw plumes of black smoke billow from the vertical exhaust as it lumbered towards the gate. Beyond it, the front of the house was a frenzy of people, and wagons moved up and down the road.

I moved back into the wall of green, applied Safe and started checking up at the canopy as I unravelled the string on the weapon to make a sling. I found a suitable tree about six yards in: it would have a good view of the house, looked easy to climb, and the branches were strong enough to support my weight. I took out the strapping that was going to be my seat, got the bergen on my back, slung the weapon over my shoulder, and started to clamber up.

When I was about twenty feet up I tried the Nokia again, and this time got a signal. Fastening the straps between two strong branches, I hooked the bergen over another next to them, settled into the seat facing the house, then spread one of the mozzie nets over me. I was going to be here for a while, until things had quietened down, so the net had to be hung out onto branches so it wasn't clinging to me, and tucked under to cover the straps. Finally, I hit the keypad.

Not giving him time to think or talk, I got to him in a loud whisper. 'It's me—Nick. Don't talk, Josh, just listen. Get her to safety, do it now. I've fucked up big-time. Get her away somewhere safe. She needs to be where no one can get at her. I'll call in a few days. Got it?'

'When does this stop? You're playing with a kid's life again!' The line went dead. He'd hung up. But I knew he'd take this seriously. The last time I'd put kids in danger, they'd been his own.

I felt a flood of relief as I removed the battery before the mobile went back in my pocket. I didn't want to be traced from the signal.

I knew I should have called the Yes Man, explained to him what I thought I knew, and waited out. So why hadn't I? Because a voice in my head was telling me something different.

Charlie had said Sunburn. The Yes Man had sent me to deal with a missile system that was a threat to US helicopters in Colombia. A ground-to-air missile system. That wasn't Sunburn—Sunburn was surface-to-surface. I remembered reading about the US navy flapping because their anti-missile defences couldn't defeat it. I tried to recall details. It had been in *Time* or *Newsweek*, last year on the tube to Hampstead . . . it was about thirty feet long because I'd visualised being able to fit two end to end in a tube carriage.

What else? Think, think . . . The Pizza Man . . . His team was monitoring drug movements by FARC. He'd also been at Charlie's house and maybe, if Charlie had told me the truth, he had Sunburn.

I suddenly saw what was happening. George was using Sunburn as a threat to FARC that if they used the canal to ship drugs they'd get taken out. That still didn't answer why I'd been sent here to stop Charlie delivering a ground-to-air system . . .

The noise of rotor blades clattered over the canopy. I recognised the heavy bass *wap wap wap wap*—the unique signature of American Hueys. Two helicopters shot past above me. The downwash made my tree sway as they flared into the clearing, then crept towards the front of the house. A yellow and white Jet Ranger followed.

Armed men jumped from the skids and doubled towards the house. It could have been the 101st 'Air Assault' screaming down for an attack, except these guys were in jeans.

The Jet Ranger swooped down close to the front of the house. I could see Charlie's family stream towards it from the front door.

I sat and watched through the optic as my former target comforted an older Latino woman, still in her nightgown. I looked at his young, bloody face, which showed only concern for the woman. He belonged to a different world from his father, George, the Pizza Man and me. I hoped he'd stay that way.

The air was filled with the roar of churning blades as they were bustled inside the aircraft. The two Hueys were already making height. They dipped their noses, and headed towards the city. The Jet Ranger lifted from the tarmac, and headed in the same direction. Somebody barked orders at the men on the ground. They started to sort themselves out. Their mission, I guessed, was to look for me.

Wagon after wagon left the house packed with men and M-16 assault rifles, and returned empty. Checking Baby-G, I knew I'd have to move out of here soon if I was to make maximum use of daylight.

Last light, Friday. That had been my deadline. Why? And why were the Firm involved in all this? They obviously needed Sunburn in place for tomorrow. I had been bullshitted with the ground-to-air story. I didn't need to know what it was really about because, after the London fuck-up, sending me was their last desperate attempt to get their hands on the complete system.

Last light. Sunset.

Oh God. The *Ocaso* . . .

They were going to hit the cruise liner, real people, thousands of them. It wasn't a drug thing at all . . . why?

Why didn't matter. What mattered was that it didn't happen. But what was I going to do? Contact the Panamanians? What would they do? Cancel the ship? If they couldn't find Sunburn, the Pizza Man could just fire it at the next ship that came along. Not good enough.

Go to the US embassy, any embassy? What would they do—report it? Who to? How long before someone picked up the phone to George? And there had to be some even more powerful people behind him. Even C and the Yes Man were dancing to their tune. I had to get back to Carrie and Aaron, the only two who could help.

MOVEMENT OUTSIDE THE HOUSE was dwindling: no more vehicles, just one or two bodies walking around, and out of sight the sound of a bulldozer shunting the damaged Lexus off the road.

It was time to leave the tree. I unpinned the trouser-leg pocket and pulled out the map. I bent my head down so my nose was just six inches from it and the compass on its short cord could rest on its faded surface. It took me thirty seconds to take a bearing, across green, then the white line of the loop road, more green, to the main drag into the city. As to how I got back to the house from there, I'd busk it.

Having checked that my map was securely pinned in my pocket, I clambered down. Once the bergen was on and the string back round the weapon, I headed east towards the loop, taking my time, focusing on the wall of green, butt in the shoulder, safety off, finger straight along the trigger guard, ready to react.

I could have been back in Colombia again, looking for drug-manufacturing plants, carefully moving foliage out of the way, avoiding cobwebs, watching where I stepped to cut noise and sign, stopping, listening, observing before moving into dead ground.

I wanted to travel faster, desperate to get back to Aaron and Carrie, but I knew this was the best way to make that happen. They'd no longer be thrashing about or firing blindly; they'd be waiting, spread out, static, for me to bumble into them. Tactical movement in the jungle is so hard. You can never use the easier high ground or tracks, never use water features for navigation. The enemy expects you to use them. You've got to stay in the shit, follow a compass bearing, and move slowly. It's worth it: it means you survive.

It took me two hours to reach the loop. I dumped the bergen and moved forward again. As I neared the road it was time to apply Safe and get down on the jungle floor. Using elbows and the toes of my Timberlands, I dragged myself to the edge of the canopy.

No more than forty yards away was one of the wagons from the house, a gleaming black Land Cruiser. Leaning against the bonnet was a body with an M-16 in his hands. He was maybe in his twenties, in jeans, T-shirt and trainers. A vehicle was my fast-track out of here—but did the body have mates?

There was only one way to find out. I inched back into the tree line, then got onto my hands and knees and crawled to the bergen. Shouldering it, I removed Safe and slowly closed on the wagon by paralleling the road. Each time my foot touched the jungle floor and crushed the leaves, the sound seemed a hundred times louder than it really was. Each time a bird took flight I froze in midstride.

Twenty painstaking minutes had passed when I was brought to a halt once more. From the other side of the wall of green came the sound of his weapon banging against the side of the Land Cruiser. It seemed to be no more than about eight yards away. I stood still and listened. There was no talking, no radio traffic, just the sound of metal panels buckling. He was standing on the roof or the bonnet.

I wanted to be in a direct line with the wagon, so I moved on a little further. Then I lowered myself to my knees and applied Safe, the metallic click sounding in my head as if I'd banged two hammers together. Finally I laid down the weapon and took off my bergen one strap at a time, continually looking in the direction of the wagon. Once the bergen was on the ground I rested the rifle against it. Then I extracted my machete. The blade sounded as if it was running along a grinding stone instead of just gliding past the lip of the sheath.

Down on my stomach once more and with the machete in my right hand, I moved carefully forward on my toes and elbows. I neared the edge of the tree line at a point about five yards short of the wagon.

I edged forward a little more. Another few feet and the bottom of the door sills and the front wing came into view. My eyes strained in their sockets as I tried to look up. I heard the coughing up of phlegm and spitting; he was definitely outside, definitely up there somewhere. He was going to hear me soon. I didn't even want to swallow: I was so close I could have reached out and touched the wheel.

I still couldn't see him, but he was above me, sitting on the bonnet, and his heels had started to bang rhythmically against the wing furthest away from me. I checked I was holding the machete with a good firm grip, and that the blade was facing the right way. I took one last deep breath and sprang to my feet.

He was sitting on the opposite wing with his back to me, weapon on the bonnet to his left. He heard me, but it was too late to turn. I was already leaping towards him, my thighs striking the edge of the bonnet, my feet in the air. My right hand swung round and jammed the machete across his neck; with my left I grabbed the blunt edge of the blade and pulled tight, trying to drag his head onto my chest.

The M-16 scraped over the bodywork as he moved back with me over the wing, my bodyweight pulling us both towards the ground. His hands came up to grab my wrists, trying to pull the machete away. I fell backwards off the wagon. The air exploded out of me as my back hit the ground and he landed on top of me.

His hands were round the machete and he writhed and kicked like a madman. I wrapped my legs round his waist as I pushed the weapon against his neck. I worked my head down to his ear. 'Ssssh!'

The blade must have penetrated his neck a little; I felt warm blood on my hands. I shushed him again and he seemed to get the message. He wasn't struggling any more.

I forced him over to the right, pulling back on the blade, murmuring, 'Come on, over you go,' not knowing if he could even understand me. Soon my chest was on his head, pressing his face into the leaf litter, and I was able to look behind me for the M-16. It wasn't far away; I got my foot into the sling and pulled it within reach. The safety catch was on, which meant the weapon was ready to fire.

There was snorting from his nostrils, and the movement of his chest made me feel I was on a trampoline. Apart from his breathing he was motionless—exactly as I would have been in this situation because, like him, I'd be wanting to come out of it alive.

I kept the pressure on his neck with the machete, and used my left hand to grab the M-16. Then, keeping the blade against his neck, I slowly got up, shushing gently until I was hovering over him and could take away the blade. Once free, I jumped back and got the M-16 on him with just my left hand. I spoke gently. 'Hello.'

His eyes locked on mine, full of fear. I nodded for him to get to his feet. He complied slowly, keeping his hands up as I steered him back into the jungle. I needed to retrieve Carrie's rifle.

We reached the bergen site and I got him to lie face down while I hurriedly shouldered the Mosin Nagant and sheathed the machete.

I smiled. 'Speak English?' There was a nervous shaking of his head as I moved a few paces towards him. '*Cómo estás*?'

He nodded shakily as I got the bergen on. '*Bien, bien*.'

I put my thumb up and gave him a smile. 'Good, good.' I wanted to bring him down a bit. People who think they have nothing to lose can be unpredictable—but if he thought he was going to live, he'd do as he was told.

I wasn't really sure what to do with this boy. I didn't want to kill him, and there wasn't any time to tie him up properly. I didn't want to take him with me, but I couldn't just let him run wild—not this close to the house, anyway. I jerked my head. '*Vamos, vamos*.'

He got to his feet and I pointed towards the Land Cruiser with the M-16. '*Camión, vamos, camión*.' He caught my drift and we moved. At the wagon it was a matter of shoving the bergen and rifle into the back, then manoeuvring him into the passenger footwell with the M-16 muzzle twisted into his shirt and lying across my lap. The safety catch was on automatic, and my right index finger was on the trigger. He got the message that any movement on his part would be suicide.

The key was in the ignition. I turned it and selected Drive, and we were moving. As we headed for Clayton and the city I looked down at my passenger and smiled. '*No problema*.'

The rain was coming early today by the look of the multiple shades of grey shrouding the green peaks in the distance. What was I to do with my new mate? I couldn't take him through the toll.

We passed one of the playgrounds between the married quarters and I stopped, got out and opened his door. He stared down the barrel of the beckoning M-16. 'Run. Run.'

He looked at me, confused, as he climbed out, so I kicked him on and waved my arm. 'Run!' He started legging it past the swings as I got back into the driver's seat and headed for the main drag. By the time he found a phone and made contact, I'd be in the city and well out of the area. I was certainly safe from the air: nothing was going to be flying when the skies opened. I checked the fuel: just under full. I had no idea if that was enough, but it didn't matter, I had cash.

TWELVE

The 4x4 pitched and rolled along a waterlogged jungle track, launching walls of water and mud in all directions. I was just glad to be doing it with windows closed and air conditioning humming. Maybe ten more minutes until I reached the clearing and the house.

The rain had started as soon as I hit El Chorrillo. By the time I joined the Pan-American Highway, it was dropping from the sky like Niagara Falls. After that, the cloud had stayed really low and threatening all the way to Chepo.

Bouncing along the track, I came into the clearing to see that the cloud had lifted. As I got nearer the house I saw Carrie come to the mozzie door and stare out. I parked the Land Cruiser and climbed out. She opened the mozzie screen for me as I stepped onto the verandah, clearly trying to work out the Land Cruiser.

'I'll explain that later,' I said. 'There's been a fuck-up—Charlie handed over the guidance system last night . . . There's more.'

My boots clumped on the verandah boards as I passed her and entered the living room. I wanted them both together before they got the news. The fans were blasting away and Aaron was sitting in an armchair facing me, leaning over a mug of coffee on the table.

'Nick.'

I acknowledged him as the screen slammed.

He kept his voice low, twisting in the chair to check the computer-room door was closed. 'Michael dead? She told me all about it.' He turned back and took a messy, nervous swig from the mug.

'No, he's alive.'

'Oh, thank God, thank God.' He slumped back in the chair.

Carrie, too, let out a sigh of relief. 'We've been so worried. My father stood you down last night, missed us by an hour. He went totally crazy at Aaron when he found out you'd already gone.'

I turned to her. 'He's crazy all right. I think he's planning a missile attack on the *Ocaso*, tomorrow. It's going to happen once it's in the Miraflores. If he succeeds, thousands of people are going to die.'

Her hand shot to her mouth. 'No, no, no, my father wouldn't—'

'George isn't pressing any buttons.' I pointed towards the fridge. 'But *he* is, the one with the scar on his stomach. You know, the beach babies, your favourite picture.' They both followed my finger. 'I saw him at the Miraflores, running as soon as he saw Aaron and the Mazda. He was also at Charlie's house on Tuesday, and then here last night. He stayed in the wagon, he didn't want to be seen . . . Charlie just told me that he was the one who took delivery . . .'

'Oh God. Milton . . .' She leaned against the wall. 'Milton was one of the Iran-Contra procurement guys in the 80s. They sold the weapons to Iran for the Lebanon hostages, then used the money to buy other—weapons—for—the—Contr— Oh shit.' Her hands fell to her sides. 'That's his job, Nick, that's what he does.'

'Well, he has just procured himself an anti-ship missile and I think he's going to use it tomorrow on the *Ocaso*.'

'No, he couldn't, you must be wrong,' she stammered. 'My father would never let that happen to Americans.'

'Yes, he would.' Aaron had something to say. 'The DeConcini Reservation. Think on it, Carrie. George and those guys . . . they are going to take down that ship so the US has just cause to come back.'

Carrie slid down to the floor, maybe realising at long last what her dad had really got up to all his life.

I turned to the rasp of bristles being rubbed. 'She gets into the locks at ten tomorrow morning—what are we going to do?'

But the question hadn't been addressed to me. His eyes were still fixed on her.

Carrie was opening her mouth, but if words came out I didn't hear them. From above us came an unmistakable *wap wap wap wap*.

We all looked up. The noise was suddenly so loud it was as if the roof wasn't there at all.

Both of them rushed towards the computer-room door. 'Luz!'

I moved to the mozzie screen and pressed my nose against the mesh. The two dark blue Hueys were hovering above the house, having already disgorged their payload. Pairs of jeans carrying M-16s were closing in on the verandah. Michael must have made the connection with Aaron from the meeting at the locks.

I ducked back into the room just as the other two came running in with Luz. Aaron's face was stone, glaring over Luz's head as they knelt on either side of her, curled up in the armchair, her eyes shut tight in fear. Both of them cuddled and tried to reassure her. From the storeroom behind them came shouts in Spanish.

It was all over. I dropped to my knees and threw my arms up in surrender, yelling at Aaron and Carrie, 'Just be still! It'll be all right!'

I didn't have a clue what was going to happen. But you've got to accept that when you're in the shit you're in the shit. There is nothing you can do but take deep breaths, keep calm, and hope.

Men spilled into the room from the back of the building at the same instant the mozzie screen burst open. There was crazed shouting between them as they tried to make sure they didn't shoot each other. Over their civilian clothes they were wearing black nylon chest harnesses for their spare mags. Four of them surrounded Aaron and Carrie, still crouched around the armchair comforting Luz.

I stayed on my knees, making sure I looked scared—which I was. But I knew we were being kept alive for some reason, otherwise we'd have been shot on sight. The weapons I could see were on Automatic.

The sole of someone's boot kicked me between the shoulder blades to get me down on the floor. I went with it, flat onto my stomach. I was roughly searched and lost everything out of my pockets.

The clatter of rotors slowed gradually and there was the high-pitched whine of the turbos as both engines closed down.

But then came the sound of lighter rotors. My stomach churned. Maybe the reason we hadn't been killed on sight was that Charlie wanted to see to it in person. As the Jet Ranger's rotor blades cut out, I heard the barking of orders and bodies rushed from the room. Three remained covering us.

Outside on the verandah I could hear a lot of warp speed jabbering. Calmer and more controlled Spanish came from the rear of the house. I tilted my head very slightly and screwed my eyes to the top of their sockets to see what was happening.

Charlie, dressed in a navy track suit and white trainers, had three or four others buzzing round him like presidential aides as he strode into the room. He walked towards me, looking as if he had need of nothing, not even oxygen. I felt scared. There was nothing I could do physically about things at the moment. If I saw the chance to get away I would grab it; but right now I just had to look away from him and wait. Whatever happened, I knew it was likely to be painful.

He was called by one of the bodies still in the computer room, and the group turned and headed back. I glanced up and saw them hunched round the PC as the screen flickered and slowly rolled down the image of the lock. One of the crew came back into the living area. He'd had a change of kit since I stole his Land Cruiser, and now boasted a clean, shiny black track suit. His neck was covered with a gauze dressing, held in place by surgical tape.

He crouched down so we could have eye-to-eye. '*Cómo estás*?'

I nodded. '*Bien, bien*.'

He gave the thumbs up with a smile. 'Good, good.' He returned to the PC, then addressed a few remarks to Charlie, probably telling him I was indeed the same man—and maybe confirming I was the only one on the ground earlier. Then he left via the storeroom.

Seconds later, one of the Hueys sparked up, turbos whining. Some of the lads were being lifted out. The heli took off, thundering over the roof, as the staff meeting came to an end. They streamed back into the living area, Charlie in the lead, my bag of docs in his hand.

He crouched down with a crack of his knees and grabbed my hair. Our eyes met. His were bloodshot, no doubt due to the force of the explosion. His skin was peppered with scabbed-up pockmarks from the shattered glass, and the side of his neck was dressed like that of the guy from the Land Cruiser.

'Why are you people so stupid? All I wanted was some assurance the device wouldn't be used inside Panama. Then you could have had the launch control system. Some form of assurance, that's all.' He threw my docs to the floor. 'Instead, I have my family threatened . . .'

I let my eyelids droop as he shook me about.

'So I comply and take the rest of your money, you then assure me everything is fine, just business. But still you try to kill my family.'

He held me, looking at me, his eyes giving nothing.

'You are going to use Sunburn against a ship in the Miraflores—that's the target, isn't it?' He shook me again. 'Why you are doing it, I don't care. But it will bring the US back—that I care about.'

As my face moved from side to side I glimpsed my passport and wallet, discarded in their plastic on the floor by the bookshelves.

Charlie brought his mouth to my ear. 'I want to know where the missile is, and when the attack will take place. If not, some of my people here are only a few years older than that one in the chair and, like all young men, eager to display their manhood . . . That's fair, isn't it? You set the rules—children are now fair game, aren't they?'

I looked into his eyes and they told me what I needed to know: that none of us was going to leave here alive, no matter what we said.

It was Aaron who broke the silence: 'He's just the hired help.' His voice was strong and authoritative. 'He was sent here to make you hand over the guidance system, that's all. He doesn't know a thing. None of us knows where Sunburn is, but I can get online at eight thirty tonight and find out. I'll do it—just let these three go.'

Carrie went ballistic. 'No, no—what are you doing?'

Aaron cut in. 'Shut up. I've had enough. It's got to stop—now!'

Charlie released my head and I let it fall to the floorboards.

Aaron followed him with his eyes. 'Eight thirty—that's when I can make contact and find out. Just let them go.' He stroked Luz's hair.

Charlie muttered instructions as he walked towards the kitchen area. Aaron and Carrie obviously understood what was going on and started to rise with Luz as two guards crossed the floor.

Carrie tried to talk some sense into Aaron. 'What are you doing? You know he'll just—'

He was tough with her. 'Just shut up!' He kissed her on the lips. 'I love you. Stay strong.' Then he bent down and kissed Luz, before the guards dragged him towards the computer room. 'Remember, Nick,' he said, laughing, 'once a Viking, always a Viking. Some things never change.' He disappeared, jabbering some kind of explanation or apology in Spanish to the men who pulled at his arms.

Commands were shouted at the boys on the verandah. The other two were herded into Luz's bedroom, and the door was closed.

Charlie came back towards me. 'The Sunburn—I want it back. Do you know how much you have paid for it? Twelve million US dollars. I'm thinking of reselling it. I should imagine FARC would appreciate the opportunity to buy Sunburn, to prepare, let's say, for when the Americans send a carrier fleet to support their troops.' He smiled.

I was pushed towards Luz's bedroom and opened the door to see both of them lying on the bed in a huddle. The door slammed shut. I moved over to the bed and sat down beside them with my finger to my lips. 'We've got to get out of here before these kids get organised.'

'What's he doing?' she whispered. 'George won't say a—'

'I don't know, sssh . . .' I was only just beginning to understand what Aaron was doing, but I wasn't going to tell her.

I got up and went to the window, which was protected by a wire-mesh mozzie screen on the outside. The windows, side-hinged types, opened inwards. The screen was held in place by wooden pegs that swivelled on screws.

I looked out and studied the tree line 200 yards away. There was intermittent chat coming from the verandah to my left. My mind was still on Aaron. He wasn't as naive as I'd thought. 'Once a Viking, always a Viking.' They slash, they burn, they pillage. They never change. He'd told me that. He'd come to the same conclusion as I had. No way was Charlie letting us out of here alive.

I went over to the bed. 'Here's what we're going to do. We're going to get out through the window and get ourselves into the trees.'

Luz's head jerked towards me. 'What about Dad?'

'I'll come back for him later. There's no time for this. We've got to go right now.'

'We can't,' Carrie said. 'We can't leave him. What will happen when they find us gone? If we stay put and don't antagonise anyone, we'll be all right. We don't know anything. Why should they harm us?'

The whine of the turbos on the Jet Ranger started up and the rotors were soon turning. I waited until they reached full revs before putting my mouth to Carrie's ear.

'Aaron knows we're all dead whatever happens—even if George does tell him the location. You understand? We all die.'

The heli took off as her head fell onto Luz's. I followed to keep contact with her ear. 'He's buying me time to save you two. We must go, for Luz's sake, and for Aaron's. It's what he wants.'

Her shoulders heaved with sadness as she hugged her daughter and the noise of the Jet Ranger disappeared over the canopy.

THERE WAS STILL MORE than an hour to go till last light but I had made my decision. We had to get out of there as soon as we could.

Mumbling still drifted from the front of the house. If somebody was on stag at the edge of the verandah, we'd be in full view for the entire 200 yards. It would take us at least ninety seconds to make that distance, and that's a long time for an M-16 to have you in its sights. But who knew what the next hour held? The three of us could be split up, killed, or put into the remaining Huey and flown out. By waiting we could end up squandering the chance Aaron had given us.

As I looked through the glass and mesh, it was easy enough to confirm our route—half right towards the dead ground, then into the tree line. We'd be moving at an angle away from the front of the house, but there'd come a point where we cleared the corner at the back and were in the Huey's line of sight. Would there still be people aboard? Maybe the pilot carrying out his checks?

Once absorbed by the wall of green we'd be relatively safe; we'd just have to contend with a night out on the jungle floor, then spend the next day moving through the canopy. We'd cross the tree graveyard at night, hiding under the dead wood in the day, until we made Chepo. From there, who knew? I'd worry about that then. As for Aaron, I doubted that he'd last much past eight thirty.

I went over to the bed and whispered, 'We're going to go for the trees. The thing to remember is that we must spread out when we're running, OK? That way it's harder to be seen.'

Carrie looked up from her child and frowned. She knew that wasn't the reason. She knew a single burst from an M-16 could kill all three of us, and if we were spread out, we'd be harder to hit.

Luz tugged at her mother's arm. 'What about Daddy?'

I could see Carrie fighting back the tears and put my hand on her shoulder. 'I'll come back for him, Luz, don't worry. He wanted me to get you two into the jungle first. He wants to know you're safe.'

She nodded reluctantly.

'If we get split up,' I said quietly, 'I want you two to carry on into the trees without me, then make your way towards the far right corner and wait for me there.' To Luz I added, 'Don't come out if anyone calls for you, even if it's your dad—it'll just be a trick. Just my voice, OK? Once you're safe, I'll come back for him.' I'd cross that bridge when I came to it. 'Ready?'

Both heads nodded. I looked at Luz. 'Me first, then you, all right?'

I moved back to the window. Carrie followed, looking out to the tree line, listening to the laughter out front.

'They're outside, on the deck, Nick. How are we going to get to the trees without—'

'Just get her ready.'

How were we going to make it? I didn't know. All I knew was that there wasn't any time for fancy plans. We just had to get on with it.

Pulling open the windows let in the sounds of the boys on the verandah. The wooden pegs squeaked as I swivelled them to release the mozzie screen. It rattled in its frame as I pushed. I froze, waiting for the murmuring to change to shouts. It didn't happen. I pushed again and the screen came away. I carefully lowered it to the ground.

I clambered out before beckoning Luz, not even bothering to check the noises—I'd know if they saw me. Her mother helped her, and I guided her down beside me into the mud. Using one hand to hold her against the wall, I held out the other for Carrie as the boys on the verandah appreciated a punch line.

Carrie was soon beside me. I got her to stand next to Luz against the wall, and pointed to the tree line to our half right. I gave them the thumbs up but got no reply so, taking a deep breath, I took off.

Within just a few strides the mud had slowed our run into not much more than a fast walk. Instinct made all three of us hunch low in an attempt to make ourselves smaller. I kept motioning to them to spread out, but it wasn't working. Luz ran close to her mother, and it wasn't long before they were actually holding hands.

We covered the first 100 yards. The heli came into view to our right. There didn't seem to be anyone in or around it. We pushed on.

There were maybe thirty yards to go when I heard the first shots.

'Run!' I yelled. 'Keep going! I didn't look behind; it wouldn't help. The rounds started to zero in on us. 'Keep going, keep going!'

They lunged into the jungle, slightly ahead and to my right. Almost at once, I heard a scream.

More rounds ripped into the jungle. I dropped to my hands and knees, gasping for breath. 'Luz! Call to me—where are you?'

'Mommy, Mommy, Mommy!'

'Luz! Lie down! Keep down! I'm coming!'

The single shots became bursts as I started crawling. The M-16s were firing into the entry points in an effort to hose us down; we needed to move offline to the right, downhill into dead ground.

Just a few yards into the foliage I found them. Carrie was on her back, eyes wide open and tear-filled, her cargos bloodstained on the right thigh, with what looked like bone pushing at the material. Her injured leg appeared shorter than the other, and the foot was lying flat with the toes pointing outwards. A round must have hit her in the femur. Luz was hovering over her, not knowing what to do.

I grabbed Carrie by the arms and started to drag her into the dead ground. Luz followed on her hands and knees, sobbing loudly. Carrie cried out as her injured leg got jarred and twisted. At least it meant she could feel pain, a good sign, but the two of them were making such a racket it was only a matter of time before we were heard.

I jumped up, grabbed Carrie's wrist, and heaved her over my shoulder in a fireman's lift. She screamed as her damaged leg swung free before I held it in place. I pushed through the vegetation with long, exaggerated strides, trying to keep the leg stable with one hand and keeping a tight grip on Luz with the other.

Frenzied shouts came from behind us. Short bursts from M-16s randomly stitched the area. They were at the entry points.

We crashed our way through wait-a-while and Carrie's leg got snagged. She screamed and I half turned, pulled it free, knowing there was a chance that the broken ends of her femur could act like scissors, cutting into muscle, nerves, tendons, ligaments—or, worst of all, sever the femoral artery. She'd be history in minutes if that happened. But what else could I do?

We crashed on, and began a gentle descent. I could still hear people hosing the place down behind us, but the jungle was soaking up a lot of it and we seemed to be out of the initial danger area.

I pushed towards the tree line until I could see the beginning of the open ground, then dragged Luz back with me so we were just behind the wall of green. At last I was able to lay Carrie down, making sure as I did so that her feet were pointing at the tree line.

Carrie lay on her back taking short, sharp breaths, her face contorted. Luz was bent over her on her knees. I gently straightened her. 'You've got to help your mum and me. I need you to kneel there, behind me. If anyone comes you just turn round and give me a tap—not a shout, just a tap, OK? Will you do that?'

Luz looked at her mother, then back at me.

'That's good—this is really important.' I positioned her behind me, facing the tree line, then turned to Carrie.

There was blood. Her femoral artery wasn't cut or litres of the stuff would have been pouring out over her leg, but if she kept leaking like this she would eventually go into shock and die. The bleeding had to be stopped and the fracture immobilised.

I got down at her feet and started to work with my teeth at the frayed hem of her cargos. I made a tear, and ripped the material upwards. As the injury was exposed I saw that she hadn't been shot. She must have fallen badly and overstressed the femur: the bone was sticking out of what looked like a rack of raw beef. But at least there was muscle there to contract, it hadn't been shot away.

I wanted to reassure her. 'It looks a lot messier than it is,' I whispered. 'I'll make sure it doesn't get worse, then get you to a doctor.

Really, it's not that bad. You haven't lost much blood. It's a clean break, but I've got to fix it so the bone doesn't move about and cause more damage. It's going to hurt more while I sort it out. I need you to hold on to the tree behind you when I say, OK?'

Forcing the words out, she sobbed, 'Get on with it.'

I gently eased Carrie's webbing belt through the hoops of her cargos and put it down by her feet. Then I took off my sweatshirt and ripped a sleeve away from its stitching. I pulled off some large waxy leaves that drooped about us. 'In a minute, I'm going to move your good leg next to your bad one. I'll do it as carefully as I can.'

As the odd Spanish shout penetrated the canopy, I rolled up the leaves into big cigar shapes, and gently packed them between her legs, to act as padding between the good leg and the bad. Then I picked up her good leg. 'Here we go.' I brought it gently over towards her injured one, just as the first splatter of rain hit the canopy.

I pushed the sleeve through the mud below Carrie's knees and laid it out flat, then ripped the rest of the sweatshirt into strips to improvise bandages as the rain notched itself up to monsoon strength.

I leaned over her, right up to her ear. 'Grab hold of the tree behind you.' I guided her hands round the thin trunk. 'Grip hard and don't let go, no matter what.' I decided not to explain what I was going to do next; she was in enough pain without anticipating more.

I crawled back down to her feet and fed the belt under both her ankles. Then, kneeling in front of her, I gently picked up the foot of the injured leg. Her whole body tensed.

'It's going to be OK, just keep hold of that tree. Ready?'

Slowly but firmly, I pulled her foot towards me. I rotated it as gently as I could, stretching the injured leg out straight to stop the taut muscles from displacing the bone any more. Every movement must have felt like a stab from a red-hot knife. She gritted her teeth and for a long time didn't make a sound, then finally it all became too much. She screamed as her body jerked, but didn't release her grip as the exposed bone started to retract from the open wound.

I continued with the traction, pulling her leg with all my weight. 'Nearly there, Carrie, nearly there . . .'

Luz came over and joined in the sobs. I just let her get on with it. I started to feed the canvas belt over Carrie's ankles with my left hand, and then over her sandalled feet in a figure of eight. 'Keep your good leg straight, Carrie, keep it straight!' Then I pulled back on the ends of the belt to keep everything in place, tying a knot with the belt still under tension to keep her feet together.

Carrie had been jerking like an epileptic, but still held on to the tree and kept her good leg straight. 'It's OK. It's done.'

It was getting so dark I could hardly see, and the fracture still had to be immobilised. I folded over the sweatshirt sleeve lying under her knees and tied the ends together with the knot on the side of her good knee. Lumps of bright green leaf protruded between her legs now that they were getting strapped together.

I placed strips of sweatshirt firmly and carefully over the wound. I fed the material under her knees and then worked it up before tying off on the side of the good leg. I wanted to immobilise the fracture, and put pressure on the wound to stem the blood loss. But I had to make sure that the sweatshirt wasn't tied too tight. I couldn't tell if the blood supply was reaching below the ties; without light I couldn't see if the skin was pink or blue, and finding the pulse was a nightmare. There was really only one option.

'If you feel pins and needles, you've got to tell me, OK?'

I got a short, sharp 'Yep.'

I couldn't even see my hand in front of my face now as I checked Baby-G. The dial illuminated and it was 6.27.

I was starting to feel cold. Not too sure where their heads were I called out into the darkness, 'You two must know where the other is all the time—never let go of each other.' I put my hand out and felt wet material: it was Luz's back as she cuddled her mother.

I was kneeling there in the rain when I heard Luz speak up. 'Nick? You going to get Daddy now?'

THIRTEEN

It seemed I had come to that bridge.

'I'll be no more than a couple of hours.' She wasn't wearing a watch, but some kind of timing would be something to cling on to.

'Eight thirty, Nick, eight thirty' Carrie fought between short, sharp breaths, as if I needed reminding.

'If I'm not back by first light,' I said, 'get out into the open ground and make yourself known. You'll need taking care of. They can use the heli to get you to hospital.' Maybe, maybe not: I didn't know what they'd do, but there was no other way if I didn't return.

Going back to the house had been a simple choice to make. Carrie needed medical attention. I needed a wagon to get her to Chepo. I had to go and get one, and that meant I needed to have control of the house and the people in it first.

I checked Baby-G: 6.32. Less than two hours till Aaron's bluff was called. 'I'll see you both soon.'

I drew an imaginary straight line down her body to her feet. She hadn't shifted position since I'd laid her down, so I knew that that was the way to the tree line. I started crawling, feeling my way over the wet leaf litter, and soon emerged into the open ground.

Here, the dull pounding of rain into mud took over from the almost tinny noise of it hitting leaves. It was just as dark, however.

I ripped an armful of palm leaves from the trees at the edge and laid them out on the ground at my entry point, throwing mud on top to keep them in place. Then, with the heel of my boot, I scraped deep score marks into the mud for good measure.

I set off towards the house, conscious that the helicopter would be somewhere to my left. I was tempted to make my way over to it and have a look for a weapon. But what if they had somebody on stag? I couldn't take the chance of a compromise so far from the house.

As I crested the high ground, I saw a glimmer of light from the single bulb in the shower area. There was no other lighting.

I moved back down the slope and, avoiding the helicopter, made my way round to the other side of the house. Eventually moving up to the left of the house, I crested the high ground again.

Approaching the tubs, I became aware of the chug of the generator, and at that point got onto my hands and knees and began to crawl. The chug was soon drowned out by the rain beating on the lids of the plastic tubs. There were no signs of life from the house, and it wasn't until I drew level with the storeroom that I made out a sliver of light coming from beneath the door. I kept moving, and eventually saw a dull glow filtering through the mozzie screen on the window between the bookshelves, but no movement inside.

There was no need to crawl any more as I got to the end of the tubs and drew level with the verandah and wagons. Covered in mud, I stood up and moved cautiously towards the Land Cruiser.

Through the haze of rain and screens I could see three guys sitting at the kitchen table. Weapons lay on the floor. Two of them wore chest harnesses. They seemed to be having a sober conversation—probably trying to make up the story of how we'd got away.

There was no sign of Aaron. I checked Baby-G. Less than ninety minutes to go before they discovered he knew jack shit.

My priority was to check if the Mosin Nagant or M-16 were still in the Land Cruiser. There'd been no light, movement or steamed-up windows in any of the three wagons. It was safe to approach.

I wiped the water from the side windows and checked inside. No sign of either weapon or machete. It was a long shot, but I'd have been making a basic error if I hadn't checked.

I went to the rear of the wagon and pressed the release button, opening the glass top section of the rear gate just enough for the interior lights to come on, then scanned the luggage area. No weapons, no bergen. I pushed the section back down until it killed the lights.

I moved towards the storeroom. As I passed the bookshelf window I saw that all three were still sitting at the table. Moving round the water butt, I could now see the light under the storeroom door. I got on my hands and knees, then shoved my right eye against the gap.

I saw Aaron at once, sitting in one of the director's chairs. A man, maybe mid-forties, in a green shirt and with no chest harness or weapon visible, was sitting next to him in the other canvas chair.

Beyond them, sitting at Luz's computer, was a younger man, in blue. I guessed by the primary colours darting about the screen and the frenzied movement of the mouse that he was playing a game. An M-16 was resting against the table beside him.

Green got up and said something to Blue, who didn't bother to turn from the game, just raising his free hand instead as Green went into the living room to join the other three.

Aaron turned on his chair to look at Blue playing Luz's game.

Shit! What's he up to?

I leapt back and scrambled behind the water butt just as the door burst open and light flooded the area. Aaron launched himself off the concrete into the mud, followed by startled Spanish screams.

As he ran and slithered into the darkness towards the tubs there was a long burst of automatic fire from within the storeroom.

I made myself as small as possible as yells echoed from the living room, together with the sound of feet pounding on floorboards.

Aaron had already faded into the darkness when Blue got to the door, hollering in panic, and took aim with a short sharp burst.

I heard an anguished gasp, then chilling, drawn-out screams.

His pain was quickly drowned by panicky M-16s opening up through the window between the bookshelves to my right, just blasting away into the night. Blue was screaming at the top of his voice—probably to cease firing, because that was what happened.

I stayed curled up to conceal myself behind the water butt as Blue moved out into the rain towards Aaron. The rest withdrew inside.

I had to act: now was my time. I stepped into the rain after him, keeping to the right of the door to avoid the light.

Blue advanced on the dark, motionless shape of Aaron on the ground a few yards ahead of him. The M-16 was in his right hand.

I was no more than five paces behind him. I kept moving.

I leapt, jamming my left leg between his, bodychecking him, grabbing at his face with my left hand. The weapon fell between us as his hands came up to snatch my hand away. Pulling hard, I arched him backwards, yanking back his head, presenting his throat. I raised my right hand and swung down hard to chop across his throat. He dropped like a stunned pig in an abattoir, taking me with him.

I kicked myself free, scrambling over him until I lay across his chest, feeling the hard alloy of the magazines between us. My right forearm jammed into his throat and I leaned on it with all my weight. He wasn't dead.The chop had got the nerves that run each side of the trachea and messed him up for a while, that was all.

Looking up, I could see into the storeroom. The others were probably still in the living room, trying to come to terms with the even bigger nightmare they were now facing, waiting for Aaron's body to be dragged back by this fuckwit who'd let him escape.

I looked down on him, his eyes closed, no kicking or resistance. I eased off and put my ear to his mouth. No sound of breathing. I double-checked by digging the middle and forefinger of my right hand into his neck to feel the carotid pulse. Nothing.

I rolled off him and felt for Aaron. My hands were soon warm with his blood as I felt for his neck. He, too, was dead. I scrabbled around in the mud for the M-16, then removed Blue's chest harness.

With the harness in one hand and the M-16 in the other, I ran to the back of the house for cover and light. I didn't have much time before they came out here to see what was taking their friend so long.

I took out a fresh thirty-round mag and pushed my thumb into it to make sure it was full. I removed the old magazine, then pushed the fresh one home. I cocked the weapon and applied Safe, quickly checking the other three mags in the pouches of the nylon harness—I didn't want to slap on a half-empty one. I put the harness on, the pouches across my chest, and clipped the buckle at the back, while listening for shouts that would tell me they'd discovered Blue.

Pulling a magazine from the harness, I held it in my left hand, ready to ram it into the magazine housing if this one became empty. Then I grabbed the stock, wrapping my left hand round the whole lot. I thumbed the safety, pushing past the first click—single rounds—and all the way to Automatic, my index finger inside the trigger guard, then moved out into the rain once more.

I stepped up onto the concrete and into the storeroom, lifting my feet high to avoid the cans, spilt rice, and other stuff strewn across the floor. I could hear them in the kitchen area. The talking was heated. There was movement, a chair scraping, boots walking towards the computer room. I froze, finger on the trigger, waiting . . .

I was going to have the upper hand for no more than two seconds. After that, if I didn't get this right, I was history.

The boots appeared. Green turned, saw me, his scream cut short as I squeezed. He fell back into the living room. I followed him through the doorway, stepping over his body into the room. They were panicking, screaming out at each other, reaching for their weapons.

I moved off to the left, squeezing short sharp bursts, aiming into the mass of movement. I squeezed again . . . nothing.

I fell to my knees to present a smaller target, tilted the weapon to the left to present the ejection opening, and looked inside. There were no rounds in the magazine, no rounds in the chamber.

I hit the release catch and the empty mag hit my leg on its way to the floor. Two bodies were sprawled, one moving with a weapon, one on his knees trying to get the safety off. I locked onto it.

I twisted the weapon over to its right and presented the magazine housing. The fresh magazine was still in my left hand; I rammed it into the housing, banged it into position from the mag bottom, and slapped my hand down hard onto the locking lever. The working parts went forward, picking up a round as I fired on my knees.

Another mag and it was all over.

There was silence as I reloaded, apart from the rain hitting the roof and the kettle whistling on the cooker. Two of the bodies were on the floor; one was slumped forward over the table. Everybody I had seen was accounted for, but the bedrooms had to be checked.

Getting to my feet, butt in my shoulder, I gave three short bursts through the door to Luz's room then forced my way in, and then the same with Carrie and Aaron's. Both were clear.

I turned to the kitchen and took the kettle off the ring. I poured myself a mug of tea from a tin of sachets on the side. It smelt of berries. I threw in some sugar and stirred it as I stepped into the computer room and closed the door behind me.

Seated in a director's chair, I slowly sipped the sweet, scalding liquid, my hands shaking a little.

Tilting the mug for the last drops of the brew, I got to my feet and went to Aaron and Carrie's bedroom. I pulled off the harness and changed into an old black sweatshirt. I put the harness back on, gathered up their bedsheet, and went to the Land Cruiser with the M-16. I checked that the keys were still inside, lowered the rear seats ready for Carrie, then climbed into the Mazda and fired it up.

The headlights bounced up and down as I bumped through the mud to Aaron. He was heavy to retrieve, but I finally got him into the back of the Mazda and wrapped him in the sheet. As I tucked one corner over his face, I thanked him quietly.

Closing the tailgate, I dragged Blue and hid him among the tubs before walking back to the house. I turned off the living-room lights and closed the door before kicking Blue's empty cases under the desk and storeroom shelving. Luz didn't need to see any of that: she had seen enough already today.

Finally, using a torch from the storeroom shelves to light me, I dragged the cot out into the rain and threw it into the back of the Land Cruiser. It just fitted on the opened lower half of the tailgate. Then I headed for the dead ground and the tree line.

The wipers pushed away the flood with each stroke, only for it to be instantly replaced, but not before I glimpsed the entry point in the tree line as the headlights hit on the palm-leaf markers.

I left the lights and engine running, grabbed the torch from the passenger seat, ran round and dragged out the cot. Gripping one of the legs as it trailed behind me, I broke through the tree line.

'Luz! Where are you? Luz! It's me, it's Nick, call to me!'

'Over here! We're over here! Nick, please, please, Nick!'

I pushed towards her, dragging the cot. Just a few feet more and the torch beam landed on Luz, kneeling by her mother's head.

Luz looked at me. 'Where's Daddy? Is Daddy at the house?'

I looked down, pleased that the weather, distance and canopy would have soaked up the sounds of automatic gunfire. I didn't know what to say. 'No, he went to get the police . . .'

Carrie coughed and screwed up her pale face, smothering her child into her chest. She looked at me quizzically over her head. I closed my eyes, put the torchlight onto my face and shook my head.

Her head fell back and she let out a low cry, her eyes shut tight. Luz's head jumped up and down as her chest convulsed. She tried to steer her mother's thoughts elsewhere, thinking it was only physical pain. 'It's OK, Mom, Nick's going to get you back to the house.'

'Luz, you've got to help me get your mum on the cot, OK?' Moving the torch slightly so as not to blind her, I looked at her face, nodding slowly. 'Good. Now get behind your mum's head, and when I say, I want you to lift her from under the armpits. I'll lift her legs at the same time and we'll get her on the cot in one go. Got it?'

I shone the torch above Carrie's head as Luz knelt behind her mother's head, then I jammed the torch into the mud. On my knees, I slid one arm under the small of Carrie's back and the other under her knees. 'OK, Luz, on my count of three—are you ready?'

A small but serious voice answered, 'Yes, I'm ready.'

I looked at what I could see of Carrie's face. 'You know this is going to hurt, don't you?'

She nodded, her eyes closed, taking sharp breaths.

'One, two, three—up, up, up.'

Her scream filled the night, but at least that phase was over. As soon as she landed she started breathing quickly and deeply through gritted teeth as Luz tried to comfort her. 'It's OK, Mom . . . ssssssh.'

I pulled the torch from the mud and placed it on the cot next to Carrie's good leg so that it shone upwards. 'The hard bits are done. Luz, grab your end, just lift it a little and I'll lift this end, OK?'

She jumped to her feet, then bent to grip the aluminium handles.

'Ready? One, two, three, up, up, up.'

The cot lifted about six inches and I immediately started crashing backwards through the vegetation. I kept checking behind me and soon made out the lights of the Land Cruiser penetrating the foliage. Just a few paces later we were out in the open.

We lifted Carrie into the back of the vehicle, her legs protruding onto the tailgate. 'You need to stay with your mum and hold on to her in case we hit a bump, OK?'

There was going to be no problem with that. Carrie pulled her child down and mourned covertly into her wet hair.

I drove very slowly towards the house and we pulled up by the storeroom door. We waddled with the cot into the brightly lit computer room. As we lowered her to the floor near the two PCs, I looked to Luz. 'You need to go and turn the fans off.'

She looked confused but did it anyway. The fans would produce a chilling effect. Carrie was in enough danger from shock as it was.

As soon as Luz left us, Carrie pulled me down to her, whispering at me, 'You sure he's dead, you sure? I need to know . . . please?'

Luz made her way back as I looked Carrie in the eye and nodded.

She let go of me and stared up at the slowing fans.

The medical case was on the shelf. I collected it, then knelt at the side of the cot and searched through to see what I could use. She'd lost blood, but I couldn't find a giving set or fluids. I guessed they would have depended on a heli coming to get them in the event of serious illness or accident. That wasn't going to happen tonight, not with this downpour—but at least it was keeping Charlie at bay. As long as it kept raining so hard he wouldn't be able to fly back to find out why contact had been broken.

I found the dihydrocodeine. The label might have said one tablet when required, but she was getting three, plus an aspirin. Without needing to be asked, Luz announced she was going to fetch some Evian. Carrie swallowed eagerly, desperate for anything to deaden what she was feeling. She was studying the wall clock. 'Nick, tomorrow, ten o'clock . . .' She turned to me, her expression pleading.

'First things first.' I ripped the cellophane from a crepe bandage and started to replace the belt and bits of sweatshirt in a figure of eight around her feet. She had to be stabilised, then we needed to be out of this house before the weather improved and Charlie fired up his helis. 'The clinic in Chepo, where is it?'

'It's not really a clinic, it's the Peace Corps folks and—'

'Have they got a surgery?'

'Sort of.'

I pressed the soles of her feet and her toes and watched the imprint remain for a second or two until her blood returned.

'Two thousand people, Nick. You've got to talk to George, you must do something. If only for Aar—'

Luz returned with the water and helped her mother with the bottle.

I didn't disturb the dressings over the wound site, or the foliage packed between her legs, but just gradually worked my way up her legs with the four-inch bandages. I wanted to get her looking like an Egyptian mummy from her feet up to her hips.

Carrie mumbled to Luz, 'What's the time, baby?'

'Twenty after eight.'

Carrie squeezed her hand. 'We're late. We've gotta get Grandpa . . . He'll be worrying . . . Talk to him, Nick. Please, you've got to . . .'

Luz got up and went over to her PC.

'No, not yet,' I said. 'Get a search engine—Google, something like that.' My eyes darted between them. 'Just do it, trust me.'

Luz was already clicking the keyboard of her PC at the other end of the room. I heard the sound of the modem handshaking.

'I got it, Nick—I got Google.'

I took her place on the chair, and typed in 'Sunburn missile'. It threw up a couple of thousand results, but even the first I clicked on made grim reading. The Russian-designed and -built sea-skimming missile (NATO code-name 'Sunburn') was now also in the hands of the Chinese. The line drawing showed a rocket-shaped missile, with fins at the bottom and smaller ones midway up its thirty feet. It could be launched from a ship or a trailer-like platform.

There was a defence analyst's review:

> The Sunburn anti-ship missile combines a Mach 2.5 speed with a low-level flight pattern. After detecting the Sunburn, the US Navy Phalanx point defense system may have only 2.5 seconds to calculate a fire solution before impact—when it lifts up and heads down into the target's deck with the devastating impact of a 750lb warhead. With a range of 90 miles, Sunburn . . .

Devastating wasn't the word. After the initial explosion, which would melt everyone in the immediate vicinity, everything caught in the blast would become a secondary missile.

That was all I needed to know. I moved off the chair and walked towards the other two. 'Luz, you can get your granddad now.'

I knelt down beside Carrie. 'The banjo you were talking about, is it a river? Is that why they have a boat?'

The drugs were kicking in. 'Banjo?'

'Where they came from last night, remember? Is it a river?'

She fought hard to listen. 'Oh, the Bayano? East of here, not far.'

'Do you know where they are exactly?'

'No, but . . .' She motioned me with her head to bend closer. When she spoke, her voice was shaking. 'Aaron next door?'

I shook my head. 'The Mazda.'

She started to cry very gently. I didn't know what to say.

'Grandpa! Grandpa! You gotta help . . . There were these men, Mom's hurt and Daddy's gone for the police!' Luz was getting herself into a frenzy. I moved over to her. 'Go and help your mum, go on.'

I found myself facing George's head and shoulders in the six-by-six-inch box in the centre of the screen. I plugged in the headset and put it over my ears.

'Who are you?' His tone was slow and controlled over the crackles.

'Nick. A face to the name at last, eh?'

'What's my daughter's condition?' His all-American square-jawed face didn't betray a trace of emotion.

'A fractured femur. You need to sort something out for her at Chepo. Get her picked up from the Peace Corps. I'll—'

'No. Take them both to the embassy. Where is Aaron?'

I looked behind me and saw Luz, close to Carrie but within earshot. I turned back and muttered, 'Dead.'

There was no change of expression in his face—nor in his voice. 'I repeat, take them to the embassy, I'll arrange everything else.'

I shook my head slowly. 'I know what's happening, George. You can't let the *Ocaso* take the hit. You have to stop it.'

He took a breath. 'Listen up, son, don't get yourself involved in something you don't understand. Just do exactly what I said. Take my daughter and Luz to the embassy, and do it right now.'

He hadn't denied it. He hadn't asked, 'What's the *Ocaso*?'

I needed to finish my piece. 'Get it stopped, George, or I'm reaching out to anyone who will listen. Call it off and I'm silent for life.'

'Can't do that, son.' He leaned forward. His face took up a lot of screen. 'Reach out all you want, no one will be listening. Too many people involved, too many agendas. You're getting into ground you wouldn't be capable of understanding.' He moved back. 'Take them to the embassy. I'll even get you paid off, if it helps.' He paused, to ensure I'd get the message. 'If not, take my word for it, the future won't look bright.'

I listened, knowing that as soon as I was through those embassy gates I'd be history. I knew too much and wasn't one of the family.

I shook my head and pulled off the headset, looking round at Carrie with a shrug of exasperation.

'Let me speak to him, Nick.'

I went over to them both and grabbed one end of the cot with both hands. 'Luz, we need blankets and water for your mum. Just pile them up in the storeroom for the journey.'

I pulled the cot back so Carrie was within reach of the headset, and placed it over her head, repositioning the mike so it was near her mouth. Above us, George's face still dominated the screen.

'Hi, it's me.'

The face on the screen was impassive, but I saw the lips move.

'I'll live . . . all those people won't if you don't call it off.'

George's mouth worked for several seconds, but his expression remained set. He was arguing, rationalising, probably commanding. The one thing he still wasn't doing was listening.

'Just once, just for once in my life . . . I've never asked you for anything. Even the passport wasn't a gift, it came with conditions. You have to stop it. Stop it now . . .'

I looked at George, and his cold, unyielding face as he spoke. It was now Carrie's turn to listen. She slowly pulled the headset from her face, her eyes swollen with tears, and let it drop on her chest.

'Disconnect it . . . get him out of here . . . It's over . . .'

George had already cut the comms himself. That was because he'd be getting onto the missile crew using the relay.

I followed the black wires from the dishes, down from the ceiling and out under the tables, looking like spaghetti as they jumbled up with white wires on their way to feed the machines. Sliding under the desk, I started to pull out anything that was attached to anything else as I shouted at Carrie,. 'Where's the relay board?'

I got a weak reply. 'The blue box. It's near you somewhere.'

Under the mass of wiring, I found a blue alloy box. There were three coaxial cables attached, two in, one out. I pulled out all three.

There was mumbling behind me. I turned just in time to see Luz heading for the living-room door. 'Stop! Stay where you are! Don't move!' I jumped to my feet and grabbed her. 'Where you going?'

'Just to get some clothes. I'm sorry . . .' She looked over to her mother for support. I let go so she could be at her mother's side, and as I turned I noticed a small pool of blood that had seeped under the door. I ran into the storeroom and grabbed a half-empty fifty-pound sack of rice. I placed it like a sandbag against the bottom of the door. 'You can't go in there—it's dangerous, there could be a fire. The oil lamps fell when the helicopters came, it's everywhere. I'll get your stuff for you Luz, just stay here, OK?'

I nearly gagged when I opened the door and stepped over the rice bag. The smell of cordite had gone, replaced by a smell like a bad day in a butcher's shop. Once the door was closed I turned on the light. The four bodies lay among the splintered wood and smashed glass, their blood in congealed pools on the floorboards.

Stepping carefully, I went and got a spare set of clothes for Luz and a sweat top for Carrie. Opening the door, I threw them out into the computer room. 'Get changed, help your mum. I'll stay in here.'

I pulled a chest harness from under Green. It was dripping with blood. That didn't matter; what did was the mags inside. I wrenched off the other harnesses. Hefting them, all filled with fresh mags, I rescued my docs from the floor and collected 212 bloodstained dollars from the bodies. I secured them in my leg pocket before checking the bookshelf for mapping of Chepo and the Bayano. I found what I was looking for, and she was right: it was to the east of Chepo.

There was no time to ponder, we had to leave. The weather might clear at any minute. If the Peace Corps couldn't do anything for her, they could at least get her to the city.

I ran through onto the verandah, and out into the rain. As soon as I got to the Land Cruiser, I dumped the kit in the footwell, then jammed the M-16 down between the passenger seat and the door before I closed it. I didn't want Luz seeing it. I went round to the other side and checked the fuel. I had about half a tank. I grabbed the torch and headed for the Mazda. When I lifted the tailgate, the light beam fell on the bedsheet covering Aaron. I dragged out one of the heavy jerry cans and slammed the tailgate shut.

I emptied the fuel into the Land Cruiser and threw the container into the footwell on top of the harnesses. I might need it later.

I walked back to the computer room. Luz was sitting on the floor beside the cot, stroking her mother's brow.

I bent down and retrieved one of the crepe bandages from the floor and put it into my pocket. 'Time to go.'

We both had our hands on the cot, Luz at the feet end, facing me. 'Ready? One, two, three. Up, up, up.'

I steered us while she shuffled backwards, ploughing through the storeroom. We squelched through the mud and slid her once more into the back of the wagon, head first. I sent Luz back into the storeroom for the blankets and Evian while I used the bandage to secure the cot legs at the head end to anchorage points to stop it sliding around on the journey. Carrie turned her head towards me, sounding drowsy on her cocktail of dihydrocodeine and aspirin.

'Nick, Nick . . . What am I going to do now?'

I knew what she was getting at, but this wasn't the time. 'You're going to Chepo and you'll both be in Boston before you know it.'

'No, no. Aaron—what am I going to do?'

I was reprieved by Luz returning with water and an armful of blanket, which she helped me arrange over Carrie.

I jumped off the tailgate back into the mud and went round and climbed into the driver's seat. 'Luz, you've got to keep an eye on your mum—make sure she doesn't slide about too much, OK?'

She nodded earnestly, kneeling over her as I started up and turned the Land Cruiser. The main beams swept over the Mazda. Carrie eventually saw it in the red glow of our taillights as we crept past.

'Stop, stop, Nick—stop . . .'

I put my foot gently on the brake and turned in my seat. Her head was up, neck straining to look out of the gap at the rear. Luz moved to support her. 'What's up, Mom? What's wrong?'

Carrie just kept on staring at the Mazda as she answered her daughter. 'It's OK, baby—I was just thinking about something. Later.' She pulled Luz close and gave her a hug.

I waited for a while as the rain fell, more gently now, and the engine ticked over. 'OK to go?'

'Yes,' she said. 'We're done here.'

FOURTEEN

Saturday, September 9

The journey to Chepo was slow and difficult as I tried to avoid as many potholes and ruts as I could. Once we hit the road, which looked more like a river in places, we were making no more than about eight miles an hour. Glancing round, I saw Luz kneeling by her mother, comforting her. I fished in my pocket for the dihydrocodeine. 'Here, give your mum another of these. Show the doctors or whoever the bottle. She's had four in total and an aspirin. Got that?'

Eventually the fortified police station came into view and I called for directions. 'Where's the clinic? Which way do I go?'

Luz was on top of this now. 'It's kinda behind the store.'

We passed the restaurant and the jaguar wasn't even curious as we drove on into the dark side of town. I took a right just before the breeze-block store. 'Luz, this the right way? Am I OK?'

'Yep—it's just up here, see?' Her hand passed my face from behind and pointed. About three buildings down was another breeze-block structure with a tin roof and the circular Peace Corps sign—stars and stripes, only instead of the stars a dove or two.

I pulled up outside. Luz jumped out of the back and banged on the door. A painted wooden plaque read: AMERICAN PEACE CORPS COMMUNITY ENVIRONMENTAL EDUCATION PROJECT.

As I climbed out of the Land Cruiser, heading for the tailgate, a woman in her mid-twenties wearing a track suit appeared on the threshold. Her eyes darted about rapidly as she took in the scene.

'What's wrong, Luz?'

Luz launched into a frenzied explanation as I got into the rear and undid the security bandage. 'We're here, Carrie,' I said.

She murmured as the young woman came to the rear. 'Carrie, it's Janet—can you hear me?'

There was no time for hellos. 'Got trauma care? It's an open fractured femur, left leg.'

Janet began to ease the cot out of the wagon. I grabbed the other end and between us we lugged Carrie inside.

The office was barely furnished, just a couple of desks, cork boards, a phone and wall clock. 'Can you treat her? If you can't, you need to get her into the city.'

The woman looked at me as if I was mad.

People were emerging from the rear of the building, three men in different shades of disarray, and a rush of American voices. 'What's happened, Carrie? Where's Aaron? Ohmigod, you OK, Luz?'

A trauma pack appeared and a bag of fluid and a giving set were pulled out and prepared. They knew what they were doing. I looked at Luz, sitting on the floor holding her mother's hand once more as Janet read the label on the dihydrocodeine bottle.

According to the wall clock it was 12.27—nine and a half hours to go. I left them to it and went back to the wagon. Once in the driver's seat I hit the cab light and unfolded the map to get my bearings on the Bayano. It snaked towards the Bay of Panama on the edge of the Pacific. The river's mouth was in line of sight of the entrance to the canal and, a little further in, the Miraflores. If this was the river they were on, they had to be at the mouth. Sunburn couldn't negotiate high ground: it was designed for the sea. The range to the canal was about thirty miles. Sunburn's range was ninety. It made sense so far.

I studied the map, wondering if Charlie was doing the same before getting out there to look for it. He didn't know what I did so he'd be scanning the sixty to seventy miles of jungle shoreline that fell within Sunburn's range and could be used as a launch point. That was a lot of jungle to sift through in less than ten hours. I hoped it would mean the difference between me destroying it and him repossessing it so he could hand it straight over to FARC.

The map indicated that the only place to launch from was the east bank as the river joined the sea. The west bank also had a peninsula, but it didn't project far enough out to clear the coastline. It had to be the east, the left-hand side as I went downriver.

The Bayano's nearest reachable point was four miles south, according to the map, via a dry-weather, loose-surface road. From there, the river wound south, downstream to the coast for about six miles. In reality it would be more, because of the river's bends.

That was all I knew. But I had to work with the information I had.

I went to the rear of the wagon and closed the tailgate, then got back behind the wheel, fired the engine, and moved off, trying to head south using the compass still round my neck. It was only then that I realised I hadn't said anything to Carrie and Luz. Carrie wouldn't have heard but, still, it would have been nice to say goodbye.

After an hour of the dry-weather track, now just a mixture of mud and gravel, I saw a river in the tunnel of light carved out immediately ahead of me. Stopping, I jumped out of the wagon with the torch and picked my way down the muddy bank.

Running along the bank, I checked for a boat, anything that would get me downstream quickly. There wasn't even a jetty—no ground sign, nothing, just mud, rough grass, and the odd tree.

I scrambled up the bank, got into the wagon and checked the map once more. I drove back up the track towards Chepo, checking each side of me for somewhere to hide the Land Cruiser, but even after two miles the ground looked bare. The loggers had been here. I finally parked up on the side of the road, dragged out the dried-out chest harnesses, the M-16 and jerry can, then tabbed back towards the river with the kit dangling off me like a badly packed Cub Scout.

I sat against a tree as the Bayano rumbled past me out there in the dark. I thought about what I was doing here. Why hadn't I just killed Michael and had done with it in the first place?

With only half an hour to push before first light and a move to the target, I knew I was bullshitting myself. I would have done this regardless. It wasn't just that so many people—real people—were at risk: it was that maybe, just for once, I was doing the right thing.

I could hear the weak but rapid *wap wap wap* of a Huey somewhere in the darkness. Maybe Charlie had been back to the house. But for the time being he'd have those aircraft search the coastline for Sunburn rather than us three.

Invisible birds started their morning songs as a yellow arc of sunlight prepared to break the skyline and yield up a hot morning. I'd repacked my docs and map in the two plastic bags, tying each one off with a knot. I checked the Velcro flaps on the mag pouches of the harnesses. Finally, I made sure all my clothing was loose, with nothing tucked in that might catch water and weigh me down.

I undid the plastic clips for the back straps of the harnesses and fed the ends through the handle of the jerry can before refastening them. I did the same with the neck straps, through the carrying handle of the M-16. More soldiers get killed negotiating rivers than ever die in contacts under the canopy. That was why everything was attached to the empty jerry can and not to me.

I dragged the whole lot down to the edge of the tepid, rusty-brown water. I waded in up to my thighs, then heaped the three harnesses and weapon on top of the floating jerry can, which wanted to go with the current. Freshly dislodged foliage sped past as the jerry can bobbed in front of me, now more than half submerged with the weight of its load. I pushed on into gradually deepening water, forearms over the weapon and harnesses, until eventually my feet began to lose touch with the riverbed. I let myself go with the flow, kicking off from the mud like a child with a swimming float. The stream carried me with it, but I kept contact with the bottom to keep some control, alternately kicking and going with the current.

After about half an hour, the jungle began to sprout up on either side of me. The opposite bank got further away and the jungle gave way to mangrove swamp. As I rounded a particularly wide, gentle bend, I could see the Pacific Ocean lying just half a mile further downstream. In the far distance I could see two container ships. I kept my eyes peeled for anything that would help me locate Sunburn.

Maybe 200 yards from the river mouth was a small, open-decked fishing boat that had been dragged up onto the bank and left to rot. As I got closer I could see, in a clearing beyond the boat, a small wooden hut in a similar state of decay.

I floated past, eyes scanning the area. There had been fresh movement. I could clearly see the dark underside of some large ferns just up from the bank, and some of the two-foot-tall grass growing around the boat was interlaced where it had been walked through.

I carried on for another fifty yards, until the canopy took over and the boat disappeared. I touched bottom and guided the jerry can ashore. Dragging the kit into the canopy, I unbuckled the harnesses and M-16. A brief dip in a river wasn't going to stop it working.

I donned the first chest harness and adjusted the straps so that it hung low, virtually round my waist. Then I put on the second, above the first, and the third one higher still. I rechecked that all the mags were stored facing the correct way, so that as I pulled them out with my left hand they'd be ready to be slapped straight into the weapon. Finally, after rechecking chamber on the M-16, I checked Baby-G. It was 8.19. I jumped up and down to check for rattles and that everything was secure. Then I removed the safety catch, pushing past single rounds, all the way to Automatic.

I moved towards the hut, pausing every few paces, listening for warnings from the birds and other jungle life, butt in my shoulder, trigger finger against the guard, ready to shoot and scoot. I had to check the area around the hut, because it would be my only escape route. If the shit hit the fan it would be a case of down to the river, pick up the jerry can, jump in and go for it, down to the sea.

I stopped just short of the clearing, went slowly onto my knees in the mud and foliage, and listened. The only man-made sound was the water dripping from my clothes onto the leaf litter.

The track leading into the canopy had been used recently, and something had been pulled along it that cut a groove through the mud and leaves. Either side of that groove were footprints. I hadn't seen any sign in the mud I floated past, because it had been covered with dead leaves. Past the bank, though, the sign was clear to see. I got up and started to parallel the track.

Within twenty paces I came across the Gemini inflatable boat, with a Yamaha 50 on the back. It had been dragged up the track and pulled off to the right, blocking my way.

I could still see ground sign heading in both directions as the track meandered round the trees. Still paralleling the track to my left, I started to move deeper into the canopy. I patrolled on, stopping, listening, checking left, right and above me, trying to keep up speed but at the same time not compromise myself by making too much noise.

There was a metallic clang in the trees. I froze, straining an ear.

For several seconds all I could hear was my own breath, then the clang rang out again. It came from ahead and slightly off to my left.

Applying the safety catch, I went down onto my stomach. It was time to move slower than a sloth, but Baby-G told me it was 9.06.

I inched forward on my elbows and toes, with the weapon to my right. I was having to lift my body higher than I'd have wanted to stop the harnesses dragging in the mud. The crawl was hard work. I moved through the undergrowth six inches at a time. I stopped, lifted my head, looked and listened for more activity but still heard only my own breath. I was looking for alarm trips—wires, pressure pads, infrared beams or maybe even string and tin cans.

There was noise, and I froze. Another clunk of metal on metal—then a faint, fast murmur above the noise of the cicadas. I closed my eyes, leaned my ear towards the source, opened my mouth to cut out internal noises and concentrated.

The inflection in the voices wasn't Spanish. I strained to listen, but just couldn't work it out. They seemed to be talking at warp speed, accompanied now by the rhythmic thud of full jerry cans.

It was 9.29. I had to get closer and not worry about the noise or the people making it. I needed to see what was happening so I could work out what I had to do within the next twenty minutes.

I lifted my chest from the mud and slithered forward. Soon I began to make out a small clearing beyond the wall of green.

The black-shirted guy who'd been on the verandah crossed the clearing, carrying two black bin liners, half full. He wore a US army webbing belt with two mag pouches hanging from it.

The voices came again from my right, a lot clearer. They were Eastern European, maybe Bosnians.

The small cleared area in the trees was about the size of half a tennis court. I couldn't see anything, but heard the unmistakable hiss of fuel under pressure being released in the vicinity of the voices.

One more slow, deliberate bound and now I heard the fuel splash. I strained my eyes to the top of their sockets. Black Shirt was to my half right, six or seven yards away, standing with the little guy who'd been with him that night. The jerry cans were being emptied over the assembled contents of their camp: camouflage netting, US army cots, a generator on its side, bin liners full and tied, all piled into a heap. It was nearly time to leave, so they were destroying evidence.

Holding my breath, I edged forward another few inches, my eyes glued to the two at the rubbish dump just a few yards away.

As the area to my right opened up a bit I saw the backs of the two Bosnians, dressed in green fatigue tops and jeans. They were bent over a fold-down table, studying two screens inside a green metal console. There were two integrated keyboards below each screen. That had to be the guidance system. To the right of it was an opened laptop. Beside them on the ground were five civilian rucksacks, two M-16s with mags on, and another jerry can—probably to deal with the electronic equipment after the launch.

I watched the two Bosnians point at the console screens, then look over at the laptop as one hit the keyboard. Beyond them I could see cables running down from the rear of the console and into the jungle. The Sunburn had to be at the river's mouth. The guidance system was separated from the missile. They wouldn't have wanted to be right on top of shedloads of rocket fuel when it went off.

A fifth member came out of the canopy behind the console. He, too, was dressed in a green fatigue top, but had black baggy trousers, an M-16 over his shoulder and belt kit. He watched the Bosnians and lit a cigarette. Sucking in deeply, he used his free hand to wave the bottom of his shirt to circulate some air around his torso. Even if I hadn't recognised his face, I'd have known that pizza scar anywhere.

All of a sudden the Bosnians began to jabber and their voices went up an octave as Pizza Man bent in towards the screens. Stuff was happening. There must be only minutes left. I had to make my move.

I pushed up onto my knees, my mud-caked thumb shifting the safety to Auto as the weapon came into the shoulder. I squeezed with both eyes open, short, sharp bursts into the mud by the dump.

Unintelligible screams mixed with the sound of rounds on auto as the Bosnians panicked and the other two went for their weapons. The fifth just seemed to vanish.

My shoulder rocked back with another short burst as I held the weapon tight to stop the muzzle rising. I didn't want to hit the Bosnians: if they could fly the thing, they could stop it. The mag emptied as I kept on squeezing. The working parts stayed to the rear.

I got to my feet and moved position before they reacted to where the fire had come from. I ran to the right, towards the table, using the cover, pressing the magazine-release catch with my forefinger, shaking the weapon, trying to remove the mud-clogged mag. I felt it hit my thigh as I fumbled at the lower harness and pulled out a fresh one. I smacked it on and hit the release catch. The working parts screamed forward as long bursts of automatic fire came from my left, from the clearing.

I dropped instinctively and crawled to the edge of the clearing in time to see the Bosnians disappearing down the track, their terrified voices filling the gaps between bursts of gunfire. I also saw Pizza Man on the other side of the clearing, in cover, shouting at them to come back. 'It's just one man, one weapon! Get back!'

It wasn't happening, the other two were following the Bosnians, firing long bursts into the jungle.

'Assholes!' Weapon in the shoulder, he took single shots at them. Fuck that, I wanted them alive.

Flicking safety to single rounds, I took aim centre mass of what little I could see of him, stopped breathing and fired. He dropped like a stone, disappearing into the foliage without a sound.

I changed mags and crossed the clearing towards Pizza Man, weapon in the shoulder, moving fast but cautiously.

He was alive, panting for breath and holding his chest, eyes open but helpless. Blood flowed gently between his fingers.

I tossed his weapon to one side and kicked him. 'Close it down!'

He just lay there, no reaction.

I grabbed his forearm and dragged him into the clearing, and it was then that I saw the exit wound gaping in his back.

His eyes were shut tight, taking the pain of the round and movement. I dropped his arm as he mumbled, almost smiling, 'We're coming back, asshole . . .'

I leaned over him, butt in the shoulder, and thrust the muzzle into his face. 'Stop it! Fucking stop it!'

He just smiled beneath the pressure of the metal. 'Or what?'

He was right. I ran to the table, checking the track for the others, checking Baby-G. Just three minutes to go.

The left-hand VDU was full of Russian symbols, the other was a radar screen with a hazy green background peppered with white dots as its sweeping arm moved clockwise. The laptop displayed the webcam image of the locks. A cable led from it, along the ground and up a tree, where a small satellite dish was clamped to a branch.

I looked back at the laptop. I could see the band playing, girls dancing and crowds in the seats and more standing against the barriers. The *Ocaso* was in pride of place on the screen. Passengers thronged the decks, clutching cameras and handycams.

Scrambling round to the back of the table, I fell to my knees and started pulling out the mass of wires and cables that led from the back of the console towards the sea. Some were just slotted in, some had a bracket over them, some were screwed into their sockets.

A high-pitched whine started within the canopy, like a Harrier jump jet before takeoff. Within seconds the noise surrounded me.

Four cables to go. The more I tried to pull or unscrew them, the more I lost it. I gave one big tug in frustration and despair. The console slid off the table and landed in the mud. The high-pitched whine became a roar as the rocket engines kicked in.

In almost the same instant there was a deafening, rumbling boom, and the ground began to shake under my feet. The missile left its platform and surged out of the jungle. The treetops shook and debris rained down around me.

I released my grip on the cables and spun the laptop round, catching the last glimpse of the ship as the image faded.

The screen was blank and there was nothing I could do but wait, wondering if I'd be able to hear the explosion, or if the sound would get swallowed up by the jungle and distance.

I waited for the screen to refresh—or stay blank for ever as the camera would surely be taken out as well.

Slowly, lazily, the image unfolded and I braced myself for the scene of carnage, trying to convince myself that the camera being intact was a good sign, then thinking I didn't know how far the camera was from the locks, so maybe not.

The picture refreshed itself. The ship was intact, everything was intact. The dancing girls were throwing their batons in the air and passengers were waving at the crowd on shore. What the hell had happened? It should have made it there by now: it travelled at two and a half times the speed of sound. I didn't trust what I was seeing. Maybe it was the image that had been captured just before the explosion, and I was going to have to wait for the next cycle.

The top of the next image began to unfold and this time I saw smoke. I sat in the mud, more exhausted than I'd ever been in my life.

Then, as the image filled the screen, I saw that the ship was still there. The smoke was coming from its funnels.

The sounds of the jungle returned. Birds screeched above me as they settled back in their roosts. Then came the distinctive *wap wap wap* of much bigger birds. The sound got louder and then came the rattle of rotors as a Huey zoomed straight over me, its dark blue underbelly flashing across the treetops. I could hear others circling.

I jumped to my feet and grabbed a jerry can, dousing the console with fuel, making sure it poured into the cooling vents at the back. I picked up two rucksacks and threw them over a shoulder, hoping that whatever made them weigh so much was stuff I could use in the jungle. Finally grabbing the weapon, I moved to Pizza Man. He looked at me with a satisfied smile.

'It didn't work,' I shouted. 'It didn't make contact, you fucked up.'

He didn't believe me and hung on to the smile, eyes closed, coughing blood. I reached into his pocket and pulled out the Zippo.

The heli had returned and was over by the river, flying low and slow. Others were now closer. There were long, sustained bursts of automatic fire. They had found the escaping Gemini.

'That's Charlie's people. They'll be here soon.'

His eyes flickered and he fought to keep the smile through the pain.

'Believe me, it didn't work. Let's hope they keep you alive for Charlie. I bet you two have a lot to talk about.'

Hearing heli noise almost directly overhead, I ran over to the console and flicked the lighter. The fuel ignited instantly. It mustn't fall into Charlie's hands; then all he would need was another missile and he would be back in business.

I turned and ran from the flames. I heard shouts from the track. Charlie's boys were here.

As the roar of the Hueys became almost deafening, I shouldered the rucksacks, picked up the weapon, and ran into the jungle.

FIFTEEN

Friday, September 15

I watched through the dirty windscreen as passenger after passenger was dropped off outside departures, and the roar of jet engines followed an aircraft into the clear blue sky. There'd been enough anti-surveillance drills en route to the airport to throw off Superman, but still I sank into the seat and watched the vehicles that came and went, trying to remember if I had seen them or their drivers earlier.

The dash digital said it was nearly three o'clock, so I turned the ignition key to power up the radio, scanning the channels for news. A female American voice was soon informing me that there were unconfirmed reports that FARC were behind the failed missile attack, which appeared to have been aimed at shipping in the Panama Canal. It was old news now and low down the running order, but it seemed that after it launched, fishermen saw the missile fly out of control before falling into the bay less than half a mile from the shore. The US had already re-established a presence in the republic as they were now trying to fish out the missile and set up defences to stop any such further terrorist attacks.

I flicked it back onto the Christian channel and hit the off switch before cutting the ignition. It was the first bit of news I'd heard about the incident. I had done my best to avoid all media these past six days, but hadn't been able to resist any longer the temptation to find out what had happened.

It had taken three long, wet and hot days to walk out of the jungle, clean myself up, and hitch a ride into Panama City. The rucksacks had contained no food, so it was back to jungle survival skills and digging out roots. But at least I could lie on the rucksacks and keep out of the mud, and though they didn't fit very well, the spare clothes helped keep the mozzies off my head and hands at night.

Once I'd reached the city, I dried out the two hundred-odd dollars I'd lifted from the guys in the house in the sun and the blood flaked off them like thin scabs. I bought clothes and the dirtiest room in the old quarter that didn't care as long as I paid cash.

Until Tuesday, four days ago, my credit card still hadn't been cancelled, so it looked as if things were still OK with the Yes Man. After I'd cleaned myself up, I went into a bank and took out the max I could on it, $12,150, before using my ticket to Miami. From there I took a train to Baltimore, Maryland. It had taken two days on four trains, never buying a ticket for more than $100 so as not to arouse suspicion. I hadn't minded the Yes Man knowing I was out of Panama as he tracked me to Miami, but that was all I'd wanted him to know. But now, three days later, Sundance and Trainers might already be sightseeing in Washington.

I heard the door handle go and Josh was at the window of his black, double-cabbed Dodge gas-guzzler. One hand pulled open the driver's door, the other cradled a Starbucks and a can of Coke.

I took the coffee as he climbed into the driver's seat and muttered, 'Thanks,' as I placed the paper cup in the centre console holder.

Josh's eyes stayed on the entrance to the long-term multistorey car park, on the other side of our short-term one. 'Still thirty minutes to push until we're due,' he said. 'We'll drink them here.'

I nodded, and pulled back on the ring-pull as he tested the hot brew. Anything he said was OK by me today. He had picked me up at the station, driven me about for the last two hours, and had listened to what I was proposing. And now here we were, at Baltimore International Airport, where I should have arrived from Charles de Gaulle in the first place, and he had even bought me a Coke.

He still looked the same: shiny brown bald head, still hitting the weights, gold-rimmed glasses that made him look more menacing than intellectual. From my side I couldn't see the scar on his face.

After a while he turned towards me. I knew that he hated me: he couldn't hide it. I would have felt the same, in his shoes.

'There'll be rules,' he said. 'You hear what I'm saying? You are first going to sort out this shit you've got us all in, man. I don't care what it's about or what you have to do—just finish it. Then, and only then, you call me. This is how it's going to be—like a divorced couple, a couple that do the right thing by their kids. You hearing me? It's the last chance you're ever getting.'

I nodded, feeling relieved.

We sat for another ten minutes, watching vehicles. Josh gave occasional sighs as he thought about what he had agreed to. He was certainly not happy, but I knew he would do it anyway, because it was the right thing. He finished the Starbucks and we drove out of the car park and followed signs for long stay, eventually turning into the multistorey. I bent down into the footwell as if I'd dropped something as we approached the barrier and ticket machine. The last thing Josh needed was a picture of us together at this time.

I could see plenty of empty spaces but we drove straight up the ramps to the second-to-last floor. The top floor was probably uncovered, and open to observation. There wouldn't be many vehicles coming up this far, and those that did would be easier to check out.

We pulled into a space and Josh nodded at a metallic green Voyager with Maine plates and a mass of cartoon-character baby sunscreens pulled down, effectively blacking out the rear. 'Five minutes, got it? This is dangerous. She's my sister, for God's sake.'

I nodded and reached for the handle.

'Just remember, man, she missed you last week.'

I got out and as I approached the Voyager the front window powered down to reveal a woman in her thirties, black and beautiful, with hair pulled back in a bun. She gave an anxious half-smile and indicated for me to go round to the sliding door as she got out.

'I appreciate this.'

There was no answer from her as she went over to Josh's wagon and climbed in next to him.

I felt some apprehension at seeing Kelly. I hadn't done so for just over a month now. I slid the door across. She was strapped into the rear seat, staring at me, a little confused, maybe a little wary, as I got inside to conceal us both.

It's incredible how much children seem to change if you don't see them every day. Kelly's eyes and nose seemed more defined somehow, and her mouth a bit larger, like a young Julia Roberts. She was going to be the spitting image of her mother.

I put on my smiley face, moving toys out of the way to sit down in the row in front of her. 'Hello, how are you?' I sat between two baby seats and looked back at her. I wanted to throw my arms round her, but didn't dare risk it. She might not want me to.

Something the size of a Jumbo was taxiing upwind of us. I could hardly hear myself think and stuck my finger in my ear and made a funny face. At least I got a smile from her.

I pulled myself over the backrest and kissed her cheek. There wasn't any coldness in her reaction, but nothing in the way of exhilaration either. I understood: why get excited, only to be let down?

'It's great to see you. How are you?'

'Fine . . . what are those lumps on your face?'

'I got stung by some wasps. Anyway, what are you up to?'

'I'm on a vacation with Monica—are you going to stay with us? You said you were coming to see me last week.'

'I know, I know, it's just that . . . Kelly, I . . . Listen, I'm sorry for not doing all the things I said I would with you. You know, call, come visit when I said I would. I always wanted to do those things, it was just, well, stuff, you know.'

She nodded as if she knew. I was glad one of us did.

'And now I've mucked it up again and have to go away for a while today . . . but I really wanted to see you, even if it was only for a few minutes.' The jumbo thundered down the runway. I waited, frustrated that I couldn't say what I wanted to until the noise died.

'Look, maybe I was jealous of Josh when you started to live with him, but now I know it's the right thing, the best thing. You need to be with his gang, having fun, going to Monica's for a holiday. So what I've worked out with Josh is, once I come back from sorting some stuff out, I'll be able to do things—you know, coming to see you, calling, going on holiday. I want to do all those things with you, because I miss you so much and think about you all the time. But it has to be like this now, you have to live with Josh. That make sense?'

'We will go on vacation? You said we would one day.'

'Absolutely. Not immediately, though. I have to sort out . . . well . . .'

'Stuff?'

We smiled. 'That's right. Stuff.'

Monica opened her door with a wide smile for Kelly. 'We gotta go, honey.'

Kelly looked at me, and for one terrible moment I thought she was going to cry. 'Can I talk with Dr Hughes?'

Concern must have been written all over my face. 'Why's that?'

Her face conjured up an enormous grin. 'Well, my dad just divorced my other dad. I got issues.'

Even Monica laughed. 'You been watching too much Ricki Lake, honey!' She closed the door on a smiling Kelly and drove out.

Josh spoke through his window as I walked back. 'You'll get the transportation for the train station outside arrivals.'

I nodded and turned towards the lift with a small wave, but he wanted to say more. 'Look, man, maybe you ain't quite the dwarf I thought you were. But you still gotta sort your shit out, get a grip of your life, man, get some religion, anything.'

I nodded as he drove out, two vehicles behind the Voyager.

She was messed up enough and the way I acted made it worse. But I was no longer going to sign her over to Josh and walk away. That was the easy way out. She not only needed but deserved two parents, even if they were divorced. I hoped that me being there, if only a little, was better than not at all. Besides, I wanted to be there.

So that was the plan. Once I had sorted out the 'stuff', I'd come back here and we'd do it correctly. Sort out visitation rights, and a system that gave Kelly what she needed, structure to her life and the knowledge that the people around her were there for her.

However, the 'stuff' wasn't going to be easy. Two obstacles had to be overcome if I wanted to stop me, Kelly, and even Josh and his lot, from being targets—now and for ever. George and the Yes Man.

The long-term solution to this problem had to be through George. He'd be able to call off the dogs. And the way to contact him would be through Carrie.

First I needed to get to Marblehead, and the two trains I was taking would get me there by six tomorrow morning. It shouldn't be hard to find Carrie, or her mother. The place wasn't that big.

As for the short-term problem of the Yes Man, he had to be dealt with quickly, in case Sundance and Trainers were already on their way. I still had the security blanket, which I'd tell George about, and Kelly was safe. The left-luggage ticket was valid for three months and hidden behind one of the payphones at Waterloo. I would have to go and get it before then and put it somewhere else.

No way was I going to call him yet, though. The call would be traced. I'd do that tomorrow.

Then I thought, Why bother going back to the UK at all? What was there waiting for me apart from the sports bag? I started to fantasise and thought that maybe, if I played my cards right, George could even fix *me* up with a US passport. After all, I had stopped the system getting into FARC's hands and maybe sticking out of the top of an aircraft carrier. I'd say that was pretty Stars and Stripes.

Who knows? Maybe while I was sorting stuff out, Carrie would let me sleep on her mother's couch.

ANDY McNAB

Having served in the SAS for many years, Andy McNab is familiar with the dangerous and murky world of undercover operations in which his hero, Nick Stone, moves. At every turn, Stone's missions are prone to unexpected developments that throw him back on his own resourcefulness. Is that how it was when McNab was in the SAS? 'Things always do go wrong on jobs,' McNab replies. 'The Regiment's work is not a science and, as Napoleon once said, if your enemy has only two options, you can always be sure he'll take the third.'

McNab left the service in 1993 and now works as a freelance adviser to security agencies here and in the USA. Asked what he finds hardest about civilian life, he says without hesitation, 'People not being direct, not saying what they mean. Particularly politicians. In the army, I always felt people didn't mince their words. If they felt something, they just said it outright. In civilian life, all this hinting and alluding to things gets right up my nose—I wish people would tell it like it is!'

The Panama Zone, where Nick Stone ventures in this latest book, is a region that McNab knows well. 'I spent time in Panama, attached to the US Army's school of Jungle Warfare, and it was my job to show a group of Green Berets how the SAS operates in the jungle. I revisited the area to research *Last Light* further as, obviously, the political situation had changed somewhat after the US withdrew from the country.'

In *Last Light*, Nick Stone is starting to question some of the things he has to do in the line of duty. Is he due for a change of career or lifestyle? 'Not at all,' McNab says. 'Nick may be starting to grow emotionally, but he still has a long way to go before he starts tree-hugging and giving it all up to become a yoga instructor. In fact, Miramax have just bought the rights to all the Nick Stone novels, so I expect everyone will be seeing a lot more of him in the future, in both books and films.'

中華中
氣功學
O.M.&
胃腸
中醫華
保健
陳杰 大夫
53號二樓二0二室
中醫李祖鑾大夫
三樓3D室
聖羅蘭集團

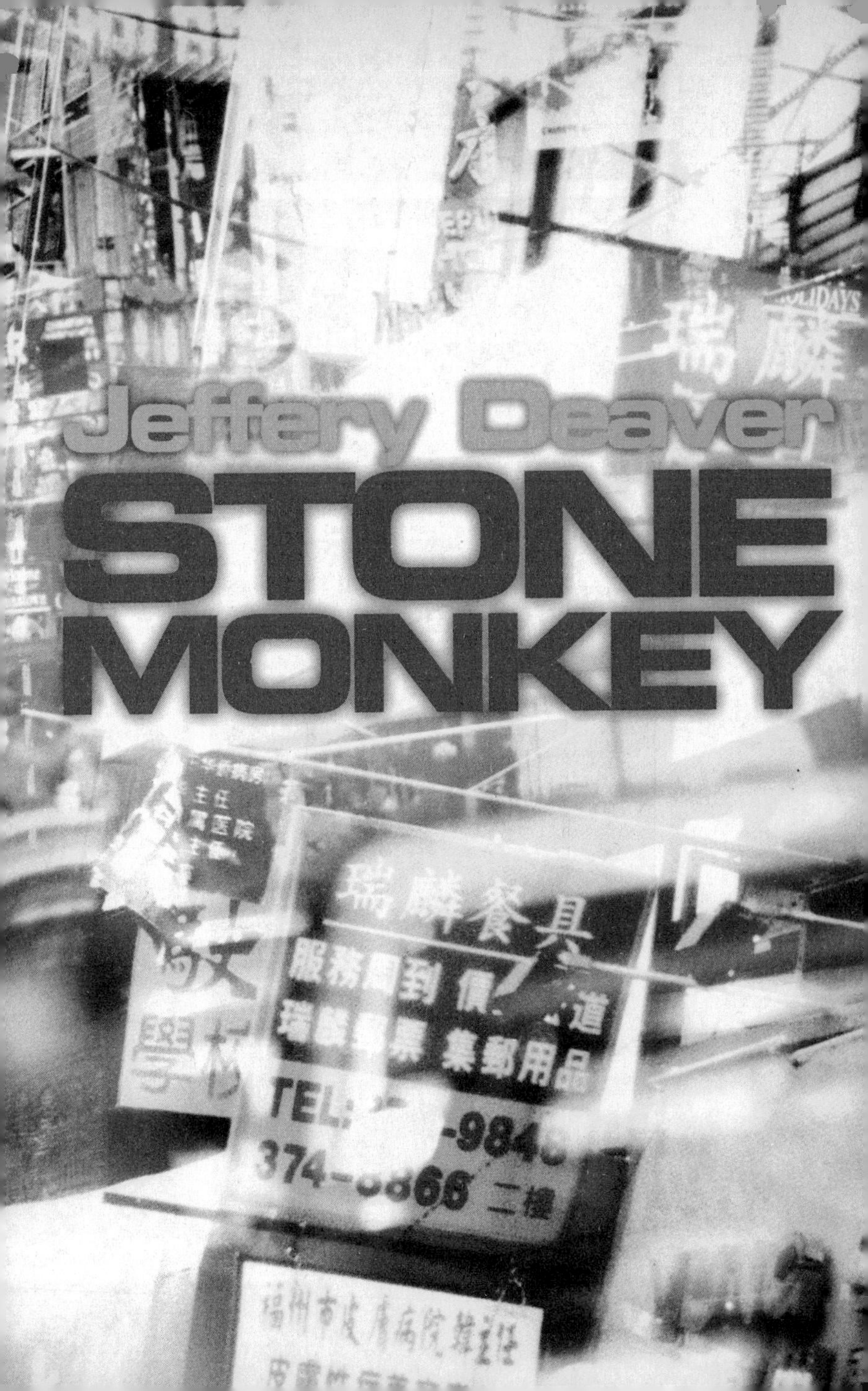
瑞麟
Jeffery Deaver
STONE
MONKEY
瑞麟餐具
集郵用品
二樓

The Chinese illegal immigrants who are hiding in the Fuzhou Dragon's hold, weary and uncomfortable from their long voyage, are filled with hope and fear about the new life that lies ahead of them in a new land.

Then, suddenly, when they are just miles from the US coastline, they hear an explosion tear through the ship . . .

Chapter One

They were the vanished, they were the unfortunate.

To the human smugglers—the snakeheads—who carted them round the world like pallets of damaged goods, they were *ju-jia*, piglets. To the US Immigration agents who interdicted their ships and arrested and deported them, they were undocumenteds.

They were the hopeful. Who were trading homes and family and a thousand years of ancestry for the hard certainty of risky, laborious years ahead of them. Who had the slimmest of chances to take root in a place where freedom and money and contentment were, the story went, as common as sunlight and rain.

They were his fragile cargo.

And now, legs steady against the raging seas, Captain Sen Zi-jun made his way from the bridge down two decks into the murky hold to deliver the grim message that their weeks of difficult journeying might have been in vain.

It was just before dawn on a Tuesday in August. The stocky captain, whose head was shaved and who sported an elaborate bushy moustache, slipped past the empty containers lashed as camouflage to the deck of the 236-foot *Fuzhou Dragon* and opened the heavy steel door to the hold. He looked down at the two dozen people huddled there in the grim, windowless space. Trash and children's plastic blocks floated in the shallow tide under the cheap cots.

Despite the pitching waves, Sen—a thirty-year veteran of the seas, walked down the steep metal steps without using the handrails and strode into the middle of the hold. The air was vile with the smell of diesel fuel and humans who'd lived for two weeks in close proximity.

Unlike many of the captains and crew who operated human smuggling ships, who sometimes even beat or raped the passengers, Captain Sen didn't mistreat them. However, most of the immigrants assumed he was in league with the snakehead who'd chartered the *Dragon*: Kwan Ang, known universally by his nickname, Gui, the Ghost. Sen's efforts to engage the immigrants in conversation had been rebuffed and had yielded only one friend. Chang Jingerzi—who preferred his Western name of Sam Chang—was a forty-five-year-old former college professor from Fuzhou in southeastern China. He was bringing his entire family to America: his wife, two sons and Chang's widower father.

Captain Sen now saw Chang sitting on a cot in a forward corner of the hold. The tall, placid man frowned, a reaction to the look in the captain's eyes, and rose to meet him.

Everyone around them fell silent.

'Our radar shows a fast-moving ship on course to intercept us.'

'The American coastguard?' Chang asked.

'I think it must be,' the captain answered. 'We're in US waters.'

Sen looked at the frightened faces of the immigrants. Like most shiploads of illegals that Sen had transported, these people—many of them strangers before they'd met—had formed a close bond of friendship. They now gripped hands or whispered among themselves, some seeking, some offering reassurance. The captain's eyes settled on a woman holding an eighteen-month-old girl. The mother—her face scarred from a beating at a re-education camp—began to cry.

'What can we do?' Chang asked, troubled. Captain Sen knew he was a vocal dissident in China and had been desperate to flee the country. If he were deported he'd probably end up in one of the infamous jails in western China as a political prisoner.

'We're not far from the drop-off spot. We're running at full speed. It may be possible to get close enough to put you ashore in rafts.'

'In these waves?' Chang said. 'We'd all die.'

'There's a natural harbour. It should be calm enough for you to board the rafts. At the beach there'll be trucks to take you to New York. Now tell everyone to get their belongings together. But only the most important things. Your money, your pictures. Stay below until the Ghost or I tell you to come up top.'

Captain Sen hurried up the steep ladder to the bridge, dodging a wall of grey water that vaulted the side of the ship.

He found the Ghost standing over the radar unit, staring into the rubber glare shade. Some snakeheads dressed as if they were wealthy gangsters, but the Ghost always wore the standard outfit of most Chinese men: simple slacks and short-sleeved shirts. The Ghost was muscular but diminutive, clean-shaven, hair longer than a typical businessman's but never styled with cream or spray.

'They will intercept us in fifteen minutes,' the snakehead said. Even now, facing interdiction and arrest, he seemed as lethargic as a ticket seller in a rural long-distance bus station. 'I timed the distance they've travelled since we spotted them.'

The throttles were full forward. If the Ghost was right they would not be able to make the protected harbour in time. At best they could get within half a mile of the nearby rocky shore—close enough to launch the rafts but subjecting them to merciless pounding by the tempestuous seas.

Ships under Sen's command had been stopped and boarded twice before—fortunately on legitimate voyages, not when he was running immigrants. But the experience had been harrowing. A dozen armed coastguard sailors had streamed onto the vessel while another one, on the deck of the cutter, had trained a two-barrelled machine gun on him and his crew. He told the Ghost what they might expect.

The Ghost nodded. 'We need to consider our options.'

The man seemed placid but, Sen supposed, he must have been enraged. No snakehead he'd ever worked with had taken so many precautions to avoid capture and detection as had the Ghost on this voyage. The two dozen immigrants had met in an abandoned warehouse outside Fuzhou and waited there for two days, under the watch of a partner of the Ghost's. The man had then loaded them onto a chartered Tupolev 154, which had flown to a deserted military airfield near St Petersburg in Russia. There they'd climbed into a shipping container, been driven seventy-five miles to the town of Vyborg and boarded the *Fuzhou Dragon.* Sen himself had meticulously filled out the customs documents—everything according to the book. The Ghost had joined them at the last minute and the ship had sailed on schedule. Through the Baltic Sea, the North Sea, the English Channel, then southwest towards Long Island.

There was not a single thing about the voyage that would arouse the suspicion of the US authorities.

'How did they do it?' the captain asked angrily.

'What?' the Ghost responded absently.

'Find us. No one could have. It's impossible.'

The Ghost straightened up and pushed outside into the raging wind, calling back, 'Who knows? Maybe it was magic.'

'WE'RE RIGHT ON TOP of 'em, Lincoln. The boat's headin' for land but are they gonna make it? Nosir, no how. Wait, do I hafta call it a "ship"?' I think I do. It's too big for a boat.'

'I don't know,' Lincoln Rhyme said absently to Fred Dellray. 'I don't really do much sailing.'

The tall, lanky Dellray was the FBI agent in charge of the federal side of the efforts to arrest the Ghost. Neither Dellray's canary-yellow shirt nor his black suit, as dark as the man's lustrous skin, had been ironed recently—but then no one in the room looked well rested. These half-dozen people clustered around Rhyme had spent the past twenty-four hours virtually living here, in this improbable headquarters—the living room of Rhyme's Central Park West town house, which resembled not the Victorian drawing room it had once been but a forensics laboratory, full of tables, equipment, computers, chemicals and hundreds of forensic books and magazines.

The team included both federal and state law enforcers. On the state side was Lieutenant Lon Sellitto, homicide detective for the NYPD, far more rumpled than Dellray—stockier too. Young Eddie Deng, a Chinese-American detective from the NYPD's Fifth Precinct, which covered Chinatown, was trim and stylish, sporting glasses framed by Armani and black hair spiked up like a hedge-hog's. He was serving as Sellitto's partner.

Assisting on the federal portion of the team was fifty-something Harold Peabody, a close-lipped, pear-shaped senior middle manager at the Manhattan office of the INS—Immigration and Naturalization Service. After the *Golden Venture* incident—in which ten illegal immigrants drowned after a smuggling vessel of that name ran aground off Brooklyn—the President had ordered that the FBI take over primary jurisdiction from the INS on major human smuggling cases. The INS had far more experience with human smuggling and didn't take kindly to yielding jurisdiction to other agencies—especially one that insisted on working shoulder-to-shoulder with the NYPD and, well, alternative consultants like Lincoln Rhyme.

Assisting Peabody was a young INS agent named Alan Coe, a man in his thirties with close-cropped dark-red hair. Energetic but sour and moody, Coe was an enigma, saying not a word about his personal life and little about his career. The only time he grew talkative was when he'd give one of his spontaneous—and tedious—lectures on the evils of illegal immigration. Still, Coe worked tirelessly and was zealous about collaring the Ghost.

Now, at 4.45am on this stormy morning, Lincoln Rhyme manoeuvred his powered Storm Arrow wheelchair through the cluttered living room towards the case status board, on which was taped one of the few existing pictures of the Ghost, a bad surveillance shot, as well as a picture of Sen Zi-jun, the captain of the *Fuzhou Dragon*, and a map of eastern Long Island and the ocean surrounding it. During his days of self-imposed retirement after a crime scene accident turned him into a C4 quadriplegic, Rhyme had been bedridden. He now spent half his waking hours in his cherry-red Storm Arrow, outfitted with a state-of-the-art touchpad drive controller. The pad, on which his one working finger rested, gave him far more flexibility in driving the chair than the older sip-and-puff controller.

Rhyme frequently worked as a consultant for the NYPD, but most of his efforts were in classic forensic detection—criminalistics, as the jargon-happy law enforcement world now preferred to call it. This assignment was unusual. Four days ago Sellitto, Dellray, Peabody and Alan Coe had come to him at his town house. Rhyme had been distracted—the consuming event in his life at the moment was an impending medical procedure—but Dellray had snagged his attention by saying, 'You're our last hope, Linc. We got us a big problem and don't have a single idea where else to turn.'

Interpol—the international clearing-house on criminal intelligence—had issued one of its infamous Red Notices about Kwan Ang. According to informants, the Ghost had surfaced in Fuzhou, China, flown to the South of France, then gone to some port in Russia to pick up a load of illegal Chinese immigrants, among them the Ghost's *bangshou*, or assistant, a spy masquerading as one of the passengers. Their destination was supposedly New York. But then the Ghost had disappeared.

Dellray had brought with him the only evidence they had—a briefcase containing some of the Ghost's personal effects from his safe house in France—in hopes that Rhyme could give them ideas where his trail might lead.

'Why all hands on deck?' Rhyme had asked, surveying the group, which represented three major law enforcement organisations.

Peabody had explained, 'The Ghost's probably the most dangerous human smuggler in the world. He's wanted for eleven deaths—immigrants and police and agents. And we know he's killed more. Illegals are called "the vanished"—if they try to cheat a snakehead, they're killed. If they complain, they're killed. They just disappear, for ever.'

Coe added, 'And he's raped at least fifteen women immigrants—that we know of.'

Dellray said, 'The only reason he's bringin' these folk over personally is 'cause he's expandin' his operation here.'

'Well, why me?' Rhyme asked. 'I don't know a thing about human smuggling.'

The FBI agent said, 'We tried ever-thing else. But we came up with nothin'. 'Cept that.' A nod towards the attaché case.

'I'll do what I can. But don't expect miracles.'

Two days later Rhyme had summoned them back. Thom, his aide, handed agent Coe the attaché case.

'Was there anything helpful in it?' the young man asked.

'Nup,' Rhyme replied cheerfully.

'Hell,' muttered Dellray. 'So we're outta luck.'

Which had been a good enough cue for Lincoln Rhyme. He'd leaned his head back into the wheelchair and spoken rapidly. 'The Ghost and twenty to thirty illegal Chinese immigrants are on board a ship called the *Fuzhou Dragon*, out of Fuzhou, Fujian Province, China. It's a two-hundred-and-thirty-six-foot combination container and break-bulk cargo ship, twin diesels, under the command of Sen Zi-jun—that's family name Sen, given name Zi-jun—and has a crew of seven. It left Vyborg, Russia, at 0845 hours fourteen days ago and is presently—I'm estimating—about three hundred miles off the coast of New York. It's making for the Brooklyn docks.'

'How the hell d'you figure that out?' Coe blurted in astonishment. Even Sellitto, used to Rhyme's deductive abilities, barked a laugh.

'Simple. I assumed that they'd be sailing east to west—otherwise he would have left from China itself. I asked a friend on the Moscow police to call all the harbourmasters in ports in western Russia. He pulled some strings and got all the manifests from Chinese ships that left port in the past three weeks. We found that only one ship took on enough fuel for an eight-thousand-mile trip when the manifest reported it was making a four-thousand-four-hundred-mile one. Eight thousand would get them from Vyborg to New York and back to Southampton, England, for refuelling. They were going to drop off the Ghost and the immigrants then scoot back to Europe.'

'Maybe fuel's too expensive in New York,' Dellray had offered.

Rhyme had shrugged—one of the few gestures his body allowed him. 'There's more: the *Dragon*'s manifest said she was transporting industrial machinery to America. The draught—that's how far the hull sinks into the water—was listed at ten feet. But a fully loaded ship her size should draw at least twenty-five feet. So she was empty. Except for the Ghost and the immigrants. Oh, I say twenty to thirty immigrants because the *Dragon* took on enough fresh water and food for that many, when—like I said—the crew was only seven.'

'Damn,' the otherwise stiff Harold Peabody had offered with an admiring grin.

Later that day, spy satellites had picked up the *Dragon* about 280 miles out to sea, just as Rhyme had predicted.

The ship was now in US waters and the Coast Guard cutter *Evan Brigant*, with a boarding party of twenty-five sailors, backed up by twin fifties and an 80mm cannon, was in pursuit. The plan was to take control of the *Dragon* and arrest the Ghost and the ship's crew. The Coast Guard would sail the ship to the harbour at Port Jefferson, Long Island, where the immigrants would be transferred to a federal detention centre to await deportation or asylum hearings.

A call was patched through from the cutter's radio.

'Agent Dellray? This is Captain Ransom on the *Evan Brigant*.'

'I'm readin' you, Captain.'

'They've spotted us. The ship's turned hard for shore. We need direction on the assault plan. We're worried about casualties. Over.'

'Among who?' Coe asked. 'The undocumenteds?' The disdain in his voice when he used the word for immigrants was clear.

'Right. We were thinking we should just make the ship come about and wait until the Ghost surrenders. Over.'

Dellray reached up and squeezed the cigarette he kept behind his ear, a memento from his smoking days. 'Negative on that. Follow your original rules of engagement. Stop and board the ship and arrest the Ghost. The use of deadly force is authorised. You copy that?'

'Five by five, sir. Out.'

A moment later Rhyme's private line rang. Thom took the call. He listened for a moment then looked up. 'It's Dr Weaver, Lincoln. About the surgery.' He glanced at the roomful of tense law enforcers. 'I'll tell her you'll call her back.'

'No,' Rhyme answered firmly. 'I'll take it.'

Chapter Two

The winds were stronger now, the waves arcing high over the sides of the intrepid *Fuzhou Dragon*. Kwan Ang, the Ghost, scanned the rear of the ship but he could not find his *bangshou* anywhere. Turning towards the bow, he squinted into the wind and could see no land, just restless mountains of dark water.

He climbed to the bridge deck and pounded on the window of the rear door. Captain Sen dutifully walked outside into the rain.

'The Coast Guard will be here soon,' the Ghost shouted over the raging wind. 'Leave those men on the bridge and you and the rest of the crew go below with the piglets. Hide with them.'

'But why?'

'Because,' the Ghost explained, 'you're a good man. Too good to lie. I'll pretend to be the captain. I can look a man in the eye and he will believe what I tell him. You cannot do that.'

'This is my ship.'

'No,' the Ghost shot back. 'On this voyage the *Dragon* is *my* ship. I'm paying you in one-colour cash.' Meaning US dollars, which were far more valuable than Chinese yuan.

'You are not going to fight with them, are you?'

The Ghost gave an impatient laugh. 'How could I? There are dozens of them.' A nod towards the crewmen on the bridge. 'Tell them to follow my orders.' When Sen hesitated, the Ghost leaned forward with the placid yet chilling gaze that so unsettled everyone who looked into his eyes.

Sen stepped onto the bridge to give the instructions.

THE TEN JUDGES of hell . . .

The man crawled along the main deck to the stern of the *Fuzhou Dragon*, stuck his head over the side and began retching again.

He'd been lying beside a life raft all night long, ever since the storm picked up and he'd fled from the stinking hold to purge his body of the disharmony wrought by the rocking sea. His gut was in agony because of the dry heaving and he was as cold and miserable as he'd ever been in his life.

He was called Sonny Li, though the name bestowed upon him by his father was Kangmei, which meant 'Resist America'. It was typical of children born under Mao's reign to have such politically correct given names. Still, as often happened with youngsters from coastal China—Fujian and Guangdong—he'd taken a Western name too. His was Sonny, after the dangerous, bad-tempered son of Don Corleone in the movie *The Godfather*.

Judges of hell . . . He was ready for them to take him. He'd own up to everything bad he'd done in life, all the foolishness, all the harm. Just stop this sickness! Li glanced towards the bridge of the ship and thought he saw the Ghost but immediately he had to turn back to the railing. Sonny Li forgot about the snakehead, forgot about everything except the ten judges of hell gleefully urging demons to prod his dying belly with their spears. He began heaving once again.

THE TALL WOMAN leaned against her car, the contrasts stark: her red hair tossed by the fierce wind, the yellow of the old Chevy Camaro, the black nylon utility belt securing a black pistol to her hip.

Amelia Sachs, in jeans and a hooded windcheater on the back of which were the words NYPD CRIME SCENE, looked out over the turbulent water of the harbour near Port Jefferson, on the north shore of Long Island. The INS, the FBI, the Suffolk County Police and her own shop had cordoned off a parking lot that would normally have been packed with families. The tropical storm, however, had kept vacationers away.

Parked nearby were two large Department of Corrections prisoner buses the INS had borrowed, a half-dozen ambulances and four vans filled with tactical officers from the various agencies. In theory, by the time the *Dragon* arrived here, it would be under the control of the *Evan Brigant* and the Ghost and his *bangshou* would be in custody. But the Coast Guard might not be able to search the ship effectively before it arrived and the snakehead and any assistants might try to shoot their way to freedom.

Sachs's job was to 'walk the grid', to sweep the ship for crime-scene evidence that would bolster the various cases against the Ghost.

Her cellphone rang and she dropped into the tight seat of the Chevy to answer it. The caller was Rhyme.

'We think they're on to us, Sachs,' he said. 'The *Dragon* turned towards land. The cutter'll get there before they make it to shore but we're thinking now that the Ghost is gearing up for a fight.'

When Rhyme paused, Sachs asked him, 'Did she call?'

A hesitation. Then he said, 'Yes. About ten minutes ago. They have a slot open at Manhattan Hospital next week. She's going to call back with the details.'

'Ah,' Sachs said.

The 'she' was Dr Cheryl Weaver, a renowned neurosurgeon. And the 'slot' referred to an opening for some experimental surgery that might improve Rhyme's quadriplegic condition.

An operation Sachs was not in favour of.

'I'd get some extra ambulances,' Rhyme said. His tone was now curt—he didn't like personal subjects intruding into business.

'I'll take care of it.'

'I'll call you back, Sachs.' The phone went silent.

She ran through the downpour to one of the Suffolk County troopers and arranged for more med techs. She then returned to her Chevy. Thinking about Rhyme's operation put her in mind of a recent conversation with another doctor, one who had nothing to do with his spinal cord surgery. Two weeks ago in a hospital waiting room, the white-jacketed doctor had addressed her with a chilling solemnity. 'Ah, Ms Sachs. Here you are. I've just been meeting with Lincoln Rhyme's physician.'

'Yes, Doctor?'

'I've got to talk to you about something.'

Her heart pounding, she'd said, 'You're looking like it's bad news.'

'Why don't we sit down over there in the corner?'

'Here's fine,' she'd said firmly. 'Let me have it straight.'

A gust of wind now rocked her and she looked out over the harbour again, at the long pier, where the *Fuzhou Dragon* would dock. Sachs flicked her Motorola to the Coast Guard's frequency to keep her thoughts from returning to that scaldingly bright waiting room.

'HOW FAR FROM LAND?' the Ghost asked the two remaining crewmen on the bridge.

'A mile, maybe less.' The slim man at the helm glanced quickly at the Ghost. 'We'll turn just before the shallows and try for the harbour.'

The Ghost could just see the line of light grey land. He said, 'Steer straight on course. I'll be back in a moment.'

The wind and rain lashed his face as the Ghost made his way down to the container deck and then to the one below it, to the metal door that opened into the hold. He stepped inside and looked down at the piglets. Their faces turned towards him with fear and distress. The pathetic men, the frumpy women, the filthy children. He scanned the piglets for his *bangshou*. But there was no sign of him.

He stepped outside again and closed the door, then screwed down the latches so that the door couldn't be opened from the inside.

As he hurried back up the stairs towards his cabin he took from his pocket a battered black plastic box. He opened it and pushed one button and then a second. The radio signal zipped through two decks, down to the duffle bag he'd placed in the aft hold below the water line. The signal closed the circuit and sent an electrical charge from a nine-volt battery into a blasting cap embedded in four pounds of Composition 4 explosive.

The detonation was huge, much larger than he'd expected. The Ghost was thrown off the stairs onto the main deck. He lay on his side, stunned.

Too much explosive! he realised. Already the ship was starting to list as she took on sea water. He'd thought it would take half an hour for the ship to sink. Instead, she would go down in minutes. He looked towards the cabin where his money and guns sat, then once again scanned the other decks for his *bangshou*. No sign of him. He rose and scrabbled across the listing deck to the nearest rubber life raft and began undoing the tie-down ropes.

THE SOUND had been deafening. A hundred sledgehammers on a piece of iron. Nearly all the immigrants had been thrown to the cold, wet floor. Sam Chang climbed to his feet and picked up his younger boy, who'd fallen into a puddle of greasy water. He then helped up his elderly father, Chang Jiechi, and his wife, Mei-Mei.

'What happened?' he shouted to Captain Sen, who was struggling to the door that led up to the deck.

The captain called back, 'Either the Ghost has blown up the ship or the Coast Guard is firing on us. I don't know.'

'What is happening?' asked a panic-stricken man. He was Wu Qichen, the father of the family that had camped out in the hold next to the Changs. His wife lay on a cot nearby. She'd been feverish and lethargic throughout the voyage and now seemed hardly aware of the chaos.

'We're sinking!' the captain called, and together he and several of his crewmen struggled to open the door latches. 'He's jammed them!'

Sam Chang and several of the crew joined the captain and tugged. But the thick metal bars wouldn't give.

The *Dragon* was listing sharply. Cold sea water was shooting into the hold from seams in the metal plates. Desperate men, women and children were hugging one another, sobbing, screaming for help, praying . . . The scar-faced woman clutched her young daughter. A powerful groaning from the dying ship filled the stale air, and the brown, vile water grew deeper.

The men at the hatch were making no headway. 'This won't work,' Chang said to the captain. 'We need another way out.'

Captain Sen replied, 'There's an access panel on the floor, in the back of the hold. It leads to the engine room.'

Using Sen's flick knife, Chang and the captain managed to undo the screws securing the access door. Chang pushed hard and it fell into the other room. Water was filling the engine room too but it wasn't as deep as in the hold. Chang could see steep stairs leading to the main deck.

Screams and shouts as the immigrants saw the open passageway. They pushed forward, crushing some people against the metal walls.

Chang cried, 'No! One at a time or we'll all die.'

'Through the engine room and up the ladder,' the captain instructed. 'There are rafts on the deck.' He nodded to the immigrants closest to the doorway and they crawled outside. The first was John Sung, a doctor and a dissident. Then two others, a young husband and wife. Sung stopped outside the doorway to help the others out.

Chang motioned to Chang Jiechi, his father, and the old man went through the door, John Sung gripping him by his arm. Then Chang's sons: teenage William and eight-year-old Ronald. Next, his wife. Chang went last and pointed his family towards the ladder. He turned back to help Sung get the others out.

The Wu family was next. Qichen, his sick wife, their teenage daughter and young son.

Chang reached into the hold to take the hand of another immigrant but a crewman raced for the doorway, knocking aside the scar-faced woman and her little girl. Another followed, pushing Sung to the floor. Chang helped the doctor to his feet. 'I'm all right,' Sung shouted and clutched a charm he wore round his neck.

The ship lurched hard. Water flooded in, filling the hold. The screams soon mixed with the sound of choking. She's going down, Chang thought. The diesel engines stopped running and the lights went out. Chang turned to the doorway to try to rescue one or two more. Through the roiling water now bubbling into the engine room he could just see Captain Sen's face. Chang motioned for him to climb out but the captain disappeared into the blackness of the hold. A few seconds later, though, he swam back to the doorway and shoved something up through the fountain of sea water.

Chang reached into the frothy water to take what the captain offered. He closed his hand around cloth and pulled hard. It was a young child, the daughter of the scarred woman. The toddler was choking but conscious. Chang held her to his chest firmly, slid to the stairwell, and climbed through to the deck above.

Turbulent waves were already covering half the listing deck. Wu Qichen and Chang's father and sons were struggling to untie a large orange inflatable launch. Chang stumbled forwards, handed the baby to his wife and began to help the others undo the rope. But soon the knot securing the raft was underwater. Chang dived under the surface and began to tug futilely on the hemp. Then a hand appeared near his. William was holding a long, sharp knife. Chang took it from his son and sawed on the rope until it gave way.

Chang and his son helped his family, the Wus, John Sung and the other couple into the raft, which was quickly drawn away from the ship by the massive waves. Chang turned to the outboard motor and yanked the cord until the motor buzzed to life. He turned their small craft into the waves. It bucked furiously. He steered in a circle, heading back through the fog and rain towards the dying ship.

'Where are you going?' Wu asked.

'The others,' he gasped. 'We have to find the others.'

That was when the bullet snapped through the air no more than a couple of feet from them.

THE GHOST WAS FURIOUS. He stood at the bow of the sinking *Fuzhou Dragon*, his hand on the lanyard of the forward life raft, and looked back to sea where he'd just spotted some of the piglets who'd escaped.

He fired his pistol once more. Another miss.

The Ghost surveyed the distance to the bridge deck, on which his cabin was located, where he had his machine gun and his money. He wondered momentarily if he could make it back to his cabin in time. As if in answer, a huge spume of venting air broke through the hull and the *Dragon* began to sink even more quickly. Well, the loss hurt but it wasn't worth his life. He climbed into the raft and pushed away from the ship. Nearby, two heads bobbed up and down, their arms waving frantically, fingers splayed in panic.

'Here, here!' the Ghost shouted. 'I'll save you!' The men turned to him, kicking hard to rise from the water so he could see them better. They were two of the crew members. He lifted his Chinese military Model 51 automatic pistol and killed them with one shot each.

Then the Ghost got the outboard motor going and turned his raft towards where he'd last seen the piglets.

SAM CHANG, reluctant captain of the fragile life raft, looked over his passengers. The two families—his own and the Wus—huddled in the back of the raft. In the front were Dr John Sung and the two others who'd escaped from the hold. Chang's wife, Mei-Mei, took off her sweater and wrapped it round the tiny daughter of the scar-faced woman. The girl, Chang recalled, was named Po-Yee, which meant Treasured Child; she'd been the good-luck mascot of their voyage.

'Go!' Wu cried. 'Go for shore. He's shooting at us!'

Chang looked at the boiling sea. 'We'll go soon. But we have to rescue anyone who can be saved. Look for them!'

Seventeen-year-old William struggled to his knees and squinted through the sharp spray. 'There!' he cried. 'I think I see somebody.'

Chang could see a dark lump thirty feet from them. A head perhaps. He steered closer and indeed it was a man, pale and choking, thrashing air. Sonny Li was his name, Chang recalled. He'd sat alone for the entire voyage, sullen, glaring at the noisy children around him. There'd been something ominous about him.

Still, Li was a human being in need and Chang would try to save him. He turned the raft into a large wave to keep from tipping over. By the time they were stable again, Chang could see a flash of orange about fifty yards away, rising and falling. It was the Ghost's raft. The snakehead started towards them. A wave rose between the two crafts and they lost sight of each other momentarily.

Chang gunned the throttle and turned towards the drowning man. 'Down, everybody down!'

As they reached Li, Chang leaned over the thick rubber and grabbed the immigrant, pulling him into the raft. A gunshot. A burst of water flew up near them as Chang sped the raft round the *Dragon*, putting the sinking ship between them and the Ghost.

A minute later, a huge, unearthly groan filled the air. The *Fuzhou Dragon* turned on her side and vanished under the water.

'Stay down, everyone!' Chang aimed the raft towards the shore and turned the motor up full.

Another shot. The bullet struck the water nearby. The massive wave created by the sinking ship rolled outwards like the shock ring from a bomb blast. The immigrants' raft was too far away to be affected but the Ghost's was much closer to the ship. The snakehead veered away and was soon lost to sight. Chang thought for a moment that Guan Yin, the goddess of mercy, might have interceded on their behalf.

But only a few seconds later John Sung, who was facing backwards, shouted, 'He's still there. The Ghost is coming after us.'

So, Guan Yin is busy elsewhere today, Sam Chang thought bitterly. If we're going to survive we'll have to do it on our own.

'HE SCUTTLED the ship.' Lon Sellitto's voice was a whisper.

Dellray stopped pacing and Peabody and Coe stared at each other.

Sellitto listened once more into the phone and then looked up. 'Linc, the ship's gone. With everybody on board. The Coast Guard picked up an underwater explosion and ten minutes later the *Dragon* vanished from the radar.'

Rhyme stared at the map of Long Island. 'How far offshore?'

'About a mile.'

Rhyme's mind had run through a half-dozen logical scenarios of what might happen when the Coast Guard interdicted the *Fuzhou Dragon*, some involving injury and loss of life. But drowning everyone on board? No, that thought had never occurred to him.

He'd listened to the INS's little mystery as if it were a diverting game at a cocktail party. Then he'd drawn his conclusions and given them the solution. And he'd let it go at that—never thinking that the immigrants might be at such terrible risk.

Lincoln Rhyme was furious with himself. He should have anticipated this. He closed his eyes. Give up the dead, he often told himself. But he couldn't give up these people. Here were whole families dead because of him. He knew he couldn't abandon the case. The hunter within him had to find this man and bring him to justice.

Dellray's phone rang and he answered. After a brief conversation he snapped off the call with a long finger. 'Here's the deal. The Coast Guard thinks a coupla motorised rafts are headin' towards shore. They're guessin' they're goin' to land in twenty minutes.' He pointed to the map. 'Prob'ly around here. Easton—little town on the road to Orient Point. They can't get a chopper in the air with the storm being as nasty as it is, but they got some cutters on the way to look for survivors and we're going to get our people at Port Jefferson out to where the rafts are headed.'

Rhyme debated for a moment then said into his stalk mike, 'Command, telephone.'

SQUEEZING THE LEATHER-CLAD steering wheel in her fingers, Amelia Sachs drove the Camaro Super Sport convertible eastbound on the Long Island Expressway at 130 miles per hour. She had a blue flasher on the dash—a suction cup doesn't stick well to convertible roofs—and weaved perilously in and out of the traffic.

As she and Rhyme had decided, when he'd called and told her to get out to Easton ahead of the FBI, who were heading there from fifty miles away, Sachs was one half of the advance team. If they were lucky, they might get to the beach at the same time the Ghost and any surviving immigrants did. The other half of the impromptu team was the young officer from the NYPD Emergency Services Unit sitting next to her.

Her phone rang. She juggled the unit and answered it.

'How's the progress, Sachs?' Rhyme asked.

'Doing the best I can. Any survivors?' she asked.

'Nothing further. Looks like most people didn't get off.'

Sachs said, 'I hear that tone, Rhyme. It's not your fault.'

'Appreciate the sentiment, Sachs. You driving carefully?'

'Oh, yeah,' she said, calmly steering into the spin that took the car forty degrees off centre. The ESU cop closed his eyes.

Rhyme paused. Then said, 'Search well but watch your back.'

'I like that. We'll print it on T-shirts for the Crime Scene Unit.'

The expressway ended and she skidded off onto a smaller highway. Twenty-five miles to Easton. She kept her foot near the floor.

AS THE LIFE RAFT smashed through the water, closer to the shore, the rocks grew more distinct. And more jagged.

'He's still there, behind us,' Wu shouted.

Chang looked back and saw the orange dot of the Ghost's raft. It was heading directly for them but making slower progress than theirs. There should be time to find the trucks that were waiting to take them to Chinatown, Chang estimated. He would tell the drivers that the Coast Guard was after them and order the men to leave immediately. If they insisted on waiting for the Ghost, then Chang, Wu and the others would overpower them and drive the trucks themselves.

Suddenly, the motor cut out. Chang grabbed the lanyard and tugged hard. A chug, then silence. Again, a dozen times. His older son scrabbled forward and tipped the gasoline can. 'Empty.'

Weak with fear for his family's safety, Chang looked in the direction they were headed and saw a line of rocks just ahead. The water caught the raft like a surfboard and carried it forward fast. They struck the rocks with stunning force, bow first. The rubber shell ripped open with a gasping hiss and began to deflate. Sonny Li, John Sung and the young couple in the front were pitched out into the turbulent water just past the rocks and swept away in the surf. The Wus and the Changs were in the rear of the raft, which remained partially inflated, and they managed to hold on.

They struck the rocks again. Wu's wife was thrown hard into a ledge of stone but she didn't go overboard; screaming, she fell back into the raft, blood covering her arm, and lay stunned. Then the raft was past the rocks and headed towards shore, deflating quickly. They were trapped in the surf now, being dragged towards the pebbly beach.

'The shore,' Chang shouted, coughing water. 'Now!'

The distance wasn't great but the swim took for ever. Even Chang, the strongest of them, was gasping for breath before he reached land. Finally, he felt stones under his feet and stumbled out of the water.

Exhausted, they all collapsed on the dark sand, coughing water, crying. Sam Chang finally managed to stand. He gazed out to sea but saw no sign of the Ghost's raft, or of Sung, Li and the other immigrant couple, who'd been swept overboard.

He sank down to his knees. They had at last finished the endless journey that had taken them halfway around the world to their new home, America: *Meiguo*, the Beautiful Country.

Chapter Three

A quarter of a mile out to sea, the Ghost hunched over his cellphone. The reception was bad, but he managed to get through to Jerry Tang, who was waiting somewhere on the shore nearby to pick him up. The Ghost described more or less where he'd be landing—about 300 yards east from what seemed to be a strip of stores and houses.

'The Coast Guard,' Tang told him, the transmission lost in static and the sound of the wind, 'they're on . . . have to get away.'

The Ghost shouted, 'If you see any of the piglets, kill them. They're on the shore near you. Find them! Kill them!'

'Kill them? You want—?'

But a wave washed over the side of the raft. The phone went dead. Disgusted, the Ghost flung it to the floor.

A wall of rock loomed and the Ghost steered round it, making for a broad beach to the left of the small town. The raft slammed into the shore in an explosion of surf and tossed its occupant onto the beach. The propeller tipped out of the water and the motor screamed as it raced. The Ghost, afraid the sound would give him away, crawled frantically back to the engine and managed to shut it off.

He saw Jerry Tang, in a silver four-by-four BMW on a sandy road about twenty yards from the shore.

Tang caught sight of him and drove forward. 'We have to go!' He nodded at a police scanner. 'They're sending the police to search.'

'The others?' the Ghost snapped. 'The piglets?'

'I didn't see anybody else. But—'

'I can't find my *bangshou* either. I don't know if he got off the ship.' The Ghost scanned the shoreline.

'I haven't seen anyone,' Tang said, his voice high.

From the corner of his eye the Ghost saw motion near the surf: a man in grey cloth was crawling on the rocks away from the water, like an injured animal. The Ghost stepped away from the truck and pulled his gun from his belt. 'Wait here.'

'What are you doing?' Tang asked desperately. 'We can't stay!'

But the Ghost was paying no attention. The piglet looked up and saw the Ghost approaching, but the man had apparently broken his leg in the landing and couldn't even stand, much less flee. He began to crawl desperately back to the water.

AT THE SOUND the families paused.

'A gunshot,' Wu Qichen said. 'He's tracking us down and killing us.'

'I know,' Sam Chang snapped. His heart cried for whoever had just died, but what could he do?

There'd been no trucks waiting for them. Chang supposed that as soon as the Ghost decided to scuttle the ship he'd called and had them return. Chang and Wu had spent several minutes calling for Sung and Li and the others who'd been washed overboard. But then Chang had seen the orange raft of the snakehead approaching and he'd led the two families off the road into bushes, where they'd be out of sight, and they made their way towards some lights.

The beacons that drew them turned out to be a line of restaurants, a gas station, stores selling souvenirs, ten or twelve houses, a church.

The hour was perhaps 6.00am, but there were some signs of life: a dozen cars were parked in front of the two restaurants, including a driverless small sedan with the motor running. But Chang needed a vehicle with room for ten.

He told the others to wait behind a tall hedge of bushes and motioned William and Wu to follow him. Crouching, they moved behind the buildings. 'Stay out of the mud,' Chang ordered. 'Walk only on the grass or branches or stones. I don't want to leave footprints.' They moved on, through bushes and trees whipped by the wind, and finally came to the last building on this strip of habitation: a small church. Behind it they found an old white van.

Chang knew a little English but these words he didn't understand. Both his sons had studied the language though. William explained, 'It says, "Pentecostal Baptist Church of Easton".'

'Hurry!' Wu said anxiously. 'See if it's open.'

But the van's door was locked. Chang scanned the rain-pelted ground, found a piece of metal pipe and swung it into the window of the van. The glass shattered. He climbed into the passenger seat and looked through the map box for keys. He couldn't find any.

He heard a loud snap. William was crouched in the driver's seat and had shattered the plastic housing of the ignition lock with a kick from his boot. The boy pulled out wires and began brushing them against each other. Suddenly the engine fired up.

Chang stared in disbelief. 'How did you know how to do that?'

William shrugged.

Wu clutched Chang's arm. 'Let's go! We have to get our families and leave. The Ghost is looking for us.'

'No,' Chang said. 'Have them come here. Follow our path.'

Wu hurried off to get them.

In the van William found maps and studied them carefully.

Chang asked him, 'Do you know where to go?'

'I can figure it out.' The boy looked up. 'Do you want me to drive?' Then he added bluntly, 'You're not very good at it.'

Like most urban Chinese, Sam Chang's main means of transportation was a bicycle. He damped down his fury at the boy's insolence and said, 'Yes, you drive.'

HE'D KILLED two of the piglets: the injured man and a woman. But there'd been about a dozen people in the raft. Where were the rest? A horn blared. It was Jerry Tang, his gestures frantic.

The Ghost scanned the beach once more. Where had they got to? Maybe they'd—

With a squeal of tyres Tang's four-by-four pulled into the road, accelerating fast.

'No! Stop!' Seized by fury, the Ghost aimed his pistol and fired. The slug hit the rear door but the vehicle continued. The Ghost stood frozen. He was eighty miles from his safe houses in Manhattan, he had no money and no cellphone. Dozens of policemen were on their way. And Tang had just abandoned him.

Not far away a white van suddenly appeared from behind a church and turned onto the road. It was the piglets! The Ghost lifted his pistol but the vehicle disappeared into the fog.

The Ghost took several deep breaths. After a moment he grew serene. He was plagued by troubles at the moment, yes, but he'd experienced far worse than this. A reversal, he'd come to learn, was merely a temporary imbalance and even the most horrific events in his life had ultimately been harmonised by good fortune. For the moment the piglets' deaths would have to wait. His abiding philosophy was found in one word: *naixin*. This translated as 'patience' but meant something more in the Ghost's mind. The English equivalent would be 'all in good time'.

He put his old pistol into his pocket and trudged through the rain and wind along the beach towards the lights of the small town. The closest building was a restaurant, in front of which was a car with its engine running. So, some good fortune already!

And then, glancing out to sea, he saw yet more good luck: not far offshore another piglet, a man struggling to stay afloat. The Ghost pulled his gun from his pocket and started towards the shoreline.

SONNY LI opened his eyes and thanked the ten judges of hell because, for the first time in two weeks, the slippery twist of nausea within his gut was virtually gone.

When the raft had hit the rocks, he and John Sung and the young couple had been thrown into the water and swept away. Li had lost sight of the other three and had been dragged down the beach until he'd been able to kick his way onto the sand. He'd lain motionless under the pounding rain as the seasickness dissipated. Now, struggling to his feet, eager to find the ghost, Li started slowly towards the road.

Stumbling onto the rainswept asphalt, he pushed forward as best he could towards the lights of a small village, afraid that the snakehead would leave before Li found him.

A moment later he received the reassurance that the man was still here: several gunshots.

Li struggled up a hill and peered into the streaming wind and rain but he could see no one. Then he saw a small orange life raft sitting on the beach. He started towards it, but as he took a step off the road a flashing blue light appeared. It was moving rapidly towards him along the road. INS? Security bureau officers?

Li hurried into some dense bushes. He crouched and watched the light grow brighter as the vehicle in which it was mounted, a sporty yellow convertible, materialised out of the rain and skidded to a stop a hundred yards away. Li moved slowly towards it.

AMELIA SACHS STOOD on the rainswept beach, staring down at the woman's body, slumped in the grotesque pose of death.

'He's killing them, Rhyme,' Amelia Sachs, dismayed, whispered into the headset mike of her Motorola SP-50 handy-talkie. 'He's shot two of them, a man and a woman. In the back. They're dead.'

The ESU officer trotted towards her, holding his machine gun ready. 'No sign of him,' the man shouted over the wind. 'People in that restaurant up the road said that they'd heard gunshots and somebody stole a car about twenty minutes ago.' The officer gave Sachs the description of the Honda sedan and the tag number and she relayed it to Rhyme.

'Lon'll put it on the wire,' he said. 'Was he alone?'

'Think so. I found some footprints in the mud, where he was standing to shoot the woman. He was by himself then.'

'So we'll assume his *bangshou*'s still unaccounted for.'

Amelia scanned the scenery. 'We're going to look for survivors.'

'Good luck, Sachs. Call me back when you start on the grid.'

The two officers trotted along the beach. They came across a second raft beached 100 yards from the first. Sachs's immediate impulse was to search it for evidence but she stayed true to her mission. Her arthritis had been bad lately and pain stabbed her joints as she ran with the wind at her back, scanning the landscape for the immigrants—and signs of an ambush or a hidey-hole where the Ghost might have gone to ground. They found neither.

Then she heard sirens in the distance and saw the carnival of emergency vehicles speed into town. The first mission of a crime scene officer is controlling the scene so that contamination is minimal and evidence doesn't vanish. Sachs reluctantly gave up her search—there were plenty of other people to do that now—and ran to the NYPD crime-scene bus to direct the operation. As the CS techs roped off the beach with yellow tape, Sachs pulled the latest in forensic couture over her soaked jeans and T-shirt: the NYPD's new crime scene overalls, a hooded full-body suit made of white Tyvek.

It fell to Amelia Sachs—and Lincoln Rhyme—to wring from the crime scene whatever information might reside here. And what a crime scene it was. A mile of beach, a road and, on the other side of the asphalt strip, a maze of scruffy brush. Millions of places to search. And possibly still populated by an armed perp.

'It's a bad scene, Rhyme. The rain's let up a little but it's still coming down hard and the wind's twenty miles an hour.'

'I know. We've got the Weather Channel on.' His voice was calm. 'All the more reason to get on with the search, wouldn't you say?'

'It's just . . . Everything's too big. There's too much here.'

'How can it be too big, Sachs? We *love* big scenes. There are so many wonderful places to find clues.'

Wonderful, she thought wryly. And, starting closest to the large deflated raft, she began walking the grid, the technique for physically searching a crime scene for clues that Rhyme insisted Sachs use—just as he'd done with the officers and techs who worked for him at NYPD forensics. It entailed covering the ground in one direction, back and forth, like mowing a lawn, then turning ninety degrees and covering the same ground again. The theory is that you see things from one angle that you might miss when looking at them from a different angle.

For the next hour, through the wind and rain, she searched, like a child hunting for seashells. She examined the intact raft, in which she found a cellphone, and then the deflated one, which two ESU officers had muscled up onto the beach. Finally she assembled her evidence: shell casings, blood samples, fingerprints and Polaroids of footprints.

She paused and looked around. 'Something's funny, Rhyme.'

'That's not helpful, Sachs. "Funny"? What does that mean?'

'The immigrants . . . ten or so of them, they just vanish. I don't understand it. They leave the beach then cross the road and hide in the bushes. I see the prints in the mud on the other side of the road.

Then they just disappear. I guess they've gone inland to hide but I can't find any tracks. No tyre treads, either.'

'All right, Sachs,' Rhyme said in a lulling voice. 'You're the Ghost now. You're a human trafficker—a snakehead. A killer. You've just sunk a ship and killed over a dozen people. What's in your mind?'

'Finding the rest of them,' she answered immediately. 'Finding them and killing them. I'm not sure why but I have to find them.' For an instant an image jolted her mind. She *did* see herself as the snakehead, filled with lust to find the immigrants and kill them. The sensation was harrowing. 'Nothing,' she whispered, 'is going to stop me.'

'Good, Sachs,' Rhyme replied softly, as if he was afraid of breaking the thin wire that was connecting a portion of her soul to the snakehead's. 'Now, think about the immigrants. They're being pursued by someone like that. What would *they* do?'

It took her a moment to transform herself from a heartless murderer and snakehead into one of the poor people on that ship, appalled that the man she'd paid her life savings to had betrayed her and was now compelled to kill her.

'I'm getting the hell out of here as fast as I can. We need a ride.'

'But you said no one reported any other vehicles stolen. So, where would you get a vehicle?'

'I don't know,' she said, feeling the frustration of being close to an answer, yet having it evade her.

'Any houses inland?' he asked.

'No.'

'Anything else?'

Sachs scanned the street. 'Nothing.'

'There can't be *nothing*, Sachs,' he scolded. 'These people escaped *somehow*. The answer's there. What do you see?'

She sighed and began reciting, 'I see a stack of discarded tyres, I see a sailboat upside-down, I see a carton of empties—Sam Adams beer. In front of the church there's a wheelbarrow—'

'Church?' Rhyme pounced. 'Get over there, Sachs. Now!'

Stiffly she began to walk towards the place.

Rhyme explained, 'How do you think churches get their youth groups to and from events? Minivans, Sachs. Minivans—with room for a dozen people.' And, as so often happened, he was right.

She walked round to the back of the church and examined the muddy ground: footprints, broken glass, the pipe.

'Got it, Rhyme. A bunch of fresh prints. That's smart . . . They walked on rocks, grass and weeds to get here. To avoid the mud so they wouldn't leave prints. And it looks like they got into the van and drove it away through a field before it turned onto the road.'

Rhyme ordered, 'Get the scoop on the van from the minister.'

A few minutes later the details came back: it was a white Dodge, five years old, with the name of the church on the side. Sachs took down the tag number then relayed this to Rhyme, who said he would tell the Port Authority police to pass the word to the toll takers at the bridges and tunnels, on the assumption that the immigrants were headed for Chinatown in Manhattan.

She walked the grid carefully behind the church but found nothing else. 'I don't think there's much more we can do here, Rhyme. I'm going to log the evidence in and get back.' She disconnected the call.

Sachs told the techs to get everything to Rhyme's town house ASAP. She wanted to make another sweep for survivors.

After fifteen minutes of not finding any sign of more immigrants, she started towards her Camaro, which was the only vehicle left on the beach. She was alone; the ESU officer who'd accompanied her had opted for a safer ride back to the city. She dropped stiffly into the front seat, found some paper and began to write notes of what she'd observed to present to Rhyme.

Sachs happened to glance up in time to see a spume of sea water flying ten feet into the air as it hit a jutting black rock. She squinted hard. What is that? Some wreckage from the *Fuzhou Dragon*?

No, she realised with a start: it was a man, clinging to the rock.

Sachs grabbed her Motorola and radioed the Suffolk County Rescue at Easton Beach: 'I'm a half-click east of the town. I've got a vic in the water. I need some help.'

'K,' came the reply, 'we're on our way. Out.'

Sachs stepped out of the car and started down to the shore. She saw a large wave lift the man off the rock and pitch him into the water. He tried to swim but he was injured. He slipped under the waves.

'Oh, brother,' Sachs muttered. She knew the basic lifesaving rule: 'Reach, throw, row, then go.' Meaning, try to rescue a drowning victim from the shore or in a boat before you yourself swim out to save him. Well, the first three weren't options at all.

Ignoring the searing pain of arthritis in her knees, she ran towards the ocean, stripping off her gun and ammo belt. At the shoreline she unlaced her shoes, kicked them off and, eyes focused on the struggling swimmer, waded into the cold, turbulent water.

CRAWLING FROM THE BUSHES, Sonny Li got a better look at the woman with the red hair as she ploughed towards somebody struggling in the waves. He'd been studying this woman from his hiding spot since she'd arrived at the beach over an hour ago. She intrigued him. She'd arrived in her bright yellow car, accompanied by a soldier with a machine gun. Li had glimpsed NYPD on her windcheater, and he'd watched her search for survivors and clues.

Sexy, he'd thought. And that hair! What a colour! He gave her a nickname, whispering, 'Hongse,' Chinese for 'red'.

Looking up the road, Li saw a yellow emergency truck speeding towards the parking lot. He had to act now, before she returned. He waited until the rescue workers' attention was on Hongse and then scrabbled across the road and up to the yellow car. He wasn't interested in stealing the car; he just wanted a gun and some money.

Opening the passenger door, he eased inside and began going through the map box. No weapons. No cigarettes either. He then went through her purse and found about fifty dollars. Li pocketed the cash and looked at some paper she'd been writing on. His spoken English was good but his reading skills were terrible. After some stumbling, he recognised the Ghost's real name, Kwan Ang, in English. He folded this paper up and slipped it into his pocket too, then scattered the rest of the sheets on the ground outside the driver's open side door, so it would look as if the wind had blown them away.

Crouching, he made his way back to the road. He glanced out into the turbulent sea, observing now that Hongse seemed to be struggling. But that wasn't really his concern: finding the Ghost and simply staying alive were his priorities now.

THE EFFORT OF SWIMMING against the battering surf to reach the drowning immigrant had nearly exhausted Amelia Sachs and she found she had to kick furiously to keep them both above water. Her knee and hip joints protested in pain. The immigrant himself was no help. He kicked lethargically and his left arm was useless, thanks to a gunshot wound in his chest. As she fought her way back to the shore, the water blurred her vision, but she could see on the sand two medics with a stretcher motioning for her to swim towards them.

The undertow was fierce and, despite her massive effort, they'd swum only about ten feet from the rock. Sachs kicked harder. A cramp seized her calf and she cried out and sank fast. The murky grey water, filled with seaweed and sand, swallowed her up. She held her breath. Oh, Lincoln, she thought. Going down . . . further into the grey linen water.

Then some sort of a black eel shot out of the foggy water and grabbed her round the chest. It tugged her upwards and seconds later she was on the surface, sucking sweet air into her stinging lungs.

The Suffolk County Rescue diver in a black wet suit spat a regulator from a bottle of compressed air out of his mouth and said, 'It's OK, miss, I got you. It's OK.'

A second diver was gripping the immigrant, keeping his lolling head out of the water.

'Cramp,' Sachs gasped. 'Can't move my leg. Hurts.'

'Just relax. I'll take you in.' He began to tow her. His powerful legs, aided by the flippers, moved them rapidly towards shore.

Finally Sachs felt pebbles under her feet. She staggered onto the shore and took a blanket from one of the medics. After catching her breath, she walked over to the immigrant, who was lying on the stretcher, an oxygen mask over his face. His eyes were dazed but he was conscious. His shirt was open and the medic was cleaning a bloody wound with disinfectant.

Sachs brushed as much sand off her feet and legs as she could, then replaced her shoes and hooked her gun belt around her once more. 'Can I ask him a few questions?'

'Just the minimum for now,' the first paramedic said.

'What's your name?' Sachs asked the immigrant.

He lifted away the oxygen mask. 'John Sung.'

'I'm Amelia Sachs, with the New York City police department.' She showed him her shield and ID. 'What happened?'

'I was thrown out of our raft. The snakehead on the ship—we call him the Ghost—he saw me and came down to the shore. He shot at me and missed. I swam underwater but I had to come back for air. He was waiting. He shot again and hit me. I pretended to be dead and when I looked again I saw him get into a red car and drive off. I tried to swim to the beach but I couldn't. I just held on to those rocks.'

Sachs studied the man. He was handsome and appeared to be in good shape.

'How are . . .?' He coughed. 'How are the others? Are they safe?'

It wasn't NYPD procedure to share information with witnesses but she saw his concern and said, 'I'm sorry. Two are dead.'

He closed his eyes and with his right hand clutched a stone amulet that he wore on a leather strap round his neck.

'How many were on the raft?' she asked.

He thought for a moment. 'Fourteen altogether.' Then he asked, 'Did he get away? The Ghost?'

'We're doing everything we can to find him.'

The medic handed her the immigrant's wallet. Most of the contents were turning to mush from the sea water. But one card that was still legible identified him in English as Dr Sung Kai.

'Kai? Is that your first name?'

He nodded. 'But I use John mostly.'

'You're a doctor? A medical doctor?'

He nodded again.

Sachs was looking at a picture of two young children, a boy and a girl. She felt a jolt of horror, thinking that they'd been on the ship.

'And your . . .?' Her voice faded.

Sung understood. 'My children? They're at home in Fujian. They're living with my parents.'

'Dr Sung, do you have any idea where the Ghost might be going?'

'No. He never talked to us. He treated us like animals.'

'How about the other immigrants? Do you know where they must've gone?'

Sung shook his head. 'No, I'm sorry. We were going to houses somewhere in New York but they never told us where.'

A black car joined the rescue vehicle on the sand. An INS agent stepped out and crunched through the sand towards them. Sachs handed him Sung's wallet. He read through it and crouched down.

'Dr Sung, I'm with the US Immigration and Naturalization Service. Do you have a valid passport and entry visa?'

'No, sir,' Sung replied.

'Then I'm afraid we're going to have to detain you for illegally entering United States territory.'

'I'm seeking political asylum.'

'That's fine,' the agent said wearily. 'But we're still going to have to detain you until the bond hearing.' He turned to the medic. 'How is he?'

'He'll be all right. We need to get him to a trauma centre.'

Sachs interrupted to ask the INS agent, 'Can he go to your Manhattan detention centre? He's a witness in the case and we've got a joint task force working there.'

The INS agent shrugged. 'Doesn't matter to me.'

Still absently clutching the amulet around his neck, Sung studied her and said, 'Thank you, miss.'

'For what?'

'You saved my life.'

She nodded, holding his dark eyes for a moment. Then the medic replaced the oxygen mask.

A flash of white caught her eye and Amelia Sachs looked up to see that she'd left the door of the Camaro open and that the wind was blowing her notes out to sea. Wincing, she trotted back to her car.

Chapter Four

The life of a tolbooth operator guarding the portals to New York City is not particularly glamorous. But the operator sitting in a Queens Midtown Tunnel booth that stormy morning just after 8.00am—a retired transit cop—was excited that something had happened to break the monotony: all the tolbooth operators in Manhattan had got a priority call about a ship that'd sunk off the coast of Long Island. The word was that some of the Chinese illegal immigrants on board were now headed into town, as was the smuggler himself. They were in a white van bearing the name of a church and in a red Honda. Some of them were reportedly armed. The police and FBI had got permission to shut down all the express pass and exact change lanes, so that the perps would have to go through a manned booth.

The ex-cop had never thought that he'd be the one to spot the immigrants. But he was now wiping his sweaty palms on his slacks and watching a white van, some writing on the side, driven by a Chinese guy, easing towards *his* booth. Ten cars away, nine . . .

He pulled his old service piece from its holster, a Smith & Wesson .357 with a four-inch barrel, and rested the pistol on the far side of the cash register. If they acted evasive, he'd pull his weapon and order them out of the van, then call for help. If one of them reached under the dash or between the seats . . . he'd shoot.

AT FIRST SAM CHANG had worried that the long line of cars meant a roadblock but then he saw the booths and decided this was some kind of a border crossing. In panic he looked for an exit but there was none—the road was surrounded by high walls.

William said calmly, 'We have to pay.'

'Pay—why?' Sam Chang asked the boy.

'It's a toll,' he explained, as if this were obvious. 'I need some US dollars. Three and a half.'

In a money belt, Chang had thousands of soggy yuan, but he hadn't dared change the money into US dollars, which would have tipped off public security that they were about to flee the country. They now searched the van and found a five-dollar bill in the plastic divider between the front seats.

The van crawled slowly forward. Two cars were in front of them. The man in the booth kept glancing at the van. One car ahead of them now. The man in the booth studied them carefully.

'I don't like this,' William said. 'He suspects something.'

'There's nothing we can do,' his father told him. 'Go forward.'

William eased the van to the booth and stopped. The man in the booth swallowed and gripped something next to a large cash register. Was it a signal button of some kind? Chang wondered.

Then William held out the US money. The officer seemed to flinch.

What was wrong? Had he offered too much? Too little?

The man took the bill, leaning forward to do so, and glanced at the side of the van, on which were the words: THE HOME STORE.

As the man counted out change he looked into the back of the van. All he could see—Chang prayed—were the dozens of saplings and bushes that Chang, William and Wu had dug up in a park on the way here from the beach and packed into the van to make it look as if they were delivering plants for a local store. The rest of the families were lying on the floor, hidden beneath the foliage.

The officer gave him the change. 'Good place, The Home Store.'

'Thank you,' William replied. He eased the van forward, then accelerated. A moment later they plunged into a tunnel.

Well, his idea had worked. Chang had realised that the police here might set up roadblocks. So they'd stopped at a huge shopping centre, in the middle of which was The Home Store. It was open twenty-four hours and—with few employees so early in the morning—Chang, Wu and William had no trouble slipping in through the loading dock. From the stockroom they stole some cans of paint, brushes and tools, then slipped outside again.

Chang told William, 'I'm taking these things now for our survival. But I'm going to pay them back.' When he got his first pay envelope or converted some yuan, he would send them the money.

He'd found a colourful newspaper in a large pile on the loading dock. Struggling with the English, he realised that this was a sales flier and that it had the address of a number of Home Stores on it.

They'd returned to the van and found a truck parked nearby. William swapped the number plates and then they drove until they found a deserted factory. Chang and Wu painted over the name of the church. After the white paint dried, Chang, a calligrapher, expertly painted the words THE HOME STORE on the side in a typeface similar to that in the flier.

They now sailed out of the tunnel into the streets of Manhattan. Through dense rush-hour traffic, they drove along a river whose shade perfectly matched the ocean they had just survived.

The grey land, Chang reflected. Not highways of gold and a city of diamonds, as the unfortunate Captain Sen had promised. As Chang looked around him he wondered what now awaited them.

In theory he still owed the Ghost a great deal of money. In his contract, Chang had agreed to pay the Ghost's debt collectors monthly until the fee for being smuggled to the USA was settled. Many immigrants worked directly for the snakehead who'd smuggled them into the country. But Chang didn't trust snakeheads. So he had made his own arrangements for jobs for him and William and had located an apartment in New York through the brother of a friend back in China. Chang had always intended to pay his obligation. But now, with the sinking of the *Fuzhou Dragon* and the Ghost's attempts to murder them, the contract was void and they were out from under the crushing debt—if, of course, they could stay alive long enough for the Ghost and his *bangshous* to be captured or to flee back to China, and this meant going to ground as soon as possible.

Chang looked back at the others in the van. Wu's wife, Yong-Ping, was in a bad way. Her arm was shattered from their collision with the rocks and the wound was still bleeding. Wu's pretty teenage daughter, Chin-Mei, was clearly frightened. Her brother, Lang, was the same age as Chang's younger son, and the two boys, with nearly identical bowl-shaped haircuts, sat close to each other, staring out of the window and whispering. Chang Jiechi sat motionless in the back with his legs crossed, thin white hair slicked back, saying nothing, but observing all through eyes half covered by drooping lids.

The van slowed to a stop because of the traffic. William pressed the horn impatiently.

'Quiet,' his father snapped. 'Don't draw attention to us.'

The boy hit the horn once more.

Chang glanced towards his son. He asked in a harsh whisper, 'The van . . . how did you learn to start it that way? You've done it before.'

'I only steal from party undersecretaries and commune bosses. That'd be all right with you, wouldn't it?' The boy grinned in a snide way. The comment was a reference to Chang's anticommunist political writings, which had caused the family so much pain in China—and necessitated the flight to America.

'You do *what*? How can you be so disrespectful?'

'If I didn't know how to start the engine,' the boy answered angrily, 'we'd probably be dead now.'

Chang turned away, feeling as if he'd been physically assaulted by the boy's words. Oh, certainly there'd been problems with William in the past. As he'd neared his late teens he'd grown sullen and angry and withdrawn. When he'd brought home a letter from his teacher, reprimanding him for bad grades, William had said that he was persecuted at school because his father was a dissident who'd flouted the one-child rule, spoke favourably about Taiwanese independence and was critical of the CCP, the Chinese Communist Party. But neither his behaviour nor this explanation for it had seemed very serious. Why was the boy suddenly behaving so differently?

Suppressing a burst of anger, Chang forced himself to say, 'You're right. I wouldn't have been able to start the car myself. Thank you.'

Twenty minutes later they were in Chinatown, driving down a broad road that was named in both Chinese and English, 'Canal Street'. It was thronging with people and lined with grocery and souvenir shops, fish markets, jewellery stores and bakeries.

'Where should we go?' William asked.

'Park there,' Chang instructed, and William pulled the van to a kerb. Chang and Wu climbed out. They walked into a store and asked the assistant about the neighbourhood tongs. These associations were made up of Chinese people who practised the same trade or profession or who came from a particular geographic area. Chang was seeking a Fujianese tong, since the two families were from Fujian Province. He was surprised to learn that there was one only a few blocks away. Chang and Wu walked through the crowded streets until they found the place.

PAINTED RED and sporting a classic bird-wing roof, the dingy three-storey building might have been transported directly from Fuzhou. Jimmy Mah, President of the East Broadway Fujianese Society, wearing a grey suit dusted with cigarette ash, greeted them and invited them into his office. A hundred or so Chinese books sat on a bookcase; on the wall were faded posters of Chinese landscapes.

'Sit, please,' Mah said in Chinese. He looked over their filthy clothes, their mussed hair. 'Ha, you two look like you have a story to tell. I would like very much to hear it.'

Chang indeed did have a story. It was fictional. He had decided not to tell any strangers that they'd been on the *Fuzhou Dragon* and that the Ghost might be searching for them. He said to Mah, 'We've just come into the port on a Honduran ship.'

'Who was your snakehead?'

'We never learned his name. He called himself Moxige.'

'Mexican? I don't work with Latino snakeheads.'

'He took our money,' Chang said bitterly, 'then he just left us on the dock. He was going to get us papers and transportation. I have two children and a baby. My father too. He's old. And my friend here, his wife is sick. We need help.'

Chang had told Wu to let him talk to Mah. On the *Dragon*, Wu had drunk too much and often grew impulsive. He'd been careless about what he'd told the immigrants and crew in the hold.

'What kind of help do you want? What do you need?'

'Papers. ID papers. For myself, my wife and my elder son.'

'Sure, sure, I can do some of them. Drivers' licences, social security cards. But you won't be able to get a real job with them.'

'I've got an arrangement for work,' Chang said. 'My father needs to see a doctor.' A nod towards Wu. 'His wife too. Can you get us health cards?'

'No, they're too easy to trace. You'll have to go to a private doctor. But if you don't have money go to a city hospital. They'll take you.'

'All right,' Chang said. 'For the other documents. How much?'

'Fifteen hundred one-colour.'

In the money belt round his waist Chang had about $5,000 worth of Chinese yuan. It was all the cash that his family had left in the world. Shaking his head, he said, 'No, impossible.' After a few minutes of haggling they settled on $900.

'You too?' Mah asked Wu.

The gaunt man nodded but added, 'Only for myself.'

Mah drew heavily on his cigarette. 'Five hundred.'

Wu tried to bargain too but Mah held firm. Finally Wu agreed.

'We also need a van. Can I rent one from you?' Chang asked.

'Of course, of course.' After more bargaining, they agreed on a rental. 'Give me the names and address for the documents.' Mah turned to his computer and, as Chang dictated the information, he typed with fast keystrokes. 'So you'll be staying in Queens?'

'Yes. A friend arranged a place for us.'

'Don't you think my broker could do better?'

'He is my best friend's brother. He has already arranged the lease.'

'Ah, friend's brother. Good.' Mah nodded towards the computer screen and asked Wu, 'You're both at this address?'

Chang started to say that they were but Wu interrupted. 'No, no. I want to stay in Chinatown. Can your broker find us a house?'

Mah said, 'He has temporary rooms. You can get a place today and then stay there until he finds you a permanent home.'

As Mah typed, Chang put his hand on Wu's arm and whispered, 'No, Qichen, you must come with us.'

'We're staying in Manhattan.'

Chang whispered, 'Don't be a fool. The Ghost will find you.'

But Wu was adamant. 'No. We are staying here.'

Mah then wrote a note, handed it to Wu. 'This is the broker. You'll pay him a fee.' Mah made arrangements for the van to be brought round. 'There. That concludes our business.'

They rose in unison and shook hands.

Mah asked, 'One thing. This Mexican snakehead? There's no reason for him to come after you, is there? You're even with him?'

'Yes, we're even.'

'Good. Aren't there enough demons after us in this life?' Mah asked jovially.

IN THE DISTANCE, sirens pierced the early morning air.

The sound grew louder and Lincoln Rhyme hoped it would mark the arrival of Amelia Sachs. A young tech had already delivered the evidence she'd gathered at the beach.

Sachs herself had been diverted to run a secondary crime scene. The church van stolen at Easton had been found in a Chinatown alley. The van had slipped past the roadblocks because it had stolen plates and the name of the church had been replaced by a good facsimile of the logo for a local home-improvement store.

'Smart,' Rhyme had said.

INS director Harold Peabody was gone, but agent Alan Coe and Fred Dellray remained, as did Lon Sellitto and the hedgehog-haired detective Eddie Deng. An addition as well: one of the NYPD's top forensic lab workers, Mel Cooper, slim, balding, reserved. He was assembling equipment and laying out the evidence from the beach.

At Rhyme's request Thom, his aide, taped a map of New York City next to the map of Long Island and the surrounding waters, which they'd used in following the *Fuzhou Dragon*'s progress.

A moment later the door opened and Amelia Sachs hurried into the room. Her hair was matted and flecked with bits of seaweed and dirt and her jeans and work shirt were damp and sandy.

'Had some free time,' she said. 'Went for a swim. Hi, Mel.'

'Amelia,' Cooper said, shoving his glasses higher on his nose.

Sachs handed more evidence bags to Cooper and started for the stairs, calling, 'Back in five.'

A moment later Rhyme heard the shower running and, indeed, five minutes after she'd left, Amelia was back, wearing some of the clothes she kept in his bedroom closet: blue jeans and a black T-shirt, running shoes.

Cooper was laying the bags out, organising them. Rhyme felt the excitement of a hunt that was about to begin.

'OK,' he said. 'Let's get to it.' He looked around the room. 'Thom? Thom! Where is he? He was here a minute ago. Thom!'

'What, Lincoln?' The harried aide appeared in the doorway, with a pan and a dishtowel in his hand.

'Be our scribe . . . write our pithy insights down'—a nod at the whiteboard—'in that elegant handwriting of yours.'

'Yes, bwana.' Sighing, Thom set down the pan and cloth. He tucked his purple tie into his shirt to protect it from the marker and walked to the whiteboard. He knew the drill. He now asked Dellray, 'You have a name for the case yet?'

Dellray said, 'Nup. Nothing yet. How 'bout the name of our boy? GHOSTKILL. That spooky enough for everybody?'

'Plenty spooky,' Sellitto agreed.

Thom wrote this at the top of the whiteboard.

Rhyme said, 'We've got two scenes: the beach in Easton and the van. The beach first.'

Dellray's phone rang and he took the call. After a brief conversation he hung up and told the team what he'd just learned: 'No other survivors so far, but the Coast Guard did recover some bodies out to sea. Two shot, one drowned. ID on one of them had merchant papers. They're sending prints and pictures to us and copies to China.'

'OK,' Rhyme said curtly. 'The beach. Tell us what happened, Sachs.'

She consulted her notes. 'Fourteen people came ashore in a life raft about a half-mile east of Easton.' She walked to the wall and touched a spot on the Long Island map. 'As they got closer to shore the raft hit some rocks and started to deflate. Four of the immigrants were thrown into the water and were washed down the beach. The other ten stayed together. They stole the church van and got away.'

'Photos of the footprints?' Rhyme asked.

'Here you go,' Sachs said, handing Thom an envelope. He taped up Polaroids. 'Nine sets of footprints. And I found some patterns that looked like a crawling child.'

'OK,' Rhyme said, studying the shoe sizes, 'looks like we've got seven adults and/or older teens, two young children and an infant. One of the adults could be elderly—he's shuffling. I say "he" because of the shoe size. And somebody's injured—probably a woman, to judge from the size of *her* shoes. The man next to her is helping her.'

Sachs added, 'There were bloodstains on the beach and in the van.'

'Samples of the blood?' Cooper asked.

She found the bag containing a vial. Handed it to him.

The tech prepared samples for typing and gendering and filled out a form for the serology lab at the Medical Examiner's office.

Sachs continued her scenario. 'Now, the Ghost landed about two hundred yards east of where the immigrants did.'

Her fingers disappeared into her abundant red hair and worried the flesh of her scalp. Rhyme knew he was driven by the same kind of tension. The difference was that he didn't have her safety valve of fidgety motion to bleed off the stress.

'Then,' she continued with a splinter of emotion in her voice, 'then he started tracking down the immigrants and killing them. He found two who'd fallen off the raft and killed them. He wounded one. The fourth's still missing.'

'Where's the wounded one?' Coe asked.

'They were taking him to a trauma centre then to the INS Manhattan detention facility. He said he doesn't know where the Ghost or the immigrants might've been going once they got here.' Sachs again consulted her soggy handwritten notes. 'Now there was a vehicle on the road near the beach but it left—fast, spun the wheels and skidded to make a turn. I think the Ghost took a shot at it. So we may have a witness, if we can track down the make and model.'

'Wait,' Rhyme interrupted. 'What was it near? The car?'

'Near?' she asked. 'Nothing. It was just parked by the roadside.'

Rhyme frowned. 'Why would somebody park there on a stormy day before dawn? I think the driver was there to pick up the Ghost but, when the snakehead wasn't in any hurry to leave, he took off.'

Sachs handed a sheet of paper to Mel Cooper. 'Dimensions of the wheelbase. And here are pictures of the tread marks.'

The tech scanned the marks into the computer and then sent the image, along with the dimensions, to the NYPD's VI—Vehicle Identifier—data base. 'Shouldn't be long,' Cooper's calm voice reported.

'What about the other trucks?' Coe asked. 'The terms of a smuggling contract include land transport too. There should've been some trucks to take the immigrants back to the city.'

Sachs shook her head. 'I didn't see any sign of them.' She looked over the evidence bags again. 'I found this . . .' She held up a bag containing a cellphone.

'Excellent!' Rhyme said. 'Fred, get your people to look it over.'

'Gotcha.' Dellray made a call and arranged for an agent to take the cellphone to the federal forensic lab.

Rhyme said, musing, 'No sign of the mysterious assistant, Sachs?'

'No,' she answered. 'I'm sure the Ghost was the only one in the second raft, and the only one shooting.'

The criminalist then asked, 'What about ballistics?'

Sachs held up a plastic bag of shell casings for Rhyme to examine.

'Seven point six two millimetre,' he said, 'but the brass is an odd length. And it's uneven. Cheap. Check out the casings online, Mel.'

When Rhyme had been head of NYPD forensics he'd spent months putting together data bases of evidence standards—samples of substances along with the sources they came from, like motor oil, thread, fibres, soil—to facilitate tracing evidence found at crime scenes. One of the largest, and most often used, data bases was the compilation of information on bullet shell casings and slugs.

'Back to your captivating narrative about the beach, Sachs.'

She continued. 'The Ghost knew the Coast Guard had a rough idea of his location. He found the third immigrant in the water, John Sung, shot him, then stole the Honda and left.' She glanced at Rhyme. 'Any word about it?'

An emergency vehicle locator notice had gone out to all nearby law enforcement agencies. But there'd been no word, he told her, then added, 'The Ghost's been to New York before, though, plenty of times. He'd know the transit system. He's got to be here by now.' Rhyme noticed a frown of concern on the FBI agent's face. 'What is it, Fred?'

'My people are feeding me reports that he's got a nice, tidy network in town. Tongs and street gangs in Chinatown, course. But it's way beyond that—even got people in the government on his 'roll.'

'Government?' Sellitto asked, surprised.

'What I hear,' Dellray said.

So, Rhyme reflected, we've got a sociopathic snakehead killer and his unidentified assistant, *and* now spies within our own ranks. It's never easy but really . . . He glanced at Sachs. 'Friction ridges?' he asked. The technical name for finger-, palm- and footprints.

'I got a few partials from the outboard motor, the rubber sides of the rafts and the cellphone.' She held up the cards of the prints she'd lifted. 'The quality's pretty bad.'

Rhyme called, 'Scan 'em and get them into AFIS.' The Automated Fingerprint Identification System was a huge network of digitised federal and state fingerprint files.

'I also found this.' She held up a metal pipe in a plastic bag. 'One of them used it to break the window of the van.'

Mel Cooper took the bag, pulled on cotton gloves and extracted the pipe, holding it only by the ends. 'I'll use VMD.' Vacuum metal deposition is considered the Rolls-Royce of fingerprint-raising systems. It involves binding a microscopic coating of metal to the object to be printed and then radiating it. After a few minutes Cooper had a razor-sharp image of several latent prints. He handed the pictures to Thom, who pinned them up.

'That's about it for the beach, Rhyme,' Sachs said.

The criminalist glanced at the chart. The evidence told him little yet. But he wasn't discouraged; this was how criminalistics worked. It was like dumping a thousand jigsaw puzzle pieces on the table—incomprehensible at first; only after trial and error and much analysis did patterns begin to appear. He said, 'The van next.'

Sachs pinned up pictures of the van on the whiteboard.

'What'd you find in it?' Rhyme asked her.

'They'd dug up a bunch of plants and had them in the back. To hide the others, I'm guessing, and make it look like they were a couple of employees making deliveries for The Home Store. But I only got the fingerprints, some rags and the blood; the spatter was on the window and door so I'm guessing the injury was above the waist. Arm or hand probably.' She shrugged. 'That's it.' She handed Cooper the cards and Polaroids of the fingerprints she'd lifted from the van.

Rhyme studied the chart for a moment the way a sculptor sizes up a raw piece of stone before he begins carving. Then he turned to Dellray and Sellitto. 'How do you want to handle the case?'

Sellitto deferred to Dellray, who said, 'We gotta split the effort. One, we'll be going after the Ghost. Two, we gotta find those families 'fore he does. We'll do the command post thing from here, if that's OK.'

Rhyme nodded. Whatever it took, the criminalist was going to find the man who'd ruthlessly taken so many innocent lives.

'Now here's what I'm thinkin',' Dellray said. 'I'm gettin' a dozen more agents assigned to the case here in the Southern and Eastern Districts and I'll get us a SPEC-TAC team up from Quantico.'

SPEC-TAC was short for Special Tactics. This little-known outfit within the FBI was the best tactical unit in the country. Rhyme was glad to hear that Dellray was beefing up their side.

Coe's phone rang. He listened for a few moments, nodding his head. After he hung up he said, 'That was INS Detention in Midtown—about that undocumented, John Sung. He was just released on bond by one of our hearing officers.' Coe raised an eyebrow. 'Everybody who's caught coming ashore tries for asylum—it's standard procedure. But it looks like Sung may just get it. He's a pretty well-known dissident in China.'

'Where is he now?' Sachs asked.

'With the lawyer he was assigned from the Human Rights Law Center downtown. He's going to set Sung up at some apartment off Canal Street. I've got the address. I'll go interview him.'

'I'd rather go,' Sachs said quickly. 'He trusts me. I saved his life.'

Coe reluctantly handed her the address. She showed it to Sellitto. 'We should have an RMP baby-sit outside his place.' Meaning a Remote Mobile Patrol—coptalk for squad car. 'If the Ghost finds out Sung's still alive he'll be a target too.'

The detective jotted the address down. 'Sure. I'll do it now.'

'OK, everybody, what's the theme of the investigation?' Rhyme called out.

'Search well but watch your backs,' Sachs responded with a laugh.

'Keep that in mind. We don't know where the Ghost is. We don't know where—or who—the *bangshou* is.' Then Rhyme's quick eyes made the circuit of the evidence. He gazed intently, as if imploring the inanimate material assembled before him to come to life, give up whatever secrets it might hold and guide them to the killer and the unfortunate prey that he was hunting.

CHAPTER FIVE

Showered and dressed in clean, unobtrusive clothes, the Ghost sat on the leather couch and looked over New York Harbor from the eighteenth-floor apartment that was his main safe house in New York. It was in a fancy high-rise near Battery Park City, in the southwest corner of Manhattan, not far from Chinatown. Now that he'd survived the sinking of the ship, his thoughts were returning to his normal priorities: he needed a woman badly.

He resumed fantasising about a woman he called Yindao, the Chinese word for female genitals. The nickname was contemptuous, of course, but the Ghost thought of all women solely in terms of their bodies. A number of images came to mind about the liaison he had planned with Yindao: her lying beneath him, the distinctive sound of her voice in his ear, his hands gripping her beautiful long hair . . . For a moment he thought about forgetting the Changs and the Wus. But, of course, it wasn't in his nature to do that. First, the piglet families would die. Then he would be able to spend long hours with her. *Naixin*. All in good time.

A glance at his watch. It was nearly 11.00am. Where were the three Turks? he wondered.

When the Ghost had arrived he'd used one of the stolen cellphones he kept here to call a community centre in Queens with which he'd done business several times in the past. He'd hired three men to help him find and kill the piglets. Ever paranoid and wishing to keep his connections between himself and his crimes as distant as possible, the Ghost hadn't gone to any of the traditional tongs in Chinatown: he'd hired Uigurs.

Racially the majority of mainland China is Han, tracing their ancestry back to the dynasty of that name. The other eight or so per cent of the population is made up of minority groups such as the Tibetans, Mongolians and Manchus. The Uigurs (pronounced 'wee-gurs') of western China were one such minority. Their native region is in central Asia and before being annexed by China was called East Turkistan. Hence the Ghost's name for them: 'Turks'.

Ten minutes later they arrived. Hands were shaken and they gave their names: Hajip, Yusuf, Kashgari. Dark, quiet, thin, small in stature, they wore black suits, gold bracelets or necklaces and fancy cellphones on their hips. Uigurs spoke Turkic, a language the Ghost didn't understand, and they weren't comfortable with any of the Chinese dialects. So they settled on English. The Ghost explained what was needed and asked if they'd have any trouble killing people who were unarmed—women and children too.

Yusuf was the spokesman. He said, 'No problem. We do that. We do what you want.' As if he killed women and children regularly.

And perhaps, the Ghost reflected, he did.

SONNY LI sat on a Long Island Commuter Services bus, which was nudging its way through the rain-spattered early morning traffic, as the skyline of Manhattan slowly grew larger. He had never seen any vehicle like this behemoth—it was huge and luxurious, with thick padded seats, clean floors and spotless windows.

After he'd fled from the beach, Li had begged a ride from a trucker at a rest stop on the highway. After a half-hour or so the trucker dropped him at a sleek bus station. Here, the driver explained, Li could take a commuter bus to where he wanted to go: Manhattan.

Li had handed one of the twenty-dollar bills he'd stolen from red-headed Hongse's car to the clerk and enunciated, 'New York City, please,' in his best American accent. He'd gone to a newsstand connected to the station and bought a razor and comb. In the men's room, he'd shaved and washed the salt out of his hair. Then he brushed as much sand off himself as he could and joined the well-dressed commuters on the platform.

Now the bus emerged from a long tunnel into the city itself. Ten minutes later it parked on a busy commercial street. Li climbed out.

His first thought: Where can I buy some cigarettes? He found a kiosk selling newspapers and bought a pack. Ten judges of hell! Nearly three dollars for a single pack! He smoked at least two packs a day. He'd go broke in a month living here, he estimated.

Li asked a pretty Asian woman how to get to Chinatown and was directed to the subway. He jostled his way through the mass of commuters and bought a token. He walked through the turnstile and waited on the platform. A few minutes later the train roared into the station and Sonny Li got on board as if he'd been doing it all his life.

At Canal Street Li stepped out of the carriage and climbed up the stairs into the bustling, early morning city. This neighbourhood was just like any small city in China: movie theatres showing Chinese films, bakeries selling tea buns and rice pastries, smoked ducks hanging in the greasy windows of restaurants, herbalists and acupuncturists. And somewhere near here, he was hoping, would be something else he was very familiar with.

It took Li ten minutes to find what he sought. The telltale sign was a guard, a young man with a cellphone, smoking and examining passers-by as he lounged in front of a basement apartment with black-painted windows. It was a twenty-four-hour gambling hall.

He walked up and asked in English, 'What they play here?'

The man looked at Li's clothes and ignored him.

'I want play,' Li shouted angrily. 'Let me inside!'

'You Fujianese. I hear your accent. You not welcome here.' And he pulled aside his jacket, revealing the butt of an automatic pistol.

Excellent! This is what Li had been hoping for.

Appearing frightened, he started to turn away then spun back with his arm outstretched. He caught the young man in the chest with his fist, knocking the wind out of him. The boy fell hard to the pavement. He lay there, gasping, while Li delivered a kick to his side.

Taking the gun, ammunition and the man's cigarettes, Li looked up and down the street. It was empty. He took the man's wristwatch too and about $300 in cash.

'If you tell anyone I did this,' Li said to the guard, speaking in Mandarin, 'I'll find you and kill you.'

The man nodded.

Li hurried back to one of the crowded commercial streets. There he found a cheap clothing store and bought a pair of jeans, a T-shirt, trainers, socks and a thin Nike windcheater. He changed in the back of the store, paid for his purchases and tossed his old clothes into a trash bin. Li then went into a Chinese restaurant and ordered tea and a bowl of noodles. As he ate he pulled out of his wallet a folded piece of paper that he'd stolen from Hongse's car.

From: Harold C. Peabody, Assistant Director of Enforcement,
US Immigration and Naturalization Service
To: Det. Capt. Lincoln Rhyme (Ret.)
Re: Joint INS/FBI/NYPD Task Force in the matter of Kwan
Ang, AKA Gui, AKA the Ghost

This confirms our meeting at 10.00am tomorrow to discuss the plans for the apprehension of the above-referenced suspect. Please see attached material for background.

Stapled to the memo was a business card, which read:

Lincoln Rhyme
345 Central Park West
New York, NY 10022

He flagged down the waitress and asked her a question. She nodded and gave him directions to Central Park West.

'YOU LOOK BETTER,' Amelia Sachs said. 'How are you feeling?'

John Sung motioned her into the apartment. 'Very sore,' he said and, closing the door, joined her in the living room. The apartment that his immigration lawyer had arranged for him to stay in was a dingy place on the Bowery. Directly below, on the ground floor, was a Chinese restaurant. The smell of oil and garlic permeated the place.

Sung walked slowly, hunched over from the wound. Watching his unsteady gait, Sachs felt sympathy for him. In his life in China, as a doctor, he would have enjoyed some respect from his patients and—even though he was a dissident—may have had some prestige. But here Sung had nothing. She wondered what he was going to do for a living: drive a taxi, work in a restaurant?

'I'll make tea,' he said.

There was no separate kitchen, but a stove, half-size refrigerator and a rust-stained sink lined one wall of the living room. He put a cheap kettle on the sputtering flame and took a box of Lipton tea from the cabinet over the sink.

Sachs asked, 'The INS let you out on bond?'

Sung nodded. 'I've formally petitioned for asylum. I spent two years in a re-education camp, and I've published articles attacking Beijing for human rights violations. My lawyer downloaded some as evidence. The examining officer said there's a good case for asylum.'

Sachs watched his hands as he took two cups from the cabinet and carefully washed, dried and arranged them on a tray. There was something ceremonial about the way he did this. He tore open the bags of tea and put them in a ceramic pot and poured the hot water over them then whisked the brew with a spoon. He carried the pot and cups over to her, sat stiffly. He poured two cups.

'Is there any word on the others?' he asked.

'They're in Manhattan somewhere, we think. We found a truck they stole abandoned not far from here. I'd like to ask you about them. Names, descriptions . . . anything.'

'Of course. There were two families—the Changs and the Wus—and a few other people who escaped. I don't remember their names.'

Sachs tried her tea. It seemed to taste very different from the grocery-store beverage she was used to. My imagination, she told herself.

'And the Ghost? Can you tell me *anything* that might help us to find him?'

He shook his head. 'The little snakeheads in China—the Ghost's representatives—said that once we landed, we'd never see him again.' Sung grew grave and seemed to be considering something. He said, 'One thing . . . I don't know if it will help you but I heard the captain of the ship talking about the Ghost and using the expression "*Po fu chen zhou*" about him. It translates "break the cauldrons and sink the boats". You'd say, I suppose, "There is no turning back". It refers to a warrior from the Qin dynasty. After his troops had crossed a river to attack some enemy, that's what he ordered his men to do: break the cauldrons and sink the boats. So there'd be no possibility of either encamping or retreating. If they wanted to survive, they had to push forward and destroy the other side. The Ghost is that kind of enemy.'

So he won't stop until he kills the families, Sachs reflected uneasily. On impulse she asked, 'Your wife is in China?'

Sung looked into her eyes and said evenly, 'She died last year in a re-education camp. The officials said that she got sick. But they never told me what her illness was.'

'I'm sorry. She was a dissident too?'

He nodded. 'That's how we met. At a protest in Beijing ten years ago. Before she was arrested we were going to come here together, with the children.' Sung's voice faded. Finally he continued, 'I couldn't stay in the country any longer. I decided to come here, apply for asylum and then send for my children.' A faint smile. 'After my mourning is over I'll find a woman here to be the mother to my children.' His hand went to the amulet he wore. Her eyes followed it. He noticed and took the amulet off his neck and handed it to her.

'My good-luck charm. Maybe it works.' He laughed. 'It brought you to me when I was drowning.'

'What is it?' she asked, holding the carving close.

'It's a carving from Qingtian, south of Fuzhou. The soapstone there is very famous. It was a present from my wife.'

'It's broken,' she observed, rubbing the fracture with her nail. Some of the soft stone flaked off.

'It got chipped on the rock I was holding on to when you saved me.'

The design was of a monkey, sitting on his haunches. The creature seemed humanlike. Wily and shrewd. Sung explained, 'He is a famous character in Chinese mythology. The Monkey King.'

She handed the amulet back to him. He replaced it and the charm dropped back against his muscular, hairless chest. Suddenly she was keenly aware of Sung's presence, inches away from her. She felt an inexplicable comfort coming from him—this man who was virtually a stranger.

'I have to get back to Lincoln.'

'To—?'

'The man I work with. Lincoln Rhyme.' She rose, felt a stab of pain in her knee.

'Wait,' Sung said. He took her hand. She felt a serene power radiating from his touch. He said, 'Open your mouth. I'm a doctor. I want to look at your tongue.'

Amused, she did.

'You have arthritis,' he said, releasing her hand and sitting back.

'Chronic,' she said. 'How did you know that?'

'As I said, I'm a doctor. Come back and I will treat you. Western doctors, they have their place. Chinese medicine is best for curing chronic pains and discomfort. There are things I can do that will help. You saved my life. I would be shamed if I didn't repay that. So please, you will come back and let me help you?'

She hesitated for a moment. But then, as if prodding her to act, a bolt of pain shot through her knee. She took out her pen and gave Sung her cellphone number.

STANDING on Central Park West, Sonny Li was confused. What was with the public security bureau here? Hongse drove that fast yellow car, bang, bang, like a TV cop, and now, it seemed, the officers were hunting the Ghost from a building as luxurious as *this*?

Li tossed his cigarette away, and then walked quickly across the street into the alley that led to the rear of the building. He found the back door open. A young blond man stepped out. He carted two green plastic trash bags with him, which he tossed into a large blue metal container. The man glanced around the alley, then returned inside, pulling the door closed. It didn't, however, latch.

Thank you, sir. Sonny Li slipped into the basement. The young man's footsteps ascended the stairs. Li waited behind a stack of boxes for him to return, but the man had apparently gone on to other chores.

Li left his hiding place. Up a flight of stairs, walking slowly. He paused behind the door at the top and pushed it open slightly.

Then several loud voices: 'We'll be back in a couple of hours, Linc. We'll have forensics call . . . Hey, Lincoln, you want one of us to stay? It might be better to have somebody with a weapon. The Ghost's vanished. His assistant too. You said yourself to watch our backs.'

Another voice, irritated, responded. 'But how's he know where on God's green earth I live? I don't need anyone to baby-sit me.'

'OK, OK.' They left and the front door closed.

Sonny Li listened for a moment: silence. He pushed the door open fully and glanced out. In front of him was a long corridor. To Li's right was the door to a living room. He looked in quickly. An odd sight: the room was filled with scientific equipment, computers, tables, test tubes, charts and books of all kinds.

But what was more curious was the dark-haired man sitting in a complicated red wheelchair in the middle of the room, looking at a computer screen, talking to himself, it seemed.

So, was this creature Lincoln Rhyme?

Lifting the gun, Sonny Li stepped into the room.

LI HAD NO IDEA where the men came from.

One of them—far taller than Li—was black as coal and was wearing a suit and bright yellow shirt. He'd been hiding against the wall inside the room. In a seamless motion he swept the gun from Li's hand and pressed a pistol against his temple.

Another man, short and fat, flung Li to the ground and knelt on his back. Handcuffs were ratcheted on.

'English?' the black man asked.

Li was too shocked to answer.

A Chinese man, who'd also been hiding in the room, stepped forward. He wore a stylish dark suit and had a badge dangling from a chain round his neck. He asked the same question in Chinese.

'Yes,' Li responded breathlessly, 'I talk English.'

The man in the wheelchair spun round. 'Let's see what we've caught.'

The black man hauled Li to his feet. Holding him with one hand he began patting his pockets with the other. He pulled out cash, cigarettes, ammunition, the sheet of paper Li had stolen from the beach. 'Ah, looks like this boy here borrowed something he shouldn'ta from Aye-melia. Shame on him.'

'So that's how he found us,' Lincoln Rhyme said, eyeing the sheet of paper with his card attached. 'I *was* wondering.'

The blond man appeared in the doorway. 'So you got him,' he said without surprise. And Li understood then that this young man had spotted him in the alley, and had left the door open on purpose. And the other men had made a noisy show of departing, pretending to leave Lincoln alone.

The man in the wheelchair noticed the disgust in Li's eyes. He said, 'That's right—Thom here spotted you when he took the trash out. And then . . .' He nodded at the computer screen and said, 'Command, security. Back door.'

On the computer screen a video image of the back door of the building and the alley popped up.

Li suddenly understood how the Coast Guard had located the *Fuzhou Dragon*: this man. Lincoln Rhyme.

'Judges of hell,' he muttered.

The fat officer laughed. 'Don'tcha just hate days like this?'

Then the black man pulled Li's wallet out of his pocket. He squeezed the damp leather. 'Our li'l skel here been swimming, I *de*-duce.' He handed it to the Chinese officer.

The fat man pulled out a radio and spoke into it. 'Mel, Alan, come on back in. We got him.'

Two men, probably the ones Li had heard leaving a few moments ago, returned. A balding, slight man ignored Li, walked to a computer and began to type frantically. The other was a man in a suit with dark red hair. He blinked and said, 'Wait, that's not the Ghost.'

'His missing assistant then,' Rhyme said. 'His *bangshou*.'

'No,' the red-headed man said. 'I know him. Some of us from INS were at a meeting last year in the Fuzhou Public Security Bureau—about human smuggling. He was one of them.'

'One of who?' the fat officer grumbled.

The Chinese officer held up an ID card from Li's wallet, comparing Li's picture with his face. 'One of *us*,' he said. 'He's a cop.'

Rhyme too examined the card and the driver's licence, both of which had pictures of the man. They gave his name as Li Kangmei, a detective with the Liu Guoyuan Public Security Bureau.

The criminalist said to Dellray, 'See if any of our people in China can confirm it.' A tiny cellphone appeared in the agent's hand.

'Li is your first or last name?' Rhyme asked.

'Last. And I not like Kangmei. I use Sonny, Western name.'

'What are you doing here?'

'Ghost, he kill three people in my town last year. We try to arrest him but he has very powerful . . .' He sought for a word. Finally he turned to Eddie Deng and said, '*Guanxi*.'

'That means connections,' Deng explained.

Li nodded. 'No one willing testify against him. Then evidence in shooting disappear from headquarters office. My boss lose interest.' Li's eyes were hard ebony discs. 'I want make sure he come to trial.'

Dellray asked, 'How'dja get on the ship?'

'I have lots informants in Fuzhou. Last month I find out Ghost kill two people in Taiwan, big guys, important guys, and was leaving from China for month until Taiwan NSB stop looking for him. He going to South of France then taking immigrants from Vyborg in Russia to New York on *Fuzhou Dragon*.'

Rhyme laughed. This small, scruffy man's information had been better than the FBI's and Interpol's combined.

'So,' Li continued, 'I go undercover. Become piglet—immigrant.'

Coe said, 'But what were you going to do? We wouldn't extradite him to China.'

Perplexed, Li said, 'Why I want him extradited? You not listen. *Guanxi*, I'm saying. In China they let him go. I going to arrest him when we land. Then give him *your* public security bureau.'

'He had his *bangshou* with him, the crew of the ship. Little snakeheads. They would've killed you.' Coe laughed.

Now Li laughed. 'Risky, you saying? Sure, sure. But that our *job*, right?' He reached for the cigarettes Dellray had relieved him of.

Thom said, 'No smoking here.'

Li grudgingly put the pack away.

A faint beeping from across the room. Mel Cooper turned to his computer. He spun the screen round so that everybody could look. The FBI's Singapore office had sent an email confirmation that Li Kangmei was indeed a detective in the Liu Guoyuan Public Security Bureau of the People's Republic of China. A picture of Li accompanied the message. It was clearly the man in the room before them.

Li then explained how the Ghost had scuttled the *Dragon*. Chang and Wu and their families, along with Dr Sung, two other immigrants and the baby of a woman on the ship got away in a life raft. Everyone else drowned. 'Sam Chang become leader on raft. Good man, smart. Save my life. Pick me up when Ghost shooting people. Wu Qichen father of second family. Wu smart too but not balanced. Liver–spleen disharmony. Too emotion. Does impulse things.'

Rhyme frowned. Being the physical scientist that he was, he had no time for disharmonious spleens. 'Let's stick with facts,' he said.

Li then told them how the raft hit the rocks and he, Sung and the others were washed overboard. They were swept down the shoreline. By the time Li made it back to where the raft had beached, the Ghost had killed two of the immigrants. 'I hurry to arrest him but by time I get there, he gone. I saw woman with red hair rescue one man.'

'John Sung,' Rhyme said.

'Dr Sung.' Li nodded. 'Sat next to me on raft. He OK?'

'The Ghost shot him but he'll be all right. Amelia—the woman you saw—is interviewing him now.'

'Hongse, I call her. Hey, pretty girl. Sexy, I'm saying.'

Sellitto and Rhyme shared an amused glance.

'I get address from her car and come here, thinking maybe I get stuff that lead me to Ghost. Information, I'm saying. Evidence.'

'Steal it?' Coe asked.

'Yes, sure. *Have* to get it for myself. Because, hey, you not let me help, right? You just send me back. And I going to arrest him.'

Coe said, 'Well, you're *not* helping us. You may be a cop in China. But here you're just one more undocumented. You *are* going back.' He reached for his cuffs. 'Li, you're under arrest for entering the United States—'

But Lincoln Rhyme said, 'No, I want him.'

'What?' the agent asked in shock.

'He'll be a consultant. Like me. Anybody who goes to this much trouble to nail a perp—I want him working on our side.'

'You bet I help, Loaban. Do lots, I'm saying.'

'What did you call me?'

Li explained to Rhyme, '"Loaban".It mean "boss". You got keep me. I can help. I know how Ghost think. We from same world.'

'No way,' Coe blurted. 'He's an undocumented. As soon as we turn our back he'll just run off, get drunk and go to a gambling parlour.'

Li ignored Coe. 'In my country we got four classes people. Not like rich and poor, stuff like you got here. In China what you do more important than money you got. And know what highest honour is? Working for country, working for people. I good cop, I'm saying.'

Coe said, 'How do we know he's not on the Ghost's payroll?'

Li laughed. 'Hey, how we know *you* not working for him?'

'Fuck you,' Coe said. He was furious.

The young INS agent's problem, Rhyme assessed, was that he was too emotional to be an effective law enforcer. The criminalist often heard contempt in his voice when he spoke about 'undocumenteds'.

As well as his derisive attitude towards aliens, the agent had a troubling personal stake in collaring the Ghost. Several years ago, Coe had been stationed in Taipei, the capital of Taiwan, running undercover agents in mainland China, trying to identify major snakeheads. During an investigation of the Ghost, one of his informants, a woman, had disappeared and presumably been killed. Later it was learned that the woman had two young children; the INS would not have used her as an informant if they'd known this. Coe was suspended for six months. He'd become obsessed with collaring the Ghost. To be a good cop you've got to tuck personal feelings away.

Dellray said, 'Juss settle down. Li stays with us for's long as Lincoln wants him. Make it happen, Coe. Call somebody at the State Department and get him a temporary visa.'

Coe muttered, 'Well, keep him. But I'm not taking any heat for it.'

'You make good decision,' Sonny Li said. 'I help lots, Loaban.' Li walked over to the table and picked up the gun he'd been carrying.

'Nup, nup, nup,' Dellray said. 'Get your hands offa that. No guns.'

'Welcome on board, Sonny,' Rhyme said, then glanced at the clock. It was just noon on Tuesday—six hours since the Ghost began his relentless pursuit of the immigrants. He could be closing in on the poor families even now. 'OK, let's start on the evidence.'

'Sure, sure,' Li said, suddenly distracted. 'But I need cigarette first. Come on, Loaban. You let me?'

'All right,' Rhyme snapped. 'But outside.'

Chapter Six

Wu Qichen wiped the sweat off his wife's forehead. Shivering, burning with fever, soaking with perspiration, she lay on a mattress in the bedroom of their tiny apartment. The basement rooms, down an alley off Canal Street in the heart of Chinatown, had been provided by the broker that Jimmy Mah had sent them to—a robber, Wu had thought angrily. The apartment stank, the place was virtually unfurnished, and roaches roamed the floor in the diffuse light bleeding in through the greasy windows.

Wu studied his wife with concern. The raging headache Yong-Ping had suffered on board the *Dragon*, the lethargy, the chills and sweats had persisted. He glanced through the doorway and saw his teenage daughter, Chin-Mei, hanging laundry on a line strung through the room. After they'd arrived the family had showered then dressed in the clean clothes that Wu had bought at a discount store on Canal Street. Chin-Mei had washed their salt-encrusted clothing.

He rose and walked into the living room.

'Is she all right?' the teenage girl asked.

'Yes. She'll be fine,' he said. 'I'm going to get her some medicine.'

Wu walked down the busy streets of Chinatown, hearing a cacophony of languages. He gazed at the stores and shops, the piles of merchandise, the huge high-rises ringing the city. Forty-year-old Wu Qichen had nurtured a dream all his life: he was going to become a wealthy man, the richest ever in his family. Seduced by the fat opportunities in the Beautiful Country, he had risked emigrating illegally. He wouldn't let the Ghost drive him from the city of money.

He found a Chinese medicine store. He stepped inside and talked to the herbalist about his wife's condition. The doctor listened carefully, and diagnosed deficient *qi*—the life spirit—and obstructed blood, both of which were aggravated by excessive cold. He then put together a bundle of herbs.

Leaving the herbalist, Wu turned in the direction of his apartment but began meandering through the side streets. The day had been a nightmare. He was concerned about his wife, he'd nearly been killed in a shipwreck, he'd lost all his possessions. He needed some diversion.

It took only a few minutes to find a Fujianese gambling den. After showing his money to the guard in front he was admitted. He sat silently for a time, playing thirteen points, smoking and drinking *baijiu*. He won a little money, had another cup of the powerful, clear spirit, and began to feel better.

Eventually he struck up a conversation with the men around him and, from the thirty dollars he won, he bought them drinks.

He lifted his cap. 'Here is to Zai Chen,' he announced drunkenly. This was the god of wealth.

'You're new here,' an old man said. 'When did you come over?'

Pleased that he had the spotlight, Wu bragged, 'Just this morning. On the ship that sank.'

'The *Fuzhou Dragon*?' one man asked. 'It was on the news.'

'Ah,' Wu said, 'the snakehead tried to kill us all but I got a dozen people out of the hold. And then I had to swim underwater to cut a life raft off the deck. But I managed to get us to shore.' He looked down sadly. 'I couldn't save them all. But I tried.'

Another asked him, 'Is your family all right?'

'Yes,' he answered.

'Are you in the neighbourhood?'

'Up the street.'

Then Wu fell silent as he realised he probably should not be saying these things. He changed the subject. 'Can someone tell me? There's a statue I want to see. It's of a woman and she's holding her accounts.'

'Accounts?' another man asked.

'Yes,' Wu explained. 'You see her in movies. She's on an island somewhere, holding in one hand a book of her business accounts and a lantern in the other so she can see how much money she has at any time of the night or day. Is that here in New York?'

'Yes, she's here,' one man said with a laugh. 'You go down to Battery Park and take a boat out to see the statue.'

Another man said, 'To the lady of accounts.' Laughing, they all emptied their glasses and then resumed the game.

AMELIA SACHS RETURNED from the witness's apartment in Chinatown and Rhyme was amused to see the harsh look with which she studied Sonny Li when he announced with pride that he was a 'detective with public security bureau in People's Republic of China'.

'You check him out?' she asked, closely studying the man.

'They checked me out good, Hongse. I'm clean.'

'*Hoankseh?* What the hell's that?' she barked.

He held up his hands defensively. 'Means "red". Only that. Nothing bad. Your hair, I'm saying. I saw you on beach, saw your hair.'

'He's OK, Amelia,' Dellray confirmed.

Sachs shrugged and turned to the Chinese cop. 'What'd you mean about the beach? You were spying on me?'

'Afraid you send me back. Wanted chance to get Ghost too.'

Sachs then told the team what the witness—John Sung—had said. Rhyme relaxed a bit more about his decision to keep Sonny Li when he heard that Sung confirmed the information Li had given them. He was troubled, though, when Sachs mentioned John Sung's story about the captain's assessment of the Ghost.

'*Po fu chen zhou*,' Li said, nodding grimly. 'That describe Ghost good. Never relax or retreat until you win.'

Sachs helped Mel Cooper log in the evidence from the van. She was bagging the bloody rags she'd found when Cooper looked at the sheet of newsprint on the table underneath the bag she was holding. He frowned. Using a magnifying glass, he looked it over carefully.

'This's odd,' he said. 'I missed these fragments. Look.'

Rhyme couldn't see anything.

'Some kind of porous stone,' Cooper said. 'How could I miss it?'

'Oh, hell,' Sachs muttered. Blushing, she held up her fingers. 'That was from me. I picked it up without gloves.'

'Without gloves?' Rhyme asked, an edge in his voice. This was a serious error by a crime scene tech.

'I'm sorry,' Sachs said. 'I know what it's from. John . . . Dr Sung was showing me this amulet he wore. It was chipped and I guess I picked at it with my nail.'

Li nodded and said, 'I remember . . . Sung let children on *Fuzhou Dragon* play with it. Qingtian soapstone. Good luck.' He added, 'It was of Monkey. Very famous in China.'

But Rhyme wasn't interested in myths. He was trying to catch a killer. And trying to figure out why Sachs had made a mistake of this magnitude. The mistake of someone who's distracted. What's on her mind? he wondered.

'Throw out the top sheet of newsprint,' Rhyme said. 'Let's move on.'

As the tech tore off the sheet his computer beeped. He read the screen. 'We've got the blood types back. All samples are from the same person—presumably the injured immigrant. It's type AB negative and the Barr Body test confirms that it's a woman's blood.'

'Up on the wall, Thom,' Rhyme called. And the aide wrote.

Before he was finished, Mel Cooper's computer summoned them again. 'It's the AFIS search results.'

They were discouraged to find that the fingerprint search came back negative. But Rhyme observed something unusual about the prints they'd lifted from the pipe used to break into the van. They knew these were Sam Chang's as they matched prints on the outboard motor and Li had confirmed that Chang piloted the raft. 'Look at those lines,' he said.

'Whatcha see, Lincoln?' Dellray asked.

The arrow of the cursor stopped on an indentation on the pad of the index finger of Chang's right hand. There were similar ones on his middle finger and his thumb.

Rhyme instructed Thom to write the observation down on the

board. He then took a call on the speaker phone from Special Agent Tobe Geller, one of the FBI's computer and electronics gurus. He'd completed his analysis of the Ghost's cellphone.

'Now, let me tell you, this is an excessively interesting phone.'

'Howsat?' Dellray asked.

'First of all, it's virtually untraceable. The memory chip's been deactivated so the log features are out completely. And it's a satellite phone. The signals are relayed through a government network in Fuzhou. The Ghost hacked into the system to activate it.'

Dellray snapped, 'Juss call somebody in the People's Republic and tell 'em this bad guy's using their system.'

'We tried that,' Geller said. 'But the Chinese position is that nobody can hack their phone system so we must be mistaken. I mentioned Kwan Ang by name. They still weren't interested. Meaning they were probably paid off.'

Guanxi. Score one for the Ghost, Rhyme thought angrily.

They were more successful with the firearms data base. Mel Cooper found that the shell casings matched two weapons, both dating back nearly fifty years: a Russian Tokarev 7.62mm automatic was one type. 'But,' Cooper continued, 'I'm betting he was using the Model 51, a Chinese version of the Tokarev.'

'Yeah, yeah,' Sonny Li said. 'Gotta be 51, I'm saying. I had Tokarev but lost it in ocean. More peoples in China got 51s.'

A messenger arrived with an envelope. Sellitto took it and extracted a handful of photographs. He glanced at Rhyme with a raised eyebrow. 'The three bodies the Coast Guard recovered from the water. Two shot. One drowned.' There were fingerprint cards too.

'Those two,' Li said, 'they crew members. Other guy, one of immigrants. Down in hold with us. Don't know name.' He muttered something in Chinese.

'What was that?' Rhyme asked.

He glanced at the criminalist. 'I said "judges of hell". Just expression. We have myth in China—ten judges of hell decide where your name go in *Register of Living and Dead*. Judges decide when you born and when you die. Everybody in world, name is in register.'

Rhyme thought momentarily of his upcoming operation. He wondered where his own name was entered in the *Register* . . .

Then another beep from the computer. Mel Cooper glanced at the screen. 'Got the make of the driver's car at the beach. BMW X5. It's one of those fancy four-by-fours.'

'Put it on the chart.'

As Thom wrote, Li asked, 'Whose car that?'

Sellitto said, 'We think somebody was at the beach to pick up the Ghost. That's what he was driving.'

'What happen him?' Li asked.

'The Ghost shot at him but he got away,' Deng said.

Rhyme ordered, 'Run the make through Motor Vehicles. New York, Jersey and Connecticut too.'

'Yup.' Cooper logged online. 'More popular car than I'd hoped,' he said moments later. 'Hundreds.'

'What are the names?' Sellitto asked. 'Any Chinese?'

Cooper scrolled through the list. 'Looks like two. Ling and Zhao. But neither of them are close to downtown. One's in White Plains and the other's in New Jersey.' The tech continued to scroll through the list. 'Here's a possibility—there are about forty X5s registered to corporations and another fifty or so registered to leasing agents.'

'Any of the corporations sound Chinese?' Rhyme asked, wishing he himself could pound on the keys and scroll quickly through the list.

'Nope,' Cooper replied. 'But they're all pretty generic—holding companies. You know, it'd be a bear but we *could* contact them all.'

'Waste of resources,' Rhyme said. 'It'll take days. Have a couple of officers from downtown check the ones closest to Chinatown but—'

'No, no, Loaban,' Sonny Li interrupted. 'You got to find that car. Number one thing you do. Fast.'

Rhyme lifted a querying eyebrow.

The Chinese cop continued emphatically, 'Find it *now*. Beemer, right? You call them Beemers. Put lots people on it. The Ghost, he going to kill that driver. That what he doing now, looking for him. Very clear. Get that driver. He lead you to snakehead.'

'And what, Sonny,' a testy Lincoln Rhyme muttered darkly, 'is your basis for that conclusion? Where are the data to support it?'

'When I on bus coming to city this morning I saw sign.' Li reached absently for his cigarettes then left them untouched when he saw Thom's sharp glance. He continued, 'I saw crow on road picking at food. Another crow tried steal it and first crow not just scare other away—he chase and try to peck eyes out. Not leave thief alone.'

'And?'

'I remember that crow now and I start thinking about Ghost and about driver—man in fancy Beemer. He is *enemy* to Ghost. Like crow stealing food. The Wus, the Changs—they not do anything bad to him personal, I'm saying. The driver . . .' Li frowned and spoke to Deng, who offered, "Betray"?'

'Yes, *betray* him. He now Ghost's enemy.'

Lincoln Rhyme tried not to laugh. 'Noted, Sonny.'

'I see your face, Loaban,' Li said. 'I not saying gods come down and give me sign. But remembering crows make me think different way, open up my mind. Get wind flowing through it. You got to find that driver, Loaban.'

Sellitto intervened. 'How 'bout if we put Bedding and Saul on it, give 'em a half-dozen guys from Patrol, Linc? They can check corporate and lease X5 registrations in Manhattan and Queens.'

'All right, all right,' Rhyme said angrily. 'Now, if it's not too much to ask, can we get back to some *real* police work?'

Chapter Seven

The family name Chang means archer.

His father, wife and children sitting around him, Sam Chang drew the Chinese characters for this name on a slat of broken wood he'd found. The silk case holding his prized brushes, ink stick and stone well had gone down with the *Fuzhou Dragon* and he was forced to use a dreadful American plastic pen. Still, Chang had learned calligraphy from his father when he was young and had practised the art all his life, so the strokes were perfectly formed.

Chang took the piece of wood and rested it on the impromptu cardboard altar sitting on the fireplace mantel in the living room of their new apartment. 'There,' he announced. 'Our home.'

Chang Jiechi shook his son's hand. 'Better than some.'

Despite the man's words, though, Sam Chang felt a wave of shame that he was subjecting his father to such a mean place as this. The strongest duty after that owed to the ruler of the government, according to Confucius, is that which a son owes to his father. Ever since Chang had planned their escape from China he'd worried about how the trip would affect the elderly man. Ever quiet and unemotional, Chang Jiechi had taken the news of their impending flight silently, leaving Chang to wonder if he was doing the right thing in the old man's eyes. And now, after the sinking of the

Dragon, their life wasn't going to get better any time soon. This apartment would have to be their prison until the Ghost was captured or went back to China.

A firm knock at the door. For a moment no one in the family moved. Then Chang looked out through the curtain and relaxed. He opened the door and broke into a smile. Joseph Tan walked inside and the men shook hands.

Chang glanced outside into the street and saw no one who looked like enforcers for the snakehead. In the air was a foul smell; the apartment, it turned out, was not far from a sewage treatment plant.

Tan, the brother of a good friend of Chang's in Fujian, had come over here some years ago and travelled freely between China and New York. Last spring Chang had shared with Tan the news that he was bringing his family to the Beautiful Country. Tan had volunteered to help. He had arranged for this apartment and for Chang and his elder son to work in one of Tan's businesses—a quick-print shop. In China, Chang had been a professor of art and culture until his dissident status had got him fired, and like many of the calligraphers and artists who'd lost their jobs during the Cultural Revolution of the 1960s he'd taken a job as a printer.

They sat down to tea.

'We heard about the ship on the news,' Tan said. 'The TV said the snakehead was the Ghost.'

Chang replied that it was and that he'd tried to kill them even after they came ashore.

'Then we will have to be very careful. I will not mention your name to anyone. But I have people around the shop who will be curious. I had thought you should start work right away but with the Ghost . . . It would be better to wait. Maybe next week.'

They spoke for a time about life in China. Then Tan asked to meet William. Chang opened the door to the bedroom. William was not there. Chang strode to the back door and found it was unlocked. He said to Tan in a panic, 'I must go find my boy.'

He and Tan walked outside, and Tan pointed him towards the shops before leaving. Chang glanced into the shop windows as he walked past and didn't see William in any of them. He prayed that the boy had merely gone for a walk and not met someone and told them how he'd come here.

Then, happening to glance down a dim alley, he saw his son. The boy was talking with two young Chinese men, both wearing black leather jackets. William handed one of them something Chang couldn't see. The man slipped a small bag into William's hand. Then the two turned quickly and walked back down the alley.

No! Chang thought in shock. His son was buying drugs?

He ducked back out of the alley and, when his son stepped out, grabbed the shocked boy.

'How could you do this?' Chang demanded.

'Leave me alone.'

'Don't you know that the Ghost is looking for us?'

'I wanted to go outside. It's like a prison.'

'You can't disobey me like this.'

The boy said nothing. Chang had learned today that the iron cables of obligation and honour that had so absolutely guided Sam Chang's life meant little to the boy.

At the front door to the apartment William started to walk past his father, but Chang reached into the boy's pocket, pulled out the bag and looked inside, stunned at the sight of a small silver pistol.

'What are you doing with this?' he whispered viciously. 'Tell me!'

'I got it so I can protect us!' the boy shouted.

'I will protect us. And not with this.'

'You?' William laughed with a sneer. '*You* wrote your articles about Taiwan and democracy and made our life miserable. *You* decided to come here and the snakehead tries to kill us all.'

'Why do you dishonour me like this?' Chang asked angrily.

Pushing inside the apartment, William shook his head, a look of exasperation on his face, and walked brusquely into the bedroom. He slammed the door.

Chang Jiechi asked, 'Where did he go?'

'Up the street. He got this.' He showed his father the gun and the elder Chang took it in his gnarled hands and examined it closely. As he handed the gun back to his son, the old man winced in pain.

'Sit, Baba,' Chang said, alarmed. He hid the weapon on the top shelf of the front closet and led the old man to the musty couch.

One of their few possessions that had survived the sinking of the *Dragon* was the nearly full bottle of Chang Jiechi's morphine. It was tightly sealed and no sea water had got inside. He now gave his father two more pills and placed a blanket over him. The man lay back on the couch and closed his eyes.

Sam Chang sat heavily in a chair. Their possessions gone, his father desperately needing treatment, a ruthless killer their enemy, his own son a criminal . . . So much difficulty around them. Regret would serve no purpose, though. All Chang could now do was pray that the stories about life here were true—that the Beautiful Country was indeed a land of miracles, where evil was brought to light and purged and where generous liberty fulfilled its promise that troubled hearts would be troubled no more.

AT 1.30PM the Ghost was in Chinatown. He'd come to the merchants' association where the Turks awaited him. Inside the large office, he found Yusuf and the two other Turks. It hadn't taken much—a few phone calls, a threat—to find the name of the man who was now sitting, nervous to the point of tears, in front of his own desk.

The snakehead pulled up a chair and sat beside him. He took Mah's hand casually and felt the trembling of muscles.

'I didn't know they came in on the *Dragon*. They didn't tell me! I swear that. They lied to me.'

The Ghost continued to hold the man's hand, adding slight pressure but saying nothing.

'Are you going to kill me?' Mah asked in a whisper.

'The Changs and the Wus. Where are they?'

Mah's eyes glanced at the Turks, and he wondered what kind of terrible weapons they had on them. But in the end it was the faint pressure of the Ghost's palm that loosened his tongue.

LON SELLITTO ANNOUNCED to the GHOSTKILL team, 'We've got a body in Chinatown. Detective from the Fifth Precinct's on the line.'

Alarmed, Rhyme looked up at him. Had the Ghost tracked down and killed another of the immigrants?

But Sellitto hung up and said, 'Doesn't look related to the Ghost. Vic's name's Jimmy Mah.'

'Know him,' Eddie Deng said. 'Heads a tong.'

Rhyme asked, 'Why don't you think it's related?'

Sellitto said, 'There was a message painted on the wall behind his desk, where they found the body. It said, "You call us wops, you take our homes." It was written in Mah's blood.'

Nodding, Deng said, 'Major rivalry between the third-generation Mafiosi and the tongs.'

Sachs looked at Rhyme. 'Maybe the Ghost killed Mah and made it look like an organised crime hit. Should I run the scene?'

Rhyme debated for a moment. 'No, I need you here,' he said. 'But send a special team from Crime Scene.' He turned to Deng. 'Call Dellray and Peabody at the Federal Building. Let them know about the killing.' Dellray had gone downtown to arrange for the extra agents. He was also wielding his influence to get the SPEC-TAC team on site, which Washington was reluctant to do. Still, Dellray was a tough man to say no to and if anyone could get the much-needed force up here it'd be the lanky agent.

Rhyme manoeuvred the chair back to the evidence and the white-boards. What else can we do? he wondered. What haven't we exhausted? Scanning the board . . . Finally he said, 'Let's look at the blood some more.' He looked over the samples from the injured immigrant woman. Lincoln Rhyme loved blood as a forensic tool: it retained its important evidence for years. 'Let's see if our injured woman's got a drug habit or is taking some rare medicine. Call the ME's office and have them do a complete workup.'

As Cooper was talking to the office, Sellitto's phone rang. Rhyme could see in the detective's face that he was receiving some bad news.

'Fifth Precinct again. Chinatown,' Sellitto said, wincing. 'Another killing. This time it's *definitely* the Ghost.' He glanced at Rhyme and shook his head. 'It's not good. They're saying it's unpleasant, Linc.'

Unpleasant was not a word that one heard often from a hardened NYPD homicide detective.

Sellitto hung up the phone and glanced at Sachs. 'Suit up, Officer, you've got a scene to run.'

'HEY, HONGSE,' Sonny Li began nervously as the crime scene bus Sachs was driving skidded round a taxi at seventy miles an hour. But he quickly fell silent.

In the back seat were Eddie Deng and agent Alan Coe.

'Which way, Eddie?' Sachs asked.

'The Bowery, turn left, two more blocks then a right.'

'Ten judges of hell,' Li muttered after another skid.

Three minutes later the crime scene bus stopped in front of an alley. The front door to what seemed to be a small warehouse was open. Sachs climbed out, followed by Deng, who called, 'Hey, Detective,' to a blond man in a suit. He nodded and Deng introduced her to a homicide detective from the Fifth Precinct.

Sachs asked, 'What is this place?'

'Warehouse. Owner's clean, looks like. We've contacted him and he doesn't know anything except that the victim—name was Jerry

Tang—worked here. Mostly he drives getaway.' He nodded at the silver BMW four-by-four in the alley. An X5.

A patrol officer responding to some screams had noticed a late model BMW four-by-four next to the building where the commotion had come from. Then he'd seen the bullet hole in the back and, with his partner, they'd entered the warehouse. And found what was left of Jerry Tang. He'd been tortured with a knife or razor—skin was missing, including his eyelids—then killed.

Sonny Li had been right: the Ghost's first mission *had* been to kill the man who'd abandoned him.

'Who's been inside?' Sachs asked the blond detective.

'Only one uniform—to see if the vic was alive.' The detective beckoned to a uniformed patrolwoman.

'You wanted to see me?' she asked.

'Just your shoe.'

The woman slipped it off and handed it to Sachs, who shot a picture of the tread and noted the size of the sole so that she could differentiate it from the prints of the Ghost and his accomplices.

She then put rubber bands round her own shoes to distinguish her footprints. Looking up, she noticed Sonny Li standing in the doorway of the warehouse. 'Excuse me,' she said testily.

'Sure, sure, Hongse. That big room. Man, lot to look at. But you know Confucius, right?'

'Not really,' she said, concentrating on the scene.

'He write, "Longest journey must begin with first step." I *think* he write that. Maybe somebody else. I read Mickey Spillane more than Confucius.'

'Could you wait over there, Officer Li?'

'Call me Sonny.' He stepped aside.

Sachs walked into the warehouse. The headset went on and she clicked the Motorola handy-talkie to life. She scanned the carnage. 'Rhyme, this is a mess.'

'Tell me,' he said. 'Give me the blueprint first.'

'Warehouse and office combined. Thirty by fifty feet, more or less, office area about ten by twenty. Four metal desks, eight chairs; no, nine—one's overturned.' The one that Tang had been tied to when the Ghost had tortured and killed him. 'Rows of metal shelves, stacked with cardboard boxes, food inside. Canned goods and cellophane packages. Restaurant supplies.'

'OK,' Rhyme said. 'Start on the grid, Sachs.'

She began to search the scene. But twenty minutes of one-step-at-a-time searching revealed nothing that would lead them directly to where the Ghost might be hiding out in New York.

Sachs jumped when Rhyme's voice popped into her ear. 'Talk to me, Sachs. I don't like it when you're quiet.'

'The place has been ransacked, drawers opened, glasses smashed. Vandalism, I'd say.'

'What are their shoe treads like?' Rhyme asked.

'All smooth.' He was, she knew, hoping for some dirt or fibres that might lead them to the Ghost's safe house, but smooth-soled shoes lose trace quickly.

'OK, Sachs, keep going. What do the footprints tell you?'

'I'm thinking that—'

'Don't think, Sachs. That's not the way to understand a crime scene. You know that. You have to *feel* it.'

His seductive, low voice was hypnotising and with each word he spoke she felt herself uneasily being transported back to the crime itself, as if she were a participant.

'Jerry Tang is at his desk and we kick the door in. He runs towards the back door but we get him and drag him back to his chair.'

'Let's narrow it down, Sachs. You're the Ghost. You've found the man who's betrayed you. What are you going to do?'

'I'm going to kill him.' *First crow not just scare other away—he chase and try to peck eyes out.* Suddenly she was filled with a burst of unfocused anger. It nearly took her breath away. 'It's like his death is secondary—what I really want is to hurt him.'

'What do you do? Exactly.'

'I'm having trouble with this one, Rhyme. There's something about him, about the Ghost.' She hesitated. 'It feels really bad there.'

A place where families die, where children are trapped in the holds of sinking ships, where men and women are shot in the back.

'Go there, Sachs,' he murmured. 'Go on. I'll get you back. You've found your betrayer. What do you do?'

'The other men with me tie Tang to a chair and we use knives or razors on him. He's screaming. We're taking our time.' Then, suddenly, the phantom anger vanished, replaced by a shocking eerie serenity. Breathing hard, she was possessed suddenly by the foul spirit of the Ghost. She felt what he had experienced: a visceral satisfaction at the sight of his betrayer's pain and slow death.

And with that thought came another: 'I'm . . . *I'm* not the one torturing Tang. I want the others to do it. So I can watch. And I have them cut his eyelids off first so Tang has to watch me watch him.'

A whisper. 'Ah, good, Sachs. And that means there's a place you're watching *from*?'

'Yes. There's a chair there, facing Tang, about ten feet away from the body.' Her voice cracked. 'I'm watching,' she whispered. 'I'm enjoying it.' She felt sweat pouring from her scalp.

'How you doing, Sachs?'

'OK,' she said.

But she wasn't OK at all. She was trapped where she didn't want to be. Suddenly everything good in her life was negated and she slipped further into the core of the Ghost's world.

Then she realised the criminalist wasn't saying anything. 'Rhyme?'

No response.

'You OK?' she asked.

'Not really,' he finally answered. 'What good does knowing where he sat do us? What kind of evidence is there. I can't think. There's got to be *something*.' She heard the frustration in his voice.

'I don't know,' she said, her voice weak.

'Hell,' Rhyme said, 'I don't know either. Is the chair upright?'

'The one the Ghost sat in to watch from? Yes.'

'But what do we *do* with that fact?' His voice was discouraged. This wasn't like Lincoln Rhyme.

Sachs focused on the chair. 'Hold on.' She walked closer and looked beneath it. 'There are scuff marks here, Rhyme. The Ghost sat down and leaned forwards—to see better. He crossed his feet under the chair. That means that any trace in the seam between the uppers and his soles might've fallen out. I'll vacuum underneath it.'

'Excellent, Sachs,' Rhyme said. 'Get the Dustbuster.'

She started for the door, then stopped and gave a faint laugh. 'You got me, Rhyme.'

'I did what?'

'Don't sound so innocent.' He'd known there was trace beneath the chair, she realised. But he'd recognised that she was lost in the Ghost's terrible world. He'd pretended to be frustrated to draw her attention back and ease her out of the darkness. 'Thanks, Rhyme,' she said.

'I promised I'd get you back. Now, go do some vacuuming.'

Sachs vacuumed the floor under and around the chair and then placed the vacuum filter in a plastic evidence bag.

'What happens next?' Rhyme asked.

She judged the angle of the blood spatter from the bullets that killed Tang. 'Looks like when Tang finally passed out from the pain the Ghost stood up and shot him. Then the assistants trashed the place.'

'Good.'

Sachs said, 'I'm going to do electrostatic prints of the shoes.'

She stepped outside and returned with the equipment. As she was crouching down, she smelt cigarette smoke. Sonny Li was wandering through the office.

'What are you doing here?' she raged. 'You're contaminating the scene!'

'What I doing? I investigate too.'

'What?' She took him by the arm and walked him to the door. She called to Deng and Coe. 'Keep him out.'

After half an hour of diligent work, Sachs told Rhyme, 'I've got everything here. I'll be back in twenty minutes.'

She was just at the doorway when her cellphone rang. She was surprised to hear John Sung identify himself.

'How are you?' she asked.

'Fine. The wound itches some.' He then added, 'I wanted to tell you—I got some herbs for your arthritis. There's a restaurant downstairs in my building. Could you meet me there?'

Sachs looked at her watch. What could it hurt? She wouldn't be long. Handing off the evidence to Deng and Coe, she told them she had a stop to make and would be at Rhyme's in half an hour.

Chapter Eight

Amelia Sachs pulled the crime scene bus into an alley near John Sung's apartment. Climbing out, she glanced at a hand-painted sign in the florist shop on the ground floor of his building, next to the restaurant: NEED LUCK IN YOUR LIFE? BUY OUR LUCKY BAMBOO!

She then noticed Sung through the window of the restaurant, went inside and sat opposite him in a booth.

'Tea?' Sung poured it and pushed the small cup towards her. 'Have you found him yet? The Ghost?'

Disinclined to talk about an investigation, she demurred and said only that they had some leads.

'I don't like this uncertainty,' Sung said. 'I hear footsteps in the hall and I freeze. It's like being in Fuzhou. Someone slows down outside your home and you don't know if they're neighbours or security officers the local party boss sent to your house to arrest you.'

'After all the press about the *Fuzhou Dragon*,' she said, 'you'd think the Ghost'd go back to China.'

Sung reminded, '"Break the cauldrons—"'

'"—and sink the boats."' She nodded. Then she added, 'Well, he's not the only one who's got that motto.'

Sung assessed her for a moment. 'You're a strong woman. Have you always been a cop?'

'Naw, I went to the police academy after I'd been working for a few years.' She told him about her stint as a model for a Madison Avenue agency. 'I was young. Was mostly my mother's idea. I remember once I was working on a car with my dad. He was a cop too, but his hobby was cars. We were rebuilding an engine in this old Thunderbird. And I was, I don't know, nineteen or something, I'd been doing modelling in the city. I was under the car and he dropped a crescent wrench. Caught me on the cheek.'

'Ouch.'

A nod. 'But the big ouch was when my mother saw the cut. I don't know who she was madder at. Me or my father.'

Sung asked, 'And your mother? Is she who watches your children when you work?'

A sip of tea, a steady gaze. 'I don't have any.'

He frowned. 'You . . . I'm sorry.' Sympathy flooded his voice. 'In China children are very important to us. You know our language is based on pictograms. The Chinese character for the word "love" is brush strokes that represent a mother holding a child.'

Sachs felt an urge to tell him that, yes, she wanted children very badly. But suddenly she felt like crying. Then controlled it fast. None of that. She looked down, sipped her tea.

'Are you married?' Sung asked.

'No. I have someone in my life, though.'

'That's good,' he said. 'I sense he's in the same line of work. Is he by any chance that man you were telling me about? Lincoln . . .'

'Rhyme.' She laughed. 'You're pretty observant.'

'In China, doctors are detectives of the soul.' Then Sung leaned forward and said, 'Hold your arm out. Please.'

She did and he rested two fingers on her wrist.

After a moment he sat back. 'My diagnosis is correct. I see from your tongue and your pulse that you have excessive dampness on the spleen. That results in arthritis.' He pushed a bag towards her. 'I got you these.' She opened it and found dried herbs inside. 'Make them into tea and drink it slowly over two days. I can also do massage. I think you call it acupressure. It's very effective. I'll show you. Lean towards me.'

Sung leaned over the table, the stone monkey swinging away from his chest. His hands found spots on her shoulders and pressed into her skin hard for five seconds or so, then found new places and did the same.

After a minute of this he sat back. 'Now lift your arms.'

She did and, though there was still some pain in her joints, it seemed less than she'd been feeling lately. She said a surprised, 'It worked. Thank you.' She glanced at her watch. 'I should be getting back.'

'Wait,' Sung said, an urgency in his voice. 'I'm not through with my diagnosis. In China doctors look and touch and talk to determine what is ailing a patient. It's vital to know their frame of mind.' He looked carefully into her eyes. 'There's disharmony within you. You want something you can't have. Or you think you can't have it. It's creating these problems.' He nodded at her torn nails.

'What harmony do I want?'

'I'm not sure. Perhaps a family. Love. Maybe that man you work with is the source of the problem,' Sung said quietly, studying her.

'Why do you say that?' she asked uneasily.

'I would say that you are the yang—the side of a mountain with the sun on it. Yang is brightness, beginnings, soft. But you seem to inhabit the world of yin—the shadowy side of the mountain, introspection, hardness, the end of things. The yin and yang should not compete; they should complement each other. I think perhaps the disharmony is that you have let the yin too far into your life.'

'I . . . I'm not sure.'

'I've just been meeting with Lincoln Rhyme's physician.'

'Yes, Doctor?'

'I've got to talk to you about something.'

Her cellphone rang and Sachs jumped at the sound. She reached for the phone and answered, 'Hello?'

'Officer, where the hell are you?' It was Lon Sellitto.

She was reluctant to say but she glanced at the patrol car across the street and had a feeling that they might have told the detective where she was. She said, 'With that witness, John Sung. Just needed to follow up on a few things.' Not a lie. Not exactly.

'Well, finish following up,' the man said gruffly.

What's eating him? she thought. 'I'll be right there.'

She disconnected the line and said to Sung, 'I have to go.'

A hopeful expression on his face, the doctor asked, 'Have you found Sam Chang and the others from the ship?'

'Not yet.'

As she rose he startled her by asking quickly, 'I'd be honoured if you would come back to see me. I could continue my treatment.'

She hesitated only a moment before saying, 'Sure. I'd like that.'

'HOPE WE DIDN'T interrupt anything important, Officer,' Lon Sellitto said gruffly when she walked into Rhyme's living room.

She began to ask the detective what he meant but Rhyme began sniffing the air. He glanced at the bag she carried and wrinkled his nose. 'And what is that? It stinks.'

'Medicine. For my arthritis. You make it into tea.'

'Hope you enjoy it. *I'll* stick to Scotch.' He examined her closely for a moment. 'How's Dr Sung doing?'

'Better,' she answered.

'Talk much about his home in China? Where he travels? Whom he spends time with?'

'What are you getting at?' she asked cautiously.

'I'm just curious if what occurred to *me* occurred to *you*.'

'And that would be?'

'That Sung was the Ghost's *bangshou*. His assistant.'

'What?' she gasped. 'But he *can't* have any connection with the Ghost. I mean—'

'As a matter of fact,' Rhyme interrupted, 'he doesn't. We just got a report from the FBI office in Singapore. The Ghost's *bangshou* on the *Dragon* was Victor Au. The prints and picture match one of the three bodies the Coast Guard found this morning. The one who'd drowned. Sung's clean. But we didn't know that until ten minutes ago. I told you to be careful, Sachs.'

'Sorry,' she muttered.

What *was* distracting her? Rhyme wondered again. But he said only, 'Back to work, boys and girls.' He then nodded at the electrostatic shoe prints from the Tang crime scene that Thom had mounted on the evidence board.

'Now, what about the trace that was in the Ghost's shoes, Mel?'

'OK, Lincoln,' the tech said slowly, looking over the screen of the chromatograph. 'We've got something here. Very old oxidised iron flakes, old wood fibres and ash and silicon—looks like glass dust. And then the main act is a dark, low-lustre mineral in large concentrations—montmorillonite. Alkaline oxide, too.'

OK, Rhyme mused. Where the hell did it come from? He closed his eyes and began, in his mind, to pace.

When he'd been head of the Investigation and Resources Division of the NYPD, the forensic unit, he'd walked everywhere in New York City. He carried small bags and jars in his pockets for the samples of soil, concrete, dust and vegetation he'd collect. A criminalist must know his territory in a thousand different ways: as sociologist, cartographer, geologist, engineer, botanist, zoologist, historian.

Rhyme continued to walk intently through, then fly over, the various neighbourhoods of the city: over the Columbia University tower, Central Park, through the streets of Midtown, the decaying parts of the Bronx . . . Soaring, soaring . . . Until he came to one place.

His eyes opened. 'Downtown,' he said. 'The Ghost's downtown. Battery Park City or one of the developments around there.'

'How'd you figure that out?' Sellitto asked.

'That montmorillonite? It's bentonite, a clay used as slurry to keep ground water out of foundations. When they built the World Trade Center they sank the foundation sixty-five feet down to the bedrock. The builder used millions of tons of bentonite. It's all over the place down there.'

'And it's only twenty minutes from Chinatown,' Deng pointed out.

Thom wrote this on the evidence chart.

Sonny Li was pacing, walking in front of the board. 'Hey, Loaban, I was at crime scene too.'

'Yeah,' Sachs said, giving him an exasperated look. 'Walking around, smoking.'

Rhyme explained, 'Anything that comes into the crime scene after the perpetrator can contaminate it.'

'Hey, Loaban, you think I don't know that? Sure, sure, you pick up dust and dirt and put in gas chromatograph and then spectrometer and use scanning electron microscope.' The complicated English words fell awkwardly from his tongue.

'You know about forensic equipment?' Rhyme asked, surprised.

'Know about it? Sure, we use that stuff. Hey, we not back in Ming

Dynasty, Loaban. I got my own computer—Windows XP.'

'OK, Sonny, got the point. What did you see at the scene?'

'Disharmony. The Ghost torture man who betray him, kill him and leave. But remember, Hongse? Place all destroyed. Posters of China torn up, statues of Buddha broken. Han Chinese not do that. No, probably Ghost left and then those men work for him, they vandal the office. I'm thinking he hire ethnic minority for his *ba-tu*.'

'Muscle. Thugs,' Deng translated.

'Yeah, yeah, thugs.' Li continued, pointing at the board, 'You want evidence? OK, here evidence. Shoe prints. Smaller than Ghost's. Han—Chinese—not big people. Like me. But people from west and north minorities—Mongols, Manchus, Tibetans, Uigurs—lot of them even smaller than us. So find some minorities. You get lead to Ghost.'

Rhyme glanced at Sachs and he could tell she was thinking the same thing. What can it hurt?

Rhyme snapped, 'I want to follow up on it. How?'

'Tongs,' Li said. 'Tongs know everything.'

'Is there anybody we can talk to?' Sachs asked.

Eddie Deng thought for a moment. 'I'd give Tony Cai a call. He helps us some and he's one of the best connected *loabans*. But he won't want to be seen around the police, not with the Ghost in the area.'

A thought occurred to Rhyme. 'Tell him we need his help and that the governor's office is sending a limo to pick him up.'

Deng nodded, turned to the phone and made a call to Cai's association. He hung up. 'OK. He'll do it.'

Sonny Li seemed uneasy. 'Hey, Loaban, I ask you something. Maybe you do me favour? I make phone call? Back to China. Cost some money I not have. But I pay you back.'

'Who are you calling?' Coe asked bluntly.

'Call is to my father.'

'That's all right.' Rhyme nodded at Thom, who got an international operator on the line and placed the call. He handed the receiver to Li.

Rhyme suddenly saw a different Sonny Li. The man was obsequious, slumped, nervous, nodding as he spoke. Finally he hung the phone up and stood looking down at the floor for a moment.

Sachs asked, 'Something wrong?'

He shook his head and turned back to Rhyme. 'OK, Loaban, what we going do now?'

'We're going to look at some harmonious evidence,' Rhyme replied.

HALF AN HOUR LATER the doorbell sounded and Thom vanished into the hall. He returned with a heavyset Chinese man in a grey suit.

'I am Mr Cai.'

Rhyme introduced himself. 'We have a problem, Mr Cai, and I hope you can help us.'

'You work for governor?'

'That's right.' In a sort of way we do, Rhyme thought.

As Cai sat down, Rhyme explained about the *Fuzhou Dragon* and the immigrants hiding in town. He nodded to Deng, who told Cai about the killers and their suspicion that the men were from a Chinese ethnic minority group.

Cai nodded, considering this. Beneath large, wire-rimmed bifocals his eyes were quick. 'The Ghost, we know about him. He does much harm to all of us here. I will help you. I have many connections. If your driver can take me back now I'll make some calls immediately.'

But as Cai walked towards the door Sonny Li said abruptly, '*Ting!*'

'He said, "Wait,"' Eddie Deng explained to Rhyme in a whisper.

Cai turned round, a frown on his face. Li strode up to him and spoke harshly, then the two began an explosive conversation.

The tong leader finally grew quiet. As Li continued to speak, more calmly now, Cai began to nod. The tong leader extended his hand and they shook. Cai then left.

'What on earth was that?' Sachs asked.

'Why you let him leave before?' Li said gruffly to Rhyme. 'He not going to help you.'

'Yes, he was.'

'No. Dangerous for him help us. He know governor not involved.'

'But he *said* he'd help us,' Sellitto said.

'Chinese not like say no,' Li explained. 'Easier for us to find excuse or just say yes and then forget it, I'm saying.'

'What did you say? What were you fighting about?'

'No, no, not fight. We negotiation. You know, business. Now he going to look for your minorities. You pay him money.'

'What?' Sellitto asked.

'Not so much. Only cost you ten thousand. Dollar, not yuan.'

'No way,' Alan Coe said.

'We can't pay—' Sellitto began.

Rhyme laughed. 'It's OK—I'll sign the chit myself.'

'I take break, Loaban? I need good cigarettes. Get some food too.'

'Go ahead, Sonny. You earned it.'

SONNY LI HAD FOUND some very good cigarettes indeed. Camels, without filters on the end, which tasted pretty close to the brand he regularly bought in China. He inhaled deeply and said, 'Bet five.' He pushed the chips forwards and watched the other poker players consider how to respond.

The gambling parlour was on Mott Street, in the heart of Chinatown. The parlour was large, populated mostly with Fujianese, and dark, except for dim lights over the tables. Such a long trip probably wasn't what Loaban had in mind when he gave Li permission to buy some smokes. But no matter. He'd return soon enough.

He won the hand and laughed, then poured *mao-tai*, China's version of moonshine, into the glasses of everyone at the table. He struck up conversations with the men around him.

A bottle of liquor and a dozen Camels later Sonny Li estimated his net loss to be merely seven dollars. He decided against another glass and rose to go. This particular gambling parlour had turned out to have little for him and he wanted to try another.

THE STOLEN CHEVROLET sped down the alleyway that led to the rear of the Changs' apartment in Queens. The Ghost gripped his Model 51 in one hand, the steering wheel in the other. The Turks were poised to leap from the van.

They burst from the alley into a large parking lot.

The Ghost glanced at the Turks, who were looking around with frowns. They were confused, troubled.

'Where it is?' asked Yusuf. 'The Changs' apartment?'

There were no residences anywhere around here.

The Ghost checked the address. The number was correct; this was the place. Except that it was a large retail shopping centre.

The Ghost spat out an obscenity.

'What happened?' one of the Turks in the back asked him.

What had happened was that Chang hadn't trusted Jimmy Mah, the Ghost realised. He'd given the tong leader a fake address. The Ghost glanced up at the big sign over their heads: THE HOME STORE—YOUR SOURCE FOR EVERY HOUSE AND LAWN NEED.

The Ghost considered what to do. The other immigrant, Wu, probably hadn't been so clever. He had used Mah's broker to get an apartment. The Ghost had the name of the broker.

'We'll get the Wus now,' he said. 'Then we'll find the Changs.'

Naixin. All in good time.

SAM CHANG hung up the phone. Numb, he stood for a moment, staring at a TV show, which depicted a family very different from his own. He glanced at Mei-Mei, who was looking at him with a querying glance. He shook his head and she dutifully returned to Po-Yee, the baby. Chang then crouched down beside his father and whispered to him, 'Mah is dead. The *loaban* in Chinatown who helped us.'

'The Ghost? That was who killed him?'

'Who else?'

His father asked, 'Did Mah know where we are?'

'No.' Chang hadn't trusted Mah. So he'd given the address of one of the Home Stores in the flier he'd found. The Changs were, in fact, not in Queens at all but in Brooklyn, a neighbourhood called Owls Head, near the harbour.

Then Chang had a troubling thought. 'The Wus! The Ghost can find them. They got their apartment through Mah's broker. I have to warn Wu.' He stepped towards the door.

'No,' his father said. 'Don't go yourself. Use the phone.'

Chang picked up the phone and spoke again to the woman from Mah's office. He asked her to get a message to Wu.

So many things to do, precautions to take. For a moment Chang was overwhelmed by the hopelessness of it all. But his eyes then fell on his family and the burden lessened somewhat.

William laughed at something on the television. He was laughing in genuine good spirits at the frivolous show. Ronald too. Chang then looked at his wife, completely absorbed in the child, Po-Yee.

In China families pray for a son to carry on the family name. Chang of course had been proud and delighted when William had been born, and Ronald after him. But Mei-Mei's sadness at not having a daughter had been a source of sorrow for him, too. Mei-Mei had been very ill during her pregnancy with Ronald. The doctors urged, for her health, that she not have any more children. She had accepted this stoically.

Out of this terrible plight, though, the gods or the spirit of some ancestor had bestowed Po-Yee on them, the daughter that they could never have, and restored the harmony within his wife.

Yin–yang. Light and dark. Deprivation and gift.

Chang rose and walked to his sons and sat down to watch the television with them. He moved very slowly and quietly, as if any abrupt motion would shatter this fragile familial peace like a rock dropping into a still, morning pond.

Chapter Nine

It was now early evening and Wu Qichen had bathed his wife's forehead for the past hour. His daughter had brewed the herbal tea he'd bought and had fed the hot liquid to the feverish woman. But there seemed to be no improvement. Wu was frightened. For the first time, he began to think about losing her.

He stood up. 'Chin-Mei,' he snapped. 'Come here.'

His daughter appeared in the doorway. 'Yes, Baba?'

'Bring me some of the new clothes for your mother.'

The girl returned a moment later with a pair of blue stretch slacks and a T-shirt. Together they dressed Yong-Ping.

Wu then went to the electronics store next door. He asked the assistant where the closest hospital was. The man wrote down the address in English, as Wu asked. When he returned to the apartment he said to his daughter, 'We'll be back soon. Listen to me carefully. You are not to open the door for anyone. Lock the door after we leave.'

Wu opened the door and held his arm out for his wife to cling to and then stepped outside. Then they started down Canal Street, filled with so many people, so many opportunities, so much money—none of which meant much of anything to the small, frightened man at the moment.

'THERE!' the Ghost said urgently, as he eased the Chevrolet to the kerb on Canal Street. 'It's the Wus.'

Before he and the Turks could find their ski masks and climb out of the vehicle, though, Wu helped his wife into a taxi. He climbed in after her and the cab drove away.

The Ghost parked in a space directly across from the apartment whose address, and front-door key, Mah's real-estate broker had given him half an hour earlier—just before they'd shot him to death.

'Where do you think they've gone?' one of the Turks asked.

'I don't know. She looked sick. Maybe to a doctor.'

The Ghost surveyed the street. He measured distances and noted particularly the large number of jewellery stores here at the intersection of Mulberry and Canal streets. It meant that there would be dozens of armed security guards; if they killed the Wus before the stores closed they might expect one of them to hear the gunshots and come running. Even after hours they'd have to move fast and wear the ski masks.

'Here is how I think we should handle it,' the Ghost said.

AFTER HER FATHER and mother had left, Wu Chin-Mei made some tea for her brother and gave him a tea bun and rice. She sat eight-year-old Lang down in front of the television with his food.

Chin-Mei sat for a few minutes, studying the outfits of the American actresses on a sitcom. Then she heard the click of a key in the latch. Was her father back already?

Just as she got to the door it opened and a small swarthy man pushed inside and pointed a pistol at her.

Chin-Mei screamed and tried to run to Lang but the man leapt forward and grabbed her round the waist. He flung her to the floor. He dragged her sobbing brother to the bathroom, pushed him inside and pulled the door shut.

'Shut your mouth. If you scream again I'll kill you.' The man took a cellphone from his pocket and made a call. 'I'm inside. The children are here.'

Wu Chin-Mei began to cry.

IN LINCOLN RHYME'S town house, grey and gloomy thanks to the storm's early dusk, the case wasn't moving at all.

Sachs sat calmly sipping that disgusting-smelling tea of hers, which irritated the hell out of Rhyme for no particular reason.

Fred Dellray was back, pacing and squeezing his unlit cigarette. 'I wasn't happy then and I ain't happy now. Not. A. Happy. Person.' He was referring to what he'd been told were 'resource allocation issues' within the Bureau, which were delaying their getting more agents on the GHOSTKILL team. Dellray's take was that nobody in the Justice Department thought human smuggling was particularly sexy and therefore worth much time.

They were having no better luck with the evidence from any of the crime scenes.

'I want a drink,' Rhyme said, discouraged. 'It's cocktail hour.'

'Dr Weaver said no alcohol,' Thom pointed out.

'She said *avoid* it, Thom. Avoidance is not abstention.'

'I'm not going to argue Webster's here, Lincoln. No booze.' The aide was adamant.

Rhyme closed his eyes, pushed his head back into the chair angrily. Imagining—a moment of absurd fantasy—that the operation would fix the nerves that operated his entire arm. He told no one this—not even Amelia Sachs—but he often fantasised that the surgery would actually let him lift things. He pictured grabbing the bottle of Macallan. He could almost feel his hands round the cool glass.

He silently sent out a plea to Dr Weaver: *Do something for me. Release me just a little from this terrible confinement.* Then he slammed the door on these personal thoughts, angry with himself.

A clink on the table beside him made him blink. The astringent smoky smell of whisky engulfed him. He opened his eyes. Sachs had placed a small glass of Scotch on the wheelchair armrest.

'It's not very full,' the criminalist muttered to her. But the subtext both Lincoln and she understood, was: thank you.

He enjoyed the liquor but found that it did little to dull the urgency and frustration he felt at the slow pace of the case. His eyes fell on the whiteboard. One entry caught his eye.

'Sachs,' he called. 'I need a phone number. Fast.'

THE GHOST HELD his Model 51 pistol against his cheek. The hot metal gave him reassurance. This was a good-fortune gun, one he'd had for years.

It had been nearly an hour since Kashgari had gone inside to make sure the Wus' children stayed put. The shops had closed along this part of Canal Street—the armed guards were gone, he was sure, and the sidewalks were deserted. Let's get on with it, the Ghost thought.

At the end of the block, he saw two people climb from a cab, keeping their heads down. The Wus. They walked into a drugstore, the husband clutching the wife round the waist, her arm in a cast.

Five minutes later the Wus left the drugstore.

The Ghost said to Hajip, 'You stay with the car. Keep the engine running. He and I'—a nod towards Yusuf—'will follow the Wus inside. I want to bring the daughter with us. We'll keep her for a while.' Yindao would, he knew, forgive this infidelity.

The Wus were now five yards from their doorway.

The Ghost found his cellphone and called Kashgari in the Wus' apartment. 'The Wus are close to the building. Where are the children?'

'The boy's in the bathroom. The girl's with me.'

'As soon as they walk into the alley we'll come in behind them.'

The Ghost and Yusuf pulled their masks over their faces and

climbed out. As Hajip slipped behind the wheel of the Chevrolet, they sprinted across Canal Street, guns at their sides. The Ghost felt the rush of excitement he always did before a kill.

It was at this moment that a loud crack echoed through the street and a bullet slammed into a parked car just behind the Ghost.

'Jesus,' a man's voice called from somewhere. 'Who fired?'

'Hell,' came another voice. 'Cease fire!'

The Ghost's head was swivelling. He gripped Yusuf's arm.

A man's voice cried through a loudspeaker, 'Kwan Ang! Stop. This is the United States Immigration Service!'

The snakehead scrabbled backwards, his gun up, as he looked for a target. 'It's a trap,' he raged to Yusuf. 'Back to the car!'

Chaos now filled Canal Street. Shouting, passers-by and store assistants diving for cover. Up the block, the doors of two white vans opened and men in black uniforms, carrying guns, leapt out.

And what was this? The Wus themselves were drawing weapons! Then the Ghost realised that they weren't the Wus at all. They were decoys. Somehow the police had found the couple and sent these people back in their place to lure him out of cover.

The Ghost fired five or six shots at random, to stoke the panic. As he crouched beside their four-by-four, he heard: 'Who fired? . . . Back-ups aren't in position . . . What happened?'

'Kwan Ang,' came an electronic shout from a loudspeaker, 'this is the FBI. Put down—'

He shut up the agent by firing twice more in his direction. Hajip got out of the car. The three men ducked. They heard ring after ring as bullets struck the front of the vehicle.

For a moment there was a lull. The Ghost looked behind him. 'This way!' The three men ran to the back alleyway of the fish market behind them, where they found an old man standing beside a delivery truck. Seeing the guns and the masks, the man dropped to his knees and lifted his arms.

'Inside,' the Ghost shouted to the Turks. They leapt into the truck. The snakehead looked behind them and could see several officers cautiously approaching the fish store. He turned and fired several shots in their direction. They scattered for cover.

FIVE MINUTES LATER Amelia Sachs arrived at the scene. She ran towards the Wus' apartment, her pistol in her hand. She found Fred Dellray crouching over an officer who'd been shot in the arm.

'What the hell happened?'

Dellray was furious. 'We were an inch away from him. *A half*-inch. He stole a delivery van from that fish market 'cross the street. We got everyone in town with a badge looking for it.'

Sachs closed her eyes in dismay. All Rhyme's brilliant deductions—and the superhuman efforts to put together a takedown team in time—had been wasted.

Rhyme, frustrated by the lack of leads, had called the lab at the Medical Examiner's office. The lab had found several things in the injured immigrant's blood: the presence of bone marrow, indicating a severe bone fracture; sepsis, suggesting a deep cut or abrasion; and the presence of a bacteria responsible for Q fever, a zoonotic disease—one transmitted from animals to people. The bacteria were often picked up in places where animals were kept for long periods, like pens at seaports and the holds of ships. Which meant that the immigrant was one very sick woman.

Rhyme had had Sellitto and Deng put together a team of canvassers from Police Plaza downtown and the Fifth Precinct. They began calling all the hospitals to see if any female Chinese patients had been admitted with Q fever and a badly broken, infected arm.

After only ten minutes they'd received a call from one of the officers manning the phones downtown. It turned out that a Chinese man had just brought his wife into the emergency room of a clinic in Chinatown; she fitted the profile perfectly: advanced Q fever, multiple fractures. She'd been admitted. Her name was Wu Yong-Ping.

Officers from the Fifth Precinct had sped to the hospital—along with Sachs and Deng—to interview the couple. The Wus had told the police where they were living and that their children were in the apartment. Then Rhyme had got the AFIS results from the Mah killing: some of the prints matched those found at prior GHOSTKILL scenes; the snakehead *had* committed the crime. When Wu explained that Mah's broker had got them the apartment, Rhyme realised that the Ghost knew where the Wus were staying and was probably on his way to kill them.

But because of one premature gunshot, the whole effort was wasted.

Dellray snapped to another agent, 'Anything more on the fish-store van? How come nobody's seen it? Somethin'. Ain't. Right.'

The agent glanced back at the fish store and his gaze settled on an old man, whose eyes dropped immediately to a dozen grey-pink flounders resting on a bed of ice.

'He told you the Ghost stole the van, right? Well, he was lying.'

Dellray and Sachs ran to the shop and into the alleyway behind it. Hidden behind a large Dumpster, they found the van.

Returning to the front of the store Dellray said to the old man, 'Tell me what happened.'

'He going kill me,' the man said, sobbing. 'Make me say they stole van. Had gun at my head. Don't know where go.'

A moment later an officer called in, saying that there'd been a report of a carjacking. Three armed men in ski masks had run up to a Lexus at a stop light, ordered the couple out and sped off.

'Who was it?' Sachs asked Dellray. 'Who fired the shot that spooked him?'

'Dunno yet. I'm gonna look this one over with a magnifyin' glass.' But he didn't need to look too far. Two uniformed officers walked up to Dellray and conferred with him. The FBI agent's face compressed into a frown. He looked up and strode over to the guilty party. It was Alan Coe.

'What in the living hell happened?' Dellray barked.

Defensive but defiant, the red-haired agent replied, 'I *had* to fire. The Ghost was going to shoot the decoys, didn't you see?'

'No, I did not. His weapon was at his side.'

'I'm getting sick of you lecturing me, Dellray. It was a judgment call. If you had everybody in position we still could've collared him.'

'We set it up to take him down on the sidewalk, without innocents around, not in the middle of a crowded street.' Dellray shook his head. 'Thirty li'l tiny seconds and he woulda been tied up like a Christmas package.' Then he nodded at the big Glock on Coe's hip. 'An' even if he *was* moving on somebody, how the hell couldja miss with a piece like that from fifty feet?'

Coe's defiance slipped and he said contritely, 'I thought it was the right thing to do under the circumstances.'

Dellray plucked the unsmoked cigarette from behind his ear. 'This's gone way far enough. From now on INS is advisory only.'

'You can't do that,' Coe said, an ominous look in his eyes.

''Cording to the Executive Order I can, son. I'm going downtown and doing what I gotta to put that in place.' He stormed off.

Sachs watched Dellray climb into his car, slam the door and speed off. She turned back to Coe. 'Did anybody get the children?'

'The Wus' kids? I don't know,' Coe said dismissively. He turned and walked back to his car without another word.

Sachs then called Rhyme and gave him the bad news.

'One of our people fired before we were in position. The street wasn't sealed and the Ghost shot his way out . . . Rhyme, it was Alan Coe who fired the shot. Dellray's bumping the INS down a notch.'

'Oh, no.' Then he asked, 'Casualties?'

'Nothing serious.' She noticed Eddie Deng. 'I've got to get the Wus' children, Rhyme. I'll call you back after I run the scene.'

She disconnected the call and said to Deng, 'Need some translation help, Eddie. With the Wus' kids.'

'Sure,' Deng said. He walked ahead of Sachs, down the few steps that led to the basement apartments. Garbage littered the alleyway. 'What's the number?' he asked.

It was then that Sachs noticed a key in the front-door lock of the Wus' apartment.

Deng reached for the knob.

'No,' Sachs cried, unholstering her weapon. 'Wait!'

But it was too late. Deng was pushing the door open. He leapt back—away from the slight, dark man holding a sobbing teenage girl in front of him, a pistol pressed against her neck.

The man started forward very slowly, motioning them back, muttering in his unintelligible language.

Neither Sachs nor the young detective moved.

Sachs spoke in a cooing voice and very slowly: 'Put the gun down.'

The man didn't respond. Sachs and Deng backed away. The assailant and the terrified girl stepped outside the door.

'You,' the man barked to Sachs in crude English, 'on ground.'

'No,' Sachs said, 'we're not lying down. I'm asking you to put your gun down. You can't get away. Hundreds of police.'

The man glanced behind him, up the dark alley. He shoved the gun harder against the girl's neck. She screamed.

Then Deng reached for his sidearm.

'Eddie, don't!' Sachs cried.

The assailant thrust his gun forward, firing into Deng's chest. The detective grunted violently and fell back, knocking Sachs to the ground. Deng rolled onto his belly, retching—or coughing blood; she couldn't tell. The round might have pierced the body armour. Stunned, Sachs struggled to her knees. The gunman aimed at her before she could raise her weapon. But he hesitated. There was some distraction behind him. In the darkness of the alleyway Sachs could make out a man speeding forward, a small figure, holding something in his hand.

The perp released the girl and spun round, lifting the gun, but, before he could shoot, the figure clocked the man in the side of the head with what he was carrying—a brick.

'Hongse!' Sonny Li called to Sachs. He pushed the girl to the ground and turned to the stunned assailant, who clutched his bleeding head. But suddenly he lifted his pistol towards Li, who stumbled back against the wall.

Three fast shots from Sachs's gun dropped the attacker like a doll onto the cobblestones and he lay motionless.

'Judges of hell,' Sonny Li muttered. He stepped forward, checked the man's pulse and lifted the gun out of his lifeless hand. Then Li turned back to the girl, helping her up. Sobbing, she ran down the alley, into the arms of a Chinese officer from the Fifth Precinct.

Medics ran to Deng to check him out, but his body armour had indeed stopped the slug. 'I'm sorry,' he gasped to Sachs. 'I just reacted.'

'Your first firefight?'

Deng nodded.

She smiled. 'Welcome to the club.' A medic helped him up.

Sachs and two ESU officers cleared the apartment and found a young, panicked boy, about eight, in the bathroom. With the help of a Chinese–American cop, the medics checked the siblings out and found that neither of them had been hurt or molested by the Ghost's partner.

Nearby, Li patted his pockets and finally located his cigarettes.

PUTTING ON HER Tyvek suit to search the crime scenes, Amelia Sachs glanced up to see Li walking towards her. 'How d'you figure out the Wus were there?' she asked.

Li finished one cigarette and lit another. 'Way I work in China. I go places, talk to people. Tonight I go three gambling halls. Lose some money, win some money, drink. And talk and talk. Finally meet guy at poker table. He tell me about man come in earlier, nobody know him. Complain to everybody 'cause wife sick. Then he say he on *Dragon* this morning and rescue everybody when it sink. Had to be Wu. Liver–spleen disharmony, I'm saying. He say he live close to gambling parlour. I look around, ask people, and find out family—just like Wus—move in today. I look through back window and see guy with gun. Hey, you look in back window first, Hongse?'

'No, I didn't.'

'Maybe you should done that. That good rule.'

'I should have, Sonny.'

Li smiled. 'Hongse, how *you* find Wus?'

Sachs told him how they'd found the Wus through the wife's injury. Li nodded, impressed with Rhyme's deductions. Sachs then explained about Coe's premature gunshot and the snakehead's escape.

'I not like that man Coe. When he over in China at meeting we not trust him much. Not like us. Talk like we children, want to do case against Ghost by himself. Talk bad about immigrants.'

Sachs got Li to promise he'd stay out of the crime scene, then processed the dead gunman's body, walked the grid inside the apartment and finally searched the Ghost's bullet-riddled SUV.

Then she and Li drove back to the clinic, where she found the Wu family reunited in a room guarded by two cops and a woman INS agent. Wu gave them some information about the Changs.

Sachs said to the INS agent, 'Do you have a problem putting them in one of our safe houses?' The NYPD had several high-security town houses in the city, used for witness protection. The Ghost would be expecting the Wus to go to an Immigration facility and, with his *guanxi*, might pay someone in the detention centre to try to kill the family again.'

'Fine with us.'

The town house in Murray Hill was free, Sachs knew. She gave the agent the address.

THE MANHATTAN Federal Plaza building and the garage beneath it, closed to all but the most senior government officials, were virtually impregnable; but the parking garage annexe in an underground structure across the street, constructed for other employees, was far less so. There was still security in the annexe, of course, but since the garage sat beneath a small park, even the worst bomb damage would be limited.

That night, at 9.00pm, the security was not at its best because the guard on duty was watching a car fire on Broadway. So he didn't notice the slight man dressed in a suit and carrying an attaché case hurry down the ramp into the half-deserted garage.

The man had memorised the licence-plate number of the car he sought and it took him only five minutes to find it. After a fast glance around the garage he pulled on cloth gloves, quickly drove a wedge between the window and the side of the door, slipped a slim-jim tool inside the space and popped the lock.

He opened his attaché case and took out a heavy-duty paper bag containing a cluster of foot-long yellow sticks. Wires ran from a detonator in one of the sticks to a battery box and from there to a pressure switch. He placed the bag under the driver's seat, unwound a length of wire and slipped the pressure switch between the springs of the seat. Anyone weighing more than ninety pounds would complete the circuit and set off the detonator simply by sitting down.

The man flicked the power switch on the battery box from OFF to ON, locked the car door, closed it as quietly as he could and left the garage, walking matter-of-factly past the still-oblivious security guard.

Chapter Ten

They sat in silence, watching the small television set, William translating those words that his parents didn't understand.

The special news report didn't give the names of the people who'd nearly been killed on Canal Street but there was no doubt that it was Wu Qichen and his family; the story said they'd been passengers on the *Fuzhou Dragon* that morning. One of the Ghost's confederates had been killed but the snakehead himself had escaped.

The story ended and commercials came on the television screen. William rose and walked into the bedroom. Ronald flipped through channels on the television.

Mei-Mei finished stitching together a small stuffed animal for Po-Yee—a cat. The woman made the toy pounce onto the arm of her chair and the girl took it in both hands, studying it with happy eyes.

Chang heard a moan on the couch, where his father rested. He rose immediately, found the man's medicine and gave him a tablet of morphine. He held the cup of cold tea so that the man could take the pill. A doctor in China had diagnosed cancer, but Chang's dissident status had kept his father waiting at the bottom of the list in the hospitals' huge queues for treatment. Chang had been able to find a 'barefoot doctor' in the countryside, one of those individuals proclaimed by the government to be paramedics. The man had prescribed morphine to ease the Chang Jiechi's pain but there was little else he could do. The bottle of the drug was large but it wouldn't last more than a month and his father was quickly worsening.

As he gazed at his father the old man suddenly opened his eyes. 'The Ghost is angry now that they've killed one of his own people.

And that he's failed to kill the Wus. He'll come after us.'

This was his father's way. To sit and absorb then give his assessments, which were invariably right. And he was right now, Sam Chang thought in despair.

Outside, a screech of brakes. Chang, his wife and father all froze.

'Shut the lights out. Quickly,' Chang ordered. Mei-Mei scurried through the apartment, dowsing them. Chang walked to the closet and pulled William's pistol out. He looked out through the curtained front window. 'It's all right,' he said. 'A delivery across the street.'

But then he looked through the dim apartment, detecting the vague forms of his father, his wife, the infant. His smile of relief faded and he was consumed with intense regret for what his decisions had done to these people he loved so much. So this is to be the life I've brought to my family: nothing but darkness and fear.

SITTING ON A BENCH in Battery Park City, the Ghost was watching the lights of the ships on the Hudson River. There was a break in the rain but the wind was still rowdy, pushing low purple clouds quickly overhead, their bellies lit by the vast spectrum of city lights.

How had the police found the Wus? the Ghost wondered. Probably through the broker he'd killed and through Mah; the investigators hadn't believed that the Mafia had killed the tong leader.

The Ghost had yet more proof that his adversaries were relentless and talented. There was something very different about the people who were after him this time. And who was this Lincoln Rhyme that his intelligence source had told him about?

Well, he believed he was safe now. He'd worn the mask at the Wus, no one had followed them from the shooting and Kashgari had had no identification on him to link him to either the Ghost or the community centre in Queens. Tomorrow, he would find the Changs.

The Ghost pulled out his phone and called Yindao. They arranged to meet later. He wouldn't have much time tonight to see her—he was exhausted from this endless day. But how badly he wanted to be close to her, touching her, eradicating the shock and anger of the near-disaster from earlier on Canal Street.

AT 9.30PM Fred Dellray stood in the FBI's Manhattan office and stretched. Time to call it a night.

He flipped through the report about the shoot-out on Canal Street. It was mostly finished but he knew he'd have to revise it tomorrow. He glanced at the pages, all the while wondering why, exactly, he was working on GHOSTKILL.

Frederick Dellray, with degrees in criminology, psychology and philosophy, was to undercover work what Rhyme was to criminalistics. Dellray's talent, however, had proved his undoing. Little by little his reputation had spread within the underworld. It became too dangerous to put him into the field. He was promoted and put in charge of running undercover agents in New York.

Being assigned to GHOSTKILL had confused Dellray at first; he'd never run any human smuggling cases before. He found himself dealing with a type of crime he had little experience with. But after his efforts tonight at the office he felt much better. Tomorrow he'd bully and connive his way into getting the teams the case needed.

Dellray called his own number, his apartment in Brooklyn.

'Hello,' a woman's voice answered.

'I'll be home in thirty,' he told Serena softly.

Walking through the halls of the Bureau's headquarters, he nodded at two agents in shirtsleeves. They waved good night. Then down in the elevator and out of the front door. He crossed the street, heading for the federal parking annexe.

He found his government-issue Ford and unlocked the door, opened it and tossed in his battered briefcase.

As Dellray started to climb inside the Ford he noticed the window weather stripping on the driver's side of the car was unsealed. He glanced down and saw the wires protruding from under his seat. He lunged for the top of the door with his right hand to keep from putting all his weight on the seat and compressing what he knew was the bomb's pressure switch.

But it was too late.

'THE CHANGS are somewhere in Queens,' Sachs said, writing this bit of information on the whiteboard. 'Driving a blue van.'

'Do we have anything specific about it?' Rhyme muttered.

'Wu couldn't remember.'

Sonny Li sat nearby, rummaging through a large shopping bag he'd brought back from Chinatown a short while earlier. Lon Sellitto was on his phone, scowling.

Sachs, Mel Cooper and the criminalist then turned to the trace evidence she'd found in the Ghost's stolen Chevrolet: a few small greyish carpet fibres under the brake and accelerator pedals that didn't match the Chevy's carpet or carpet in any of the prior scenes.

'Burn 'em and let's check the data base.'

Cooper ran two of the fibres through the gas chromatograph. As they waited for the results there was a knock on the door.

It was Harold Peabody, his face grim. Behind him another man appeared. Rhyme recognised him as the assistant special agent in charge—the ASAC—of the Manhattan office of the FBI. He too was grim-faced. Then a third man appeared. His crisp navy-blue suit and white shirt suggested to Rhyme that he was Bureau as well, but he identified himself tersely as Webley from State.

So, the State Department was now involved, Rhyme thought. That was a good sign. Dellray must have indeed used his *guanxi* in high places to get them reinforcements.

'Sorry to intrude, Lincoln,' Peabody said.

The ASAC: 'We need to talk to you. Something happened downtown tonight. We don't think it's related, but it's going to have some implications, I'm afraid.'

'What?' Get on with it, Rhyme thought impatiently.

'Someone planted a bomb in the garage across from the Federal Building. It was in Fred Dellray's car.'

'No!' Sachs cried.

'A bomb?' Sellitto blurted, snapping closed his cellphone.

'He's OK,' the ASAC said quickly. 'The main charge didn't go off. Only the detonator fired.'

'Why don't you think it's related?' Rhyme asked.

'Anonymous 911 call about twenty minutes before the blast. Male voice, Russian accent, said the Cherenko family was planning some retaliation for the bust last week.'

Dellray, Rhyme recalled, had just finished running a huge covert operation in Brooklyn, the home of the Russian mob. Dismayed, he suddenly understood the 'implications' the ASAC had been referring to. 'And Fred wants off the Ghost case, right?'

The ASAC nodded. 'The thing with his partner, you know. He's already cleared the decks.'

The partner killed in the Oklahoma City bombing, Rhyme remembered. He could hardly blame the agent. But he said, 'We'll need some help. Fred was getting a SPEC-TAC team together, and some more agents.'

The ASAC said reassuringly, 'We'll have a new field ops agent for you in the morning and some more news about SPEC-TAC.'

Peabody said, 'I heard what happened with Alan Coe—at the Wus' apartment, I mean. I'm sorry.'

'We would've catch the Ghost,' Li said, 'if Coe not fire shot.'

'I know. Look, he's a good man. He's just impulsive. I try to cut him some slack. Had a tough time after an informant of his disappeared. I guess he blamed himself. After his suspension he took a leave of absence. He won't talk about it but I heard he went overseas to find out what happened to her. Finally came back to work and's been going like a greyhound ever since. One of my best agents.'

Peabody, the ASAC and Webley from State left.

'OK, back to work,' the criminalist said to Sellitto, Sachs, Cooper and Li. Eddie Deng was home, nursing his badly bruised chest. 'What else did the Wus tell you, Sachs?'

She gave them the details she'd learned in the clinic. The Wus included Qichen, his wife, Yong-Ping, a teenage daughter, Chin-Mei, and a young son, Lang. The Changs were Sam, Mei-Mei, William and Ronald as well as Chang's father, Chang Jiechi. Then she said that the family also had a baby with them, whose mother had drowned on the *Dragon*. 'Po-Yee. It means "Treasured Child".'

Rhyme noticed a certain look in Sachs's eyes. He knew how much Sachs wanted a child—and wanted a child with him. He secretly liked the idea, though part of his motive wasn't paternal. Amelia Sachs was one of the best crime scene searchers he'd ever seen. Most important was her empathy. She had the ability to transport herself into the mind of the perpetrator and, in that persona, find evidence that most other officers would have missed. What drove her to perfection at crime scenes drove her into danger. A champion pistol shot, an expert driver, she was often first on the scene at takedowns, ready to pull her weapon and engage a perp. Rhyme would never ask her to give that work up. But with a child at home he hoped she'd restrict herself to the crime scene work where her true talent as a cop lay.

Mel Cooper interrupted his thoughts. 'Chromatograph results from the carpet.' He'd matched them to the FBI's carpet-fibre data base, and the results appeared on the screen. 'It's Lustre-Rite brand and the manufacturer's Arnold Textile and Carpeting in Wallingham, Massachusetts. I've got phone numbers.'

'Get somebody calling them,' Rhyme said. 'We want to know about installations in Lower Manhattan.'

'I'll do it,' Sellitto said. 'Only don't hope for miracles.' He nodded at the clock. It was nearly 11.00pm.

Rhyme said, 'There's probably a night shift. And a night shift means a foreman, and a foreman'll have the boss's number at home.'

Cooper was testing the trace Sachs had found in the Chevrolet. 'What do you think, Lincoln? Is this mulch?' He looked up from the microscope.

'Command, input, microscope,' Rhyme ordered. The image that Cooper was looking at came up on Rhyme's computer screen. The criminalist recognised traces of fresh cedar mulch.

'Lot of landscaping around Battery Park City,' Sellitto pointed out, referring to the large residential development in downtown Manhattan, where the trace evidence they'd found earlier had suggested the Ghost might maintain his safe house.

'Long shot, but it's something.' Then Rhyme asked, 'How about the body?'

'Not much,' Sachs said. She explained that the man had had no identification on him.

Sonny Li pointed to a Polaroid of the face of the corpse. 'Hey, Loaban, his face—check it out. He's Kazakh, Kirgiz, Tajik, Uigur. A minority, like I telling you, remember?'

'I remember, Sonny,' Rhyme said to him. 'Call our friend from the tong—Cai. Tell him that we think the gang is of those minorities. Might help him narrow things down.' Then he asked, 'Ballistics?'

'The Ghost was still using his Model 51,' Sachs said. 'I found some nine-millimetre casings too.' She held the evidence bag up. 'But no distinctive ejection marks. Probably a new Beretta.'

'And the dead guy's weapon?'

'I processed it,' she explained. 'His prints only. It was an old Walther PPK.'

'Where is it?'

A look passed between Sachs and Sonny Li—a look decidedly not for Lon Sellitto. She said, 'I think the feds have it.'

Rhyme knew immediately that Sachs had slipped the Chinese cop the weapon. Well, good for him, the criminalist thought. If not for the Chinese detective, then Deng, Sachs or the Wus' daughter might've been killed tonight. Let him have some protection.

Sellitto called, 'Just got through to a senior VP at Arnold Textile. That particular carpeting is for commercial sale only and it's the top of their line. He gave me a list of twenty-six distributors in the area.'

Rhyme glanced at Sellitto and said, 'Get somebody on it.'

Sellitto made a call to some detectives and faxed the list to them.

Then Rhyme's private line rang and he answered it.

'Lincoln?' a woman's voice asked through the speaker-phone.

He was thrilled to hear his neurosurgeon's voice. 'Dr Weaver.'

'I know it's late. Am I interrupting anything? You busy?'

'Not a thing,' Rhyme said.

'I've got the details for the surgery. Manhattan Hospital. Week from Friday at ten a.m. Neurosurgery pre-op. Second floor.'

'Excellent,' he replied.

Thom jotted the information down and Rhyme and the doctor said good night.

Sachs said nothing. Rhyme knew that she would prefer him not to have the operation. Most of the successes with the technique had occurred with patients whose injuries were less severe than Rhyme's. The surgery would probably produce no discernible benefit and was risky—it might even make him worse. But Sachs understood how important it was to him and was going to support him.

'So,' she finally said, a stoic smile on her face, 'we'll make sure we nail the Ghost before next Friday.'

Rhyme noticed that Thom had been studying him closely.

The aide took Rhyme's blood pressure. 'Too high. And you don't look good.'

'Well, thank you very much,' he snapped.

'It's quitting time,' the aide said firmly.

Sellitto and Cooper also voted to call it a night.

Rhyme did feel oddly tired. He supposed he should be concerned about it but he believed it was nothing more than the demands of the case, which had been consuming him for days.

'Sonny,' Rhyme said. 'You'll stay here tonight.'

'Not got other place to go, Loaban. Sure.'

'Thom'll make up a room. I'll be upstairs, taking care of a few things. Come up and visit if you feel like it.'

Rhyme wheeled into the elevator that ran between the ground and first floors. Sachs joined him and closed the door. Rhyme glanced at her face. It was thoughtful but in a way that didn't have to do with the case, he sensed. 'Anything you want to talk about, Sachs?'

Without answering, she pressed the UP button.

IN CHINESE many words are combinations of their opposites. For instance, advance-retreat means 'to move'. And the word for 'doing business' literally translates as 'buy-sell'.

This was what the four men sitting in the smoky storefront office of the East Broadway Workers' Association were now engaged in, late on this stormy August night: buying and selling. That the object of the negotiations was human life—selling the Ghost the location of Sam Chang's family—didn't appear to give these men any qualms.

At nearly midnight, the three leaders of the workers' association sat on one side of the table, across from a man who could be very valuable—since he knew where the Changs were hiding.

There were, of course, many legitimate tongs in Chinatown and they provided many important services for their members. But this particular tong had one speciality: to serve as a base of snakehead operations in New York.

'How do you know these people?' the director of the association asked the man, who'd given only his family name, Tan.

'Chang is a friend of my brother in China. I got them an apartment and Chang and his boy a job.'

'Where is the apartment?' the director of the tong asked casually.

Tan, gesturing abruptly, said, 'That's what I'm here to sell. If the Ghost wants it he has to pay for it. I deal only with the Ghost.'

'It's dangerous,' the director said to Tan. 'What will you pay us to put you in touch with the Ghost?'

'Ten per cent of whatever he pays me.'

The director waved an arm. 'Half.'

The battle lines being drawn, they got down to business. Finally, they agreed on thirty per cent, provided it was US dollars.

The director pulled out a cellphone and placed a call. The Ghost came on the line and the director identified himself. 'I have someone here who rented an apartment to some of the survivors of the *Dragon*, the Changs.'

The Ghost was silent for a moment, then said, 'Tell him to prove it.'

The director relayed this request to Tan, who replied, 'The father's Western name is Sam. There is an old man too, Chang's father. And two boys. Oh, a wife. Mei-Mei. And they have a baby. She isn't theirs. She was on the ship. Her mother drowned.'

The Ghost considered. 'Tell him I'll pay one hundred thousand one-colour for the information.'

The director asked Tan if this was acceptable. He said immediately that it was.

'Send him to see me tomorrow morning at eight thirty. You know where.' The Ghost hung up.

HIS HANDS SHAKING, his breath fast, Sam Chang left the storefront of the East Broadway Workers' Association. He laughed to himself. What an appalling idea—he was actually bargaining with these men over the price of his family's life.

Sitting in their apartment several hours earlier, Chang had been thinking: So this is to be our life . . . darkness and fear.

His father's keen eyes had narrowed. 'What are you thinking of doing?' he'd asked his son.

'The Ghost is looking for us. He won't expect *me* to be looking for *him*.'

'And what would you do if you found him?'

He said to the old man, 'Kill him.'

To his surprise, his father asked only, 'You would be able to do that?'

'Yes, for my family.' Chang then pulled his windcheater on. 'I'll see what I can do to find him.'

Chang reflected that he would probably die. He'd shoot the Ghost immediately—as soon as he opened the door. But the man would have associates, who would in turn kill him. His thoughts strayed to William, his first-born son, the guardian of the Chang name. In his mind, the father now heard his son's insolence, saw the contempt in his eyes. Oh, William, he thought. Yes, I neglected you. But I did so in the hopes of making a better homeland for you. And I brought you here to give you what I couldn't back home. Love shows itself in discipline, example and sacrifice—even giving up one's own life.

AMELIA SACHS WAS DRIVING downtown, uncharacteristically close to the posted speed limit. She heard the doctor from several weeks ago.

'I've just been meeting with Lincoln Rhyme's physician.'

'Yes, Doctor?'

'I've got to talk to you about something.'

'You're looking like it's bad news.'

'Why don't we sit down over there in the corner?'

'Here's fine. Tell me. Let me have it straight.'

Her whole world in turmoil, everything she'd planned for the future altered completely. What could she do about it?

Well, she reflected, pulling to a stop, here's one thing . . .

Amelia Sachs sat for a long moment. This is crazy, she thought. But then, impulsively, she climbed out of the Camaro and, head down, walked quickly round the corner and into an apartment building. She climbed the stairs. And knocked on the door.

When it opened she smiled at John Sung. He smiled back and nodded her inside.

Suddenly she felt a huge weight lifted off her shoulders.

MIDNIGHT. Sonny Li walked into Lincoln Rhyme's bedroom, carrying a shopping bag. 'When I down in Chinatown with Hongse, Loaban, I buy some things. Got present for you.'

'Present?' Rhyme asked from his new Hill-Rom Flexicair bed.

'Look what I got here.' In his hands was a jade figurine of a man with a bow and arrow, looking fierce. Li looked around the room and put the figurine on top of a table against the wall. Then he returned to the bag and took out some sticks of incense.

'You're not going to burn that in here.'

'Have to, Loaban. Not kill you.'

He set the incense into a holder and lit it. He found a paper cup in the bathroom and filled it with Macallan Scotch.

'What are you doing, making a temple?'

'Shrine, Loaban. Not a temple. This is Guan Di—god of war. We make sacrifice to him.' Li bowed towards the icon and whispered some words in Chinese. He sat in the rattan chair by Rhyme's bed, filled a paper cup for himself and then filled one of Rhyme's tumblers and fitted a straw inside. Li nodded towards the impromptu sacristy. 'Guan Di is the god of detectives too, I'm saying.'

'You're making that up.'

'No, we got gods for everything.' The Chinese cop continued, 'That surgery you talk about. That make you better?'

'It might. A little. I could regain a little movement.'

'How it work?'

He explained to Li about Dr Cheryl Weaver, whose neurology unit was performing experimental surgery on spinal cord injury patients. He could still remember almost verbatim the doctor's explanation of how the technique worked.

The nervous system is made up of axons, which carry nerve impulses. In a spinal cord injury those axons are cut or crushed and they die. So they stop carrying impulses and the message doesn't get from the brain to the rest of the body. In the peripheral nervous system—like our arms or legs—damaged axons can grow back. But in the central nervous system—the brain and the spinal cord—they don't. But we're learning to do things that can stimulate regrowth.

Our approach is an all-out assault on the site of the injury. We use traditional decompression surgery to reconstruct the bony structure of the vertebrae themselves and to protect the site where your injury occurred. Then we graft into the site of the injury some of the patient's own peripheral nervous system tissue and some embryonic central nervous system cells.

'From a shark,' Rhyme added to Sonny Li.

The cop laughed. 'Fish?'

'Exactly. Sharks are more compatible with humans than other animals are. Then,' the criminalist continued, 'I'll take drugs to help the spinal cord regenerate.'

'Hey, Loaban,' Li said, 'this operation, it dangerous?'

Again, Rhyme heard Dr Weaver's voice.

Of course there are risks. Any C4 quad is going to have lung impairment. With the anaesthetic there's a chance of respiratory failure. Then the stress of the procedure could lead to blood pressure elevation which in turn could lead to a stroke or a cerebral event. There's a risk of surgical trauma to the site of your initial injury.

'Yes, it's dangerous,' Rhyme told him.

'Sound to me like "*yi luan tou shi*". Words translate: "throwing eggs against rocks". Means doing something bound to fail. So why you do this operation?'

It seemed obvious to Rhyme. To move a step closer to independence. To scratch his head. To be closer to Amelia Sachs. To be a better father to the child that Sachs wanted so badly.

He said, 'It's just something I have to do, Sonny.'

Li shook his head. 'No, no. You should not do this. Embrace who you are! Embrace your limitations.'

'But why? When I don't have to?'

'Doctors in China, they not use all this science you have here in *Meiguo*. They put us back in harmony.'

'You think I'm in harmony like this?' Rhyme asked.

'Fate make you this way, Loaban. And make you this way for a purpose. Maybe you best detective you can be because of what happen. Your life balanced now, I'm saying.'

Rhyme had to laugh. 'I can't walk, I can't pick up evidence . . . How the hell is that better?'

'Maybe your brain, it work better now. Maybe you have stronger will. Your *jizhong*, your focus, maybe is better.'

'I want to walk again,' Rhyme whispered adamantly, wondering why he was baring his soul to this strange little man. 'That's not too much to ask.'

'But maybe *is* too much ask,' Li responded. 'Listen, Loaban, look at me. I could wish to be tall and look like Chow Yun-Fat, have all girls chase me. Could wish to be Hong Kong banker. But not my nature. My nature is being good cop. Maybe you start walking again, you lose something more important.'

Li downed the glass and poured another. 'Listen, Loaban, you know the *Tao*? English name is *Way of Life*. In it, Lao-tzu, he say what is best is for each person follow the way of life on his own. Find harmony and nature. *Tao* all about you, Loaban.'

'About me?' Rhyme asked.

'In *Tao*, Lao-tzu say, "There no need to leave house for better seeing. No need to peer from window. Instead, live in the centre of your being. The way to do is to be." '

The men fell silent for a minute. Finally the conversation resumed and Li talked at length about life in China.

'What kind of crime is there in your home town?' Rhyme asked.

'In Liu Guoyan? Lots bribes, protection money. Other crime too. Kidnapping women big problem in China—have more men than women. For every hundred women, we got hundred twenty men. So lots kidnappers take girls and women, sell them for brides. I find six last year. Record in our office. Good feeling to arrest kidnapper.'

Rhyme said, 'That's what it's all about.'

They drank in silence for a moment, Rhyme thinking that he was feeling content. Most of the people who came to visit treated him like a freak. They meant no unkindness. But either they struggled to ignore his 'condition', as most of them referred to it. Or they celebrated his disability, making jokes and comments about it to show how closely they connected with him. These people never got below the appearance of a relationship. But in Sonny Li's face Rhyme could see complete indifference to Rhyme's state.

He realised then that nearly all the people he'd met over the past few years, with the exception of Amelia Sachs, had been merely acquaintances. He'd known the man for less than a day but Sonny Li already seemed more than that.

'You mentioned your father,' Rhyme said. 'When you called him before, it didn't sound like a good conversation. What's his story?'

'Ah, my father . . .' He drank some more Scotch. 'My father . . . He not like me much. I not live up to what he wants.'

'Why not?'

'Ah, lots things. Give you our history in acorn.'

'Nutshell.'

'My father, he fought with Mao. October 1949, he standing with Chairman Mao at the Gate of Heavenly Peace in Beijing. Oh, Loaban, I hear that story a million times. Big patriotic time. So my father, he got *guanxi*. Connections high up. He become big guy in Communist Party. Want me to be too. But I see what communists do in 1966—destroy everything, hurt people, kill people. Government and party not doing right things. I not care about party. What I like is police work. I like catch criminals . . .' His face grew dark. 'Other bad thing is I not have son—no children—when I married.'

'You're divorced?' Rhyme asked.

'My wife, she die. Some fever, bad thing. Only married few years but no children. My father say it my fault. We try, just not have child.' He rose and paced to the window, stared at the lights. 'Never what I did was good enough for him. I good student. Got medals in army. Marry nice, respectful girl, become detective. Come visit my father every week, give him money, pay respect at mother's grave. But never anything I do is enough.'

'Maybe your father thinks more of you than he's letting on.'

'No, he just not like me. Nobody to carry on family name—that very bad thing.' Li looked out of the window again. 'Maybe I stay here. I speak English good. I be cop here.' He laughed and said what they were both thinking. 'No, no, too late for that. No, we get Ghost, I go home and keep being good detective. Solve big crime and get my picture in paper in Fuzhou. Maybe my father watch news and see and he think I not be such bad son.' He turned back to Rhyme. 'OK, I drunk enough now—you and me, we play game, Loaban.'

'I can't play most games, Sonny. Can't exactly hold the cards, you know.'

'Ah, card games?' Li said, sneering. 'Only good for make money. Best games are games where you keep secrets in head. *Wei-chi*? You ever hear it? Also called *go*.'

Rhyme believed he had. 'Like checkers or something?'

Li laughed. 'Checkers, no, no.'

Rhyme surveyed the board that Li took from the shopping bag and set up on the table beside the bed. It was a grid with a number of perpendicular lines on it. He then took out two bags, one containing hundreds of tiny white pebbles, the other black ones.

Suddenly Rhyme had a huge desire to play and he forced himself to pay careful attention to Sonny Li's animated voice as he explained the rules and object of *wei-chi*.

'Seems simple enough,' Rhyme said. Players alternated putting their stones on the board in an attempt to surround the opponent's and eliminate them from play.

'*Wei-chi* like all great games: rules simple but winning hard.' Li separated the stones into two piles. Then he said, 'OK, we play. You see how you like. Can last long time.'

'I'm not tired,' Rhyme said.

'Not either,' Li said. 'Now, you never play before so I give advantage. Give you three piece extra. Seem like not much but big, big advantage in *wei-chi*.'

'No,' Rhyme said. 'I don't want any advantages.'

Li glanced at him and must have thought this had to do with his disability because he added gravely, 'Only give you advantage because you not play before. That only reason. Is customary.'

Rhyme understood and appreciated Li's reassurance. Still, he said adamantly, 'No. You make the first move. Go ahead.' And watched Li's eyes lower and focus on the wooden grid between them.

Chapter Eleven

Chang awoke to find his father in the back courtyard of their Brooklyn apartment going through the slow movements of Tai chi. He watched the elderly man for a few moments and a thought occurred to him: Chang Jiechi's seventieth birthday was in three weeks. Sam Chang would not make it to the party but his spirit perhaps would. He looked down at his wife, still asleep, and next to her the little girl, who slept with her arm round the white stuffed cat Mei-Mei had sewn for her. He gazed at them for a while. Then he cocked his head, hearing the sounds of clanking metal in the kitchen. Alarmed, he climbed out of bed, pulled the pistol from beneath the mattress and walked cautiously in to the main room of the apartment. He laughed. His father was making tea.

Chang Jiechi lifted the iron pot, and poured. The two men sat.

Last night, when Chang had returned, he and his father had taken a map and located the Ghost's apartment building.

'When you get to the Ghost's apartment,' his father now said, 'if he has bodyguards, they'll search you.'

'I'll hide the gun in my sock. They won't search carefully. They won't be expecting me to be armed. I will come back,' Chang said firmly. 'I will be here to take care of you, Baba.'

'You are a good son. I could not have asked for a better one.'

'I have not brought you all the honour I should have.'

'Yes, you have.' The old man poured more tea. 'I named you well.' Chang's given name, Jingerzi, meant 'shrewd son'.

They lifted their cups and Chang drained his.

Mei-Mei came to the door.

'Wake William,' Chang told her. 'There are some things I want to say to him.'

But his father waved for her to stop. 'No. He will want to come with you.'

'I'll tell him no.'

Chang Jiechi laughed. 'And that will stop him? That impetuous son of yours?'

Chang fell silent for a moment then said, 'I can't go off like this without talking to him. It's important.'

But his father asked, 'What is the only reason that a man would do something like you are about to do?'

Chang replied, 'For the sake of his children.'

His father smiled. 'Yes, son, yes. Keep that in mind, always.' Then he grew stern. 'It's my wish that you don't wake William.'

Chang nodded. 'As you say, Baba.' He looked at his watch and said to Mei-Mei, 'I have to leave soon. But I wish that you come sit by me.'

She sat beside her husband, lowering her head to his shoulder.

Sam Chang was content to sit in silence. And then it was time to leave and go to his death.

RHYME SMELT cigarette smoke. 'That's disgusting,' he called.

'What?' asked Sonny Li. The hour was 7.30am.

'The cigarettes,' Rhyme explained.

'You should smoke,' Li barked. 'Relaxes you. Good for you.'

Mel Cooper arrived and Lon Sellitto and Eddie Deng not far behind him. The young Chinese-American cop walked very slowly.

'How are you, Eddie?' Rhyme asked.

'You should see the bruise,' Deng said, referring to his run-in with a lead slug yesterday during the shoot-out on Canal Street.

Sellitto carried a handful of pages from the overnight team who'd been canvassing recent contractors that had installed grey Arnold Lustre-Rite carpet in the past six months. Thirty-two separate installations in and around Battery Park City.

'Hell,' Rhyme muttered, 'thirty-two.' He'd hoped there'd be no more than five or six.

INS agent Alan Coe arrived, walking brightly into the lab. He didn't seem in the least contrite and began asking questions about the investigation as if the Ghost hadn't escaped, thanks to him.

More footsteps in the corridor outside.

'Hey,' Sachs said, entering the room. She kissed Rhyme. He started to tell her about the list of carpet installations but Sellitto interrupted.

'I tried you at home about one last night. Had some questions for you.' The detective's voice had a definite edge to it.

'Well, I got home at two,' she answered, a flare in her eyes. 'I went to see a friend.'

'I couldn't get in touch with you. Your cellphone was off.'

'You know, Detective,' she said, 'I can let you have my mother's phone number. She can give you some pointers on checking up on me. Even though she hasn't done it for about fifteen years.'

'Watch yourself, Patrolman,' Sellitto said to Sachs.

The argument mystified Rhyme. True, when she was working, Rhyme insisted that she be instantly available. But after hours it was different. Amelia Sachs was independent. Just as there were times when he ordered her away. When he needed time alone. To consider little questions like, Do I want to kill myself today?

Rhyme's phone rang. He snapped, 'Command, answer phone.'

A Chinese-accented voice asked, 'Mr Li, please.'

Li sat down and began to talk rapidly in Chinese. Then he hung up and smiled. 'That was Cai, from the tong. He ask around about minorities. There this group of Chinese called Uigurs. They Turks. Tough guys. Cai finds that Ghost hires people from Turkistan Community Center of Queens. The guy Hongse shot, he one of them. Hey, was I right, Loaban? I say he from minority.'

'You sure were, Sonny.'

'Should we raid it?' Sellitto asked.

'Not yet. Might tip off the Ghost. I've got a better idea,' Rhyme said. 'The Ghost called the centre at some point yesterday morning —presumably to arrange for his muscle. We'll check out all incoming and outgoing calls to the number of the place after, say, nine a.m.'

In half an hour the phone company had provided a list of about thirty numbers. Most of those they could eliminate, but four were cellphones with local exchanges. Because the phones were stolen, there was no billing address where the Ghost might be. But the cellphone providers were able to give information about where the callers were located when each call had been made or received. One phone had been in the Battery Park City area, in a wedge about half a mile square near the Hudson River.

'Now,' Rhyme shouted, feeling the excitement of narrowing in on his prey, 'did any of the buildings in that area have Arnold Lustre-Rite carpet installed?'

Finally Sachs looked up from the list and shouted, 'Yes! Got one.'

'That's the Ghost's safe house,' Rhyme announced.

She said, 'A new building: 805 Patrick Henry Street. Not far from the river.' She circled it on the map. Then she sighed, looking over the information from the Arnold company. 'Hell,' she muttered. 'They installed carpet on nineteen floors.'

'Then,' Rhyme said impatiently, 'you better get going.'

THE GHOST STOOD at the window of his apartment on Patrick Henry Street and watched the boats sailing through the harbour below him.

He had learned from his sources that the Wus were in an NYPD safe house. Yusuf had talked to a colleague who would check out the place and see what the security was like, perhaps even kill the Wus. As for the Changs—they'd be dead by nightfall, betrayed by this Tan fellow, whom the Ghost would, of course, kill after the man revealed the family's address. His luck was changing.

These meditations were interrupted by a knock on the door.

The betrayer had arrived.

The Ghost nodded towards a Uigur, who pulled his gun out of his waistband. He opened the door slowly.

The man in the hallway said, 'I am Tan. I am here to see the Ghost.'

'Come in,' the Ghost said. 'Do you want some tea?'

'No,' the old man replied. 'I won't be here long.'

JUST AHEAD of Amelia Sachs, driving her bee-yellow Camaro at seventy miles an hour, was the building that contained the Ghost's apartment. The structure was huge, many storeys tall and wide.

A sharp crackle in her Motorola speaker. 'Be advised, all RMP units in the vicinity of Battery Park City, we have a ten-thirty-four, reports of shots fired. Stand by . . . Have a location. Eight zero five Patrick Henry Street.'

The very building she was now bearing down on. The Ghost's. Was it a coincidence? She doubted it. What had happened?

A few seconds later, Sachs's Camaro was up on the kerb. Two other responding cars pulled up out front and the uniformed officers ran inside. Sellitto and Li were behind them.

'We heard the ten-thirty-four,' Sellitto said. 'This's his building, right? The Ghost's?'

'Yep,' Sachs confirmed.

'There've got to be three hundred apartments here,' the homicide detective muttered.

Sachs's Motorola clattered again. 'Sachs, are you there?' Lincoln Rhyme's voice said.

'Yeah, go ahead. I'm here with Lon and ESU.'

'Listen,' the criminalist said, 'I've been talking to dispatch. It looks like the shots came from either the eighteenth or nineteenth floors.'

'We're going to sweep, Rhyme,' she said. 'I'll call you back.'

Sachs and a group of officers stepped into one of the elevators and started up to the eighteenth floor. When the door opened one officer looked out with a metal mirror attached to a wand. 'Clear.'

Out they stepped, moving cautiously. Bracketed by two large cops, machine guns ready, Sachs picked a door and knocked.

The door opened. A tiny, grey-haired woman looked up at them. 'You're the police, here about those firecrackers I complained about.'

'That's right, ma'am,' Sachs said. 'We're trying to find out where the sounds came from.'

'I think it's 18K, up the hall. That's why I thought they were firecrackers—because an Oriental man lives there. They use firecrackers in their religion.'

'OK, ma'am, thank you.'

An officer knocked hard on the door of 18K. 'Police, open the door!'

No response.

The officers eased a battering ram back and then swung it forward hard into the door near the knob. The lock gave way immediately and the door slammed inwards. Half a dozen officers raced into the room. Amelia Sachs moved in fast behind.

The Ghost was gone.

But, just like at Easton Beach, he'd left death in his stead. In the living room was the body of a man who bore a resemblance to the Uigur Sachs had shot outside the Wus' apartment. He lay near a leather couch that had been riddled with bullets. A cheap chrome automatic lay on the floor. The other body was in the bedroom. He was an elderly Chinese man, lying on his back, his eyes glazed. There was a bullet wound in his leg. Sachs could see no other wounds.

Sachs studied him. Then leaned forward. 'Ah, got it,' she said, nodding at the man's hand, in which was clutched a brown bottle. Sachs worked it out of his fingers. The characters on the label were in both Chinese and English. 'Morphine,' she said. 'Suicide.'

This might have been one of the immigrants on the *Dragon*—perhaps Sam Chang's father, who'd come here to kill the Ghost. She speculated about what had happened: the father had shot the Uigur but the Ghost had jumped for cover behind the couch and the old man had run out of ammunition. The Ghost was going to torture him to learn where the rest of the family was but the immigrant had killed himself.

Crime Scene arrived—two techs carrying large metal suitcases. Sachs donned the Tyvek suit and then announced, 'I need to process the room. Could I have everybody out of here please?'

As she finished the search, Sachs was aware of cigarette smoke. She looked up to see Sonny Li standing in the doorway, surveying the room. 'I know him from boat,' Li said, shaking his head with a sadness in his eyes. 'That Sam Chang's father.'

'I figured. Why'd he try it?'

'For family,' Li said quietly. 'For family.'

'I suppose you want to run the scene too?' she asked.

'What you think I doing, Hongse? I walk grid in my mind now.'

Sort of like Rhyme does, Sachs reflected.

Chapter Twelve

Chang Mei-Mei set a cup of tea in front of her groggy husband.

He blinked at the pale green cup, but his attention, like that of his wife and sons, was wholly on the television set. The news story, they learned with the translation assistance of William, was about two men found dead in Battery Park City.

One of the men was an Eastern Turkistani immigrant from Queens. The other was an elderly Chinese national, believed to have been a passenger on the *Fuzhou Dragon*.

Sam Chang had awoken from his heavy sleep half an hour ago. As soon as he noticed the gun was gone he'd understood what his father had done: the tea Chang Jiechi had given him had been generously laced with the old man's morphine. Chang stood up and stumbled to the door.

But Mei-Mei had stopped him. 'It's too late.'

'No!' he'd cried, falling back onto the couch. He raged at Mei-Mei, 'You helped him, didn't you? You knew what he was going to do!'

The woman said nothing.

Chang had then sat for a long time as the drug wore off, racked by worry. The television report confirmed the worst.

The Turkistani had been shot to death, the reporter explained, by the elderly man, who had then died of an overdose of morphine, apparently a suicide. The apartment was believed to have been a hideout for Kwan Ang, the human smuggler wanted in connection with the sinking of the *Fuzhou Dragon* early yesterday. Kwan had escaped before the police arrived and was still at large.

Sam Chang was seized with bottomless anger. 'I am going to kill him!' he screamed. 'I found him once and I'm going to find him again. This time—'

'No,' Mei-Mei said firmly. 'What will happen to us if you die? Have you thought about that? You won't avenge his death. You'll stay here with us, in hiding, until the Ghost is captured or killed.' She wiped her face, from which tears streamed. 'I loved him too, you know. It's my loss as well as yours.'

Chang sat for a long time in silence, staring at the shabby red and black carpet on the floor. Then he motioned to his younger son. He asked Ronald, 'Son, do you know the warriors of Qin Shi Huang?'

'Yes, Baba.'

These were thousands of full-size terracotta statues of soldiers, charioteers and horses built near Xi'an by China's first emperor in the third century BC and placed in his tomb. The army was to accompany him to the afterlife.

'We're going to do the same for Yeye.' Yeye was the affectionate term for grandfather. Chang nearly choked on his sorrow. 'We're going to send some things to heaven so your grandfather will have them with him.'

'Will that work?' the boy asked, frowning.

'Yes. But I need you to help me. Take some paper there and that pencil.' He nodded towards the table. 'Why don't you draw a picture of his favourite brushes—the wolf-hair and the goat. And his ink stick and well. You remember what they looked like?'

Ronald bent over the paper and began his task.

'And a bottle of the rice wine he liked,' Mei-Mei suggested.

Then Chang was aware of someone behind him. He turned to see William looking at his brother's drawing. 'When Grandmother died,' the teenager said sombrely, 'we burned money.' It was a tradition at Chinese funerals to burn slips of paper printed to look like million-yuan notes, so that the deceased would have money to spend in the afterworld. 'Maybe I can draw some yuan,' William added.

Chang was swept with emotion but he didn't embrace the boy, as he wanted desperately to do. He said simply, 'Thank you, son.'

When the children had finished their drawings, Chang led his family outside into the back yard and, as if this were Chang Jiechi's actual funeral, he set two burning incense sticks in the ground to mark the spot where the body would have lain and then set light to the pictures his sons had drawn, watching the smoke disappear into the grey sky.

'SOMEBODY MADE another move on the Wus,' Lon Sellitto said, glancing up at Rhyme from his cellphone.

'What?' Sachs asked, astonished. 'In our Murray Hill safe house?'

Rhyme wheeled round to face the detective, who said, 'A dark-complexioned man, slight build, spotted on one of the security cameras in the alley. Two of our people went after him but he got away.'

The criminalist asked, 'How the hell did the Ghost find out where they were?'

Sachs considered this. 'After the shoot-out on Canal Street, one of his *bangshous* could've followed me to the clinic then followed the Wus to the safe house. Hard to do but possible.' She walked to the white-board and tapped an entry. 'Or how 'bout this? "Ghost is reported to have government people on payroll." Nobody at the Bureau knew we sent them to Murray Hill. Dellray had left by the time I thought of it. That leaves somebody at the INS or NYPD.'

'Well,' Sellitto said, 'I'll have the Wus taken to a witness protection facility upstate. And *that* information doesn't leave this room.'

Rhyme was growing impatient. 'Somebody check with the Bureau.

Where the hell is Dellray's replacement? Eddie, make the call.'

Deng got in touch with the Bureau's ASAC. It turned out that there'd been some delay in getting the additional agents to work on GHOSTKILL.

'Don't they know there's a killer out there?' Rhyme asked caustically.

'You want to call them back?'

'No,' he snapped. 'I want to look at the evidence.'

Sachs's search of the crime scene at Patrick Henry Street had mixed results. One discouraging fact was that the cellphone that had been instrumental in tracking down the Ghost had been left there. It meant that he'd probably figured out that this was how they'd found him and would now be more careful when calling on mobiles.

Rhyme's gaze then slipped to close-up pictures of the old man's hands. 'Look at that.'

Sachs squinted. 'Indentations!' She pulled the print-out of Sam Chang's fingerprints off the wall and held it close to that of his father's hand. The indentations on Sam Chang's fingers and thumb were similar to the lines clearly evident on his father's.

'What's it mean?' Mel Cooper asked. 'Genetic?'

'No, can't be,' Rhyme said. He closed his eyes for a second, then looked at Sachs. 'They're painters! Father and son are both artists. Remember the logo on the van? One of them painted it. The marks came from holding brushes or pens.'

'No,' Li said, looking at the photo. 'Not painters. Calligraphers. Hold brush like this.' He grabbed a pen and held it perfectly vertical. When he released it, the red indentations on his fingers and thumb were identical to those on the hands of Chang and his father.

'We know the Changs are in Queens,' Rhyme said. 'And Wu said the Changs had a job lined up here. Let's get as many Chinese-speaking officers to call printing or sign-painting companies that have just hired anyone illegal.'

Deng made a call to his headquarters.

Mel Cooper had run some of the trace from Patrick Henry Street through the gas chromatograph. 'Something interesting. From Chang's father's shoes. Nitrates, potassium, carbon, sodium . . . Biosolids.'

This caught Rhyme's attention. Biosolids: processed human waste. The fourteen waste-treatment plants in New York City produced more than 1,000 tons of biosolids a day. For there to be significant amounts on the victim's shoes meant that the Changs were probably living close to one of the plants.

'Can we search house by house near the treatment plants?' Sellitto asked.

Rhyme shook his head. A door-to-door search would take for ever.

The rest of the evidence didn't help much. But Amelia Sachs was not the only cop to run the crime scene.

Sonny Li said, 'Hey, Loaban, I found things too when I search Ghost's place. Got some good stuff, I'm saying. OK, there a statue of the Buddha across from door, facing it. Hallway painted white. Had statue of eight horses. All mirrors very tall so they not cut off part of head when you look in them. Had brass bells with wooden handles—keep them in western part of room. Figure it out, Loaban?'

'No,' Rhyme said, sighing.

'Feng shui, I'm saying.'

Impatient, Rhyme said, 'What's the evidentiary point, Li?'

'The point, Loaban? The Ghost hire somebody to arrange his room. Maybe know other places the Ghost has apartments. I go check feng shui men in Chinatown.'

'OK,' Rhyme said. 'That's useful.'

The Chinese cop left, and the team returned to the evidence, but made no headway. As he gazed at the whiteboards, Rhyme felt a too-familiar sensation: the desperate hope that evidence picked over long ago would yield just one more nugget. Then his head swivelled fast towards the map of Long Island. He looked at the tiny red dot about a mile off the coast of Orient Point.

'Goddamn,' he whispered. 'We have another crime scene. And I forgot all about it. The *Fuzhou Dragon*.'

'SOMEBODY CALL the Coast Guard, patch me through to whoever's in charge of the rescue out there.'

Lon Sellitto finally got through and put the call on speaker-phone.

'This is Fred Ransom speaking. I'm captain of the *Evan Brigant*.' The wind whistled loudly over the mouthpiece of his radio mike.

'This is Detective Sellitto, NYPD. I'm here with Lincoln Rhyme. Where are you now?

'Just above the *Dragon*. She's about eighty, ninety feet down. We're still looking for survivors but haven't had any luck.'

'You have divers available who can check out the interior?' Rhyme asked. 'I'm talking about searching for evidence.'

'I see. We could send some folks down. The thing is, though, that my divers've never done that. They're Search and Rescue.'

Then Amelia Sachs's voice interrupted. 'I'll search it.' She said into the speaker-phone, 'Captain, I can be down in Battery Park in thirty minutes. Can you have a chopper get me out to your location? I'm PADI certified.' Meaning she had been trained in scuba diving by the Professional Association of Diving Instructors.

'But you haven't been diving for years, Sachs,' Rhyme pointed out.

'Like riding a bike.'

'But, Miss—'

'That'd be Officer Sachs, Captain,' she said into the speaker-phone.

'Officer, there's a big difference between recreational dives and what it's like down there today,' the captain said. 'My people've been diving for years and I wouldn't feel real comfortable sending *them* into an unstable wreck under these conditions.'

'Sachs,' Rhyme said. 'You can't do it. You're not trained for that. We'll walk them through it.'

'There are a million things they'd miss. You know that.'

Rhyme hesitated for a long moment. But then nodded, indicating that he'd back her up.

'Will you help us out here, Captain?' Rhyme asked. 'She needs to be the one who goes down.'

'OK, Officer.'

'I'll be at the pad in thirty minutes,' Sachs said. She hung up and glanced at Rhyme. 'I'll call you with what I find.'

There was so much Rhyme wanted to say to her and yet so little he was able to. He settled for 'Search well—'

'—but watch my back.'

She stroked his right hand—the one whose fingers couldn't feel any sensation whatsoever. Not yet, at any rate. Maybe after the surgery.

OK, I CAN DO THIS.

Amelia Sachs stood on the rippled metal floor of the Coast Guard's Sikorsky HH-60J helicopter. Beneath them was the cutter *Evan Brigant*. It had never occurred to her that the only way to get to the ship would be by winch down onto the bobbing deck.

Encased in an orange vest and battered helmet, Sachs gripped the handhold near the open doorway. Then out she went. She swung wildly from the momentum of stepping out of the door. In a moment the motion slowed and she started down, buffeted by the wind and the powerful downdraught from the rotor blades.

A shroud of fog suddenly enveloped her and she was disorientated.

But then the cutter grew visible beneath her. Her feet touched the deck towards the rear of the ship.

On the bridge the captain, Fred Ransom, welcomed Sachs. He showed her underwater photos of the *Fuzhou Dragon* and told her where the bridge was and where the cabins were located—on the same deck but down a lengthy corridor towards the stern.

'Now, one thing, Officer, just to warn you,' he said delicately. 'We understand there are about fifteen bodies inside. It could be pretty grim . . .' But his voice faded as he looked into her eyes.

Sachs said, 'Appreciate the warning, Captain. But I do run crime scenes for a living.'

'All right, let's get you into your gear.'

She was introduced to a man and a woman wearing wet suits, the chief dive officer and his second-in-command.

'Understand you did PADI,' the man said. 'Well, we're going to walk you through all the steps again, like you're a novice.'

'I was hoping you would.'

'Your deepest?' the woman dive officer asked.

'Eighty feet.'

'That's about the same as here.'

Behind a screen she stripped and put on a wet suit. Then they geared her up with the rest of the equipment: weights, mask and the air tank, attached to the BCD—buoyancy control device. Also attached was a primary regulator—the one that she'd breathe through—and then a secondary one that could be used by a fellow diver to breathe off her tank if the buddy's air supply was cut off. They also fitted a head-mounted spotlight to her hood. They ran through the basic hand signals.

The dive chief handed Sachs a large mesh bag for stowing any evidence she found. Into this she placed plastic bags she'd brought for evidence collection. Then he and his assistant donned their equipment and all three walked to the stern of the heaving ship. Shouting over the noise of the wind the dive chief said, 'We'll get into the raft, put our flippers on and then fall backwards into the water.'

They climbed into the yellow raft, which reared up and down like a bucking horse. Twenty feet away was an orange buoy. The dive chief pointed to it and said, 'There's a line from there that goes straight down to the vessel. We'll swim over to that and follow the line down. What's your plan for the search?'

She called back, 'I want to search the bridge and cabins alone.'

'OK,' the dive chief said uneasily. Then he continued. 'Now, sounds don't work well underwater but if you're in trouble bang on your tank with the knife in your BCD and we'll search for you.' He held up her SPG—submersible pressure gauge—which showed how much air was in her tank. 'You've got three thousand pounds of air. You'll burn it fast because you're going to be pumped up on adrenaline. We leave the bottom with five hundred. No less than that. That's an iron-clad rule. No exceptions.'

The dive chief gave the 'OK' sign—middle finger and thumb in a circle—and Sachs responded the same way. The diver gestured for her to roll backwards.

One, two, three . . . Backwards into the churning water.

In a few minutes they'd swum to the buoy. Then a thumbs-down sign, which meant descend. For a moment Sachs was struck by the absolute peace of life underwater. Then she looked below her and saw the *Fuzhou Dragon*, dark, jagged and foreboding—and containing the bodies of so many innocent people. A huge coffin, she thought.

The three divers continued downwards. As they got closer to the ship she began to hear the noises—grating and moaning as the ship's thick metal plates scraped on the rocks.

At the site of the explosion, Sachs used her knife to scrape residue from the outwardly curled metal. She placed some of the black ashy material into a plastic bag, sealed it and put that in the mesh collection bag. OK, Rhyme, here we go.

And the pressure gauge gave her its message: 2,350 pounds. At 500 they left the bottom. No exceptions.

Because the ship was on her side the bridge door now opened upwards. It was metal and very heavy. The two officers struggled to lift it and Sachs swam through the opening and down into the bridge. They lowered the door. It clanked shut with a chilling boom and Sachs realised that she was now trapped inside the ship.

She clicked on the light mounted on her wet-suit hood and swam away from the bridge down a dark corridor that led to the cabins. *I don't like this, Rhyme*. But then she thought about the Ghost searching for the Changs, about Po-Yee, the Treasured Child. *Think about that, not the darkness or confinement*. Amelia Sachs swam forward.

SHE WAS IN HELL. No other word described it.

The black hallway was filled with fish with piercing yellow eyes. The sounds were harrowing: the scraping and groaning, moans like human voices in agony, pings and snaps, the clank of metal on metal.

She found herself looking at two dull human eyes in a white lifeless face. She screamed and jerked back. The body of a man, barefoot, his arms above his head, floated nearby.

She thought of the Chang family. She thought of the baby.

Clank, clank.

The rooms above her, facing the surface, were not, she deduced, the Ghost's: two didn't appear to have been occupied on the voyage and one was the captain's; in this she found seafaring memorabilia and pictures of the bald, moustachioed man she recognised as Captain Sen from the pictures tacked up on Rhyme's wall.

Sachs swam downwards to check out the rooms facing the bottom. Three cabins hadn't been occupied on the voyage. That left only one more—it had to be the Ghost's.

The cabin door was closed. She gripped the knob and twisted. The latch released and the heavy wooden door eased downwards.

In front of her a man floated in the black space, eyes closed. What must have been a thousand $100 bills floated in the water, filling the room, like flakes in a plastic souvenir snow globe.

The bills explained the man's death. His pockets were filled with money and she deduced that he'd run to the cabin to get as much of the Ghost's cash as he could but he'd been trapped here.

Sachs eased further into the room, the bills swirling in her wake. She couldn't see more than a few feet past the cloud of bills. She grabbed several handfuls for evidence. Then she noticed an open attaché case and found more currency inside—Chinese. A handful of these bills went into the collection bag.

Clank, clank.

She then located an Uzi machine pistol and a Beretta 9mm. The Uzi's serial number had been etched out. There was a number on the Beretta, though, so she slipped it into her evidence bag. A glance at her pressure gauge: 1,800 pounds of air. She was going through it fast.

Clank, clank . . . clank.

Ignoring the spooky moans and the clanking, Sachs looked around her. In a tiny room like this, where would one hide things? She glanced at the closet. His clothes? Maybe. She kicked towards it.

She began to go through the clothes. Nothing in any pockets. But she found a slit in the lining of an Armani jacket. She reached in and extracted an envelope containing a document. Into the bag.

OK, I'm outta here.

Clank clank clank . . . clank . . . clank . . . clank.

But then she stopped, gripping the doorway.

Amelia Sachs realised something about the eerie banging she'd been hearing. Three fast bangs, three slow.

It was Morse code for S-O-S. And it was coming from somewhere deep within the ship. Somebody was alive! The Coast Guard had missed a survivor.

Should she go and find the other divers? That would take another ten minutes.

Less than 1,200 pounds of air left. Sachs turned towards the darkness and kicked hard. Follow the clanking.

When she came to the end of the black corridor, training the light on the wall she discovered a door about two feet square. She opened it and gazed into the bowels of the ship. The shaft was a dumbwaiter, presumably to cart supplies up from the lower decks.

Oh, man . . . Can't do it. No way.

Do it. Sachs eased forwards along the shaft, which was just wide enough to accommodate her. The clanking was grew louder. She continued down to the very bottom of the dumbwaiter and out into what was the galley of the *Dragon*.

Above, she saw the shimmering surface of a large air pocket and a man's legs in the water, dangling downwards. A bald man with a moustache was clinging to a rack of shelves that were bolted to the wall—now the ceiling of the kitchen. Sachs noticed the name on his jacket, Sen Zi-jun. This was Captain Sen of the *Fuzhou Dragon*.

He was so blue he looked cyanotic—the colour of an asphyxia victim. Pulling the secondary regulator off her vest, she stuck it into Sen's mouth. He breathed deeply and began to revive somewhat. Sachs pointed down into the water. He nodded.

A fast glance at the pressure gauge: 700 pounds of pressure. And two of them were using her supply now. She released air from her BCD and they sank to the bottom of the galley.

She eased the captain into the shaft before her, feet first, then followed him. Another glance at the gauge: 400 pounds of pressure. *We leave the bottom with five hundred. No exceptions.*

Then they were out of the dumbwaiter and floating into the main corridor. She swam beside the captain, holding him by his belt.

The captain suddenly went into a seizure. He kicked out hard, struck her in the face with his foot. The spotlight went out and the regulator popped from her mouth. The blow pushed her backwards.

How could she let the Coast Guard divers know she was in trouble?

Holding her breath, Sachs reached in the evidence bag and pulled out the Beretta 9mm. She pulled the slide to chamber a round, pressed the muzzle close to the wooden wall and pulled the trigger. A flash and loud explosion and a powerful recoil. She dropped the gun.

Please, she thought . . . Please . . .

Lights burst on silently as the dive chief and his assistant kicked fast into the corridor. Another regulator mouthpiece was thrust between her lips and Sachs began to breathe again. The dive chief got his secondary regulator into the captain's mouth. The stream of bubbles was faint but at least he was breathing.

Then the foursome made their way out of the bridge and to the orange rope. Calmer now, Sachs concentrated on ascending slowly, breathing, deep in, deep out, as they left behind the ship of corpses.

SACHS LAY in the cutter's sickbay while the chill subsided. When she felt well enough, she climbed up to the bridge to call Rhyme. She told him that she'd found some evidence. 'And maybe a wit.'

'A *witness*?'

'Found somebody still alive in the ship. The captain. If we're lucky he'll be able to give us some leads to the Ghost's operation in New York. He's unconscious now. The hospital will call as soon as they know something.'

'Hurry back, Sachs. We miss you.'

The royal we from Lincoln Rhyme, she knew, really meant 'I'.

CHAPTER THIRTEEN

Feng shui, which literally means wind and water, is the art of trapping good energy and luck and repelling bad. Because of the astonishing number of rules, there are very few truly talented feng shui practitioners. The Ghost's apartment had clearly been done by a master. Sonny Li had no idea who here in New York could have prepared the Ghost's apartment so expertly. But rather than race around like Hongse in her yellow car to track down someone who could help him, Li remained true to his Taoist way. *The way to use life is to do everything through being.*

And so Detective Sonny Li went into the fanciest tea shop he could find in Chinatown, sat down at a table and slouched back in the chair. Sitting, sipping tea . . . Forty-five minutes passed.

His patience was finally rewarded. An attractive Chinese woman walked into the tea shop, found a seat near him and ordered a tea.

The woman wore a beautiful red dress and high, narrow heels. He looked at her and decided, Yes, she's the one. Li walked to her table and introduced himself. He said casually, 'The reason I troubled you—forgive me—but perhaps you can help. The man I work for has bad luck. I believe it is because of how his apartment is arranged. You obviously have a good feng shui man.'

He nodded at the emblems that had told him that she indeed followed feng shui diligently: an ostentatious bracelet of nine Chinese coins, a pin in the likeness of the homely goddess Guan Yin and a scarf with black fish on it. This was why he had selected her—and because she was rich, which meant that she would go to only the best practitioners of the art, men that the Ghost too would hire.

The beautiful woman smiled and dug into her purse. 'Mr Zhou,' she said, nodding at the card. 'He is one of the best in the city.'

'SACHS!' Rhyme looked up from the computer screen. 'Guess what the Ghost blew the ship up with?'

'Give up,' she called, amused.

Mel Cooper answered, 'Grade A, brand-new Composition 4.'

This had put Rhyme in a good mood because C4 was rare. The substance was available only to the military and a few select law-enforcement agencies. That meant that there were relatively few sources for high-quality C4, which in turn meant that the odds of finding a connection between that source and the Ghost were far better than if he'd used any of the commercially available explosives.

Cooper had sent the trace results to Quantico. 'Should hear back in the next few hours.'

Eddie Deng arrived. 'Got here as soon as you called, Lincoln.'

'Excellent, Eddie. Put your reading specs on. You've got to translate for us. Amelia found a letter in the Ghost's sports jacket.'

'It's hard to read,' Deng murmured, squinting. The characters had been bleached out by the sea water and were barely visible. 'OK, OK . . . It's to the Ghost. The man who wrote is named Ling Shui-bian. He's telling the Ghost when the charter flight will be leaving Fuzhou and when and where to expect it at the Nagorev military base outside St Petersburg. Then he says he's wiring money into an account in Hong Kong—no number or bank. It then says part of the money is enclosed—in dollars. Finally, there's a list of the victims—the passengers on the *Dragon*.'

'Have some of our people in China check out that guy Ling,' Rhyme told Sellitto. 'How much money was there, Sachs?'

'A lot. Maybe a thousand hundred-dollar bills. It was hard to tell. And there were about thirty packs of yuan this size.'

'Thirty stacks, given the exchange rate,' Eddie Deng estimated, 'equals about twenty thousand dollars US.'

A cellphone rang and Sachs pulled the unit off her belt.

'Amelia?'

She recognised John Sung's voice. 'John.'

'I was just wondering if you might have time to stop by later.'

'I think that'll work out. But can I call you in a bit, John? I'm at Lincoln's right now and it's a little crazy. I'll call you later.'

She hung up and saw Lon Sellitto looking at her with what could only be described as a glare.

'Detective,' she said to him, 'can I talk to you outside?'

Sachs walked into the corridor and Sellitto followed. She spun round, hands on hips. 'Why've you been on my case for the past two days, Detective? You have something to say to me, say it to my face.'

A pause. Finally he said, 'I know where you were last night. The baby-sitters outside Sung's apartment told me you went there after you left here and you didn't leave till one forty-five.'

'My personal life is my own business.'

The burly cop whispered vehemently, 'But it's *not* just your business any more, Amelia. It's Rhyme's business too. He's tough. But the one thing that'll break him into little pieces is you—if you keep going the way you're headed.'

She was bewildered. 'Headed?'

'Look, you're the centre of his life. He's let down all his defences with you. You're going to break him. And I'm not going to let that happen.' His voice dropped even further. 'Just think about it: if you keep seeing this guy, it's going to kill Rhyme. It's—'

'You're talking about me and John Sung?' Sachs began shaking with laughter. 'Oh, Lon . . .' Then she turned away quickly because the laughter turned into tears. Finally she caught her breath. 'It's not what you're thinking.'

'Amelia, what—?'

'You know Rhyme and I've talked about having kids.'

'Yeah.'

She gave a sour laugh. 'I wasn't getting pregnant. I was worried that there was something wrong with Lincoln. So a few weeks ago we went in and we both had checkups.'

'Yeah, I remember he went to the doctor.'

She thought back to that day in the waiting room.

'I've just been meeting with Lincoln Rhyme's physician.'

'Yes, Doctor?'

'I've got to talk to you about something.'

'You're looking like it's bad news.'

'Why don't we sit down over there in the corner?'

'Here's fine. Tell me. Let me have it straight.'

'Well, Lincoln's doctor tells me that the results of his fertility workup are within normal levels. A slightly diminished sperm count, which is typical of someone in his condition, but nowadays that's a very slight hurdle to pregnancy. I'm afraid, though, that you have a more serious problem.'

'Me?'

She now told Sellitto about this conversation. Then she added, 'I've got something called endometriosis. I've always had problems but I never believed it was as bad as what the doctor told me.'

'Can they cure it?'

Sachs shook her head. 'No. They can operate, do hormonal therapy but it wouldn't really help the fertility thing.'

'I'm sorry, Amelia.'

Sachs offered a hollow laugh. 'That's what I was doing at John Sung's. He examined me and gave me an acupressure treatment. And he's getting some herbs that he thinks'll help. It turns out a lot of Western doctors recommend that women with endometriosis use Chinese medicine to treat it. Last night, when I took Lincoln upstairs we talked about it. He thought it was pretty silly but he'd noticed how upset I've been. So we decided I'd go ahead and see what Sung could do for me.' She fell silent. 'There's so much death around me, Lon . . . I wanted to have some *life* around us, Lincoln and me. Don't you know what he and I are to each other? How could you think I'd do something like that?'

'I'm sorry, Officer. I didn't know. I shoulda thought better.' Sellitto extended his hand. She shook his huge palm, and they returned to Rhyme's living room.

'FRED,' RHYME SAID as Dellray walked into his living room. 'You gave us a hell of a scare.'

'Just what I myself was feeling, settin' my ass down on a few sticks of Mr Nobel's creation.' He looked around. 'Where Dan?'

'Dan?' Rhyme asked.

'Guy who took over for me. Dan Wong. From our San Francisco office. Wanna thank him for taking over.'

Rhyme and Sachs looked at each other. The criminalist said, 'Nobody took over for you. We're still waiting.'

'Still *waitin'*?' Dellray whispered in disbelief. 'He was gonna call you an' be out here on an army jet this morning. What about SPEC-TAC?'

'No word.'

With a snarl Dellray pulled his phone off his belt. 'This is Dellray . . . What happened to Dan Wong? . . . Jee-sus.' He clicked the phone off. 'Dan got some emergency assignment in Hawaii,' he snapped. 'This ain't good. I'ma get it taken care of when I get back to the office. No excuse for this.'

Sellitto asked, 'Where are you with the bomb investigation?'

Dellray dug out a plastic bag containing a bright yellow stick of explosive and tossed it across the room to Sachs.

She caught it one-handed. 'Holy Mother, Fred,' she called.

'S'only dynamite. And if it din't go off with a detonator it sure ain't gonna go bang with a little lob to left field.'

Sachs examined the stick of dynamite. There were numbers on it.

'Any friction ridges?' Sellitto asked.

'Wiped clean. No prints. And the numbers turned up nothin'. Our boys said it was too old to trace. Too old for marker additives, too.'

'Probably is,' Rhyme said, 'but I want to test it anyway.' He shouted to Mel Cooper, 'Get it over to the lab ASAP. I want it analysed.'

THE GHOST, wearing his windcheater to conceal his new Glock 36, was walking down Mulberry Street. He'd just got the news from the Uigur that Yusuf had hired to break into the Wus' special safe house. The security was better than he'd expected and the guards had spotted him. Undoubtedly the police had moved the family again. A brief setback but he'd eventually find out where they were.

Down one alley, then another, then across a busy street. Into yet another dim cobblestoned alley. Finally he arrived at his destination. He walked through the doorway, waving hello to his feng shui expert, Mr Zhou, who sat in the back of the Lucky Hope Shop.

SONNY LI lit another cigarette and continued down the street called the Bowery. He walked past the bustling crowds and the fish markets and came to the Lucky Hope Shop, a small place but packed with merchandise: jars of twisted ginseng root, dried cuttlefish, noodles, spices, melon seeds, oyster sauce, lotus, frozen tea buns and tripe.

In the back he found a man sitting at a desk, smoking, reading a Chinese-language newspaper.

'You are Zhou?' Li asked.

'Yes, that's right.'

Li said, 'I'm honoured to meet you, sir. I was at the apartment of a friend at 805 Patrick Henry Street. I believe you arranged it.'

Zhou's eyes narrowed, then he nodded cautiously. 'A friend.'

'That's right, sir. I need to get in touch with him and he is no longer in that apartment. I was hoping you could tell me where he might be. His name is Kwan Ang.'

Zhou nodded. 'He was here not five minutes ago. He left just before you walked in.'

'What? Which way did he go?'

'Outside the store I saw him turn left. If you hurry you can find him. He is carrying a yellow bag with my store's name on it.'

Li sprinted out of the store and turned left. He looked around frantically. Then, about a hundred yards away he saw a man of medium build, with short, dark hair, carrying a yellow shopping bag. His gait was familiar. Yes, Li thought, it's the Ghost.

He supposed he should try to call Loaban or Hongse. But he couldn't risk the man's escaping. So Li sprinted after him, gripping the loaded German automatic pistol in his pocket.

Before the snakehead realised he was being pursued, Sonny Li was on him, grabbing his collar and shoving his gun into the man's back.

The killer dropped the yellow bag and started to reach under his shirt. But Li took a large pistol from the Ghost's belt and slipped it into his own pocket. Then he roughly spun the snakehead round to face him. 'Kwan Ang,' he intoned then recited the familiar incantation: 'I'm arresting you for violation of the organic laws of the People's Republic of China.'

But as he was about to continue he glanced at the neck of the Ghost's shirt, which had been tugged open as he'd reached for his pistol. Dangling there from a leather cord was a soapstone amulet in the shape of a monkey.

His eyes wide in shock, Sonny Li stepped back, holding the pistol level at the Ghost's face as he tried to figure out what was happening.

Finally he whispered, 'You killed John Sung at the beach and you took his papers and the stone monkey. You've been pretending to be him!' Ten judges of hell, Li thought. Hongse had no clue that the 'doctor' was the snakehead himself. 'You were using the police woman to find out where the Changs and the Wus were.'

The Ghost nodded. 'I needed information. She was happy to provide it.' He now examined Li more closely. 'Why did you do this, little man? Why did you come all the way after me?'

'You killed three people in Liu Guoyuan, my town.'

'Did I? I don't remember. Listen, little man, I'm tired and I don't have much time. So, one hundred thousand one-colour,' the Ghost said. 'I can give it to you in cash right now.'

'You are under arrest,' Li growled. 'Lie down on your belly. Now.'

The Ghost knelt on the cobblestones. Suddenly Li realised that the shopping bag was between them and that the Ghost's right hand had disappeared behind it.

'No!' he shouted.

The Lucky Hope Shop bag exploded towards Li, as the Ghost fired through it with a second gun he had hidden in an ankle holster or a sock. The bullet zipped past Li's hip. By the time he was thrusting his own pistol forward the snakehead had knocked it from his hand. Li grabbed the Ghost's wrist and tried to pull the Model 51 from his fingers. Together they tumbled to the slick cobblestones and this gun fell to the ground too.

Desperately they clutched at each other, wrestling and trying to reach one of the weapons that lay on the cobblestones. The Ghost struggled towards the pistol.

Stop him, stop him, Li raged to himself.

He seized the leather thong around the Ghost's neck, the one that held the stone monkey amulet, and began to pull hard. The Ghost's hands flailed uselessly and from his throat came a gurgling noise. The snakehead began to quiver. Li pulled harder.

Until the leather snapped.

The monkey figurine fell to the ground and shattered. Li stumbled backward, falling hard into the alley, striking his head on the cobblestones. He nearly passed out. Judges of hell . . .

The cop could faintly see the Ghost, also on his hands and knees, gasping and coughing, holding his throat with one hand as the other patted the ground for a weapon.

An image came to Li's mind: his father reprimanding him for some foolish comment. Then another one: the bodies of the Ghost's victims in Li's town in China.

Sonny Li rolled to his knees and began crawling towards his enemy.

AMELIA SACHS, her face grim, jumped out of the crime scene bus, accompanied by Alan Coe and Eddie Deng. They ran through the pungent alleyway towards the cluster of uniformed officers.

Sachs gazed down at the body. Sonny Li was lying on his stomach on the filthy cobblestones, palms flat beside him. Sachs paused, filled with the desire to drop to her knees and grip the man's hand.

Look past it, ignore who the victim is. Remember Rhyme's advice: give up the dead.

Well, that'd be tough to do. For Rhyme especially. Sachs had noticed that Rhyme had formed an improbable bond with this man, as close as he'd come to a friendship since she'd known him. But then she thought of Po-Yee, soon to be another victim of the man who'd committed this crime if they didn't find him. And so Sachs put the pain away.

Agent Coe walked slowly up to her. 'I'm sorry,' the INS agent said, though there seemed to be little genuine sorrow in his voice. 'He was a good man.'

'Yes, he was.' She said this bitterly, thinking: And he was a hell of a better cop than you are. She motioned to the other officers. 'I've got to run the scene. Could I have everybody out of here?'

She pulled her headset on and made the call to Rhyme.

A click. 'Yes?' Rhyme asked. She sensed him trying to keep the hope out of his voice.

'He's dead. I'm sorry, Lincoln,' she said softly.

Rhyme gave no response for a moment. 'I see.' His voice nearly caught. 'All right, get going. Run the scene.'

A half-hour later she'd finished bagging everything, and assembled the evidence. She made another call to the criminalist.

'Go ahead,' Rhyme said grimly.

'Sonny was shot three times in the chest but we've got four casings. One casing's from a Model 51. The others are .45. He was killed with that one, it looks like. There was trace on his leg—yellow paper flecks and some kind of dried plant material. And there was a pile of the same material on the cobblestones.'

'What's your scenario, Sachs?'

'I think Sonny spots the Ghost leaving a store, carrying something in a yellow bag. Sonny follows him. He collars him in the alley here and gets the Ghost's new gun, the .45. He assumes that's his only weapon. Sonny relaxes and tells the Ghost to get onto the ground. But the Ghost pulls out his back-up—the Model 51—and shoots through the bag, spattering the plant material and flecks of paper on Sonny. The bullet misses but the Ghost jumps him. There's a fight. The Ghost gets the .45 and kills Sonny.'

'You want to canvas the stores there to see who has yellow bags?'

'No, that'd take too long. I think we need to find out what the plant material is first. It's probably Chinese herbs. I'm going to stop by John Sung's apartment with a sample of it. He should be able to tell me right away what it is. He only lives a few blocks from here.'

Chapter Fourteen

He stared out of the window at the grey dusk. His head drooped forwards, heavy, immobile—not from damaged fibres of nerve but from sorrow. Rhyme was thinking of Sonny Li.

Li: a small man who wanted nothing more than to offer the citizens on his beat some justice, some comfort in the aftermath of evil. The lone cop had travelled to the ends of the earth to collar his suspect. And for his reward Li was content to enjoy a good hunt, a challenge and, perhaps, just a little respect from those he cared about.

'OK, Mel,' Rhyme said evenly. 'Let's put this one together. What've we got?'

Mel Cooper was hunched over the plastic bags that a patrolman had raced here from the crime scene in Chinatown. 'Footprints.'

'We sure it was the Ghost?' Rhyme asked.

'Yep,' Cooper confirmed. 'They're identical.'

Rhyme agreed. This was evidence and it belonged on the board. 'Thom . . . Thom!' he shouted. 'We need you!'

The aide appeared immediately. He picked up the marker and walked to the whiteboard.

Cooper then opened Li's clothes over a large sheet of clean, blank newsprint. He examined the trace that had fallen onto the paper. 'Dirt, flecks of paint, the yellow paper particles from the bag and the dried plant material that Amelia mentioned.'

'She's checking out the plant stuff right now,' Rhyme said.

'Fingernail scrapings,' Cooper announced, examining the label on another plastic bag. He mounted the trace on a slide.

'Project it, Mel,' Rhyme said and turned to the computer screen. A moment later a clear image appeared.

'Tobacco,' the criminalist said, laughing sadly, thinking of the cop's addiction to cigarettes. 'What else? What are those minerals there? What do you think, Mel? Silicates?'

After a few moments the chromatograph results came back—magnesium and silicate.

'That's talc, right?'

'Yep.'

'Go on-line and find out everything you can about talc and magnesium silicate.'

As Cooper was typing, Rhyme's phone rang. Thom put the call on the speaker.

'This is Dr Arthur Winslow at HuntingtonMedical Center.'

'Yes, Doctor?'

'There's a patient here, a Chinese man. His name is Sen. He was medevaced to us after the Coast Guard rescued him from a sunken ship off the North Shore. We were told to contact you with any news about him.'

'That's right.'

'Well, I think there's something you ought to know.'

JOHN SUNG HAD CHANGED clothes. He was wearing a turtleneck sweater—which seemed odd in the heat—and new workout pants. He was flushed and he seemed distracted, out of breath.

'Are you all right?' Amelia Sachs asked.

'Yoga,' he explained. 'I was doing my exercises. Tea?'

'I can't stay long.' Alan Coe was waiting for her downstairs.

He held up a bag. 'Here's what I wanted to give you. The fertility herbs I told you about last night.'

She took the bag absently. 'Thank you, John.'

'What's wrong?' he asked, searching her troubled face.

'That police officer from China, the man who helped us? He was found dead about an hour ago. The Ghost.'

'Oh, no, I'm sorry.'

'I am too,' she said brusquely. She reached into her pocket and withdrew a plastic bag of the plant material she'd collected. 'We found this where he was murdered. We think it's some herbs that the Ghost bought.'

'Let me see it.' Sung opened the bag, then shook out some of the contents. He inhaled the aroma and examined the substance. Finally he handed the bag back to her. 'I smell astragalus, ginger, poria, maybe some ginseng and alisma.' He shook his head. 'I'm afraid you can buy this at any herbalist. You could check the stores closest to where the policeman was killed,' Sung suggested.

She nodded. 'That's what we'll have to do. Maybe we'll get a break.' She started to stand and winced as pain shot through her shoulder.

'Taking your medicine?' he asked, chiding her.

'Yeah, I am. But you know how disgusting it tastes.'

'Here, sit down.'

She lowered herself painfully to the couch. He moved close behind her. Then she felt his hands on her shoulder as they began squeezing—softly at first then harder, more probing. It was relaxing, yes, but she felt momentarily disconcerted when the palms and fingers nearly encircled her throat.

'Relax,' he whispered in that calm voice of his.

She tried to. His hands slid again to her shoulders then down her back. They moved forward along her ribs but stopped before he touched her breasts and returned again to her spine and neck.

'Why don't you take off that gun belt of yours?' he whispered. 'It's interfering with your circulation.'

She reached for the buckle and started to undo it. But then a harsh sound interrupted them: her cellphone ringing. She eased away from him and pulled the unit off her belt. 'Hello? This is—'

'Sachs, get ready to roll.'

'What do you have, Rhyme?'

'The captain of the ship, Sen, is conscious. Eddie Deng's on the other line, interviewing him . . . Hold on.' Voices, shouts. 'Listen, Sachs, the captain overheard Chang talking with his father. Looks like some relative or friend arranged for an apartment and job for the family in *Brooklyn*.'

'Brooklyn? What about Queens?'

'Sam Chang's the clever one, remember? I'm sure he said Queens to lead everybody off. I narrowed down the area where I think they are—Red Hook or Owls Head.'

'How do you know?'

'The biosolids on the old man's shoes. Remember? There are two waste treatment facilities in Brooklyn. I'm leaning towards Owls Head. It's more residential and close to the Chinese community. I want you over there. I'll let you know as soon as I have an address.'

She glanced up at Sung. 'John, Lincoln's found the Changs' neighbourhood. I'm going over there now.'

'Where are they?'

'In Brooklyn.'

'Oh, very good,' he said. 'May I come? I can help translate. Chang and I speak the same dialect.'

'Sure.' Sachs said into the phone, 'John Sung's coming with me and Coe. He's going to translate.'

They hung up. Sung stepped into the bedroom and a moment later he came out, wearing a bulky windcheater.

'It's not cold out,' Sachs said.

'Always keep warm—important for the *qi* and blood,' he said. Then Sung took her by the shoulders. 'You have done a very good thing, finding those people, Yindao.'

She looked at him with a faint frown of curiosity. 'Yindao?'

He said, 'It's my pet name for you in Chinese. "Yindao." It means "close friend".'

Sachs was very moved by this. She squeezed his hand. Then stepped back. 'Let's go find the Changs.'

ON THE STREET in front of his safe house the man of many names—Ang Kwan, Gui, the Ghost, John Sung—reached his hand out and shook that of Alan Coe, who was, it seemed, an INS agent. This gave him some concern, for Coe, he believed, had been part of a group of Chinese and American law enforcers pursuing him overseas. But apparently Coe had no idea what the Ghost looked like.

Yindao explained what Rhyme had learned and the three of them got into the police station wagon—Coe climbing into the back before the Ghost could take that strategically better seat. They pulled away from the kerb.

From what Yindao was telling Coe, the Ghost understood that there would be other cops and INS agents present at the Changs' apartment. But he'd already made plans. When he'd gone to get his gun and windcheater a few moments ago, Yusuf and another Uigur had been in the bedroom. He'd told them to follow Yindao's police car. In Brooklyn the Turks and the Ghost together would kill the Changs.

He quickly lost himself in his continuing fantasies about Yindao, which had grown ever more powerful since he'd first seen her on the beach—swimming out to save him. It was more than a desire to possess her physically. There was something else about Yindao: he recognised something of his own soul within her.

But he wouldn't hesitate to do what he'd planned: take her to a deserted warehouse or factory and spend an hour or so fulfilling this relentless fantasy. And kill her afterwards, of course. As Yindao herself had told him, she too would break the cauldrons and sink the boats; after she learned that he was the Ghost she would not rest until she had killed or arrested him. She had to die.

TEN MINUTES LATER Lon Sellitto's phone rang.

Rhyme stared at it rapt in anticipation.

The detective took the call. Listened. Then his eyes closed and he broke into a smile.

'They found the Changs' address!' he shouted, and hung up. 'That was one of the patrolmen down at the Fifth. He found a guy in Owls Head who owns two quick-print shops. Name's Joseph Tan. Our guy gave him the line about the family'd be dead in a couple hours if we didn't find out where they were. Tan broke down and admitted he'd got Chang and his kid a job and set 'em up in an apartment. Two blocks from the sewage treatment plant.'

Rhyme wheeled into position in front of the whiteboards. He gazed at the chart, the pictures of evidence.

Sellitto said, 'I'll call and get everybody going.'

'Hold on a minute,' the criminalist said.

'What's the matter?'

'An itch,' Rhyme said slowly. 'I have an itch.'

Rhyme's head moved slowly as he took in Thom's careful jottings and photographs and other bits of evidence from this case—each adding to the grim story, like hieroglyphs in ancient Egyptian tombs.

Here's the answer, Rhyme thought, staring at the entries. The only problem, though, is that we don't know the question.

'What are you thinking?' Sellitto asked.

Rhyme didn't answer. He mentally followed the trails of evidence that they had collected, some of them wide as the East River, some as narrow and frail as thread; some helpful, some as seemingly useless as the broken nerves that ran from Lincoln Rhyme's brain south into his still body. But even these he didn't neglect.

THE HIGHWAY took a sweep around the Brooklyn army facility and Yindao steered the station wagon onto an exit ramp, and descended into a pleasant neighbourhood of tidy yards and red-brick buildings.

The Ghost glanced into the side mirror casually and noticed that Yusuf was still behind them. Then he looked at Yindao, the profile of her beautiful face, her shimmery red hair pinned into a bun, the outline of her breasts beneath her black T-shirt.

He was startled by the blare of the woman's phone ringing.

She answered it. 'Rhyme . . . yeah, we're in the neighbourhood. Go ahead.' She fell silent. 'Excellent!' She turned to the Ghost and Coe. 'He's found them.' She turned her attention back to the phone. As she listened to what Rhyme was saying, though, it seemed to the Ghost that she had tensed. 'Sure, Rhyme,' she said. 'Got it.'

The Ghost looked at her. 'So he got the exact address?'

She didn't answer for a moment. Finally she said, 'Yeah.'

Then she began talking, just chatting like a schoolgirl, about her life in Brooklyn. The Ghost saw at once that this wasn't her nature and he grew suspicious. He noticed her hand slip to her leg, which she scratched absently. She left her hand near her hip, and he realised that the gesture was merely an excuse to move her hand to her gun.

The Ghost's hand now slipped casually to his side and then curled behind his back until it was touching the grip of his Glock pistol, which rested in the waistband of his slacks.

Another turn and, looking at the house numbers, she pulled up to the kerb, pointing to a small brownstone building. 'That's it.'

The Ghost kept his attention wholly on Yindao.

Coe said, 'Let's go get this over with.'

Yindao said casually, 'Wait.' And she turned to her right to look at Coe over the seat.

She moved fast. Before the snakehead could even close his fingers around his own pistol, Yindao was swinging her gun towards him.

The Ghost involuntarily flinched, half expecting Yindao to shoot. But the muzzle of the black weapon travelled past him in a blur and came to rest on the man in the back seat.

'Not an inch, Coe. Don't move an inch.'

'What . . . what is this?' Coe asked, rearing back in shock.

'Lincoln knows. How you're the one working for the Ghost.'

The agent swallowed. 'Are you out of your mind?'

'You're protecting him. That's why you fired that shot at the Wus' place on Canal Street. You weren't trying to hit him; you were trying to *warn* him. And you've been feeding him information.'

Coe looked around nervously. 'This is bullshit.'

The Ghost struggled to control his breathing from the shock. He was sweating furiously.

'We've had reports all along that the Ghost was bribing people in the government over here,' Yindao said. 'We just never thought it'd be an INS agent. Why all the trips to China? You were meeting your boss's snakehead.'

'You're crazy, Sachs.'

Yindao snapped, 'Were you going to call the Ghost when we got to the Changs' apartment? Or were you just going to kill them yourself? . . . And us too?'

Coe swallowed. 'I want to talk to a lawyer.'

'You'll have plenty of time for that. Now, right hand on the door handle. It moves off by one inch, I'll park one in your arm. Left hand, thumb and index finger only, on your weapon, grip first.'

Disgust on his face, Coe removed the weapon and handed it to her.

Yindao pocketed it and then said, 'Out of the car.'

The Ghost watched as, on the sidewalk, she expertly cuffed the agent. He rolled down his window and nodded towards the apartment. 'Do you want me to talk to the Changs?'

'That's not their place,' Yindao said. 'It's still a few blocks from here. I lied—I had to keep Coe off guard. I picked it because there's a police precinct house round the corner. They're going to hold him for the FBI to pick up.'

Yindao roughly led Coe to the corner, where she was met by three uniformed officers, who took him into custody. The Ghost glanced behind him and saw Yusuf's van idling at the kerb.

Five minutes later Yindao returned, climbed in the car, fired up the engine. She looked at the Ghost and shook her head. 'I'm sorry. Are you all right?' She now seemed relaxed, more like herself.

'Yes.' The Ghost laughed. 'You handled that perfectly. Your friend Rhyme is quite a detective.'

Rhyme would have to die too. The Ghost knew that he also was a man who would never stop until he'd defeated his enemies. This Rhyme was just like Yindao. Too dangerous to stay alive.

She picked up her cellphone and made a call. 'OK, Rhyme, Coe's in custody . . . No, no problems. John and I are going on to the Changs' now . . . OK, I'll be there in three minutes. We're not going to wait for ESU. The Ghost could be on his way there right now.'

He could indeed, the snakehead reflected.

Yindao turned abruptly down a one-way street and stopped. She double-parked and left a police ID on the dashboard.

'That's the house there.' She pointed to a three-storey, red-brick house several doors away.

They climbed out of the car and she nodded at the front bay window. 'We'll go through the back door—if it's unlocked. They'd be able to see us from the front and might run. Come on,' she said. 'Move slow. Don't startle them. Tell them we're here to help.'

Yindao tried the door. It was unlocked. She pushed it open quickly. They walked silently through the small, stifling kitchen.

On the stove a pot of water was heating. Half an onion sat on a board, a bunch of parsley nearby. Yindao paused at the doorway of the corridor that led to the living room, gestured that he stop.

The Turks, he saw, were outside in the alley beside the house. Yindao's back was to him and he motioned them round to the front. The Ghost reached back under his windcheater and pulled his gun from the waistband of his slacks.

AMELIA SACHS stepped forward slowly into the dark corridor.

'Wait here a minute, John,' she whispered.

She hesitated only a moment and then called, 'Now.'

'What?' the Ghost asked, hesitating.

But instead of responding she spun back towards him, raising her own pistol so quickly that the motion of the black weapon was a grey blur. The abyss of the muzzle settled steadily on the Ghost's chest before he could even lift his own Glock.

Sachs's utterance had been directed to the half a dozen men and women in full combat gear—Emergency Services Unit tactical cops—who pushed into the small kitchen. They rushed in from the back door and past her from the living room, guns pointed at the shocked Ghost's face, screaming, 'Down, down, down, police, drop your weapon, on the floor!'

His pistol was torn from his hand and he was flung face down to the floor and cuffed and frisked. The Model 51 was lifted away.

'We've got the subject down,' an officer shouted. 'Scene clear. Outside, we've got two, both down and locked.' More Uigurs from the community centre in Queens, Sachs assumed.

Then Lon Sellitto and Eddie Deng joined her from upstairs, where they'd been waiting. They dragged the Ghost into the living room and pushed him into a chair. Eddie Deng read him his rights—in English, Mandarin and Minnan—the Chinese dialect spoken in Fujian.

He confirmed that he understood, with surprisingly little emotion, Sachs observed, considering the circumstances.

'How are the Changs?' Sachs asked Sellitto.

'They're fine. Two INS teams are at their apartment.'

The town house in which they now stood, about a mile from the Changs', was neatly decorated, full of flowers: a surprise to Sachs, considering that it was inhabited by Lon Sellitto.

'So this is *your* house, Lon?' Sachs asked.

'This was the best we could do at such short notice. We figured if we drove too far from Owls Head, he'd start to get suspicious.'

'It was all fake,' the Ghost said, amused. 'You set me up.'

'Guess we did.'

Lincoln Rhyme's call had been to tell Sachs that he believed the Ghost was masquerading as John Sung. Another team of cops was on its way to the Changs' real apartment to detain them. Sellitto and Deng were setting up a takedown site at Sellitto's house, where they could collar him without the risk of bystanders getting killed.

It had taken all of Sachs's emotional strength to pretend that Coe was working for the Ghost and that the man who was supposedly her friend, her doctor, the man sitting two feet from her and undoubtedly armed, was the killer they'd been seeking for the past two days.

She thought now of the acupressure session last night—coming to him with her secret, with her desperate hope of being cured. She shivered with repulsion at the memory of his hands on her back and shoulders. She also remembered with horror that she'd mentioned to him the location of the safe house where the Wus were staying.

The Ghost asked, 'How did Rhyme know that I wasn't Sung?'

'The stone monkey,' she explained. 'I found some trace under Sonny Li's fingernails. It was magnesium silicate, like talc. Rhyme found out that it came from soapstone—which is what the amulet's carved out of.' Sachs reached out and roughly tugged down Ghost's turtleneck, revealing the red line from the leather cord. 'What happened? He ripped it off your neck and it broke?'

The Ghost nodded slowly. 'Before I shot him he was clawing the ground. I thought he was begging for mercy but then he looked up and smiled at me.'

So Li had scraped some of the soft stone under his nails to tell them the Ghost was actually Sung.

Remembering the contamination on Sachs's hands yesterday, Rhyme realised that it might have come from Sung's amulet. He'd called the officers who'd guarded Sung's apartment and they'd confirmed that there was a back entrance to the place, which meant that the Ghost had been able to come and go without their seeing him. He'd also asked if there were a gardening shop nearby—the likely source for the mulch that they'd found—and was told about the florist on the ground floor of the apartment building. Then he checked calls to Sachs's cellphone; the number of the cell that had been used to call the Uigur centre showed up in her records.

The real John Sung had been a doctor and the Ghost was not. But everyone in China knew something about Eastern medicine.

'And your friend from the INS?' the Ghost asked.

'Coe?' Sachs replied. 'We knew he didn't have any connection with you. But we needed to make sure you didn't think we were on to you. And we needed him out of the way. He might've gone after you again, like he did on Canal Street.' She looked him over and shook her head in disgust. 'You shot Sung, hid the body then shot yourself. And swam back into the ocean. What about your gun?'

'Stuffed it into my sock. Then I hid it in the hospital and picked it up after the INS officer released me.'

'Everything you told me about John Sung . . . you made it up?"

The Ghost shrugged. 'No, what I told. Before I killed him I made him tell me about himself, about everyone who was on the raft, about Chang and Wu. Enough to make my performance believable. I threw out his picture ID and kept the wallet and the amulet.'

'Where's Sung's body?'

A placid smile. His serenity was infuriating.

Sachs's phone rang. She answered. 'Yes?'

'I suppose somebody was going to call me *eventually* and let me know what happened,' Rhyme's voice said sarcastically.

'We've been a little busy here, Rhyme,' she answered, 'because we caught him.' She added, 'I tried to get him to tell me where John Sung's body is but he—'

'In the trunk of the stolen Honda,' Rhyme interrupted.

'And that's still out on the eastern end of Long Island?' she asked, understanding finally.

'Of course. The Ghost stole it, killed Sung and then drove *east* to hide it—we wouldn't look that direction. We'd assume he'd headed west—into the city.'

Chapter Fifteen

Amelia Sachs found the Chang family standing outside a run-down house near Owls Head Park. The smell of sewage was heavy in the air.

Sam Chang stood with his arms crossed, grim and silent, head down, as an INS agent talked with him, jotting notes. At his side was a woman in her forties, holding the hand of Po-Yee. Sachs felt a huge thud within her when she saw the Treasured Child. The toddler was adorable. A round-faced girl with silky black hair, she wore red corduroy jeans and a sweatshirt that was two sizes too big for her.

A NYPD detective recognised Lon Sellitto and walked up to him and Sachs. 'The family's fine. We're taking them to INS detention in Queens. It looks like with Chang's record of dissident activity—he was at Tiananmen and has a history of persecution—he's got a good shot at asylum.'

'You have caught the Ghost?' Sam Chang asked her in unsteady English as he joined them.

'Yes,' she said. 'He's in custody.'

'Thank you.' Chang thought for a moment and then said, 'I may ask you? The man, old man killed in Ghost's apartment building? My father, he must have proper funeral. Is very important.'

Sachs said, 'I'll make sure he's not moved. After you're through with the INS you can arrange to have a funeral home pick him up at the morgue.'

'Thank you.'

A small blue Dodge pulled up to the scene. A black woman in a brown trouser suit got out. 'I'm Chiffon Wilson. I'm a social worker with Children's Services.'

'You're here for the baby?'

'Right. They have no claim to her, I'm afraid. She's an orphaned citizen of another country. She'll have to go back to China.'

Sachs nodded slowly then gestured the social worker aside. She whispered, 'You know what happens to baby girl orphans in China?'

'She'll be adopted.'

'Maybe,' Sachs said dubiously.

'I don't know about that. I'm just following the law.'

She then nodded to the INS agent, who spoke in Chinese to the

Changs. Mei-Mei's face went still but she nodded and directed the baby to the social worker, then she frowned, trying to think of the English words. 'She very good baby. Lost mother. Make sure she good take care of.'

'I'll make sure.'

Wilson picked up Po-Yee, who squinted at Sachs's red hair and reached out to grip a handful of the strands with curiosity. When she tugged hard, Sachs laughed.

The social worker started for the car.

'*Ting!*' came a woman's urgent voice. Sachs recognised the word for 'wait' or 'stop'. She turned to see Mei-Mei walking towards them.

'Here. There is this.' Mei-Mei handed her a stuffed animal toy, crudely made. A cat, Sachs believed. 'She like this. Make her happy.'

The child's eyes were on the toy, Mei-Mei's on the girl.

The social worker strapped the child into a car seat and drove away.

Sachs spent half an hour talking to the Changs, debriefing them, seeing if she could learn anything else that might help shore up the case against the Ghost. Then the exhaustion of the past two days caught up with her and she knew it was time to go home.

EVEN THOUGH THE GHOST was in custody, Lincoln Rhyme and Amelia Sachs spent the next morning processing the information that continued to arrive regarding the GHOSTKILL case.

An analysis of the chemical markers in the C4 by the FBI had determined that the likely source of the plastic explosive used to blow up the ship was a North Korean arms dealer.

Recovery divers from the *Evan Brigant* had brought up the bodies of the crewmen and the other immigrants from the *Fuzhou Dragon*, as well as the rest of the money—about $120,000. They had also learned that Ling Shui-bian, the man who had paid the money to the Ghost and had written him the letter that Sachs had found in the ship, had an address in Fuzhou. Rhyme emailed the name and address to the Fuzhou public security bureau.

As Thom was writing the latest information on the board, Rhyme's computer beeped with a list of new messages.

'Ah,' Rhyme announced, 'I was right.'

The body of John Sung had been found in the trunk of the red Honda that the Ghost had stolen. As Rhyme predicted, the car had been found sunk in a pond less than a hundred yards from Easton Beach. One more murder charge against Kwan Ang.

There was another message that interested him. This one was from Mel Cooper, who was back in his office at the NYPD forensic lab.

Lincoln,
We have analysed the dynamite and it is phoney. The perp used dummy explosive—stuff used for training. Might be something to think about.

Rhyme laughed. Some arms dealer must have scammed Dellray's attacker by selling him the fake explosives.

The doorbell rang. Heavy footsteps on the stairs. Two sets. Rhyme believed they belonged to Sellitto and Dellray. He'd tell them about the fake bomb. They'd all get a laugh out of it. But then an alarm bell went off inside his head. The men had stopped outside the door and were whispering, as if debating who should deliver bad news.

A moment later the rumpled cop and the lanky FBI agent pushed into the room. 'Hey, Linc,' Sellitto said.

One look at their faces told Rhyme he was right about the bad news. He looked from one to the other. 'Well, say something.'

Dellray uttered a long sigh. Finally Sellitto said, 'They took him out of our jurisdiction—the Ghost. He's being sent back to China.'

'What?' Sachs gasped.

Angrily Dellray said, 'Bein' escorted onto a flight later today. Once it takes off he's free.'

'Extradited?' Rhyme asked.

'That's the fuzzy li'l spin they're puttin' on it,' Dellray growled. 'But we ain't seen any arrest warrant for him issued by a Chinese court.'

'What does that mean, no arrest warrant?' Sachs asked.

'That his *guanxi*'s saving his ass,' Rhyme said bitterly.

'I talked to our folk over there. The high-ups in China want him back, lemme quote, "for questioning in connection with irregular matters of foreign trade".'

Rhyme was stunned. 'He'll be back in business in a month. Fred, can you do *anything*?'

The FBI agent shook his head. 'This li'l decision got made in State Department Washington. I got no clout there.'

Rhyme remembered the man in the blue suit: Webley from State.

'He knew,' Sachs whispered. 'The Ghost knew he was safe. At the takedown he was surprised but he didn't look worried.'

'I'm not going to let this happen,' Rhyme said, thinking of the people dead in the *Fuzhou Dragon*. Thinking of Sonny Li.

IN THE FEDERAL Men's Detention Center in downtown Manhattan the Ghost sat across the table from his lawyer in a private conference room. He spoke quietly in Minnan. 'I need you to find some information for me. There is a woman who works for the police department. I need her home address. Her name is Amelia Sachs and she lives somewhere in Brooklyn. S-A-C-H-S. And Lincoln Rhyme. Spelled like in poetry. He's in Manhattan.'

The lawyer nodded.

'Then there are the two families,' he said. 'The Wus and the Changs. They might be in INS detention somewhere.'

The lawyer considered. 'When do you need this information?'

'As soon as possible.'

The Ghost dismissed his lawyer then lay back on the cot in the clean, square cell. He closed his eyes and pictured Yindao. The thought of her would get him through the difficult coming weeks.

'WE'VE HAD our differences, Alan,' Rhyme said.

'I guess.' INS agent Coe was cautious. He sat in Rhyme's bedroom. This was to be a completely private conversation.

'You heard about the Ghost's release?'

'Of course I heard about the Ghost.'

Rhyme asked, 'Tell me, what's your real interest in the case?'

Coe hesitated and then said, 'The informant of mine he killed, Julia. We were lovers. She died because of me. We should've been more careful. We went out in public some.' There were tears in his eyes now. 'I never had her do anything dangerous. Just glance at scheduling calendars from time to time. But I should've known the Ghost. Nobody could get away with even the slightest betrayal. The Ghost got her. She left two daughters behind.'

'That's what you were doing overseas during the time you took off?'

He nodded. 'Looking for Julia. But then I gave up and spent my time trying to get the children placed in a Catholic home. But the state took them and I never saw them again.' Coe wiped his eyes. 'So that's why I go on about undocumenteds. As long as people pay fifty thousand bucks for an illegal trip to America we're going to have snakeheads like the Ghost killing anybody who gets in their way.'

Rhyme wheeled closer to Coe. 'What are you willing to risk to stop him?' he whispered.

There was no hesitation as the agent said, 'Everything.'

THE SHACKLES binding his wrists felt light as silk.

They would come off as soon as he was at the doorway of the airliner that would carry him home and, because he knew that, the metal restraints had already ceased to exist.

They were walking down the corridor of JFK Airport, a curious entourage—two armed guards and the two men in charge, Peabody from the INS and Webley from the United States Department of State, now joined by two armed Port Authority guards.

'Mr Kwan . . . Mr Kwan!'

They turned to see a thin Chinese man in a suit walking quickly towards them.

'It's my lawyer,' the Ghost said.

Peabody nodded the man forward, frisked him, and let him and the snakehead step to the side of the corridor.

The Ghost turned his ear towards the lawyer's mouth. 'Go ahead.'

'The Changs and the Wus are out on bond, pending the hearing. It looks like they'll be granted asylum. The Wus are in Flushing, Queens. The Changs are back in Owls Head. The same apartment.'

'And the Sachs woman?' the Ghost whispered.

'Oh, I have her address too. And Lincoln Rhyme's.'

'Tell them to me slowly. I'll remember them.'

After three repetitions the Ghost had memorised them. He said, 'You'll find your money in the account.'

The lawyer nodded, turned and left.

The group continued down the corridor. Ahead of him the Ghost could see the gate. And through the window he glimpsed the 747 that would soon take him west. His boarding pass was protruding from his shirt pocket. He had 10,000 yuan in his wallet. He was free. He—

Somebody was moving towards him fast and the guards were pulling him aside, their weapons coming out of their holsters. The Ghost, gasping at the shock, thought that he was going to die.

But the attacker stopped short. The Ghost began to laugh. 'Hello, Yindao.' Then he focused past Yindao. Behind her was a tall black man in a white suit and noisy blue shirt. The fat cop who'd arrested him in Brooklyn was here as well, as were several city policemen. But the one person who captured his full attention was a handsome dark-haired man about the Ghost's age, sitting in a complicated, bright red wheelchair. A trim young man—his aide or nurse—stood behind him.

The man in the wheelchair was, of course, Lincoln Rhyme. The

Ghost studied the man who'd discovered the location of the *Fuzhou Dragon* at sea, who'd found the Wus and the Changs and who had succeeded in capturing the Ghost himself. Which no other policeman in the world had ever been able to do.

Harold Peabody surveyed the situation and motioned the guards back. They put their weapons away. He didn't need problems, not with this case. 'What's this all about, Rhyme?'

But the man ignored him and continued to study the snakehead carefully. The Ghost felt a trickle of unease. But he had *guanxi* at the highest level. He was immune, even to the magic of Lincoln Rhyme.

Webley, the State Department bureaucrat, said impatiently, 'All of you, now—just clear on out of here.'

'He's not getting on that airplane,' Rhyme said.

'Oh, yes, he is,' said the dour official. He plucked the Ghost's ticket from his pocket then strode towards the gate agent.

'You take one more step towards that airplane,' the fat policeman said, 'and these officers are authorised to arrest you.'

'Me?' Webley muttered angrily.

Peabody gave a sharp laugh and looked at the black agent.

'Dellray, what is this?'

'Probably oughta listen to my friend here, Harold. In your best innerest, believe you me.'

Peabody said, 'Five minutes.'

A regretful frown crossed Lincoln Rhyme's face. 'Oh, I'm afraid it may take a little longer than that.'

Chapter Sixteen

The Ghost stood shackled and surrounded by law enforcers, still in control, serene, shoulders and arms relaxed. Lincoln Rhyme understood immediately how Sachs could have been suckered by him: the Ghost's eyes were those of a healer, a doctor, a spiritual man. But, knowing the man now, Rhyme could see in the placid gaze evidence of ruthlessness and a relentless ego.

'OK, sir, what's this all about?' asked Webley from State, as the criminalist now thought of him.

Rhyme said, 'You know what happens sometimes in our line of

work, gentlemen? I mean, forensic science. We sometimes lose sight of the big picture.'

The gate agent announced pre-boarding of the Northwest Airlines flight to Los Angeles.

'My nature is to study each piece of evidence and put it where it belongs. We figured out the clues just fine.' A nod towards the Ghost. 'After all, here he is, caught, right? Thanks to us. And we've got enough evidence to convict him. But what happens? He's going free.'

'He's not going free,' Peabody rejoined. 'He's going back to stand trial in China.'

'Free from the jurisdiction where he's committed a number of serious felonies in the past few days,' Rhyme corrected sharply, and kept steaming forwards. 'Big picture . . . Let's think about it. It's Tuesday, on board the *Dragon*. You're the Ghost, a wanted man—wanted for capital offences—and the Coast Guard is a half-hour away from interdicting your smuggling ship. What would you have done?'

Peabody sighed. Webley from State muttered something *sotto voce*.

Since no one was helping him out Rhyme continued, 'I personally would've taken my money, pointed the *Dragon* out to sea full speed ahead and escaped to shore in one of the life rafts. The Coast Guard and cops and INS would've been so busy with the immigrants I could easily've got to land and been halfway to Chinatown before they realised I was gone. But what did the Ghost do?'

Rhyme glanced at Sachs, who said, 'He locked the immigrants in the hold, sank the ship and then hunted down the survivors. And he risked getting caught or killed to do it. Why would he do that?'

'Well, they were witnesses,' Peabody said. 'He *had* to kill them.'

'Ah, *why*? That's the question that nobody's asking. What would it gain him? All that the passengers could do would be to testify in one case of human smuggling. But there were already a dozen warrants against him for smuggling. Homicide charges too. It made no sense to go to all that trouble to murder them just because they were witnesses. But killing them makes perfect sense if the passengers were his *intended* victims.'

Peabody was perplexed and surprised. In Webley from State's eyes there was a different look. He knew exactly where Rhyme was going.

'"Victims",' Rhyme continued. 'That's a key word. See, Sachs found a letter when she went for her little swim in the *Dragon*.'

The Ghost, who'd been staring at Sachs, turned slowly towards Rhyme when he heard this.

'It said, more or less, here's your money and a list of the victims you'll be taking to America . . . Are we catching on to the big picture, gentlemen? The letter didn't say "passengers" or "immigrants". It said "victims". I didn't realise at first when I had the letter translated that that was the exact word the writer used. And the big picture becomes a lot clearer when we look at who those victims were—all Chinese dissidents and their families. The Ghost isn't just a snakehead. He's also a professional killer. He was hired to murder them.'

'This man is crazy,' the Ghost snapped. 'I want to leave now.'

But Rhyme said, 'The Ghost was planning all along to scuttle the *Dragon*. He was only waiting until he was close enough to shore so that he and his *bangshou* could make it to land safely. But a few things went wrong: we found the ship and sent the Coast Guard in, so he had to act sooner than he'd planned; some of the immigrants escaped. Then the explosive was too powerful and the ship sank before he could get his guns and money and find his assistant.'

'That's absurd,' muttered Webley from State. 'Beijing wouldn't hire anybody to kill dissidents. It's not the 1960s any more.'

'Beijing *didn't* do it,' Rhyme responded, 'as I suspect you probably know, Webley. No, we found out who sent the Ghost his instructions and his money. Ling Shui-bian is his name.'

The Ghost glanced desperately at the boarding gate.

Rhyme continued, 'I sent the Fuzhou police an email with Ling's name and address. But they sent back a message saying the address was a government building in Fuzhou. Ling is the Fujian governor's assistant in charge of trade development.'

'What's that mean?' Peabody asked.

'That he's a corrupt warlord,' Rhyme snapped. 'He and his people are getting millions in kickbacks from businesses all along the south-eastern coast of China. He's probably working with the governor, but I don't have any evidence about that. Not yet, anyway.'

'Impossible,' offered Webley, though with much less bluster than he'd displayed earlier.

Rhyme said, 'Not at all. Sonny Li told me about Fujian Province. It's always been more independent than the central government likes. It has the most connections with the West and Taiwan, the most active dissidents. Beijing is always threatening to crack down on the province, nationalise businesses again and put its own people in power. If that happens, Ling and his boys lose their income stream. So, how to keep Beijing happy? Hire a snakehead to kill the most vocal dissidents.'

'And more likely than not,' Sachs said, 'nobody'd even know that they died.' Nodding at Webley from State, she reminded, 'Rhyme?'

'Oh, right. Why's the Ghost going free?' He said to Webley, 'You're sending him back to keep Ling and his people in Fujian happy. To make sure our business interests aren't affected. Southeast China is the biggest site for US investment in the world.'

'That's bullshit,' the man snapped in reply.

'Well, we have the letter from Ling. But if you want more proof. Remember, Harold? You told me that other shiploads of the Ghost's immigrants disappeared in the past year or so. I checked. Most of those victims were dissidents from Fujian too. Then there's the money,' Rhyme continued. 'The smuggling fee. When Sachs went for her little paddle in the Atlantic she found a hundred and twenty thousand US dollars and maybe twenty thousand worth of old yuan. I invited a friend of mine from the INS over to my place to help me look at the evidence. He—'

'Who?' Peabody asked sharply. 'Alan Coe?'

'A friend. Let's leave it at that.'

In fact, the friend *was* agent Coe, who'd also spent the day stealing classified INS files, which would probably cost him his job.

'The first thing he noticed was the money. He told me that when immigrants contract with snakeheads they can't pay the down payment in dollars—because there *are* no dollars in China, not enough to pay for transit to the US anyway. They always pay in yuan. With a shipload of twenty-five or so immigrants, that means Sachs should've found at least half a million in yuan—just for the down payment. So why was there so little Chinese money on board? Because the Ghost charged next to nothing to make sure that the dissidents on the hit list could afford to make the trip. The Ghost was making his profit from the fee to kill them. The hundred and twenty thousand? Well, *that* was the down payment from Ling. According to the Federal Reserve, that cash was last seen going into the Bank of South China in Singapore. Which happens to be used regularly by the Fujianese government.'

The State Department official was resolute. 'He's getting on that plane and that's all there is to it.'

Rhyme squinted and cocked his head. 'How high are we now on the ladder of evidence, Sachs?'

'How about the C4?'

'Right, the explosive used to blow up the ship. The FBI traced it to a North Korean arms dealer, who regularly sells to—guess who? People's Liberation Army bases in Fujian. The *government* gave the Ghost the C4. Then there's the cellphone that Sachs found at the beach . . . It was a government-issue satellite phone.'

'The trucks, Rhyme,' Sachs reminded.

Rhyme nodded. 'I was looking at our evidence board and I realised that something was missing: the trucks to transport the immigrants. My INS friend told me that ground transport is part of the smuggling contract. But there weren't any trucks. Because the Ghost knew the immigrants would never get to shore alive.'

Webley from State leaned down and whispered viciously into Rhyme's face, 'You're in way over your head here, mister. You don't know what you're doing.'

Rhyme gazed back at him in mock contrition. 'Nope, I don't know a thing. Not about world politics. I'm just a simple scientist. My knowledge is woefully limited. To things like, say, fake dynamite.'

Which shut up Webley from State instantly.

Peabody cleared his throat. 'What are you talking about?'

'The bomb in Fred's car? Well, the results came back from the lab about the dynamite. Interesting—it wasn't dynamite at all. It was sawdust mixed with resin. Fake. Used for training. My INS friend told me that Immigration has a bomb squad, with dummy explosives on hand to teach rookies recognition and handling. The sticks in Fred's car match the samples from there. And the numbers on the detonator are similar to some he found in an INS evidence locker.'

Rhyme enjoyed the flicker of horror in Peabody's eyes.

'If you're suggesting,' said Webley from State indignantly, 'that anyone in the federal government would hurt a fellow agent . . .'

'Hurt? How could a small detonator hurt anyone. It was just a firecracker, really. No, the important criminal charge *I'd* think of would be felonious interference with an investigation—because it would seem to me that you might've wanted Fred off the case temporarily.'

' 'Cause'—white-suited Dellray took over—'I was makin' waves. Gettin' together the SPEC-TAC team. Who woulda taken the Ghost out no nonsense. Hell, I think that's why I was on the case in the first place. I din't know beans 'bout human smugglin'. An' when I arranged for an expert—Dan Wong—to take over the case, next thing we know his butt's on a plane headin' west.'

Rhyme summarised, 'Fred had to go so you could dispose of the Ghost the way you'd planned: catching him alive and getting him safely out of the country as part of a deal between the State Department and Ling in Fujian.'

'I didn't know anything about killing dissidents,' Peabody blurted. 'That was never expressed to me. I swear! All they said was that they needed to keep the Justice Department out of it.'

'Watch it,' Webley from State muttered threateningly. Then he turned to Rhyme and said in a reasonable voice, 'Look, if—I'm saying *if*—any of this is true, you have to realise there's a lot more to it than just this one man, Lincoln. The Ghost's cover's been blown. Nobody'll hire him as a snakehead after this. But,' the diplomat continued smoothly, 'if we send him back, that'll keep the Chinese happy. And with more American influence there'll be improved human rights. Sometimes we have to make hard choices.'

Rhyme nodded. 'So what you're saying is that it's essentially an issue of politics and diplomacy.'

Webley smiled, pleased that Rhyme finally understood. 'Exactly.'

'See,' the criminalist explained, 'politics are complicated, diplomacy is complicated. But crime is simple. I don't like complicated things. So here's the deal: either you hand the Ghost over to us for prosecution in this country or you let him fly back home. And if you do that we go public with the fact you're releasing a perp in a multiple homicide for political reasons. And that you assaulted an FBI agent in the process.' He added flippantly, 'Your choice. Up to you.'

'Don't threaten us. You're just city cops,' said Webley.

'Harold?' Rhyme asked.

Miserable, Peabody said, 'I'm sorry. There's nothing I can do.'

Rhyme smiled faintly. 'That's all I wanted. A decision. You made one. Good. Thom, could you please show him our handiwork?'

The young man took an envelope out of his pocket and handed it to Webley from State. He opened it. Inside was a long memo from Rhyme to Peter Hoddins, a *New York Times* reporter. It described in detail exactly what Rhyme had just told Peabody and Webley.

'Peter and I are good friends,' Thom said. 'I told him we might have an exclusive about the *Fuzhou Dragon* sinking and that it had implications all the way to Washington. He was intrigued.'

Webley from State and Peabody looked at each other for a moment. Then they retired to the corner of the now-empty gate area and each made phone calls.

Finally the two federal telephones were hung up and a moment later Rhyme had his answer: Webley from State turned without a word and stalked down the corridor to the main lobby.

'Wait!' the Ghost cried. 'There was a deal! We had a deal!'

The man kept going, tearing up Rhyme's memo as he walked, not even pausing as he tossed it towards a trash container.

Sellitto told the gate agent to close the door to the aircraft. Mr Kwan wouldn't be making the flight.

SEVERAL DAYS LATER the Ghost had been arraigned and was being held without bail. The laundry list of offences was long: state and federal charges for murder, human smuggling, assault, firearms possession, money laundering.

Rhyme and Sachs were alone in his bedroom and the policewoman was looking herself over in a full-length mirror.

'You look fine,' the criminalist called. She was due to make an appearance in court in an hour.

Amelia Sachs, who'd never looked back when she gave up modelling, called her herself a 'jeans and sweats girl'. She was now dressed in a crisp blue suit, white blouse and a pair of highly sensible navy-blue heels that boosted her height to over six foot. Her red hair was perfectly arranged on top of her head.

The phone rang and Rhyme barked, 'Command. Answer phone.'

'Lincoln?' a woman's voice asked through the speaker.

'Dr Weaver,' Rhyme said to the neurosurgeon.

Sachs sat down on the edge of the Flexicair bed.

'I got your phone call,' the doctor said. 'My assistant said it was important. Is everything all right?'

'Fine,' Rhyme said.

'I'd like you to come into the office tomorrow for the final check-up before the surgery.'

Rhyme held Sachs's eye. 'I've decided not to have the operation.'

'You're—'

'I'm cancelling. Forfeiting my room deposit,' he joked.

Silence for a moment. Then: 'You wanted this more than any patient I've ever had.'

'I *did* want it, that's true. But I've changed my mind.'

'I've told you all along that the risks were high. Is that why?'

He looked at Sachs. He said only, 'In the end, I guess, I don't see that much of a benefit.'

'I think this is a good choice, Lincoln. It's the wise choice.' She added, 'We're making a lot of progress with spinal cord injuries.

There are new things happening every week. We can think about options in the future. Or just call me to talk.'

'Yes. I'd like that.'

'I'd like it too. Goodbye, Lincoln.'

'Goodbye, Doctor. Command, disconnect.'

Silence filled the room. Then Sachs squeezed his hand, and asked, 'Are you sure about this, Rhyme?'

Embrace your limitations . . . Fate make you this way, Loaban . . . Maybe you best detective you can be because of what happen. Your life balanced now, I'm saying.

'I'm sure,' he told her. 'Are *you* sure you want to do *this*?'

He nodded towards the file on the table nearby, which contained a picture of Po-Yee, a number of affidavits and official-looking documents. The top sheet of paper was headed: PETITION FOR ADOPTION.

Then she glanced at Rhyme. The look in her eye told him that she too was sure about the decision she'd made.

SITTING IN THE JUDGE'S chambers, Sachs smiled down at Po-Yee, the Treasured Child, who sat beside her in the chair where the social worker had deposited her. The girl played with her stuffed kitten.

'Ms Sachs, this is a rather unorthodox adoption proceeding. But I assume you know that.' Justice Margaret Benson-Wailes, a heavyset woman, sat behind her desk in Manhattan Family Court.

'Yes, Your Honour.'

'Tell me, Officer, how's a girl like you get so much pull in this city?'

Apparently Sachs, too, had good *guanxi*. Her connections reached from Fred Dellray to Lon Sellitto to Alan Coe (who was, far from being fired, taking over early-retiring Harold Peabody's job at the INS). In the space of several days the miles of the red tape that accompany most adoptions had been shredded.

The justice continued, 'You understand that the welfare of this child comes first no matter what and if I'm not convinced that the disposition is in her best interest I will not sign the papers.'

'I wouldn't want it any other way, Your Honour.'

'So here's what I'm going to do. I'll grant foster guardianship for a three-month period, subject to supervision by the Department of Social Services. At the end of that time, if there are no problems, I will grant permanent adoption, subject to the standard three-month probation period. How's that sound to you?'

Sachs nodded. 'It sounds fine, Your Honour.'

The justice glanced at Po-Yee, then she jabbed her intercom button and said, 'Send in the petitioners.'

A moment later the door to the justice's chambers opened and Sam and Mei-Mei Chang cautiously entered. Beside them was their attorney. Mei-Mei's eyes went wide when she saw the child, whom Sachs handed off to her. She hugged Po-Yee fiercely.

'You are Mr Sing?' the judge asked the lawyer.

'Yes, Your Honour.'

'If you could translate.'

'Certainly.'

'Usually the adoption process in this country is arduous and complicated. It is virtually impossible for a couple of uncertain immigration status to be given adoptive custody.'

A pause while Sing translated. Mei-Mei nodded.

'But we've got some unusual circumstances here. I'm told by Immigration and Naturalization that you've applied for asylum and, because of your dissident status in China, it will probably be granted. That reassures me that you can bring some stability into the child's life. As does the fact that both you and your son, Mr Chang, are employed.'

'Yes, sir.'

'"Ma'am", not "sir",' corrected Justice Benson-Wailes sternly. The judge now repeated for the Changs what she'd told Sachs about the probation and adoption. The lawyer translated.

Mei-Mei began to cry quietly and Sam Chang hugged her. Then Mei-Mei stepped up to Sachs and hugged her. '*Xiexie*, thank you, thank you.'

The justice signed a document in front of her. 'You can take the child with you now,' she said, dismissing them.

SAM CHANG LED his family, now officially increased by one, to the parking lot near the black-stone Family Court Building. This had been his second court appearance today. Earlier Chang had testified at the Wu family's preliminary hearing. Their asylum bid was less certain than the Changs' but their lawyer was guardedly optimistic.

Mei-Mei and the children now continued on to their van and Chang remained beside the red-haired policewoman. Translating his words slowly, he said to her, 'Everything you do for us, you and Mr Rhyme . . . I am not knowing how to thank you.'

'I understand,' the woman said. Her voice was clipped and Chang realised that, though she appreciated the gratitude, she was uneasy receiving it. She dropped into the seat of her car. The engine fired up with a powerful rattling noise and she drove quickly out of the parking lot, spinning tyres as she accelerated away.

AMELIA SACHS STRODE into the living room.

'So?' the criminalist asked, wheeling to face her.

'A done deal,' she answered, disappearing upstairs. She returned a few minutes later, as jeans and sweats as she could be.

He said. 'You know, Sachs, you could've adopted the baby yourself if you'd wanted.' He paused. 'I mean, *we* could've done that.'

She considered her answer then said, 'The other day I laid some brass on the deck with a perp in a Chinatown alleyway, then I went swimming ninety feet under water, then was point on a takedown team. I can't *not* do things like that, Rhyme.' She hesitated as she thought of how best to summarise her feelings then laughed. 'There are two kinds of drivers—those who check their blind spot when they change lanes and those who don't. I'm not a checker. If I had a baby at home I'd be looking over my shoulder all the time. That wouldn't work.'

'You'd be a good mother, Sachs.'

'And you'll be a good father. It'll happen, Rhyme. But let's give it a couple of years. Right now we've got a few other things to do with our lives, don't you think?' She nodded at the whiteboard, on which were written Thom's charts for the GHOSTKILL case, the same whiteboard that had been covered with notations from a dozen prior cases and would be filled with those from dozens of future ones.

She was, of course, right, Lincoln Rhyme reflected; the world represented by these notes and pictures, this place on the edge that they shared, was *their* nature—for the time being, at least.

'I made the arrangements,' he said to her.

Rhyme had been on the phone, making plans to have Sonny Li's body shipped back to his father in Liu Guoyuan, China. The arrangements were being handled by a Chinese funeral home.

There was one more task that Rhyme needed to do. He called up a word processing program. Sachs sat down next to him.

After a half-hour of writing and rewriting he and Sachs finally came up with this:

Dear Mr Li,

I am writing to express my heartfelt condolences at the death of your son.

You should know how thankful my fellow police officers and I are for the privilege of having worked with Sonny on the difficult and dangerous case that resulted in the loss of his life.

He saved many lives and brought a vicious killer to justice—an accomplishment we alone could not have achieved. His actions have brought the highest honour to his memory and he will always have a place of great respect within the law enforcement community of the United States. I truly hope you are as proud of your son for his courage and sacrifice as we are.

Lincoln Rhyme, Det. Capt., NYPD (Ret.)

Sachs set the letter aside for Eddie Deng to translate when the young cop arrived later in the day.

'Want to get back to the evidence?' Sachs asked. There was much preparatory work that needed to be done for the Ghost's trial.

But Rhyme said, 'No, I want to play a game.'

'Sure,' she said coyly, 'I'm in the mood to win.'

'You wish,' he chided.

'What game?' she asked.

'*Wei-chi*. The board's over there. And those bags of stones.'

She set up the game on the table near Rhyme. She glanced at his eyes, which were examining the grid of the board, and said, 'I think I'm being hustled, Rhyme. You've played this before.'

'Sonny and I played a few games,' he said casually. 'Three, is all.'

'How did you do?'

The criminalist said defensively, 'It takes a while to get the feel for a game.'

'You lost,' she said. 'All of them.'

'But the last one was close.'

She looked over the board. 'What'll we play for?'

With a cryptic smile Rhyme replied, 'We'll think of something.' Then he explained the rules and she leaned forwards, raptly taking in his words. Finally he said, 'That's it . . . Now, you've never played so you get an advantage. You can make the first move.'

'No,' Sachs answered. 'No advantages. We'll flip a coin.'

'It's customary,' Rhyme assured her.

'No advantage,' Sachs repeated. Then dug a quarter out of her pocket. 'Call it,' she said.

And tossed the coin into the air.

JEFFERY DEAVER

Jeffery Deaver is a firm believer in giving good value for money. 'I try to keep one thing in mind when I'm writing: what are my readers going to enjoy most? We writers have a responsibility to give the people who read our novels something they really want in exchange for their hard-earned money. And I've learned over the years that what thriller readers want is a fast-paced book with a twisty-turny plot and lots of big surprises.'

The fact that Jeffery Deaver manages to do these things so superbly well is what has placed him firmly on the best-seller lists for many years now. He works very intensely to produce his books, spending eight or nine months outlining and researching, and then three months writing and rewriting. 'And rewriting and rewriting,' he says with a laugh. He usually works ten-hour days, six days a week, and when he's actually writing sits in a darkened room, with the phone shut off, touch typing. It's a regime that enables him to publish a book a year—good news for his fans.

Inspiration for *The Stone Monkey* came from a real-life incident. 'A Chinese smuggling ship ran aground near New York some years ago, when I was living in Manhattan, and tragically a number of illegal immigrants drowned. I thought it would be interesting to base a mystery around that and to write about a Chinese 'snakehead': a human smuggler. And it gave me the chance to create some very complex characters in the form of my illegal immigrants.'

When he's not hard at work, Jeffery Deaver likes to relax by cooking for his friends. 'I do a lot of entertaining. I'll cook anything. Probably classic French or French/American are my favourites, but I recently had a German dinner party—and I once gave a Roman banquet that included two-thousand-year-old recipes—the ingredients were fresh, however! And, yes, we wore togas!'

Dying to Tell

Robert Goddard

A man's body discovered lying on the bank of a Somerset river . . .

An old black and white photograph found hanging on the wall of a Tokyo bar . . .

The Great Train Robbery . . .

How can these things be linked to the disappearance of shipping executive Rupert Alder?

His old schoolfriend Lance Bradley is about to find out.

SOMERSET ONE

That day started just like any other for me: late and slow. I didn't draw the curtains full back at first. There looked to be too much sun out for me to face before a shower and half a gallon of strong coffee. It had no business being so bright towards the end of October. In duller weather the bills lying on the doormat wouldn't have been so obvious, nor would those shadows under my eyes that I found myself studying as I shaved.

With my thirty-seventh birthday only a few weeks away, I wasn't looking bad—for a forty-five-year-old. The fact was that I needed to take myself in hand. Or find someone to do the job for me. Neither eventuality seemed very likely.

A few minutes before noon I slid onto my usual stool at the bar of the Wheatsheaf, sipped a Carlsberg Special and applied my mind to the quick crossword as a tune-up for trying to pick a winner from the afternoon races at Chepstow. It was quiet and soothing and safe and very far from memorable.

But I do remember it. In detail. Because that was the last time my life was quiet and soothing and safe. The door of the pub was about to open. And normality was about to slip through the window.

I didn't know that, of course. It didn't feel like fate or destiny or anything significant. But it was. It most assuredly was.

I DIDN'T RECOGNISE HER at first glance. Winifred Alder had to be pushing sixty and didn't look much better for her age than I looked for mine. She was spare and gaunt, with iron-grey hair cropped jaggedly short—like she'd done it herself with scissors in need of sharpening. There was no trace of make-up, but make-up would hardly have been in keeping with her clothes—coarse grey sweater, brown shin-length skirt, a mud-stained mac and faded purple shoes, Clarks seconds, *circa* 1980. They were what joined up the memories. It had to be her.

Or her sister, of course. Mildred was a pea from the same pod. A couple of years younger, though that was unlikely to amount to much of a difference at this stage in their lives. But Winifred's direct, stern-eyed gaze made up my mind for me. Mildred had always been more of a flincher.

'Are you looking for me, Win?' I asked. (There didn't seem to be any other way to account for her presence; she wasn't likely to have dropped in for a port and lemon.)

'The waitress in that café you live over reckoned I'd find you here,' Win replied. 'I'd like a word with you, Lancelot. A private word.'

It took me aback to hear someone use my full name, I don't mind admitting. Lance was now how everyone knew me. 'We could go into the garden,' I suggested. 'Would you like something to drink?'

She ran her eye along the bar. Nitrokegs and alcopops were clearly a mystery to her. 'A small cider,' she finally announced. 'Not fizzy.'

THE GARDEN was actually a cramped back yard accommodating two rusty tables divided by a washing line sagging under the weight of half a dozen drying bar mats.

'Have you heard from Rupert?' Win asked abruptly, making no move to sit down.

'Rupe? No, I . . .' Rupert was her youngest brother. More than twenty years separated them, Rupe being something of an afterthought on his parents' part. He was in fact a few months younger than me. We'd been friends at school and at university and while we'd both been working in London. But I hadn't seen much of him in recent years; his mother's funeral was his last visit to Street that I knew of, back in '95. While he'd gone on going up, I'd gone the other way. And, to prove it, there I was, out with the empties in the Wheatsheaf's so-called beer garden, while Rupe . . . Well, yes, what *about* Rupe? 'I haven't heard from him in a long time, Win.'

'How long?'

'Could be . . . a couple of years. You know how time flies.'

I sat down and pushed out another chair for Win. She lowered herself awkwardly onto the edge of the seat. 'I'd hoped . . . you might have heard from him,' she said hesitantly.

'Haven't you?'

'No. Not even . . . indirectly.'

What she meant by 'indirectly' wasn't clear. Rupe's family led a withdrawn life, keeping themselves to themselves. His mother had been alive when I'd first known them, his father long dead. Penfrith, their ramshackle home in Hopper Lane, down at the Ivythorn Hill end of Street, had once been a farm, before their father's death had forced them to sell their cows, and most of the fields. Rupe had long since flown the coop but Winifred, Mildred and their other brother, poor simple Howard, had lived on at Penfrith, unemployed and unattached to anything much except one another, without so much as a telephone to maintain contact with the world.

'We should have, you see. Should have heard from him.'

'How long's it been . . . since you did?'

'More than two months.'

'You've written to him?'

'Oh yes. We've written. No reply, though.'

'Telephone?' (There *were* call boxes, after all.)

'No reply. Just his answering machine.' She broke off to drink some cider, wiping her mouth with the back of her hand. 'Well, it can't go on, can it?'

'I expect he's abroad. You'll hear from him soon.'

'Something's wrong. Someone's got to go to London and find out. We want you to.'

Now Win's journey to Glastonbury made sense. 'Oh, come on, Win, I can't just drop everything and go,' I said.

'He's your friend. He saved your life.'

'Yes. So he did.' It was true, though in another sense you could say he also put it at risk.

Back in the summer of 1985, Rupe had persuaded me to join him on a caving expedition in the Mendips. Once the two of us were underground, Rupe noticed signs that the water level was rising, presumably because of rain on the surface. Only then did he reveal that the weather forecast had mentioned the possibility of heavy showers. We turned back, which involved climbing a more or less vertical slope. I fell. Broke an ankle, and several ribs. The floodwater was still rising. Rupe realised that I'd drown long before a rescue party arrived if he left me where I was while he went to fetch help. So he hauled me back to a higher level. Most of the time, I was no better than a dead weight. But we made it. He put me in a survival bag and waited until the waters started going down. Then he went to get help. I've never been underground since. Not even down the Tube.

'Lancelot . . .' She leaned towards me. 'He sends us money,' she whispered. 'It's how we live.'

'Don't you get . . . social security?' No, I supposed, reading her contemptuous gaze, they didn't. They'd have called that charity.

'There's been nothing since the end of August.'

'I see.'

'Will you go, Lancelot?' She gave me a pleading look.

'Have you contacted the shipping company he works for?'

'They say he's left. "Left the company". That's all I could get out of them. Most times I called, they just . . . played music to me.'

I felt sorry for her then, fumbling with her purse in a call box while trying to make sense of a computerised telephone system she'd briefly been connected to. 'I'll phone them,' I said. 'See what I can find out. If that doesn't work . . .'

'You'll go?'

'Maybe. But I don't suppose it'll be necessary.'

'It will be. There's something wrong. I know it.'

'Let's wait and see.'

THE DAY DEFINITELY wasn't unfolding as I'd anticipated. I saw Win off on her way to the bus stop, then made a beeline back to the flat to dig out the phone numbers I needed. I got what Win had got: the answering machine on Rupe's home number and some totally unhelpful spiel from the personnel department of the Eurybia Shipping Company. 'Mr Alder is no longer with us.' How long had he not been with them? 'I'm afraid I can't say.' Who did he work for now? 'I'm afraid I don't have that information.' How could we find him? 'I'm afraid I don't know.'

But there were resources I had that Win didn't. Simon Yardley, who had been at Durham University with Rupe and me, was something big in merchant banking. The three of us had met for a drink occasionally in London when we'd all been working there. And I was pretty sure Rupe and he had gone on meeting after I'd dropped out of the picture. I rang Simon's number. It was way too early to find a merchant banker at home, but the message on his answering machine suggested trying his mobile, so I did.

'Hi.'

'Simon, it's Lance Bradley.'

'Who?'

'*Lance Bradley.*'

'Oh, Lance. Well, this is a surprise. How are you?'

'Fine. You?'

'Never better. Never busier either. Listen, could we do this some other time? I'm—'

'It's about Rupe, Simon. Can't seem to get hold of him.'

'Have you tried his office? Eurybia Shipping?'

'He's left them.'

'Really? He never hinted he was thinking of moving.'

'Have you seen him recently, then?'

'Actually, no. Sorry, Lance, but I haven't a clue. And I've got to run. Next time you're in town, give me a bell. *Ciao.*'

I rang Rupe's London flat again and left a message, asking him to contact me urgently. I even gave him the Wheatsheaf number to try. My reasoning was that he might be reluctant to speak to his family. Perhaps he'd been sacked by Eurybia. That would explain why the money had dried up. But he wouldn't need to worry about speaking to me. If I was right, he'd get in touch.

He didn't.

CHANCE IS A SLIPPERY commodity at the best of times. That's why I bet on horses, not the Lottery. I like the idea that I can think my way to a fortune. What you win by chance you can just as easily lose. Take my stressless but far from prosperous existence down in Somerset. After losing a good job, a lovely woman and an over-mortgaged house in London during the recession of the early nineties, I went to stay with my parents in Street purely as a stopgap. Then I met Ria and, instead of heading back to London, found myself living with her in a flat in Glastonbury High Street, and helping to run Secret Valley, her New Age joss-stick and Celtic charms shop. Then Ria chucked in the shop along with me and buggered off to Ireland with a Celtic charmer of the human kind called Dermot, Secret Valley became the Tiffin Café, and I went . . . nowhere.

With so much evidence to draw on, it naturally didn't escape my analytical mind that a brief sortie to London in search of a missing friend might give rise to all manner of complications. The question was: did I want a change as much as I probably needed one?

The answer was still proving elusive the following afternoon, when I caught the bus to Street to report my lack of progress to Win.

Hopper Lane still looked like a country byway. There were modern houses at the Somerton Road end but, as I pressed on, it was all overgrown orchards, weed-choked smallholdings and run-down cottages. Penfrith itself didn't look quite as bad as I'd thought it might—mainly because the house was almost completely invisible behind a forest of rhododendrons. But slates were missing from the roof and the apex had an ominous sag to it.

Bending sideways to avoid a swag of rhododendron, I reached the front door and knocked loudly. Several silent seconds passed. I was about to try again when I caught sight of Howard Alder staring at me through the bay window.

In his early fifties by now, he was unshaven, and was wearing some sort of lumpen grey cardigan over pink and white striped pyjamas.

'Bloody hell, Howard,' I shouted. 'Aren't you going to let me in?'

He made a circling motion with his hand that I eventually realised meant the door wasn't latched. I turned the knob, and went in.

My first impression of the place was that nothing had changed from how it was when Rupe and I were lads. A narrow hall led towards the stairs. A large barometer hung on one wall, opposite an ancient piece of furniture combining the rôles of mirror, coat hook and umbrella stand. The carpet and wallpaper were surely the same. Then the musty smell hit me. That was the point: nothing *had* changed. Except that decay is change. And that's what was going on in Penfrith: slow decay.

I went into the sitting room and met more of the same. The hearth-rug, the three-piece suite, the bureau, the clock on the mantelpiece: they'd mouldered in their appointed places. And they'd gathered dust. Yes, one hell of a lot of dust.

Howard was still standing in the bay window, trying to smile, it seemed, though with Howard you couldn't be sure. Next to him, on a table, was a slew of magazines, dog-eared copies of *Railway World* from his train-spotting days in the sixties, his only reading matter.

'It's Lance, Howard,' I said, smiling at him. 'Remember me?'

He nodded vigorously and made a sucking noise. Howard hadn't actually said anything as far as I knew—words, I mean, as distinct from vague noises—since August 1977.

That was the summer of his crowning madness. He was still holding down some kind of job at Clarks Shoes then. Rupe and I were thirteen-year-olds, cycling out across the moors on fishing expeditions. But Howard was ranging further afield on his moped. And in his mind . . . Well, who knows where Howard had got hold of the idea that the government was hiding a strategic reserve of steam locomotives in a vast cavern at Box, Wiltshire, in case of an oil drought or some such emergency. Anyway, he took to staging nocturnal expeditions to the area in search of clues. One loco in search of a whole lot of locos, you could say. In fact, I may have said precisely that at the time. But the joke turned sour when Howard fetched up in hospital seriously injured after somehow managing to fall down a ventilation shaft. He was lucky not to have been killed, if you can bracket luck with permanent brain damage.

'Where are your sisters?' I asked.

He pointed towards the back of the house and mimed digging.

'In the garden? Thanks. I'll try there.'

I went out into the hall and headed for the back door. The rear garden wasn't as neglected as the front. Although the grass in the orchard was waist-high, the vegetable plot was well tilled and tended. And there was Mildred Alder, lifting carrots and potatoes with tight-jawed vigour. She was remarkably similar to her sister, though not as erect. There was a panicky look in her eyes when she caught sight of me, and her breath misted in the air as she stared at me.

'Hello, Mil,' I said, walking towards her.

'Lance,' she said with a frown. 'I didn't think you'd come. What have you got to tell us?'

'Nothing, really. I can't get hold of Rupe.'

'Didn't think you would.'

'No faith in me, Mil?'

'Didn't mean that.' She looked quite flustered. There might have been a blush on her weathered face. 'Look, here's Win.'

Win had emerged from the orchard, carrying a bucket filled with apples. 'What happened?' she called as she walked round the potato patch to join us.

'Nothing,' I said. 'I've drawn a blank.'

'Only what I expected.' She stopped at her sister's shoulder and plonked down the bucket. 'And is it all you mean to do?'

'No. I think I'd better go up to London and see what the trouble is—if there is any. I'll go tomorrow.'

'That's good of you. We're grateful, aren't we, Mil?'

'Oh yes,' said Mil. 'It *is* good of you, Lance.'

'When exactly did you last hear from him?' I asked.

'Depends what you mean by "hear from him". He doesn't write. There's just the . . . money. And there hasn't been any of that since the end of August.'

'Well, when did you last speak to him?'

'Speak to him?'

'Yes, Win. *Speak*.'

'When Mother died,' said Mil. 'Not since.'

A glance passed between the sisters at that moment. But their communications had been finely honed over many years. I hadn't a hope of working out what it meant.

'Rupert's been so busy with his work,' said Win, apparently feeling that some kind of explanation was due. 'We're worried about him, Lancelot. Truly we are.'

IT WAS ONLY a fifteen-minute walk from Penfrith to my parents' house. But it was more like a hundred years in other ways. Soon I was outside 8 Gaston Close, where I had entered this life one Friday afternoon in November 1963. At that time Dad—along with most Street males of his generation, and half the females—had been working for Clarks Shoes. Much of the land away to the west was still orchards and fields then. Now the town had crept out to surround it, and when Dad retired my parents had moved to a seventies bungalow in that new area of housing, where lawns were trimmed, cars washed, woodwork painted and appearances maintained.

'Your mother's out,' were Dad's first words when he opened the door to me, implying that I'd only called to see her. 'Scrabble.'

'Still keeping that up, is she?'

'Oh yes. Every Wednesday afternoon.' He plodded off towards the kitchen and I followed. The stoop was getting worse, I noticed. All those years of bending over account books at Clarks had taken their toll. 'I was going to make some tea. Do you want a cup?'

'Why not?'

He flicked the switch on the kettle, and when it boiled he put an extra bag in the pot and poured in the water. He squinted at me through the plume of steam. 'Have you got any news?' he asked.

'Not exactly. I wanted to ask you a favour, actually. I need to catch an early train to London and I'm looking for a lift.'

Car ownership had slipped out of my life even less ceremoniously than Ria some time before.

'This for a job interview by any chance?'

'No.'

'Thought not. I mean, there'd be no time to have your hair cut, would there?'

'Good point, Dad. Well spotted.'

'How early?'

'Just early. Could you look up some times for me on the Net.'

'I suppose I could.' He smiled at some irony he detected in this. 'I'll do that while you pour the tea. I'll have two digestives.'

So off he swanned to his study while I fiddled about with mugs and milk and the biscuit tin.

I took the tea through to the lounge and found the *Daily Telegraph* lying on the coffee table, folded to display the crossword. It looked like the last few clues were frustrating him, and I'd just begun to give them my attention when he walked in.

'There's a train from Castle Cary at ten to eight. Gets into Paddington at half past nine. Early enough?'

'Sounds fine.'

'I'll pick you up at seven fifteen.'

'Thanks.'

'Well, the car needs a run.' He sat down and drank some tea. 'This isn't about a job, you say? That's a pity.'

'I'm doing someone a favour myself, as it happens. The Alders. They're worried about Rupe. They can't contact him. He seems to have, well, disappeared. So they want me to try to find him.'

'Really?' Dad looked distinctly sceptical about my qualifications for the task. 'Have you considered the possibility that Rupert may simply have washed his hands of his family? You could hardly blame him if he had. They're a sorry bunch. Should have gone on farming the land they were born on. But they abandoned it.'

'Circumstances turned against them.'

'George Alder dying without a son old enough or sensible enough to take over from him, you mean?'

'Yes. You never knew him, did you?'

'Not at all. He died in '63, before Rupert was born. Drowned himself. We'd never have known any of the family but for you befriending Rupert at school.' Dad chomped thoughtfully on his digestive biscuit. 'Strange. I'd forgotten all that.'

'All what?'

'Oh, there were some other farming deaths around the same time.

Accidents. Suicide. That sort of thing. The *Gazette* was full of it.'

The *Central Somerset Gazette* being full of something hardly made it earth-shattering news. But I was still surprised that I'd never heard of the Street farmers' deaths before. 'How many deaths?'

'I can't remember. Two or three perhaps. Mmm. Maybe I'll check up on that next time I'm in the library. It's an interesting subject.'

Two or three? I was more curious than I was letting on. Why hadn't Rupe mentioned any of this to me? He loved mysteries, great and small. And this one seemed to involve his own father. Perhaps he didn't even know about it.

Dad leaned back in his chair. 'You won't oversleep tomorrow, will you, son?'

'No, Dad. I won't.'

And I didn't.

LONDON
TWO

The train was half an hour late into Paddington, but I'm not sure that's why I felt so down as I wandered out of the station into a grey London morning. The early start definitely hadn't helped. And now it was the number 36 bus for me: a boring forty-minute trundle across town to Kennington.

Number 12 Hardrada Road was one of a terrace of three-storeyed yellow-brick Victorian houses. Smart but unpretentious, I suppose you'd say. It didn't look like its owner had run out on it. The top-floor windows were ajar. I rang the bell, feeling I ought to before trying the neighbours. Naturally, there was no answer; even if Rupe was still living there, he'd likely be out at work at eleven o'clock on a Thursday morning.

The harassed but helpful mother of two who opened the door to me at number 10 hadn't seen Rupe in months. 'I thought he was working abroad. Ask Echo. She'll know if he's due back.'

'Who?'

'Echo Bateman. His lodger. She gets home about midday.'

A lodger! Maybe getting a fix on Rupe was going to prove easier than I'd anticipated. Little Miss Echo could sort everything out for me. To celebrate this happy thought, I ambled back to a pub I'd passed on my way from the bus. Something was needed to knock out the headache too much coffee and too little breakfast had given me.

The Pole Star was your usual stripped-pine piece of nineties chic. Halfway through my drink, I decided to hedge my bets where the lodger was concerned and tap the barman for information.

'Do you know Rupe Alder? He lives just round the corner.'

'Rupe Alder? Yeah. Not been in for quite a while, though. You a friend of his?'

'From way back. More way back than recently, to be honest. That's my problem. We've lost touch and I don't know where he is at the moment.'

'Can't help you, mate. But there's a bloke who works here in the evening who knows him quite well. You could ask him.'

'And will he be here tonight?'

'If he wakes up in time, yeah. His name's Carl.'

THINGS WERE LOOKING better. They often do when my aimless ramble through life assumes the fleeting dignity of a plan. The plan I left the Pole Star with was to go back to Hardrada Road, hear what Echo had to say for herself, scout round for a cheap place to spend the night, maybe take in a film somewhere, then gravitate back to the Pole Star to catch Carl in mid shift.

A young woman was letting herself in as I hove to at number 12. Tall and broadly built, with short, spiky black hair and big bush-baby eyes, she was wearing Post Office uniform.

'Echo?'

'Christ, you made me jump.' She turned to look at me. 'Do I know you?'

'Your neighbour told me your name. I'm a friend of Rupe's. Lance Bradley.'

'You do look familiar. Have we met?'

'No. But I'm looking for Rupe. His family are worried about him.'

'His *what*?'

'Family. Most of us have one.'

'First I've ever heard of Rupe's. Anyway, you won't find him here. But . . .' She looked me up and down. 'All right. Come on in. I've seen your photo. You *are* a friend of Rupe's.'

She pushed the door wide open and went in, gesturing for me to follow. We moved past two closed doors to the kitchen. 'That's you, isn't it?' asked Echo, prodding at a picture on the wall to her left.

It was a photomontage, a collection of snapshots from Rupe's life. Some of places—Glastonbury Tor, Durham Cathedral, Big Ben. And some of people—friends I recognised, friends I didn't. Echo's prod had landed on a photograph of me sitting outside a Pennine pub during some weekend jaunt from Durham *circa* 1983.

'I'm surprised you recognised me from this,' I muttered.

'Maybe I wouldn't have if you'd had the good sense to change your hairstyle.' She filled the kettle and lit the gas. 'Now, what's this about Rupe's family? He's never mentioned any relatives.'

'A brother and two sisters. They live at Street, down in Somerset. That's where Rupe was born. Me too. We were at school together. And university. How long have you been lodging with him?'

'About a year. Not very much *with* him, though. He's been abroad most of the time. That's really why he suggested me moving in. He needed someone to look after the place while he was away.'

'Away where?'

'Tokyo. On assignment for the shipping company he works for. No mystery. I don't know why his family are worried about him.'

'Well, they don't know about Tokyo, for starters. You have some way of contacting him there?'

'A phone number. Actually . . .' She frowned at me. 'I've called him a few times lately. No answer. And he hasn't phoned back. But . . .'

'He's left Eurybia Shipping.'

'He has?' The frown deepened. 'I didn't know that.'

'Why have you been phoning him lately?'

'Things.' She seemed puzzled. 'Odd things.'

'Care to share them?'

The kettle began to sing. She took it off the boil and crooked her head at me. 'You may as well come through.' She led me back into the hall and opened the door into the front sitting room. 'My room's upstairs. This is Rupe's.'

It was sparsely but comfortably furnished, with minimal decoration. There was a well-filled bookcase in one corner, with a model sailing ship on top. As far as personal touches went, that was about it. But Rupe had never been one for surrounding himself with things.

There was a desk beneath the window, on which stood a telephone and answering machine, alongside a pile of letters. Echo walked across to it. 'I've got my own phone. Rupe was adamant I shouldn't bother to deal with any of his calls. Or his post. So, I haven't. But—'

'What?' I asked.

'I think someone's been in here and taken some of the letters. Maybe listened to his phone messages as well.'

'Somebody broke in?'

'Not broke, exactly. Slipped a latch on a window at the back. I'm pretty sure there are some letters missing. And the books have been moved. Dust disturbed. You know?'

'Have you reported this to the police?'

'What's there to report? It's not much more than a suspicion.'

I leafed through the letters. Brown window envelopes, for the most part; nothing exciting. The only hand-addressed ones were from Win. The scratchy fountain pen and Street postmark gave her away. Whatever else there'd been . . . had gone. 'You said odd *things*, Echo. Plural. What else has happened?'

'You've turned up. And you're not the first. Lately I've had three other blokes round here looking for Rupe.'

'*Three?*'

'Yeah. And liquorice allsorts they were. To start with, there was a bloke from Eurybia Shipping paying what he called a "social call".'

'Didn't he mention Rupe had left the company?'

'Nope. And he didn't seem to know Rupe was supposed to be in Tokyo either. Said he'd been abroad himself.'

'Leave a name?'

'Charlie Hoare. Pretty typical middle-aged London suit. After him came the Japanese businessman. I've written his name down there.' She pointed to a Post-it note stuck to the answering machine: *Mr Hashimoto, Park Lane Hilton*. 'He called last week. Said he wanted to speak to Rupe. I told him Rupe was in Tokyo, but I'm not sure he believed me.'

'And the third one?'

'A couple of days ago. Some old bloke. He was pretty rough. Said he was looking for Rupe. Didn't leave a name.'

'When *did* you last hear from him?'

'When I last saw him. Some time in early September. A flying visit to London, so he said. He only stayed a few nights. Then, back to Tokyo—as far as I knew.'

'Mind if we play back the messages?' I tapped the machine.

'Suppose not.'

I rewound the tape and sat down on the black leather sofa to listen to what it contained. Echo joined me. The first message was from a car dealer offering Rupe a wonderful deal, the second from a dentist's receptionist saying his six-monthly check-up was well overdue. Then Win's voice, raised and nervous. '*We haven't received anything, Rupert. Is there something wrong?*' She was on twice more, the anxiety in her tone stepping up each time. Next was a cheese-grater cockney saying, '*You said we were in business. What's with the big silence? Give me a bell. Or I'll come looking.*'

'That's the old bloke who called round,' said Echo.

'Like he said he would.'

'*Charlie Hoare here, Rupe. We really do need to talk. So, if you're hearing this, get in touch. Soon.*'

And that was it. Apart from one from me, of course. 'Where are you?' I murmured as the tape clicked off. I stood up, walked over to the telephone and dialled a number.

'Who are you calling?' Echo asked.

'The middle-aged London suit. Charlie Hoare.'

But Charlie wasn't in his office. All I could do was leave a message asking him to call me. Urgently.

I put the phone down, wandered back to the kitchen, stopped by the photomontage and looked at a picture of Rupe. It was about the most recent one on display. He was standing on a quayside somewhere, with a Eurybia container vessel unloading behind him. The glaring light and the linen suit he was wearing suggested a tropical location—the Gulf maybe, or the Far East.

'Is this bloke his brother or something?' Echo tapped a black and white photograph towards the top of the montage. 'I've looked at him a few times and wondered where he fits in. I suppose it's the black-and-white that singles him out.'

I gazed at the picture. It showed a man of thirty or so in jeans and a reefer jacket, carrying a bag over one shoulder, standing on a railway platform. His hair was short, almost crew-cut, his face pale and raw-boned, the jaw square and jutting. He was holding a cigarette in one hand, furtive cup-of-the-palm style between forefinger and thumb. The station name-board bore the words ASHCOTT AND MEARE. 'Bugger me,' I murmured.

'What's wrong?'

'Ashcott and Meare was a station on the S and D a couple of miles west of Glastonbury.' Seeing her eyes widen uncomprehendingly, I added. 'The Somerset and Dorset railway.'

'So?'

'It closed in 1966, when Rupe and me were just toddlers. This photograph must have been taken before then.'

'But not by Rupe.'

'Hardly. Howard would be my guess. His brother. Not in the picture, but taking it. A real rail nut, our Howard.'

I looked around at all the other more recent—and more colourful—photos then back at the man in the reefer jacket. 'How did Rupe come across this, I wonder? And why did he want to keep it? I don't recognise the bloke. Never seen him before.'

As I went on peering at the nameless man standing on the bare platform at Ashcott and Meare, Rupe's telephone started to ring.

'Bet you that's the suit,' I said, scooting into the sitting room and picking up the phone.

It *was* the suit. 'Mr Lance Bradley? Charlie Hoare here. You rang a few minutes ago. On Rupe's phone number, I notice.'

'I'm an old friend of his. Trying to track him down on behalf of his family.'

'Am I to understand they haven't heard from him?'

'Not for a couple of months.'

'Worrying for them. Technically, Rupe's no longer on the staff here. But I'd like to help if I can.'

'Do you have any idea where he is?'

'No. But the situation's . . . complicated.' He laughed gruffly. 'Eurybia use me as a kind of . . . trouble-shooter. I've known Rupe for seven years—as long as he's been with the company. He's developed some lucrative business for us. Eurybia has a lot of cargoes finishing in Scandinavia, not many starting. And it's the other way round in the Far East. That means empty ships, which means empty coffers. Rupe handled negotiations with Russian industrialists to close the circle—send containers on through Russia to the Far East. We posted him to Japan to smooth out that end of things.'

'And did he smooth it out?'

'Oh yes. At least, he started to. Then, suddenly, back in the summer, he resigned.'

'Why?'

'No idea.' Hoare hesitated. 'Not at the time, anyway.'

'But since?'

'Well . . .' He cleared his throat. 'That's why I'm calling you now, actually. A chap resigns without giving a reason? It's a free country.

It seemed odd, even a bit curt. All we had was a fax from Tokyo. But Eurybia didn't own him. We had no choice but to let him go. As of the 31st of August, he was off our books. And then . . . things started to happen. Weevils started crawling out of the woodwork.'

'What sort of weevils?'

'Do you know what a bill of lading is?'

'Not exactly,' I replied.

'It's a document of legal title, representing ownership of a cargo, issued by the shipper to the customer, who can use it as security against a loan if they wish. But if the shipper can somehow be persuaded—or bribed—to issue more than one bill of lading per cargo, then you might end up with several loans, all secured against the same cargo. Like Rupe did.'

'You're accusing Rupe of fraud?'

'It's pretty hard not to when there's a Eurybia container sitting out at Tilbury with eighteen tons of Russian aluminium inside it, being wrangled over by lawyers representing half a dozen different Far Eastern banks, all claiming ownership in default of loans to a will-o'-the-wisp outfit called the Pomparles Trading Company.'

'The *what*?'

'Pomparles. Does the name mean something to you?'

'Yeah. It would to any Street boy.' Briefly I told him that Pomparles Bridge was, according to Arthurian legend, the site of the original *Pons Perilis* from which the dying Arthur is said to have ordered Bedivere to cast Excalibur into the lake.

'Rupe's little joke,' he said when I'd finished. 'He's chairman, managing director, treasurer and tea boy of the Pomparles Trading Company. He issued multiple Eurybia bills of lading to his own company for a cargo of aluminium leaving Yokohama, bound for Tilbury. He used those bills of lading to raise loans. Then he resigned from Eurybia, took the money—around a hundred and twenty thousand pounds—and ran.'

'I don't believe it. Rupe's no con artist. He just isn't the type.'

'Everyone's the type. If they need to be. And that's what I'm wondering. Did Rupe need to be?'

'Why should he?'

'You tell me, Lance.'

'I can't. Anyway, like I said, I don't believe it. Besides . . .' My mind was trying to make a series of connections. What the bloody hell was Rupe up to? And why, if he was suddenly awash with ill-gotten cash, should he stop subsidising life at Penfrith?

'Look, I'm going out to Tilbury tomorrow,' Hoare said. 'Why don't you join me? Be at Eurybia's Canary Wharf offices at ten thirty and we'll drive down. There's someone I'd like you to meet.'

'Who?'

'Someone I reckon can convince you that Rupe really has put his straight-dealing days behind him. For good and all.'

He rang off before I could ask him if he knew a Mr Hashimoto. But it could wait. I put the phone down.

'You're meeting him tomorrow?' asked Echo.

I nodded. 'I'll have to find somewhere to stay between now and then. So I'd better be making tracks.'

'You can stay here if you want.'

'Really?' I looked at her in surprise.

'I could put some sheets on Rupe's bed. He won't be wanting it, will he?'

'That's kind of you, Echo. Thanks.'

'Well, it's only for a couple of nights. And if whoever searched Rupe's belongings creeps back for a second go, you'll be on hand to sort them out, won't you?'

'Yeah.' I smiled uneasily. 'There's that, too.'

I DIDN'T BUY Charlie Hoare's version of Rupe as arch-fraudster for a minute. But I wasn't about to tell him that. Bills of lading and the price of aluminium didn't turn Rupe into a villain overnight. Not in my eyes, anyway.

Still, there was no denying that a lot of people were on Rupe's trail, maybe all for the same reason, so I called the Hilton. Mr Hashimoto was still staying there, but he was out. I left a message asking him to call me—'in connection with Mr Alder'.

Echo went out, leaving me free to search Rupe's sitting room and bedroom for clues to his whereabouts. There weren't any, so I gave up and called my parents to let them know where I was staying.

After writing down the address and phone number, Mum put Dad on, saying he was keen to speak to me.

'I visited the library today, son.'

'Oh yeah?'

'Reminding myself of those farming deaths round here back in '63. You said you'd like to know what I found out, so I photocopied some of the *Gazette* articles.'

'Is there anything interesting in them?'

'Let's just say there's a surprising connection between two of the cases.'

'Meaning what?'

'Best you read them for yourself. I'll put them in the post to you first thing tomorrow.'

'Thanks. One other thing . . .' I hesitated.

'What is it?'

'Could you call in at Penfrith and tell the Alders how they can contact me?'

'For God's sake.'

'They don't have a phone, Dad. And they're anxious for news.'

'Maybe, but . . .' A slowly yielding silence settled on the line. 'All right. I'll, er . . . send your mother.'

ECHO STILL wasn't back by half eight, when I headed round to the Pole Star. The place had slipped into evening mode, with a football match playing on a big-screen telly.

'I'm Carl Madron,' a pasty-faced, hair-gelled lad said to me from behind the bar as he prised the bottle tops off a multiple order of Mexican beer. 'You the guy who was in earlier?'

'Yeah. Lance Bradley. I'm a friend of Rupe Alder's. They tell me you know Rupe quite well.'

'A bit.'

'Any idea where he might be these days?'

'No.' He broke off to take some money, then gave me his attention. 'I'm not a mate of the guy. He used to come in here quite a lot. Early evening, mostly. We'd chat a bit. That's about it.'

'I had the impression it was, well, more than that.'

'Did you? Well as it happens, I'm getting some grief over your friend. He's let someone down.'

'Who is this "someone"?'

'What's it matter to you?'

'I'm trying to find Rupe. His family are worried about him.'

'They probably ought to be. You let people down, you get into trouble.'

'Look, Carl . . .'

'Tell you what.' He fixed me with a cold stare. 'I could call that someone I mentioned. See if he wants to meet you.'

'That'd be great.'

'OK. When I get a chance. You'll hang around?'
'Yeah. Course. Thanks.'

BY CLOSING TIME, I was decidedly blurry. Two idle hours in a pub aren't exactly good for my clarity of thought. Carl, on the other hand, was getting sharper all the time. He'd made the promised phone call, with favourable results.

'Bill'—the someone had a name now—'says he'd like to see you. Wait while we close up and I'll take you round there.'

'Is it far?'

'Far enough. But I've got wheels.'

'Chauffeur service, then?'

'That's right, Lance.' Carl grinned at me. 'Door to door.'

THE CAR wasn't the sort of thing you saw being lovingly buffed outside a Mayfair casino. It was a cramped rust-bucket, with blankets covering the seats.

We headed east, aiming, so Carl told me, for the Rotherhithe Tunnel. Bill Prettyman—his surname was donated somewhere along the way—lived in West Ham. 'Famous as a hard man in his day,' according to Carl. 'My dad knows him from way back.'

Eventually we arrived at the foot of some shabby stump of high-rise housing. Carl led me in by a heavily reinforced side door, and I followed him up the urinal-scented stairs.

Prettyman's flat lay at the far end of a concrete-parapeted landing. Halfway along, Carl paused. 'Watch what you say to Bill. He's not been in the best of moods lately. Thanks to Rupe.'

'What did Rupe do to him?'

But the only answer I got was Carl's sodium-lit grin. Clearly, he just didn't have the heart to spoil the suspense.

'THIS HIM, IS IT?' were Prettyman's welcoming words as the door opened to our knock. He was a short, pigeon-chested little man with a round, frowning face and pale blue eyes. His head was shaven as closely as his jaw, doing nothing to soften the mangled jut of his sometime-broken nose. He was wearing a grubby vest and even grubbier tracksuit bottoms.

'Pleased to meet you,' I lied. 'I'm Lance Bradley.'

'Carl said you're a friend of Alder.'

'Rupe, yes.' (Rupe and Bill not on first-name terms, it seemed. Was that good news or bad?) 'I'm trying to find him.'

'Better come in, then.'

We stepped inside and Carl closed the door. Bill Prettyman lived with bare walls, cheap furniture and a huge wide-screen TV. Homely wasn't the description that sprang to mind. A panatella was smouldering in a giant onyx ashtray on top of the TV. He picked it up and took a puff. 'You boys want a drink?'

The choice looked to be Scotch or Scotch. We both chose Scotch.

'Been up to anything exciting, Bill?' Carl enquired as he sat down on the sofa and sipped his whisky.

'I'm too old for excitement. All I want is a bit of comfort.' Bill glared at me. 'What are you after Alder for?' he demanded.

'His family are worried about him. I'm trying to track him down.'

'Purely out of the goodness of your heart?'

'Something like that.'

'And where is this . . . family?'

'Street, in Somerset.'

'*Street?*' You' d have thought I'd said Baghdad by his reaction. 'He grew up there?'

'Him and me both.'

'That's how he knew, then. Fucking hell. I thought he was too young. He *was*, by rights. But he knew more than he was telling.'

'I'm not sure I—'

'*Where is he?*' Bill shouted. 'Where is he, Lance? That's what I want to know. And what's he up to?'

'That's what I'm trying to find out.'

'Why don't you let him in on what this is about, Bill?' said Carl.

'I sometimes wish your dad had taken my advice and drowned you the day you were born,' growled Bill. 'All right, you may as well fill him in. It's an itch you just can't stop scratching, ain't it?'

'Uncle Bill here is a big-time criminal, Lance,' said Carl, all eager garrulousness now. 'He had a hand in the most famous heist of the century. Well, the last century. The Great Train Robbery: August '63. You're looking at one of the blokes who laid their hands on the three million quid in used fivers, back when three million quid could buy an Arab oil state outright.'

'It was nearer two and a half,' Bill grudgingly corrected him. 'And there were a fair few of us to take our whack. I didn't come away with more than a hundred and fifty thou.'

'Which would probably be worth three million today,' Carl went on. 'If you'd stuck it in the building society and led a sensible life.'

'Yeah,' said Bill. 'Life's full of ifs.'

The Great Train Robbery? I was struggling to catch up. Even those of us still in our mother's womb at the time knew that back in August 1963 a gang of thieves stopped the Glasgow to London mail train one night in the middle of the Buckinghamshire countryside and robbed it of a medium-sized fortune in used banknotes that were on their way to the Royal Mint for incineration. Most of the gang had subsequently been caught and clobbered with thirty-year jail sentences. Some of them had escaped and been caught again. There'd been books and films, and rumours of proceeds never recovered. It had become part of the nation's folklore. But Bill Prettyman? I'd never heard that name mentioned. And he certainly didn't look like a Mr Big to me. Nor was he living like one. But that, of course, was exactly what he was griping about.

'Bill had the good sense to keep his gloves on during the divvying up at Leatherslade Farm,' said Carl. 'So he got clean away with his share of the loot. Only to have it taken off him by smooth-talking con men. Which is why he finds himself passing his declining years in this rat hole, unable even to strike a lucrative publishing deal in case the police come knocking at his door.'

'I don't like to interrupt,' I interrupted, 'but what has this to do with Rupe?'

'Good question,' said Carl. 'See, the thing is Rupe got me talking about the Great Train Robbery one night at the Pole Star and I, well, gave him the idea that I might know someone who was in on it. Nothing specific, mind. But . . . the hint was there. And Rupe was interested. Very interested. He knew a bit himself, apparently. He gave me a name. Fellow called Peter Dalton. Asked me to mention it to . . . whoever it was I knew . . . and see if he'd like to meet up and hear more about what had happened to this guy.'

'Know of him, do you?' Bill looked sharply at me.

'Can't say I do.'

'Seems he was a member of the gang as well,' said Carl, at which Bill gave a nod of confirmation. 'Also never caught. And not just your standard gang member. No, no. Dalton was there on behalf of the gang's prime informant—the mystery man who told them about the train and how much dosh might be aboard. He took an extra cut to pass on to his boss. Isn't that right, Bill?' Another nod.

'What did Rupe know about him?'

'That he was dead,' said Bill. 'Dalton was found with his head blown off at the farm he owned, near Street. Less than a fortnight after the robbery. Suicide, it was, according to the stuff from the paper Alder showed me. Suicide, my arse. The mystery man did it, of course. The source of the info.'

'Why would he kill Dalton?'

'To cover his tracks,' said Bill. 'Part of the plan all along, maybe. The cops were on to us that fast, boy. Too fast. Somebody grassed us up. And who could have done it better than the bloke who set us up in the first place?'

'Whose identity you never knew?'

'Not me. Not no one. Except Dalton.'

'And now Rupe,' put in Carl.

'Alder seemed to think he could flush him out,' Bill continued. 'He didn't say how. Nor how he knew who he was. He said the bloke was called Stephen Townley and that he had . . . ways and means . . . of tracking him down. He had a photo of Dalton, taken from the local rag. Once I said yeah, that was the same Dalton I'd last seen at Leatherslade back in '63, he seemed sure he could pull it off.'

'He had a photograph of Townley as well,' said Carl.

'*Said* it was Townley,' Bill corrected him.

'Was Townley standing on a railway station in the picture?' I asked.

'Yeah.' Bill gave me another sharp look. 'How'd you know that?'

'It's pinned up in Rupe's kitchen. The station wasn't far from Street.' My mind was racing. Rupe had no business knowing about any of this stuff. But he did. *Sure he could pull it off*. I wondered if he was so sure now. 'When did you meet Rupe, Bill?'

'It's got to be . . . a couple of months ago. Which is twice as long as he said he'd need to sort Townley.'

'Maybe Townley proved more elusive than Rupe had anticipated.'

'Or maybe he did a deal with Townley and froze me out. Maybe all he wanted me to do was ID Dalton and tie the string on his blackmail package.'

'You can see Bill's point,' said Carl. 'It does look like that.'

'Rupe's no blackmailer.' (But he was, if Bill was to be believed. That's exactly what he was. Why? He couldn't be in this for the money. Not this and the aluminium too.) 'There has to be some . . . misunderstanding,' I said.

'There's no misunderstanding,' said Bill. 'He promised me a cut of whatever he made out of Townley. So, when you find your friend, tell him he owes me.'

'Sure. *If* I find him.'

'You'll keep us posted, though?'

'Certainly. I want to sort this out as much as you do.'

'Is that a promise?'

'It's a promise.'

'Good. I'm partial to promises.' He eyed me through a puff of panatella smoke. 'I can hold people to them, see? And I do. Whether they want to be held to them . . . or not.'

'YOU KNOW, Lance,' Carl said some time later, as we started back towards Kennington in his car, 'the way I figure it, this Townley has to be a real hard case to have pulled off that stuff in '63. Too hard for Rupe to tackle any way he chose to go about it. I don't want to dash Bill's hopes—he's got little else to keep him going—but Rupe isn't coming back with a fat pay-off to share out.'

'What do you reckon's happened to him, then?'

Carl gave the question a moment's thought, then said, 'Not sure, but . . . nothing good.'

THREE

Going to bed in the small hours with a lot to think about isn't anyone's recipe for a sound dose of slumber. Was Rupe really up to defrauding Far Eastern banks and blackmailing veteran arch-criminals? I doubted it. In fact, I doubted just about everything I'd learned so far. More worryingly, I doubted it was wise to get mixed up in any of it. Cue a hasty retreat to Glastonbury? That at least made sense. And it was that comforting thought that finally lulled me into sleep.

Only to be jolted awake by a noise from the kitchen. Someone was moving about. I checked my watch. It was just gone four. Had the person who'd so carefully searched Rupe's belongings come back for a second look? My heart began to pound.

Then the toaster popped and I remembered: postal workers keep early hours.

THAT MORNING'S appointment with Charlie Hoare involved a trudge to Elephant and Castle, a bus to Shadwell and another from there to Canary Wharf. The Isle of Dogs had been transformed from a building site into a city unto itself while my back had been turned. A mall about a mile long led me to a phalanx of reception desks at the foot of the Canada Square Tower. A message was phoned up to Eurybia's perch on the umpteenth floor and ten minutes later a well-dressed man with a mop of grey hair and a fuzz of slightly less grey beard emerged from the lift to greet me.

'Glad you could make it, Lance. I think you'll find this Tilbury trip worth while. Shall we go?'

He piloted me to the underground car park, loaded me into his Lexus, weaved his way out onto the A13 and pointed the bonnet towards Essex. He seemed to feel I was in need of a potted biography of Charlie Hoare, man of the shipping world, and that took us well past Dagenham.

It had started to rain by the time we turned in through the dock gates at Tilbury. Hoare seemed to be a familiar face to the gateman who waved us past. I gazed around at the ships, at the cranes and gantries and the Lego-like towers of containers.

'I love ports,' said Hoare. 'Always have. The foreign flags. The far-flung destinations. The exotic cargoes.'

'Isn't this one of yours?' I nodded at the soaring flank of a berthed container ship we were passing. 'What are they unloading?'

Hoare glanced round. 'Frozen meat, at a guess.'

A car was parked ahead, next to a rust-red container that was standing somewhat forlornly on its own, the word EURYBIA painted on it in white. A man in a yellow safety coat was leaning against the driver's door of the car, clearly waiting for us. He had one of those round, pliable faces that fold naturally into a smile.

We pulled up and got out. 'Colin Dibley, Lance Bradley,' Hoare announced with a grin. Handshakes followed. 'Good to see you, Colin. I thought we could entice you out for a drink before we get down to business. Lance won't want to stay for that anyway.'

'Suits me,' said Dibley. 'Charlie tells me you're a friend of Rupe's, Lance.'

'That's right.'

'He's given us a bit of a headache with this baby.' Dibley crooked his thumb at the container.

'Is that the famous consignment of aluminium?'

'It is. And it's been here more than a month. It arrived a couple of weeks after Rupe's last visit. After the things he said then . . .' Dibley shrugged. 'I should have known he was letting me in for some kind of trouble. There have been lawyers to deal with. *And* Customs.'

'Suspicious about the contents?' I ventured.

'You bet. A high-value cargo from Russia always sets them thinking about organised crime. When the owner goes missing . . . naturally they want to take a peek inside.'

'What did they find?'

'Aluminium, so they tell me.'

'That isn't the mystery,' Hoare said. 'The mystery is why Rupe needed to raise so much money on his cargo.'

'And mystery's certainly what he was dealing in when he came here,' said Dibley.

'Time we made for the pub,' put in Hoare, rubbing his hands. 'I need a drink if I'm to listen to this one again.'

THE RAIN BEGAN to get its act together as we left the Docks and drove out through the dismal margins of Tilbury. Dibley asked me some desultory questions about my friendship with Rupe, patently stalling till he could get his palm round a pint. I decided to help him out by throwing in a question of my own. 'Either of you two ever hear of a guy called Hashimoto?'

'Don't think so,' said Dibley.

'Nor me,' said Hoare. 'In our line of business, is he?'

'Not sure. He called at Rupe's house last week, apparently, wanting to speak to Rupe.'

'And Rupe's been based in Tokyo this year,' Hoare mused. 'This Hashimoto must know him from there. Could well be in shipping. I'll ask around. Did he leave a phone number?'

'No,' I found myself saying. 'He didn't.' Some instinct told me to keep a few cards up my sleeve. I was fairly sure Hoare wasn't being completely frank with me. It made sense to return the compliment.

THE WORLD'S END INN was aptly named, huddled as it was in the lee of the dyke where the Essex marshes met the Thames. Inside, though, was the haven that is every decent pub. With drinks bought and lunches ordered, we drew up our chairs at a corner table and Dibley started to talk.

'I wouldn't claim to know Rupe as well as you do, Lance. But as far as work went, I'd have said he was a real asset to Eurybia.'

'I'd agree,' said Hoare.

'Anyway,' said Dibley, 'I'd not seen Rupe for quite a while, thanks to this Tokyo posting, when he turned up here at the end of August. I didn't know he'd resigned from Eurybia. In fact, I assumed Eurybia had sent him. It's certainly what he led me to believe. He said the company was worried about a client they'd been dealing with: Pomparles Trading. Had I heard any whispers about them? The answer was no. Of course, it later transpired that Rupe *was* Pomparles Trading. Anyway, we popped down here for lunch. That's when I began to notice a few . . . differences.'

'In Rupe?'

'Yeah. He was drinking more, for a start. And he was . . . well, wilder, I suppose. Talking louder than usual. Waving his arms around. I asked him about Tokyo, but he didn't want to go into it.'

'What did he want to go into?'

'The past, funnily enough.'

'Nineteen sixty-three,' murmured Hoare.

'Exactly,' Dibley went on. 'Nineteen sixty-three. He asked me what I remembered of it. Well, I was still at primary school then. A few things stuck in my mind, naturally. We had a lovely summer holiday in Cornwall. Then there was the big stuff—Profumo, the Kennedy assassination, the Great Train Robbery. Rupe seemed to be hanging on my every word. When I'd finished, he said, "Ever heard of Stephen Townley, Col?"'

Stephen Townley. So, there he was again. The man in the photograph. 'Had you?' I asked, to cover my surprise.

'Nope. The name meant nothing to me. I asked Rupe if I should have done, if this Townley had done something notable in 1963. Rupe said, "No, you shouldn't have heard of him. But, yes, he did do something notable in '63. And you will be hearing about it. I'll make sure of that."'

'What did he mean?'

'God knows. He was playing some weird game of his own. I asked him what he was getting at, and when he dodged the question, I dropped the subject. After he left I phoned Charlie and asked him if Rupe was, well, all right.'

Hoare emptied his glass. 'I told Colin that Rupe was a couple of days away from serving out his notice to us, that he hadn't gone to Tilbury on Eurybia business, that as far as we knew he was still in

Tokyo and that I'd never heard of the Pomparles Trading Company. When I looked into it, though, I found Pomparles on our system as a new client, with a container of Russian aluminium on its way here from Yokohama. I was too busy to do any more about it at the time. If Rupe wanted to play silly buggers, I reckoned that was his affair.' He gave a wry smile. 'Seems I should have taken it more seriously.'

HOARE AND DIBLEY returned to the Docks for their business meeting, dropping me at the station en route. On the slow train ride back to London I tried to kick-start my brain into thinking mode. Rupe had something big on Townley. It seemed he needed money—a lot of it—to make it count. But nothing had happened. Rupe had vanished. That was all. And Townley was as anonymous as ever.

It had begun in Tokyo. That, at any rate, was a reasonable supposition. Which pointed to the so-far elusive Mr Hashimoto. From Fenchurch Street I caught a bus to Trafalgar Square and walked across Green Park through the thinning rain to his hotel.

He wasn't in. But the receptionist asked brightly, 'Are you Mr Bradley?'

'Yes, I am.'

'Mr Hashimoto left a message for you in case you called.'

'What's the message?'

'He can meet you here at ten o'clock tomorrow morning.'

'Great. Tell him I'll be here.'

'THEY'RE A WEIRD LOT, then, are they, Rupe's family?' Echo put the question to me a few hours later, as we toyed with some appetisers in Kennington's foremost Portuguese dining establishment.

'Pretty dysfunctional, yeah.'

'And him into aluminium smuggling and great train robbers. I had no idea I was lodging with such a man of mystery.'

'It's not exactly smuggling.' (I was beginning to wonder if confiding in Echo had been a good idea. But after a couple of drinks I was bound to confide in someone.) 'As for this Townley bloke . . .' I shrugged. 'I just don't get it.'

'Perhaps Mr Hashimoto will tie it all together.'

'Maybe. But if he doesn't that'll be the end of the road. There's nothing else I can do.'

'You'll just give up?' She looked genuinely disappointed. 'I thought you meant to go on and on until you dug out the truth.'

'You've got me all wrong, Echo. I'm a natural quitter.'

'Oh yeah?' Her gaze narrowed. 'I'm not so sure.'

'Just you wait and see.' I took a big swallow of *vinho verde*.

'So what am I supposed to do if you draw a blank? Should I move out of Hardrada Road? Being lodger to an international crook could be bad for my health. Be sensible to move on, wouldn't it?'

'Might be, I suppose.'

'I reckon I will. If you pack up and go home. Has to be the safest option.' Her face crumpled into a frown. 'And then . . .'

'What?'

'Well . . .' She gazed soulfully into her wine. 'Rupe really will be lost then, won't he?'

ECHO HAD SET OFF for the sorting office by the time I surfaced the following morning. Dad's letter had been delivered, and over a cobbled-together breakfast, I examined its contents. He had done a thorough job with the *Gazette* cuttings, as I might have expected—a clutch of articles reporting sudden farm-related deaths and subsequent inquests crammed into the summer and autumn of 1963.

The sequence had started at the end of July, with Albert Crick falling off a barn roof. Then Peter Dalton had been found dead of gunshot wounds at Wilderness Farm, near Ashcott. By Howard Alder, no less. The date: Monday, August 19. Within a fortnight of the Great Train Robbery, just as Bill Prettyman had said.

The *Central Somerset Gazette* wasn't to know of a connection—if there really was one—with big-time crime in Buckinghamshire, of course. They said Dalton had inherited Wilderness Farm from his father the year before, and was thought by neighbouring farmers to be struggling to make a go of it. Shotgun suicide was lightly implied. The inquest a month later had gone along with that, despite what the coroner had called 'minor inconsistencies in the disposition of the deceased and the weapon'. What did that mean? The *Gazette* wasn't in the business of asking. As to the discovery of the body, there was Howard's name in black and white.

> Howard Alder, 15, of Penfrith, Street, was cycling along a footpath that passes through the yard of Wilderness Farm when he noticed a figure lying in the doorway of the milking shed.

In all the years I'd known Howard through Rupe, there'd never been a whisper of this event. Very strange.

And it got stranger. Andrew Moore, son of the owner of Mereleaze Farm, near Othery, had been knocked off his motorbike by a lorry and killed on the A39 on the afternoon of Monday, October 28. It was the day after the clocks had gone back; the early dusk was held partly to blame. But with Halloween in the offing, some ghoulish theories about curses and the like had done the rounds.

The fourth and evidently final death was of George Alder himself, on Sunday, November 17, the *Gazette* reported.

> Mr Alder went out early in the morning. When he did not return by midafternoon, his family grew concerned. His 15-year-old son, Howard, cycled to Cow Bridge and began looking for him along the banks of the River Brue, where Mr Alder had recently taken to walking. Howard eventually found his father's body, tangled in the reeds, a short distance west of the bridge. Mr Alder is believed to have drowned.

It was strange stuff to read. The *Gazette* had failed to point out that Howard now figured in two of the clutch of deaths. Perhaps they'd refrained out of sensitivity. And why had George taken to walking by the Brue? No suggestions. What about his wife's pregnancy? It wasn't mentioned. There was enough tragedy without dwelling on that, apparently. The inquest, just before Christmas, brought in a verdict of accidental death. The coroner emphasised that suggestions of a link between the deaths in the area were 'as absurd as they are unfeeling'.

I was born five days later, at Butleigh Cottage Hospital. And Rupe was born the following spring. We began just as all that ended. But what *had* ended? Forget a curse on the land. Howard was the connection the coroner reckoned it was absurd and unfeeling to make.

Howard had never seemed the secretive type, but now I knew better. He'd concealed plenty. OK, that could have been because it was all too traumatic to call to mind. Rupe had told me Howard was weak-minded from birth, and no doubt finding his father's body floating in the Brue speeded up his decline. What did it all mean?

It was a question that bothered Dad as well as me, as he admitted in a note attached to the cuttings:

> *Howard certainly must have had a bad time of it that summer and autumn. And Dalton's death reads oddly to me. Does it to you? 'Inconsistencies in the disposition of the deceased and the*

weapon.' What was the coroner getting at? Something other than suicide? The police officer mentioned in a couple of the reports is actually Don Forrester, who worked for Clarks for a few years after he retired from the force. I see Don quite often, pushing a trolley around Tesco. He must be eighty-odd now, but looks pretty spry. Do you want me to ask him about the deaths? It might lead nowhere, of course. Who can say? Let me know. I have nothing better to do. And it is interesting, I have to admit.

My mind was still turning all this over as I sat on the top deck of the number 36 as it lumbered towards Hyde Park Corner. The deaths of Crick and young Andrew Moore were probably not significant, but those of Dalton and Alder were much more interesting. I most certainly did want Dad to put a few questions to Don Forrester. Did he think Dalton had actually been murdered, for instance? If so, who by? As far as I could see the name of Stephen Townley had never made it into the columns of the *Central Somerset Gazette*.

It was a few minutes to ten when I entered the lobby of the Hilton hotel and headed towards the reception desk. I was early, but not too early for Mr Hashimoto. A slim, grey-suited figure bobbed into my path and I found myself looking into a calm, sad-eyed Japanese face, gold-rimmed specs glinting in the Hilton spotlights.

'Mr Bradley?' he asked, with that slight but distinctive oriental vagueness around the Rs. 'I am Kiyofumi Hashimoto.'

'Er . . . Pleased to meet you.'

We shook hands. There was a hint of a bow on Hashimoto's part.

'I'm a friend of Rupe Alder, Mr Hashimoto,' I said. 'If you can help me find him . . .'

'That is what you are trying to do?'

'Yeah. His family are worried about him. He's, er . . .'

'Disappeared.' Hashimoto nodded. 'I am looking for him also. Perhaps we can help each other.'

'Maybe we can.'

'Shall we take a stroll in the park? It will be . . . pleasanter . . . to talk there.'

THE MORNING was too cool and damp by my reckoning for strolling, even if strolling in parks had been a habit of mine, which it wasn't. Hashimoto didn't exactly seem the outdoor type either, hoisting a vast Hilton golfing brolly against the drizzle and stepping carefully through the muddy drifts of leaves in his gleaming lounge-lizard shoes.

'Are you in shipping, Mr Hashimoto?' I asked, as we wandered vaguely west towards the Serpentine.

'No. Microprocessors. My concern to find Rupe has nothing to do with business.' He glanced round at me. 'You are a good friend of his, Mr Bradley?'

'Lifelong. You, er, met Rupe in Tokyo?'

'Yes. My niece Haruko was his girlfriend. I met Rupe at my sister's home two or three times last summer. It was a typhoon romance.' Hashimoto smiled. 'Her mother was very pleased.'

'Were you?'

'Certainly. Rupe seemed . . .' He shrugged. 'Kind. Charming. Easy to like.' (That description fitted Rupe, all right.)

'What did Haruko's father think?'

'Her father is not with us.' (Did that mean dead? I hadn't the nerve to ask.) 'That is why I have to be . . . more than an uncle to her.'

'How serious was this romance?'

'For Haruko, very serious. She hoped to marry Rupe, I think.'

'And for Rupe?'

Hashimoto sighed. 'I'm sorry to say this. You are his friend. You must think well of him. But the truth is . . . he strung her along. He did not want to marry her. He wanted something else. Once he had it . . . he was gone.'

'What was it he wanted?'

'Something that belongs to Haruko's mother—my sister, Mayumi.' Hashimoto stopped and looked at me. 'Rupe stole it.'

'Stole? I don't believe it. Rupe's no—' I broke off. Whatever I'd previously have said you couldn't accuse Rupe of, his own actions seemed to tell a different story.

'Rupe used Haruko to get close to Mayumi. He knew she had this letter that he wanted. Let us call it . . . the Townley letter. Eventually, he persuaded Haruko to show him where it was hidden. Then he stole it.'

'Townley? Stephen Townley? It's a letter from him?'

'No. *About* him.'

'To Mayumi?'

'Yes.'

'From . . .'

'I do not know. Mayumi does not tell me everything. She is fifteen years older than me. Always she has thought she has better judgment than I. But her judgment is not as acute as she believes. She should not have kept the letter. She should have destroyed it.'

'What's in it?'

'I do not know.' (Was he lying? His expression gave nothing away.)

'When was it written?'

'A long time ago. Nineteen sixty-three.'

That year again. 'Did Mayumi know Townley?' (Hashimoto looked to be in his mid to late forties, which put his sister in her early sixties. The arithmetic seemed to stack up.)

'Yes. In Tokyo. When she was very young. Just after the war.'

'What was he doing there?'

'He was a soldier. American. Based in Japan.'

'And Mayumi was his girlfriend?'

'It does not matter. What matters is that the letter is dangerous to Townley. And not just to Townley. It is dangerous to Mayumi. I have to get it back. This is more than honour. This is life and death.'

'It can't be as bad as that.'

'It can. That is why Rupe wanted it. He has strayed into a very dark place.'

'Come off it.' But the dark was what I was whistling in.

'We have to find him.'

'That could be a problem, Mr Hashimoto. I haven't the foggiest where he is. The consensus seems to be—'

'Excuse me, gentlemen?'

I don't know if Hashimoto was as surprised as I was by the interruption. He certainly couldn't have been *more* surprised. A figure had materialised next to us, his approach screened, perhaps, by the brolly. He was a tall, faintly stooping bloke in a neatly tailored raincoat. He had short grey hair and a narrow, lugubrious face. His voice was soft and precise.

'My name is Jarvis. You don't know me. But I know you. Mr Hashimoto. Mr Bradley.' He nodded politely at us. 'I also know Rupert Alder. He is, let's say, an interest we have in common.'

'Did you follow us here?' Hashimoto's question had a tetchy edge to it and I can't say I blamed him.

'Forgive me. Surprise was inevitable. Antagonism is unnecessary. My card.'

He plucked two business cards out of his pocket and handed us one each. Philip Jarvis evidently represented a company called

Myerscough Udal, with an address in High Holborn. The nature of their business went unspecified.

'We handle confidential enquiries,' Jarvis continued. 'We're one of the largest operations in the field worldwide.'

'And you have been enquiring into us?' asked Hashimoto.

'Not exactly. Mr Alder is a client of ours. We, like you, are concerned about him.'

'What did he hire you to do?'

'Find a man called Stephen Townley.'

'And did you?' I pressed.

'No.' Jarvis allowed himself half a smile. 'You could say he found us, though. Let's step down to the Serpentine. Rippling water calms the mind, I find. I'll explain as we go.'

As we started along the path to the lake, Jarvis began his explanation. 'Strictly speaking, gentlemen, I ought not to be telling you any of this. Myerscough Udal's reputation has not been built on sharing its secrets. But these are exceptional circumstances. To begin at the beginning, Mr Alder engaged our services through our Tokyo office four months ago to locate one Stephen Townley, using such limited information as Mr Alder was able to give us.'

'How limited was that?' I asked.

'Mr Alder knew only that Townley was an American, probably in his sixties, who'd served in the US Army and been based at one point in Japan. He also supplied us with the names of two former acquaintances of Townley, one of them deceased.'

'Peter Dalton.'

'You have him. The other was—'

'My sister,' put in Hashimoto.

'Quite so. Mr Alder presented us with a photograph of Townley, apparently taken by his brother at a railway station near Glastonbury in August 1963. He said Townley had been a friend of Peter Dalton and our investigations have certainly shown that to be possible. Dalton committed suicide on August the 19th, 1963. Mr Alder suspected that Dalton was murdered by Townley to cover up his part in the Great Train Robbery, but since Mr Alder declined to share with us his reasons for harbouring such an apparently outlandish suspicion, it was difficult to know whether to take it seriously.

'In seeking to trace Townley, we went back to his roots and worked forward. Stephen Anderson Townley was born in Tulsa, Oklahoma, on May the 17th, 1932. An only child of a single mother, long since dead. He enrolled in the army straight from high school in the summer of 1949, and saw a good deal of action in Korea. After that he was shuttled around like thousands of other soldiers. Particularly significant for our purposes, was the year and a bit he spent in West Berlin in the mid-fifties.'

'Why's that?' I asked, as Jarvis paused, either for breath or effect.

'Because Peter Dalton, a farmer's son from Somerset, was serving with the British Army in West Berlin at the same time. We must assume the two men became acquainted during that period. Also because Townley married a German girl while based there. Rosa Kleinfurst. Rosa went back to the United States with him when he was transferred home early in 1955. Later that year, their first child, Eric, was born. A daughter, Barbara, followed eighteen months later. By then, the marriage seems to have been on the rocks. The couple separated, Rosa keeping the children. Townley transferred to Military Intelligence, which means there's very limited information on his activities from that point on. We believe he was based in Japan for the next two or three years, during which period he patronised a bar in Tokyo called the Golden Rickshaw, the proprietress of which was—'

'My mother,' said Hashimoto.

'Indeed.' Jarvis nodded. 'Who knows, Mr Hashimoto? You may have glimpsed Townley at the counter on your way home from school some days.'

'It is possible.' The admission sounded painful.

'Your sister Mayumi entertained the customers?'

'Quite innocently. She was young and pretty. People liked her.'

'And her daughter has followed in her footsteps?'

'Yes.'

'I understand the Golden Rickshaw's walls are decorated with photographs of former patrons, taken over the years, and I further understand Stephen Townley appears in one of those photographs.'

'Yes.'

'Which is how Mr Alder knew your sister was likely to have been acquainted with him, possessed as he was of another photograph of Townley, taken a few years later.'

'Yes.'

'We believe Townley left Japan in the spring of 1960,' Jarvis continued. 'Frankly, we haven't a clue what duties he was assigned to for the remainder of his service. He left the army two years later. All official trace of him ceases at that point.' (We'd reached the Serpentine by now and had begun a slow tramp towards the boathouse. The wind was raising quite a few ripples on the lake, but I was immune to their supposedly calming effect.) 'And in the absence of a single hard fact about his life after he left the army, Townley is a dead man without a death certificate. A void. If he's still alive, it's in another man's skin. And we have absolutely no idea who that man might be.'

'What about his wife? His children?'

'Although the Townleys have never divorced, that appears to be because Mrs Townley has had no way of contacting her husband since he left the army. He ceased to pay maintenance to her at that point. She has consistently claimed that she believes him to be dead. Their children take the same line.'

'They may be lying.'

'Of course.' Jarvis smiled faintly. 'There are . . . discrepancies . . . in the banking records of all three. Discrepancies that imply financial assistance from an unidentified source.'

'Townley,' said Hashimoto.

'It's possible. When I met Mr Alder on August the 30th, to review progress, he thought that was indeed the case. And he was surprisingly cheerful. He was certain that Mrs Townley and/or her children knew where Townley was, and he told me that he had procured from your sister, Mr Hashimoto, the means to force them to tell him where that was.'

'He did not procure,' said Hashimoto. 'He stole.'

'Really? I confess I am not greatly surprised.' There was the slightest sceptical twitch of Jarvis's right eyebrow, then he went serenely on. 'I have neither seen nor heard from Mr Alder since. Though I believe that, directly or indirectly, he made contact with Townley.'

'How can you be sure of that?'

'Because within weeks of that meeting our offices were broken into and correspondence relating to the Townley inquiry stolen. More or less simultaneously, an anonymous message was passed to us via a legal practice that often acts for us, warning us to drop the case or Myerscough Udal would be ruined. Our directors were persuaded that our most valuable clients would be taken from us if we persisted. We did not persist.'

'So . . .' said Hashimoto slowly, 'why are you here, talking to us?'

'An astute question, Mr Hashimoto. Why indeed?' Jarvis looked warily to right and left. 'Officially, this meeting is not taking place. If you visit or telephone me at our offices, I will decline to speak to you and deny that we have ever met. Myerscough Udal does not like to be pushed, apparent though it is that we *can* be pushed. We are seriously unhappy about this, gentlemen. We are fearful for the welfare of a client, yet in no position to aid him.' He smiled. 'But you are.'

'What are you getting at?' I asked.

'I tell you things, Mr Bradley. I give you information. What you do with it is up to you. Save to say that I hope you will do *something*.'

'Such as?'

'That really must be up to you. What I can say is this. The Townleys had two children—Eric and Barbara. Barbara lives in Houston, Texas. She's married to an oil executive, Gordon Ledgister. They have one child—a son, Clyde, born 1980, currently a student at Stanford University. Eric, meanwhile, lives with his mother in Berlin. She went back there after the Wall came down. Eric now styles himself Erich. He's gay, by the way. Rosa Townley and he share an apartment on Yorckstrasse. Number 85. You may be interested to know that airline records show a Mr R. Alder flew from Heathrow to Berlin on September the 3rd. There's no record of a return flight. And now'—he began to turn round—'I must be going. Good morning to you both.'

With that he was off, striding back the way we'd come. He'd said everything he had to say. Myerscough Udal had dropped the case. And Jarvis had washed his hands of us. He hurried on. But Hashimoto and I stayed exactly where we were.

IT WAS ELEVEN O'CLOCK by the time we got back to the Hilton, so I prescribed a drink for us both and piloted Hashimoto round the corner to a cosy little boozer in Shepherd Market.

Halfway through my second Carlsberg Special and his first Glenfiddich, Hashimoto seemed to come to some kind of decision.

'We must go to Berlin at once,' he announced.

'Don't I get a vote on that, Kiyo?'

He looked at me oddly. Maybe my Carlsberg-inspired invention of an abbreviated name for him hadn't gone down well. But if so, he didn't dwell on it. 'I must find the Townley letter. And you must find your friend.'

'I'm not sure about that. You said yourself he'd strayed into a dark place. It could be a dangerous one, too, if Townley is as powerful as Jarvis seems to think.'

'It is true. Mr Jarvis invites us to put our heads into the tiger's mouth, to see if the tiger will bite.'

'I'm sure my mother told me once never to put my head in a tiger's mouth.'

Hashimoto nodded solemnly. 'A mother would.'

'Besides, I have to go home next week. A trip to Berlin's not on.'

'Why must you go home?'

'Oh, this and that.' (A fortnightly date with the dole office was the beginning and end of my commitments, but I certainly wasn't about to admit it.)

'We may not need to be gone for long. And I will pay your expenses.'

'I still can't go.'

'Why not?'

'I've left my passport at home.'

'How far is your home?'

'A hundred and fifty miles or so.'

'Then we will go and get it. I have the use of a car. It is in the Hilton garage.'

And so at midday, my apprehension dulled by several more Carlsberg Specials, I found myself being high-speed chauffeured along the M4 and down the M5 in a courtesy BMW. And tomorrow, apparently, I was going to Berlin.

WE MADE IT to Glastonbury in a shade over two hours. Hashimoto wasn't a dawdler behind the wheel. I thought of suggesting a diversion to my parents' so that I could ask Dad to tap Don Forrester for information. But I decided to phone Dad instead, thereby dodging having to explain to him what I was up to.

On the way back we stopped at Heathrow and Hashimoto booked us aboard a Sunday lunchtime flight to Berlin (club class, no less). Then he drove me to Rupe's place, saying he'd pick me up at ten the following morning. We were all set.

We were also mad, according to Echo. 'You have absolutely no idea what you're getting into.' (A fair point.) 'I thought you said you were a natural quitter.'

'I am.'

'Then why aren't you quitting?'

'Because that's the thing with quitting, Echo: you have to choose your moment. And this isn't it.'

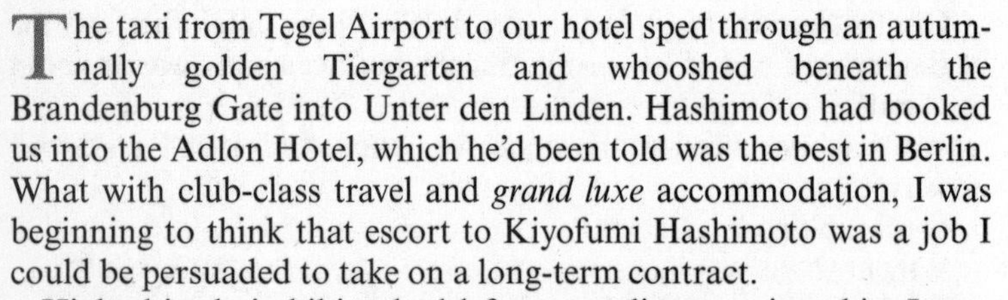

BERLIN FOUR

The taxi from Tegel Airport to our hotel sped through an autumnally golden Tiergarten and whooshed beneath the Brandenburg Gate into Unter den Linden. Hashimoto had booked us into the Adlon Hotel, which he'd been told was the best in Berlin. What with club-class travel and *grand luxe* accommodation, I was beginning to think that escort to Kiyofumi Hashimoto was a job I could be persuaded to take on a long-term contract.

High-altitude imbibing had left me needing a serious kip. I suggested we meet up in the bar at seven o'clock and Hashimoto seemed happy with that. So I stretched out on the enormous double bed in my lavishly appointed room and let the distant murmur of traffic on Unter den Linden lull me to sleep.

IT WAS DARK OUTSIDE when I woke, woozily identifying the persistent warbling in my ear as the telephone ringing on the bedside table. It was Hashimoto.

'Lance. You must come quickly.'

'Start without me, Kiyo. I'll be down in a minute.'

'I am not in the hotel,' he said. 'I am in a call box on Mehringdamm. Near the Townleys' apartment.'

'For Christ's sake. Couldn't that have waited?'

'You must come here now. I will wait for you outside Mehringdamm U-Bahn Station. Get here as soon as you can.'

'Yeah, but—' The line went dead.

THE TAXI DRIVE was a short and fast run south along broad and empty streets. We were soon at the station. Hashimoto emerged from the entrance to greet me as I stumbled out of the taxi.

'There is a café at the next corner. We will talk there,' he said.

He steered me across the road and down to the next junction. The turning to the right was Yorckstrasse. Hashimoto caught my glance at the sign, but didn't explain until we were sitting in the café.

'I decided to see where the Townleys live. It is a little way along

Yorckstrasse.' He nodded in the general direction. 'An apartment block. Expensive, I would say. As I was climbing the stairs to the door, it opened and a man came out.'

'Erich Townley?'

'I think it must be. Right age. Right . . . appearance.'

'What is the right appearance?'

'You will see for yourself.'

'How's that?'

'Listen.' Hashimoto lowered his voice. 'I followed him to a bar a little way down the street. I think he is still there now. It is a chance to speak to him. To ask him questions when he thinks all you are doing is—'

'*Why me?*'

'It will go better if you approach him, Lance. I am too . . .' Hashimoto spread his arms. 'The thing is, Lance . . .'

'Yeah?'

'I think you might be his type.'

THE BAR WAS CLOSE, as Hashimoto had promised. The interior looked dark, half empty and faintly mournful. (It was reassuring to realise that Sunday evenings in Germany weren't much jollier than in England.) Hashimoto took himself off to hover at a bus stop opposite. Leaving me, after some hesitation, to go in.

A bloke matching Hashimoto's description of the man on the stairs was sitting on a bar stool drinking some colourless spirit or other and smoking a fat French cigarette. He was wearing tight jeans and a white shirt under a three-quarter-length black coat. He was tall and thin, and his hair was too long for someone so thin on top. I didn't yet know if I was his type, but I was already absolutely certain that he wasn't mine.

I plonked myself on the stool next to Erich, ordered a Budweiser and ran a few possible chat-up lines past myself. The situation had all the makings of a grade-one fiasco.

Then a strange thing happened. Townley spoke to me.

'You American?' (He obviously was, albeit with a clipped vein of Mitteleuropa in the gravelly drawl.)

'No,' I tried to reply, but my throat wouldn't cooperate until I'd repeated the word twice. 'No, no.'

'Can't imagine why anyone who wasn't American would order a Bud. Real horse piss.'

'I didn't know there was anything real about it.'

He laughed at that. 'You're English, right?'

'Yeah.' The Budweiser arrived, and I took a swig. 'And you're American.'

'I'd have to own to that, yuh. *Half* American, anyways.'

'And the other half?'

'Local.'

'You live here?'

'Yuh. But you're just visiting, right? Vacation?'

'Business.'

'What kind?'

That was a tricky one. 'Does it matter? It's still the weekend. My name's Lance, by the way.'

'Pleased to meet you, Lance. I'm Erich.' He offered me one of his cigarettes. 'Smoke?'

'No thanks. I, er . . .'

'Believe the Surgeon-General's warning.'

'Yeah, but . . .' I caught his gaze and tried to hold it. 'I've got nothing against vice, Erich. Nothing at all.'

'You've come to the right city, then. Berlin's got it all, if you don't mind delving into dark corners.'

'Depends what I'm likely to find there.'

'Maybe you need a helping hand.'

'Maybe I do.' (This was all going too fast for my liking. What had Hashimoto got me into?) 'There are lots of things a guidebook doesn't tell you.'

'Right.' Erich took a long, thoughtful draw on his cigarette, then said, 'There's a place I know. Several places. I reckon you might enjoy them. Interested?'

'Sure.' (Horrified was nearer the mark.)

'Let's go, then.'

'OK.'

WE TURNED LEFT as we exited the bar and headed south. I didn't dare risk looking back to see if Hashimoto was following us. I felt stone-cold sober and more than a little frightened.

'I had it with the States a long time ago,' said Townley. 'Sooner or later, you have to decide where your soul belongs.'

'And yours belongs here?'

'Absolutely. What about you?'

'Still trying to decide, I suppose.'

He chuckled loudly. 'That's what I love about strangers. There's a whole . . . back-story . . . waiting to be told.'

We turned right at the next junction, and Erich started along a path that led straight into the ill-lit heart of a public park.

'We'll cut through here,' he said, as if it explained everything. I had an impression of a wooded slope in the darkness ahead of us. Dim lamps shone thinly on ponds and rockeries. I dragged my feet, to little effect. 'Keep up, Lance. It'd be easy to get lost in here.'

'Are you sure we aren't already?'

'Oh yuh. I know my way.'

'Glad to hear it.'

'What line of work did you say you were in?'

'I . . . didn't, did I?'

'Maybe you didn't. So, let me guess. Could it be . . . shipping?'

'Shipping? No. What—?'

I'm not sure what I saw or sensed first. A blur of night-shrouded movement. A scuff of shoe on asphalt. Something, anyway, brought almost instantly into focus by a sharp pain as my right arm was jerked up behind me. I was pulled backwards, struggling to stay on my feet. A hand closed round my throat—Erich was strong—far stronger than me. I tried to wrench myself free, but he held me fast. I tried to cry out for help. All I managed was a hoarse splutter.

'You are one dumb shit, Lance. You know that? You sidle up to me, all dewy-eyed and simpering, thinking I'm about to fall for your English charm. Do me a favour. Do yourself one. You're looking for your friend Rupe, right?'

His grip relaxed just enough to let me speak. 'All right . . . Yes, I am.'

'Well, you're all out of luck. Because Rupe isn't here. And you're never going to find him.' There was a noise behind me, thin and metallic—a blade being flicked from a handle. 'Your search is over, lover boy.' He released my right arm and in the same instant grasped my left shoulder and yanked me round to face him.

Into my mind flashed the acute awareness that I was about to be stabbed. But I never was.

Something struck Erich under his right arm—something powerful, moving horizontally. He grunted and fell sideways, hitting the ground hard. As he did so, I saw Hashimoto slowly lowering his left leg. He'd dealt Erich some sort of judo kick—the sort that felt like a battering ram, to judge by the effect on its victim. Erich rolled onto his side and propped himself up on one elbow.

'Stay where you are,' Hashimoto shouted. (I couldn't work out for the moment which of us he meant, so I played safe by standing stock-still.) 'Are you all right, my friend?'

'Yes. I . . .'

'Who the hell are you?' said Erich. He scrambled to his feet, breathing hard.

'Someone capable of breaking your arm or dislocating your shoulder,' said Hashimoto, and he sounded hellish convincing to me. 'Why do you seem intent on giving me the excuse to do so?'

Erich looked at me, then at Hashimoto, then back to me. 'Do you know each other?'

'Go now,' said Hashimoto, quietly but firmly.

Erich hesitated, taking the measure of himself and his opponent. There was bluff on both sides. But who was the bigger bluffer? I wouldn't have wanted to bet on it. And nor, apparently, would Erich. He pocketed the knife, turned on his heel and strode away, with a parting toss of his head.

IT WASN'T UNTIL we were back in the café at the corner of Mehringdamm that I stopped shaking and became capable—thanks to two large brandies—of coherent speech.

'He was going to kill me, Kiyo. Do you realise that?'

'It certainly seemed probable.'

'Thank God you turn out to be some kind of black-belt judoist.'

'In truth, I never progressed beyond the pupil classes. I was a great disappointment to my instructor. But I remember how to kick. For the rest, it is as well that Erich Townley did not put my technique to the test.'

'Now he tells me.'

'Would you have preferred me to mention it in Townley's presence?'

I released a long sigh. 'I'd have *preferred* not to have been in his presence at all.'

'But, Lance, think how much we have gained.'

I did think—for a moment. 'I can't see that we've gained a single bloody thing. We've learned nothing. And now he's on to us.'

'You are forgetting this.' Hashimoto slipped something from his pocket and jiggled it in his palm. It was a silver cigarette lighter. 'It fell out of his coat while he was on the ground. See the engraving?' He held it up to the light and I made out three initials on the back:

E.S.T. 'Erich Stephen Townley, I believe. This lighter is evidence against him, Lance. And I can swear that I intervened to prevent him stabbing you.'

'Swear? What are you talking about?'

'I am talking about how it would look for Erich Townley if we reported this incident to the police.'

'Are you crazy? How the hell would that get us what we want—the whereabouts of Townley senior?'

'Lance, I said *if* we reported it to the police. Obviously we do not wish to do so. But it is a question of . . . pressure.'

'Well, I've had enough pressure for one night.'

'Likewise Erich Townley, I would think. Where do you suppose he is now?'

I shrugged. 'Soothing his bruised pride in some bar or other.'

'I agree. Which means we might have an opportunity to apply some pressure to Mrs Townley.'

'You don't mean—'

'Yes, Lance.' He smiled at me. 'We have a call to make.'

NUMBER 85 YORCKSTRASSE was a classy-looking neo-Gothic apartment block, heavy on balconies, porticoes and reclining caryatids. The door—a sumptuously carved affair—was firmly closed. Hashimoto pressed the Townleys' buzzer long enough for the entry-phone to splutter into life.

'*Ja?*'

'Frau Townley?'

'*Ja.*' (The admission came cautiously.)

'Is Erich in?'

'He is not here.'

'We need to speak to you about Erich. He is in serious trouble.'

'Who are you?'

'Let us in and we will explain.'

'Go away.'

'If we do, we will go to the police. They will arrest Erich.'

'*Polizei?*' (Now she sounded worried.)

'Let us in. For Erich's sake.'

There was a lengthy silence. Then the door-release buzzed.

WE CLIMBED BROAD, marble-treaded stairs to a tall, double-doored apartment entrance on the second floor. One of the doors stood ajar and peering at us through the gap was Rosa Townley.

Frau Townley was no querulous, quavering old biddy, that was for sure. She held herself well, shoulders back, jaw square, eyes glaring above high cheekbones and a broad nose. Hers was the kind of face that actually improved with age. Her hair was thick, grey streaked with black, and she was wearing a black polo-necked sweater and trousers, simple but far from casual. 'Who are you?' she demanded.

'My name is Hashimoto, this is Mr Bradley. May we come in?'

'You have not stated your business.'

'A cigarette lighter.' Hashimoto held it up for her inspection. 'Dropped by your son as he fled after I had intervened to prevent him stabbing Mr Bradley.'

'You are lying. What do you want?'

'We want to offer you a way to resolve this matter without reference to the police.'

'Money?'

'No.' Hashimoto smiled at her. 'Let us in and we will explain.'

The drawing room was as elegant as I'd have expected of Rosa Townley's living space. Polished wood, soft leather and gleaming chandeliers. I didn't doubt this was Rosa's exclusive domain. Erich probably kept to his own quarters.

There was no invitation to sit. Rosa stationed herself by the fireplace and waited to hear what we had to say.

'Earlier this evening, Frau Townley,' said Hashimoto, 'your son assaulted Mr Bradley in Viktoriapark.' (My God, the man even knew the name of the park. You couldn't fault him for thoroughness.) 'He had his reasons, though he would find them difficult to explain to the police. They would probably infer . . . a sexual motive.'

'Tell me what you want.' Her voice was hard and unwavering.

'We want to know where your husband is.'

There was no reaction. 'My husband is dead.'

'We do not think so.'

'He is dead.'

'How do you finance your life here, Mrs Townley?' I chipped in. 'Not to mention Erich's?'

'What business is that of yours?'

'You don't work, I assume. And Erich certainly doesn't seem the industrious type. So, where's the money coming from?'

'Rupert Alder came looking for your husband,' said Hashimoto, trying another approach. 'We know this. What did you tell him?'

Without taking her eyes off us, Rosa stretched out a hand behind her to a silver box on the mantelpiece. She took out a cigarette, put it to her lips and cocked her eyebrows at Hashimoto. He hesitated, then stepped forward, struck Erich's lighter and lit the cigarette.

We waited. Rosa inhaled deeply and exhaled with studied slowness before she said, 'You do not understand.'

'Make us,' I challenged her.

'Mr Alder wanted to know how he could find Stephen.'

'Really?'

'I told Mr Alder what I have told you. Stephen is dead.'

'Did he believe you?'

'No. No more than you,' she said, adding, 'He wanted me to pass on a message to Stephen.'

'What message?'

'He said he had a letter containing damaging information about Stephen's activities in the summer and fall of 1963. He refused to say what the information was. If Stephen wanted to prevent the contents of the letter becoming public, he was to contact Mr Alder.' She shrugged. 'I told him there was nothing I could do. I told him Stephen was dead. He asked for proof.'

'And you could prove it?'

'No. I have had no contact with my husband of any kind for the past thirty-eight years.'

'Then you can't know he's dead, can you?'

She devoted a lengthy moment to her cigarette, then treated us to a heavy sigh. 'Stephen is dead, Mr Bradley. Long dead. Why do you not believe me?'

'Because your son wouldn't have been willing to kill me to protect a dead man.'

She frowned at me. 'If anyone should be going to the police, it is him, not you. And he may—if you continue to harass us.'

'Frau Townley,' said Hashimoto with sudden decisiveness, 'you have twenty-four hours to consider your position. If, after that, you still refuse to tell us where we can find your husband . . .' He shrugged, almost apologetically. 'You will leave us no choice.'

'Twenty-four hours will change nothing.'

'I hope it will change your mind. We are staying at the Adlon, if you wish to contact us. I am sure none of us wants to involve the police.'

'Then do not involve them.' Rosa made a strange tossing movement of the chin. 'As I have tried to explain to you, it is your decision.'

'AN ULTIMATUM, Kiyo,' I murmured to Hashimoto as we exited the apartment block a few moments later. 'Nice move.'

'The only move,' he said expressionlessly.

'Do you reckon it'll work?'

'It might.'

'And if it doesn't?'

He looked round at me and spread his hands helplessly. 'At least we have twenty-four hours to think about it.'

IF THINKING had to be done, I for one had no intention of starting that evening. Hashimoto went back to the hotel but I took myself off to a cinema showing undubbed movies. *American Psycho* wasn't the kind of entertainment a man in my frazzled state really needed. After a few drinks in a dire pseudo-Irish pub to restore my equilibrium, I made it back to the Adlon around midnight, confident I wouldn't have to think about anything until morning.

I was wrong.

A letter had been slipped under the door of my room. I picked it up. Then I noticed a red light glowing on the bedside telephone. *Message waiting.*

I slumped down at the desk and looked at the letter. My name was handwritten in capitals on the envelope. I didn't recognise the writing. I tore the flap open. Inside was a leaflet advertising open-top bus tours of Berlin. There was a timetable on a separate sheet of paper that slipped out of the leaflet and someone had circled the 12.15 departure from the Brandenburg Gate in red ink. Strange, I remember thinking; very strange.

I went over to the telephone, picked it up and pressed the MESSAGE button. A computerised voice told me something in German. There was a brief electronic pause. Then the message kicked in. '*What you've been told is true. I have the letter. I am in Berlin. We must meet. Tomorrow. I will let you know how. Trust me.*'

I sat slowly down on the bed, then stabbed at the MESSAGE button and listened to the recording again. There was no doubt about it. The voice was Rupe's.

BERLIN WAS LOCKED in perfect weather. The sky was a flawless blue, the air crisp, the sunshine as warm as the shadows were cool. The 12.15 Berlin City Tour bus nudged out from its stand in Pariser Platz and crawled between the scaffolded pillars of the Brandenburg Gate as the hyperactive multilingual guide hopped around at the front of the top deck, microphone in hand. Sitting beside Hashimoto at the back, meanwhile, I gave little thought to the lofty views of historical sites our twenty-five Deutschmarks had bought.

Where was Rupe? We were where he'd told us to be. But he wasn't. '*We must meet.*' He was right there. '*Tomorrow.*' Well, tomorrow had come. '*Trust me.*' I was trusting him. And Hashimoto was trusting him as well. But not exactly wholeheartedly.

'How can we be sure it is Rupe on the tape?' he'd fired as his first doubting salvo that morning.

'I recognised his voice, Kiyo.'

'But how can we be sure he is not being forced to say these things?'

'Why would anyone want to force us to go on a tourist bus trip round Berlin?'

'I do not know. It does not make sense.'

'Unless it really is Rupe.'

'But he could meet us anywhere, Lance. Why the bus?'

Which was a good question. And the only answer I could come up with was that the bus was a safe and neutral venue, with witnesses on hand. In other words, Rupe didn't trust us.

The message had been recorded at 9.27pm. Hashimoto had established that in the process of laying hands on the actual tape. (The concierge had clearly thought we were both mad, but had eventually agreed to extract it from the system for us.) Some time after 9.27pm the letter had been dropped off for me at reception. A bellboy had then delivered it to my room. All of which told us . . . very little.

But very little wasn't the same as nothing. Rupe knew we were in Berlin. How? And he knew which hotel we were staying in. How again? Maybe he was keeping the Townleys under surveillance. If Rupe had been following us, though, he'd have known I wouldn't be at the Adlon to take his call. Which implied he hadn't actually wanted to speak to me. The message had been all that mattered.

But he was going to have to speak to me soon. The route map showed a dozen or so stops on the hour-and-a-half tour. Rupe could be waiting at any one of them.

The bus cruised round to the Reichstag, where a giant snake of tourists was queuing to visit the dome, but nobody at all was waiting for the bus. As we pressed on through Tiergarten, our guide regaled us with tired anecdotes about the places we were passing—which Hashimoto greeted with rapt attention.

'We're not here to see the sights,' I grumbled as the bus circled some draughty triumphal column. 'Keep your eyes peeled for Rupe.'

'He will come to us or not, Lance,' said Hashimoto. 'Looking will not force him into view.'

This was true, of course, but unhelpful.

Once we were out of Tiergarten and back on city-centre streets, our pace slowed in the lunchtime traffic. We stopped to take on some people at the Zoo, but Rupe wasn't among them. It was pushing towards one o'clock now and the Berliners were out in force, shopping and lunching and bustling about their business. It would be easy for one man to lose himself in the crowd, to watch us drift by on the bus. This, I supposed, was how Rupe had planned it: for us to show ourselves before he had to decide whether to show *him*self.

We drew up at a stop opposite the Europa-Center shopping complex. 'There'll be a break here of twenty minutes,' the guide announced. 'If you want to leave the bus to stretch your legs, be sure to be back by one fifteen.'

Everybody else on the top deck but Hashimoto and me got off. The guide went down for a chat with the driver. 'This could be it,' I said. 'Twenty minutes for Rupe to clock us and come aboard.'

'And lots of people to obscure his approach,' said Hashimoto, glancing across at the crowded pavement on the other side of the road. 'You are right. It is the likeliest place.'

There were benches spaced along the grassed and flowerbedded central reservation, most of them occupied by workers snatching a takeaway lunch. I craned over the rail and studied each bench in turn. There was no sign of Rupe.

'I will treat Rupe leniently, Lance,' Hashimoto announced. 'I will try not to punish him for what he has done.'

'You don't need to be so generous on my account.'

'But he is your friend. And you are *my* friend. I hope you would help Mayumi and Haruko . . . for the same reasons.'

I looked round to find Hashimoto smiling at me. I reckoned this was as gushing as the guy ever got. 'I'd do my best for them, Kiyo. Sure.'

His smile broadened. 'It is all I ask.'

I looked back at the benches. 'Well, you can be as lenient with my good friend Rupe Alder as you want, Kiyo, but I'm going to tell him exactly what I think of him. Where the bloody hell is he?'

'Close, I suspect. Very—'

Something pierced the air just in front of me and Hashimoto gave a strangled gasp. I swung round towards him. The right lens of his spectacles had shattered, and there was a raw red gap where his eye should have been. As he toppled sideways into the aisle between the seats, a bullet—I didn't doubt what it was—struck the rail near my elbow and pinged past me. I dived for the deck.

Hashimoto's face drew close to mine as I crawled into the aisle. His lips sagged apart, as if he was still trying to tell me how close Rupe might be. But he was never going to tell me—or anyone else—anything, ever again. Kiyofumi Hashimoto was dead.

Another bullet struck the back of one of the seats beyond and above me. Somebody was trying to kill both of us and they weren't about to stop with the job half done. I had to get off that bus. I squirmed past Hashimoto towards the stairs, catching some object on the floor as I went and dragging it with me. I reached down and pulled it out from under me. It was the tape of Rupe's message. It must have slipped out of Hashimoto's pocket as he fell. Only then did I remember that it was Rupe who had lured us into this trap. '*Trust me*,' he'd said. And I had. Suddenly, I wanted to find Rupe more than I could ever have imagined. I gritted my teeth and made for the stairs.

Another bullet whined overhead. Then I was in the relative safety of the stairwell. I scrambled to my feet, leapt down the treads two at a time and lunged for the open door at the bottom.

People were scattering in both directions along the pavement, screaming. I saw the guide and the driver crouched by the front wheel-arch. I heard another shot and saw them flinch. Then the guide spotted me. 'Get down, behind the bus,' he shouted. 'I've called the police on my mobile. They'll be here soon.'

Maybe they would. And maybe he was safe where he was. But he wasn't the target. The bus had stopped just past a turning and the body of the vehicle would shield me as far as the corner. At least, I hoped it would. I started running.

What was I going to do? Where was I going to go? 'This is life and death,' Hashimoto had told me back in London. I hadn't believed him. I did now.

The road ended in a T-junction. I turned right, breath failing me, legs aching. We'd been set up. That was obvious. Rosa Townley had moved fast. She and Erich and Rupe too, it seemed, had plotted our execution. They were in it together, and they were all my enemies.

I had to get out of Berlin. The realisation came to me just as I spotted a taxi approaching with its light on. If I stayed, I was lost. They knew the city, I didn't. The police wouldn't believe me. If I stayed, they'd get me. I flagged the taxi down, ran across the road and jumped in. '*Flughafen Tegel*,' I shouted to the driver.

'*Flughafen Tegel. Ja.*' He started away.

Then I remembered. My passport was back at the Adlon. Without it, I was going nowhere. 'No. Not the airport. Hotel—' I stopped. They knew I was likely to go there. They could be waiting for me. But I had to get my passport. I pulled out my map. '*Komische Oper*,' I said, spotting how close it was to the Adlon; I could cut round from there to the rear entrance of the hotel.

'*Komische Oper*. OK.' The driver picked up speed.

The taxi ride wasn't as fast as I'd have liked, but in another sense it was too fast, because I had no better idea of what to do when it ended than when it had begun. Get the hell away was all my stunned reasoning process could come up with. Hashimoto was dead and I was lucky not to be dead as well. I wasn't looking for Rupe any more, or Stephen Townley, or an old letter. I just wanted out.

There didn't look to be anyone hanging around the back entrance of the Adlon. I ran across Wilhelmstrasse without waiting for the lights to change, and rushed into the hotel. I knew I ought to be inconspicuous, but I felt anything but. My shoulder was aching from the scramble off the bus, and there was a stain on my sleeve that was probably Hashimoto's blood. I made it to reception without drawing any looks, and tried to make the request for my key sound casual. The lobby and bar were busy without being crowded. If anyone was watching the front door, there was a reasonable chance they wouldn't notice me as I took the key and doubled back to the lifts. You had to have a room key to access the guest floors (by waggling it in front of a sensor in the lift). I reassured myself I was in the clear now.

I jogged from the lift to my room, opened up and rushed in, swinging the door shut behind me as I made for the safe in the corner, where I'd stored my passport and a wad of Deutschmarks Hashimoto had given me.

I was stooping in front of the safe, tapping in the combination, when I heard a rattle from behind me, as if my shove hadn't been enough to close the door. I glanced over my shoulder. And there was Erich Townley, pushing the door gently shut and leaning back against it.

'In a hurry, Lance?' he asked, smiling sourly.

I stood up slowly and turned round to face him.

'Oh, you can go ahead and open the safe, I'd like to see what you have inside. Just in case it includes the letter.'

'What letter's that?'

'Trying to be smart when you're as dumb as you are is just pathetic, Lance. You know that? Why'd you come back here?'

'Too dumb not to, I suppose.'

'I heard there was a shooting near the Europa-Center. Some Japanese tourist's on his way to the morgue.'

'Who did the shooting, Erich?'

'Wouldn't you like to know? Not Rupe. He's no marksman. But he's one hell of a decoy, don't you think?'

'Why did you kill Hashimoto?'

'I haven't killed anyone.' He moved towards me. 'Yet.'

'What's in the letter?'

'Maybe you know better than I do. Open the safe.'

'I'm afraid I can't. I've forgotten the combination.'

'Not funny, Lance.' He reached into the pocket of his coat and took something out. I'd expected it to be a knife. But it wasn't. It was a gun. He pointed it at me. 'Open up.'

I crouched down in front of the safe, tapped in the numbers and opened the door.

'Take out everything that's inside.'

This was crazy. Why the hell should he think I had the letter? It made no sense. I picked up the passport and the bundle of cash, holding the handful up for him to see. 'This is all there is, Erich.'

'Stay where you are.' He crouched down for a view past me into the safe. There was nothing for him to see. 'I guess it was an outside chance anyway,' he said, standing up again. 'Worse luck for you.'

'Why's that?'

'Work it out for yourself.' (I tried not to.) 'Now, stand up. Slowly.'

I obeyed, turning to face him as I rose.

'Empty your pockets onto the desk.'

That didn't take long. My wallet; the keys to my flat in Somerset; a grubby handkerchief; some coins; and the tape.

Erich stared at the scatter of objects for a moment, then returned his gaze to me. 'What's on the tape?'

'That tape?'

'Yeah. That tape.'

'Abba's greatest hits.'

He glared at me, then leaned forward to pick up the tape.

'Don't say you're an Abba fan too, Erich.'

'Shut up.'

He looked away for the fraction of a second it took him to grasp the tape. And that, I knew, was the only fraction of a second luck was likely to hand me. I lunged at him in as good a rugby tackle as I could manage. We both went down hard. I braced myself for the gun to go off, but it didn't. Erich hit the floor, grunting as the breath shot out of him. I heard a clunk somewhere behind us and rolled round to see the gun lying several feet away under the desk. A table lamp wobbled above me as I came to rest against the cabinet it stood on. Erich began to scramble back up, his gaze focusing on the gun. I swivelled and kicked, catching him on the side of the head. Then I was on my feet, grabbing the lamp by its heavy brass base. Erich tried to dodge the blow but I brought the lamp down fast, the rimmed base hitting him somewhere above his left eye. There was a solid crunch of brass on bone.

Erich slumped to the floor, blood oozing from a triangular wound on his brow. I put the lamp slowly back down on the cabinet. My hands were shaking. My knees were shaking. I tried to think clearly. Had I killed him? I jammed two fingers under his ear and felt for a pulse. His heart was still beating. He was unconscious, but he wasn't dead. Thank God. I didn't want to leave Berlin as a murder suspect on the run. But leave it I had to, fast. Someone deadlier by far than Erich had been responsible for shooting Hashimoto. He might already be on his way to the Adlon.

I rushed to the wardrobe, grabbed my bag and flung in the spare clothes I'd brought. Then I threw in my toothbrush and shaving kit from the bathroom, stuffed the items on the desk into my pocket, including the tape, passport and cash, and made for the door.

I stopped halfway. I needed an edge over the enemy. What did Erich have I could make use of? I stooped over him and checked his coat pockets. Some keys he was welcome to keep—and a wallet. I reckoned he'd have to live without that. I slung it into my bag, closed the zip and headed for the door again.

I LEFT THE ADLON the way I'd come in, by the back door, and picked up a taxi within a couple of blocks. As we sped through Tiergarten, I seriously wondered if I should divert to Police HQ and tell them everything that had happened. But I was sure there'd be nothing to link the Townleys with the shooting. And I'd probably end up being charged with assaulting Erich. No, I had to go.

But my run-in with Erich had changed something in my mind. Before, I'd been high on fear and the instinct for self-preservation. Now, I was beginning to feel angry. Hashimoto was my friend. He'd said so himself. He deserved to be avenged. And the people who'd killed him deserved to be punished.

But was I the man to do either? I didn't have much choice. The nameless marksman who'd snuffed out Hashimoto's life would come after me. I was sure of that. I could go back to England and try to resume a normal life, but sooner or later, he'd track me down.

I felt the tape in my pocket. Had Rupe really sold out? Or was his message a fake? *I have the letter. I am in Berlin. We must meet*. Short, simple sentences. A spliced tape, maybe, made up of parts of a previously recorded conversation. It was possible. In the right hands, it was probably easy.

If the tape *was* a fake, then it was also a clue as to what Rupe had done in Berlin. *I have the letter. We must meet.* He hadn't been talking to me. He'd been talking to the Townleys. Of course. They'd recycled Rupe's blackmail call. *Trust me* meant *You'd better believe I'm serious*. And they *had* believed him. What they'd done to neutralise the threat he posed I didn't know. But it hadn't been enough, not quite. They still didn't have the letter. Erich's behaviour proved that. They didn't have it and they were prepared to kill anyone to suppress the secret it held.

As the taxi headed west out of Tiergarten, I unzipped my bag and took out Erich's wallet. What did we have here? Credit cards that were no use to me—plastic leaves a trail and I couldn't afford to do that. What I needed was hard cash. Fortunately, Erich seemed to be a serious fan of folding money. He had about 3,000 Deutschmarks on him, plus several hundred US dollars. 'Thanks very much,' I murmured, transferring the cash to my own wallet. What else was there? Nothing much that I could see, apart from a clutch of membership cards for various clubs.

But hold on. One of them was more of a business card. Gordon A. Ledgister, Caribtex Oil, with an office address in Houston, Texas. Erich's brother-in-law—the oil executive Jarvis had said Barbara Townley had married. You never knew when I might want to contact *him*. That went into my wallet as well. The rest went into a rubbish bin at the airport.

THANKS TO ERICH'S fondness for the crinkly stuff, added to Hashimoto's generosity, I was able to pay cash for my economy-class ticket to Tokyo at the Lufthansa desk.

Sitting in the departure lounge at Tegel, trying to stop my thoughts whirling in on themselves, I suddenly realised that there were people other than myself to consider. And I badly owed a couple of them a telephone call.

The first was my father, who seemed strangely unsurprised by my urgent request for him to call me straight back on a Berlin number.

'I spoke to your friend Echo yesterday,' he explained when we were talking again. 'She told me you'd gone to Germany. What's this all about, son?'

'Too complicated to go into, Dad. We don't want to overload your phone bill, do we?'

'That's true.' (I'd known the point would appeal to him.)

'Why did you contact Echo?'

'Because you asked me to have a word with Don Forrester and let you know the outcome.'

'And what was the outcome?'

'Well . . . Don was reluctant to go into it at first, I can tell you. It took some doing to talk him round.'

'You managed it, though.'

'I did, yes. Apparently the police did consider the possibility that Peter Dalton had been murdered by a friend who'd been staying with him at Wilderness Farm. But the friend was never traced, and the pathologist narrowly favoured suicide as a cause of death, so—'

'Was the friend called Stephen Townley?'

'Townley? Might have been. Don couldn't remember the name. What he did remember, though, was that Howard Alder virtually accused this friend of murdering Dalton. The police might never have known about him otherwise, though neighbours subsequently confirmed his existence. What's more, Howard showed Don a photograph of the fellow. The photo was taken at—'

'Ashcott and Meare railway station.'

'How did you know that?'

'I've seen the photograph. On Rupe's kitchen wall. But that doesn't matter. What efforts did Don make to track down Townley?'

'None. Officially, it was never a murder inquiry. And Howard wasn't exactly a reliable witness. Although, oddly enough, he *did* come up with a motive for murder.'

'Really? What was that?'

'Howard had taken to sneaking around Wilderness Farm that summer, apparently. A few days before the shooting, he was in the farm, spying through the kitchen window, and he saw—claimed he saw—a holdall full of banknotes standing on the kitchen table. Well, there was no holdall full of cash at the farm when the police searched it. Howard suggested that it was the proceeds of a crime and that the murderer had stolen it. This was just after the Great Train Robbery, remember. The papers were full of speculation about where the robbers might have hidden the money. Don reckoned that Howard got the idea about the holdall from such stories and used it to blacken Dalton's reputation.'

'Why would he want to do that?'

'Ah, well, in some ways that's the most surprising part of the whole thing. It seems Peter Dalton was sweet on Mildred Alder. So Howard believed, anyway. And he didn't approve of Dalton as a suitor for his sister. That's why he was spying on Dalton. And why he was out to discredit him.'

'Did Don ask Mil about this . . . relationship?'

'Tried to, apparently. But George told him it was just a fantasy of Howard's and Don left it at that. Although he did say that when he called at Penfrith it was obvious that Mildred was very upset about something. But it's all a very long time ago. Don reckons the deaths were just coincidental.'

'And that George Alder drowned accidentally?'

'It hardly seems likely he would want to kill himself, does it? Not with a child on the way. Don was flummoxed. Still is, come to that.'

'I'll bet he is.' So was I.

'That's about all I can tell you, son. You could always try asking Mildred about Peter Dalton, of course. Just don't ask me to.'

'I won't. Maybe I'll do it myself when I get back.'

'When's that likely to be?'

'Not sure.'

'Do you want your mother to take a message to the Alders?'

'No, I don't want you or Mum to contact them. Just . . . drop it. Do nothing. Say nothing. It's best, believe me.'

'I was just beginning to enjoy myself.'

'Then quit while you're ahead. I wish I could.'

'What's that supposed to mean?'

'Nothing. I've got to go, Dad. Don't worry, OK? I'll be in touch.'

'Yes, but—'

'Bye.' I didn't enjoy putting the phone down on him, but cutting him off from what I'd become involved in was the best way to protect him.

And the same applied to Echo. I found her at home, resting up after her morning round. She sounded relieved to hear from me.

'Is there something wrong, Echo?'

'I had creepy Carl round here last night, asking where you were and what you were up to. I told him you'd gone away without saying where or why.'

'Good. It's a good line to stick to. Now, you remember what you said to me Friday night about moving out?'

'Yeah.'

'I think you should. As soon as possible.'

'Why? What's happened?'

'It's better you don't know.'

'I hate it when people say that.'

'So do I. But it really is better. Find lodgings somewhere else, Echo. Forget Rupe. Forget me, too.'

'I can't do that.'

'Try.'

'Don't you think you should quit now?'

'Definitely.'

'Then why don't you?'

I had to think about that for a moment. The answer, when it came, was neither illuminating to Echo nor consoling to me. But it was true. 'Because the time for quitting has come and gone.'

TOKYO FIVE

After changing planes in Frankfurt, I reached the Land of the Rising Sun the following day, just as the sun was setting. Travelling as light as I was at least meant I didn't have to hang around the baggage hall at Narita Airport. I made straight for the bureau de change, swapped my Deutschmarks for yen, then hit the information desk. The legendary courtesy of the Japanese is the only possible explanation for me going away with a street map of Tokyo on which neat red crosses marked the locations of the Golden Rickshaw bar and the Far East office of the Eurybia Shipping Company, along with a note of their addresses in Japanese.

I studied the map as the N'EX train sped me into the city. The Golden Rickshaw was in a side street a shortish distance east of Tokyo's central station. To that extent, my luck was in. Eurybia's office was quite a way to the southwest, however, so Rupe wasn't likely to have chanced on the Golden Rickshaw while sampling nearby bars. No, he'd sought it out. He'd known what he was looking for. Though what that was . . .

The Tokyo rush hour, amped up to an oriental pitch, was in full swing when I got off the train. I battled out of the station and immediately set off in the wrong direction, then had to double back and soon lost count of how many blocks I was supposed to cover. A department-store doorman eventually put me right, and I found the side street I was looking for. There were several bars along it, but no sign of the Golden Rickshaw, so I tried my luck in one of the friendlier-looking establishments. The barman studied the piece of paper on which I had the Golden Rickshaw's address written down.

'Seven doors that way, other side. But it's closed.'

'Closed?'

'Yeah. Six weeks now, must be. They closed down. Gone.'

'Gone where?'

'Hey, they don't tell me. They just go.'

'The mother and the daughter?'

'Yeah. That's right. Gone. Like smoke.'

GONE LIKE SMOKE. And so they were. The Golden Rickshaw still had its gilded emblem hanging over the door, but the bar was unlit, its bamboo blinds drawn. Thanks to the glow of a street lamp, I could see something of the interior round the edge of the blinds: a bare counter beyond a jumble of stacked tables, chairs and stools, and a slew of unopened mail. They'd gone. No question about it. And those photographs of former patrons decorating the walls? They'd gone too. I could see the nails they'd hung on.

It wasn't really surprising, I admitted to myself as I trudged back to the station. They'd known they were in danger, ever since Rupe made off with the Townley letter. If I could track them down, so could others.

But where did I go from here? There was only one answer, of course. It was the second address written on my piece of paper.

After queuing at a taxi rank for ten minutes, I got myself a cab, waved Eurybia's address under the driver's nose and barely twenty minutes later we were at the foot of some alp of a skyscraper. The driver pointed at the steps leading up to the brightly lit entrance. I filled his hand with yen and clambered out.

The Chayama Building fulfilled the office needs of several dozen corporations. Eurybia was on the ninth floor. But making it to the brushed-steel lift doors meant talking my way past a grim-looking security man. I had my doubts about whether I looked the part for office visits and it was also suspiciously late. I just had to hope Eurybia's staff were a dedicated bunch.

'Hi. Eurybia Shipping?'

The man smiled with surprising warmth. 'Who you seeing?'

'Not sure. Mr Charles Hoare of their London office said I was to call round. My name is Lance Bradley. Could you ask them if I could go up?'

'If they ask . . . what about?'

'Say . . .' An inspired notion came to me. 'Say it's about the Pomparles Trading Company.'

'Pomparles. OK.'

He picked up the phone, pressed a button and had a brief conversation with somebody in Japanese. I caught my name, and Charlie Hoare's and the agonisingly enunciated *Pomparlees*. My name was repeated—twice. Then he put the phone down. 'They say you go up.' He flapped a hand towards the lift. 'Floor nine.'

THERE WAS A BLOKE waiting for me when I exited the lift. Middle-aged, sober-tied and dark-suited, stocky going on flabby, he had slicked-back greying hair and a large, lugubrious, flat-nosed face rather like a bulldog's, with a long, diagonal crease across his forehead so prominent it could have been a scar. 'Mr Bradley?' he ventured, bowing slightly.

'Yeah. Thanks for—'

'I am Toshishige Yamazawa.' We shook hands. 'Pleased to meet you. May I see some identification, please?'

I handed my passport over and he looked studiously at my photograph, then handed it back.

'Rupe spoke about you.'

'He did?' That was a surprise. 'So, you worked with him?'

'Yes. And now I work with Mr Penberthy, Rupe's successor. I take you to meet him.'

Yamazawa led the way to a set of double doors, where he tapped out a number to gain access. Inside, we walked down a corridor into a large, starkly furnished office. About half the desks were still occupied despite the fact that seven o'clock had come and gone.

We pressed on towards a trio of larger, partitioned-off desks, behind one of which sat a thin, blue-suited European. He had fair, receding hair and dark shadows round his eyes.

'Penberthy-san, this is our visitor,' Yamazawa announced as we approached. 'Mr Bradley.'

Penberthy frowned at me. 'Bloody Charlie Hoare,' he said. 'We've had nothing from him about a visit from you. And this is a pretty odd bloody hour to come calling.'

'I'm an old friend of Rupe Alder's, Mr Penberthy. I'm trying to find out what's happened to him, on behalf of his family.'

'It's no can do as far as I'm concerned. God, if I ever hear the end of bloody Rupert Alder and his Pomparles business I think I'll be dreaming.'

'It *is* a complicated affair,' put in Yamazawa.

'Don't I know it? Complicated enough to get me targeted by burglars in this supposedly crime-free city.'

'You've been burgled?' I asked.

'Oh yes. And not just once. But—' He broke off and eyed me doubtfully. 'I'm not sure we should be discussing Eurybia business with you, Mr Bradley.'

'I would be willing to help Bradley-san,' said Yamazawa.

'Charlie mightn't like you to, old man.'

'In that event it would be my problem, not yours, Penberthy-san.' Yamazawa smiled. 'We can talk at the Nezumi. Off the record.'

'It'll be *on* the record if this goes pear-shaped. *Your* record. But go on. Do what you like.' He waved a hand expansively across his desk. 'When did my opinion ever count for anything around here?'

THE NEZUMI was a small bar a few blocks from the Chayama Building. Yamazawa seemed to be well known there, exchanging a strange Japanese version of high fives with several of the customers. Most of them were drinking and smoking at a stiffish pace, inebriation a certain destination—unless asphyxiation got them first.

Yamazawa lit up and ordered a couple of beers. '*Kampai*,' he announced, polishing off half of his in three swallows. 'We drink to health and happiness for Penberthy.'

'I get the impression you won't be seeking the presidency of Penberthy's fan club.'

'I couldn't afford to refuse it. But Rupe is my friend, Bradley-san. You could say he saved my life.'

'How?'

'A private matter.'

'OK. Though, as it happens, you could say he saved my life too.'

'Strange.' Yamazawa peered at me through his cigarette smoke. 'Rupe is more careful with his friends' lives than his own.'

'You think his life's in danger?'

'For sure. Unless . . . it is already over.'

'Pessimistic bugger, aren't you?'

'It is in my nature. Not in Rupe's, though. He always sees a bright dawn.'

'Do you know anything about the Golden Rickshaw bar?'

'It's closed. My fault, you could say.'

'How's that?'

'I introduced Rupe to it. He used to ask me about Tokyo in the old days. Fifties and sixties. Officers from the American bases used certain bars and clubs; lower ranks used certain others. They didn't mix. Except at the Rickshaw, which made it unique, gave it a strange kind of reputation. He was interested, so I took him there.'

'What was it like?'

Yamazawa shrugged. 'Like a lot of other places. Quieter than most, maybe. Mayumi Hashimoto was the *mama*. She ran it well. She was helped by her daughter. There were no Americans. That time was gone.'

'But there were photographs of that time on display, weren't there?'

Yamazawa looked surprised. 'How did you know about those?'

'I met Kiyofumi Hashimoto, Mayumi's brother.'

'Ah. He also is looking for Rupe.' Yamazawa nodded. 'Of course.' (I wondered if I ought to tell him then that poor old Kiyo was looking no more, but some instinct held me back.) 'He came to see me shortly after Rupe left Tokyo.'

'Accusing him of stealing a letter?'

'Yes. And of deceiving Hashimoto's niece, Haruko. That was a surprise to me.'

'Didn't you know about their engagement?'

'No. I did not. I never even knew Rupe had gone on visiting the Golden Rickshaw after that one time I took him there. He said nothing to me about any of it.'

'Why don't we have another beer?' I asked, glancing at our suddenly empty glasses.

'Good idea.' Yamazawa arranged that with little more than a twitch of the eyebrows. 'You like Sapporo beer?'

'It hits the spot.'

'For sure.'

'I need to find that letter.'

'But you are not the only one looking, I think. Hashimoto said his sister and niece were in danger because of it. That is why they went away. To hide. And since then . . . there have been the break-ins.'

'You mean the burglaries Penberthy complained of?'

'He lives in the flat Rupe used to live in. It is leased by Eurybia. It has been broken into twice. Nothing has been stolen. But everything has been searched. Thoroughly. Of course, Rupe left nothing there. You are his friend, so I must be honest with you. He did not take everything with him.'

'Are you holding something for him?' I asked, catching his drift.

Yamazawa nodded. 'A briefcase. He asked me to keep it safe and secret. I did not tell Hashimoto about it. But that was before the break-ins and the Pomparles scandal. Something is very wrong. I think that maybe the time has come to open the briefcase.'

'I think maybe you're right.'

'Yes.' He took a deep swallow of beer. 'We do it tonight.'

'Where is it?'

'At my flat.'

HIS FLAT was a longish taxi ride away, on the third floor of a drab, mid-rise block in a western suburb: one small living room and three windowless cupboards that the fittings suggested were bedroom, kitchen and bathroom. A couple of large beanbags and a low table were about it on the lounge furniture front.

I lowered myself onto one of the beanbags while Yamazawa hurried away into the bedroom. Then he was back, carrying a slim, black leather briefcase with four-digit combination locks—a standard-issue executive sandwich carrier. He laid it flat on the table.

'It's not going to be easy to break open,' said Yamazawa.

'Maybe we don't need to break it open.'

'You know the combination?'

'No, but I know Rupe. The combination will have some secret significance.' I tried 1963. But no joy. Too obvious, perhaps.

'His birthday, maybe?'

I tried it. 'No.'

'His father's birthday?'

'I wouldn't know when that was. But hold on . . . I do know the date of his father's death. November the 17th.'

And 1711 did the trick. The case opened to reveal a sheaf of papers and a wallet of photographs.

'What is there?' asked Yamazawa.

'Not sure. Take a look at these pics.' I handed him the wallet, then took out the papers and began leafing through them. They were all photocopies. A lot were of the same *Central Somerset Gazette* stories Dad had dug out for me, plus articles from the national press about the Great Train Robbery. Others were parts of large-scale Ordnance Survey maps of the Street area, dating from the same period. Wilderness Farm was picked out in yellow highlighter.

'Does it tell you anything?' asked Yamazawa.

'Nothing I didn't already know.' I looked up at him. 'What about the photographs?'

'See for yourself.' He spread them out on the table.

They were mostly snapshots of an attractive young Japanese woman with a trusting intensity in her gaze that convinced me she loved the person taking her picture. 'Haruko Hashimoto?'

'Yes,' said Yamazawa. 'A most charming fiancée.'

'And this must be Mayumi.' I pointed to a picture of Haruko standing next to an older woman in front of some kind of temple. There was a strong family resemblance between the two women.

'Mother and daughter taking a stroll in Ueno Park,' said Yamazawa, recognising the spot. 'Also charming.'

'Until you know Rupe's just stringing them along.'

Then I noticed one photograph in black and white. 'What's this?'

I picked it up to examine, holding it up so that Yamazawa could see as well. Three men in lightweight US military uniforms were sitting at a table in a bar. There were drifts of smoke and blurred figures in the background at other tables. One of the three had his back to the camera and was half in shadow. He was young and slim, his dark hair cropped just shy of a crew cut. He was looking across the table to his left, the light catching his chin and cheekbone. The man he was looking at was facing the camera, though apparently unaware of it. He was stockier and slightly older, with a hint of flab around his jaw, and a smile creasing his wide face as he raised a beer bottle in his hand. 'It is a photograph of a photograph,' said Yamazawa. 'One of the pictures from the wall of the Golden Rickshaw.' He was right. There were patches of sheen on the print that could only be reflections from the glass in the frame.

'Yeah,' I said. 'And I know why he chose this particular picture.' The third man at the table was thinner and grimmer-faced than his beaming companion. He was also slightly younger than in the only other photograph of him I'd seen, waiting for a train at Ashcott and Meare station. 'It's Stephen Townley,' I said.

'Who is Stephen Townley?'

'I think the letter Rupe stole concerns him.'

'Who are the other two?'

'Haven't a clue.'

'I think we do. We have a smile.' Yamazawa pointed at the grinning bloke with the beer bottle. Then he picked up another photograph and held it in front of me. 'The smile is the same.'

And so it was. Worn by a forty-or-so years older man. His hair was still short, but had turned white with age. The surplus flesh under his jaw had become a wedge of fat, but the smile hadn't altered. He was standing next to Haruko Hashimoto, grinning amiably at the camera—and hence at Rupe. 'Bloody hell,' I murmured. 'It's the same man.'

'For sure.'

'He's still here.'

'Not here, actually. That is not Tokyo.'

I looked more closely. Smiler and Haruko were standing on what was probably a balcony, its railings visible behind them. On the other side of the street below was a stone-block wall and part of what looked like a castle or palace, high-roofed and ornately eaved.

'That is Nijo-jo,' said Yamazawa. 'In Kyoto. The ancient capital. They are on the balcony of somebody's flat, I would guess, overlooking the castle.'

'Whose flat? Smiler's?'

'Probably.'

'An American who was based here as a soldier and came back. I guess he *could* be sheltering Haruko and her mother. Now.'

'It is as likely as anything else.'

'A flat near . . . what was it?'

'Nijo-jo. Quite a landmark.'

'And Smiler's probably a landmark in his own right round there. Which means it should be possible to trace him.'

'I think you would have a good chance.'

'And I haven't got a lot of chances to choose from, have I? How far's Kyoto?'

'By one of our famous bullet trains, less than three hours.'

WITH MY NEXT MOVE decided, we both relaxed. Yamazawa invited me to stay the night, which was more or less inevitable, given how late it was. He then opened a bottle of some potent spirit called *shochu*, into which we made alarmingly mind-mangling inroads as the night deepened.

I woke late the next morning on Yamazawa's lumpy guest futon to a stream of sunlight through the window and a headache for which the word 'ache' was pitifully inappropriate. Yamazawa had gone to work long since, leaving a farewell note by the front door.

Bradley-san,

I cannot give Penberthy more to complain about by being late, so I leave you sleeping like a baby. Call me on my mobile (not at Eurybia) and let me know what happens in Kyoto. The number is 90-5378-2447. Good luck and stay well.

Toshishige

THE *SHINKANSEN* super-express delivered me to Kyoto just after three o'clock. There was nothing in the least venerable about its futuristic railway station, but the taxi ride to Nijo-jo took me past a couple of ancient temples and it was pretty obvious the city beat to a less frenetic drum than its brash young cousin.

There were a couple of tour buses parked at the front of the castle and a steady stream of visitors filing in through the high-porched gate. Clutching Rupe's photograph I started off round the perimeter, following Yamazawa's directions.

It didn't take long to find what I was looking for. A double-roofed structure soared above the wall at its southeastern corner. I'd only to cross the road to the south and look up to match it to the photograph. And I'd only to turn round to see several modern blocks of flats with balconies commanding a good view of it. I was there.

At any rate, I was close. But which block *exactly* did Smiler live in? Among the bicycles propped near the entrance of one stood a big old Harley-Davidson motorbike. An exiled American's token of his easy-riding youth? Among the names next to the bells beside the combination-locked front door was LOUDON, M. I pressed the bell.

No answer. Loudon, M. was evidently out. It looked like I was just going to have to wait for Loudon to return, as he was bound to, sooner or later. At least I'd recognise him when he did.

HALF AN HOUR slowly passed. Traffic trundled by. Nobody came or went. I started to feel hungry and was giving some serious thought to shoving off in search of food and drink when Loudon, M., a white-haired and paunchy likeness of his photograph self, walked up with a stiff-hipped limp. He was wearing jeans and a tweed jacket over a checked shirt, and carried an old canvas knapsack.

'Excuse me,' I ventured. 'Mr Loudon?'

'Yuh.' He looked over at me. 'What can I do for you?'

'Not sure. But I believe you know the Hashimotos. Mayumi and Haruko.'

'You *believe*? Who are you?'

'Lance Bradley. A friend of—'

'Rupe Alder's.' He nodded grimly.

'Yes. How did you—?'

'Never mind. What in God's name are you doing in Kyoto?'

'We need to talk, Mr Loudon.'

'Call me Miller. I was hoping we'd never need to, Lance. But you're right. We do now. Not out here, though.'

Loudon's flat presumably reflected the divided nature of its owner. One of the living rooms was a tatami-matted oasis of uncluttered calm, the other a chaos of sagging armchairs, bulging bookcases and discarded coffee mugs. He led the way into the latter, and as we sat down he said, 'Mind telling me how you found me, Lance?'

In answer, I held up the photograph for him to see.

'Holy shit. Where's that come from?'

'It was among some things Rupe left with a colleague at Eurybia in Tokyo for safekeeping.'

'What colleague might that be?'

'Name of Yamazawa.'

'Never heard of him. And let's hope no one else has either.'

'What do you mean?'

'If you can follow the trail, so can others.'

He opened his knapsack and pulled out an English-language newspaper: the *Japan Times*. A second later I saw Kiyofumi Hashimoto's photograph low down on the front page. JAPANESE BUSINESSMAN SLAIN IN BERLIN ran the headline. Reading the surprise on my face, Loudon said, 'When you're on the run, you really should pay more attention to the newsstands.'

'On the run?'

'Well, what would you call it?'

'Something that doesn't sound so guilty, I suppose. OK, strictly speaking I should have stayed and helped the police with their inquiries, but I reckoned Berlin wasn't a safe place to hang around. And there was nothing I could do to help Kiyo.'

'I'm not talking about Kiyofumi.' He stopped and stared at me. 'Hold on. Are you saying . . . you didn't do it?'

'Didn't do what?'

'Kill Erich Townley.'

'He's dead?'

'Oh yeah. Erich's well and truly dead. Found battered about the head—'

'In my hotel room. Oh my God. I hit him, yes. With a lamp. But he wasn't dead when I left. Unconscious, but breathing. And it was self-defence, for God's sake. He had a gun.'

'No mention of that in the papers.'

'What do they say?'

'See for yourself.' He handed me the *Japan Times*.

> Kiyofumi Hashimoto, 47, a senior manager with the Fujisaka Microprocessor Corporation, was shot dead on Tuesday while aboard an open-top bus in the centre of Berlin. German police say the killing appears to have been the work of a professional assassin, and may be connected with another death in the city on Tuesday. Erich Townley, 45, a German-American citizen, was found dead from head injuries in a room at the Hotel Adlon. They are trying to trace Lancelot Bradley, 36, a British citizen who had been staying in the room, and who is believed to have been with Hashimoto at the time of the shooting.

'Bloody hell,' I mumbled, handing the paper back to Loudon. 'Look—none of this was my fault. It could just as easily have been me as Kiyo who died on that bus . . . I was only trying to help.'

'So Kiyofumi said.'

'He told you about me?'

'He told Mayumi.'

'Where is she?'

'I'm not sure you need to know that.'

'But you *are* sheltering her—and Haruko?'

'I'm doing my best to protect them, yuh. The question is: do I have to protect them from you? Why are you here, Lance?'

'*Why*? Because the Townleys must be stopped. Can't you see that?'

'Brave words.'

'Desperate ones, actually. I can't change what Rupe did. And I can't bring Kiyo back to life. But I can do something to stop the Townleys.' (Though God alone knew what.) 'And you can help me.'

'How—exactly?'

'By telling me what this is really all about. Beginning with what's in the Townley letter.'

'Didn't Kiyofumi let you in on that?'

'He did not. Mayumi swore him to secrecy.'

'Well, it's the same here, Lance.'

'For God's sake. We're in this together. I think I'm entitled to know what it *is* that I'm in.'

'You have a point. But it's not my decision.'

'Take me to Mayumi, then.'

'No can do.'

'Why not?'

'Because that might be just what they want.' Loudon sighed. 'Has it occurred to you that the assassin who shot Kiyofumi was almost certainly professional enough to account for you as well?'

'What are you getting at?'

'I'm getting at the disturbing possibility that you were *allowed* to escape. So you could do exactly what you have done.'

'You think I've been followed?'

'Maybe.'

'That's crazy. On the plane? Everywhere I've been? No way. Besides, if you're right, why did Erich try to kill me?'

'Disobeying orders, maybe. You and Kiyofumi *were* putting the squeeze on him.'

'All right.' I shrugged. 'In that case, what do we do?'

'We go to a little bar a few blocks from here and talk it through.' Loudon grinned. 'There are some things I *am* allowed to tell you.'

THE BAR WAS a cavernous basement under a dry-cleaner's shop. Custom was thin at just gone five on an autumn afternoon and, apart from us, entirely Japanese. 'Any strangers following us in are going to stand out like Mount Fuji on a clear day,' Loudon said.

Nobody did follow us in. We took stools at one end of the bar and ordered drinks. Sapporo for me, Coca-Cola for Loudon.

'I'll need to keep a clear head,' he explained. 'Time was when I got too buddy-buddy with Rupe and let him top me up with bourbon till I was ready to spill the beans on the Townley letter. Once bitten, twice shy, Lance.'

'How long have you known Mayumi?'

'More than forty years. Since my first visit to the Golden Rickshaw.'

'What *was* the Golden Rickshaw?'

'Just a bar. And a popular one, thanks to Mayumi. She was . . . radiant . . . back then. We came like moths to a lantern. And, like moths, one or two of us got burned.' He chewed over the past for a silent moment before continuing. 'Then again, of course, it wasn't just a bar. Townley and his outfit made sure of that.'

'What was his outfit?'

'Something linked with the CIA. Their role was to identify servicemen who had the skills and aptitude to perform special duties—during *and* after their military service. They used the Rickshaw as a place to size people up. Evaluate them when they were at their most relaxed, with a view to possible recruitment.'

'Did they recruit you?'

'Only as a scout. I was done a few favours and handed a few greenbacks in return for acting as a talent-spotter.'

'What sort of talent were you looking for?'

'Oh, the grim, dedicated, intensely anticommunist, faintly manic kind, of course. What other kind?'

'To do . . .'

'Dirty work, Lance. Very dirty work. I never asked for the specifics, but I didn't need to. I understood that killing people was going to be on the agenda. All in the noble cause of defending the United States of America against its enemies.'

I took out the photograph of him with Townley and some other guy as young military men and showed it to him again. 'Is this one of those recruits?' I pointed to the third man.

'Yuh.' Loudon gave a rubbery grimace. 'Townley certainly had his eye on him. No question about that.' He squirmed in his seat, as if this particular subject made him uncomfortable. 'Look, Lance, it pans out like this. Townley and his sinister band of brothers make me feel . . . important, I guess. So, I do a few things for them. I oil some wheels. Then I move on. Out of the army. Back to college. I forget Townley. I even *try* to forget Mayumi. I put it all behind me. End of story. Or should be.'

'Why did you come back here?'

'Because the country had got its claws into me. Well, the people had. They're so gentle, so . . . private. I guess the American way of life just wasn't for me. So now I teach English Lit at Doshisha University. This isn't my home. But it is where I belong.'

'Townley obviously didn't feel the same way.'

'No. He left as soon as he could and never came back.'

'Leaving behind only his face in this photograph, which Rupe spotted on the wall of the Golden Rickshaw,' I began reasoning. 'He recognised Townley, who he was already interested in because of his connection with Rupe's own family.'

'I know nothing about that.'

'It doesn't matter. The point is that Rupe saw his chance to find Townley by romancing Haruko. And she no doubt soon let slip that one of the other people in the photograph was living here, in Kyoto.'

'I got back in touch with Mayumi when I came back here. So, yuh, Haruko mentioned me when Rupe showed an apparently innocent interest in the picture and the history of the bar. Then Rupe suggested a visit. I was pleased to see them.'

'Certainly looks like it.' I held out another photograph for him to see—the snapshot of him with Haruko on the balcony of his flat.

'Yuh. There I am, grinning like the sap he played me for.'

'At some point, you told him about the Townley letter.'

'I was boasting. That's the truth of it. Making myself feel important by shooting my mouth off about the old days. So thanks to me—and Haruko's blindly adoring trust in him—Rupe was able to steal the letter and make his move on Townley. Which put Mayumi and Haruko—and me, for that matter—in more danger than you can possibly imagine.'

'Me too now, I assume.'

'Yuh. That's right, Lance. You too. Oh, he put himself in danger too, I grant you. But that was his choice. We didn't get a choice.'

'When can I meet Mayumi?'

'Not sure. If you've been followed, taking you to her would be the stupidest thing I've ever done. And anyway, what will you do if you find out what was in the letter?'

'Go to the authorities, make a case. Strike back at Townley any way we can.'

Loudon leaned back on his stool and stretched, then relaxed again. 'OK. Let's lay it on the line. Everything we do from here on in is risky. Even doing nothing is risky. And temperamentally, I'm a retaliatory kind of guy. I'll speak to Mayumi. She'll decide.'

'You're going to see her?'

'Yuh. I'll ride out there tonight. And if I'm followed, well, on that road I'll surely know it.'

'And if not?'

'Then I'll come back for you in the morning. You can bed down at my apartment. I'll phone Mayumi from there and set it up.'

'When did you decide all this?'

'Oh, around the time you walked up and introduced yourself.'

'Then why have you been giving me such a hard time?'

'Because I wanted to see what you had to offer in the way of a game plan before I committed myself.'

'So, I've persuaded you, have I?'

'No, Lance. Not remotely.' He gave me the same grin he'd worn in Mayumi's photograph—and in Rupe's. 'But I'll do it anyway.'

SIX

Loudon's biggest and saggiest armchair unfolded into a bed. He showed me how to lock it into place, then phoned Mayumi. He conversed with her in Japanese, thereby freeing himself to say what he liked about me; certainly my name *was* mentioned several times.

Pausing only to show me where I could find the coffee and the bourbon, he then shucked himself into his Harley-Davidson leathers and made ready to leave. 'If I don't phone at eight tomorrow morning it'll be because I'm on my way back, in which case I'll be here by nine. Got it?'

'Got it.'

'You'll know it's me on the phone because I'll give it three rings and hang up, then call again. Don't answer it otherwise, OK?'

'OK.'

'Good. If you want some bedtime reading, there's a copy of *For Whom the Bell Tolls* on my bedside table. A dip into that could be kind of appropriate.'

'I'll think about it.'

'Do that. And now I have to get rolling. While I'm gone . . .'

'Yeah?'

'Try to relax.'

I WATCHED THROUGH the chink in the blinds as he roared away into the night. There was no sign of a car going off in pursuit.

I gave *For Whom the Bell Tolls* a miss. I was bone weary and not far short of brain dead, and with the help of my absent host's Jack Daniel's, I nodded off into dreamland.

When I came to, daylight was seeping between the slats of the blinds and there was less than an hour to go to the time Loudon had said he'd call. I took a shower and ate some toast to soak up the black coffee.

I looked again at the article in the *Japan Times*, which Loudon had left behind. *German police . . . are trying to trace Lancelot Bradley, 36 . . . believed to have been with Hashimoto at the time of the shooting.* How had they worked that out? It had to be the airline records. But the German police had moved fast, no doubt about it, and they'd probably asked their British opposite numbers to check my home address by now. It could only be a matter of time before they ended up at my parents' door. Maybe I ought to phone Mum and Dad to warn them. It was around half past ten the previous evening in England. Mum would just be making the cocoa, blithely unaware of the trouble her son was in. If I didn't phone now, I mightn't get the chance for quite a while.

But that chance slipped through my fingers sooner than I'd expected. Suddenly, the doorbell rang. I rushed to the balcony and stepped outside, craning over the railings for a view. But the entrance was obscured by the porch. Who the hell could it be?

I'd just decided to go back in and wait for them to go away when a figure emerged from the overhang of the porch and looked straight up at me. He was a tall, rangy, middle-aged guy, with fair, thinning hair and a moustache, dressed in a short leather jacket, black T-shirt and jeans. He smiled, and held up a hand in greeting. 'Hi,' he drawled with an American accent. 'You must be Lance.'

'Who are you?' I responded.

'Steve Bryce. A colleague of Miller's from Doshisha. He asked me to pick you up.'

'He did?'

'Yuh. Trouble with his bike. But what can you expect? More rust in the tank than gas. So, I had my arm twisted. Your taxi awaits.'

'Miller hasn't phoned me about this.'

'He'll still be wheeling his bike back to the farmhouse.'

'The farmhouse?'

'Yuh. Where we're going. It's OK. I know where it is. Miller called me from a payphone. Out in the sticks, they only take coins. He did say he wouldn't have enough to call you as well. We're kind of lucky he made any contact at all.'

'I . . . suppose so. But—'

'Now I don't want to hurry you, Lance, but I have to be back at Doshisha by ten and it must be an hour's drive to the farmhouse, so could we move this along? Hell, I'm doing you guys a favour.'

So he certainly appeared to be. But appearances could be deceptive. I looked down at his blandly smiling face and asked myself the obvious question: could I trust him? Loudon hadn't mentioned any friends at Doshisha to me. But if his motorbike had let him down and time was of the essence (as it was), I wouldn't be helping anyone by sitting tight. The farmhouse was presumably where Mayumi and Haruko were hiding. And I wanted to speak to them—badly.

'Is there a problem, Lance?'

'No.' I'd made my choice. 'I'll be right down.'

BRYCE'S SMALL white saloon didn't have any of the glamour of Loudon's Harley-Davidson. But, as Bryce pointed out, it had just chalked up a points victory for reliability. We drove northwest out of Kyoto, sunlight dappling the wooded mountains ahead. Bryce asked a stream of questions about my connection with Loudon and the urgent need for me to be ferried out to the back of beyond, but he got no change out of me and had given up probing for information by the time we left the city limits.

We zigzagged up an ever-steeper road between thick stands of conifers until Bryce turned off onto a rough, unmetalled side road.

'I guess I'd better check the map,' he said, pulling over under the trees. 'Hold on while I fetch it from the trunk.'

He clambered out, walked round to the back and opened the boot.

I heard him shifting things around, then it went quiet. I wound down the window and leaned out. 'You OK?'

'Not exactly,' he replied. 'You better come and look at this.'

'What is it?'

'Just come see.'

'All right.' I sighed and climbed out. 'So, what's the—?'

The words died in my mouth as I rounded the rear wing of the car and glanced into the boot. Miller Loudon was lying there on his back, a dark, blood-clotted bullet hole in the middle of his forehead.

'I thought she wasn't pulling right,' said Bryce. 'Here's the reason: two hundred and seventy pounds of dead weight.'

I stared at him, horrified. A gun was in his right hand, trained on me. 'Journey's end, Lance. Turn round and start walking into the forest. I'll tell you when to stop.'

I didn't move, just looked down at Loudon's body, trussed with ropes, then back up at Bryce. Still no words came.

'Come on, Lance. One foot in front of the other. Get moving.'

'Who are you?'

'Just move.' He slammed the boot shut and raised his right arm, pointing the gun at my head. 'OK?'

All my choices had been pared away. There was nothing left but to do what I was told. I turned and started walking.

I'd gone about twenty yards when Bryce told me to stop. I was near the foot of a tall, red-leafed maple standing among the pines. As I waited, a single leaf fluttered slowly down to rest at my feet. Was he going to kill me here? Was this where it ended?

Suddenly, something hard and heavy struck me round the back of my neck. I don't remember hitting the ground.

PAIN AND CONSCIOUSNESS met up some time later. Speech and coherent thought were late for the party, though. I was sitting at the foot of the maple tree, my back resting against the trunk, unable to move. Bryce was standing a few yards in front of me, flicking through the contents of my wallet. Then I became aware of the ropes holding me tight against the tree. And Bryce noticed me make a futile effort to struggle free.

'Hi, Lance,' he said, smiling at me. 'Welcome back.'

'What . . . what the—?'

'A few minutes ago you asked who I am. But it turns out you already know.' He tossed the wallet aside and held up a small white card. 'Gordon A. Ledgister, Caribtex Oil. Pleased to meet you.'

'Ledgister?'

'That's right. Although, if you asked the agency I hired the car from, they'd say that my name is Lance Bradley.' His smile widened. 'With poor old Miller in the trunk, I guess somebody will be asking them that question sooner or later. But, hey, let's not worry about it.'

'You . . . followed me from Berlin?'

'Got it in one. Stifling my grief at the demise of my brother-in-law Erich, I tagged along as you Hawkeyed your way here.'

'You shot Hashimoto?'

'Never mind him. It's the living I want to talk to you about. Where are they, Lance? Where are Mayumi and Haruko?'

Clumsily, my thoughts grasped the point that Ledgister was making. He'd followed Loudon to the farmhouse. But Mayumi and Haruko hadn't been there. Why? There could only be one answer. Loudon had told them to clear out in his phone call the previous evening. He must have reckoned it was odds-on I'd been followed, so he'd decided to flush out whoever was doing the following. He'd put Mayumi and Haruko out of harm's way. But not himself.

'I asked Miller, of course. You bet I did. Very . . . forcefully. But he wouldn't tell me. In the end, I lost patience. So now I want you to help me, Lance. If you can't help me, our relationship isn't likely to last very long. Now, let's try again. Where are Mayumi and Haruko?'

'I don't know. I don't even know where they *were*.'

'Come on. This isn't auguring well for your future, Lance. You do realise that, don't you?'

'Yeah, I do.' But there I'd told him my first lie. Because I'd just seen a man threading softly through the trees behind Ledgister—a slim, lithely built Japanese man dressed in a blue tracksuit. His hair was short and flecked with grey, his face raw-boned and pale. His gaze was fixed on Ledgister. And he was carrying a gun, clasped in both hands in front of him.

'I don't have the leisure to prolong this conversation indefinitely,' said Ledgister. 'So maybe I ought to—'

'Put your gun down.' The man in the tracksuit had spoken.

Ledgister half turned and saw him. 'Who the—?'

'Put it down.'

'OK.' Ledgister lowered himself onto his haunches and laid his gun on the ground. 'No problem.'

'Stand up. Untie Mr Bradley.'

'Who is this guy, Lance?' Ledgister glanced round at me. 'Shouldn't you introduce us?'

'Untie him. Now.' Tracksuit moved closer still, his gun pointing straight at Ledgister.

'OK, OK. I'll do it.'

Ledgister walked slowly round to the other side of the tree. The ropes slackened and fell away. I scrambled to my feet.

'Sit in Mr Bradley's place,' said my anonymous saviour, his voice unwaveringly calm. 'Tie him up, Lance.'

Ledgister sat down at the foot of the tree and I gathered up the ropes. Ledgister's question had been a good one. Who *was* this guy?

'Luck like yours doesn't last for ever,' Ledgister whispered as I tied his hands behind his back. 'When it runs out, I'll be waiting.'

I tightened the ropes until I'd forced a grunt out of him.

'Good,' said Tracksuit as he checked the knots. 'We go now.' Then he checked Ledgister's pockets, presumably for concealed weapons. He didn't find any. But as he looked, Ledgister noticed something.

'Hey, you're missing a pinky, friend.' He was right. The little finger on the man's left hand ended at the first joint. 'You're *Yakuza*, aren't you?' He got no reply beyond a brief glare. 'You've taken out some expensive insurance, Lance. I hope you can afford the premiums.'

'Enough.' Tracksuit stood up and looked at me. 'We go.'

I hesitated, scanning the ground for my wallet. There it was, not far from where Ledgister had dropped the gun. I moved towards it.

'Don't touch it. Leave the gun where it is.'

I stopped and looked round. 'It's my wallet I want.' I pointed to where it lay.

'OK. Take it and walk to the road.'

I did as I'd been told, stopping only when I reached Ledgister's car. I turned round. Tracksuit was still within a stride of me, his gun no longer in view. 'My car is back along the road,' he said. 'A short walk.'

'Do you know what's in the boot of this car?'

'Yes. I saw. I heard. Do you know where the ladies are?'

'Not a clue. They were being sheltered in a farmhouse apparently. But they're not there now.'

'They may return there.'

'But I don't know where it is. Only Ledgister knows that.'

'He will not tell us. Check the car. There may be something.'

I opened the driver's door and checked the side pocket and dashboard shelves. Nothing. I leaned across and yanked open the glove compartment. Inside was a folded map. I lifted it out and stared at a jumble of roads, rivers and contour lines, labelled in Japanese. Then I saw it: a cross in red ink, added by hand. 'This could be it.'

'Yes.' He peered over my shoulder. 'Near Kamiyuge. About fifteen kilometres from here. Good. Bring the map with you.'

'What about Loudon?'

'He is dead.' The man stared at me blankly. 'We must go.'

'Ledgister hired this car in my name.'

'But the description the agency give to the police will fit him, not you. And a bullet from his gun killed Loudon.'

'Yes, but—'

'I could kill Ledgister, but that would make the police think you killed both men. You understand? This is the best way. We will call the police and send them here. OK?'

'Are you . . . *Yakuza*?'

'Yes. But I'm not here for them. I'm here for my brother. Toshishige.'

'You're . . . Yamazawa's brother?'

'Yes. Shintaro Yamazawa. That is me. We have to go, Lance. It is dangerous for us here. If we are seen . . .'

'All right. I understand.'

I didn't, of course. Not the half of it. But leaving made sense. Yamazawa led the way back down the track. His green Range Rover was parked under the trees beyond the second bend. We climbed in, he threw it round in a five-point turn and we drove away.

'Did Toshishige tell you what this is about?' I asked, wondering just what he and his brother were up to.

'He told me some. Your friend put the Hashimotos in danger. The American, Loudon, was hiding them. Toshishige was worried about you. He asked me to watch your back. But he should have been more worried about them. You brought the danger with you.'

It was true. I'd trailed a line behind me and Ledgister had followed it. He'd killed twice that I knew of. And if it hadn't been for Loudon's self-sacrifice, it would have been more. 'I have to find Mayumi and Haruko.'

'If they've gone back to the farmhouse, we will find them. But we cannot wait there long. You must not be seen in places that connect you to this.'

'I can't just walk away.'

'Better than being carried, I think.'

WE REJOINED the main road and headed north. Within a few miles, we descended into a valley and came to a village, where Yamazawa stopped at a call box and phoned the police with his anonymous tip-off about Loudon's body. Then we carried on.

'Do you often do Toshishige favours like this?' I asked, when some of the shock had begun to drain out of me.

'Never one like this before. It is a . . . special case. Your friend Rupert Alder . . . Did not Toshishige tell you this?'

'Not sure. What was it?'

'Toshishige and I both had a fine education, Lance. Our father was specially keen for us to learn to speak English fluently. He thought it would help us make good careers. You can guess I was a disappointment to him. He forgot there are openings for fluent English speakers in organised crime as well as big business. He was proud of Toshishige, though. A respectful son, an honest guy and a hard worker. But when his wife left him, he changed. He got to like the wild side, started drinking and gambling. He needed money. More than he earned, you understand? So I set up a few deals for him.'

'What sort of deals?'

'Smuggling, mostly. A brother in shipping can be useful. Then . . . your friend found out.'

'Rupe knew?'

'Yes. He stopped it, of course. But he didn't report Toshishige. He let him off. It was their secret.'

'Toshishige said Rupe had saved his life.'

'Could be true. Prison would have finished him. Maybe your friend realised that.'

We went through another village, this one smaller and more scattered, then turned off along a side road where the woods were thinner, the views more open and extensive of the mountains around us. Yamazawa stopped where a track led down off the road and checked the map. We were in a shallow valley, with overgrown fields to either side and a wood bordering them.

'The farmhouse must be down this track,' Yamazawa announced. He nosed the Range Rover cautiously off the road and we rolled gently through the potholes as the track wound round the wood.

The farmhouse, which had clearly long ceased to play host to active farming, appeared ahead of us. The roof was partly thatched, partly tiled, and there was a verandah out front, with weed-choked flowerbeds beneath it. To one side was a rusty-roofed barn. In its open doorway stood a Harley-Davidson motorbike.

We pulled up in the yard and got out. The sliding door leading into the house was half open. We moved towards it, then stopped at the sight of what were obviously bloodstains on the floor of the verandah, smudged as if someone had been dragged across them.

Yamazawa stepped gingerly past the marks and slid the door fully open. There were more stains inside. 'Loudon died here, I guess,' he said. 'Then Ledgister dragged him to his car.'

'Mayumi and Haruko?'

'Gone. That is certain. But I will check. You stay here.'

Yamazawa went inside, leaving me to stare down at the bloodstains and across at Loudon's abandoned motorbike. He was back within a couple of minutes. 'There is no one here,' he announced.

'Loudon telephoned them last night. The conversation was in Japanese. But he must have told them to clear out. They're hiding somewhere, probably waiting for a call from him.'

'If you are right, they will not return here. They will wait and wait. But there will be no call. And then they will learn what has happened—from the TV, the newspapers.'

'We must find them.'

'You may be safer on your own.'

'I can't just leave them to fend for themselves.' (Besides, there was still the question of the Townley letter. More than ever, I needed to know what was in it.)

'You are determined to look for them?' Yamazawa frowned at me, as if weighing me up.

'Yes.'

'Then ask yourself: what did Loudon plan? He must have realised he was in danger. So, he must have thought about what would happen to them without him. Who would he ask to protect them?'

'There's no one that I know of. Except me.'

'But he did not tell you where he was sending them.'

'Of course not. He was afraid that—Hold on.' I stopped and thought. The only way Loudon could have pointed me in the right direction was to give me a cryptic message that I wouldn't recognise as such until after the event. Then, if he didn't come through, I'd be able to work out what he meant. 'He recommended a book to me. *For Whom the Bell Tolls.*'

'Ernest Hemingway.'

'You know his work?'

'No. But I am an Ingrid Bergman fan. Therefore I have seen the film. It is disappointing, of course, with that terrible haircut she has in it. But the story is OK.'

'Hemingway's not really my cup of tea. Frankly, Loudon should have been able to tell that . . .' I stopped. Of course. Loudon had chosen something he'd been sure I'd ignore—until I turned his remarks over in my mind later. That was the whole point. 'We have to look at that book. It's at the flat.'

'Going there is too risky.'

'I have no choice.'

BACK IN KYOTO, Yamazawa parked two streets south of the apartment block. We approached it on foot, from the rear, hopping over a low fence into a compound used to store rubbish bins.

'We should be doing this at night,' Yamazawa complained, wrenching back the door of a service lift. 'I am breaking all my own rules for you, Lance.'

We exited the lift into a concrete stairwell, then pushed through a fire door into a carpeted corridor and made for Loudon's flat.

Yamazawa glanced cautiously around, then took out of his pocket a small, right-angled metal tool. He slid the blade in round the jamb next to the Yale keyhole and, after no more than a few seconds' manipulation, slipped the latch.

I made straight for Loudon's bedroom, Yamazawa keeping pace behind me. A dogeared old paperback of *For Whom the Bell Tolls* stood on the bedside cabinet. As I picked it up, I noticed one page had been folded down at the top corner. I opened the book at that page. In the rows of print, only one thing stood out. A name, underlined in pencil—*Maria*.

I showed it to Yamazawa. 'Mean anything to you?'

'There is a famous hotel called the Maria, in Arashiyama.'

'That's a coincidence.' But it was no coincidence at all.

Yamazawa didn't think so either. 'We go,' he said, turning towards the door.

ARASHIYAMA lay out to the west of Kyoto, where the hills subsided to the plain on which the city was built. There was a pretty bridge across a river, a scatter of temples and a sprawl of trinket shops.

'Is it always like this here?' I asked as Yamazawa nudged the Range Rover through the mobs of tourists clogging the pavements.

'No. But the gardens of Tenryu-ji are specially beautiful in the fall. And this is a public holiday. *Bunka-no-hi*. Culture Day.'

Yamazawa pulled into a car park in front of a modern building, glaring plainness relieved by a dazzling abundance of chrysanthemums, in borders and window boxes. 'Here's the Maria.'

'Why would Loudon send Mayumi and Haruko here?'

'Because, as you see, Arashiyama's crowded. Good choice, I think. A crowd is safe if you don't want to get noticed.'

'They may well have booked in under false names.'

'Yes. But they are not experts at the running game. They give themselves away.'

'What do you mean?'

'See that Nissan?' He pointed to a small, mud-spattered red hatchback in a corner of the car park. 'Tokyo number plate. And it looks like it's been down more farm tracks than any other car here.'

'It could be theirs, I agree, but—' We'd surged into motion. 'What are you doing?'

Yamazawa didn't answer. He threw the Range Rover round to the left, then reversed straight across the car park and crunched solidly into the Nissan's rear wing.

'What the hell are you doing?'

'Wait here.' Yamazawa opened his door. 'I think I need to report this to the owner of the car.' And with what I could have sworn was a wink, he climbed out.

AFTER YAMAZAWA had vanished into the hotel, I got out too and wandered round the car park, struggling to prepare myself for the encounter that was surely about to happen. I was the best friend of the man who'd betrayed Haruko and I'd played a part Mayumi couldn't be expected to understand in her brother's death; a part also in a second death she didn't yet know about. What was I going to say to them? What were *they* going to say to *me*?

Five minutes later the hotel door slid open and Yamazawa came out with a woman I recognised instantly as Mayumi. A small, trim, erect figure in a beige trouser-suit, she had her grey-black hair gathered in a bun, emphasising a gauntness that I didn't remember from Rupe's photograph of her and Haruko. She was frowning, too, and looked as worried as she had every right to be. But still in her face there was the shadow of her youthful beauty.

They had reached the cars and were looking at the damage,

discussing it in Japanese, when I came up behind them. I hesitated for a moment, then said, 'Mayumi Hashimoto?'

I saw her flinch as she turned. There was fear written starkly on her face as she stared at me.

'I'm Lance Bradley,' I said. 'I'm here to help you.'

She didn't respond. She just went on staring. Nothing in her expression suggested that she believed me. To be honest, I couldn't blame her. But I meant it. If it was the last thing I did—which it easily could be—I *was* going to help her.

YAMAZAWA DID MOST of the talking at first, explaining the grievous realities of the situation to Mayumi as swiftly and as sensitively as possible. (I had to take that on trust, of course, since they conversed in Japanese.) Mayumi scarcely said a word, glancing often at me as he spoke. I couldn't have judged from her expression the moment at which she realised Loudon was dead. But, after she'd gone to fetch Haruko, Yamazawa told me he'd held nothing back.

'She is a proud woman, I think. But frightened also, though she will not show it. That is why she has accepted my offer of shelter.'

'Where are you going to shelter them?'

'At my home. They cannot stay here. Neither can you, Lance. And there is nowhere else to go.' He shrugged. 'It is best.'

I didn't have any choice but to trust him. Nor did Mayumi and Haruko. We loaded their belongings into the Range Rover, leaving the dented Nissan where it was, and set off, crossing the river and heading towards the western outskirts of Kyoto.

'We will take the Meishin Expressway to Ashiya,' Yamazawa said. 'That is where I live. On the coast, between Osaka and Kobe.'

Mayumi and Haruko sat in the back, saying nothing beyond the odd whispered exchange between themselves. I glanced as often as I dared at their reflections in the mirror on the back of the sun visor. Mayumi's composure never slipped, but Haruko was less self-controlled, clutching her mother's hand and dabbing at her eyes with a handkerchief to staunch the tears of grief and fear.

The coastal strip west of Osaka was an undistinguished urban sprawl of which Ashiya looked to be the most prosperous part. Yamazawa's house was in the foothills of the mountains above the town, where high walls and conspicuous security devices suggested twitchy residents with a lot to be twitchy about. I spotted a couple of Rottweilers patrolling the adjacent garden, as we waited for the automatic door leading to the garage to slide slowly up.

'You are thinking that crime pays well,' Yamazawa said.

'It's none of my business,' I replied, as we drove in.

The house was vast and bare. Yamazawa spoke to his housekeeper, evidently hired for her inscrutability, then took Mayumi and Haruko off to their quarters. I was left alone, padding round a huge tatami-matted lounge in a pair of fluffy cream guest slippers.

I'd been alone there for twenty minutes or so, wondering what was to happen next, when Yamazawa came in to join me, frowning ominously. 'I have spoken to my contact in the Kyoto police,' he said. 'What he has told me is not good.'

'What is it?'

'Ledgister has escaped.'

'You're joking.'

'I do not joke.' (Ever, I assumed he meant.) 'It seems two men from the local station got there first. After they had untied Ledgister, he snatched a gun . . .' Yamazawa snorted irritably. 'He shot one of them and lost the other in the forest. I should not have relied on the police.'

'Could he have followed us here?'

'Not possible. He has no car. He does not know the mountains. He is free. But he cannot know where we are.'

'That's something.'

'But not enough. The police will probably think he is you. He hired the car in your name. By now the German police will know you flew to Toyko. It will look bad for you. Very bad. You should leave the country as soon as possible.'

'What about Mayumi and Haruko?'

'They are safe here.'

'For the moment. But you can't shelter them for ever. Besides, how can I leave? I'd be stopped at the airport.'

'I could get you out.'

'To go where? I don't even know what I'm up against, but I think Mayumi can tell me. I have to find out, Shintaro. Do you understand?'

He looked out of the window and sighed. 'I will tell her about Ledgister. Then I will ask her to speak to you. You can ask her then, Lance. She is my guest, so . . . I do not think she will refuse.'

SHE DID NOT REFUSE. The housekeeper brought tea and, a few minutes later, Mayumi came into the room, expressionless and outwardly calm. We sat down and she poured tea for both of us.

'Kiyofumi said you are a good man, Bradley-san.'

'Not as good as he was. And, please, call me Lance.'

'You are involved in this only because you are Rupe's friend?'

'Yes. I suppose it comes down to that.'

'Haruko loved him greatly. She thought he loved her too.'

'I can't undo anything he did.'

'I know. But . . . he broke her heart.'

'I told your brother I'd do everything in my power to help you.'

'And, unlike your friend, you keep your promises.'

'The question is, Mayumi: how *can* I help you?'

'Save Haruko. That is all I ask now. I have lost so much. I must not lose her.'

'Why is she in danger, Mayumi? Why are we all in danger? What's in the Townley letter?'

She sipped some tea. 'The only way to save Haruko is to make Stephen stop hunting us.' (It was quite a shock to hear her refer to Townley by his first name.) 'We must communicate with him.'

'But even if we could find him, he wouldn't listen.'

'Stephen was trained to kill people, Lance. He was a dangerous man when I knew him. But he is not evil. And he is old now. He is probably as frightened as I am. I think his son-in-law, Ledgister, is acting without his knowledge.'

'Why would he do that?'

'Because it is not only about Stephen. Being in the oil business, Ledgister would be in danger too. Miller—' She broke off and looked away, taking time to compose herself. 'Miller explained the consequences to me. There seems no end to it. But there must be.'

'No end to what?'

She gazed at me, her calmness restored. 'I know you think it will be better if you understand. But it will not be. It will destroy you.'

'Mayumi—'

'Please listen.' She held up a hand to silence me. 'You may have guessed—I do not know—but Miller was Haruko's father.' (I supposed I had guessed, though until she'd said it I hadn't been conscious of doing so.) 'When he came back to Japan, twenty-five years ago, we were together for a while. Then . . . we parted. Haruko does not know this. I would not let him tell her. That is why he told Rupe about the letter. To make himself matter to Haruko and the man she would marry. He did not know what was in the letter. He did not know how dangerous it was until I told him, *after* Rupe had stolen it.

I kept it in a safe-deposit box at my bank. Haruko had things in the box also. Things inherited from her grandmother. She had access to it. Rupe persuaded her to let him see the letter. She would have done anything for him. She did not know he meant to steal it. How could she? She loved him. And now I have to trust what my instincts tell me. Stephen has lost his son. I have lost my brother. It is enough. I think Stephen will understand that. I cannot give him the letter. I do not have it. But I will never tell anyone what is in it. I ask you to be the proof of that.'

'Me?'

'I want you to take a message to him from me. I want you to ask him to end this. Before we all lose everything.'

'How can I do that?'

'Kiyofumi told me that Stephen has a grandson at Stanford University, in California.'

'Clyde Ledgister. What about him?'

'I want you to speak to Clyde, persuade him to take you to Stephen. You must see him face to face. Tell him he has to stop. I will never reveal his secret. That is all I can offer him. But he will believe me, I think. Because even my messenger will not know what the secret is.'

I was caught in a velvet vice. I wanted the truth. But I also wanted to help Mayumi, to repair the damage Rupe had caused. Mayumi's plan, desperate as it was, was the only plan in town. Keeping me in ignorance just might win Townley over.

'I am sorry to have to ask you to do this, Lance,' Mayumi said. 'But there is no one else I can ask. You do not have to do it. I would understand if you refused.'

There was, of course, no way I could refuse.

Yamazawa didn't see it that way. In fact, when we talked later in his study, it was pretty obvious he thought I was mad.

'I get the impression you don't think what I am proposing is a very smart idea.'

'You have to decide what is best for you to do, Lance. But there will be nobody to watch your back in California.'

'I offered to help her. This is the help she's asked for.'

'Then I will see what can be done. You will need a new name and passport. Also safe passage. Stanford is near San Francisco, right?'

'So I believe.'

He thought for a moment. 'I will need to speak to some friends.

The airports will be watched, for sure. So, safe may be slow, OK?'

'I'm in your hands, Shintaro.'

'But soon you may be in Townley's hands. You should think about that, Lance. You should think hard.'

AS IT TURNED OUT, I had plenty of opportunity for thought over the next twenty-four hours. Yamazawa was absent most of the time, making arrangements on my behalf. Mayumi and Haruko kept themselves largely to themselves, although they came to watch the news bulletins on the television regularly. We didn't even eat together. I couldn't leave the house, of course, and neither could they. We were prisoners by choice *and* necessity. All we knew for sure was that Ledgister was still on the loose.

Finally, Yamazawa returned, and called me back into his study. He handed me my passport (which he'd borrowed earlier). As I took it, I noticed it was closed around a second passport. An American one.

'Your photograph's been scanned onto the details of Gary Charlesworth Young,' he said.

'Who's he?'

'He was born in New York on May 26, 1961. And he does not require his passport any more.'

'We're sure about that, are we?'

'The source of this passport is most reliable, Lance. Asking questions is not part of the transaction.'

'I'll bet it isn't.'

'Container ship *Taiyo-Maru* leaves Kobe, Monday morning, bound for Europe. It calls at Busan, in South Korea, on Tuesday, to take on cargo. You can get off there and—'

'I'm leaving by ship?'

'Slow but safe, like I told you.'

'How slow?'

'Train from Busan to Seoul and an evening flight to San Francisco. With the time change, it will still be Tuesday when you arrive.'

'But that's three days from now.'

'These arrangements are secure, Lance. If you try to fly direct, I estimate a seventy-five per cent chance you will be picked up.'

'There's been nothing on the television news about me.'

'Maybe not. But I have spoken to Toshishige. The police have been to see him.'

'How did they get on to him?'

'His boss at Eurybia. He contacted the police as soon as he read about you in Thursday's *Japan Times*.'

'That bastard Penberthy! What did Toshi tell the police?'

'As little as possible. But they will have made the connection with Loudon's murder by now. So, we have to be careful. It is possible—just possible—that the police will suspect Toshishige of helping you. If they do, they might decide to investigate his friends and . . .'

'His family.'

'Exactly. I do not think they would be able to trace me, but we cannot take the risk. Mayumi and Haruko can stay. They have nothing to fear from the police. But you must leave. Tonight.'

He was right, of course. 'OK. Where do I go?'

'I have booked Mr Gary Young into the Hotel Umi in Kobe. I will drive you there as soon as it is dark. Tomorrow night, at twenty-two hundred hours, a man called Ohashi will call for you. He will take you to the container terminal and put you aboard the *Taiyo-Maru*. Officially, you are an employee of the ship's owners. There is a crew of twelve—Japanese master, mate and chief engineer, the rest are Filipinos. None of them speaks English. But the master has his instructions. There will be no problem. From Busan . . .' He handed me a thickly filled brown envelope. 'There is enough here in US dollars for your needs.'

'I can't accept that.'

'You must.'

And he was right yet again.

LATER, AFTER AN EXCHANGE of stilted but hopeful farewells with Mayumi and her daughter, I set off with Yamazawa in his Range Rover. As we were cruising along the empty expressway towards Kobe, he handed me a slip of paper.

'This is a cellphone number which you can reach me on,' he said. 'Mayumi and Haruko will be anxious to hear what happens.'

'Won't you be?'

'You have an American passport, Lance. And money in your pocket. When you get to California, you will have a choice.'

'I don't intend to run out on them. I'm going through with this.'

'They will be safe even if you don't. I will make sure of that.'

'I'm still going through with it.'

'OK.' He fell silent as the car surged on towards the lights of Kobe, then said, 'It's your choice.'

SAN FRANCISCO SEVEN

Touchdown in San Francisco, with the passport of a native New Yorker wedged in my pocket, was an experience registering fairly high on the scale of surreality. I'd left Kobe forty-eight hours before and crammed a cruise across the Sea of Japan, a train ride through South Korea and a flight over the Pacific Ocean into that time. Thanks to crossing the International Date Line, however, forty-eight hours had been magically reduced to twenty-four, and I was about to live Tuesday, November 7, all over again.

I could have taken a cab from the airport, except that then I'd have had to specify a destination. Tricky when you don't have one. I didn't have much luggage either, which made the SamTrans bus into the centre an attractive option. It was slow, but I was in no hurry.

I'd bought a *San Francisco Chronicle* before boarding the bus and leafed idly through it as we trundled up the freeway, with autumn sunlight winking off the waters of the bay to the right. I was looking for affordable accommodation, but as I searched past the sits vac for living space to let . . .

> ALDER, Rupe.

My gaze had already drifted beyond the name when recognition reached my brain. Suddenly I was alert, jet lag banished, eyes wide as I backtracked up the page. A mistake, surely? A trick of blurred vision. But no. It wasn't.

> ALDER, Rupe. We met briefly at Kimball Hall, Stanford, September 15. If you're still here, please call me urgently. Mobile 144671789.

I rang the number from the bus terminal and got a recorded message telling me the phone I was calling was switched off.

A COUPLE OF RAGIN' RIVER ales in a nearby bar soothed my temper, but couldn't stop my thoughts racing off into the wilder realms of speculation. Rupe had been to Stanford to see Clyde Ledgister.

There could be no other explanation. But who'd placed the ad? And why? I tried the number again on the bar payphone.

And this time there was an answer.

'Hi.' The voice was female, soft and husky.

'I'm calling about your ad in this morning's *Chronicle*.'

'Who are you?'

'I might ask you the same question.'

'I'm Maris.'

'OK, Maris, I'm Gary. I'm a friend of Rupe Alder's . . .'

'You are?'

'Yes. Why are you trying to contact him?'

'I can't get into that on the phone.'

'Perhaps we could meet, then.'

'Maybe.'

'I don't think you're going to get any other response to your ad. You're lucky I saw it.'

There was a brief silence, then she said, 'OK, Gary, point taken. When do you suggest we meet?'

'Right away suits me. I could come to you now.'

'Where are you?'

'Downtown San Francisco.'

'OK. Do you know how to get to Stanford's bookshop?'

'Not exactly. I just got into town.'

'Then I *am* lucky, aren't I?'

'I said you were. Now, how do I get to Stanford?'

AN HOUR'S RIDE on the CalTrain to Palo Alto turned out to be the answer, with a courtesy bus laid on at the station to ferry students, staff and visitors to the university campus.

The bus dropped me outside the main quad and I made my way through an elegant maze of honey-stoned colonnades to the university bookshop, where the mysterious Maris had said she'd meet me in the in-store café prior to a three o'clock seminar. I'd know her by her hair, she'd assured me. 'Red, and lots of it.'

It was true. I had no trouble spotting her, sipping cappuccino, distractedly turning the pages of a fat textbook. The hair was long and lustrous and very conspicuous. She was wearing a baggy grey sweater and cropped trousers. She glanced at her expensive-looking wristwatch a fraction of a second before noticing me.

'Hi. I'm Gary Young. We spoke on the phone.'

'Hi. Maris Nielsen. Do you want a coffee?'

I glanced round at the long queue to the counter. 'Forget it.' I sat down. 'We don't have that much time, do we?'

'Guess not.' Maris put her book away and gave me her attention. 'So . . . Gary . . .'

'I'm an old friend of Rupe's.'

'From England?'

'Actually, I'm American by birth.' (It seemed a good idea to flag up my cover story early.) 'But I grew up in England. Rupe and I were at school together.'

'What brings you to San Francisco?'

'This is where Rupe was when his family last heard from him, back in mid-September. Which is when you met him, I believe.'

'Oh, it's when I met him, all right. But could I just get something straight first? I don't want Clyde hearing about the ad.'

'Clyde?' I raised my eyebrows.

'My boyfriend. Clyde Ledgister. Did Rupe mention him to you?'

'I don't think so.'

'Only I got the impression . . . well, that Rupe had come here to see Clyde. Specifically, I mean.'

'Why was that?'

'I don't know. That was the whole point of . . .' She glanced at her watch. 'I don't have that long, I'm afraid.'

'Why not just tell me why you're so keen to speak to Rupe, then?'

'OK. But if Clyde ever finds out . . .'

'Mightn't he see the ad?'

'Not really. He's out of town at the moment. His uncle's died.' (And Uncle Erich was no doubt being buried in Berlin. Yes, Clyde was well away.)

'That's why you put it in today?'

'All this week, actually. Clyde won't be back till next week.'

'So this was a good opportunity to see if Rupe was still around.'

'Yuh. I mean, OK, it was a long shot, but . . . I'm worried about Clyde. What else could I do to find out what in hell's going on? He's not been the same since that day—September 15. I knew there was something wrong when I walked in on them in Clyde's room. I had the feeling your friend was . . . threatening Clyde. After he'd gone, Clyde just tried to brush it off, said there was nothing I needed to bother about. But he couldn't fool me. He was scared of something. Something Rupe had told him. He was real scared. And then . . .'

'What?'

'After Rupe's visit he got to be . . . secretive. And oftentimes absent, without explanation. Most everyone lives on campus here. Stanford's a self-contained community. Clyde and I never went into the city much. But after your friend's visit, that altered. I wouldn't be able to find Clyde, then someone would tell me they'd seen him heading for the train station. When I asked him where he'd been, he'd just shout at me to stop interrogating him. So, I stopped.'

'But you went on wondering.'

'Yuh. The more I thought about it, the more it led back to the quietly spoken Englishman I'd met in his room—Rupe Alder. So, what can you tell me about him, Gary?'

'Nothing that'll answer your questions. He's a professional guy, single, thirty-six years old. Lives in London. Works for a shipping company. *Did* work for a shipping company, I should say. Resigned at the end of August. Nobody knows why. Nor why he came here. What he was up to—what he wanted with Clyde—is a total mystery.'

'There must be some clue to his intentions.'

'Not really. Except . . .' I sensed the moment had arrived when, if I volunteered something, however meagre, I might get a little more in return. 'There's a photograph he seems to have been interested in, pinned up in his kitchen, of someone nobody close to Rupe recognises. It's possible that he's looking for that person.'

'Do you have the photograph with you?'

'Er . . . yeah.' I burrowed in my bag and produced the snap Rupe had taken of the picture of Townley with Loudon and another man at the Golden Rickshaw. 'It seems that it's the guy on the right that Rupe was interested in.' I tapped at Townley's face with my finger.

'So, how old would this guy be now?'

'Oh, sixty-five, seventy.'

'Sixty-five, seventy.' The computation had given her food for thought. 'That's kind of interesting.'

'Why?'

'Because . . .' She looked away, chewing her thumb pensively.

'Do you know who the guy in the photograph is?'

'No. Not exactly. One day, a couple of weeks after Clyde had started going missing, I . . . followed him. I saw him getting on the shuttle bus. It goes out round by the shopping mall on its way to the station, so I knew if I cycled down Palm Drive I'd get there first. I kept out of sight when the shuttle pulled in. Clyde got straight on the train, without paying any attention to me and a few others boarding the bike car. At the depot at San Francisco he got on a bus, I tagged along behind on my bike. I guess you don't know the city well?'

'Not at all.'

'OK. Well, with the number of stops plus the traffic congestion, it's no problem to keep up with a bus on a bike. Clyde got off in Chinatown and hopped onto a California Street cable car. He rode that all the way to the terminus on Van Ness, then walked up into Pacific Heights. That's a pretty exclusive neighbourhood. He crossed Lafayette Park and went into an apartment block. A smart-looking place, portered and all. I couldn't follow him in.'

'So what did you do?'

'I sat in the park, sheltered by the trees, with a good view of the entrance to the block, and waited. After about twenty minutes, Clyde came out. And there was this . . . old guy with him.'

'Did he look like him?' I pointed to the main in the photo.

'Maybe.' She peered at Townley's face. 'It's possible. That's about all I can say. They crossed over to enter the park, so I had to hightail it out of there. I never got a close view of the guy. He looked old—white hair and beard, cut short—but good for his age: upright, holding himself together well. That's all I can give you.'

'Have you seen him since?'

'No. I went up there a few days ago—after Clyde had gone away—hoping I might see him coming or going. But he never showed. That's when I decided to place the ad and see if I got an answer.'

'Well, you did.'

'Yuh, but not quite the one I was hoping for.'

'Don't be so despondent, Maris. Seems to me I can do something you're not really in a position to do.'

'What's that?'

'Well, if you started asking questions at the apartment block, you're worried that word might get back to Clyde, right?'

'Right.'

'So, let me ask the questions for you.' I smiled benignly at her. 'All you have to do is give me the address of the block.'

THE AUTUMN LIGHT was failing by the time I got off the train back in San Francisco, and started to retrace the route Clyde had taken the day Maris had followed him.

At the end of the cable-car tracks on Van Ness Avenue, finding myself at the door of a Holiday Inn, I trailed in after a clutch of tourists and booked a room. From there I called Maris to let her know where I was staying. Her number was unavailable again, so I had to leave a message. Then I headed back out and walked the two blocks to Lafayette Park as night closed over the city.

Egret Apartments stood close to the northwestern corner of the park. It was a tall, slender Art Deco block, presenting a broad and handsome frontage to Laguna Street.

The porter, who I could see leafing through an evening newspaper behind the counter in the lobby, wasn't going to volunteer information about the residents to a stranger for no good reason, so I wandered on west to the neighbourhood shopping street, where the scents of coffee and cinnamon wafting out of a wayside café reminded me that I was more than a little hungry. I sat on a stool near the door, munching a waffle and sipping a hot chocolate while I formulated a plan. If I was to contact Townley, finding out what he called himself was the obvious way to start. But how?

An answer came to me as I watched customers coming and going at the bookstore next door. After I'd drunk the last of my chocolate, I went in and bought a glossy tourist guide to Japan. A plastic bag bearing the name of the shop came with it. Then I dug out the Tokyo street map I'd been given at Narita Airport, marked with the names and locations of the Golden Rickshaw and Eurybia Shipping, and slipped it inside the cover of the book. I reckoned that was sure to get Townley's attention.

Back at Egret Apartments, the porter was still absorbed in his newspaper. He looked up as I entered. 'Good evening, sir.'

'Good evening. I wonder if you can help me with a tricky little problem. Last week, I got chatting to a guy in a café down on Fillmore Street who happened to mention that he lives here. We'd both bought books at the bookstore next door and, when we left, well, our books got mixed up. We took the wrong ones. He got mine, I got his.' I flourished the bag. 'Easy mistake to make.'

'You want to do a swap, right?'

I nodded. 'But unfortunately, I didn't get the gentleman's name.'

'What did he look like?'

'Well, knocking on, but in good nick. Short white hair and beard. Carried himself well. Sixties, seventies—that sort of age.'

'Sounds like Mr Duthie. He's out of town for a few days. If you care to leave his book, with a note of your name and phone number . . .'

'OK. Do you have a piece of paper?' He handed me a sheet and I scribbled on it: *I know who you are. I guess you know who I am. We need to talk. I will phone after your return.* I slipped that in beside the map and passed the bag to the porter. 'I can't be reached on the phone, I'm afraid. Maybe I could call Mr Duthie when he's back?'

'Here's the general number.' He gave me a small card. 'There's always someone here.'

'Thanks a lot.' I'd hoped for Mr Duthie's personal number, but I'd hoped for too much. Smiling, I made my exit.

BACK AT THE HOLIDAY INN, I checked the phone book, but I found no Duthie listed at Egret Apartments. Somehow that wasn't a surprise. Then I called Maris again. This time, her phone was switched on.

'Clyde's friend is called Duthie. He's also away at the moment. I'll speak to him when he gets back at the end of the week.'

'How will you explain tracing him without dragging me in?'

'I'll say Rupe mentioned his name.'

'And then?'

'I'll see what he says in response.'

'What if he says nothing?'

'I don't plan to give him that option.'

BRAVE WORDS. Chronic stress and a haywire body clock were playing havoc with my normally acute instinct for self-preservation. I went out in search of a congenial bar, settled for an uncongenial one instead, and, two-thirds of the way through my second Ragin' River, was hit by fatigue. A totter back to the hotel was swiftly followed by a descent into sleep several levels deeper than the norm.

Half of Wednesday had vanished when I rejoined the ranks of the conscious. Since my itinerary wasn't exactly clogged, this represented no problem whatever. After a large lunchtime breakfast, I became a tourist for the afternoon, riding the cable cars to Fisherman's Wharf and shelling out for a boat trip round the Bay.

Back at the Holiday Inn, Maris was waiting for me. And it was obvious from her expression that it wasn't to reassure herself that I'd enjoyed the sights.

'I got another answer to my ad,' she said.

'Who from?'

'Mr Duthie.' There was an accusation detectable in her voice. 'He wants to meet me. Eight o'clock, in the bar of the Fairmont Hotel.'

I knew her apprehensiveness about the encounter would turn to terror if I told her what really lay behind it. Even so, she seemed grateful to me for volunteering to take her place.

'He's *bound* to tell Clyde about this, Gary.'

'Hold on. He doesn't know you're Clyde's girlfriend.'

'It won't take him long to work that out.'

'I think it might.'

'Why?'

'Because, when he meets me, your involvement will fall right off the top of his agenda. I promise.'

THE BAR OF THE FAIRMONT was quiet—too late for cocktails, too early for after-dinner drinks. Spotting Mr Chester Duthie wasn't difficult. He looked at his ease, if not in his element, dressed in a dark blue suit and open-neck maroon shirt—an outfit that emphasised the whiteness of his hair and beard, as well as the robin's-egg blue of his eyes. His face was lined, but the set of his shoulders and the tilt of his chin suggested he'd made few compromises to age—or indeed very much else. Even sitting in a leather armchair, he had an unmistakable physical presence. It would have been easy to feel afraid of him. And that's exactly what I did feel.

For a man expecting to meet a twenty-year-old girl, Duthie met my approach with a noticeable lack of surprise.

'Mr Duthie?'

'Yuh.' He drew on his cigarette. 'You must be the guy I met in a café on Fillmore Street last week. I believe your name's Lance Bradley.'

A denial would have been pointless. 'And I believe your name's Stephen Townley,' I said, trying to recover the ground I'd lost.

'Why don't you sit down?'

'OK.'

'How about a drink?'

'Fine.'

He summoned the waiter. 'Another large J and B on the rocks for me and the same for the gentleman.'

'I don't take ice in my whisky,' I said as the waiter bustled away.

'Time you started.'

'If you say so.'

'Let's hope you take the same line on some other recommendations I have for you.'

'Can't promise.'

'No? Well, promises are cheap. Look at Miss Nielsen's promise to meet me here.'

'She's just worried about Clyde. Nothing else.'

'I guessed that. Just like I guessed you'd turn up in her place.'

'Glad not to have disappointed you.'

'You should be. I don't take disappointment well. And as for a death in the family . . .' He paused while the waiter returned with our drinks, but kept looking at me till the bloke had gone again. 'I take that even worse.'

'I'm sorry about your son. I didn't mean to kill him.'

'I believe you. But he *is* dead. And the German police seem to think you're responsible.'

'It was self-defence.'

'No, Lance. It was murder. But you didn't do it.'

'What do you mean?'

'We'll come back to what I mean later. You wanted to meet me. That's what the farrago with the book was all about. So, you're meeting me sooner than you'd hoped, thanks to my early flight home. The porter smelled a rat right off, incidentally. He's not likely to see me with a bookstore carrier bag under my arm if we both live to be a hundred. As for talking to strangers in coffee shops, that's not my style. Now, what do you want to say to me?'

'I have a message from Mayumi.'

'Deliver it.'

'She'll never reveal the contents of the letter to anyone if you agree to leave Haruko and her in peace.'

'I have to trust her on that, do I?'

'Yes. I think you know you can. The only two people she did tell—Miller Loudon and her brother—are dead.'

'Didn't she tell you, Lance?'

'No.'

'I believe you. You know why? Because, if you knew what was in the letter, you wouldn't have come to San Francisco. You'd have run for your life.'

'Why don't *you* tell me?'

He allowed himself a smile. 'You have a sense of humour, Lance.'

'Do you accept Mayumi's offer?'

'Offer? Sounds more like a plea for mercy to me.'

'And are you a merciful man?'

'What do you think?'

'I think . . . not.'

Townley stubbed out his cigarette. 'Honest as well as humorous. You have a lot going for you. More than your friend Rupert Alder.'

'Where is Rupe?'

'He threatened me, Lance. And when I showed him I wasn't prepared to yield to his threats, he threatened my grandson Clyde. I don't know what he thought I'd do about that. But ask yourself: what should I have done? What choice did he give me?'

'What did you do?'

Townley dropped his voice. 'I killed him.'

They were the words I'd half-expected to hear, but they still sent a chill through me. 'You killed him?'

'Let's be accurate here. I'm retired from that line myself. I had my son-in-law handle the job. Gordon enjoys the work. He lured Rupe to a rendezvous in Buena Vista Park. The official cause of death was a cocaine overdose. The police evidently thought he got the bump on the head falling over in a drugged stupor. Some tourists found him.'

I couldn't seem to frame a response. All this way and all this struggle, for the bleak reward of Townley's deadpan report on how he had neutralised the threat Rupe posed to them.

'Gordon removed anything that could have identified Rupe, of course, and checked him out of his hotel room. At that point, your friend dropped off the edge of the world. Well, the edge of the continent, anyhow, on account of the fact that bodies unclaimed after thirty days are cremated and their ashes scattered in the ocean. Sadly, though, he didn't leave my life so neatly. Gordon searched his clothes and his room. But all he found was a photocopy of the letter, which was all Rupe had shown me. Rupe must have hidden the original. The question is: where?'

'You think I'd tell you if I knew?'

'I do. You see, Rupe wanted me to go public with the whole story. But that would have been suicide. Worse, it would have endangered my family. I had to defend them. I tried talking him out of it. I tried buying him off. None of it did any good. Your friend was determined to blow everything that happened back in 1963 wide open. He had to be stopped. He *was* stopped.'

'So, you murdered Rupe because he was blackmailing you.'

'That's what it amounts to, yuh.'

'And Peter Dalton? What was your justification for murdering him, all those years ago?'

'Money. I needed it pretty badly then. I was preparing for my very early retirement. I could see what was coming up and I knew I'd have to drop conclusively out of sight. Rupe would never have traced me if I'd stuck to my soundest principle: solitude is safety. I've invested wisely over the years. I own Egret Apartments, though as far as the lessees are concerned I'm just another one of them. The only unwise thing I've done is the most human. I stayed in touch with my family. But for that, no one would ever have found me.'

'Does Clyde know what happened to Rupe?'

'No. Nor why. And I'd like to keep it that way.'

'I won't tell Maris, if that's what you mean.'

'That's considerate of you.'

'I'm considering *her*.'

'Of course. What a gent in disguise you are. Unlike Rupe. You know, Clyde didn't even know he had a grandfather until Rupe told him. He made it clear that I wasn't exactly your footstool-and-slippers kind of grandpappy. Left me with a lot of ground to make up. I'd appreciate being allowed to tackle the task the best I can.'

'Am I missing something here?' I certainly felt I was. Townley wasn't what I had expected, though whether that made him more dangerous or less I couldn't decide. 'You still haven't given me your answer to Mayumi?'

'Let's get out of here.' He turned towards the bar, where the waiter was refilling the ice bucket. '*Check!*'

'I'm not sure I—'

'Don't worry. I'm not taking you to Buena Vista Park.'

WE DIDN'T in fact go further than the square separating the Fairmont Hotel from Grace Cathedral, where we walked slowly round the perimeter of the small park occupying the western half of the square. There were cars and people about. The street lighting was good, the location as safe as they come.

'I don't doubt Mayumi's sincerity, Lance. The problem is the letter. In among all this sympathy for her and her daughter, you might ask yourself why she was so stupid as to keep the letter in the first place. If it fell into the wrong hands, the consequences are unthinkable.'

'Mayumi doesn't have the letter any more.'

'No. But fortunately, however, you are in a position to resolve the situation.'

'I am?'

'We're both in trouble, Lance. You're a murder suspect in two continents. I'm a nobody who wants to stay that way. I can prove you didn't murder anyone. You can guarantee the continued anonymity of Chester Duthie. I see the making of a deal there, don't you?'

'How can you prove anything—or me guarantee anything?'

'OK. Listen. I chose Gordon as a husband for Barbara because I thought she might need protection when I could no longer protect her myself. Of course, she never knew. The downside of protection is that sometimes the guard dog can turn on its owner. Gordon contracted the hit against Hashimoto in Berlin to a pro called Ventress. There's a protocol in these things Gordon doesn't understand. When I explained to Ventress that I was his contractor-in-chief, he was willing to tell me everything that occurred. It seems Gordon added a second hit to the list. He'd followed you to the Adlon and knew Eric had already disobeyed orders by taking a personal hand against you. Just before taking off after you, Gordon instructed Ventress to make sure Eric didn't survive that act of disobedience.'

'So you're saying . . .'

'Ventress finished Eric off, on Gordon's orders. My son-in-law decreed that my son had become a liability. The question now is: what am *I* going to do about it?'

'What's the answer?'

'That's where you come in, Lance. You see, I could tip the authorities off in Germany *and* Japan. I could tell them Gordon Ledgister is the man they're really looking for. Forensic evidence would nail him for Miller Loudon's murder, no question. And since he could also be shown to have been on the scene in Berlin, your version of events would be believed over his. Leaving you in the clear and Gordon . . . where he deserves to be. Eric *was* a liability. Gordon was right about that. But he was also my son. The man who killed him must be made to pay for it. And I don't mean Ventress.'

'Aren't you afraid Gordon will implicate you?'

'Don't worry about Gordon. I made him. I can break him.'

'What do you want?'

'The letter. What else?'

'I don't know where it is. I can't give it to you.'

'I think you can. You were Rupe's best friend, weren't you? His best and oldest friend. That means you know the way his mind worked. Which also means you have a better chance than anyone else of figuring out where he hid it.'

'*I don't know.*'

'Not yet. But I'm backing you to learn. Find the letter, Lance. And deliver it to me. Then I'll accept Mayumi's offer. And you'll get your life back.'

WHEN TOWNLEY and I parted, I took a roundabout route back to Maris at the Holiday Inn. I couldn't decide whether I'd just been handed a lifeline or not. Townley's reasoning was sound as far as it went. I probably did stand a better chance than anyone of working out where Rupe had hidden the letter. But if I found the letter and read it, I'd know at long last what secrets it contained. And I knew what had happened to those who'd learned Townley's secret. That could well be the fate he had in mind for me too, even if he did mean to let Ledgister take the rap for the murders. Two for the price of one was a bargain that would appeal to him. I couldn't trust him.

And yet I had no choice but to act as if I did.

'CHESTER DUTHIE is Clyde's grandfather. A bit of a rough diamond, banished from his grandson's life by Clyde's mother. Rupe was trying to squeeze money out of them by threatening to tell her they'd got together. They paid him off and he left town. That's all there is to it. Chester assures me he won't tell Clyde about your ad.'

Maris looked at me with scepticism. 'How come a stranger from England found out about this obscure family difficulty?'

'Business dealings with Chester, apparently. The old boy wouldn't go into details. Probably because they were . . . legally iffy.'

'And it just so happens that, since then, Rupe has disappeared.'

'Left town. Coincidentally. I'll have to look for him elsewhere.'

'It doesn't have anything to do with the death of Clyde's uncle?'

'Nothing whatever.'

'Look, Gary. I'm going to lay it on the line for you . . . and for Chester. I'll go along with this, for Clyde's sake. I'll let it lie. But there's one thing I want you to know.'

'What's that?'

'I don't believe a single word you've said.'

I COULDN'T BLAME Maris for doubting me. I could only hope she did what she'd said she'd do: let it lie.

The uncongenial bar was still open when I got there and the proprietor seemed happy to ply me with drinks at the rapid rate I set.

There's a world of difference—in mood and reason—between getting drunk slowly and getting drunk fast. This was a fast occasion. I had a friend to mourn and to curse. I did both, more or less simultaneously, as midnight slurred into the early hours.

I WAS AT THE Public Library when it opened the following morning. It took me no more than twenty minutes to find what I was looking for in a back copy of the *San Francisco Chronicle*, on an inner page of the local news section for Saturday, September 23.

> DEATH IN BUENA VISTA PARK
> The body of an unidentified Caucasian male, approximate age 30–35, was found yesterday morning in Buena Vista Park. A police spokesperson said the death appeared to be drug-related. Anyone with information regarding his identity is asked to contact the Police Department.

That was it. One short paragraph. Not much of an obituary. But it was the only one Rupe was going to get.

I walked out into the plaza filling the square between the Library and City Hall and made my way slowly round the rectangular pond at its centre. Sunlight sparkled in the fountain and a cool breeze sent fallen leaves rushing past me.

Where was the letter? Where could it be? A bank vault seemed the obvious bet. But Rupe would have had some sort of receipt in that case, some documentary proof of ownership. Ledgister had found nothing in his pockets or belongings. He'd drawn a blank at Rupe's house in London and his flat in Tokyo as well. Rupe had chosen his hiding place well. That much was certain.

It was clear to me he wouldn't have left the letter in Tokyo, since he'd not have wanted to go back there. Nor would he have carried it with him during his dealings with the Townleys in Berlin and San Francisco. A photocopy was all he'd needed to show them.

So, London it had to be, the only other place he'd been after stealing the letter and before his fatal appointment in Buena Vista Park. It was waiting for him there somewhere. Waiting patiently. All I had to do—such a little thing—was find it.

Going back to London was risky, of course, even with the protection of my new identity. There was probably a warrant out for the arrest of Lancelot Bradley. I just had to hope I found the letter before the police found me.

LONDON EIGHT

At Paddington, I made a phone call. It was my second attempt to contact Echo and I got the same result as I had at Heathrow: no answer. My last piece of advice to her had been to move out. Maybe she'd already acted on it. That would explain why there was no answerphone cut-in. Not that I'd have left a message if there had been. I didn't want any record of Lance Bradley's return home.

I sat in the station café, drinking my way through a couple of espressos to ward off jet lag and trying to apply some cool logic to the problem of where Rupe had hidden the letter. The odds were still on a safe-deposit box. But where was the key—or whatever he needed to access it? Number 12 Hardrada Road had to be the likeliest answer. Cunningly concealed, obviously, since the house had already been searched to no avail. But I couldn't just roll up there unannounced, especially in daylight. The neighbours might have been asked about me by the police. I had to speak to Echo first.

I booked myself into the suitably anonymous Hotel Polaris in Craven Road, and tried her again from the lobby payphone, only to draw a third blank. My next move wasn't exactly risk-free either, but with the weekend about to close on my window of opportunity I couldn't really opt for delay.

THE OFFICES of Myerscough Udal were part of a drab seventies block, out of which early leavers eager for the weekend were already trickling when I took up position behind an *Evening Standard* in the next doorway. I had Philip Jarvis down as a five-thirty man, maybe five on a Friday. He also struck me as about the likeliest person to know where Rupe had squirrelled away the document.

On the dot of five thirty he emerged into the dank autumn evening, and with a twitch of his raincoat collar he turned and strode towards Holborn Underground station.

I let him put a bit of distance between us and Myerscough Udal before quickening my pace to overhaul him. 'Mr Jarvis,' I called.

He stopped and looked round, instant recognition lighting his features. Then suddenly it changed, like a switch being flicked. He tensed and drew back. 'What?'

'Mr Jarvis, I have to speak to you. It's really very important.'

'Who are you?'

'You know who I am. We met in Hyde Park with Mr Hashimoto.'

'Who?'

'Hashimoto. Come on. There's no need to play games.'

'I have no idea who you are or what you want.' He raised his voice, as if to make a point to some unseen observer. 'Leave me alone.' He turned on his heel and strode away.

'Jarvis,' I shouted. 'For God's sake.' I started after him, but stopped within ten yards. There was no point pursuing him. Of that I was certain. Maybe Myerscough Udal was being pressurised by some corporate entity far more powerful than they were. But *who* were we talking about? Caribtex Oil? Or a giant corporation of which they were just a minor subsidiary?

It wasn't what I'd expected, but somehow, now that it had happened, I felt unsurprised. Even the fear that had quite clearly gripped Philip Jarvis was, in its way, predictable. It was also more than a little familiar. I was beginning to know the look.

I'D DECIDED what to do next, but the time to do it hadn't yet arrived, so I sat through a thoroughly unmemorable film until it was time to get a taxi to Kennington. I asked the cabbie to wait for me in the next street east from Hardrada Road and made my final approach on foot. With early starts at the sorting office, Echo was no night bird. If she was still living at number 12, she'd be home by now.

But she wasn't. The house was in darkness and there was no response to a succession of lengthy stabs at the bell. What was more conclusive was that the curtains were open on all the windows. I squinted through the letterbox. All I could make out was emptiness.

NEXT MORNING, dull and early, I was on an empty 36 bus as it trundled southwards over Vauxhall Bridge. Soon I was trudging down Wandsworth Road in thickening drizzle towards the sorting office. It was still only seven o'clock.

The enquiry desk didn't open till eight, according to the sign next to the shuttered door, so I cut round to the loading yard at the back, buttonholed a bloke just going into the sorting office and talked him into asking postperson Echo Bateman to step outside for a word.

'I KNEW IT HAD to be you,' she remarked as she emerged into the yard. 'I've been wondering if I'd ever hear from you again.'

'The past ten days have been kind of hectic.'

'More than hectic, Lance. The police contacted me.' She rolled her large eyes at me.

'You moved out of Hardrada Road.'

'Your idea, as I recall.'

'Yeah. The thing is, Echo, I need to, er, take a look inside.'

A van started up nearby, followed by a series of loud warning honks as it began to reverse. 'I haven't got the keys. Not on me. And I've got to get out on the round. Come to my new place around midday and we can talk then. Actually . . .' She hesitated. 'Maybe it would be better if we met somewhere else.'

I shaped a smile. 'I think it's probably a sensible precaution.'

THE FERRET AND MONKEY was far enough into Clapham to guarantee Echo and me total anonymity amid the young and noisy Saturday lunchtime crowd.

'The police wouldn't tell me anything, Lance. But it was obvious you were in serious bother. That clinched it for me about moving out. Now, why do you want to look in the house?'

'Rupe hid something there. I have to find it.'

'What is it?'

'Can't tell you. Honestly, Echo, I'm glad you moved out. I'm glad you're not involved. Stay that way. I wish I could.'

'Too late to quit?'

'Far too late.'

'Have you learned anything about Rupe?'

'He's not coming back, Echo.'

'Never?'

I shook my head and mouthed 'Dead' at her.

'Bloody hell.'

'What about the keys?'

She stared at me for a moment, then took the keys out of her pocket and plonked them on the table. 'You'll be careful, won't you?'

'Oh yes.' I grinned. 'Don't worry about me.'

'I will worry.'

'That's nice to know. Look, I'd better be going.'

I picked up the keys and we both stood up, smiling awkwardly. Echo's smile turned to a frown. 'I nearly forgot. You have another

Japanese friend. The neighbours sent him round from Hardrada Road the day before yesterday. He's anxious to contact you.'

'Name?'

'I wrote it down.' She handed me a crumpled piece of paper, on which was written, in capitals: *TOSHISHIGE YAMAZAWA—ARUNDEL HOTEL, MONTAGUE ST., WC1*. '*Is* he a friend?'

'I think so.'

'Well, seems to me you need every one of them you can get.'

'I certainly do.'

'I'm one too.'

'I know.'

She leaned forward and kissed me on the cheek. 'Good luck, then . . . quitter.'

AS FAR AS I COULD TELL, I made it to the door of 12 Hardrada Road unobserved. I let myself in with a sigh of relief and closed the latch carefully behind me.

Minus Echo's possessions, Rupe's house looked noticeably sparse. The photomontage still hung in the kitchen. I took it down and prised off the backing. There was no letter hidden behind the photographs. I'd searched Rupe's sitting room and bedroom before—albeit without knowing what I was looking for—and turned up nothing. I went over them again, though, with painstaking thoroughness. The result was the same.

I decided to try the loft next and was halfway out of the cupboard under the stairs with the stepladder when the doorbell rang.

I crouched back into the cupboard out of sight, but caught the top of the ladder on the lintel above my head, lost my grip and winced helplessly as it crashed against the wall.

The bell rang again. I stayed where I was, hoping the caller had somehow failed to hear the noise. The letterbox creaked open.

'I know you're in there, Lance.' The voice belonged to Carl Madron. 'Why don't you stop mucking about and let me in?'

IT'S NOT NICE when somebody has you at a disadvantage. When that somebody has the leery smile and rodent-like gaze of Carl Madron, the experience is excruciating.

'I somehow thought you'd be back, Lance, you know that? I've got an instinct for these things.'

'What do you want, Carl?'

'A friendly little chat would be nice. Least you owe me, really, seeing how I put you on to Bill Prettyman. You were supposed to keep us posted. So, how is it I have to rely on a nosy neighbour to tip me off that you've shown up again after two weeks of silence?'

'There's been nothing to keep you posted *about*.'

'Is that a fact? Not according to the filth, it isn't. They reckon you've been a very busy boy. A trail of murder and mayhem leading halfway round the world is the tale they tell. But I'm sure you'd rather not talk about that, so what's it worth for me to stay shtum about you being back in town?'

'Why don't you tell me? I'm sure you've already decided.'

'Comes down to this, Lance. You're caught up in something big. Something huge, as a matter of fact. I know one of the dead guys in Berlin was called Townley, so don't bother to deny there's a tie-in with the Townley that Rupe was looking for. That means there's also a tie-in with the Great Train Robbery. What are we talking about here? The high rollers behind it crawling out of the woodwork—or being pulled out? I know a guy from one of the Sundays. He's talking serious money for an exclusive on the whole can of worms. By serious I mean there's a lot of noughts on the end. Here's my proposition, Lance. I'll keep my mouth shut if you'll open yours.'

'How could I resist a sales pitch like yours, Carl?' (Easily was the truth, but Carl would believe everybody's motives to be as base as his.) 'But I have to fit one last piece into the jigsaw first. A piece that could multiply those noughts for you.'

'What is it?'

'A letter, implicating Stephen Townley in the robbery.'

'Rupe hid it here, did he?'

'It's the only place left to look.'

Carl glanced at the stepladder. 'Attic job, is it?'

'Maybe. Want to give me a hand?' I was skating on thin ice now, but the only way to get rid of him was first to convince him I was willing to go along with him. And then . . .

'You carry on, Lance. I'll watch.'

'We could be here a fair while.'

'That's OK.' He grinned. 'I'm in no hurry.'

AS IT HAPPENED we soon found what we were looking for. *I* found it, actually. Carl confined his contribution to telling me where to try next. He was observing my dusty scramble between the joists from the platform of the stepladder, his head and shoulders above the level of the loft hatch, when the beam of the torch I was using to supplement the single light bulb fell on something I recognised.

It was a short strip of red and white caving tape. Rupe and I had encountered taped stretches in the cave system he'd led me into that day in 1985 that had nearly ended in my death. 'They're to protect vulnerable areas,' he'd explained. 'Keep-out signs, if you like.'

Keep out—or come hither? The strip was nailed to a rafter, low down near the eaves, where headroom was minimal, deep in the shadow cast by the water tank. When I trained the torch on the area around the tape, I couldn't see anything. I explored with my hand the insulation-filled gulley under it.

And there it was. A small padded envelope, parcel-taped to the side of the joist. I smiled to myself in a small moment of satisfaction as I ran my fingers across it. But what to do next? I wasn't sure Carl could be shaken off, and I couldn't bring myself to leave the house without the envelope, so I just ripped the envelope free of the joist and backed away until I could stand upright.

'I think I've got something,' I said, turning towards Carl.

'You have?'

'Yeah. An envelope. Let's go down and take a look.'

'OK.'

Carl started to descend as I reached the hatchway. Wedging the envelope into the waistband of my jeans, I sat down on the hatch frame and lowered myself towards the platform of the stepladder. Even as I did so, I saw my chance. Carl glanced down to check how many steps there were to the floor. Bracing my arms, I swung my feet and struck him a solid blow around the jaw. He grunted and fell, hitting the floor with a thump and lying where he'd fallen, shocked and winded. I kicked the stepladder, which toppled onto him, then I jumped down and turned towards the stairs, while Carl moaned and rolled over, struggling under the stepladder.

I took the stairs two at a time and had already reached the bottom when Carl bellowed after me, 'You bastard.' But I was way ahead of him. I pulled the keys out of my pocket, yanked the front door open, plunged out into the street, slammed the door behind me and turned the mortise key in the lock to slow him down.

Glancing round, I saw the woman from number 10, laden with children and shopping, staring at me in bemusement. 'Hi,' I found myself saying. Then I turned and legged it.

LUCKY IN LOVE, unlucky in cards. Well, I've never had a lot of luck in either department. But buses are a different matter. My faithful stand-by, the 36, was just pulling away from the Harleyford Road stop when I jumped aboard. Looking back from the platform as it accelerated away, I could still see no sign of Carl.

I paid my fare, slumped down on the first empty seat, and tugged the envelope free of my jeans. There was nothing written on the outside to give a clue to the contents, but I could feel something small and hard inside. I edged a finger under the flap and tore it open.

The small, hard object was a key, with a number stamped on the bow: 4317. Round it was folded a letter. But it wasn't the kind of letter I'd been expecting.

12 Hardrada Road
London SE11

International Bank of Honshu
164–165 Cheapside
London EC4

August 29, 2000

Dear Sirs,

This is to confirm the authorisation I gave you today to afford access to safe-deposit box 4317 to Mr Lancelot Bradley of 18A High Street, Glastonbury, Somerset.

Yours faithfully,
Rupert Alder

I stared at Rupe's immaculately word-processed, one-sentence letter as the bus trundled up Vauxhall Bridge Road. It made no sense and yet it made perfect sense. If he never came back—as he never would now—there'd be this, waiting to be found by the only friend likely, in the end, to look hard enough. Not the Townley letter itself, but secure means to lay hands upon it.

I got off the bus at Victoria and took a cab to Cheapside. I had no realistic expectation that the International Bank of Honshu would be open for business on a Saturday afternoon, but I couldn't resist taking a peak at the place. It was a slab of matt steel and bronze-tinted glass, its interior all gleaming marble and clean-lined wood. That was as much as I could glean from the pavement. And the pavement was as far as I was getting until 9.30 on Monday morning, as a discreetly displayed statement of banking hours made clear.

It was beginning to get dark. I hopped on a bus to Oxford Circus, grateful for the slow going it made in the thickening traffic. I had some thinking to do. I couldn't be certain the safe-deposit box contained the Townley letter, but I *felt* certain. The way things stood gave me an excellent chance to deliver it to Townley in circumstances where he could be confident I hadn't read it. I'd never find out what his secret was, of course, but if I'd learned anything in the past few weeks it was the value of not knowing that particular secret.

The Hotel Polaris didn't boast in-room telephones and the lobby payphone was no place for making confidential international calls, so I got off the bus and walked up into the fringes of Bloomsbury. Thanks to the note Echo had given me, I thought I knew a hotel guest in the vicinity who might let me swell his phone bill.

But Mr Yamazawa was out, the friendly receptionist at the Arundel informed me, so with a sigh I wandered off down the road, reckoning the pub on the corner would be as good a source as any of the mound of coins I'd need to call the States from a phone box.

THE PUB WAS FULL, the bar hard to see for backs. As I squeezed through the ruck, I felt my sleeve being tugged and heard a voice I recognised saying, 'Lance. Here, Lance.'

I turned to see Toshishige Yamazawa grinning up at me from a chair at one of the tables along the wall opposite the bar. He was wearing some kind of plastic mac over the sort of shirt I'd last seen on Elvis Presley in an afternoon TV showing of *Blue Hawaii*. On the other side of the table, also smiling at me, was a stockily built, grizzle-haired black guy of fifty or sixty, dressed smart-casually in powder-blue jeans, maroon turtleneck and tweed jacket.

'What are you doing here, Lance?' piped Yamazawa.

'I could ask the same of you, Toshi.'

'We've both got some explaining to do, for sure.'

'Sounds like you've got a lot to talk over,' said the other bloke. 'I'll leave you to it.' He drained his glass and stood up.

'Gus and I have just got back from the Tower of London,' Yamazawa explained. (As if that explained everything.)

'Yuh. Pleased to meet you, Lance.'

'You too, Gus.' I shook his hand.

'I'll catch you later, Toshi.' With that Gus manoeuvred his large frame with surprising ease through the crowd to the door.

'I didn't expect to see you, Lance,' Yamazawa said as I sat in the chair Gus had vacated. 'I contacted Miss Bateman on the half-chance.'

'Yeah? Well, it's only a half-chance I came here after drawing a blank at your hotel.' I looked at his glass. 'What are you drinking?'

'Old Peppered Hen. Excellent.'

'Speckled. You want another?'

'Good idea.'

I got up, struggled to the bar and returned a couple of minutes later clutching two pints. 'Shintaro must have told you what happened in Kyoto.'

'Yes, he did. But London is a long way from San Francisco. Does this mean you took my brother's advice and abandoned the ladies?'

'No, it doesn't. There's good news on that front. I'll explain in a minute. Why don't we start with you. Who's Gus?'

'Oh, Gus is from New Jersey. He is here for a holiday, staying at the Arundel. We are both alone. He suggested going to the Tower of London today. Most enjoyable.'

'Are you on holiday as well?'

'In a way of speaking, yes.'

'What's that supposed to mean?'

'Well, like you know, Penberthy told the police you came to see us. I had to answer lots of questions. So did Penberthy. He complained to Charlie Hoare. Charlie summoned me here to explain why I had assisted you. I could not explain, of course. The Board were not happy. It seems I was already marked down for'—he lowered his voice theatrically—'bad attitude.'

'They didn't sack you, did they?'

'Yes. That is it, Lance. They sacked me. Cheers.' He took a deep swallow of beer. 'Instant dismissal. I recommend the experience. Very liberating. They did not want me to work my notice, so . . .' He grinned at me again. 'I take a holiday. Now, what is this good news?'

HALF AN HOUR LATER, with Yamazawa snoring gently on his bed at the Arundel, I sat at the small desk in his room and put a call through to Stephen Townley.

His phone rang six times before he picked it up.

'Glad to hear from you, Lance. Where are you?'

'London.'

'Uh-huh. And why are you calling me?'

'I've got the key to a safe-deposit box. And authority to access it. I've little doubt the box contains what you want.'

'And you're proposing that I join you for the opening ceremony?'

'It's in a bank vault, which means I can't get to it before Monday morning.'

'OK. In that case, I *will* join you. Where's the bank?'

'Cheapside. Near St Paul's Cathedral.'

'OK, Lance, I'll meet you outside the west front of St Paul's at nine fifteen, Monday morning. Does that suit?'

'Yes. I—' But the line was dead. Townley had hung up. Even at my expense (well, Yamazawa's), he'd chosen not to waste his words.

YAMAZAWA WOKE UP for long enough to assure me he'd phone his brother in the morning and let him know what I was planning. I could have phoned him myself there and then, but 3.30am, as it was in Japan, struck me as no time to be calling anyone. So, leaving the old fox to sleep off his hens, I walked round to an Italian restaurant I remembered at the top of Shaftesbury Avenue and forked down some pasta, then wandered back to the Polaris via a couple of pubs in Marylebone. With each drink the prospect of getting my life back looked brighter. Things were definitely looking up.

They didn't look so bright the following morning, but I put that down to a hangover, the squalid ambience of the Polaris and my genetically programmed aversion to Sundays.

Jet lag was still gumming up my body clock into the bargain, so going back to sleep for a few hours seemed like a good idea. It was a lot later than I'd intended when I called Yamazawa from a payphone at Paddington Station, and I wasn't surprised to be told he was out. He'd mentioned visiting Hampton Court with Gus, and now I almost wished I'd gone along with them.

Phoning my parents at that point was a spur-of-the moment decision. I owed them a call, if only to reassure them that their son was alive and well. As they knew, he was also in a lot of trouble. But I reckoned I could afford to hint that he might soon be out of it.

My father answered. 'Who is it?' His voice was even more peremptory than usual.

'It's Lance, Dad.'

'Lance? My God. Your mother's sick with worry. What the hell's going on? The police have been here. They mentioned . . . murder.'

'It's all one big misunderstanding. You don't seriously think I'm capable of murder, do you?'

'Of course not. But—'

'I need a few days to put myself in the clear, Dad. Then I'll go to the police and explain the whole thing.'

'Perhaps you'd like to explain to *us* while you're about it.'

'Of course. Soon, I promise. You didn't mention the Alders to the police, did you, Dad?'

'No, son, I didn't. We said we knew nothing about what you might be up to. It went against the grain, but it seemed . . . best.'

'It was, believe me. I'm grateful, Dad. Honestly.'

'So you should be. We're had Winifred round here twice, asking if we've heard from you. I don't like having to cover for you. But I do it. So does your mother. And we're not the only ones. What about poor Miss Bateman? Have you spoken to her?'

'Yes. Echo's fine. I saw her yesterday.'

'She didn't *sound* fine this morning.'

'This morning?'

'Yes. She phoned while we were having breakfast. She asked if we'd heard from you and, if so, how she could contact you.' (I hadn't told her where I was staying, of course, reckoning it was safer for her not to know.) 'She said she needed to speak to you. Urgently.'

'HELLO?' It was a woman's voice, but not Echo's.

'Is Echo there?'

'Who's calling?'

I had to take a deep breath before answering. 'Lance Bradley.'

'Ah. She said you might call. I'm Karen. She's lodging with me.'

'Right. Can I speak to her?'

'No. You see . . . When I got back and saw the state she was in—'

'What *state*?'

'I gather you know the bastard who did this to her.'

A sickening guess sprang into my mind. 'Carl Madron?'

'So she said.'

'What did he do?'

'It could have been worse, I suppose, but—'

'*What did he do*?'

THE A AND E UNIT at St Thomas's Hospital was the usual scrum of walking wounded. After a certain amount of wrangling with the receptionist, a message came back that I could go through.

Echo was in a curtained cubicle in an assessment ward, fully dressed but lying on a bed, her face distorted by a black eye and a swollen bruise to the jaw. Whether she could have smiled at me if she'd wanted to I don't know, because she didn't try.

'Are you all right, Lance?' she lisped.

'Am *I* all right? What about you?'

'It's just what you can see, plus a loose tooth and some blurred vision. They're going to keep me in for observation.'

'What happened?' I sat down on the chair next to the bed. 'I had a run-in with Carl yesterday and I should have realised he might take it out on you. This *was* Carl, right?'

'Oh yeah. It was Carl. But keep your voice down. I'm saying I was mugged by a stranger. A nice policeman was here an hour ago.'

'For God's sake. Why didn't you tell them who did it?'

'Because if they took Carl in, he'd bring you into this, wouldn't he? He'd be bound to.'

'Let me worry about that.'

'You don't understand, Lance. There were two of them. They're after you.'

'Two of them?'

'They must have been waiting for Karen to go out. She jogs every morning. When I answered the door, they burst straight in. Carl . . . and this other guy.'

'What did the other guy look like?'

'Middle-aged but muscular. Thinning fair hair and a 'tache. American.' She must have seen my jaw drop. 'You know him?'

'Yeah. I know him. But . . . he was with *Carl*?'

'He was. And pulling the strings, as far as I could tell.'

'This doesn't make any sense.' (Gordon Ledgister, in London, and in cahoots with Carl. What it did make was my flesh creep.)

'I thought they were going to kill me, Lance. The American had a knife. And he was deadly serious. He threatened to slit my throat if I didn't tell them where you were.'

I noticed then that her hand was shaking. I reached out and closed mine around it. Maybe it was the gesture—or the memory of Ledgister's threat—that brought tears suddenly to her eyes.

'Sorry. God, this keeps happening.' She fumbled for a tissue and dried her eyes. 'Sorry.'

'Please don't say that. I'm the one who should be apologising for landing you in this.'

'Well, maybe we should both be apologising to Mr Yamazawa.'

'Why?'

'I didn't know where you were. If I *had* known, I'd have told them. That's the truth. But I had to tell them something. I had no choice, Lance. I've never been so frightened in my life.'

'You told them about Toshi?'

'Yeah. I said he knew where you were.' She took another deep breath. 'And they went looking for him.'

THE NEAREST phone was outside the A and E waiting room. I grabbed the handset and dialled.

'Arundel Hotel. Miranda speaking. How may I help you?'

'I need to speak to one of your guests urgently. Mr Yamazawa.'

'Hold on.' There was a pause of several seconds, then she was back. 'I'm afraid Mr Yamazawa's out. Who's calling?'

'My name's Lance Bradley.'

'Ah. Mr Yamazawa phoned earlier, saying you might call. He left a number where you can contact him.'

'THAT YOU, Lance?' The voice was Carl's.

'Where's Yamazawa?'

'Right here. Why don't I put him on?'

'Hello, Lance.' It was Toshi. 'I never got to Hampton Court.'

'Are you OK?'

'They have not harmed me.'

'Yet,' said Carl, coming back on the line. 'That's the operative word.'

'You bastard.'

'Shut up, Lance, and listen. I reckon you know who else is here. He wants the letter. Meet him on Hungerford Bridge one hour from now. Have the letter with you. If you don't hand it over, your chum Yamazawa commits involuntary harry-karry. Get it?'

I got it.

AN HOUR LATER I was walking north over Hungerford Bridge beneath a gunmetal sky from which the light was already fading. The Thames was a brown, rain-swollen surge. To my left, trains rumbled into and out of Charing Cross. Ahead, a figure was leaning against the railings, smoking a cigarette and gazing downstream.

'Hi, Lance,' Ledgister said, without looking round.

'You must be desperate to go into partnership with Carl,' I said, resting my elbow on the railings a foot or so away from him.

'I doubt even he thinks of it as a partnership.' Ledgister turned to face me. 'Now, I suggest we get straight down to business. Toshishige Yamazawa is the brother of that *Yakuza* asshole who got in my way last time we met. It'd be no hardship for me to despatch him into the Shinto afterlife, so I advise you not to strain my tolerance. To wrap it up for you, Lance, where's the letter?'

'Here.' I took the envelope out and handed it to him.

'You've read it?'

'Yeah.'

'Unwise, my friend, very unwise. That means you know what my trigger-happy father-in-law was mixed up in.' He slid the letter out of the envelope. 'I'm sure you—'

He stopped as his gaze ran down the sheet of paper. Then, gritting his teeth, he smiled. 'You'll be the death of me, Lance, you know that? Such a funny guy, aren't you?' He peered into the envelope. 'I see we have a key as well. Rupe thought of everything, didn't he?'

'I'm your open sesame. I can empty the safe-deposit box as soon as the bank opens tomorrow morning and deliver the contents to you in exchange for Yamazawa.'

'That's how you see it working, is it?'

'A straight swap. Yeah.' Actually, how I saw it working wasn't so much obscure to me as invisible, but there seemed nothing else for it but to string Ledgister along in the hope that I'd think of some way to play him and Townley off against each other.

'I'm sorry to disappoint you.' He slid the letter back into the envelope. 'I'll keep this. Then, tomorrow morning I'll be at the bank to relieve you of the contents of the box just as soon as you open it.'

'What about Yamazawa?'

'When I'm satisfied Rupe has no more posthumous tricks to pull, I'll call Carl and have him set Tokyo Joe loose.'

'How can I be sure you'll do that?'

'You can't. What time does the bank open up?'

'Nine thirty.'

'Nine thirty it is, then. I'll meet you there. And I'll give Yamazawa the same sort of burial Rupe got if you fail to keep our date.'

'I'll be there.'

'Yuh. I reckon you will.' With that he moved away from the railing and started walking.

I stayed where I was, watching as he strode on along the bridge towards Charing Cross. This was bad. Very bad. In fact, it couldn't be worse. Ledgister thought he had me where he wanted me. So did

Townley. And they were both right. But they couldn't both win. And whatever happened, I was going to lose.

Which would have been bad enough, but for the fact that several other people stood to lose with me.

I WALKED UP to the Arundel through the leaden afternoon, a ramshackle idea forming in my head. If I could glean some clue to where they were holding Yamazawa, it might give me a slender advantage. It had struck me that Gus just might know something.

The receptionist identified him from my description as Gus Parminter. But Mr Parminter, apparently, had signed up for an all-day coach trip to Salisbury and Stonehenge. He'd left early and would be returning late. He clearly wasn't going to be able to tell me anything, so I made my way back to St Thomas's, where I found Echo installed in a general ward, looking slightly better.

'How's Mr Yamazawa?'

'Don't ask,' I said. 'When do you reckon you'll get out of here?'

'Tomorrow. I'd probably be out now if it wasn't Sunday.'

'OK. Could you do me a favour when you've been discharged?' I leaned towards her. 'Go to the police and change your story. Tell them about Carl. In fact . . . tell them everything.'

I LEFT THE POLARIS at first light and walked all the way to St Paul's through the damp beginnings of the day. Commuters were out in force, heading for their computer screens and office intrigues. Ordinarily, I'd have pitied them. Today was different, though. Today, I'd have happily swapped places with any one of them.

'You're on time,' said Townley as I reached the top of the steps in front of St Paul's. 'I like that.' He turned up the collar of his raincoat. 'The weather I don't like, though.'

'You'll like something else even less. Your son-in-law's meeting me at the bank. He has the letter of authorisation and the key to the safe-deposit box.'

Townley looked at me expressionlessly for a moment, then said, 'You shouldn't have allowed Gordon to involve himself in this, Lance. It was supposed to be between you and me.'

'I had no choice. He's holding a friend of mine hostage.'

'I've never had any friends. Maybe now you can understand why.'

'But you do have family.'

'Yuh. And I thought I could trust them.'

'I'm not saying you can't. Gordon's probably planning to hand the letter over to you, as agreed. He doesn't know our deal.'

'He was never planning to stand by me, Lance. I can see that now. He has his own side deal. Sensible, from his point of view. But dangerous. I don't care to be crossed.'

'I'm not crossing you. I'm just trying to—'

'What you're trying to do is have your cake and eat it. Seldom possible, in my experience.'

'There has to be a way out of this.'

'Oh, there is. You meet Gordon at the bank. You open the box for him. You let him carry off the booty.' Townley fixed me with his cold-eyed gaze. 'And you leave the rest to me.'

LEDGISTER WAS RELAXING in an armchair, perusing a complimentary copy of the *Financial Times*, when I entered the foyer of the International Bank of Honshu at 9.32am.

'Good morning, Lance.' He discarded the paper and stood up. 'Your friend Toshi passed a comfortable night, by the way.'

'Let's get on with it.'

He took the letter of authorisation out of his pocket and handed it to me. 'Lead on, why don't you?'

I was required to produce my passport and driving licence by way of identification, then Rupe's letter of authorisation was taken away for comparison with the bank's records. When the back office was satisfied, a polite gentleman, whose lapel badge proclaimed him to be Toru Kusakari, escorted us in the lift down to the vault.

It was a gleaming chamber of solid steel, with banks of numbered lockers along the walls. A doorway at the far end led to a small inner chamber furnished with a desk and two chairs.

Kusakari located locker 4317, opened it and lifted out the shallow metal box inside. He handed me the box and pointed to the inner chamber, then withdrew.

I carried the box to the desk and plonked it down. Ledgister slid the key into the lock and turned. The box sprang open.

Inside, was a single white envelope, with my name printed on it. Ledgister snatched it up and ripped open the flap, then stepped back so I wouldn't be able to read the letter inside.

It was immediately obvious that what I was missing wasn't good news. He glared at me. 'Take a look at this.'

The letter was on Pomparles Trading Company stationary, and

was dated August 29, the same as the authorisation letter. This one was signed by Rupe in his capacity as managing director of the company. It was addressed to Colin Dibley at Tilbury Freeport.

Dear Colin,

By the time you receive this you will be well aware of my company's ownership of a consignment of aluminium due to be delivered to Tilbury by Eurybia Shipping (whose employment I will by then have left) on September 14.

Notwithstanding any legal restraints that may be placed on onward movement of the cargo, I should remind you that this company remains owner of first title pending the resolution of any and all counterclaims and must be afforded access to the cargo for inspection purposes.

This letter authorises my associate, Mr Lancelot Bradley of 18A High Street, Glastonbury, Somerset, to exercise such right of access at any reasonable time.

Thank you for assisting him in this regard.

Yours ever, Rupe

'It's in the container,' I murmured, my words lagging behind my thoughts. Of course. That was what the whole Pomparles fraud had been about. Not aluminium. Not money. But a means of keeping a small item safe and secure, camouflaged by a big cargo that was in turn immobilised by a transnational legal dogfight. Safe, while Rupe carried out his hazardous tilt at the Townleys.

'That's certainly how I read it,' said Ledgister. 'Concealed in the impounded cargo of aluminium. And *you* have to be there to get it. Seems you and I need to take a ride to the coast, Lance. Right now.'

I TRIED NOT TO LOOK around for Townley when we left the bank and headed east along Cheapside. Ledgister had a car parked in a nearby side street, an anonymous white saloon. He walked round to the driver's side and tripped the locks. As I went to get in on the passenger's side, I suddenly saw his expression change. He froze, the driver's door half open, his eyes fixed on something behind me.

'Stephen,' he said slowly. 'What are you doing here?'

I turned, feigning surprise as best I could.

Townley smiled neutrally. 'Looks like a case of great minds, Gordon. You reckoned Lance was the key to this. So did I. Hasn't he told you about our deal?'

'No,' said Ledgister. 'That he hasn't.'

'I'd heard nothing from you since Kyoto. I didn't have much option but to put together a fall-back position.'

'I'm sorry not to have been in touch, Stephen. There was a lot of heat on me in Japan. I figured it was safer for you if I stayed underground until I could deliver the goods.'

'And can you deliver them?'

'Reckon so. Jump in and I'll explain as we go.'

I COULDN'T HELP admiring the way Townley and his son-in-law both rewrote their own recent pasts to reflect a perfect accord. As we drove east along the Commercial Road, Ledgister told some twisted tale about how he'd got out of Japan and headed for London because that was where he'd figured I'd end up. He'd strung Carl Madron along with money and a promise of more to come, and grabbed Yamazawa to force me to cooperate.

Townley, for his part, reported half of our agreement accurately enough—the letter in exchange for an undertaking to let Mayumi and Haruko live in safety. Naturally, he made no mention of the other half—letting Gordon take the rap for a trio of murders.

Somewhere along the way, Ledgister tossed me his mobile phone and told me to call Dibley. 'Negotiate an entrée for us, Lance. A wrangle at the gate we don't need.'

How Dibley would react to my improbable transformation into Rupe's business partner, I didn't like to ask myself. So it was just as well that Dibley was in Felixstowe for the day, leaving his assistant, a mild-sounding bloke called Reynolds, to mind the shop.

WE REACHED the main gate of Tilbury Docks a little over half an hour later. Reynolds had booked us in and we were sent through with directions to the admin block, where he was expecting us.

Townley and Ledgister stayed in the car while I went up to Dibley's office, where Reynolds was presiding for the day. We chewed over some polite nothings and he perused Rupe's letter. Then he telephoned someone at the Customs House.

'Dave Harris will meet you at the container,' Reynolds announced, putting the phone down. 'I, er, assume you know where it is.'

'Yes,' I said, forcing a smile. 'As a matter of fact, I do.'

I returned to the car and we drove the short distance to the container, still held in its own concreted patch of limbo. Dave Harris, a big man wearing a yellow anorak, was waiting for us, clipboard in hand.

There were some desultory introductions and I was required to sign a form. 'As you can see, gentlemen,' said Harris, 'nothing's been done since the cargo arrived, aside from our inspection of the contents. You'll find everything's in order.' Then he produced a pair of bolt cutters and a torch from his car, snapped the official Customs and Excise seals and swung the doors open.

Inside, looking rather like so many silver loaves of bread, ingots of Russian aluminium sat neatly stacked on pallets, waiting to be turned into fizzy drink cans and wheel trims. On the way over, Ledgister had said he'd look after Harris while Townley and I searched for the letter. It was no surprise to me, therefore, that he struck up a conversation with the big man, slyly manoeuvring so that, to talk to him, Harris had to turn his back on the container.

Meanwhile Townley and I tracked slowly along the sides of the pallets, in search of a clue to where Rupe might have lodged the letter, exchanging shakes of the head as we drew progressive blanks.

I had the torch, and soon needed it, as visibility deteriorated the further we went. We were about two-thirds of the way along when I saw a strip of red and white caving tape wrapped round the strut of a pallet. I crouched down and shone the torch in and around the area beneath the pallet. There didn't seem to be anything there. I lay on my side for a closer look. And then I saw it.

A square of brown, thick-gauge plastic was parcel-taped to the underside of the pallet. I stretched my hand in and peeled off a length of the tape, then pulled the rest away. The plastic square was in fact a sealed packet. I could feel a slim, flimsy object inside. I stood up, forced a hole in the plastic with my finger and tore it open.

There was a letter inside. This one wasn't addressed to me. I didn't have a doubt that it was *the* letter, as the torch beam fell across the face of an airmail envelope. *Mayumi Hashimoto, Golden Rickshaw, 2-10-5 Nihombashi, Chuo-ku, Tokyo, Japan,* was written in a scratchy, looping hand. There were two US five-cent stamps on the envelope, and the postmark: DALLAS, TX, NOV 22, 1963.

I think I knew it all then. As if I'd entered a darkened room and the light had suddenly come on, revealing the cobwebs, thick as a forest, that hung around me. There was fear, like a clutch at the throat. And fascination, like a beckoning finger. I turned the envelope over in my hand. The flap was no longer stuck down. I hesitated, then lifted it.

'Don't do it, Lance.'

Townley's voice, so close to my ear, made me jump with surprise. I whirled round and saw him standing less than a foot away.

'I really do advise you not to.' He held out his hand. 'Give it to me.'

What else could I do? I passed it to him and watched as he slipped a single sheet of paper out of the envelope and held it up to the light.

'Good,' he said, sliding it back into the envelope. 'Secure at last.'

'I want the letter back, please.'

There was a faint widening of his eyes. 'You do, huh?'

'When I see Yamazawa alive and well, I'll hand it over for keeps.'

'If I refuse?'

'I reckon I can kick up enough of a fuss to have you stopped at the gate. I'm sure you don't want that to happen.'

'There are two of us, Lance. We can overpower you any time we like.'

'And I can tell Gordon about our deal any time *I* like. Can you be certain he won't believe me?'

Townley thought about that for a second, then nodded. 'OK.' He handed the letter back to me. 'Keep it until we pick up Yamazawa.'

'Right.'

'Now, let's go.'

OUR DEPARTURE, once Townley had signalled to Ledgister that we had what we'd come for, was swift. We left a bewildered Harris to reseal the container, got into the car and drove away.

'You're sure it's the original?' said Ledgister.

'I'd stake my life on it,' Townley calmly replied.

'That's what you are doing, Stephen. Me too.'

'Lance is keeping it for us until you reunite him with his Japanese friend. But he hasn't read it, I can assure you.'

'Good. Better still for him.'

'And he's not going to ask us any of the questions the date and place it was mailed from have planted in his mind. Are you, Lance?'

'I have no questions,' I said levelly.

'Smart of you.' Ledgister glanced across at me. 'Real smart.'

I HAD QUESTIONS, of course—dozens of them, swarming inside my head. Dallas, Texas, November 22, 1963. One of the most famous dates of the century. The ultimate hit. And the day I was born.

Who had Mayumi known in Dallas? Why was he or she writing to her—that day of all days? The answer was there, nestling in my pocket. Maybe the answer to *all* the questions.

I remembered the photograph from Rupe's briefcase of Townley, Loudon and a third man drinking at the Golden Rickshaw. I remembered it so clearly I could almost have been staring at it closely. At the third man. At the side of his face. A face that would never turn to meet my stare. Because if it did . . .

'MAKE THE CALL.'

We were on the dual carriageway slicing through Dagenham when Townley broke the silence. Ledgister pulled his mobile out of his pocket and jabbed at some numbers with his thumb.

'It's me,' Ledgister growled into the phone. 'Yuh, I know . . . It hasn't been straightforward, but it's OK now . . . We'll be there within a half-hour. Have everything ready. OK? . . . Good.' With that, he rang off. 'That was Carl, Lance. He's looking forward to our arrival. Not as much as Yamazawa is, though, I'll bet. It'll be a sweet parting for all of us. A straight swap. OK by you?'

'Just fine.'

We covered more miles through the grey sprawl of East London.

What would I learn if I pulled the envelope out of my pocket and read the letter? What would I understand about Townley that made him more dangerous than ever? I remembered a night out with Rupe and Simon Yardley at Durham to celebrate my twentieth birthday, back in November 1983. It had been the twentieth anniversary of the Kennedy assassination as well, of course. I remembered arguing with Simon about the hoary old question: did Oswald do it, or was it a conspiracy? Simon had favoured the lone nut theory. Even as a student, he'd been an establishment man. I'd gone for conspiracy, just to annoy him. The truth was that I'd never bothered to study the evidence. But Rupe had. 'There can't be any serious doubt there was a conspiracy,' he'd said, reeling off an army of facts about ballistics and forensics and dead witnesses and God knows what. 'The only question that really counts is: who were the conspirators?'

I glanced over my shoulder at Townley. Neither of us spoke. Then I looked back at the road.

IT WAS A SURPRISE when we left the A13 at Canning Town and pulled over in front of the Underground station. This couldn't be the handover point, I reasoned. It was too public.

'Stephen and I need to have a private word, Lance,' said Ledgister. 'Why don't you step out for a moment?'

'That would probably be best,' agreed Townley.

'But don't go far, hey? Stay where we can see you.'

'OK.' I got out, slammed the door behind me and strolled ten yards or so ahead. When I looked back, Townley was leaning forward between the front seats, watching me and listening as Ledgister spoke. Their private word lasted no more than a couple of minutes, then Townley got out of the car and came to meet me.

'Gordon feels—and I agree—that it would be . . . inadvisable . . . for me to be seen by Madron. Best for me to maintain a low profile. So I'll go on from here by subway and meet up with Gordon later.'

'What about the letter?'

'Surrender it to Gordon when Yamazawa's free. As agreed.'

'You know what I mean.'

'Everything's under control, Lance. Get back in the car.' I almost believed a smile was flickering at the edges of his mouth, but I couldn't be sure. 'You can trust my son-in-law.'

'But—'

'Get back in the car!'

I GOT BACK IN. And watched Townley vanish into the entrance to the Underground station as we drove away. He had apparently consented to an arrangement that could let Ledgister walk away with the letter. It made no sense. Yet I knew that, somehow, it must.

'Not far now,' said Ledgister as we headed down the approach to the Blackwall Tunnel. 'Our business will soon be concluded. And don't worry. It'd be crazy—even if kind of satisfying—to kill you and Yamazawa once I've got the letter. I aim to leave London without a trace that I've ever been here.'

'Don't you mean "Once *we've* got the letter"?'

Ledgister just chuckled. 'Not trying to come between me and my father-in-law, are you, Lance? That's a bad habit of yours.'

He took the first turning off after the tunnel and followed a winding route into the industrial wasteland of North Greenwich. Away to the east I glimpsed the roof of the Millennium Dome. Someone had told me the Dome had revitalised the whole area, but all I saw was a dismal sprawl of disused warehouses and derelict chemical works.

We drove along an alley between a couple of such premises, then turned through a seemingly purpose-cut gap in a security fence into the loading yard of an abandoned depot. Ledgister cut the engine.

'It had to be select accommodation, Lance, seeing as Yamazawa's a friend of yours.'

'Where is he?'

'Patience, patience.' Ledgister gave the horn three short blares. 'We'll soon have you back together. See?'

Carl Madron appeared on the loading platform of the warehouse, raised a hand in acknowledgment, then scuttled back inside.

'Let's get out,' said Ledgister. 'He won't be long.'

We got out of the car and walked slowly round in front of it. A few seconds passed. Then Carl reappeared, this time with Yamazawa. Toshi looked tired and unshaven, but otherwise none the worse for his experience. He hurried down the steps from the loading platform and started across the yard towards us, Carl following.

'I'll take the letter now, Lance,' said Ledgister. 'If you please.'

I took the letter out of my pocket and handed it over.

'Thank you kindly.' Ledgister prised the letter open inside the envelope and peered down at it, as if checking I hadn't removed it earlier. He nodded in satisfaction. 'That's it all right.' He glanced over at Carl. 'Get in the car. We've got what we wanted.'

Carl kept his distance as he moved past me. What sort of deal he'd struck with Ledgister I didn't know, but I doubted there was much of a chance Ledgister would honour it.

Carl got into the passenger seat of the car and slammed the door. That was the cue for Ledgister to pocket the letter. 'Good day, gentlemen. It's been a pleasure doing business with you.' He got in the car, started up, then drove out through the gap in the fence.

'I am in your debt, Lance,' said Yamazawa, smiling wanly. 'Thank you for doing whatever you had to do to free me.'

'No problem,' I said, watching the car pick up speed. 'It was a—'

My voice was drowned in a sudden, deafening roar. Instinctively, I crouched down, squeezing my eyes shut. When I opened them a couple of seconds later, I saw a vast plume of smoke rising beyond the warehouse roof. Fragments of metal and other debris were raining down onto it. Seagulls filled the sky, their screeches of alarm slowly drowning the fading roar.

'What was that?' said Yamazawa.

'It sounded like a bomb.'

'To me also.'

I ran towards the fence, Yamazawa following, and through the gap into the alley. There wasn't much left of the car beyond its wheels. The rest was twisted metal, shattered glass and black smoke fed by hungry flames. Somewhere close to the heart of the fire I could see two dark shapes that had been the driver and his passenger, but were now just melting flesh and charring bone. And the letter in Ledgister's pocket . . . was ash on the breeze.

'TOWNLEY,' I shouted. 'Where are you? Show yourself.'

'What are you saying, Lance?' Yamazawa stared at me, clearly in some doubt about my sanity.

'Isn't it obvious? We've been driving around all morning with a bomb on board. Townley must have followed us from Canning Town somehow and waited until he could get Gordon and Carl in one hit before setting it off. Which means he must be close by.'

I watched and waited. The gulls wheeled and swooped above us. But Townley didn't step obligingly into view. Maybe, I thought, he was already making his escape. Ledgister was dead and the letter destroyed. Townley had finished the job. And now he'd slipped back into the shadows Rupe had stupidly tried to flush him out of.

'If we stay here, Lance,' said Yamazawa, 'the police will find us. They will come soon, I think.'

He was right. We couldn't afford to linger. We had to go.

WE COULD ALREADY hear the wail of approaching sirens when we reached the riverside path and struck south towards Greenwich. I tried to give Yamazawa a coherent account of what had happened, holding nothing back except the chilling suspicion I had about the author of the letter I'd had so briefly in my possession. What use was the suspicion, anyway, now the letter was gone for ever?

'What happens now, Lance?' Yamazawa asked me.

'I was afraid you'd ask me that.'

'Is it over?'

'For Townley it is. He's neatly disposed of a treacherous son-in-law and an incriminating letter. He's in the clear. Which means he won't go after Mayumi and Haruko now.'

'And what about you, Lance?'

'I'd rather not think about that. Not yet.'

We caught a bus heading for Russell Square and sat on the top deck as it trundled west through Rotherhithe. Yamazawa recounted how he'd been abducted—grabbed and bundled into the boot of a car by two men he now knew to be Ledgister and Carl Madron as he wandered down Kingsway on Sunday morning, bound for Hampton Court. After the phone call that they'd forced him to make to the Arundel, he'd been gagged and chained in the derelict warehouse—and convinced that they meant to kill him.

'It was strangely calming, Lance, to know that, if it was going to happen, there was nothing I could do to prevent it. But not knowing *why*—that I did not like. Do you know what the letter was about?'

'Are you sure you want me to tell you?'

'Of course.'

'OK.' I leaned towards him and whispered into his ear. 'The Kennedy assassination.'

His eyes widened. He turned and stared at me. 'Truly?'

'I think so, yeah,' I looked ahead. 'For what that's worth now.'

'DO ME A FAVOUR when you get back to the Arundel, Toshi, will you?' I asked as the bus started across Waterloo Bridge.

'Sure. What is it?'

'Phone your brother. Ask him to tell Mayumi the letter's been destroyed and she and Haruko are safe. They can go back to Tokyo and live in peace.'

'And maybe take on a redundant shipping executive as a washer-up at the Golden Rickshaw?'

'They could do worse. When will you go back to Japan?'

'Soon, I think.'

'I probably won't see you again before you leave.'

'I still don't know what you are going to do, Lance.'

'Maybe that's because I don't know either.'

'Would it help if I wished you luck?'

'It wouldn't do any harm.'

'Good luck then, my friend.'

We parted at the bus stop in Russell Square. Yamazawa headed straight for the Arundel and I took a bus to the Polaris, where I devoted all of five minutes to packing and checking out, then walked across to Paddington Station. On the way, I passed a newspaper stall and couldn't help noticing the headline on the late edition of the *Evening Standard*: CAR BOMB NEAR DOME KILLS TWO. I decided against buying a copy.

I got to the station just in time to catch a train for the West Country. Flooding on Sedgemoor meant I'd have to take a bus from

Taunton to finish my journey. It might be late—it might be very late—when I got where I was going. Not that it really mattered. Because, in so many other ways, it was already far too late.

SOMERSET
NINE

It wasn't, as it turned out, that late when I reached Street. But a wet Monday night in November isn't exactly carnival time, and it might as well have been midnight as the middle of the evening in Hopper Lane. I groped my way through the dripping rhododendrons to the door of Penfrith, and spotted Howard through the sitting-room window, slumped in a chair staring vacantly at the television.

Howard's response to the knocker was to jump like a startled rabbit and run for cover. When the door was opened—by Win—I could see him behind her, peering out from the sitting room.

'Best come in out of the rain, Lancelot,' Win told me.

'Hello, Howard,' I said as I stepped inside. He grinned in return.

'Go back to your programme, Howard,' said Win. 'We'll be in the kitchen.'

Howard slowly turned and did as he'd been told.

'Sorry to call so late,' I said as he vanished from view.

'We've been worried about you.' Win didn't look worried, but then her basic expression—stern and practical—had never encompassed a wide range of emotions.

'There have been problems, Win. Keeping in touch . . . just wasn't possible.'

'Have you any news of Rupert?'

'Yes, I have. Where's Mil?'

'Behind you.'

Mil was indeed standing directly behind me, having presumably come down the stairs without my noticing. 'Lance,' she said simply.

'Hello, Mil.'

'Let's get out of the hall,' said Win. 'It'll be warmer in the kitchen.'

This much was undeniably true, thanks to the range, although that was the full extent of the room's attractions. Washing-up was piled in the sink, the tap dripping percussively into a soiled saucepan.

'Will you have some tea, Lancelot?'

'Yeah. Thanks. Why not?'

'See to that, Mil.'

'Before you do, there's something I've got to tell you. Perhaps you should sit down.'

Both sisters stared at me in a taut moment of silent scrutiny. I took a chair on one side of the table. Win first, then Mil, sat opposite me.

'What have you to tell us, Lancelot?' Win asked.

'Rupe's dead.'

At first, there seemed to be no reaction. They went on staring at me. Then Mil stifled a sob. Tears filled her eyes. Win swallowed hard. For her, tears apparently weren't an option. 'How did it happen?'

'He was murdered. In San Francisco.'

There was another sob from Mil. To my surprise, Win crossed herself and whispered something in Latin. Then she turned to her sister. 'Make the tea, dear.' Calling Mil 'dear' was, I reckoned, as much as she could manage by way of sisterly consolation.

Mil got up and moved to the range.

'I'm sorry,' I said to Win.

'Thank you.' She seemed to remember something important. 'He was your friend as well.'

'He was.'

'Who murdered him?'

'A man called . . . Townley.'

Mil gasped and grabbed the rail of the range. Win looked round sharply at her, then back at me. 'Townley?'

'Stephen Townley. Recognise the name?'

'No.'

'Come on, Win. It's pretty obvious Mil does, even if you don't.'

'Mil knows nothing.'

'*Nothing?*' The word came out of Mil's mouth almost as a wail. There was horror as well as grief in her face. 'How can you say that?'

'Keep your voice down. Do you want Howard in here?'

'I'll keep *my* voice down,' I said levelly. 'You sent me to find your brother. That's what I did.'

'We're grateful.'

'I don't want your gratitude. Going after Rupe got me—and others—into a lot of trouble. He's not the only one to have been murdered. There have been five other deaths, Win. *Five*. Just think about that. I don't blame you. Rupe did the damage. But why? Why did he go after Townley? He was trying to blackmail the man. That's how he came to be murdered. But *why*? What was it really all about?'

'I don't know what you mean.'

'Peter Dalton. It goes back to him, doesn't it?'

'Peter?' gasped Mil.

'Control yourself,' said Win. 'Brew the tea.'

'Forget the tea,' I said. 'Just tell me.'

'This can't have anything to do with . . .'

'I think you know it has. Dalton died in August '63. Officially, he committed suicide. But he was more likely murdered—by Townley. Maybe for money. Train Robbery money? Howard told the police he saw a holdall full of banknotes at Wilderness Farm, a few days before Dalton's death.' I looked up at Mil. 'You knew Peter Dalton pretty well, didn't you, Mil?'

She gaped at me helplessly. 'It was Mum's fault,' she murmured. 'If she hadn't told Rupert—'

'That's enough,' snapped Win. 'Don't say another word.' She was on her feet now, staring at her sister. 'You'll not blame Mother for anything. Hers wasn't the fault, was it?'

'No, Win. I'm sorry.' Mil wiped away her tears with a dishcloth that had been drying on the range. 'It's just . . . so hard.'

'I think you should go upstairs, Mil,' said Win, quietly but firmly. 'I can explain. It'll only upset you more to hear it said.'

Mil bowed her head, replaced the dishcloth on the range, then moved slowly to the door. Just as she was about to leave the room, she stopped and turned to me. 'I'm truly sorry, Lance,' she said, 'for any trouble I've brought you.'

'That's all right, dear,' said Win. 'Leave this to Lancelot and me.'

Mil nodded dolefully and left. Win waited until she saw her sister climbing the stairs, then closed the door, stooped to a low cupboard and got out a dusty bottle of Johnnie Walker whisky. She poured us a couple of fingers each in grimy glasses and sat back down again.

'Rupert tried to blackmail Townley, you say?'

'There was a lot to blackmail him with.'

'More than the Train Robbery?'

'That wasn't the half of it.'

'And Townley killed him?'

'Not personally. But . . . effectively, yes.'

She sighed. 'Mil was right. If Mother hadn't left that letter for him, none of this would have happened. If I'd known what she'd done . . .'

'What letter was this?'

'She lodged it with the solicitor, to be handed to Rupert after her death.'

'What was in it?'

'The family secret. And a shameful one it was, Lancelot. Rupert was Mil's son.'

'What?' I gaped at her in astonishment.

'There it is. I've said it. Yes, my brother Rupert was born to my sister. It's true. Mother thought he had a right to know and feared we would never tell him. So, she decided to ensure that after her death the secret would be revealed to him.'

'How did he react?'

'Like you, he could hardly believe it. There were harsh words. Rupert . . . But there, I couldn't blame him. It was a terrible thing for him to learn. He's never set foot in this house since.'

'I don't understand. How was this kept secret originally?'

'Before Mil began to show, Mother took her away to Bournemouth. We told people Mother was expecting and needed special treatment on account of her age and that Mil had gone to keep her company. They came straight back after Rupert's birth and registered him here as Mother's child. Illegitimacy then was a real scandal. Mil would have been shunned. It seemed best to arrange it as we did. It worried Father, though. Whether he'd have allowed us to go through with it if he'd lived . . . I'm not sure.'

'Did he kill himself because of this, Win?'

'Nobody knows what happened. It wouldn't have helped to think of his death as anything other than an accident.'

'But he was depressed at the time, because of what was planned?'

'Yes. He thought it was wrong.'

'Who was Rupe's father, then? Peter Dalton?'

Win nodded. 'Mother named him in her letter. Rupert made lots of enquiries about him after reading it. He dug it all up.'

'And his investigations led him to believe that his real father had been murdered by Stephen Townley, before he was born.'

Win nodded again. 'If Peter Dalton had been alive and willing to marry Mil when she admitted she was with child, it would all have been different.'

'And Rupe held Townley to blame for that. The man he went after was his father's murderer.'

I thought about that for a moment and felt sorry for Rupe for the first time since setting off in search of him. The woman he'd always thought of as his sister was actually his mother. And the people he'd always thought of as his parents were actually his grandparents. No wonder Rupe had wanted to take revenge for the guilt-riddled chaos of his family relationships. And there was Townley, a deserving target for whatever revenge he could contrive.

'Rupe had a photograph of Townley, taken by Howard. How did he get hold of that, Win?'

'Howard must have given it to him. We drummed it into Howard to keep quiet about what he reckoned he'd seen that summer for fear he'd blurt out something about Mil and Peter. But he may have told his tale to Rupert.'

But how had he got started on Townley's trail? 'Would the letter your mother left for Rupe have told him anything about Townley?'

'I never read it. How can I say? All she would have known about him, from Mil, was that he was an American friend Peter made during his time in the army. She knew precious little about Peter, come to that. There wasn't much she could tell Rupert about him beyond his name. Mil had nothing of his. Except,' Win frowned, 'a small china cat that sits on her bedside table. Peter gave it to her. It's a good-luck charm from Japan.'

'Japan? Peter Dalton had been to Japan?'

'At some point, I suppose.'

Yes, it had to be. That was the connection. Mrs Alder probably had referred to it in her letter. Even so, Rupe wouldn't have made much of the reference at first. Then Eurybia sent him to Tokyo, where he had the opportunity to look for traces of Dalton's army friend. Bingo! At the Golden Rickshaw, haunt of a certain brand of American military man *circa* 1960, he chanced on another photograph of Townley. From that moment on there was no turning back.

'Is it important, Lancelot? Is Townley threatening you?'

'Let's just say I've lived to regret making his acquaintance.'

She didn't ask why. 'Have you seen your parents?'

'Not yet. I thought I'd go round there now.'

'Please give them my regards.'

'Will do.' I glanced up as the clock began to strike nine—the strong, unhurried strikes of a Victorian farmhouse timepiece, probably bought by Win's grandparents. 'I'd better be on my way. They go to bed early these days.'

Win saw me to the door. Howard didn't stir from his chair in front of the television as I passed the sitting room. There was no sign of Mil. I glanced up the stairs, half expecting to see her watching me from the landing, but she wasn't there.

'It's stopped raining,' said Win, as I stepped out into the cool, damp air.

'So it has.'

I heard the door close behind me as I barged my way back through the sodden barrier of rhododendrons. I turned into the lane—and pulled up sharply.

A man was standing directly in front of me—a broadly built figure, raincoated, his face deep in shadow.

'Hi, Lance.'

I recognised his voice, but doubted my recognition. It couldn't be him. Not here. 'Gus Parminter?'

'Got it in one.'

'What the bloody hell—?'

'Am I doing here? Good question.'

'Is Toshi with you?'

'No. Toshi has no idea where I am. I'd checked out of the Arundel by the time he got back there.'

'But . . .'

'I followed you here, Lance. Parminter's not my real name.'

'It isn't?'

'No. Nor's Ventress. But that's the name you know me by.'

If a fissure had opened in the earth beneath my feet, I think I'd have been rather less surprised than I was by the realisation that Yamazawa's laid-back drinking buddy from New Jersey, Gus Parminter, was actually a hired assassin.

'Let's take a walk along the lane. We need to talk, you and me. It looks private enough hereabouts. And like the lady said . . . it's stopped raining.' Gus laid a large, firm hand on my shoulder and turned me round. We started walking, slowly.

'You're . . . Ventress?' I asked, struggling to get the words out. 'Ledgister hired you . . . to kill Hashimoto and Erich?'

'He did. Then Townley hired me . . . to kill Ledgister.'

'You planted the bomb?'

'And set it off. Yuh. Neat work, if I say so myself. I reckoned Yamazawa was bound to lead me to you. And therefore to Ledgister. Townley's instructions were clear. Terminate Ledgister and that low-life he'd taken up with—Madron. Plus destroy the letter. Three birds with one stone. Not bad, hey?'

If he was expecting a compliment, he'd come to the wrong man. But why had he come to me at all? 'What do you want?'

'I want to tell you something very important, Lance. You see, Townley's instructions didn't finish at Ledgister, Madron and the letter. He wants a clean slate. He wants to rule out any possibility of another Rupe Alder disturbing his retirement. He wants the thread Rupe followed cut at the source and wound in. Which means . . .'

We stopped. Staring at him in the pallid gleam of one of Hopper Lane's very few street lamps, I hadn't the slightest doubt as to what he meant. 'You've come here to kill me.'

He nodded. 'Plus the Alders. The brother and the two sisters.'

'Oh my God.'

'A more pious response to the imminence of death than some manage, Lance. I'll give you that. But consider: why am I telling you this? You surely don't think I gave Ledgister any notice of his demise. And you know I didn't give Hashimoto any.'

I swallowed hard. 'Why, then?'

'Because Townley's not the only one who could use a clean slate. I hadn't a clue what Ledgister was getting me into when he hired me. I have now. And to clean the slate I need to close down the whole Townley connection. And I reckon that's best done at the other end.'

'What . . . do you mean?'

'I mean to take Townley out. And you can help me. In return for which, you and your hillbilly friends . . . get extended leases on life.' A glimmer of lamplight told me he was smiling. 'Tell you what. My car's stowed further along the lane. Why don't we go over the details there? I think it could be starting to rain again.' He moved on and I fell in beside him, my thoughts struggling to keep pace.

'Hold on.' A point suddenly struck me. 'I thought you said you followed me here. You can't have done that in a car.'

'An exaggeration, I admit. As soon as you got on the train it was obvious where you were headed. Hertz beats public transport any day. I was here way ahead of you.' (In more ways than one, I was rapidly coming to understand.) 'There's the car.'

A small, dark-painted hatchback was parked on the verge ahead, overhung by trees. Ventress opened the passenger door for me, then went round to the driver's side and got in beside me. 'Hell of a damp climate you got here, Lance. I'm surprised you don't have gills.' He looked round at me. 'I don't mind if you laugh at my joke.'

'Is it compulsory?'

He laughed for me—a deep, rumbling sound of apparently genuine amusement. 'OK. Let's quit horsing around. This is no bedtime story I have to tell you. This is reality. If you saw the letter Townley and Ledgister so badly wanted, you're one up on me. But I made my own enquiries. It pays to watch your back in my line of business. So I asked around and got some disturbing answers. Townley was one of the Dallas boys—the Kennedy hit team, back in '63. I mean, that is hall-of-fame stuff in my profession. But it's not what you'd call enviable status. Was there or wasn't there a conspiracy? People have been debating that all your life and two-thirds of mine. Well, the big problem for conspiracy theorists is that no one's ever held their hand up and said, hey, yeah, I was part of it, and this is what it was and how it went down. Now, why do you suppose that might be, Lance?'

'You tell me. Why hasn't anyone?'

'Because they're already dead. Dead and buried. They all got taken out. Like so many of the witnesses. Culled, to save the herd. The hit men were hit.'

'Except Townley.'

'He saw it coming and had an escape route ready and waiting. We have to figure he was more than a foot soldier. He was on the recruitment side of things in Japan. Hell, he may even have recruited Oswald while the guy was serving there with the Marines. He and Townley certainly knew each other. So when Oswald saw Townley in Dallas the day before Kennedy's visit—I'm guessing now—he realised that Townley was involved in what was going on and decided to warn Mayumi Hashimoto of the danger she might be in after the event, as a mutual acquaintance—or a mutual whatever she was to them. So he wrote her a letter and mailed it on his way into work. Or after the assassination. It doesn't matter. It got mailed. And, because of it, here we are.'

'You believe Townley's escape route involved Great Train Robbery money?'

'It involved money big time. Disappearing's an expensive business. But he'd already set aside his disappearance fund. Peter Dalton was a friend of his who'd got into trading information in the British underworld. I think he may have had Mafia connections. Anyhow, Townley was sent over here in the spring of '63, apparently to sever any embarrassing links between the brewing Profumo scandal and the sensitive parts of US Intelligence that Townley's group had dealings with. Funny how all these things get kind of interconnected. Townley was already looking for vanish money because he'd got wind of what was planned for the fall. Dalton had just picked up some choice dope about trainloads of used banknotes snaking down the country with zero security. Put the two together and what have you got? Motive and means.

'They set the heist up—or they set up the people who set it up. Dalton had recently inherited Wilderness Farm—a handily out-of-the-way place for Townley and him to do the planning and coordinating. Dalton probably trusted him. Big mistake. Townley killed him, set it up to look like suicide, saddlebagged the loot and rode off into the sunset. Three months later, straight after the Kennedy hit, he black-holed his entire life to date.'

'Why not do that right away—in August?'

'I think he believed in the cause. He wanted the conspiracy to succeed and stayed on to do his bit towards ensuring it did. It was an article of faith for him—an expression of his twisted brand of patriotism. There were plenty who thought like him in '63. Getting back in touch with his family years later wasn't so smart, though. Understandable, of course, but risky. Not that it would have mattered—not if Rosa stuck to her story that he was dead—but for your friend Rupe Alder. There's just no factoring-in a guy like that.'

'So how are you going to get to Townley?'

'Easy. I called him while I was waiting for you to show up earlier. I told him things went wrong after the car bombing. I had the cops on my tail. Accordingly, I had to let him down where you and the Alders were concerned and get out of the country in double-quick time. He wasn't happy. He was seriously *un*happy. But he believed it. My panic turn is surprisingly convincing. So what's he going to do? Fly back to San Francisco leaving unfinished business behind him? I don't think so. No, he'll come here. First thing tomorrow, I'd guess. He'll stake out the Alder joint during the afternoon and make his move some time after nightfall. But I'll be waiting.'

'His . . . *move*?'

'The triple hit, Lance. Quadruple, counting you. Get with it, will you? We don't have an infinite amount of time. But we have enough.'

'Enough for what . . . exactly?'

'For you to persuade the Alders to take in a couple of house guests. For the very short duration.'

I SPENT THAT NIGHT closeted in damp and chilly Penfrith, trying to hold the nerves of Win, Mil and Howard together while we waited for what I was only marginally better equipped to anticipate.

Win alone of the three had a clear grasp of the situation we were in. She listened in silence as I explained why putting our trust in Ventress made sense—why, in fact, there was nothing else we could do. 'The police can't protect you from a man like Townley, Win. Ventress really is our best hope.'

'We can't leave here,' she said when I'd finished. 'If trouble must come in Rupert's wake, then we must meet it.' She paused, then ventured, 'Townley killed Rupert, didn't he?'

'Yes.'

'Then why wouldn't I harbour the man who promises to kill Townley? The Old Testament records the ways of our hearts in this, Lancelot. An eye for an eye is a fine balance. I shall speak to Mil and make Howard understand that he's to keep to his room. Then you can bring Mr Ventress in.'

HOWARD, THEN, was dispatched to his bedroom and told to stay upstairs. Mil consented to whatever Win thought best, as was her habit. She was still numb with the shock of learning that Rupe, her secret son, was dead. After fetching some blankets for Ventress and me—we were destined to sleep as best we could in the sitting room—she took herself off to bed.

Win made us cocoa (the supposedly soothing effects of which seemed strangely absent). Then she went to bed, too, leaving Ventress and me to the fusty delights of the sitting room. My cocoa was reinforced by then with a slug of Johnnie Walker. I offered Ventress some, but he declined on professional grounds.

'I don't touch the juice when I'm working, Lance. A steady hand and a clear head are my sword and shield.'

'I thought you said he wouldn't come tonight.'

'He won't. But I'm already in training for when he does.'

Ventress took the armchair, assuring me he'd catnap through the night and be roused by any suspicious noises. 'I sleep light, Lance, and hear like an owl. Which means you can sleep easy. And hear nothing till morning.'

The doors were locked, the windows fastened, and I was happy to take Ventress's razor-sharp reactions on trust. But still his restful prognosis didn't quite do the trick. The lumpiness of the Alders' sofa wasn't really the problem. I was simply too anxious, my thoughts too crowded, for a good night's sleep to be a realistic option.

I nodded off at some point, though, and slept until Ventress woke me with the weight of his hand on my shoulder. Twilight was seeping through the curtains behind him, but a tension in his stance told me that he hadn't come over to ask whether I wanted tea or coffee.

'What's wrong?'

'Nothing major. It's the loony brother. He came down to the kitchen a couple of minutes ago. He's probably just raiding the refrigerator, but why don't you go check? He's likely to take serious fright if I creep up on him.'

'OK.' I struggled up, put my shoes on and headed out into the hall. The kitchen door was closed, but I could hear a squeaking, rattling noise from the other side. What the hell was Howard up to? I grabbed the knob and pushed the door open.

Just in time to see him scrambling out through the open window. The back door was locked, the key lodged in the sitting room. But that hadn't stopped him. He was leaving.

'Howard!' I shouted. 'Wait!'

Wait he did not. He crouched for a fraction of a second on the sill, then jumped out onto the path skirting the house.

I ran to the window and leaned out. His shadowy figure disappeared round the corner of the house. Guessing that he was heading for the lane, I went through the window after him.

The rhododendrons rustled ahead of me. Then I heard the chainwheel of a bicycle revolving.

'Stop, Howard! I have to talk to you.'

Too late. He was on the bike, pedalling hard, when I reached the lane. I ran after him, but he sped ahead, vanishing into the dark overhang of the trees further along the lane. I stopped, panting for breath, and listened for a moment, but Howard was out of hearing as well as sight by now. I turned and hurried back to the house.

The front door opened as I approached. Ventress stood back to let me enter, then closed it behind me. The landing light was on and I saw Win standing at the foot of the stairs.

'Did he take his bike, Lancelot?' she said at once.

'Yeah.'

'I ought to have brought it indoors.'

'Are you saying you anticipated this, ma'am?' There was a hint of irritation in Ventress's voice.

'No. But perhaps I should have done. I didn't tell him Rupert was dead, but if he eavesdropped on us last night . . .'

'Where's he gone?'

'I can't tell. He cycles all around when the mood takes him. He has his favourites, of course, but—'

'What *are* his favourites, Win?' I put in.

'Well, there's . . . Ashcott Heath. Out Wilderness Farm way.'

'We need to pick him up, Lance,' said Ventress. 'Take the car and bring him back. Any way you have to.'

'I should go with you,' said Win. 'He'll listen to me.'

Ventress sighed. 'Of all the cockamamie . . .'

'We have time on our side, Gus,' I reasoned. 'You said so yourself.'

'All right. Take her along. But don't be all morning about it. And try not to attract any attention.'

HOWARD HAD RIDDEN west along Hopper Lane, which was consistent with Wilderness Farm being his destination. I was confident we'd overhaul him in the car, but Win didn't share my confidence.

'He knows all sorts of short cuts and back tracks,' she said. 'You won't be able to drive the route he'll take.'

It was soon obvious that she was right. There was no sign of him along Brooks Road, or out on the A39. If Howard had taken to field paths and secret ways, all we could do was drive to Wilderness and wait for him to turn up.

'How much does Howard understand, Win?' I asked. 'Is it that he simply can't communicate? Or is there nothing to communicate in the first place? I never was sure about that.'

'Howard can't take in new events or new people. But his memories before the accident are clear. So he knows you as Rupert's friend. And he knows Wilderness Farm as the place where Peter Dalton died.'

'Does that mean he'd recognise Stephen Townley?'

'He'd know who Townley was. Whether he'd recognise him after thirty-seven years is doubtful. But if Howard heard us talking about him—'

'He'd have known who we were referring to?'

Win nodded. 'Oh yes. I think so.'

I pulled over at the end of the lane that led to Wilderness Farm. The farm buildings were visible beyond the straggling hedge. Twenty minutes slowly passed. The sky grudgingly lightened. But there was still no sign of Howard.

I turned to look at Win. 'Where else could he have gone?'

'I don't know.' She thought for a moment. 'I'm sure it would be somewhere connected with what's happened.'

'And where might that be?'

'Well, if he was listening to us, he'll have heard us speak of Peter and Mil . . . and Mother . . . and Father.' Win's eyes widened with alarm. 'He might have gone to Cow Bridge. Where he found Father.'

I started the car.

'That was a November day too.'

I DROVE NORTH to Meare, then southeast along the B road to Glastonbury. The bypass looked to be pretty snarled with early rush-hour traffic, so I took the back way round the Abbey to Butleigh Road. It was less than half a mile from the edge of town to Cow Bridge. As I accelerated towards its humped span, Win gasped. 'There's his bike.' She pointed, and I saw it too, propped against the right-hand parapet. It was a bike, certainly, and I was ready to back Win's judgment as to whose it was.

I pulled over just short of the bridge and started to get out, only to recoil smartly as a lorry sped by. Win had already jumped out on her side. I watched as she dodged between the traffic in her haste to reach the bike.

By the time I caught up with her, she was leaning on the parapet scanning the brown, swollen course of the Brue as it swept westwards towards Pomparles Bridge.

'He's gone,' she said, without looking round at me. 'The river's taken him. As it took Father.'

'You can't know that.' Couldn't she? Win knew Howard better than I did. And from where he'd left the bike, directly above the middle of the stream, it would have been a short jump into a long hereafter for any but the strongest of swimmers. And as far as I knew Howard couldn't swim at all. 'Win—'

'I must go back to Penfrith and tell Mil.' She turned away from the river and I saw the frozen certainty on her face. 'There's just the two of us left now.'

THERE WAS NO REASONING with Win in her present mood. We went back to the car and drove towards Street. What would happen when we reached Penfrith, I couldn't summon the strength of mind to imagine. We could hardly continue to lie low in such circumstances.

But what else were we to do? Ventress's trap would be sprung before it was properly set if we contacted the police. Yet I couldn't just abandon Howard to whatever fate had overtaken him.

'Why are you stopping?' challenged Win as I pulled into the lay-by next to a call box a few hundred yards further on.

I didn't bother to answer. I dialled 999 and asked for the police. 'I think a man may have fallen into the Brue near Cow Bridge, on the Butleigh road south of Glastonbury. The river's in spate and—'

'We know the state of the river, sir.'

'Right. Well, search the banks west of the bridge, will you? He's a bit soft in the head. He needs help.'

'You know him, then, do you, sir?'

'Just do something, for God's sake.'

'Where are you—?'

'IT'S NO GOOD,' said Win when I got back into the car. 'Howard's beyond saving.'

'We don't know that.'

'I do. It's plain to me now. When he realised Rupert was dead, he decided to go to Cow Bridge and end it. He knows what he did—and what it led to. There, most of all.'

'There?'

'Where Father died. Howard won't have forgotten his guilt.'

'Howard's guilt? What are you talking about?'

'Not just his. Mil's too. And mine, for letting the lie stand.'

'What do you mean, Win?'

'I should have told Rupert the truth long ago. Then none of this would have happened. Now Howard's gone, too, it can't hurt either of them. Rupert was his son, Lancelot. Howard's son, by his own sister.'

At first, I couldn't grasp what she'd said. Then, when I did, I couldn't believe it. And my disbelief must have been clear to see.

'Mil set her cap at Peter Dalton, but he didn't look twice at her. Howard was jealous even so. And not straight in his thoughts. His feelings ran away with him. He forced himself on her. Mil told me how it had been when she admitted to me that she was carrying his child. But what was she to do? Brand her brother the worst of monsters, when he was only really a butter-brained booby who couldn't control himself? She told Mother and Father that Peter had got her with child because Peter was dead by then and couldn't deny it. She bought the china cat she claimed he'd given her from a gewgaw stall at Glastonbury Market. It seemed to me at the time that it was better to blame Peter than have the truth destroy our family. But I was wrong. After Mother had taken Mil away to Bournemouth, Howard grew anxious and remorseful. Eventually, he confessed what he'd done to Father. I could never tell Father a direct lie. When he asked me what I knew, I told him. That was the night before he drowned. Thirty-seven years ago, almost to the day.'

I stared out through the windscreen. And then I laughed. It was funny, in its way, though God knows I didn't feel amused. In looking for his father's murderer, Rupe had got the wrong man. Not the wrong murderer, of course, but the wrong father.

'There's nothing to laugh at, Lancelot.'

'Isn't there? Let me just check this with you, Win. Your mother told Rupe that Peter Dalton was his father because she thought he had a right to know. But what she told him was actually a lie cooked up by you and Mil to protect Howard.'

'To protect all of us.'

'You didn't do a very good job, then, did you? Your father drowned himself and now you think Howard's done the same. Rupe's dead as well. And you and Mil—along with me, incidentally—are running scared from a ruthless killer.'

Win stared at me, but she said nothing. Not a word. Perhaps, after all, there was nothing left for her to say.

I started the car and pulled out into the traffic.

QUITE WHAT I was going to say to Ventress—quite what I was going to suggest we do about Howard's disappearance—I still had no idea when I parked the car in Hopper Lane. A fatalistic lethargy had settled on my thoughts. As for Win, I couldn't even summon the curiosity to consider what she was thinking.

I opened the front door and she followed me in. I'd vaguely expected Ventress to be waiting for us in the hall, but he wasn't there. Nor was Mil. 'Gus?' I called. There was no answer 'Mil?' Still none. I walked along to the kitchen and pushed the door open.

And there was Ventress, spread-eagled on the floor, with a slack look of surprise on his face, a neat, round bullet hole in the centre of his forehead, and blood on the flagged floor beneath his head. There was no sign of his gun. Then I noticed the cracks radiating from a hole in one of the panes of the window next to the range, at about his standing height. The unhelpful thought came into my mind that he might as well have had a nip of Johnnie Walker in his cocoa after all.

Win was at my shoulder, staring like me at Ventress's corpse. 'Where's Mil?' she murmured, close to my ear.

'Upstairs.'

The voice had come from behind us. We turned to see Stephen Townley standing in the hall, pointing a gun at us. He was wearing jeans and a brown leather jacket. His blue eyes sparkled. He looked younger than when I'd met him in London—he was back in harness.

'I wondered when you'd get back. I'm glad I didn't have to wait too long.'

'What have you done to my sister?' said Win, strangely uncowed by the experience of having a gun trained on her.

'You can go up and see her, Miss Alder. I don't mind. Lance and I have a couple of things to discuss.' He stepped to one side.

With a fleeting glance in my direction, Win moved forward and past him, then started slowly up the stairs.

'Back up, Lance,' said Townley, nodding for me to retreat into the kitchen. I took six paces back until I felt the range rail behind me. 'Good enough.' He moved into the doorway.

'We have nothing to discuss,' I said, surprised by how calm I felt. 'Why don't you just get on with it?'

'There's a case for that. But I'm ahead of schedule. Ahead of Ventress's schedule, for sure. He obviously wasn't expecting me so soon. As for Howard, well, who knows what he was expecting?'

'What do you know about Howard?'

'He made it easy for me, taking an early-morning stroll by a swollen river. Just one push was all it needed.' (Win's feeling was right, then, but her conclusion wrong.) 'So now, while Win says a few prayers over her departed sister—pending their early reunion—I want to know, Lance: what was this about? Why did Rupe come gunning for me?'

'It was a mistake.'

'A mistake?'

'Yeah. He thought you'd killed his father.'

'I never even knew his father.'

'Like I say: a mistake.'

'A pretty goddamn far-reaching one. Where's the photograph?'

'Photograph?'

'You know the one. Rupe's snapshot of the picture of Miller Loudon and me at the Golden Rickshaw.'

'Of you and Miller *and* Lee Harvey Oswald, you mean?'

'Where is it, Lance?' (In my bag was the simple answer.) 'It's a loose end I really do need to tie up.'

'I don't know what you're talking about.'

'I'll find it anyway.'

'And you'll kill me anyway too, won't you? So, why should I do you any favours?'

'Because there's a difference between dying—and dying slow.'

The barrel of the gun dropped fractionally as he fired. There was a flash of heat and pain in my left knee. Then I was on the cold floor, my head resting against one of Ventress's legs. A jolt of something way beyond the dictionary definition of agony hit my brain. I grabbed at my knee and felt a mess of smashed bone and torn flesh that I could hardly believe was part of me.

Townley loomed into view. 'Tell me where the photograph is and I'll make it quick, Lance. That's a solemn promise.'

I wanted to tell him then. I really did. But something stopped me—some low, lurking perversity that wouldn't let me give him everything he wanted. 'A solemn promise, from you?' I gasped. 'Is that meant to be a . . . joke?'

'Have it your way.'

He aimed the gun. I closed my eyes. There was an echoing roar of noise. But the extra pain never came. I opened my eyes.

To see Townley's toppling figure hit the range and slide down to rest against its base. The right rear side of his head was missing.

I looked across to the doorway and saw Win slowly lowering a rifle, the barrel smoking faintly. The weapon must have belonged to her father. I'd once seen her shooting rabbits with it. The memory only returned to me as I lay there, staring woozily up at her. Rupe and I had watched her from the top of Ivythorn Hill, bagging bunnies for the pot in a field below Teazle Wood. When would that have been? 1974 or '75. Some time around then.

'She's a good shot, your sister, isn't she?' I'd said.

'You bet,' Rupe had replied, smiling. 'Never misses.'

ROBERT GODDARD

The South Sea Bubble, the Spanish Civil War and now the Great Train Robbery, are just some of the history-making events that Robert Goddard has turned into page-turning mysteries during his impressive fifteen-year writing career. And so skilfully does he weave fact with fiction that readers are usually left wondering where does one end and the other begin. It's a response the author relishes. 'I do try to convince my readers that everything in my books could be real,' he says.

It is often the question marks surrounding historical events that inspire Goddard, who is a Cambridge history graduate, the most. 'There are so many puzzles in the past that when I'm writing a new book all I have to do is invent a plausible explanation for what might have happened.' For *Dying to Tell*, Goddard looked at the loose ends surrounding the Great Train Robbery of 1963. 'I read all the memoirs and accounts of the robbery that I could get hold of, and so many contradictions and mysteries still remain.'

Weaving those contradictions and mysteries into best-selling mysteries seems to come effortlessly to Goddard, but he reckons he has been practising the skill since childhood. He regularly used to read local newspaper articles aloud to his grandmother and, much to her delight, make up the endings in an effort to 'spice them up a little. But I never suspected that I would be able to make a career out of my habit of fantasising and making up plots,' Goddard adds.

With the help of his wife, Vaunda, Goddard researches his stories meticulously, drawing on all kinds of sources, including photographs and maps, in his efforts to make his books as authentic as possible. Vaunda also helps by transcribing Goddard's longhand scripts onto a computer, line-editing as she does so. It's a working relationship they both enjoy. 'It's good to have someone to discuss the books with,' the author says, 'because writing can be such a solitary business.'

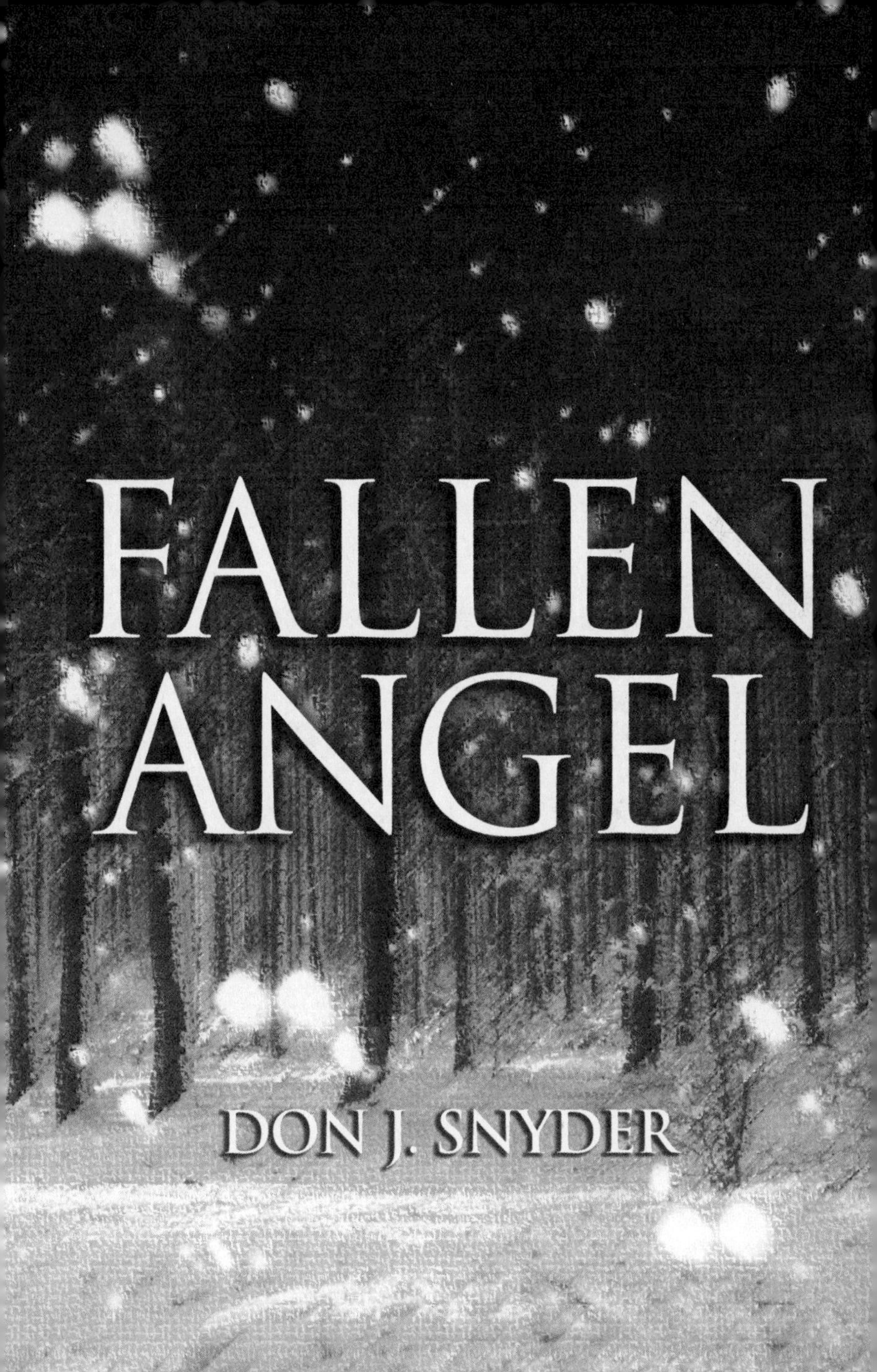
FALLEN
ANGEL
DON J. SNYDER

As he looks around his father's workshop, trying to come to terms with the old man's death, Terry McQuinn finds a note that stirs up very mixed emotions: Open 'Serenity' for Christmas. Thirty years ago, the two of them had opened up the Halworths' house together, eagerly awaiting the arrival of the owners and Katherine, their little girl. But that was before the tragic accident that left the house shrouded in darkness.

Now, thirty years later, Katherine wants to return.

PROLOGUE

This is always with me now. The way I saw her that first morning as she came up from the shore, across the ice-glazed granite rocks that stood at the opening of the harbour. A long blue denim dress. Dark hair, black as ink, in a thick braid lying across her left shoulder. She was holding the hand of a small child in a green cloth coat. They were both wearing silly red puddle boots, so inappropriate for a winter day in Maine. There was a yellow dog running out ahead of them. Or was it later, at the cottage, where I first saw the dog?

This is the difficulty I am up against, trying to recall her precisely as I first saw her, just the plain and exquisite portrait of her when she was still a stranger to me. Her shape, a few brush strokes outlined against the bruised, winter sky behind her, before I knew the thousand things I would come to learn about her. When I go back and stand alone in the emptiness before she entered my life, I see that I was a blind man. Blind to the mystery that surrounds us. Blind to the holiness of this world, to the way the wind collects our voices then scatters them across the open fields of memory and time. Maybe you were standing beside me that first morning in the ordinary light of the vanishing stars, when she was still distinct and separate from the story she gave to me, and I am giving to you now.

There is a deep loneliness in life that can take our breath away and leave us weary. I saw the loneliness in her and could tell that she had come a long way to that shore in Maine. Didn't I see her weariness right away that morning? The way her shoulders were pitched forward slightly in her jacket. And before she turned and walked away down the snow-covered lane, still holding the child's hand, she leaned against a fence post and bowed her head and I was struck by her weariness.

But beyond that, what could a blind man have known then? That we are made whole by our fears and desires? That the passage of time is indifferent to our dreams? If you were standing there would you have seen that she and I, in our separate ways, held the broken ends of an old story, and that we had come together in those cold winter days in Maine, drawn out from our dark history, free to finally join the broken ends together?

CHAPTER ONE

I was eight years old the year our story began, just a boy, but I can place its beginning in the moment my father came to pick me up from Mrs Fisher's third-grade class. I looked up from my desk and there he was, standing in the doorway of the classroom in his royal-blue carpenter's overalls that zipped up from the knees to his chin. I had never seen my father in my school before.

The school was calling parents to come and collect their kids that morning. My mother must have taken the call and then reached my father over the two-way radio in his pick-up truck, or on the telephone in his workshop.

I was holding his hand. His boots, I remember, were caked with mud and we were leaving a trail along the glassy corridor. When we passed the principal's office she was standing at her window with her head bowed, crying. I remember her shoulders were shaking, and I was still thinking about this when my father lifted me into his truck and said, 'The President's been shot, Terry, everybody's going home.'

For the next week we ate supper in the living room on TV trays, watching the evening news. In those days my father kept some of his carpenter's tools in a honey-coloured wooden chest in the kitchen next to the copper boiler. The chest was a perfect cube, three feet long by three feet wide by three feet deep, with little trapdoors and secret compartments and folding shelves. Lift the lid and you found a crosscut saw and a coping saw fastened by bronzed wing nuts to the other side. A bevel with a mahogany handle in a vertical drawer. A set of flat files lined up by ascending heights. That week, when there was so much sadness and my mother kept crying in front of the TV in her curlers, I daydreamed of being inside my father's big tool chest, stretching out against a bronze level, resting my head in the curved hemlock handle of a block plane.

You remember the picture on television that November of John John saluting his father's coffin? I think that picture was the reason my father began taking me to work with him on the days I wasn't in school. He'd never taken me with him before, and I came to believe that my father's way of coping with the President's death was to pull me closer to him.

On the way to work we would stop at Bridie's Hardware in Oak Hill for whatever supplies my father needed. It would still be dark when we loaded our supplies into the back of the truck and drove down to the end of the Blackpoint Road, where the town of Ellsworth turned into Rose Point. There was an electric gate my father opened with a key, and beyond the gate a world you couldn't really believe even when you were there. A high promontory of open fields and meadows set just back from the ocean, surrounded by giant fir trees, lime-coloured bluffs that looked out over a mile-long strand of beach, and twenty-two cottages hidden along narrow gravel lanes. Designed by the famous Indiana architect, Leslie Woodhead, and built at the turn of the century by Pennsylvania steel and oil barons, these cottages were mansions really, sprawling four-storey places, timber-framed and cedar-shingled, with turrets and gabled roofs and screened balconies that faced the sea.

It was one of Maine's private colonies, a summer place that was abandoned to the care of my father during the off season. He had keys to each house, and the owners employed him to repair the damage done by the fierce storms that battered Rose Point all winter. Beside the thirteenth green of the golf course, he had a small workshop where he kept his tools and, in a set of pigeon-hole boxes salvaged from the old summer post office when it was remodelled, the keys to each house under a named slot. This was one rule of Rose Point, that each proprietor must name his house and print this name in discrete black letters on a rectangular oak board, which my father varnished every spring and hung from the front-porch eaves. *Northwinds. The Ark. Fair Haven. Kettle Cove.* I suppose the idea was that a name on your house could make you feel less temporary about yourself.

I went inside all the houses with my father that winter. In *Long Rest* there was a photograph of the owner standing beside President Eisenhower. The chandeliers in *Homeward* came from the Spanish ocean liner *Queen Isadora*, when she was decommissioned at the turn of the century. In the marble-floored entrance hall of *Last Light*, Clark Gable once greeted evening guests. In *Maine Stay* my father once filled all five claw-footed bathtubs with bottles of champagne and ice before a party. The back yard of *Right Way* had been transformed into a miniature replica of Yankee Stadium, with every detail, including the dugouts and outfield walls, built to scale. For twenty-nine years my father cut the infield grass wearing soft leather slippers and using a lawn mower with wheels he had covered with felt.

From Memorial Day in May until Columbus Day in October, the lanes at Rose Point were swarming with summer people from far away. Sailing was their main activity; each house had a boat, and regattas were held four times a week. Following an old tradition, the skippers sailed in dark blue double-breasted coats with gold buttons and striped ties. Evening lectures were held in the stone library, and picnic lunches at the beach house.

After Columbus Day weekend my father locked up the houses for the long winter. He drained the pipes and shut off the electricity and capped the chimneys. He covered the furniture in white sheets. And then in the spring these chores were reversed. Putting the cottages to bed and then waking them up was how my father described this. He preferred the winter, when he had free run of the Point and could come and go like a proprietor. When the summer people were there, he was just hired help and he had to use the servants' entrances and do his work without being seen or heard.

THAT WINTER of 1963, two weeks before Christmas, my father got word that he was to open the *Serenity* cottage. He told my mother and me about it at dinner one night.

'Backward,' he said. 'No heat. Pipes will freeze. Rich people are silly sometimes.'

'Not only rich people,' my mother reminded him.

He didn't acknowledge her. 'But if they want me to open the place, I'll open it.'

My father was a man who hurried through life, leaving behind him the doubters of the world, the cautious and the circumspect. He was the only man I ever knew to wrap his legs outside the rungs of ladders and slide down full speed, stopping himself just before he hit the ground. And so I have remembered clearly how we entered the cottage without making a sound, my father *so careful*, using both hands to ease the door closed behind us. We followed his flashlight and walked slowly from room to room. Slowly and silently, with reverence, the way you would walk through an empty church.

Inside the cottage it was as dark and cold as a cave. In the library, my father ran his hand along the spines of a row of books, centring them on the shelf. He stepped back from a painting in the dining room to make sure that it was straight on the wall. Because he never took even a passing interest in the appointments of his own house, where he often tracked a trail of mud and sawdust, the time I spent with my father at Rose Point taught me that a certain dignity attends the work we do to earn our living.

It took two days to fill every room with light. There were more than seventy windows and doors, each covered with a sheet of plywood, fastened with screws in all four corners. My father had to climb a ladder to reach the windows on the upper floors. I stood at the bottom, holding the ladder for him and watching the soles of his boots move up and down above my head. It was so cold we had to stop every hour and sit in my father's truck with the heater roaring. After we finished the last window and went back inside and stood in the lighted rooms, it was as if music had been turned on inside the cottage.

Because the cottages were so close to the ocean, none of them had basements. Beneath *Serenity* there was a crawl space in the earth. I held the flashlight for my father while he dragged in bales of hay to insulate the water pipes. He built a box round the water pump and wired a light bulb inside it to keep the pump from freezing.

On the fourth or fifth day we made one last trip to Bridie's Hardware after the owner of *Serenity* had called my father, instructing him to build a skating rink in the front yard. 'That takes the cake, Paul, if you ask me,' Bridie said to my father.

We bought a tarpaulin and put the plough on my father's truck to clear away a square in the deep snow. We laid the tarp down in the square and hammered two-by-sixes into the frozen ground around the border. That night my father hooked up a hose and let water trickle onto the canvas. By morning the ice was an inch thick and smooth as glass. Years later I learned that the owner of the cottage had been an All-American hockey player at Harvard, and captain of the United States Olympic team that competed in Innsbruck, Austria.

The last thing we did in the cottage before the owner arrived with his family was bring in Christmas trees for the three living rooms and the library on the ground floor and one for the glassed-in widow's walk on the ridge of the roof. This one we decorated with coloured lights. The moment we plugged it in, a stillness fell over us. I saw a look of wonder on my father's face, the way an artist might gaze upon a finished painting that turned out to be more beautiful than anything he ever believed he could paint. My father turned me towards the glass windows and pointed to the black ocean. He told me that there were ships out there in the darkness and men on board who would see the lighted tree. 'You never know, son,' he said, 'this may help some poor soul find his way home.'

THREE DAYS before Christmas, a northeaster began tracking across the Atlantic, on gale-force winds from Nova Scotia, that drove temperatures along the Maine coast to twenty-five below zero. My father worked forty-eight-hour shifts helping lobstermen haul their boats out of the cove before their wooden hulls were crushed.

When the Maine turnpike was closed to traffic late in the afternoon of the 23rd, my father said he was sure that the Halworths wouldn't be able to make the trip, and that all our work had been for nothing. But on Christmas Eve morning word came that Mr Halworth had hired a man with a truck and a plough in Kittery for an escort, and they were driving up Old Route 1 through the storm. I remember my father staring out of the window at the blowing snow after he hung up the telephone. 'Someone should tell them to turn back,' my mother said. 'Don't they have a child with them?'

'How do you tell a rich man he can't do something?' my father said. 'You know these people.'

He was in the hall, ready to go to the Point, when he stopped and asked me if I wanted to come along with him.

'You'll be careful?' my mother said.

He opened the front door and didn't look back.

IT TOOK US OVER an hour to drive seven miles. Every few minutes the windscreen wipers iced up and my father had to climb out of the truck and clean them off.

After we passed through the electric gate at the entrance to the Point, my father told me to move closer to him. We dropped the plough and he held me back against the seat as he gunned the engine. All the way down Winslow Homer Lane the tall cedar trees were bending low in the wind, and the mansions kept appearing and then dissolving in the blowing snow. At *Serenity* cottage we ploughed the driveway open, and then shovelled a path to the front porch.

Inside we turned on all the lights and laid in newspaper, kindling and logs in all seven fireplaces. I remember opening the refrigerator and being shocked to find its shelves stocked with food. My father always waited in his truck in the parking lot of the supermarket when my mother went grocery shopping. He'd always claimed that the displays of food made him dizzy. I couldn't imagine how he had known what to buy for a family he knew so little about.

We were halfway down Winslow Homer Lane, heading home, when my father remembered one more thing he wanted to do. He found his way to the skating rink and ploughed off the snow, our tyres sliding sideways.

SHORTLY BEFORE NOON we returned home. I was watching *Lassie* on television when Sheriff Kane came by in his cruiser with Christmas presents for us: a bottle of Scotch for my father, a box of chocolates for my mother, and for me a small box that my father told me to put under the Christmas tree. The year before, Sheriff Kane had presented me with a real deputy badge, and I was dying to see what he'd brought me this year.

'Let him open it now,' my mother said.

'Sure, why not?' the sheriff agreed.

It was a container about the size of a cigarette box. One half held an ink pad and little sheets of onionskin paper. The other side, white powder and a small brush. The sheriff waited until I figured it out.

'A fingerprinting set,' I said.

He knew how pleased I was. 'That's no toy, Terry,' he said to me as I was examining it. 'That's the real McCoy, the same little number that my deputies and me keep at the station.'

I was so thrilled with it that I brought it with me when my father and I returned to the *Serenity* cottage late in the day. Charles Halworth, a tall man with wide shoulders, made a big deal out of it when he saw it in my hand. 'Well, that *is* something,' he said. There was a kind of melody in his voice that matched the quick, graceful way he moved. He had his daughter on his shoulders when he knelt down in front of me and held his hand out. 'Do me the honours, won't you?' he said. I looked at my father, who stood off a little way with his hat in his hand. Then I took Mr Halworth's fingerprints while his daughter looked down silently at me.

'Thanks,' he said, giving me his other hand to shake. 'Now, if I ever get lost you'll be able to track me down.'

I was drawn to the man the way children are always drawn to those rare adults who do not condescend to them. His wife, on the other hand, was busy in the kitchen and didn't pay any attention to us.

'Say, here's the reason I called you over,' Mr Halworth said as he led us upstairs. He told my father that his wife had lost a diamond earring two summers before in the cracks between the wide pine floorboards in one of the bedrooms. 'All the way up this morning I had a feeling I was going to find it, and the minute I stepped into the room—bingo!' he said enthusiastically. 'See, look right down here.'

He needed my father to prise up a board so he could retrieve it.

My father went to his truck to get a hammer. While he worked on the floorboard I knelt beside him, and we looked at each other when we heard Mrs Halworth raising her voice about something in another room. 'Not *that* again,' I heard her say. A door was slammed a moment later and the cottage seemed to fill with a sadness that remained even after Mr Halworth appeared in the doorway dressed in a Santa Claus outfit.

I was so surprised that what happened next seemed oddly disconnected from me. There was my father handing Mr Halworth the diamond earring. And Mr Halworth telling us how he had a tradition of making an appearance as Santa Claus in the children's hospital near their winter home every Christmas Eve. And Mrs Halworth commenting that her husband had spent most of his adult life apologising for being wealthy. And my father agreeing to let me ride to the Maine Medical Center in Portland with Mr Halworth and his daughter. In this regard my father was reluctant.

'I'll bring him home straight away,' Mr Halworth declared.

I saw him place some money in my father's hand, though my father tried to conceal it from me.

THEN WE WERE RIDING through the snowstorm in Mr Halworth's big Cadillac. Me in the back seat with his daughter, too scared to speak.

We spent almost an hour in a toy store in Cape Elizabeth, where everything was made by hand, going up and down the aisles with shopping baskets and store clerks helping us. 'Two of those!' he exclaimed. 'Three of these!'

So much snow had fallen by the time we reached the city that half the streets were closed and it was like driving through a maze to find our way to the hospital. At one intersection a car had slammed into a telephone pole.

Mr Halworth rolled down his window and his face grew tense as we passed the wrecked car.

'I'll get us home in just a few minutes,' he said, as if he was reassuring himself.

By the time we had parked and walked to the front doors of the hospital, he had recovered his excitement. He practically danced by the security guards at the main entrance.

In the children's cancer ward he decorated the kids' noses with whipped cream, while his daughter and I passed out gifts. In one room, where the children were too sick to get out of bed, he knelt down beside each of them and whispered something. He gave a kite to a boy whose face was as white as paper. And ballet shoes to a girl with a swollen head and a rubber hose running from one ear.

When we left, nurses and patients were dancing in our wake. Even after the elevator doors closed I could hear them calling 'Merry Christmas' to us.

The snow had changed to sleet, coating the streets and the car's windscreen with ice. The defroster was blowing at top speed when we pulled out of the parking lot. 'Homeward bound,' Mr Halworth said, reaching back over the seat and patting his daughter's knee. 'You look like a young man who knows how to ice-skate. Am I right?' he asked me.

'I've never skated,' I replied.

'Never skated? What do you think of that, Katie?' he exclaimed, turning to smile at his daughter. She smiled back at him, glanced at me, then quickly turned away. 'Tomorrow Katie and I are going to get you up on skates,' Mr Halworth said.

It was dark by now. You could barely see anything through the car windows. When we turned onto State Street, which was a steep hill running all the way down to the entrance to the highway, Mr Halworth rolled his window down and stuck his head out to see what was ahead of us. I could see the lighted sign of the Acme supermarket through his open window, and it was only after the sign began spinning that I realised we were going sideways down the hill. 'Oh God,' I heard Mr Halworth exclaim. He began pumping the brake pedal as we picked up speed. He was hunched over the dashboard, stomping harder on the brake, when a mailbox crashed through the window next to his daughter. She screamed and he jerked the steering wheel hard to the right, and then the left. A second later we hit something and his arms flew up in the air. There was a jangling sound, like we were dragging a chain, just before we crashed into a snowbank.

We had barely stopped moving when Mr Halworth threw open his door and jumped out of the car. For an instant he stood perfectly still, and then he ran beyond the car. I looked over the front seat and saw him drop down to his knees as if something had knocked him off his feet. I could see only the top of his red Santa Claus hat, which suddenly seemed silly and worthy of Mrs Halworth's scorn.

I remember trying not to be afraid and not daring to look at Katie for fear that she might be crying. I looked down at the floor, which was dark except for a narrow band of light that fell through the open car door.

When I looked up again, Mr Halworth's red cap was gone. There was no sign of him. I wondered if his daughter had watched him disappear and I turned to look at her. Her eyes were wide open and her head was bowed. She was staring at her shoes. They were shiny shoes, reflecting a streetlight behind us, and she was holding them up off the floor, staring hard at them. I saw at once that one of her shoes had slipped off her heel and was balancing from her toes. She was trying not to move her foot. I looked into her eyes again and saw how determined she was to keep the shoe from falling off. As if we were from different parts of the world and shared no common language, we sat in silence.

In minutes there were police cars and an ambulance with their lights flashing. Except for a fireman who stuck his head inside the car and looked surprised, no one paid any attention to us. We sat there long enough for me to begin to feel responsible for Mr Halworth's daughter. At last I moved close enough to her to reach down and slide the shoe back on her foot. Her heel was cold in the palm of my hand.

Eventually Sheriff Kane took us to his cruiser and told us that he was going to drive us home. 'Where's my daddy?' Katie asked him.

'He'll be home soon,' the sheriff told her.

I didn't know that we had hit someone until it came over Sheriff Kane's radio.

When we pulled up to the cottage, Mrs Halworth was standing on the porch in a long fur coat. My father was in his truck at the end of the driveway and the light went on when he opened the door. He called me over and I got in. He started the truck as soon as the sheriff led the little girl and her mother inside the house.

My father backed out into the lane. I wanted in the worst way to stay there. I didn't know why, I just wanted to stay until Mr Halworth came back.

THOUGH I HAD been riding in the car, I was one of the last people in town to learn what had happened. 'It's one of those things,' my father said to me when he explained that Mr Halworth's car had struck and killed a woman and her baby. 'An accident. No one is to blame.'

It was my mother who finally told me that Mr Halworth had disappeared. 'He's probably still in shock. They'll find him,' she said.

Christmas Day the city newspaper reported the details on the front page. My father had been wrong; the woman's baby was still alive, in a coma at the Catholic hospital, where the chaplain had begun a prayer vigil. For several days there were reports on television of the baby's condition and of prayer groups organised across the city. This was all everyone was talking about in our town. It seemed to capture people just as the President's assassination had.

I was in my bedroom, dressing for school on the first day back after vacation, when my father told me he didn't want me saying anything about the accident to the kids at school. 'It's better that way. Do you understand?'

I told him I did, but I didn't. 'What's going to happen to the man?' I asked him.

'Nothing,' he said.

'But where is he now?' I asked, hoping the way a child hopes that he was back with his daughter and her mother.

'He turned himself in,' my father said. 'There are no charges against him. He's not in any trouble.'

So he *had* come back, just as my mother had said he would. This gave me reason to believe that everything would turn out all right.

The baby lived another week. In the newspaper there were pictures of the funeral, too sad to look at really. And then more sad news that winter when my father told us that there was going to be a divorce between Mr and Mrs Halworth and that she had sent a crew of men to clean out the cottage and ordered my father to close it up.

IT WAS SPRING and the story had faded away by the time I had the chance to see the cottage again. My father was working down the lane at another place, putting in underground hoses for a sprinkler system. He wasn't paying any attention to me and I just walked away.

There were flowers blooming in the front gardens at *Serenity* and the lawn was freshly cut. But sheets of plywood, painted grey, covered all the windows and doors. That sad contrast between the bright flowers and the dull grey boards meant even more to me as I grew older and observed the same contrast between my mother's persistent attempts to please my father and his growing indifference. She brought the light into our world and he turned his back to it.

CHAPTER TWO

I moved to California. Los Angeles, which is, in every respect, as far from Maine as you can get. And that was my intention: to put as much distance between myself and my old man as I could. I think about this when I make my way out to Santa Monica beach at sunrise each morning. I think about how we get lost in this life, and then how we find ourselves again. We make plans, take vows, believing what we need to believe in order to keep marching. And then, without thinking, we turn slightly and suddenly there it is, the real story of our life, what we will be remembered for, and what we will remember most vividly at the end. I'm forty years old now, you might say old enough to know better. But I still hold on stubbornly to the belief that our lives are more about fate than accommodation.

Having said that, here's my confession: on the lookout for fate to take hold of me, I spent a lot of time waiting for my life to begin. Time I won't ever get back.

ONE MORNING, as I passed through the dawn haze along the shore, I was having a difficult time hearing the sea above the dull, persistent roll call of names that was drumming inside my head: *Tom Cruise.*

Tom Hanks. Tom Petty. Tom, Dick and Harry. Just names to me. The names I drop at parties and in restaurants. Names that The Company represents and that I spend my days promoting.

I found my way to The Company ten years ago. It was a long road. I was a banker in St Paul. A fundraiser in Des Moines. A systems analyst in Chicago. I sold time-share vacations on the western shore of Lake Michigan, persuading people to swear their faith in an unknown future. I spent another five years as a book scout in Manhattan, putting together million-dollar deals for studios on the West Coast. Then this head-hunter showed up at my office and offered me five times as much money doing pretty much the same thing in Hollywood.

It's the kind of work that can take over your life, and that morning, as I walked past the scenic overlook at Ramsdale Point, I was surprised to see a Christmas tree in a coffee-shop window. It could have been Easter or Halloween as far as I knew. I had long ago become disconnected from the seasons. Or, to be more precise, once I joined the legions of men and women for whom time is money, every day of the week became the same to me.

I didn't give it another thought that morning at the office. Christmas, I mean. But late in the afternoon, Peter Billings asked me if I wanted to join him and a few of the other guys on a Christmas skiing trip to the French Alps. We were pumping away on the Nautilus in a mirrored room at The Club on Bishop Street, trying to hear each other above some piped-in top forties hit by Cher.

'Who else is going?' I asked him.

'Meaning, for chicks?' he said. 'Five hot ones from the Merrill Lynch typing pool.'

'They still have typing pools?'

Billings finished ten reps at the bench press, then stood in front of the mirrors pushing his thinning hair over his bald spot. 'If I died tomorrow,' he said suddenly, 'who would give a damn that I've spent most of my youth filling the pockets of meat-eating producers with trophy girlfriends? I mean, what's it all worth, anyway?'

Just turned thirty, I said to myself. A few hairs on his pillow in the mornings and the big questions begin to roll in like dark clouds.

Then he turned to me and asked what I would do for Christmas if I didn't go skiing in the Alps.

'Work,' I said.

Later, as I drove down Beverly Boulevard, Bing Crosby was singing

'White Christmas' on the radio. At the Myrna Loy building on the Sony lot in Culver City, I dropped off a pair of silver high heels left at my place by a woman I'd stopped dating, then headed home.

A DEAL CAN GO down at any time. A few years back I closed a $40-million feature with Overland Films in the middle of an earthquake. At home that night I took a shower, got out of one suit and into another, and returned a call to Max Anaman at Boulevard Pictures.

I had already burned up more than an hour that morning pitching a script to Max. He was one of those guys who had seventeen ways to say no without saying no. I was listening to him talk and checking to see if there was anything decent on at the cinema tonight, when the call-waiting began beeping.

'Max, I need to take another call,' I said. 'Can I get back to you?'

'Take your call; I'm going bowling,' he said.

Before I tell you what happened next, I should explain why I hadn't heard my father's voice in ten years. But such a thing can't really be explained. Ten years before, my mother passed away. I flew home for the funeral, and, rather than sleep one night in the same house or the same town or the same state as my father, I drove back to the airport and spent the rest of the night waiting at the gate.

We split up because of money, I think. Money and pride. As I grew up I began to see that my old man really had no life of his own, and he deprived my mother of a life as well. He closed the door on every possibility for her and resented her for asking. He called himself a caretaker at Rose Point, but for giving every day of his life to the rich summer people, I called him a servant. Once to his face. And when he took a swing at me for it, I stepped back and then caught him on the chin with a punch that knocked him over the foot of my bed. After that, there was no turning back for either of us. The months turned into years, and then I said goodbye to my mother.

Tonight it was my father on call-waiting. 'I've got my doctor here,' he said. 'He wants to talk to you.'

That was it. I could have hung up.

'Your father's in the hospital,' the doctor told me. 'I don't think he's going to make it.'

TWO HOURS LATER I was on the red-eye flight, drinking a vodka tonic and remembering my trip home to Maine when my mother was in the final stages of cancer. I had spent the last hours of her life in a chair by her bed. Exhausted from the trip, I had nodded off, and to my surprise she woke me up and asked me to come closer. She patted my head and said, 'My boy, my boy.' I looked into her bloodshot eyes and knew in that instant that I was one of those sons who had made a far better boy than a man.

Tonight, as the plane rose into the night sky, I started making phone calls to cover for my absence the next day. The in-flight movie was one I'd packaged seven years ago, and knowing the people who were stabbed in the back to get the film made took the fun out of it for me.

I looked around at the other first-class passengers and I wondered, as I often do, how many of these people had become prosperous on their own, the way I had. It's one of the hazards of a competitive life like mine, this kind of measuring, and it always leaves me feeling anxious. But I can't help it; it means a lot to me that I worked my way to the top without the benefit of a trust fund or a helping hand. I earned my way through Brown University playing football. I've got screws in one ankle to show for it. I fought my way to the top. And what does it say about me that I still draw some kind of cold consolation from it?

Some men take satisfaction, I suppose, in becoming more successful than their fathers were. What I wanted was to reach a point where I could afford to *hire* my father *to work for me* if I wanted. And those rich summer people from my boyhood? I was still trying to measure up to them. Which is why I paid a lot of money to fill my driveway in Beverly Hills with crushed seashells the way the cottage driveways are at Rose Point.

AT THE AIRPORT in Boston I bought a newspaper, had my shoes shined, and waited for a small commuter plane to take me the rest of the way to Portland. When the plane was ready for boarding I dropped my ticket in a trash can. It just came over me that I didn't want to get there that quickly. I needed time to think. I rented a car and drove north on Route 1. It was cold, that relentless New England cold that makes your bones feel brittle.

I had just crossed the New Hampshire state line into Maine when I realised that I couldn't picture my old man. His face had vanished from my consciousness.

I took Mud River Road through Biddeford (the long way), and when the medical centre appeared up ahead I turned off onto the shoulder and sat there. I wondered if anyone ever succeeds in outrunning his past. One of the few remaining miracles about America is that you can start a new life in the blink of an eye. We don't even have to say goodbye to our neighbours, because we never knew them. And we won't be homesick, because in the new place there will be an identical strip mall with Big Macs and office supplies from Staples to make us feel safe.

ON THE WAY to the hospital I stopped at a grocery store and bought a tin of cashews. That was the only thing I could ever give my old man. Cashews on his birthday. Cashews on Father's Day, and Christmas. He was a neat man, meaning he hated clutter, and I think a gift of cashews was perfect because he could eat them and throw the tin away, and that would be that. No trace of his son's gift, no awful neckties or ceramic ashtrays to hold on to until his child went off to college.

A heavyset woman at the visitor's desk went down a list of patients' names. She lost her smile and told me it would take another minute. She made a call and, just as she finished telling me that it looked like we would have a white Christmas, a woman in a plaid jumper appeared and told me she was very sorry, but my father had died in the night. I knew I had heard her correctly, but I asked anyway. 'He died? Are you sure?'

She told me that she was sorry, and said yes, she was sure.

I made my way to the hospital morgue. Seeing my father in the drawer that pulled out of the refrigerator, his body so much smaller than I remembered it, and holding his folded khaki shirt and trousers in my hands, I felt small. And alone. When your parents are alive you feel that you still have a long way to go on this earth. When they're gone, you know that the umbrella of immunity has been lifted from your head.

The technician in a white lab coat asked me if I wanted burial or cremation. It was up to me to decide this for a man who had always decided everything for himself, and for his wife, and for me when I lived under his roof. I'm getting even now, Pop, I thought.

I chose the less time-consuming of the two.

'You can pick up the remains tomorrow by four,' he said.

'Not till then?' I asked.

He looked surprised. 'Can you mail them to me?' I said. He took my address, and I left the tin of cashews on a chair.

LATER THAT MORNING, a man from the auction house on Payne Road met me at my father's house.

'I could write you a cheque for three thousand, for everything, right here,' the man said.

'I was thinking more along the lines of eight thousand for everything,' I told him.

He grimaced. 'I'm including the cost of getting rid of some of it. They closed down the dump here, maybe you didn't know that.'

That edgy tone—right out of some correspondence course in negotiations offered by a no-name business school.

The difference of five thousand was about what I tacked on to my expense account every month. 'All right,' I said. 'But I want everything out of here by the end of today.'

He grimaced again. 'Today? I don't know.' He looked around as if he was thinking it over. I knew he wasn't going to walk away.

'How soon can I start removing stuff?' he asked.

'Right now.'

After he left I picked up the photograph of my mother that stood in a frame on an end table. In the picture she was about my own age now, and even from where I stood I could see myself in her face. The same nose. The same creases at the corners of her eyes. My colour hair. It's funny how you think of your life as pretty much a straight line until you see it begin to bend into a circle.

IT WASN'T A BIG JOB; my father was not a man to save. In the meantime, I spent two hours with an estate agent, another two with a lawyer who would settle my father's estate—his cash assets were just under $20,000, my base monthly income—had a quick lunch, and by the time I returned to the house everything but the rugs was gone.

I could have left then, and flown home. Instead I walked through the empty rooms, listening to the echo of my footsteps. I thought of my mother starting her life in this house. In her early twenties, just married to Pop. What had she wanted then? What had she dreamed of having and doing in this world?

There were ghosts in the empty rooms. Over there, by the door that opened to the attic stairs, is where my mother kept her sewing machine. I remembered the spring my father promised her a vacation to the Finger Lakes after the summer people had gone home. All summer she sewed new outfits for the trip. Sometime in late August the sewing machine broke and my father refused to give her the money to repair it. By then he had decided to pull the plug on the vacation, anyway. I was working as a lifeguard on Higgins Beach that summer, and snuck the sewing machine out of the house and paid to have it fixed. My mother was pleased, but I never saw her sitting at the machine again.

On the back of a closet door were the pencil markings she made to measure my height from year to year. Standing before this door, I recalled her pleasure in this ritual. How she smiled, and how eager I was to turn round and see how I had grown.

I touched the mark for September 1967. Five foot, four inches. I closed my eyes and there is my mother standing in front of me in her red plaid housedress as she makes the mark on the door.

In the kitchen I saw my father. The way he was always checking to see that I hadn't left a burner on or the refrigerator door open. If he could slide a dollar bill into the freezer after I'd closed the door, then I hadn't closed it tight enough and was costing him money.

It was two o'clock when I left the key in the estate agent's lock-box and walked away from the house. I drove my father's truck to the town Mobil station and asked if I could leave it with a for-sale sign in the windscreen. 'I'll give you a twenty per cent commission on whatever it sells for,' I told the red-haired boy behind the counter, who took this offer eagerly and then gave me a ride back to my car. I noticed the dirt under his fingernails. The calluses on his palms. Working hands like my old man's. Not like my own.

I WAS ON THE INTERSTATE heading south when I remembered that I had left the photograph of my mother on the table in the living room; it had been carted away with all the rest of the furniture. From the moment I had stepped onto the plane to fly east, all I had in mind was a clean break. I turned round at the next exit.

The auction house was closed when I got there. I called the number that was stencilled on the glass door and pleaded my case to a man with a soft voice; he told me to wait there. He would meet me in ten minutes.

'It's silly, I know,' I said when he arrived.

'It isn't silly at all,' he said. 'People change their minds all the time. About ten years ago we started a practice of keeping everything in the back barn for forty-eight hours before we dispose of it.'

From the moment I held my mother's picture in my hand, I knew what I wanted to do with it. Instead of heading to the interstate, I drove out to Rose Point. I left my car outside the locked gate and walked the six or seven hundred yards to my father's workshop.

It was a small act of defiance on my part, and I did it for my mother. During the forty-nine years my old man worked at Rose Point this workshop was his kingdom, a place my mother was never welcome. I found the key in an old soup can under the third step. All I planned to do was hammer a nail into one of the studs and hang the picture on it so that whoever was hired to take over my old man's caretaking position would look up from time to time at my mother, and wonder. Just wonder, that's all.

The door swung open on its bronze hinges, and I could not move. I smelt oil and wood shavings. On the floor in front of me, my father's footprints in sawdust. I turned away and stared out at the ocean to try and clear my head. Suddenly I wanted to be back in California, drinking vodka tonics in the bar at the Beverly Hills Hilton, watching the supermodels chain-smoke to keep thin. I tried to picture myself there, thinking that I would never have to return to Maine again.

But the moment I stepped inside I felt all of that fall out of me. I stood in my father's world, in a stillness that seemed to have descended just as I opened the door.

I walked to the band saw, with its dull green casing. Another two steps to the table saw, then the mitre box, where my father had taught me to cut angles. The grinding wheel where we sharpened our chisels in a shower of white sparks. The overhead racks of mahogany and cedar. The old oak roll-top desk, its drawers filled with hardware. With my eyes closed I could still name everything in those drawers.

It was a tidy workshop, all the tools within reach like the galley of a ship. I walked solemnly, breathing in the scent of pine. As a boy I had stood in this room with my father. Hadn't I dreamed of one day becoming my father before we became so angry at one another? He was an uncomplicated man who had grown up on a potato farm in Canada, a day's drive from here but a million miles away. In the privileged world of Rose Point he must have felt out of place, and yet lucky to have found a way to earn his passage in such a quiet and beautiful place. His own boss, so to speak. This desk, these tools that became the centre of his life, had satisfied whatever desires had carried him from his father's world. This was his Hollywood. I saw that now for the first time. Seeing this, and letting it sink into my consciousness, opened some part of me. It was a small opening, but I felt it.

There was the telephone at the workbench with the numbers worn off the dial. And across the double windows that gave my father an ocean view, a length of twine with clothespegs hanging from it where he clipped his work orders, on slips of paper, like a short-order cook.

One slip of paper still hung there. I thought it must be the job he would have finished next if he hadn't died. How unlike my father to leave a job unfinished.

I won't say that I had a premonition about what was written on that slip of paper. But in my father's left-handed script were words that stopped my heart: Open 'Serenity' for Christmas.

Below these words, a telephone number.

I backed away, a step or two, then turned and ran, the way a boy would run, straight out of the door without stopping to close it behind me. I ran without looking at the snow-covered ground to see if there was anything in my way. At the end of the lane I could see the bare flagpole in front, and I was expecting to see that my father had opened the cottage. But it stood exactly as I remembered it, boarded up, abandoned.

For a long time I stood in the falling snow, looking at the cottage, thinking about how far I had ventured from this place and the person I had been when I had last seen it. The years now seemed to have passed quickly. Summers lost and gone. I wondered if my father had felt the same loss at the end, if he had been surprised at how quickly his time had passed.

My plane was going to leave Boston in three hours. Back home in LA I had suits to pick up at the dry-cleaner's in the morning and at least a dozen people I needed to call. And tennis at the club tomorrow night. A busy life that suddenly felt like it didn't belong to me.

CHAPTER THREE

I took the work order from the line of string and a carpenter's pencil from the desk drawer and then I dialled the number my father had written down. The area code was for New York City. After four rings there was a taped message in a child's voice. 'Nobody is here. Leave beeps for Mommy.'

Leave beeps. I laughed out loud. There are no children in the world that I inhabit, and this child's voice had caught me by surprise.

'All right,' I said. 'Here are my beeps—*beep, beep*. Please have your mommy call the caretaker at Rose Point.' I paused, and then added stupidly, 'In Maine.'

Then I clipped the work order back on the string where my father had left it. I turned it so I could read the words while I sat in my father's chair and waited.

I waited fifteen minutes. I told myself I would wait fifteen more. The workshop was cold and growing colder. There were a few dry logs in one corner of the room. I split them into kindling with my father's axe and started a fire in the woodstove.

I checked my watch again. Fifteen more minutes. Another hour and I would miss my flight.

Because in my life I never sit still, I was fighting back the persistent urge to get up and do something. The trick to living alone is to keep moving from the minute you open your eyes in the morning, charging ahead at full speed, so that at the end of the day you're too exhausted to think about anything, especially what you might have missed. If there's another way to keep from being lonely, I haven't found it.

Finally, I walked across the room and stood in the doorway of the workshop listening to the stillness around me. A kind of universal quiet that made me feel awkward and nervous. I thought for a moment and then yelled at the top of my lungs, 'Merry Christmas to all!' I had somehow forgotten how alone you could be in Maine, and how it felt to be so alone. I yelled once more, half expecting my words to change something this time. But they disappeared into the sky, and the stillness returned.

Back to the desk. Back to the chair.

Five more minutes and I gave it up. I went outside with a bucket that I filled with snow to douse the fire in the woodstove.

I was on my knees putting snow on the hot coals when the telephone rang. In the world I know, eagerness is seen as weakness and so my habit is to let the telephone ring twice. And then a third time.

I answered and heard a woman's voice speaking my father's name.

'Paul McQuinn, please?' she said.

My father had always been known by the summer residents of Rose Point as Mr Mac.

'I'm his son,' I said.

'His son?' she said. 'When I spoke with your father he didn't tell me he had a son working with him.'

'I don't work here,' I told her. 'I'm here from California because my father died.'

'*Mr McQuinn?*'

'Yes. I have a flight out tonight and I'm just here tying up loose ends.'

'I just spoke with your father on Monday. *Now he's gone?*'

She said this with such compassion that it caught me off guard and I couldn't think of what to say to this. 'I liked your message,' I told her.

'Message?'

'On the answering machine.'

'Oh. Yes. That's my Olivia.' For a moment she said nothing. Then, 'I'm just so sorry to hear about your father.'

'His heart was bad,' I said, a little too glibly.

There was only silence. And then she replied. 'I'm . . . I'm so sorry,' she said quietly.

I heard the loneliness in her voice. Or was it sadness, I wondered. A genuine sadness for my father's death. 'Did you know my father?' I asked.

'I never knew him,' she told me. 'But as I said, we spoke on the telephone on Monday.'

'Yes. So you own *Serenity* cottage?'

'Well,' she said, and then she hesitated. 'It's a long story.' Suddenly everything was so quiet I could hear her breathing. 'Is it beautiful there?' she asked me.

'It is,' I said. 'Some people think there's no more beautiful place in the world. Didn't your . . .' I paused, and then decided to ask. 'Didn't your father ever tell you about Rose Point?'

'My father?' she said.

And it was how she turned those two words into a question—*my father?*—that made me know at once that this was Charles Halworth's daughter, the little girl preserved so clearly in my memory that I could still picture her in her shiny shoes. I stood up at my father's desk and closed my eyes. Then I sat down again. Here I was, hearing, against all odds, a woman's voice that belonged to the daughter Charles Halworth called Katie thirty years ago when he promised that the two of them were going to teach me to skate on Christmas Day. I had spent perhaps five hours with her, sitting beside her in her father's big car, walking next to her in the toy store, following her down the hospital corridors. Five hours, thirty years ago. The past. The past suddenly returning to me with such force of emotion that I can no longer think of the past as merely a time, but also a place.

'Yes,' I said.

'I'm afraid I only found out about Rose Point a few weeks ago. I explained it to your father. He and I had a good laugh together,' she said. 'The cottage belonged to my mother. When she remarried last month and moved to England with her new husband, she went through her things. As she put it, it was time for house-cleaning. You'd have to know her to appreciate that.'

I smiled at this and felt a kind of anticipation rising inside me, the same boyish excitement that had sent me running to the cottage when I first saw the work order. 'And she gave the cottage to you?'

'Yes. She said it was an old, musty place too close to the sea to ever get the bath towels to dry properly.' She laughed. 'That's my mother through and through, Mr McQuinn.'

'And your father?' I asked her again.

'That was part of my mother's house-cleaning as well,' she said. 'My father left her before I was born, but he and my mother once spent time at Rose Point. I suppose that's why she forgot about the place. Bad memories and all. In any event, Mr McQuinn, I need to come and see this place now that I know the truth about it.'

The truth, I thought, was a lie.

'What did my father say when you told him?' I asked her.

'Just that he understood.'

'And did he say he would open the cottage for you?'

'Yes,' she said.

'For Christmas?'

'Yes. For Christmas.'

Her voice faded with the mention of Christmas. And I thought I detected a contradiction in her, as if she were hoping and giving up at the same time.

'Then I'll have the place ready for you,' I said.

'I don't know,' she said. 'How can I ask you to do this, with your father dying? And you need to go home.'

'You didn't ask me. I offered.'

'But are you sure?'

I was no longer listening. 'When do you want to arrive?'

'Well,' she said, 'I had planned to drive up on the twentieth. And stay until the day after Christmas.'

'Fine,' I said.

'What's your name?' she asked.

'Excuse me?'

'Your name?'

'Terry,' I said.

'I'm Katherine,' she said. 'You're very kind, but if our visit is too much of an imposition . . .'

'No, it won't be. It's not going to be an imposition.'

'So, I'll get to meet you then?'

'I'll be waiting with your keys.'

'Oh,' she said, 'I have keys; I nearly forgot. My mother gave me keys.'

'I'll have to guess on which rooms to make up. The cottage has twelve bedrooms.'

'Twelve! That's a little daunting.'

'Daunting, yes. How many rooms should I make up?'

'Two,' she said.

'Two,' I said. One room for the child. One for the mother and father. The wife and husband.

'I'll make up two rooms with ocean views, how's that? Just like a five-star hotel.'

She laughed at this, and I could tell she was happy. 'You'll call me if this becomes too much,' I heard her say.

'I will.'

I gave her my cellphone number, she thanked me again, and we said goodbye. I hung up the telephone. Across the room the dark window held my reflection. Beyond it a plane moved across the sky from star to star. I thought of the plane that would take me back home, and my car waiting in the parking lot, and my office. All of that suddenly felt far away, separated from me by more than miles and hours, more than space and time. The voice of Charles Halworth's daughter had crossed life's wide arc of possibilities and reached me as I always believed it would.

I glanced at the work order that I had been writing on while we talked. And I saw that I had written a list of names. The names of actresses who could play Katherine, and actors who would play her father, and the two studio producers I trusted to handle this movie sensitively.

I called Peter Billings, the only friend I trusted at The Company.

'Where are you?' he asked.

'Maine.'

'Maine?'

I laid out the story of Katherine Halworth and her father.

'Amazing,' Billings said. 'It would be meat on the table for Crossworth at Sunmount. Say it again?'

'It is about a daughter who finds the father she never knew she had.' When it comes to the idea behind a great movie, you know you have something if you can describe it in one declarative sentence.

'Yeah, wonderful, that is truly wonderful.'

'And it would be true, Peter,' I said. 'All of it.'

'So, the father's come back to Maine? Have you met him?'

I told him that part we would have to make up.

'We'd have to get Anthony Terrell to play the father.'

'I agree,' I said.

'OK. I'm moving on it. We'll talk again soon.'

'Right,' I said.

I drove into town to see about finding someone to help me.

At the hardware store on Main Street I asked the old man behind the register for a name. 'I've got to open up one of the cottages at Rose Point,' I told him.

He looked puzzled. 'What about McQuinn?' he said. 'He's the caretaker out there.'

'He died last night,' I told him.

'*What?*'

'He's my father, that's what *I'm* doing here.'

'Oh man, I'm sorry to hear that,' he said. 'Your father was a tough old sonofabitch, but I liked him.'

'Thanks,' I said. 'Do you know anybody?'

He thought for a minute, then told me there was a guy in Old Orchard Beach who used to come into the store with my father from time to time. 'Older guy. He bought the carousel at the fairgrounds a few years ago. I think your father was helping him restore the place. I can try to get in touch with him if you want.'

'Great,' I said. 'Call me.' I gave him my cellphone number. 'And have you got the number for my father's workshop?'

'It's around here somewhere,' he said. 'I'll call you.'

I CHECKED INTO A ROOM in a motel on Route 1, but it felt wrong. It could have been anywhere, which meant that it was nowhere. If I was going to make a movie, I needed to be close enough to the story for some of my blood to run into it.

I did some shopping in a Kmart at the outskirts of town. It had been my mother's favourite store. I was thinking about her red purse when a woman in a brown smock with a name tag rang up my purchase, a sleeping-bag.

I wasn't really paying attention, but she hesitated when she read the name on my credit card and when I looked at her she was holding back a smile.

'You don't remember me?' she said.

Our eyes met. There were so many names in my life. 'I should remember you,' I said to be polite.

'Algebra with Miss Dunne?' she said.

'Miss Dunne. Yes, there's a name I remember. Miss Dunne. But, no, I apologise.'

She looked down at her name tag. 'After a ten-hour shift I have to remind myself. Gwen Stevens,' she said.

I could tell she was a little hurt. 'I do remember you,' I lied. 'How are you?'

'I heard about your father. I'm sorry.'

I nodded and thanked her.

'I was painting houses at Rose Point the other summer,' she said. 'I used to see your father almost every day. He told me that you were working in Hollywood. He was very pleased, I could tell.'

This took me by surprise, and I didn't know what to say.

'Hollywood. That's something,' she said. 'I could tell even back in ninth grade that you were going places.'

'It's not as glamorous as it sounds.'

'Don't tell me,' she said, with a smile. 'Don't spoil it for me. So, where are you going now, Terry?' She gestured to the sleeping-bag.

For a moment I thought I wouldn't tell her anything. Keep it fast. Make my exit. But then I told her that I was going to stay at my father's store. 'I'm doing some work out at Rose Point that my father couldn't finish,' I said. 'It's the place that's been boarded up.'

'Oh, wow!' she exclaimed. 'Your father told me the story of that house. Amazing, isn't it? You know, that's just so nice of you to care. Your father would really be proud of you.'

She was nodding her head the whole time I was telling her that I wasn't so sure he would be.

Then she said, 'Sure he would. I mean you've been out in Hollywood for all this time, and here you are willing to get your hands dirty to help your father, and these people you don't even really know. Not many people would do that, do you think?'

'Well—'

'Hey,' she said, 'maybe you can turn this into a movie?' Then she quickly laughed. 'God, can you imagine?'

A man in a shirt and tie passed by us, eyeing her.

'My manager,' she said.

I grabbed the bag and we said goodbye. The top of my head was burning and I felt like my legs were going to give out. I had to stop at the door and take hold of it to keep from either falling down or racing out of the store.

I don't remember parking outside the gate at Rose Point that night, or walking to my father's workshop to drop off the things I'd bought in town. Suddenly, it was midnight, and I was standing in the snow looking up at the cottage. Above the highest roof peak a sickle of moon lay on its back. The tall cedar trees were tossing in a light breeze off the ocean. I began thinking about everything my old high-school classmate had told me. What would she think if she knew the truth about me? That my first impulse when I heard Katherine Halworth telling me her story was no more honorable than a shark going for blood. That I was always looking out for myself, for a way to distinguish myself from all the people who lead unremarkable lives. Wasn't that the reason I went to Hollywood in the first place? And hadn't I come home *for myself* as well? There wasn't anything I had wanted to say to my father; I was just coming home to hear *him* say something *to me* before he died. Maybe that he was sorry.

Soon my mind was racing through everything that had happened in the last twenty-four hours. I thought about Katherine Halworth as a small child, riding in the back seat of her father's car. I couldn't know why people had lied to her about her past, why she was told she had never been to Rose Point. Maybe her mother had some good reason for this. Maybe Charles Halworth just never loved his daughter enough to remain a part of her life. All these years, I had been transforming his disappearance into some epic Hollywood saga, when really he might be just another person who cared only about himself.

I tried calling Billings on the cellphone to tell him to forget the movie, but his line was busy. I watched a red fox dash across the crusted snow and made a mental note to call him back later. I walked back to my father's workshop, put the work order in his drawer, and fell asleep in his chair, wrapped in the sleeping-bag.

SOMETIME DURING THE NIGHT I must have laid down on the floor, because in the morning I woke with my head just a few inches away from the woodstove. As soon as I opened my eyes, all the confusion from the day before returned and my mind began racing, tearing round the corners of stupid ideas and beautiful ideas, running into walls of doubt. I just lay there on the floor with everything turning to dust in my head.

I stumbled into the bathroom to pee, and then remembered the toilet wasn't working.

Outside, the whole world of Rose Point was frozen solid. Fresh snow had fallen during the night. Every standing thing—each bush and tree, each porch column and flagpole, the cottages themselves—looked like they were about to crack and fall to pieces in the snow. I turned my head slowly, taking in everything, because this morning it seemed like it had been created just for me. As I stood there, the confusion began to recede, and I said out loud, 'Just be of some use here before you leave. Just do the work and then go home.'

I walked to the cottage with my father's snow shovel and, wearing his work boots and blue overalls, I made tracks in the snow. And when I stopped once to look back at them, I felt like I was alone for the first time in my life. Truly alone, but not lonely, in this world that the summer people and my father no longer inhabited. It was just me now, a man with work to do.

I began to feel strong in a way I hadn't felt in years, and when I came to the cottage it was as if I were seeing it for the first time. I stood in the lane that ran along the front of the property. *Just look at this place*, I said to myself. It was magnificent. The pitched roof with five matching gables. Half a dozen balconies attached to turrets and decks. The elegant wraparound porch with its sky-blue ceiling. The carriage house covered in cedar shingles like the main cottage. Even though all her windows and doors were boarded up with plywood shutters painted grey, none of her beauty was diminished.

I confess that even after what my old high-school classmate had said to me, even after I had renounced my idea of a movie, I could picture where the platform of lights would stand when shooting the evening scenes. I would have lined the balconies with rocking chairs, with one small one for Olivia. There would be a skating rink on the back lawn, and it would be on the rink where Mr Halworth would see his daughter again for the first time in thirty years. He would take her in his arms and skate her across the ice.

Just thinking about this now made me see that yesterday I had been a little crazy. Making a movie out of this family's misery? Maybe my father's death was getting to me.

I BEGAN SHOVELLING snow at the cottage that morning, and by noon I had a portion of the porch and two brick walkways cleared. I ate a peanut-butter-and-jelly sandwich in my father's workshop and called my secretary.

'You missed lunch today with Elizabeth Tisdale,' she reminded me. 'And tomorrow there's a—'

I didn't hear the rest. 'I need you to clear the decks for me for five days, Marylou.'

'What should I say?' she asked.

'Tell them that my father died,' I told her.

'All right,' she said, and I could tell by the flatness of her voice that she accepted this as just another run-of-the-mill lie.

'Marylou,' I said. 'It's true. My father *did* die.'

She still didn't believe me. 'OK,' she said. 'Winfield Marshall's calling for you every fifteen minutes.'

THE TELEPHONE WOKE ME at six the next morning. It was the man from the hardware store calling to say he hadn't been able to reach the guy at Old Orchard Beach he'd told me about.

I drove out to Route 1 and headed south to Old Orchard Beach myself. As soon as I turned onto Ocean Drive and saw the pier, I began to feel calm for the first time since I had left LA. Up ahead was the amusement park where my mother had taken me each summer on my birthday. She'd had neither a driver's licence nor a set of car keys in her life, so Dottie Hunter would drive us in her truck with the windows rolled down so we could hear the carnival organ from half a mile away. These trips were a secret my mother and I shared—and kept hidden from my father. You couldn't have paid him to go to an amusement park.

As I drove along, the sounds began returning to me like something from a dream. The shrill whistle of the miniature train. The amplified voices of the barkers. The screeching iron wheels of the roller coaster. The nearer I got to the place, the more real these sounds became, so that when I parked on the side of the road and stepped out of the car into silence, I felt lost. The amusement park had never been more than a few ramshackle buildings, but now they were gone.

I walked slowly through the ruins. All that remained of the Ferris wheel was a rusted skeleton swaying in the wind. The bingo hall and souvenir shops had collapsed into the sea. I remembered, suddenly, that this world with its doughnuts and its fortunetellers, its tattoo parlours and its hoopla galleries, was as far from Rose Point as the moon, and that was why my mother and I had loved it.

Up ahead was the low-slung, whitewashed building that held the carousel. Protected by the dunes, it stood exactly as I remembered it, attached to a one-room cabin where the owner had lived. I began walking towards it slowly, remembering how my mother always tied a bandanna round her head before she climbed onto her horse with the silver stirrups. And how I always rode the horse with the cherry-coloured saddle.

I was walking round the building, trying to find a way to look inside, when a car pulled up and a man in a Boston Celtics wind-cheater got out. 'You an antique dealer?' he hollered.

I took a few steps towards him. 'Not me,' I said. He was a man of about seventy, I thought, with a nice smile and a wiry build. There was a warmth and a toughness about him that reminded me of so many older men in my hometown.

He studied me. 'No,' he said. 'You don't look like one. Sorry.'

'No problem,' I said. 'I used to come here as a kid, years ago.'

'Yeah?' he said, nodding his head. 'I get visitors all the time who tell me that. I bought the place eleven years ago after I retired from the marines. You know, something to tinker with in my old age. I bought it off a fellow named Stintson from up in Bucksport. He bought it from one of the Kelly brothers right here in Old Orchard.'

'Kelly,' I said. 'That's the name. He had a red moustache.'

'Yep. And he wore crazy silver cowboy boots.'

'Yes, I remember.'

He seemed pleased. He looked at me for a few seconds, not saying anything. Then he reached into his pocket and pulled out a bunch of keys. 'If you've got time, I'll let you have a look around.'

'You don't have to do that.'

'I know I don't,' he said.

I watched him unlock the double doors and push them back on their rails. And I know this sounds crazy, but for an instant I thought I heard the organ music starting up.

'It smells like summer,' I said, as I walked inside with him. He had all the horses wrapped in burlap covers.

'*Smells* good,' he said, 'but I couldn't make a go of it as a business. Some out-of-state people built a fancy place on Route One with water slides and go-carts. That was the end of this old fire hazard.'

He asked if I wanted to see one of the horses.

'I don't want to take any more of your time,' I told him.

'I've got plenty of time,' he said. As he was untying the burlap bag, he told me that antique dealers came by all the time, offering him money for the place. 'This carousel was built in 1914 by the Carousel and Taboggin Company of Willowgrove, Pennsylvania,' he said. 'These horses are carved from solid white oak. Take a look.'

I stared into the lifelike black eyes of the white stallion with a golden mane.

'Did you have a favourite horse?' he asked. 'Most people who come by tell me they had favourites.'

'Mine had a cherry-coloured saddle,' I said.

He pointed across the planked stage. 'That one over there,' he said. 'A few years ago one of its front legs fell off. Had to hire a carpenter to fix it. You want to take a look?'

We knelt down in the frozen sawdust, and he explained the whole procedure to me, showing me how the carpenter had repaired the broken leg with wooden dowels. My father's work. I could tell by how perfectly it had been done. I didn't say anything, I just listened and followed him from horse to horse as he uncovered them. In the end, when he finished telling me his stories, all the burlap covers were on the ground and the carousel looked exactly as it had when I was a boy.

'Do you want me to help you cover the horses before I go?' I asked him as we neared the door.

'No, no. I'll cover them later. It'll give me something to do. That's one of my problems now, son, I don't have enough to do. I'm still learning how to be an old man.'

'Well, I have some work for you if you're interested,' I told him. 'My name's Terry McQuinn. My father was the caretaker at Rose Point. A man at the hardware store told me you two knew one another.'

He looked at me. 'My name's Warren,' he said softly, and we shook hands. 'Your Mac's son?'

'I am, yes.'

'You said your father *was* the caretaker?'

'He died,' I told him.

His eyes opened wide. He looked like he had something to say, and I waited. I didn't intend to tell him anything else; it just came out of me. 'The truth is,' I said. 'I didn't get home in time. He died before I could see him.'

I had turned away when I told him this. When I looked back at him I saw his eyes close.

He sighed, then looked at me. 'That's rough,' he said. His voice was low. 'I'm sorry.'

'Thanks,' I said. 'Would you want the work? I've got to open one of the big cottages by December twentieth.'

'For a summer person?'

'Coming up for Christmas,' I said.

Now he stared at me. 'For Christmas? Why would they want to come up here for Christmas?'

'It's a long story,' I said, remembering that Katherine Halworth had said the same thing to me. 'I was hoping maybe you were a carpenter, too,' I said.

'No,' he said. 'I'm sorry.'

He made a gesture with his hand that was part-wave, part-salute and quickly turned away. I could see that he was in a hurry. 'Do you know anyone who could help me?' I called to him.

'Sorry,' he said, without looking back at me.

I watched him go inside his cabin. I wondered if something I had said had offended him. Or if it was the mention of my father that had bothered him. Maybe he'd had a run-in with my old man. OK, I thought, I'll do the work myself.

CHAPTER FOUR

When I got back to Rose Point, I swore at the locked gate and walked through the snow to the store, determined to find my father's key. I started emptying boxes and old coffee tins. I'd been at it maybe ten minutes when I cut my thumb just below the knuckle on a rusted razor blade at the back of a drawer. I thought it was nothing at first but, when I looked closely, the cut was open all the way to the bone, and I knew I needed stitches.

I wrapped my hand in a cloth and then cursed all the way to the hospital. My second trip to the hospital in two days.

I counted twelve people ahead of me in the emergency room. All I could do was sit and wait. The hospital was doing a brisk business. The automatic doors never really closed all the way before they opened again. Did I remember these doors, how they reflected the falling snow that Christmas Eve? And if I tell you that Mr Halworth stopped to gaze into the glass to adjust the Santa's cap on his head, am I making this up? How can we say with certainty what we remember from our past and what we invent to bridge the distance?

I PASSED OUT COLD when they stitched up my thumb. A nice nurse pushed me to the lobby in a wheelchair. 'It's the rule,' she said.

I was surprised to see that it was already dusk. I asked the nurse for directions to the men's room, then thanked her and wished her a Merry Christmas.

Inside the men's room there was an Asian man dressed in a Santa Claus costume. He was standing at the mirror adjusting his fake beard. 'Can't get it to stick on right,' he complained.

The sight of him did something to me. I walked back to the ER to find the nurse, knowing it was a long shot.

'I was here one Christmas Eve a long time ago,' I said to her. 'A man I knew, dressed as Santa Claus, brought gifts for the children.'

She had been on the telephone about to make a call. She put the phone down. 'You knew him?' she asked, surprise in her eyes.

'He owned a cottage out at Rose Point,' I said. She was nodding her head. 'My father worked there.'

'He came here one Christmas and there was an accident,' she said. Her voice was steady and thoughtful. 'And you're looking for him?'

I didn't think about what I would say next. It just came to me. 'His daughter is looking for him,' I told her. A small lie. Disbelief passed across her face. 'It's true,' I said.

'After all these years?'

'Yes.'

Then, as if she was disclosing a great secret, she looked behind her to make sure no one was coming. 'I had a teacher at nursing school who was in love with him,' she said.

THE TEACHER'S NAME was Callie Boardman, and she lived only a few blocks from the nursing school at the Maine Medical Center, where she had taught for more than twenty years. I parked outside her terraced house in Vaughn Street, waiting for her to return from wherever she had gone. It had begun to snow again. For two hours I watched the snow mount on the roof of the building, and thought about the weight of the snow on the roof of the *Serenity* cottage. I thought of all the winter nights when the cottage stood alone, waiting for someone to open the doors and windows again.

She came on foot from up the street, in a long green winter coat with a pale yellow scarf round her neck. There was something solitary and completely without expectation about the way she approached her front door, opened her bag and took out her keys that told me she lived alone and had for a long time.

'By choice,' she said to me after she had shown me into the living room. 'I've lived alone by choice. But I've had my work, you see.'

I told her that I *did* see. Completely.

She knew why I was there, she said. The young nurse at the hospital had called her for me. I watched her walk into the next room and turn on a lamp. There was a table with a basket of apples sitting on a square of white linen. She began to walk back towards me, but then stopped at the table. She unwrapped her scarf and her long silver hair fell over her shoulders. She was, I thought, a woman who looked much older than her age.

After a long silence she looked up at me. 'I need to catch my breath,' she said. 'Please sit here.'

We sat across the table in straight-backed chairs, a narrow space dividing us. 'Now that I'm here,' I said, 'I don't know what to say.'

'I think I know,' she said. She folded her hands in front of her. There was a peacefulness in her eyes. 'Thirty years ago, on Christmas Eve, when Charles went to the hospital with gifts for the children, his daughter was with him. And there was also a little boy. The son of the caretaker at Rose Point. He would be about your age now. He grew up and left Maine and never came back.'

'Yes,' I said.

'Until now. I had a feeling we would meet some day,' she said. 'Why have you come home now?'

I told her that I had flown home to see my father. 'But he died before I got here,' I said. 'I was just going to leave, to go back to California, but before my father died, Mr Halworth's daughter called him and asked him to open the *Serenity* cottage.'

Callie took a deep breath, tipped her head back, closed her eyes, and then opened them slowly.

'For Christmas, with her daughter,' I said. 'I've spoken with her, and I'm going to open the cottage for them.'

'Why?' I heard her say.

'Because she asked my father to.'

I said a few more things about shovelling the pathways to the cottage, but I could tell she wasn't really listening any more. She had become distracted, or uncomfortable.

She got up and went to the chair where she had left her coat and scarf. 'You have to walk with me,' she said.

THERE ARE SOME MEN, many, I suppose, who could turn away from a child, leaving her behind in a discarded life. But not Charles Halworth. In this respect I had been right about him all these years. As I walked through the snow, much lighter now, with the woman who knew him best, I began finally to learn his story.

'You understand that I came to love him very much,' she said. 'And because of this, there are things I can't share with you, or with anyone else.'

'Yes, of course,' I told her.

'I met him four years after the accident,' she went on, 'It was almost four years.'

I interrupted her without knowing why at first. 'I'm sorry,' I said, 'but . . . I guess I need to tell you that I never forgot him. Or his daughter. I ran away from here, and I always told myself that I was running away from my father, because we didn't get along. But now that I'm here, I mean, standing here with you, I know I ran away because I gave up.'

'Gave up what?'

I tried to find the best words. 'I gave up ever seeing them again. No, not just seeing them, but being part of their life. You have to understand: my father worked for the people at Rose Point. He was never really allowed to just be there in that beautiful place. And neither was I. But that night, that Christmas Eve, Charles Halworth made me feel different about things. About myself. He made me feel like I was good enough. I guess because I was only a kid it was possible for me to believe that his daughter and I might become friends. That I might be able to come and go in their big cottage, in a way that my father never could.'

I saw that she was smiling at me. 'What is it?' I asked.

'It was the same thing with Charles,' she said. 'The big summer house, the big life, the money. None of that was his, you see. It all belonged to his wife. All he ever was good at, he used to tell me, was skating. He grew up in Maine, in Bangor. He came from nothing. But he played ice hockey well enough to get a scholarship to a prep school in Boston. Then, after that, it was Harvard. That's where he met his wife. He was beautiful then. A gifted athlete. She was at Radcliffe, an attractive girl from a wealthy family. Incredibly wealthy. Whatever they had in common—I don't know . . . youth, I suppose—turned out not to be enough. The trip to Maine that Christmas had been his idea, one last effort to try to win her back by spending Christmas at Rose Point.'

Somehow we had taken backstreets unfamiliar to me, and we ended up at the hospital. We went to a rear entrance and took an elevator to the fifth floor. The nurses there knew Callie by name, and they smiled and said hello and Merry Christmas as we passed down the corridor.

We stopped at a room with a glass wall. On the other side were rows of newborn babies, each in a wheeled basket with transparent sides. They all wore tiny knitted hats that made them look as if they were travellers together who had taken a long journey to arrive here. One had a kind of half-smile on his face as he slept.

'I met Charles here,' she told me. 'He was pushing a mop along the floor here, and when he stopped and gazed at the babies I fell in love with him . . . with whatever was in his eyes. I was very shy. Young and shy. He worked nights, and whenever I was on the late shift I would wait to see him.'

She took me to another elevator and we rode to the top floor. When the door opened we were in a kind of storage room. She walked down a narrow aisle between tall shelves, to a window. The snow clouds had swept out to sea.

'On a clear night like tonight you can see a long way. There's the back cove, there. And the lighthouse at Cape Elizabeth. And there, there's Rose Point.'

It was amazing to me.

I told her that, though my parents had told me Charles had returned after the accident, I had believed as a child that he was in trouble. 'I mean, for leaving,' I said. 'My father told me there were no charges against him. I guess that's true or he wouldn't have been able to get a job here.'

She told me that my father had told me the truth. 'Charles was running for a long time. Not from the police, though. He was running from himself.' She paused.

'Like me.'

She smiled at this. 'Even when we were together, he never really stopped running,' she said. 'He worked here for seven years, and we were together for that time. We often stood at this window. He was always hopeful that he would see his daughter again. You see, he spent those four years after the accident in New York City, trying to earn his way back to his daughter.

'But his ex-wife made it impossible. Then he became desperate . . . he tried to take Katie. The charges were dropped, but after that, it was over for him. Yet he still had this hope. I think his hope was the deepest thing inside him. The hope of a child, really. I think that's why he loved children so much. I carry the guilt for ending his hope.' She wiped tears from her eyes. 'I'm the one who finally convinced him to give up ever seeing Katie again. I was afraid it would kill him. I think of it every day. Because I can *tell* you I did this for him, but really I did it for myself. I was selfish, you see? I wanted him to live. To live for me. And in the end, I lost him anyway. I lost him to his terrible sadness.'

BEFORE I LEFT HER, we walked down State Street, to the intersection where the accident had taken place. I looked down at the slush in the street, and I heard again the sound of what I had learned later was the baby carriage dragging beneath the car. I closed my eyes, and it all came back to me. The damp scent of the cloth seats. Mr Halworth's arms flying up in the air. The flashing red and blue lights. A coldness ran through me as if I were standing barefoot in the snow. Then I felt her taking hold of my hand.

She looked past me in silence before she told me that in the years when Charles Halworth was with her they came here together every Christmas Eve. 'Twelve years ago he disappeared from my life,' she recounted. 'I came alone that Christmas. I still do. It's something . . . I don't know, I should forget him. But I can't. When something terrible happens to someone you love, your friends tell you that in time you will get over it. To me that always seemed like the saddest thing. I mean, when someone you love is gone and you finally stop thinking of them. The idea that I might go through a whole day without thinking of Charles . . .'

Finally, I asked her what I should tell his daughter.

'Do what your heart tells you to do.' She looked into my eyes. 'Charles is dead. He had a brother who knew about me. He came to see me and he told me that Charles had died.'

She told me that she hoped I would stop running away, and that I would find peace. I couldn't say anything. I'd grown prosperous by never showing any emotion. By never really caring too much about any of the projects I pretended to be willing to die for. And now I was crying in the street.

I SLEPT AGAIN on the floor of my father's workshop. If you can call it sleep. My thumb throbbed all night long. I hadn't put enough logs in the woodstove to keep it going, and I was frozen to my bones. Sometime before daybreak I got up and stood at the window, thinking how sad it was that Charles Halworth would never see the sun rise over Rose Point again. It left me feeling hollow inside, as if something precious had been taken from me.

Finally, I got the woodstove going again and, to take my mind off things, I began devising a kind of platform bed. I sketched it out on my father's workbench. Then I set the table saw whirring and grimly got to work. The whole time I thought of Callie Boardman's last words to me: 'Do what your heart tells you to do.' I didn't know what my heart was telling me. So much sadness. Far better, I thought, if his daughter lives with her mother's lie.

When I finished the bed I stood there and looked at it disdainfully. Here was something my old man could have made in twenty minutes. It had taken me two hours and a lot of cursing. I had tools scattered on the floor.

I kicked the table saw and walked away. When I looked up, my mother's face was there, her eyes staring back at me. I took the photograph in my hands and sat down with it. The rose-patterned dress. She was wearing that dress the time we went grocery shopping and I begged her for cherries. She told me they were too expensive, that my father would be angry with her for spending so much money. All I wanted was a handful, but she couldn't grant me this. And she clung to her purse as if she were afraid I would try to take it from her.

'Oh, God,' I said, as I felt the same old anger and frustration rising inside my chest. The feeling that I was trapped in a long, dark corridor of resentment. It was something that had been a part of me for so many years that I could no longer name its point of origin. My mother's voice calling to my father as he walked away from her? The first time he shook his fist at me? The way he could fill a room with silence, silence that dared you to speak? Or maybe it was just his damned coldness. Put a colour to that coldness and it would be the cobalt blue of the winter sky this morning. I have been afraid of that coldness, afraid that it inhabits me and that I would pass it on were I to get married and have a family. I have been in love a number of times. There was a girl I would have married. Her name was Nicole and we were together three years. In the end she left me because I could not stop thinking about myself. *My* fears, *my* desires. *My* work. *My* future. She made me see that the world would be better off if men as self-centred as I didn't have families. If they had the courage to live alone.

I HUNG THE PHOTOGRAPH back in its place. For once I was just plain tired of being angry over things that had happened so long ago. This was a new morning. There was a pink light out over the sea, and in the distance a small parade of fishing boats was heading out into the bay. I thought of the men on those boats, the risks and dangers they faced, and the families they were providing for.

When I opened the door and stepped outside I said to myself, This is where it stops. The anger and the resentment stop here. Right now. Kick yourself in the butt and get back to work.

But it wasn't until I had found the key to the gate and had pulled the rental car to the end of the driveway at *Serenity* cottage, opening all the doors with the radio blasting, that I began to find my way into the work. A radio station was playing the old soul music of Percy Sledge, and soon I was shovelling happily to 'When a Man Loves a Woman' and 'Try a Little Tenderness'. All the words came back to me from somewhere, and before long I was singing at the top of my lungs and shovelling to the cadence of the bass runs.

When I reached the bare grey floor of the porch, I found the boards in surprisingly good condition. My father must have painted this porch fifteen or twenty times in his life, and he must have been paid by Mrs Halworth. I imagined her ambivalence as she wrote out cheques for a house she no longer visited.

Soon Mr Halworth's daughter would walk across this porch again. She would climb the stairs I had shovelled and she would walk to the front door and push it open for the first time since she was a little girl. And now she had a little girl of her own.

I turned and looked at the mailbox by the front door. The same mailbox, painted red, with the word 'POST' stencilled in white letters, just as it had been when I was eight years old. The corners were mitred so perfectly I knew at once that my father had built it. I could see where he had carefully caulked the seams with silicon to keep out rain and moisture. I would have been in grade school when he built it. And he would have been about the age I was now. 'Build everything out of clear cedar, no knots in the wood, and it will last for ever,' he used to say. 'Learn a trade and you will never go hungry.'

Learn a trade. He had been preaching that to me since junior high school, and I had turned my back on his advice from day one, when I enrolled in the college prep programme rather than what was called 'industrial arts' in my school. I can still remember autumn afternoons on my way to football practice when I would pass the high-school hoods from industrial arts sitting out behind the workshop, hunched over their cigarettes, with their go-to-hell sunglasses and motorcycle boots. I looked down on them. To me they were boys who would grow up to become my father's kind of men. Hourly wage, no ambition, two weeks off a year, classic American working stiffs. As soon as I was old enough to see how the world worked, I began working hard to escape my father's life. Like a man fleeing a fire, I never looked back.

Until now.

Standing on the Halworths' porch it felt like all the years I was running I had been merely taking the long way home. And nothing I had done in my life, no contract with my initials on it, no commission on another person's work, seemed as substantial as my father's wooden mailbox.

When I raised the lid, I saw that there was a hole in the bottom as wide as my thumb, and a nest, made from small twigs and bits of straw, in one corner. I suppose some animal had bored its way into the mailbox, and then left it for a bird to build a nest there.

I finished all the shovelling just before dark, clearing the four brick pathways, the wraparound porches and the driveway. I took the mailbox back to the workshop with me to repair the hole in the bottom board. Removing that one damaged piece without destroying the rest was not easy, and it was very late when I finally finished. I painted the bottom with oil primer and caulked the seams the way my father had, and then placed the mailbox on a stool beside the woodstove to dry.

I sat in my father's chair, listening to the wind race across the roof and rattle a loose pane of glass in the window above my head. I went through all the things I had to do at the house, counting and recounting the more than seventy windows and doors, the shutters of which I would begin removing in the morning. Then I would have to get the water and electricity running and insulate the copper pipes beneath the house so they wouldn't freeze. Inside, at least a whole day of cleaning. After thirty years it had to be a mess inside.

I ate baked beans from the can, and half a pumpkin pie. Twice, before I fell asleep, I got up to check the mailbox, to reassure myself that I had made the repairs well enough. In the end I set the bird's nest inside, concealing the seam so that you couldn't tell where my father's work ended and my own began. I had just turned out the light on my father's desk when I heard a car coming up the lane. I went to a window and watched as the car neared the store. It came to a stop, and then quickly turned and drove away. Someone with a key to the gate, I said to myself.

I OPENED MY EYES to sunlight and someone shaking my arm. 'Wake up, Mr McQuinn. Wake up. It's me, Warren, from the carousel. You're going to freeze to death out here, kid.'

'The carousel?' I said.

He opened the woodstove and stirred the coals.

'Wait,' I said. 'What are you doing here?'

'What am I doing here? I'm making sure you live to see sunny California again.' He was throwing wood into the fire. 'You've got to get some heat in this place.'

'OK, I give up. But what are you doing here?'

'Bill Walters,' he said, 'the guy at the hardware store. He told me you were staying out here. I couldn't believe it. I'm here to help you.' He nodded his head solemnly. 'Where do you want to begin?'

It took us almost two hours to get the plumbing working.

LATER, AFTER WARREN and I had filled my father's workshop with cigar smoke to celebrate the small miracle of a flushing toilet, I remembered how, yesterday at the carousel, after I'd told him who I was and that my father had died, he had suddenly seemed eager for me to leave. Now he was in no hurry. He began telling me how badly he had missed cold weather during the war when he was stationed in the Philippines with the marines. 'I made a promise that if I ever got back to Maine in one piece, I'd never curse the cold again,' he said.

'I'll tell you what else the war taught me though, son,' he added. 'To appreciate the little things. The smell of coffee. The chance to sit and talk like we are this morning.'

'That's nice, Warren,' I said. 'And for helping me here, I want to pay you.'

'That's silly,' he said. 'Anyway, I still owe your father for a job he did on one of my horses.'

'Well, your time is valuable,' I said.

He waved this idea aside. 'I've got too much time, already told you that.'

'Nope,' I said, 'no one has too much time. I wonder how many bathrooms the cottage has.'

'Six,' he said, nodding his head.

I looked at him for a second. 'You know?'

'No, no, no, I'm just guessing. Six at least. Every place out here must have at least a half dozen bathrooms.'

'Yeah, I guess so,' I said. I was trying to remember if I'd told him yesterday which cottage I was opening for Christmas. 'Have you ever spent any time out here, Warren?' I asked him.

'Here?' he said, raising his hands in the air to dismiss the very notion. 'Three or four times with your father, that's all.'

'Is there anybody around here who might have a key to the gate?' I stared right into his eyes.

'This gate?' he said.

'Yeah.'

'I wouldn't know, son,' he said.

I watched him sit up straight. *Nervous,* I thought.

'Someone drove in here last night,' I said. 'Now that I think of it though, I probably left the gate open.'

'I'm forgetting things all the time,' he said, shaking his head.

'Where'd you park?' I asked him.

'Park?' he said.

I had him, and I knew it. 'This morning,' I said.

'Oh,' he said. 'You confused me. Outside the gate. It was locked when I drove up.'

'Locked,' I said. 'So I didn't leave it open last night? That's a mystery. Like life itself, right?'

'Right you are, son,' he said, with relief. 'You want to start opening up that cottage?'

If you give liars enough time, their lies will lead you to the truth they are trying to conceal. For this reason alone I might have decided not to challenge Warren. I had another reason as well. I needed his help to open the cottage.

This morning, as we walked towards *Serenity*, he walked behind me.

'Here she is,' I said, when we were standing in front of the cottage. He tipped his head back in the early morning light.

'Imagine,' he said, softly, almost as if he were talking to himself. 'Imagine living in such a beautiful house.'

We opened the widow's walk first, and from the top rung of my ladder I could see the outline of the hospital far off across the cove. It was snowing again, big fat flakes swirling slowly through the grey sky. I was afraid to look down to watch them land. Warren was below, holding the ladder.

Just as I figured, my father had fastened the shutters across each window with galvanised screws. I worked slowly, using a cordless drill. One window and then the next. Like taking the coins off a dead man's eyes.

It wasn't until I had all eight windows uncovered on the widow's walk that I looked inside. The centre of the floor was open to a set of stairs that ran down to the second floor below, just as I remembered. An elaborate set of cobwebs reached from the tops of the windows to the sills, trapping the shells of dead flies and moths. In one corner of the room I saw a Christmas tree stand with seven strands of lights beside it, each neatly coiled. My father's work, I could tell. Finally, I saw the angel in a white box on the floor. I remembered my father letting me stand on a chair to put her on the tree. She had a tiny light bulb on her back that illuminated her gauze wings.

'Warren,' I said when I came down the ladder, 'can you believe my father put caulking on each shutter to keep out the dampness? I expected the house would be crumbling inside, but it's going to be in perfect condition.'

'That's something,' he said.

I saw that his lips were blue with cold.

'Let's go and warm up in the workshop,' I said.

'I'd like to, but I have to be home before noon.'

'Sure,' I said. 'I'll leave the gate open for you in the morning.' I looked into his eyes for something.

'Right,' he said, nodding his head.

I spent the afternoon on my back beneath the cottage, wrapping insulating tape round the water pipes until it grew too dark to see. That night, before I slept, I couldn't help walking back to *Serenity.* Looking up at the windows from the front lawn, seeing the moonlight reflected off the glass now that the shutters were gone, I began to feel that I was drawing near to all I might yet know.

CHAPTER FIVE

The sky was overcast all the next morning and the temperature never got above the single numbers. We pulled off thirty shutters and then stopped for lunch. I climbed down and told Warren that by this time tomorrow we would be inside the cottage.

While we ate our sandwiches on the porch, the sun broke through and the lawns and open fields for as far as you could see looked like they were covered with splinters of glass. Warren had a far-off look in his eyes. He began talking about the marines again.

'By the time Vietnam came around,' he said, 'the corps wouldn't let me see combat. Stuck me in a desk job. The worst duty I ever pulled. I had to write letters home. Not for the dead marines, but for the wounded ones.' He stopped for a moment, then went on. 'Terry, dying isn't the worst thing that can happen to you. Some of those boys were shot up so bad. I mean, some medic in the field just stuffed them back together as best he could. Then I got to write to the mother or wife telling her that the boy she loved would be on his way home soon. Times it would have been more compassionate to just list the boys as dead, the shape they were in.'

I waited until he was finished talking. 'Did my father ever tell you anything about this cottage?' I asked him. 'About what happened here a long time ago?'

'No,' he said. 'I only saw your dad here and there and that was to drop off my horses that needed to be repaired. Dry rot, you know. He was a fine carpenter.'

While we worked that afternoon I told him everything I knew about Charles Halworth and Callie, and Charles's daughter. By dusk we had finished all but the front door.

'We're going in together,' I said to Warren. As soon as I took out the first screw, I knew that the board had been removed recently. The caulking had been cracked and the screws came out too easily. And when I pushed the door open I saw snow on the floor of the entrance hall. You could see plain as day that the snow had fallen off someone's boots.

'Look at this footprint,' I said.

I knelt down. Warren was standing behind me.

'Who would have been in here?' I said. I turned and looked at him. He shrugged his shoulders.

I stood up and walked ahead, glancing into the big room on my left. 'I suppose my father might have come in after he got the call to open the place, right?' I turned and looked back at Warren again.

'To tell you the truth, I don't feel comfortable,' he said. 'I mean, walking in here, in somebody else's house.'

'It's all right,' I said. 'Let's find the fuse box so we can see where we're going.'

We found the door to the basement and went down together. The main switch was on a wall across from the stairs. An overhead bulb lit up above our heads when I threw the switch. To the right there was a laundry room, to the left a giant room with shelves on every wall, from floor to ceiling, all of them completely empty.

On the ground floor it was the same. Empty. A kind of emptiness I had never seen or felt before. There were oriental rugs on the floors. The furniture was still there, all of it arranged neatly. But there was nothing personal in any of the rooms, not even a book in the walnut-panelled library.

On the first floor the mattresses on the beds were covered with sheets of newspaper. I leaned over a picture of Lee Harvey Oswald on one bed. In the room across the landing, pictures of Jack Ruby and Jackie Kennedy. Newspapers my father used in December 1963 when he closed the cottage. I counted sixteen beds in the twelve bedrooms, all the mattresses covered by similar photographs.

We were on our way downstairs when I opened what I thought was a closet door. Inside was a narrow set of stairs with snow on them and more boot prints. 'My father was here,' I said, 'I'm sure of it.'

We followed the stairs to a room hidden somewhere above the kitchen. On one wall there was a panel of bells. 'Maids' quarters,' I said. 'Look at this, Warren.'

I found the old wiring still connected.

'Excuse me for a minute,' he said. 'I'll be right back.'

I heard him leave, and when I turned round I saw a white bureau with some things set on top. The first sign of life in the cottage.

A pair of leather slippers. Gold-framed glasses. An appointment book with the year 1964 printed in gold on the front cover above the Brooks Brothers logo. When I opened it I saw Charles Halworth's signature. I turned the pages, slowly at first, and then hurriedly. They were all empty except for a notation on July 7, printed in black ink. *Katherine's sixth birthday*.

When I opened the top drawer there were framed photographs of Charles Halworth and his daughter. The two of them in a sailboat with the child at the tiller. A young Charles in a hockey uniform leaning against the goal on some rink. Katherine as an infant asleep on a couch with a dog sleeping next to her. Katherine and her father holding croquet mallets.

The other drawers were empty. I followed the narrow stairs the rest of the way down to the kitchen. Warren was standing at the sink, looking out of the window.

'There are some things upstairs,' I said to him. 'Sad. They made me sad, Warren . . . I feel like taking a break. Will you have dinner and a couple of beers with me?'

He turned and we looked at each other. 'A man shouldn't drink by himself,' he said.

'OK,' I said. 'Give me half an hour. I'll pick up some burgers and we'll eat and then start in on the plumbing.'

AS SOON AS I DROVE away, my cellphone rang. The office, I thought. I almost didn't answer it.

'Mr McQuinn, is that you?'

When I heard Katherine's voice I felt relieved that I no longer had any designs for making a movie of her life. Instead, I could just listen to her voice, delighting in it as if I were listening to music.

'And how are you, Mr McQuinn?' she asked.

'Call me Terry,' I said.

'Thank you, Terry.'

'I'm fine,' I said. 'Doing well. And you?'

'Olivia and I are getting more and more excited each day. We'll probably drive you crazy when we get there.'

I smiled and wondered what it would be like for her when I showed her the photographs of her and her father. I would have to tell her as soon as they arrived, and then go up the hidden stairway with her to stand beside her.

'Well, here's a silly question,' she said. 'I'm just wondering if we should bring linens. Sheets and towels. Blankets.'

I told her that I hadn't come upon any in the cottage so far.

'So you've been inside? How is it?'

'Empty,' I said.

'We'd better bring linens.' She thanked me again for all my work.

'You're welcome,' I said.

'I've been telling Olivia that our first day in Maine is going to become our best 'live-over' day. It's a thing she and I do together. Pretend that we're going to have the chance to live over the best days we ever had. Live-over days. You only get five, so you have to choose carefully.'

I was trying to decide on my own live-over days while I waited in line at Burger King. I still didn't have one when I stopped at the hardware store for insulation to cover the water pump and the hot-water heater.

The owner called to me: 'Hey, how are things at the cottage? Did Warren Halworth ever stop by to help you?'

I turned and looked at him. For a few seconds there was a loud rushing noise in my head and I couldn't speak.

'What did you say?' I asked at last.

'You know, the old-timer from the carousel?'

I RACED BACK to the point, rehearsing how I was going to question Warren, shifting the sentences in my mind and trying to find my anger. When I got to the cottage, the lights were on, but there was no sign of him. He knew that I had gone to town for our dinner. I checked the workshop, but the lights were off.

I found him at the carousel. He had taken the burlap off the horses and was cleaning them with a cloth.

I stood in the open doorway with the dark winter sky behind me. 'Tell me who you are,' I said. I was surprised that my voice was even and low. I felt only a strange kind of disappointment.

He wouldn't turn and look at me. 'I'm a bad liar,' he said. 'Always was.'

'I'll wait right here, then, for the truth,' I said.

He turned slowly and faced me. He was folding the cloth in his hands. Folding and unfolding it. 'I wish you hadn't come home from California,' he said. Then he shook his head and dropped his hands to his sides. 'No offence to you. But this isn't easy for anybody.'

'What isn't easy?'

He thought a moment. 'The truth,' he said. 'Those things in the bureau. I saw them in your father's workshop the first time I met him.' He spoke in slow, measured words. 'Mrs Halworth hired people to clean out the cottage, but your father got in there ahead of them and saved those things. When he showed them to me, he said, "Nobody should ever be completely forgotten." The week before last he told me that Katherine had called and was coming up, and he said he was going to put the things back in the cottage for her to find.'

Warren stopped and looked at the ground a moment. 'I told him I thought it was best if she never found out anything about her father, but your dad felt different. He was going to put the things back where he'd found them thirty years ago. He gave me keys to the gate and the front door. He told me that if I wanted the things gone, then I could come and take them.' Warren turned his head and smiled a half-smile. 'Your father went by the book, son. But I guess you already know that.'

'I guess I know it as well as anyone,' I said, with a touch of scorn in my voice.

'You shouldn't be so hard on him,' he said. 'Fathers make mistakes.'

'Sometimes they abandon their children,' I said.

I saw a look of shock cross his face, but it instantly transformed itself into something else. 'Terry,' he said, the way a patient father would speak to a child, 'you've got it all wrong.'

Then I stared hard at him. I wanted an honest answer to a thirty-year-old question. 'Tell me what really happened.'

He looked away from me, and I thought he might not answer this. 'You'll have to come with me so I can show you.'

I DIDN'T ASK HIM where we were going. We drove into the city. He turned onto Congress Street and drove slowly past Monument Square, where a tall blue spruce tree had been decorated for Christmas. The centre of the city was lit up with coloured lights and bustling with shoppers. They reminded me that it was Christmas; somehow I'd forgotten again.

'Maybe I was wrong before. Maybe I'm glad you came home,' Warren said to me, as he turned into a multistorey car park on Exchange Street. He stopped at a lighted booth, where a man with a bow tie handed him a ticket.

'How are you, Phil?' Warren asked.

'Freezing,' he replied. 'This is a good night for it.'

'It is,' Warren said.

'A good night for what?' I asked him.

'You'll see, son,' he said. We drove through a labyrinth of ramps and concrete columns until we reached one of the top floors and parked in a far corner. Warren kept the motor running. He checked his watch. 'The symphony starts in twenty minutes.'

Then he changed the subject. 'I used to go out to Rose Point every Thursday morning in the winter to play cribbage with your dad.' He looked at me. 'He understood better than most people, I think, because he came from nothing. There he was with the keys to paradise at Rose Point. All those wealthy people surrounding him.'

'Understood what?' I asked him.

'Understood Charles. I think he understood him better than I did. To me, though he was twelve years younger, I idolised him as I was growing up. He had everything. He looked like a movie star. And it wasn't just ice hockey that he was good at. He turned down a baseball scholarship, too. Colleges from all over the country. Coaches would come all the way to Maine, just to take him out for lunch. I knew I wasn't ever going to leave Maine, there wasn't anything special about me. But Charles had the whole world just waiting for him. Harvard . . . I went down to see him there. I saw him play half a dozen times. Then came the Olympics. Her father or grandfather was on some committee that picked the athletes, that's how they met.'

He paused and took a knitted hat from under the seat and put it on. 'But he was a simple man at heart. What he wanted was to be a carpenter like your dad. But that wasn't what his wife had in mind for him. For a while she tried to make him into a stockbroker or some such thing. He didn't have the heart for it. I guess I knew from the start that it wasn't going to work between them.'

He stopped suddenly and sat up straight. I watched him point over the dashboard. 'It's almost time,' he said.

A steady stream of cars had begun pulling into the garage—a procession of Mercedeses, Volvos, and the occasional Lexus. 'Just like you have in Hollywood, I bet,' he said to me. 'The symphony should thank God for doctors.'

The men and women getting out of these cars were dressed in long cashmere overcoats and evening gowns. I could hear the women's heels on the concrete as they hurried into elevators and disappeared. The garage was silent again.

'Here they come,' Warren said, just above a whisper.

I never see homeless people without thinking of the brilliant movie *Ironweed.* Tonight was no exception. But in my life I only drive past the homeless, and so I was unprepared for what I saw next. Each man and woman in rags took a different car and spread out on the bonnet of the engine.

'What are they doing?' I asked Warren.

'Keeping warm,' he said. 'On a cold night like this, they go from one indoor car park to the next.'

I counted thirteen men and women. Most of them lying with their arms out at their sides, as if they were trying to embrace the cars. 'I think of them as fallen angels,' Warren said, softly. 'When they lie like that, I mean . . . You know, I bought the carousel so I could be near him.'

He was distracted then, and I watched him as his eyes moved from one car to the next. Finally, he nodded. 'This is the hard part,' he said. He turned and looked at me. Then he pointed to a man lying across the hood of a silver station wagon. 'There,' he said. 'There's my brother.'

Though he must have only been in his late fifties, he had a grey beard, and a ragged navy-blue coat that reached almost to his ankles.

'That's Charles?' I said. 'He's your brother?'

Warren reached in front of me and rolled down my window. 'It's up to you,' he said. 'Maybe I'm wrong. Call his name if you want. Leave those things in the cottage. Do whatever you think is right. But you have to promise me one thing. You won't tell Callie. She believes he's dead. And there are things worse than that, remember?'

I DRANK TOO MUCH Scotch that night, staring at the telephone on my father's desk, trying to get up the courage to call Katherine to tell her. *Tell her what?* That I had to leave before she arrived? Yes, that was it. There were a hundred excuses, a thousand small lies I could tell her so that I wouldn't be here pretending I didn't know anything. Even *I* wasn't a good enough actor to pull off that deceit.

I thought about what Warren had told me, what my father had done here after Katherine called him to open *Serenity*, trying to reinstate Charles and Katherine in the cottage where they had last been happy in one another's presence.

Finally, I dialled Katherine's number. As soon as I heard her voice on the line I apologised. 'It's late,' I said. 'I'm sorry.'

She told me it was all right, that she was up anyway. 'Is it snowing there?' she asked.

I could see only my own reflection in the dark windows. 'I'm not sure,' I said. 'I'm sitting here in my father's workshop, but you don't know where that is, do you? And you never met my father, did you?'

'Are you all right?' she asked.

'And you never met me, Katherine. I'm just a voice on the telephone. I figured out about an hour ago that I am exactly thirty-eight years, seven months, and four days old, and I am trying to calculate what my father was doing at exactly this same age. Have you ever done that? I'm sorry, you don't have to answer that. I've been drinking.'

'I think I could tell.'

'I don't often drink.'

'Well, that's probably good.'

'I have to let go of you, Katherine.'

'Let go of me?'

'I mean, let you go. I have to let you go because it's late and the only reason you're awake is because some idiot called you from Maine. I just called to tell you that I can't be here when you arrive. I have to go back to California.'

'Oh,' she said. 'I'm sorry.' Her voice was a whisper.

'It's time for me to go home, that's all.'

She thanked me for everything I had done. 'I want you to send me a bill for your time.'

'No, that's silly.'

'I insist,' she said. 'I want you to write down my address and send me a bill.'

I wrote it down.

She said that she hoped we would meet someday. And this lingered with me while I slept in my father's chair with my head down on his desk.

AT FIRST LIGHT a throbbing pain in my head woke me. I drank two mugs of coffee and went to work.

Halfway through the morning, as I was running the vacuum cleaner across the tiled hall of the cottage, I heard someone shouting at me. The temperature was in the teens outside, but I had all the windows and doors wide open to air the place out. I turned and looked into the face of a tall, lanky kid who was breathing hard.

'They told me some old guy would meet me at the gate.'

'What are you talking about?'

'The tree,' he said, gesturing behind him. 'The Christmas tree. I tried not to drag it too much. There was supposed to be a guy to meet me at the gate. I've been out there for two hours freezing my tail off.'

'Do you have the guy's name?'

'McQuinn. Something McQuinn,' he said.

'That would have been my father. I'm sorry, kid. He died a few days ago.'

His face turned red. 'Oh Jeez,' he said.

'No, never mind,' I told him.

We drove back down Winslow Homer Lane in my car. I made him sit for a while so the heater could warm him.

'Do you have a bill?' I asked.

He pulled out an invoice that had the name and number of a tree farm in Waterville, Maine, about two hours north of Rose Point. The tree cost forty-seven dollars. Stapled to the back of the invoice was my father's cheque.

He followed in the truck. I knew where my father had planned to put the tree. As we carried it through the rooms of the cottage, I saw him looking around at everything. 'I've never seen a house like this before,' he said. 'You work here?'

'No, I'm just finishing up a job for my father.'

'Who owns the place anyway?' he asked.

'A woman from New York City.'

'Figures,' he said.

I heard myself in that remark. 'You'd like her,' I said.

Together we got the tree into the metal stand. It fitted the room perfectly.

'Enough room on top for an angel,' the kid said.

I told him that my father was a man who would have made his measurements carefully. '"Measure twice, cut once" was a motto he lived by.'

I thought about my father going to the trouble of ordering a Christmas tree for Charles Halworth's daughter. The date of the invoice showed that he had ordered the tree for her the day she told him she was coming to the cottage for Christmas.

I spent so much time vacuuming and mopping that by the time I returned from town late that afternoon with the plastic tarpaulin and the timber to build the skating rink, I had to use the car's headlights to see what I was doing.

WARREN MET ME at *Serenity* to help put down the rink. The stars overhead were so low and bright that they seemed to be moving as you stared at them. I told Warren that I didn't see stars like those in LA. I stared up at them until I was dizzy. I wondered aloud if I would ever learn to name them.

He told me that he knew it wasn't easy for me to leave. 'You want to see them back together, anyone would,' he said. 'But it's not that simple . . .' His hands were at his sides, nervously drumming his thighs. 'I just want you to know,' he went on, 'that I *have* tried to save my brother. I would gladly change places with him if that would help. People don't understand how anyone can live the way he lives, but he's found something with those people, I think. He takes care of the younger ones. I bring him to my place as often as he'll let me and get him cleaned up, dressed in decent clothes. I always try to keep him from going back.'

He stopped, and I told him that I understood.

'No,' he said, 'nobody can understand, really. Sometimes *I* don't understand.'

THE LAST THING we did was take the things from the bureau in the maid's room and put them in Warren's car. I told him that it was really none of my business what happened in this cottage. 'I think I blew it all out of perspective over the years. I made it into some beautiful, romantic thing. I'm going home where I belong.'

He just nodded and looked into my eyes. He said that next summer he might talk to whoever was in charge of hiring my father's replacement. 'The caretaker's job would be a way for me to keep an eye on my brother's daughter. To see that she always has what she needs.'

I asked him if he would shut down the cottage after Christmas.

He nodded. 'Don't worry, I'll close the place up.'

I thanked him for his help. 'Take care of yourself.'

'You too,' he told me.

IN THE MORNING I packed up my things. The bed frame I left as it was. And the sleeping-bag.

It was in honour of my father's memory that I took the time to decorate the Christmas tree in the widow's walk as he and I had done together once. When I finished I stood at the windows looking back towards the city, then out over Rose Point. At the white strand of beach where waves were running up onto the shore. I saw the yacht club with its grey docks pulled up onshore. The tall, pitched roof of the library. The open fields where the snow lay evenly. And the stately cottages standing in the wintery light. I wondered if I would ever see this place again.

I walked through the cottage one more time, feeling a part of myself in the rooms, along with my father. It was a good feeling, which surprised me and made me think that I had changed in some way in the days since I'd returned here.

AS SOON AS I GOT IN the car and turned on the radio, there was news of the storm. It was sweeping up the eastern seaboard; gale warnings had been posted for all of coastal Maine. Half a foot of snow had already fallen in Philadelphia, and in Providence and Hartford snow was falling at a rate of one inch per hour.

The highway south was clear all the way to Kittery, and I didn't let the car slip below eighty miles per hour. I was driving fast to try to keep myself from losing my resolve. I wanted to honour Warren's wishes, and I knew that if I didn't leave Rose Point behind me I wouldn't be able to keep myself from telling Katherine about her father. *This time, a clean break from the past*, I kept telling myself. I had held on long enough to the world at Rose Point, a world that had never included me except in my illusions.

When I crossed into Massachusetts the sky darkened and the snow began coming down hard on a slanting wind. As soon as the signs for Logan Airport appeared, the traffic grew heavy, and I had a sense that something was wrong.

Just outside the Ted Williams Tunnel, two state troopers were stopping cars.

'Airport's closed,' one of them said to me.

'For how long?'

'Indefinitely. A plane skidded across the main runway.'

'Can I get a flight to LA from anywhere else?'

'Providence will be shut down by the time you get there. New York's your only shot.'

Normally you figure Boston to New York is a four-hour drive, four and a half at the most. I knew it might take me twice as long today, which would make it six in the evening when I reached JFK Airport.

I lost an hour just getting back through the tunnel. On the highway I couldn't go faster than twenty miles an hour without the back end of the car fishtailing right and left. The blowing snow and the cadence of the windscreen wipers made me feel disconnected from time and more awake than the world around me.

It grew dark and I hadn't reached the border of Connecticut, impossible as this was for me to comprehend. I began to press down on the accelerator, but for some reason I was unable to close the distance; the miles seemed to be dividing and multiplying while I was frozen in place on a road that kept moving out ahead of me, pouring out of itself and spreading further and further into the distance.

I GOT AS FAR as the rental desk at JFK to return my car. I opened the car door and looked at the airport terminal, snow piled high on its flat roof. For some reason I began to divide the airport roof into sections, trying to calculate how long it would take me to shovel all the snow off. I thought of Warren telling me what my father had said to him, how no one should ever be completely forgotten. I thought about what Callie Boardman had said to me, how she hoped that I could stop running away.

It was three in the morning. I began driving north, through the snow and frozen slush, back to Maine.

CHAPTER SIX

When I saw the gate to Rose Point up ahead of me, I felt like I was coming out of a fever dream, stunned by the miles and hours without sleep, the numbing effect of driving blind, staring into swirling snow. I had driven hard, bearing down on the peaceful stillness of Rose Point and the woman who was a little girl when I last saw her.

It was late morning. The storm had blown offshore, and a hard amber light had seeped through the clouds. I was walking to my father's workshop for the key to the gate when I heard a sound enter this silent world, the sound of a dog barking.

From behind the snow-covered pine trees on a small promontory overlooking the harbour, I saw a black limousine parked at the shore alongside the granite rocks that protected the east side of the harbour. There was a white rowing boat tied to its roof.

Just beyond, I saw a woman and a child. 'It's them,' I said out loud. In an instant I felt the exhaustion leave me, replaced by such a surge of hope that I had to concentrate to catch my breath.

Katherine was holding the hand of her small child in red puddle boots that matched her own. She wore a long denim dress and a navy-blue coat that fell below her waist. Her dark hair was in a braid. How could I help but wonder at once about her husband? Perhaps he and I would shake hands. He would thank me for the work I had done.

These thoughts knocked something down inside me. What right had I to be here except my father's right, the right of the caretaker?

There was a yellow retriever running round them in wild, ecstatic loops, dipping its nose in the waves, biting at the snow, then charging back to lick the child's face and bark encouragement. I remembered what Katherine had told me when we spoke last. How she believed her days at the point would be live-over days for Olivia and for her. I hadn't really known what she had meant until I saw them on the shore where, it seemed, some aspect of them was being completed even as I watched.

Katherine looked happy, as you would expect. But I saw her weariness as well. She sat down on the rocks, not bothering to clear away the snow. She took the child into her arms and stared out at Pumpkin Island, which lay half a mile offshore. She rocked her daughter slowly, laying her cheek against the top of the child's head.

Then the driver came out of the limousine, a tall, barrel-chested man, as big as an opera tenor, dressed in black and wearing a chauffeur's cap. He untied the ropes that held the boat on the roof, then slid it onto the ground. He took oars from the boot and then stood quietly a moment with his hands clasped behind his back. Like a soldier, I thought, someone hired not simply to drive Katherine and her daughter from here to there, but to protect them.

Carefully Katherine took the child by both hands and led her to the boat one step at a time, then lifted her and placed her inside it. She kept one hand on the child's arm as she stepped into the boat herself. She took hold of the oars and placed the child's hands beside her own, and together they pretended to row. After a moment Katherine waved to the driver, and then the child waved too. The driver called to them, and this made the child wave even harder. He lingered a few moments before Katherine gestured for him to drive on. He returned to the car and drove away, slowly.

I had a sense that there was something wrong with Olivia, though I couldn't have known for sure. When it was just the two of them I saw more clearly that there was some inexplicable pattern to their movements, like they were bound awkwardly to one another, as if the child were falling and the mother were trying to catch her before she struck the ground.

Olivia placed her hands against her eyes. Katherine reacted at once, moving them away from her face. She leaned forward and said something to her before she stepped out of the boat. Then she took the child's hands and helped her out. I expected Olivia to run down the beach to the breaking waves. But she knelt in the sand for a little while, and then Katherine lifted her and carried her back up the rocks before they disappeared down Winslow Homer Lane.

THE STREETS OF PORTLAND were piled high with snow. Along the sidewalks a narrow path had been cleared for shoppers, who walked with their heads down against a stiff wind that shook the street signs and traffic lights. I passed up several forlorn-looking hotels until I came to the Regency, a handsome brick building with arched doors and a circular drive lit by old-fashioned gas lamps.

I paid for six nights, through Christmas, and asked the desk clerk if the front door was locked after a certain hour.

'Midnight,' she said. 'But your key opens it.'

'I'm going to need two keys,' I said. I told her that I would be meeting a friend during my stay and that I wanted him to be able to come and go as he pleased.

'I should write his name here then,' she said, taking a journal with a leather cover from beneath the counter.

'Charles Halworth,' I said, and told her that I wanted him to be able to charge incidentals to my room account. For this I had to sign a special invoice. I had no idea, really, what I was doing.

The room was very nice. Two large beds, a mahogany desk and dressing table, and three modest oil paintings. A wall of windows overlooked the Christmas tree in Monument Square.

AT A SWANKY MEN'S STORE an irrepressible little man spent the afternoon helping me. 'Do we know the occasion?' he asked. 'Office party? Dinner party? Travel?'

'Reunion,' I told him.

I guessed at Charles Halworth's size, figuring him to be just slightly larger than me. We began with seven pairs of dark, ribbed woollen socks and seven pairs of boxer shorts, then worked our way to corduroy trousers in olive green, tan and black. Navy-blue and wheat cable-knit sweaters. Half a dozen cotton shirts, a tweed sports jacket, and a dark blue cashmere overcoat that looked like Mr Halworth's ragged one might have looked when it was new. When we were finished we laid everything out. 'What do you think?' he asked me, sweeping his hand over our selection.

'What do I think?' I said. 'I think I'm crazy.'

'Pardon me, sir?'

'Nothing. Nothing.'

I had a simple plan. The next night I would find Charles Halworth in the multistorey car park. I would tell him that I was a rich man who wanted to do something good at Christmas. How could he say no to this? I would install him in Room 603 at the Regency, where he would dress in his new clothes and wait for me to come by and take him to Rose Point, thus delivering him into the world of the blessed, into the arms of his daughter and granddaughter. And we would all spend Christmas together at the cottage.

It was, at best, a childishly simple plan. I knew it would never work, and yet I could not resist it.

If you had said to me that I was still trying to turn Charles Halworth's life into a movie, that I had prepared the set and his costume, and that I was waiting for him to act out the part of a good father, I would have said you were wrong. Watching Katherine on the shore had convinced me that she needed her father.

THE NEXT MORNING I stood outside the cottage watching her walk towards me, holding her daughter's hand. I studied her black hair, the way a few loose strands had curled in the moist air. And her long fingers. And the way the cold had coloured her cheeks red.

I heard the hard-packed snow creak beneath her feet. 'I'm Katherine,' she said, offering me her hand. She seemed pleased to see me. 'I thought we were alone here,' she said. 'Have you come to Maine for Christmas?'

It took me a moment to realise that she thought I was another resident. 'I'm Terry McQuinn,' I said, taking off my father's glove and holding out my hand for her to shake.

She looked surprised. 'You didn't go back to California?'

'The storm,' I said. 'The airports were closed.'

'Brought together by a storm?' she said, as if she were thinking out loud.

'Fate,' I said.

'Well, this is my good fortune,' she said, smiling. 'I've put you to so much trouble, though.'

'No,' I said. 'It's been good work.'

Just then I remembered the last time we spoke. 'I'm sorry about that last call. I'm not a drinker, really.'

'Don't be sorry,' she said.

She looked into my eyes, holding me in her gaze. She had those sea green eyes you seldom encounter. So green you had to look again to be sure. Then she turned and looked back at the cottage above us. 'Isn't the house something?' she exclaimed. 'What is it, Olivia?' she asked the child.

'My castle,' the child said, with delight. 'C for castle.'

'C for castle, that's right, Teapot,' Katherine said.

I watched Olivia press her fists up against her eyes. Katherine responded immediately by gently pulling them away. 'What else lives in the C book?' she asked.

'Cake. Cake and cars!' Olivia said proudly.

'Yes! Yes,' her mother said. Then, in quick succession the child's fists flew against her eyes again, and Katherine moved them, holding them back the last time.

'And curtains,' Olivia said. 'And Carmel, California.'

Katherine took her in her arms. 'Oh yes,' she said. It was as if I had vanished and it was only the two of them. She was smiling when she kissed Olivia's cheek, but when she turned and looked at me, I saw the smile fading.

I was reluctant to say anything.

'Did you freeze last night?' I asked.

'We were fine,' she said. 'Olivia and I slept in the blue room with scallop shells stencilled in gold round the ceiling. Didn't we love your grandmother's old blue bed?'

'Cambridge, England,' Olivia said.

'It's the *Encyclopedia Britannica*,' Katherine said to me. 'We made poor Lawrence bring the whole set to Maine with us.'

Lawrence. I took a chance and asked. 'Is Lawrence your husband?'

'Oh,' she replied. 'Poor, dear Lawrence. I don't think he would wish to be my husband in a thousand years. I drive him crazy as it is. He helps us get around,' she went on. 'It's just the three of us. He's in town getting warm. Lawrence has a tolerance for many things. Tobacco. Alcohol. Poker. But not for the cold. He was shivering like a schoolboy so I ordered him to town.'

Each time she smiled, it surprised me that I wished my father were here to see her. I pictured him carrying the Christmas tree lights and the angel up to the widow's walk in preparation for her visit. Placing Charles Halworth's things in the white bureau for her to discover. Setting up the stage as I had done at the hotel for her father.

'Come closer,' she said to me suddenly. 'Come and meet Olivia.'

I didn't know how close to come. I took a step, and then another when she gestured with her hand.

'Olivia,' I said. 'It's a lovely name.'

Katherine thanked me. 'You see, Mommy gave you a lovely name,' she said to her daughter. 'This is Mr McQuinn,' she said. But the child would not look at me.

I asked her to please call me by my first name. 'Whenever you say "Mr McQuinn", I think my father must be standing behind me.'

There must have been an edge to those words, because she turned and faced me with a curious expression. Then she touched Olivia's face. 'Terry opened your grandmother's castle for us.'

'I loved your message,' I said to Olivia. 'And I left you a beep. A couple, in fact. Did you hear my beeps?'

She nodded her head. I saw her eyes clearly for the first time, cloudy pools of white with just a trace of brown. Floating eyes, without light or a spark of recognition.

Katherine smiled and said she had been walking from room to room in the cottage, looking for signs that she had been there as a child. This took my breath away.

'My mother swears I never was,' she said. 'But she revises history. Still, I didn't find anything broken.'

I asked her what she meant by this. Before she answered she set Olivia down and took the child's cane from inside her coat. Without saying a word, she placed it in Olivia's hands and the little girl wandered off.

'I was the terror of the neighbourhood when I was a kid,' she said to me. 'I broke everything. There's always one like that, I've learned.'

She was laughing now. And smiling. I watched her and thought of the resilience of her spirit.

'So if you found anything broken when you were opening the cottage,' she continued, 'I must have been here.'

'But you weren't ever here before?'

'No. Apparently not.'

'And your mother just told you about the place?'

'Last month, before she and her new husband left for England. I think she felt sorry for us.'

She said nothing for a moment, and I watched with her as Olivia walked a little way away from us. She walked slowly in the deep snow. When she seemed to going straight for a birch tree, I began to say something. Katherine raised her hand. 'No,' she whispered. 'She'll find her way.'

And she did. The tip of her cane struck the tree, then Olivia reached out and touched it. She stood there for several minutes, running her hands over the bark.

'Does she see anything?' I asked.

'Not any more. Until she was one, she could see bright lights. I was teaching her colours. But we didn't finish.'

I told her I was sorry, and she looked at me as if she had just remembered that I was standing next to her.

'She's the reason I finally got to see Maine,' she said happily. 'I've always wanted to come to Maine, and we brought a skiff with us.'

'A skiff?' I said, stupidly.

'A rowing boat. You're not a sailor?'

'No, I'm afraid I never spent any time around boats.'

'You grew up here and no one ever took you sailing?'

'I lived in a different world.'

'What a shame you've never sailed,' she said earnestly. She paused momentarily, then continued to tell me that she had to row out to Pumpkin Island. 'The first thing we did when we got here yesterday was to walk on the beach and look at the island. My mother claims to have buried her pet dog on Pumpkin Island when she was a little girl. You see, when she told me about this house I was certain she was making the whole thing up. Then she told me about the dog's grave, and I assured her that I would check her story. I found life jackets in the carriage house. One small enough to fit Olivia, which must have been for my mother when she was a child. Would you like to come with us?'

I wondered briefly how many ways I could embarrass myself in a boat. 'I wouldn't miss it,' I said. 'It might be a live-over journey, especially with me aboard.'

She was so pleased with this. 'Our *live-over* days in Maine. You remembered,' she said, without taking her eyes off her daughter. By now, Olivia had found her way round to the skating rink. We watched her kneel down and touch the ice with both hands. Then Katherine spoke again as if I weren't there. 'I took my daughter to the best facility in the world for blind children. When we first arrived the director spoke to all of us in an auditorium. He told the children that they were going to have to learn to be twice as smart as sighted children. Twice as hardworking. Twice as strong. I was sitting there listening to this man, when it dawned on me that what he was really saying was that my daughter was only half a person and so she would have to try twice as hard. It broke my heart, Terry. I took Olivia's hand and we walked out of the auditorium.'

I saw her fierce determination. It seemed to deepen the green in her eyes.

'I'm not sure I did the right thing,' she said, sadly. She turned and began walking away. As the space between us widened, I wanted to call her back and tell her that she *had* done the right thing, that feeling like half a person was exactly how I had felt about myself in comparison to the summer people at Rose Point, just as I had told Callie. Even then, in the first glimpse of the instinct she carried in her heart, I didn't want her to walk away. I watched her kneel down on the ice rink and put her arm round her daughter. I was certain, the way we are about some things, that the sight of them would be enough to draw Charles Halworth back to the world of the hopeful and the loved. And so long as they were here, in the cottage, just down the lane from me, they were not lost to him. They would never be lost to him as long as I knew where they were.

CHAPTER SEVEN

I met the limousine coming the other way on the lane as I walked to my father's workshop. I waved, the car rolled to a stop, and the driver's window went down, revealing Lawrence behind the wheel. He was in his fifties, with silver hair slicked back. When I introduced myself he pointed to a shoe box beside him on the seat.

'Would you have some place to hide this until Christmas?' he asked me. He lifted the lid off the box and showed me a tiny brown rabbit, with a twitching pink nose and black eyes. I saw the yellow dog in back, his face pressed to the glass panel.

'That's Jack,' Lawrence said. 'He wants the bunny for lunch. Right, Jack?'

He introduced himself to me as he followed me into the store with the shoe box. 'Lawrence Wilson, at your service,' he said. The rabbit was for Olivia, he told me. 'She has stolen my heart,' he said. 'I also went to L.L. Bean, but I couldn't find the thing I was searching for.'

'What was that?' I asked.

'A sledge. A real sledge, not a plastic one. Are you too young to remember the Flexible Flyer?'

'No, I remember them,' I said. 'You're Katherine's driver?'

'Newly appointed, yes,' he said. 'I was eighteen years with the queen mother until she shipped off for England with husband number six.'

'The queen mother? Is that Mrs Halworth?'

'Halworth is a name she discarded five husbands ago. She's been a Tilly, a Frederick and a Constantine since I went to work for her. Before I arrived on the scene, a Wentworth.'

'And her daughter?'

'She's got Tilly's name,' he said. 'That would be the husband after Halworth.'

'I remember her when she was Halworth,' I said, waiting for him to question me.

'From where?' he asked.

'Here. Thirty years ago she and her husband spent some time at the cottage. My father was caretaker here. I helped him open their house one Christmas.'

By the way he was looking at me, I knew he had figured out what I was going to say next.

'Katherine would have been four or five? Did they bring her with them?' he asked.

'Yes,' I said. 'Why did her mother tell her she'd never been here before?'

He took off his hat and sat down beside the band saw. 'The father, I suppose,' he said. 'I'd been working for the queen for about a year when I asked her about Katherine's father. None of my business, you know, but I was curious. She told me the guy was a real bad character. He'd tried to kidnap the girl once. Her mother and her second husband were on a golf course, riding in a cart with Katherine between them. The crazy man stalked them on a golf course. Wouldn't you have to be one of the world's great idiots to try to kidnap someone on a golf course?'

'Or very desperate,' I said.

FOR A WHILE we worked together, trying to build a rabbit cage. I kept making mistakes and pretending they weren't mistakes, trying to save face. Finally, I confessed that I had none of my father's skills, and we used his tool chest for a cage, lying a screen window over the top and filling the bottom with wood shavings.

'That's a creature who'll be loved, right there,' Lawrence said, as we finished. 'You'll have to prise this bunny out of Olivia's hands. Be careful, that little pirate will steal your heart.'

I liked his smile and his enthusiasm. I thought that, when the time came, I would tell him the true story about Charles Halworth and he would understand.

I asked him about Katherine's husband.

He raised his eyebrows. 'She and Olivia are on a very small boat. There's no husband on board, my friend. No room for one.'

'*Was* there a husband?'

'There was an Oliver something the fourth. Engaged to be married, I take it. But when Katherine wouldn't give up the child, he took off.'

'Give up the child?'

'Katherine's a social worker, and there was this blind baby that no one wanted. Katherine took her—you know, just until they could find a foster home—and adopted the little pirate. Oliver wasn't a bad fellow, from what I've heard. But he didn't take to the idea of raising a blind child that wasn't even his. None of us can know what we would do in a situation like that. He left. And she bought a set of encyclopaedias.' He paused and smiled to himself. 'They don't sleep at night, you know. They study. All the way up it was *Chandelier. China. Chile.* I got an education while I drove.'

Just before he left, the workshop phone rang. It was one of the summer people, checking in to see how much snow had fallen on his roof in the storm. I told him that my father had died.

'I'm sorry to hear that,' he said. 'Will you be taking over from him?'

Before I could respond he asked me if I would be shovelling the snow off his roof today or tomorrow. 'Your father always cleared my roof first,' he said. 'Above the billiards room there's been a problem with leakage.'

'Leakage,' I said, and I hung up.

'You'll hear from every one of them now,' Lawrence told me. 'They'll call to express their sympathy for your father, but really to make sure someone's on board to do his work. I know rich people.'

LAWRENCE WAS RIGHT about the summer people. I spent the afternoon fielding calls from them. They asked me about the storm and if I was going to clear their roofs. I told them I was making a list of names and that I would do my best to get to them. Each person who called wanted to know where they were on my list.

I didn't see Katherine and Olivia again that day. I shovelled snow from the Eldredge roof, where the drifts reached up to my waist. From there I could see most of the cottages and more snow than I could have shovelled if I'd had the rest of the winter to finish.

'THEY'RE SLEEPING,' Lawrence told me when I went to the cottage the next morning to borrow a kettle. He looked at his watch. 'Is it really the twenty-second?' he asked.

'It is,' I told him.

'I've lost track of the days since I left New York. They'll be asleep for at least another two hours. They were up studying most of the night. So you're a tea man, are you?'

I was distracted by the thought of the two of them in the cottage, asleep somewhere above me. 'I'm sorry. Tea? No.'

I told him I needed the kettle for an idea I had to make a sledge for Olivia. He was curious.

'Come with me and I'll show you,' I said, and we walked back to the workshop together.

I built a wooden box long enough to hold some oak strips that my father had in a pile, then propped it up above the kettle on the woodstove as the water boiled and steam filled the box. We repeated this with six pots of water until the steam had softened the oak slats enough so we could round the ends into runners for the sledge.

'Hey,' he said with surprise. 'That's going to work, I believe.'

'My reputation is on the line here, Lawrence,' I said.

'But this is not your line of work. What do you do?'

I told him I worked in California. 'I represent people in the film industry,' I said, intending to be vague and hoping to leave it at that.

He was delighted. 'The movies? You represent actors and actresses?'

'That's it,' I said. 'Producers, directors. Writers.'

'Oh, I always wanted to act,' he said, wistfully.

The whole time we talked, I wanted to tell him what I knew about Katherine's father. Maybe I should have done so. And maybe I should have told him what I had felt when I first saw her and her daughter on the shore. But I didn't say anything because I wasn't sure how he would react. What I wanted to tell him was that standing in front of the cottage with Katherine and Olivia had made me feel that I would remember them as long as I lived, and if it took until the end of my life to reconcile Katherine and her father to their past, I would patiently try.

I CALLED MY OFFICE that afternoon. There were forty-three messages on my voicemail. In the end there was only one that I cared enough about to return, an actor I had been through good times and bad times with, mostly bad times. 'I screwed up the audition,' he said when I called him back. 'And I *had* it, Terry, I swear, they wanted to *give* me the bloody part.'

'There'll be other parts, Lewis. Have faith.'

'In what?' he asked.

'Yourself.'

'I can't,' he told me, softly.

I could feel the anguish in his voice. 'OK then, Lewis, have faith in me. I'm with you, Lewis. So hang in there. I'll make some calls.'

The truth is, there wasn't a casting person in town I could lean on to get him work. He was fifty now, at the dark turn in the road.

I caught myself talking to the rabbit about Lewis while I sanded the seat for Olivia's sledge. 'Let's see, Mr Rabbit, who still owes me a favour in the city of angels?'

Before I could come up with a single name, there was a knock at the door, and there she was. A streak of red sky behind her. She said she only had a moment and she was smiling at me in a way that made me feel she was pleased to see me.

'I went by the cottage earlier,' I said. 'Did you sleep well?'

'Like bears,' she said. 'The air is so wonderful here.'

I asked her to sit down, but she didn't. And then I wondered if she had smiled at me a moment earlier because she was glad to see me or if I had read too much into this.

She wanted to know if I had any interest in going into Portland with them tonight. 'Do you know Dylan Thomas's *A Child's Christmas in Wales*?''

Maybe I should have told her the truth, that I'd represented the director who did the adaptation for network television. 'I know the story, yes,' was all I said.

'I've always wanted Olivia to see it,' she said, 'and it's playing in the city tonight.'

We stood together on the steps of the workshop before she left. She gestured beyond the harbour towards the River Road, where there was a small development of ranch houses. 'I guess those would be the real folks out beyond the castle walls,' she said.

I named the families for her. The Sullivans, whose daughter Mary Lou once won the Miss Maine contest. Paul Joseph, who built racing cars out of wrecked cars. Link and Julie Cutler, who lived in the church one winter when their trailer burned to the ground. I had gone to school with the kids who grew up in those houses. To them the summer people had the allure of royalty.

'I ran away from those people,' I told her.

She turned and looked at me. 'To find fame and fortune?'

'I don't know any more.'

'What did you find?'

'No fame,' I said. 'A little fortune.'

'In Hollywood,' she said. 'Lawrence told me.'

'Yes,' I said.

She gazed past me. 'I don't think a movie could do justice to this beautiful place, do you?'

I thought a moment. 'I'm glad it's real,' I said.

She smiled at this and our eyes met. 'Yes, me too.'

We were silent for a while. The wind shifted and carried the scent of burning wood down the lane to where we stood.

'You got your fireplaces going?' I said.

'All seven of them. I was once a Girl Scout.'

'A Girl Scout. You look like a Girl Scout.'

'An old one, maybe. Circles under my eyes.'

'No,' I said, 'your eyes are beautiful.'

She seemed startled by what I had said. I thought how sad it was that Olivia would never see her eyes.

'Thank you.' She turned away quickly and went down the steps. 'We'll come for you at seven thirty?'

'Do I need my tuxedo?'

She smiled. 'Yes, absolutely.' She lingered a moment, then she waved. 'Goodbye,' she said.

JACK, THE DOG, sat in front with Lawrence and Olivia, with an expression on his face that said, *I could drive this thing if they'd give me a chance.* Olivia was giggling at something Lawrence had said.

'I always wonder what she would think if she knew what splendour we travelled in,' Katherine said.

'L,' I said. 'You'll get to limousine in your encyclopaedias.'

She looked at me knowingly. 'Lawrence told you,' she said. 'I'm doing the best I can.'

'She's a beautiful girl,' I said. 'And she has you.'

We drove the length of Congress Street. Among the Christmas shoppers in the square I saw two men in rags pushing a shopping cart piled with rubbish bags. Impulsively, I slid open the glass panel.

'Take a right up here,' I called to Lawrence. Another right, and two blocks later we were waiting in line at the multistorey car park Warren had brought me to.

As soon as we reached the second level I saw them waiting in the shadows. I asked Lawrence to stop. 'Just for a minute,' I said. I got out and walked towards them.

Charles was standing off by himself, shifting his weight from foot to foot to keep warm. Staring at me, I thought. Then I knew it was the limo he was looking at.

'I need to hire someone to help me,' I said to him. 'Ten dollars an hour. More if you work hard.'

I put out my hand to Charles. He didn't hesitate to shake it.

'Can I bring a few guys with me?'

'Anybody you can find,' I said. His face was drawn and the grey beard made him look like an ancient mariner. Still, there was a quickness in his manner that fitted perfectly my memory of him bounding down the hospital corridor in a Santa Claus outfit. 'I'll pick you up here at seven tomorrow morning, is that all right?'

'Yes,' he said. 'Thanks.'

'Thank *you*,' I said. 'I can use the help.'

He never asked me what he would be doing or where he would be working.

'I've got thirty roofs to shovel,' I explained when I got back in the limo. 'I've asked for some help.'

THERE WAS A MOMENT in the limousine after the show. Katherine had taken off her necklace, a single strand of pearls, and given it to Olivia to hold. The child placed the necklace in my hands and then sat beside me and rested her head on my arm. This surprised me, and I was self-conscious at first, sliding down in my seat as if I'd never sat in a car before. I saw Katherine smiling at this. I watched her taking the braid out of her hair. When she leaned across the space dividing us and kissed Olivia, her hair brushed my hand. 'You have a new friend,' she said, looking up at me.

By the time we reached the cottage, Olivia was asleep. I carried her inside, up the stairs to the pale blue bedroom where her encyclopaedias were in stacks on the floor. The moment I laid her down on the bed in front of the window she woke up and cried out. 'My C book,' she said desperately.

'I'll find it,' I said. 'It's right here.'

It took me a while. When I placed it in her hands she thanked me.

'Olivia?' I said, and she smiled at me. 'Do you know what your mommy looks like?'

Her smile never changed. 'No,' she said, 'I don't see Mommy.'

I said good night to her. She was opening the pages of the encyclopaedia. The book that would accompany her through the dark night. At the door I turned back and said, 'You have a beautiful mommy, Olivia.'

She looked up at the ceiling. 'I know I do,' she said.

I WILL REMEMBER THIS, I thought, as the gate to Rose Point swung open and Charles Halworth bowed his head, gazing at the floor of the car. He would not look out of the window. A kind of surrender, I thought.

He said nothing. Neither did the two men who had come along with him to work for me. I had stopped at the hardware store for shovels. The three of them were dressed inadequately for the bitter cold morning, but in the hardware store I could buy them only gloves and hats. I made one last stop at Dunkin' Donuts, where they were selling a special Christmas vacuum flask. I bought three, and filled them with black coffee.

For the first part of the morning I worked with them on the roof of the Eldredge place. I was never more than ten feet from Charles, watching him, waiting for him to say something to me. He shovelled with his head down, ploughing through the drifts with powerful strokes. Just once I saw him pause, stand up straight, and gaze across the Point. A moment later he was back to work.

At noon we moved the ladders to the next cottage. I told the men that I would be back to pay them before dark and to drive them into town.

Charles nodded his head and began climbing. The rubber sole of one trainer was flapping loosely. His thin khaki trousers were mended with strips of insulating tape. What was it about me, I wondered angrily, that still believed I could fix his life? This man didn't want his life to be fixed, yet I believed I could sit with him tonight in my father's workshop and tell him the daughter he lost was here, just down the road, with a limousine for him to ride in from now on.

I'm a fool, I thought. Somewhere during my years in Hollywood I had lost my sense of what was real.

'HERE ARE THESE life jackets,' Katherine said, when she greeted me on the beach that afternoon. They were the old orange stuffed ones that hung over your chest. If the sea had been anything but flat calm I would have tried to talk them out of this trip to Pumpkin Island in a boat so small.

Katherine put a life jacket on Olivia, but when she tried to tie her own, the canvas straps were twisted at the back and they wouldn't reach round her.

'Let me help,' I said. I stood behind her. Her hair smelt like apples, and I felt the warmth of her skin.

'You must tell Terry what you read last night, Teapot,' Katherine said to Olivia.

'Canada,' the child, said brightly. 'And guess what, Terry?'

I loved hearing her say my name. 'What is it, Olivia?'

'They skate on ice in Canada. Like the ice you made for me and Mommy.' She smiled with pleasure. When I looked at Katherine, she had the same smile.

'Maybe Santa Claus will bring you some skates,' I said.

'Santa Claus isn't real,' Olivia said, with a serious expression. 'He's a story, right, Mommy?'

'A lovely story,' Katherine said. 'But not real, you're right.'

We got under way. The dog laid his head on Olivia's knees as I rowed us through a cathedral of silence. Seals popped their heads up through the water like submarine periscopes. Gulls were circling overhead. 'So peaceful,' I heard Katherine say. Then she began singing to her daughter. '"There'll be blue birds over the white cliffs of Dover, tomorrow, just you wait and see. When the world is free. Just you wait and see."'

Halfway out Katherine pointed back to the shore. 'Look, you can see the men on the roof.'

I turned.

'What men?' Olivia asked.

'Terry has some nice men shovelling snow from the roof of a big green cottage,' her mother said.

'Why?' she asked.

I explained that it was the weight of the snow.

'Such a beautiful place,' Katherine said. 'I can't believe my mother's had the cottage locked up my whole life.'

'It's yours now. You can come back whenever you wish.'

'It hasn't sunk in yet,' she said. 'Could we live here year round, do you think?'

'You'd have to put in some kind of heating and insulate the pipes. But you could do it. It gets lonely here, though.'

She hugged Olivia. 'We never get lonely, do we, Teapot?'

'Would you live here with us, Terry?' Olivia asked. 'We have twelve big bedrooms!'

'You do, that's right.'

'And you should be staying with us,' Katherine said. 'Unless you're staying in your father's workshop to be close to his spirit.'

'Where is your father?' the child asked.

I almost said he was in heaven.

'Terry lost his father,' Katherine said.

'I lost my father too,' Olivia said.

'And look at Jack,' said Katherine swiftly. 'He lost his mother *and* his father.'

At the mention of his name, the dog swung his head towards Katherine, pushing his nose against her hand until she patted him.

'It's no wonder dogs try so hard to please,' she said. 'They begin their lives as orphans, taken from their mothers.'

All my life I'd been around dogs, and never once had I thought of them as orphans. But from now on they will always be orphans to me. Maybe the force of beauty is contained in its ability to surprise us. This is what drew me close to Katherine in our first hours together. If you can fall in love with someone for the things they say, then I was already in love with her.

IN TWENTY MINUTES we were there. I held my arms out to Olivia, forgetting she couldn't see me. 'May I lift you out, Olivia?' I asked.

She looked up at me, smiling like she had won something. 'Lift me, Terry,' she said, eagerly.

'Go! Run!' Katherine shouted to Jack. He jumped to his feet and charged off to explore the island.

'If he were a person,' she said, 'he'd be late for work every day and leave his clothing all over the house.'

'If I were a dog,' I said, setting Olivia down, 'I'd hope to find a little girl just like you, Olivia.'

'Blind like me?' she asked.

I saw Katherine looking at me. When I looked into her eyes she didn't turn away.

'Exactly like you,' I said to Olivia.

Katherine took her daughter's hand. She told her that there were slippery rocks on the shore and that she would have to hold her hand tightly. Then she said, 'And now we get to find out if your grandmother was telling us the truth.'

There were only three trees on the island, and it took us minutes to find what Katherine was searching for. I held Olivia again while her mother got down on her knees and dug away the snow. Below the third tree we found a round stone set in the frozen ground, with these words carved into its face: *Our Beloved Friend, Sally*.

Katherine placed Olivia's hands on the stone and helped her trace the letters.

'I asked my mother why I should believe her,' Katherine said, 'after all these years of keeping this place hidden from me. Don't get me wrong, she's not a bad person, but there have been a lot of lies in my family. I asked her why she hadn't told me about the cottage before, and she said because she was always going to sell the place. But she never followed through. It wasn't that she ever planned on coming back, but I think some part of her wanted me to have the cottage. The part of her that isn't made of slate.'

It began snowing while we walked together across the centre of the island. When we got to an open field, Katherine hooked the leash to Jack's collar and placed the other end in Olivia's hand. 'You and Jack can walk here,' she said. And then to the dog, 'Take your girl for a stroll.'

Somehow the dog knew to move cautiously. As we followed behind, I listened to Katherine talk about her life. I felt her leaning closer to me, her voice becoming calmer and more familiar. 'When I first met Olivia she was nine months old and had been in four foster homes already. Well, any mother will tell you that there's a magical time at nine months. The baby has learned how to sleep through the night, and how to eat and to sit up. It's amazing. With feet still small enough to wash in a teacup, and yet smiling at you and making intelligent sounds to try to communicate. I fell in love, and I couldn't give her away.'

We stopped and watched Olivia making a snowball. When she had finished, she threw it up into the air and the dog caught it in his mouth.

'And she's been a gift to me,' Katherine went on. 'Olivia has taught me to live in the present. That's a *great* gift, you know? She's made me a better person.'

I waited a moment, then told her she and Olivia were both lucky. 'You have each other,' I said.

She didn't seem to hear this. 'I already told you that I was the kid in my neighbourhood who broke everything,' she said. 'Well, I grew into a young woman in a broken family. And then my engagement was broken. And now I'm a mother with a broken child.' She laughed at herself. 'I never thought of this before,' she said.

IT WAS SNOWING harder when we made our way back to the shore. The wind was stronger as well. Olivia was in her mother's arms. When we reached the top of a bluff I was shocked to see that the passage between us and the Point had disappeared in fog and blowing snow.

'Where did *that* come from?' I said. 'We have to go, we have to hurry now, Katherine.'

I took Olivia from her and we ran down to the shore. We followed our footprints in the snow. They led us to where the boat had been, but the tide had turned while we were exploring, and the boat was gone. We stood looking for it through the dizzying snow. The sea was no longer calm; there were strong waves breaking on the beach.

'The tide took it,' I said, miserably. 'My damn fault.'

At last Katherine spotted it, maybe thirty feet out. I took off my boots and waded into the freezing water. The beach fell off sharply beneath my feet. I swam only a few strokes before my arms turned to lead. I had to force myself to keep moving.

It took for ever to reach the boat, and when I grabbed hold of it to pull myself up, I couldn't tighten my grip enough to keep from slipping off. It took several tries before I was able to drape my arms over the stern—first one, then the other—with great effort. I saw the sea water run off my coat sleeves and make a puddle in the bottom of the boat. I closed my eyes and tried again to tell myself what I needed to do to turn the boat round and bring it back to the island. There was a pounding in my head, and when I looked down at my hands I saw they were a deep red, as if they had been scalded. *Kick*, I told myself. *Keep kicking until you turn the boat round.* I could barely feel my legs, but slowly the bow began to turn. I was shaking violently and my eyes were closed when I felt the shore under my knees and someone taking hold of me.

'Here we are,' I heard Katherine say very softly, as if there was nothing to fear. 'Here we are, Olivia, you're going to help me get Terry into the boat now.'

I opened my eyes and saw their hands on my arms.

'We're going to make our way back to Rose Point now,' Katherine said.

They lifted and pushed me until I was on the floor of the boat. Then Katherine made the dog lie next to me, and I felt the warmth of its fur. 'Stay, Jack,' she said.

She rowed us steadily through the black waves. 'We don't have far to go,' she said. 'We'll all take nice hot baths when we get home. We'll have hot chocolate.'

'What about Jack?' Olivia called out.

'Gravy and potatoes for Jack,' Katherine said.

As we neared the point the wind grew even stronger. I saw the blowing spray off the whitecaps washing across their faces. I watched Katherine working the oars, turning us from side to side to keep us steady in the churning waves. And then she shouted to someone. 'Oh yes!' she said. 'There's someone to help us.'

I heard her yelling, 'Thank you. Thank you, sir.' Suddenly I saw Charles Halworth's face. And then his arms as he lifted Olivia out of the boat and onto his shoulders. I understood then what was happening. The waves were crashing behind us and it was only a matter of time, seconds, before a wave would lift up the back of the boat and flip us over.

'Keep rowing,' I heard Charles telling Katherine.

He had the bow against his chest and was walking backwards. Only his head and shoulders were above the water. Each time a wave ran beneath us from behind and raised the back of the boat, he lifted the front to hold us flat.

WE WERE SAFELY on the beach when Charles lifted me from the boat and laid me in the sand. I looked up and saw his face. Salt water had turned his lips white. Beside him, Katherine was holding Olivia and looking down at me. 'He saw us from the roof, Terry,' she said. 'How will we ever thank you?'

It was only a moment, The three of them together. Finally together. Three people who shared the same soul had somehow travelled across time and were standing together on this shore. Though none of them knew it.

'Up we go,' Charles said. He lifted me onto his back. I heard him tell me to talk to him and I tried, but I was slipping away. The last thing I remember was the fear that the moment had passed us by, that this group of three would now scatter in different directions, never to find one another again.

CHAPTER EIGHT

I was in the blue bedroom in the cottage with Lawrence. He had taken off my clothes, wrapped me in blankets, and put me in a stuffed chair in front of a roaring fire.

'Katherine wants me to get you in the tub,' he said.

'Not now,' I told him. 'Let me sit here. But where's Charles?'

'Who?'

'The man who helped us,' I said.

'He's downstairs with the others. I gave him some of my clothes. They want me to drive them back to the city.'

I thought of the hotel room. 'Lawrence, can you bring him up here, please? I need to tell him something.'

He left to get him. I looked into the fire and tried to piece together what had happened, how I'd got here. I remembered Charles taking me out of the boat and laying me in the sand.

Then I turned and saw Charles in the doorway.

'Are you OK?' I asked him.

'Yes,' he said. 'The others wanted me to ask for our money. I told them we could wait if you can't pay us now. Are you going to be all right?'

I looked into his eyes and thanked him. 'There's money in the workshop. It's in the drawer below the bench.'

'I don't think I can do that.'

'It's fine. Take a hundred for each of you. Would that be enough?'

'More than enough. Thank you.' He turned to leave.

'No, wait, please. Do you remember the caretaker here?'

He nodded. 'I knew the man,' he said.

'I know you did,' I said to him. He was looking right at me then. 'I'm his son.'

He didn't turn away.

I told him that he had been gone a long time. He just looked down at the floor. 'So have I,' I said. 'But we've both come back.'

I told him that I had a room he could stay in. 'The Regency Hotel,' I said. 'There's a room key in the same drawer with the money, in the workshop. You can stay there.'

He took a deep breath, then raised his head. 'Thank you,' he said, 'but I can't take handouts.'

'Think of it as a repayment, then, for saving my life.'

He thought about this. 'Could my friends use it?'

'Whatever you want,' I said. 'I left your name at the desk,' I said.

'My name?' he said.

'Charles Halworth,' I said.

It took a moment before he spoke again. 'I think you took my fingerprint once,' he said.

'A long time ago,' I said.

He lowered his eyes again. 'I never forgot.'

'I never forgot either,' I said.

He glanced out onto the landing. When he looked back at me, he said, 'I won't be back tomorrow.'

'I could use your help.'

'I'm sorry,' he said.

'Don't be sorry. I'm glad you were here today.'

He left then. I listened to him going down the stairs. I thought of going after him. If I never saw him again, I'd never forgive myself for letting him leave. But what would *he* want, I wondered. What would he want me to do? I thought over everything that Warren and Callie had told me, and I decided that I couldn't say anything until I spoke with him again and told him the truth.

Lawrence came upstairs again. 'He asked me to go into your workshop for him. He doesn't want to get the money himself.'

'Fine,' I said. 'In the drawer below the workbench. And the key.

There's a key there for Room 603 in the Regency Hotel. Can you take him there, please?'

'Done,' he said. 'Get your bath. You look awful.'

I DON'T KNOW how long I slept in the chair in front of the fire. When I awoke the house was quiet and I could feel my legs again. I got to my feet slowly. When I turned, I saw Katherine and Olivia asleep on the bed behind me. The dog was on the floor. His tail flew up for a second, but other than this he remained perfectly still. A resigned look was in his dark eyes, as if this were part of his job, to guard them and to wait patiently for them to return from wherever it was they went in their sleep.

Olivia was wearing white tights under a crimson velvet dress that was covered in dog hairs. Her mother wore a matching dress and blue woollen tights. The black braid of her hair fell over her left shoulder onto her breast. Though they were asleep, they didn't seem to be resting, as if their sleep had not carried them away from the concerns of the waking world.

When I stepped closer to them, the dog raised his head in anticipation. For a moment I had a sense that I belonged here and that I had travelled across a vast emptiness to stand in this room with them.

The day was almost over, the last of the sea light lay in a ribbon across the room. I was looking at Katherine when she opened her eyes. 'I came upstairs to help you get a bath,' she whispered. 'But you were sleeping.'

'I'm fine,' I said. 'I'm warm.'

'No,' she said, 'you need a bath.' She got off the bed slowly, without waking Olivia. I followed her along the landing, looking at her hand and wanting to take it in mine.

She went into the bathroom ahead of me, closed the door behind us and began drawing the water. 'I'm going to sit outside the door,' she said.

When the tub was full and I had turned off the water, I heard her call to me in a low voice.

'I forgot to tell you we have pink water,' she said. 'Very stylish.'

I told her it was the rust that had collected in the old cast-iron pipes. 'The pipes were drained for thirty years,' I told her. 'I helped my father close this place. I was eight years old. Kennedy had just been assassinated. It was Christmas. Your mother wanted *Serenity* opened for Christmas.' I waited, trying not to move, or make a sound that would prevent me from hearing her.

'She came to *Serenity* for Christmas? That sounds too sentimental for my mother. She has bad memories of this place. The memory of my father before he left her.'

'Well, you have the place now,' I said. 'You can make your own memories.'

'Yes. I have to get used to that. And to the fact that my father was here, in these rooms. Most of my life I've been all right with this, I mean, with not knowing my father. I had surrogate fathers. My mother's husbands, all of them very nice. But when I found Olivia—that was when I began to miss my father. I just wanted to show her to him and, for the first year we were together, I had the feeling that I was going to find him, somewhere. I'd walk down a street and there he'd be. Of course, that was silly.'

I wondered if her mother had anticipated this and had held on to *Serenity* for Katherine. I told her this.

'No,' she said. 'And I think if Olivia had been a normal child, she never would have told me about this place. Last summer we spent some time with her on the Cape. She has a mansion there. And a very big social life. We were in the way from the moment we arrived. I don't think she was doing it on purpose, but she kept leaving things lying around on the floor, and Olivia kept falling over them.'

I heard her sigh.

I told her that Olivia would grow to love Rose Point. 'She'll be safe here,' I said.

'That's the thing all parents want, isn't it, to be able to protect their children? Nothing else matters as much as that.'

'And what do parents get in return?' I asked.

'Many things. You'll see for yourself some day.'

'I don't know,' I said. 'The time is flying past.'

'Well, you shouldn't miss out on being a father. I can tell you'll be good at it. You wonder sometimes,' she said, softly. 'I wasn't going to have children. I mean, my fiancé and I had an understanding. No kids to interrupt us reading the *New York Times* each morning. Our lives were, well, you could say that our lives were . . . orderly. I guess that's the word. But a couple of other words come to mind as well. Predictable. Empty.'

'Lots of people live empty lives,' I said.

'In New York there are so many old women living alone,' she said, as though she hadn't heard me. 'I watch them. And though they are alone, they make a great effort to present themselves well. You can see past their deprivation, catch a glimpse of their elegance. So completely alone in the world and yet if they were mothers, then they were once the centre of someone's attention. Once you're a mother, no one can ever take that from you. You can lose everything else, but never the memory of being adored.'

When she didn't say anything more, I was afraid she would leave. 'I want you to know why I came back,' I said.

'Back?'

'Yes, after driving to the airport in the storm.'

'The airport was closed,' she said innocently.

'It wasn't just that,' I said. My words echoed in the room. 'I could have spent the night at the airport,' I said. 'Remember you were telling me how Olivia has taught you to live in the present tense?'

'How do you live?' she asked.

'The future, always,' I confessed. 'You are only as good as your next deal.' There was a long pause, and I decided to say something I knew I wouldn't be able to retract. 'This is the future too,' I said. 'Being here with you.'

She said she didn't understand.

'I know,' I said. 'You never knew it, but I've been waiting a long time for this, and looking for you.' There was a movement outside the door. My hands were shaking.

'Where, Terry?' she asked softly. 'Where have you been looking?'

'Everywhere,' I said.

There was only silence. I tried to picture her expression. Then I heard a sound. 'It's Olivia,' Katherine said. 'I'll be right back.'

I waited for her, but she never returned. I wrapped the towels round me and opened the bathroom door. From the landing I could hear Katherine reading to Olivia in their bedroom. And I knew she had forgotten me.

I LEFT THE COTTAGE quietly. The only thing I wanted was to find Charles in the hotel and sit and talk with him. Tell him everything before this night was over. I drove into the city, going over the sentences in my mind right up to the second I pushed the door open—and saw that the room was empty. No one had been here since I'd filled the chest of drawers and the closet with new clothes.

I saw the lights from the Christmas tree in the square reflected in the window. I walked across the room, opened the window and looked down into the square. A man with a white apron over his coat was selling coffee from a cart. Someone from the Salvation Army stood behind a black kettle, ringing a bell.

Something came over me. Anger at myself. And defiance. Not wanting to let go of the illusions that had coloured my life. I started by dropping a pair of new socks out of the window. I watched them float to the ground, where they landed in a stand of thin birch trees that had been strung with white lights. Then I dropped all the other pairs. People were looking up at me and I didn't care. I turned away from the window and quickly gathered up all of the remaining clothes, then headed for the door.

By the time I came out of the elevator and walked out of the hotel, the fight in me was gone, and with my head bowed I picked up the socks. I carried the whole bundle to the Salvation Army man. 'Would you know someone who could use all this?' I asked him.

He nodded. 'Of course. Leave that with me.'

Back in the workshop that night I worked on the wooden sledge, trying not to hurry or to think about how it was going to look, until the day had drained out of me and I was tired enough to go to sleep.

IN THE MORNING, when I gazed at the sledge I had finished, it fell far short of what I had imagined. Warren stopped by when I was waxing the oak runners with a candle.

'You're still here,' he said, walking to the workbench for a look at the sledge. 'Can Hollywood survive without you for this long?'

I didn't want to talk about that. 'Your brother was here,' I told him. 'I found him in the city and hired him.'

I don't know what reaction I expected from him. Anger perhaps. Instead he ran his palm along one runner. 'I spoke to him,' he said. 'I want to show you something.'

We walked together until we saw Charles in the distance, straddling the ridge of a snow-covered roof.

'He called me for a ride this morning,' Warren told me. 'The first thing he's asked me for in five years.' He looked at me with an expression I couldn't interpret.

'What do you want to say to me, Warren?' I asked him.

He shook his head. 'I just don't want anything to happen to him,' he said slowly. 'I don't want to lose him. He was my brother long before he had anything to do with these people out here.'

'Well,' I said. 'I think it's off to a good start.'

'But how will it end? That's what concerns me.' He looked into my eyes. 'When your father told me that she was coming up here for Christmas, I asked if he knew what kind of person she had grown up to be. Of course, he didn't know. I guess I was worried that she might be like her mother. She might hurt him. Does that make sense?'

'I think she's a good person, Warren,' I said.

He nodded. 'Will you let me be the one to tell him?'

'You're the only one who should tell him,' I said.

CHAPTER NINE

I drove to town and bought Charles a steak sandwich for lunch. When I climbed up the ladder to give it to him, I saw that Warren had given him a rope, which was tied round his waist and the base of a chimney for a safety line. He told me that he wasn't hungry.

'Well,' I said, 'you have to eat.'

He stopped and looked at me. 'What do you remember?'

'Everything,' I said.

He thought about this a moment. 'Your father pulled out a diamond earring I found in the floor,' he said.

'I know.'

'Those kids in the hospital?'

'I remember them too,' I said.

Finally I got him to take the sandwich and coffee. He sat down on the roof, leaning his back against the chimney.

'Do you know the story about the people who owned this cottage?' he asked me. 'The Rideouts?'

'The name is familiar,' I told him.

'They threw this dinner party once and hired the chef from the Plaza Hotel, New York. Your poor father had to drive him up and back.'

I smiled at him. 'I wonder what the two of them talked about for eight hours.'

'Rich people, probably,' he said.

I felt like he and I were getting close to something, so I asked him if he'd ever come back here after the accident.

'Yes,' he said. 'For a few summers I slept on people's boats in the harbour and spent the days in the woods. I thought they might come back. I was foolish. I was here when the men came and cleaned out the cottage. I watched them fill two big trucks. I never came back.'

I waited a moment, then told him I had met Callie. 'You can see this place from the hospital,' I said.

He said something, but I couldn't make it out. 'Why didn't you stay with Callie?' I said. 'She loved you. Why should she have to go through her life thinking you're dead?'

'She deserved someone better than me,' he said.

'Well, she never found anyone,' I told him. 'And who were you to decide that, anyway?'

This was all he wanted to say to me. He stood up, picked up his shovel, and started in again. Before I left him I said I thought he had been kicking himself long enough.

I IMAGINED HIM watching us from the roof later that afternoon, when we went sledging on the snow-covered dunes behind the yacht club. We posted Lawrence in his new L.L. Bean boots at the bottom of the hill to catch Olivia. Katherine and I ran alongside the sledge. 'Again!' Olivia shouted as soon as the sledge came to a stop. 'Again, Terry!'

Katherine and I rode with Olivia for the last run of the day, and the three of us landed in a heap, in each other's arms, laughing and holding on to one another. If Charles Halworth had been watching, I wondered if he would think we belonged together.

Katherine brushed the snow off my hair and told me she was sorry.

'For what?' I asked.

'Last night,' she said. 'I started reading with Olivia and I forgot.'

She took my hand. Olivia and Jack walked ahead of us. 'I feel like I've made this world for Olivia and me,' she said. 'A small world where we hide. And I hope that we'll discover something here. Something that will make life better for her. But sometimes, Terry, I feel like we live in two places, that this life is only a shadow of another, that we live in some other place, somewhere above us. And every so often, when the two come together, we catch a glimpse of the real meaning of our lives.'

'What's it like,' I asked her, 'in those moments when the two come together?'

She smiled at me and looked around us. 'Like this, Terry,' she said. 'Moments like this when we don't need anything more than what is right here, all around us.'

Like this, I thought, looking into her eyes. I realised how close our faces were. I didn't move. I drank in her attention, her closeness, thinking that maybe I had done something right to earn her touch. She smiled, then closed her eyes and kissed me.

'Maybe I shouldn't have done that,' she said.

'No,' I told her. 'It was the right thing to do.'

'Are you sure?'

'I'm sure.'

I TOOK THE SLEDGE back to the store and dried it, and was putting on another coat of varnish when Katherine knocked on the door. She stood in the doorway, holding a dish in her hands.

'Do you like pumpkin pie?' she asked.

I saw something in her eyes. She wore a light blue sweater and jeans. Her hair was down on her shoulders.

'I've got two plastic forks here,' I said.

I turned on the radio and we sat on the bed eating her pie in the dim light. One piece had been cut. She reassured me she had tested the pie on Lawrence first.

'He survived,' she said. 'But he's got a cast-iron stomach.'

'So have I,' I said.

She told me that she and Olivia had enjoyed the sledging. 'I can't believe you built the sledge right here.'

'That's the absolute limit of my carpentry skills,' I told her. 'If my father were here he could have made you a much better sledge in one-fifth of the time.'

An old song by Roy Orbison came on the radio. When Katherine told me that it was one of her favourites, I asked her to stand up. I took her in my arms and we danced. After a few moments she laid her head on my shoulder. I felt her breath on my face. 'I have to tell you something, Terry,' she said.

'What is it?'

'I'm not a person who thinks about things as deeply as I should. I keep busy; I don't dwell on things. But since I've been here I've realised there's a great amount of loneliness in me. When you have this inside you, you don't let anyone get too close, because if you come to need them or to love them and they leave, then there will be too much loneliness in your heart. So you push people away. I've become good at that. I pushed everybody away until I found Olivia, the one person who wouldn't leave me. At least, that's what I've told myself from the day I brought her home. Only now, I see how wrong that is.' She looked right into my eyes. 'I feel like I can trust you, Terry. When I kissed you today I knew what I wanted for my daughter. I want her to fall in love some day and have a full life. And this means that I must help her become strong enough to leave me.'

I listened until she was finished. I looked up at my mother's photograph and she seemed to be staring at me. I told Katherine that Olivia would always be with her, no matter where her life took her. 'Remember,' I said, 'you told me about the old women in the city, the ones who were once loved by a child?'

She raised her head and I saw that she was smiling. 'Yes,' she said. 'So, if you come into the city some day and see me crossing the street with my stick, and shoes with the old lady heels, you'll remind me?'

'I will,' I said.

WE HAD DINNER together that night, the four of us in front of a blazing fire in the dining room. I told them Hollywood stories until it was time for Katherine and Olivia to begin their nightly ritual.

'I have an idea,' I said to Olivia. 'How about tonight I tell you a story?'

I looked to Katherine. She nodded her approval. 'Mommy says it's fine,' I told the child.

Before we went upstairs, I remembered the bird's nest in the mailbox, which I had put back by the front door. We climbed all the stairs together to the widow's walk and sat beneath the Christmas tree. 'I've never told a story to a child before. You're the first, Olivia.' I placed the nest in her hands. It took a while for me to stop feeling self-conscious and to let myself be drawn close enough to her that *I* didn't matter any more. Then a story came into my head. The story of a bird named Sheila who lived in the mailbox and spent her days going from one mailbox to another and flying away with all the bad news. 'The bills, of course, but also the sad letters,' I told the child.

I went on, sentence after sentence falling into place. There was a child who befriended the bird and who opened all the mailboxes on his way from school each day. The bird trusted the child and led him to where she kept all the sad letters. And they rewrote them, taking out all the sad parts and the mean things people had never really meant to write, and writing the things that they wanted to say but somehow never got around to.

I heard Katherine's voice, and for a moment I didn't know where I was or where the voice was coming from.

'I want to know how it ends,' Katherine said, softly. She leaned close to me and looked down at Olivia.

'I'm not sure,' I told her. 'Do I have to know the ending?'

She smiled at me. 'No, maybe it's better without one,' she said.

I thought again of how Olivia had taught her to live in the present. This moment, *right now,* is all we have. Maybe this is the best way to live. Maybe a fulfilled life is just one beginning after another. No endings, just beginnings.

'Look,' I heard Katherine say to me. 'Look who's sleeping.'

I carried Olivia down to the first floor and waited for Katherine to show me which room. 'I have an idea,' she said. 'I'll be right back.'

She went into another room and returned with blankets and a pillow. I watched her make a bed for Olivia in front of the windows in the blue room. As I tucked the child in, Katherine closed the door behind us.

'Tell me,' I said. 'I've been meaning to ask you why she puts her fists against her eyes.'

She took my hands and made them into fists. 'Press them hard against your eyes, and tell me what you see.'

It took only a few seconds before I saw white flashes.

'A blind person sees the same thing. And so they want to do it all the time. It only takes a few years before the eyes are ruined and have to be removed.'

Glass eyes, then, I thought.

'Olivia is learning,' she said, hopefully. 'I don't have to tell her nearly as often as I used to.'

The room grew darker, more tranquil. In the candlelight I held her in my arms and asked her to try to go back in her mind to her earliest memory.

'I can't,' she said. 'I don't have a good memory.'

'Everyone says that. Try. You have to try. Close your eyes and think back.'

'I remember our family doctor sitting on my bed and telling me that I had the measles. I would have been five or six I guess.'

'Further,' I said. 'Back further.'

'I remember standing in the fog on the first day of school. We couldn't see the bus coming up the hill.'

'I was there,' I said.

'No, sir.'

'Yes, ma'am,' I teased her. 'I was there beside you. Always have been'

'OK then, what kind of shoes was I wearing?'

'Red boots,' I joked. 'You've always loved red puddle boots.'

She kissed my lips. 'Wrong,' she said. 'I wore my shiny shoes. I loved them. My mother says I always called my patent leather shoes my shiny shoes.'

I propped myself up on my elbow and looked into her eyes. 'I remember those shoes,' I said.

'Of course you do. You were there beside me.'

'The shoes had elastic straps that held them on. The right strap was loose and the shoe kept falling off.'

I told her this with a straight face and an even voice, looking right into her eyes. The way you would tell someone you love them. She responded at once, pulling herself up in the bed. 'You couldn't know that, Terry,' she said, emphatically. 'Tell me how you knew that.'

'I didn't know,' I lied. 'I was just making it up.'

She stared at me a moment before she told me anything more.

'I had sprained my ankle,' she said. 'I remember it was Halloween. There was a party and we played musical chairs. I tripped and hurt my ankle. For weeks I had to wear a thick bandage round my foot, and it stretched the elastic on my shoe.' She frowned at me. 'You couldn't have known this.'

In the morning, I thought. In the morning I will tell you everything.

'No,' I said as I gently pulled her close. 'I was only guessing.'

SOMETIME IN THE NIGHT I awoke beside her and saw the moonlit sky on her face. This is who I am, I thought. My life is here now beside this woman, and I am a man who will ask nothing for myself except that she never leave me. I gazed at her face on the pillow, her dark hair. I longed to see her waking, for that is when we truly know who a person is, in those first seconds before they remember where they are in the universe. I made a pledge to the white stars beyond the frosted windows, a pledge that I would never leave her, that nothing in the wide world would take me from her side. Her denim dress folded on the chair across the room, her red boots by the door, meant the end of a deep longing inside me.

SOMETIMES WE ASK what it is we have done wrong in our lives to deserve heartache and despair. I was already asking this when I awoke in the morning and heard a man speaking to Katherine in the kitchen below me. Her scent was on the pillow next to me, but I was back in LA, in my office. I had to be there because the voice I heard downstairs belonged to Peter Billings.

I walked to the top of the stairs. 'I've been on the phone ever since Terry told me about you and your father,' Billings was saying. 'We'll make a gorgeous movie, you can trust us. And are you the father?'

I heard Lawrence answer, 'No.'

'And to think,' Billings went on, 'that your father killed that woman and her baby, and all these years he blamed himself, when it was just an accident.'

I came down the stairs so fast that I was falling forward when I reached the kitchen. The first thing I saw was the bitter disappointment in Katherine's eyes.

'Wait,' I said. I turned to Lawrence. 'I can explain this,' I said. Even as I began, I was thinking that I could talk my way out of this. I could take care of this. I turned back to Katherine. 'There's no movie, Katherine. It's just a misunderstanding.'

'No movie?' she said quietly. 'Is there a father? Or did you make that up?'

'I didn't make any of it up,' I said.

'And the mother and baby?'

'No, I'm saying—'

'*What* are you saying?'

'I care about you.'

'You care about me? And the truth? When were you going to tell me the truth?' She turned her back to me, sweeping Olivia up in her arms as she walked away.

'Please,' I called to her. But she kept going.

CHAPTER TEN

Lobster traps wash up on the beaches in Maine. Mostly they are the new type made of wire, but occasionally you will find one of the old traps made of oak slats and fastened with bronze nails that give off a marvellous green flame when they're burned.

Billings and I dragged two traps back to my father's workshop. I sawed them into pieces that we burned slowly in the woodstove. I kept thinking that I should walk back to *Serenity* to plead my case.

I rehearsed what I might say, going over and over it in my mind. But then there was the memory of Katherine's face, the disappointment in her eyes. And the wrenching in my stomach. The picture of myself as an outsider here once again, as I had always been.

Billings was sitting as close to the woodstove as he could get without setting himself on fire. He was petting the rabbit, whose dark eyes seemed focused on me. I remembered that it was Christmas Eve, and tonight I was supposed to carry the rabbit to the cottage for Lawrence. He would have to come to pick it up himself.

'You're in love with her, aren't you?' Billings said.

I was on the telephone to the airlines, on hold with a children's choir singing 'Frosty the Snowman' in my ear. The wind shuddered against the windows above my father's desk. I felt something opening inside me. A vast open space was pushing through me, and with it a coldness that seemed to be searching for a permanent place to attach itself in me.

'What difference does it make?' I said.

I had spent much of the morning talking to Billings, and finally I couldn't stand the sound of my own voice. I drove into the city. I passed the hospital, which stood like a fortress. Then I turned onto State Street. There at the bottom of the hill I saw Callie standing on the corner. She wore her yellow scarf. I told her everything that had happened, and where she could find Charles. I watched her eyes fill with wonder. 'You have to see him,' I said. 'Warren will help you.'

'I don't know what to say,' she said. 'And you're going—'

'Where I belong,' I said.

She put her hands on my arms and pulled me close to her. I looked up into the empty blue sky. 'I've always thought I should have told Charles something a long time ago,' she said. 'Something about love. He told me so many times that he didn't deserve to be loved. I should have told him that no one *deserves* to be loved. Love is a gift.'

She began to cry.

ON THE PLANE back to the West Coast, Billings said, 'You know what I was looking forward to most about making this movie? It would be *ours*. I mean, we'd finally get to *make* a movie instead of just sweating over somebody else's.'

I had my eyes closed and my head back against the seat, sorting through the time I'd spent with Katherine, from the moment I first saw her on the shore with Olivia. I could see her face in each scene, the way her eyes responded to me. What I was already missing about her was the stillness that had enclosed us when we were together. How I could be quiet in her presence. Her voice replacing mine.

'I should have stayed,' I said. 'I should have tried to say something that would have convinced her.'

Billings raised his hand for the stewardess and ordered us each another drink. 'In a movie you would have.'

'I think I'll call in,' I said. I dialled my number at The Company and the first message was from my secretary telling me that she had transcribed all 187 of my phone messages.

'A hundred and eighty-seven messages,' I said. I listened to them all, wanting only to hear Katherine's voice, and feeling myself becoming the person I needed to be to survive where I was going. The kind of man who had chosen not to bury his father because it would have taken too much time. By the time the plane landed I felt cold and closed off.

And then I remembered Katherine kissing me. Leaning towards me with her eyes lit up. The plane had taxied to a stop, and Billings was standing in the aisle waiting for me. 'Go on,' I said. 'I'll see you later.'

'OK, man,' he said.

All the passengers filed out past me. The cockpit door opened and I saw the pilot and copilot putting on their dark blue jackets.

'Is everything all right?' a stewardess said to me.

I looked up at her. I wanted to tell her that everything was so far from all right that I didn't think I could stand up.

INSIDE THE TERMINAL I watched rain lashing across the big glass windows. That sad old Christmas song by Joni Mitchell was playing: 'It's coming on Christmas, they're cutting down trees . . . I wish I had a river I could skate away on.' I sat down in an empty gate area and began writing to Katherine. I kept writing until I'd said everything to her that was in my heart, trying to make it the kind of letter that she would keep for the rest of her life.

Then I walked a long way to the FedEx terminal and arranged for the letter to be delivered to the *Serenity* cottage before the end of Christmas day.

THROUGH THOSE DAYS and weeks that followed, Billings proved himself a good friend, and I opened up to him, which one does not do in Hollywood. I told him that it was the way I missed Katherine that made me certain I loved her. How I was already ordering my life around what was absent and most precious to me, waiting for her to ask me to return to her. I never took a shower without bringing my phone into the bathroom so I could hear it ring. I took it with me when I walked to the beach in the early mornings. And no matter how discouraged I was at the end of a long day of waiting, I began each new day hopeful again that, before dark, my life would change.

Billings did his best to hold me up through the winter. One night on the way home from a black-tie premiere, he confronted me. 'You look terrible,' he said.

'No sleep,' I told him.

'You can get some pills for that.'

'You don't understand. I don't want to sleep.' I explained that I didn't want to because I kept having the same dream: that when I awoke, Katherine and Olivia would be there.

'If we weren't dreamers,' he said, 'what would we be?'

'Husbands, maybe. Fathers,' I said.

WE MANAGE, even with our hearts broken. By summer I had moved out of my apartment so I could stop spending time in rooms where all I'd done was wait for the telephone to ring. I got a place off Hazwell Boulevard, paid a decorator to make it look like a men's club, and then I put my head down. What saved me was the work I did to rescue Lewis, my failing actor friend. All summer he was in and out of a mental hospital, and on Labor Day morning the police brought him to my apartment after they'd found him walking back and forth across Wilshire Boulevard, trying to step into the paths of oncoming cars.

I made him take a shower, then I sat him on my couch and swore that I would turn the city upside-down if that's what it took to find him work. The next day I began a Blitzkrieg of phone calls, emails, and faxes that lasted right through the autumn.

Nothing happened. And then, just before Thanksgiving, I heard that Max was about to sign a lucrative TV deal for a mini-series. I called him right away. 'I have to see you, Max,' I said. I told him that Lewis belonged in the lead.

'Why don't you go through your Rolodex and throw out all your clients who are older than forty-nine?' he said to me.

'Sounds a little cruel, Max, don't you think?'

'That's how you got where you're at, isn't it?'

But in the end Max came through for me, and Lewis got the part. That evening I took him to a nice place to celebrate. 'I'll never forget this,' he said. There were tears in his eyes.

'Yes, you will,' I told him. 'You'll go on to great, stunning successes that will make this look like small potatoes. But now you have to do something for me.'

'Name it,' he said.

I asked him to ride with me to a beach in Santa Monica. He stood beside me while I scattered my father's ashes into the dark sea. For some reason I had not wanted to do this alone.

On the way home, we were stopped at a red light next to a filling station, where a couple of guys were unloading Christmas trees from a truck and lining them in rows across the parking lot. I was stunned. 'I had no idea it was even close to Christmas,' I said to Lewis. 'Tell me how it can be Christmas again.'

'What do you mean?' he asked.

'Another year gone? Lewis, what am I doing with my life?'

'Helping poor slobs like me.'

Suddenly I felt the wait was over. 'Look, I've got to drop you off and get home. I've got some calls to make.'

I PACED AROUND the apartment with the phone in my hand, then I watched some of a basketball game while I rehearsed what I was going to say to her. Finally I hit the mute button and placed the call. The phone rang and rang. No answering machine. Nothing. I kept trying all night long, and by morning I was desperately afraid that she and Olivia had disappeared into the wide world and I would never see them again.

Finally, I called Warren.

'Thought I would have heard from you long ago,' he said.

'I'll tell you the truth, Warren, I've wanted to call you every day since I left Maine, but I was afraid that, once I started, I wouldn't be able to stop. I would have called every day just to see . . . Just to try . . . I've been trying to forget, instead,' I said. 'And I was doing OK until I saw these Christmas trees yesterday.'

'Well,' he said, 'I'm glad you called. I should have called you to thank you.'

'For what?'

'Listen, Terry,' he went on. 'What you did here . . . it worked. I have my brother back, thanks to you. And Charles has his daughter. It's not perfect, but it's so much more than we had before. You gave us all a chance.'

I felt grateful for this. I thanked him and told him I had tried to call Katherine in New York.

'They're in South Carolina for the winter,' he explained. 'I can give you the number there.'

'Is Charles there?'

'Yes. Callie's there too.'

I closed my eyes and pictured their faces. I didn't have what I wanted most, but this was something I could hold on to. It was a miracle, really.

Warren told me he had taken over for my father at Rose Point. 'I have *Serenity* cottage all wrapped up for winter.'

AS CHRISTMAS DREW NEAR I surrendered to Billings's plan to spend a week in the Swiss Alps skiing. 'Once you're up there in those mountains,' he said, 'you'll feel better.'

We were scheduled to fly out of LA on the morning of Christmas Eve. The day before, I was packing when I came across the invoice from the Christmas tree farm where my father had ordered the tree for *Serenity* before he died. I threw it into the wastepaper basket and then I picked it up and held it in my hand, recalling the kid who had delivered the tree.

On a whim, I picked up the phone. Moments later I got the owner on the line and asked him if he could take a tree out to the cottage.

'You know there's no one out there this time of year,' he said.

'It's something my father did,' I said to him. 'I know it's late, but I just realised that it's something I want to do, not just this year but every Christmas from now on.'

We talked for a few minutes. I told him he would have to walk in from the gate. I asked him if he could make a stand for the tree and set it on the front porch.

'I know it sounds crazy,' I said, 'but if you can do it, I'll be grateful. I'll pay you whatever you think is fair.'

'Don't worry about it,' he said. 'If I can get to it, I will. Give me your number and I'll call you back one way or the other.'

He called my cellphone the next morning as Billings and I were checking in at the airport. 'I took the tree out to the house,' he said, 'but I was a little embarrassed barging in, you know. You didn't tell me anyone would be there.'

'Who was there?' I asked quickly.

'A whole family,' he said. 'An old man was skating on a homemade rink with a little girl. He helped me carry the tree up to the widow's walk. Does a hundred dollars sound OK to you?'

I could barely speak. I spun round to Billings, but his face suggested he already knew what I was going to say. 'I've got to see her,' I told him.

'I'll call you before the end of the day to make sure you're all right,' he replied.

I stood for another beat, frozen.

'Go,' he said.

I WALKED DOWN Winslow Homer Lane in the deep silence that I remembered. Here I am, I thought. I stopped when I saw my father's workshop through the trees. I dug through the snow with my hands until I found the soup can beneath the steps. I opened the door and stepped inside. When I turned, my mother was looking down at me as if she had been expecting me to return.

I was staring into her eyes, trying to hear her voice inside my head, when my cellphone rang again. I figured Billings must have landed. And what was I going to say to him? *Here I am, waking up after another dream?* I answered the phone.

'Thank you for my Christmas tree, Terry.'

It was Olivia. I turned quickly, thinking she was standing behind me.

'I'm glad you like it.'

'I know what an elephant looks like now,' she said, as though the past year had only been a day.

'You're in the E book?'

'Yes, E for elephant!' she said.

'That's wonderful, Olivia.'

'Here's my mommy,' she said.

A wave of anxiety washed through me. I walked out of the workshop and then, when I heard her voice, I couldn't move.

'Thank you, Terry,' she said. Her voice was so close.

'Merry Christmas,' I said.

'We woke you, I'm so sorry, I didn't even think about the time difference.'

'No, I was awake,' I told her. 'You made it back to Maine.'

'Yes,' she said. 'We're all here.'

'Together,' I said. 'That's good.'

'Terry,' she said. 'I needed time to think.'

'I know,' I told her.

'But I was wrong,' she said, her voice cracking. 'I never should have let you leave.'

I started running then and I didn't stop until I saw her in the widow's walk. She was looking out to sea with her back turned towards me, but Olivia was looking down as if she could see me.

'As soon as we got here, I realised everything,' Katherine was saying.

When she said this, I was in front of the cottage, my shoes filled with snow. 'Katherine,' I asked, 'are you sure?'

'I'm sure.' She hesitated. 'But your life is out there, Terry. I know that.'

'Not any more,' I said. 'Turn round, Katherine.' I stood there looking up at her until she saw me. In my ear there was the sound of the phone falling as I watched it drop from her hand. Seconds later they burst through the front door and I saw they were both smiling when I took them in my arms.

THEIR TOUCH that morning placed a new sense of wonder in my heart. Since Katherine and I were married I have come to believe that what is common to us all in our varied lives are the things we cannot fully explain. Somehow I think we know this even while we arrange our enterprises with such care, with the illusion that we have everything figured out. We look up at the stars at night and cannot say how far the sky goes or where the true god of words and time stands watching over us.

I now live in a father's world, walking Olivia to school, down on my hands and knees hunting for toys lost under the furniture. Counting toes. Changing nappies. There is a tiny statue of Audrey Hepburn, my favourite actress, on the counter by the washbasin where Olivia helps me give her brother his baths every morning and again at night before bedtime. It's just a little plastic figure that I picked up at some shop on Sunset Boulevard. Now that the baby is teething he grabs hold of the statue and chews on it through his baths. There are his tiny teeth marks on it, and Katherine and I have spoken about how we will carry this with us for the rest of our time together, to remind ourselves how full our lives have been.

DON J. SNYDER

In Spring 1991, Don Snyder was a contented man. He'd had three books published and, as professor of English at Colgate University, upstate New York, he was teaching with a passion that had earned him the nomination of 'Professor of the Year' by his students. Then, out of the blue, came a letter of dismissal. 'My first reaction upon reading the letter was that some mistake had been made,' says Snyder. 'I knew professors, plumbers, managers and bank tellers were being laid off across the country, but I was on the inside . . . where bad news isn't about you.'

After long months of fruitless search for a university post, Snyder sold his house, and he and his wife Colleen and their four young children moved to Maine, where the couple had their roots. But Snyder's search for a teaching job in a university remained unsuccessful, and as his savings ran out, he was forced to take a job as a construction worker, a carpenter, a house painter and finally as caretaker of a summer mansion. 'To my surprise,' Snyder says, 'I found the work restful; there was a steady cadence to it that seemed blessedly to carry over to the rest of my life.' At the same time, he wrote *The Cliff Walk: A Memoir of a Job Lost and a Life Found*, recounting the shattering effect that his six years of searching for a job had had on himself and his family.

In Snyder's most recent novel, *Fallen Angel*, there are obvious parallels between the life experiences of Terry, the fictional central character of the story, and those of the author. Both are born and brought up in Maine, both leave behind a working-class background (Terry's father is caretaker of a summer house in Maine) to go to college and thence to successful, lucrative employment. But it isn't until Terry returns to his roots, and rediscovers his past, that, like the author himself, he finds his destiny.

Although Don Snyder is now an internationally recognised writer, he can still be found 'banging nails back'. 'I've found a peace in working with my hands,' he says. 'A peace I can't part with now.'

ACKNOWLEDGMENTS AND PICTURE CREDITS: *Last Light:* pages 6–8: man's face: Zefa/Powerstock; jungle landscape: Getty Images; photomontage Curtis Cozier. Page 149: © Robin Matthews; *The Stone Monkey:* pages 150–151: Getty Images; photomontage: Curtis Cozier. Page 295: © Jerry Bauer; *Dying to Tell:* pages 296–297: landscape: Gettyone Stone; sky: Getty Images/Telegraph Colour Library. Page 441: © Jane Brown; *Fallen Angel*: pages 442-443: house: Getty Images/Telegraph Colour Library; mother and child: Getty Images; photomontage: Rick Lecoat @ Shark Attack. Page 539: © Colleen Snyder.

DUSTJACKET CREDITS: Spine from top: Zefa/Powerstock; Getty Images; photomontage: Curtis Cozier; Getty Images; photomontage: Curtis Cozier; Gettyone Stone, Getty Images; photomontage; Rick Lecoat @ Shark Attack.

Printed by Maury Imprimeur SA, Malesherbes, France
Bound by Reliures Brun SA, Malesherbes, France

218AN